ARC LIGHT

ARC LIGHT

Eric L. Harry

Hodder & Stoughton
LONDON SYDNEY AUCKLAND

First published in Great Britain in 1994
by Hodder and Stoughton
A division of Hodder Headline PLC

10 9 8 7 6 5 4 3 2 1

British Library Cataloguing in Publication Data

A CIP catalogue record for this title is available from
the British Library

ISBN 0 340 63970 9

Typeset by Hewer Text Composition Services, Edinburgh
Printed and bound in Great Britain by
Mackays of Chatham PLC, Chatham, Kent

Hodder and Stoughton Ltd,
A division of Hodder Headline PLC
338 Euston Road
London NW1 3BH

To Marina, my wife and best friend:

Я люблю тебя

Contents

Chapter Four

PART TWO

Chapter Five

Chapter Six

PART THREE

Chapter Seven

PART FOUR

*At what point shall we expect the danger? By what means
shall we fortify against it? Shall we expect some transatlantic
military giant, to step the Ocean, and crush us at a blow?
Never! All the armies of Europe, Asia and Africa combined,
with all the treasure of the earth . . . could not by force, take
a drink from the Ohio, or make a track on the Blue Ridge
in a trial of a thousand years . . . If destruction be our lot,
we must ourselves be its author and finisher. As a nation of
freemen, we must live through all time, or die by suicide.*
                                                —ABRAHAM LINCOLN
                                                  January, 27, 1838

Prologue

SOUTH OF DEMILITARIZED ZONE, SOUTH KOREA
June 10, 1100 GMT (2000 Local)

'Arc Light, Arc Light,' U.S. Army Captain Bernard Weaver heard faintly
over the radio speaker's din of electronic disturbance – the words leaving
him stunned. South Korean Army Lieutenant Pak looked at Weaver
quizzically. 'What was that?' he asked in heavily accented English after
it became clear that Weaver's careful tuning of the frequency knob would
not be successful in pulling the distant signal in.

'It's . . . uh' – Weaver couldn't believe it— 'it's the radio call for a
B-52 strike.'

Pak's eyes grew wide and his jaw fell. Huddled together at the table of
the earthen Command Post, all seemed quiet. Surely, Weaver thought,
he must have misheard the call. *'Arc Light,'* the words came to him,
sending a shiver down his spine. *What the hell's going on?*

Weaver looked down at his report and picked up the hand mike. He
couldn't make contact with the rear areas, but maybe they could hear
him. 'Alpha Lima Six Six, this is India Tango Four Seven. Stand by
for OPREP-3.' It was an Operations Report that could have political
ramifications, hence he'd given it a 3. As soon as he tried the radio he
would pack up and head back on foot. The message was priority, headed
directly to the Emergency Operations Center at the Pacific Command.
'To EOCPACOM. From India Tango Four Seven. "Company-size element
NKA infantry sighted by ROK Army in DMZ fifteen miles east southeast
of Panmunjom," Weaver read, lifting his finger off the PUSH-TO-TALK

button briefly, as taught, "at approximately 1630 Zulu. Observed activity included digging."

Just then, the two men heard a single rifle crack, followed a half second later by a deluge of small-arms fire that continued to grow in volume for several seconds until it sounded as if the entire battalion had opened fire. Weaver's heart fluttered and pulse quickened with every decibel increase in the sound of fighting.

Pak grabbed his helmet and M-16 and without saying a word ran out the open entrance of the CP into the dark.

Weaver worked to calm himself and keep his wits about him as he pulled his Special Forces beret off his stubble-covered head and retrieved the Kevlar helmet from his rucksack. He had never seen action before, having still been in Special Forces training during the Gulf War and having run from skirmish to skirmish the last few days along the 'Z' firing off nothing more than the after-action reports of junior Korean officers. Now, however, he thought as he hefted the rifle into his hands and listened to the fire being poured downhill, he was in the right place at the right time.

The first heavy blasts of artillery began to burst outside. The thump vibrated up through Weaver's feet despite his distance from the barrage, and the sound roared in through the entrance. Weaver froze at the sounds. This was different. This was unlike any of the games he had heard described during the forty plus years since the war here. The barrage grew to ferocious intensity – Russian-style preparation. The vibrations shook dirt through the beams and plywood of the CP's earthen roof, and the thought passed fleetingly through his brain that this might really be it. That possibility seemed more real with each thudding burst. But PACOM had been on alert for almost a week and Marines were holding Operation Eastern Gale just offshore to rattle the saber. Surely, he thought, the North Koreans wouldn't dare . . .

Weaver returned to his rucksack and hoisted the load onto his back, settling the heavy pack that smelled of canvas and sweat into its familiar place and buckling up. The artillery was falling steadily now, and the air of the CP was thick with dust. The rounds were not being poured on – only one every three or four seconds in the immediate vicinity.

With every step he took toward the first zig of the bunker's entrance, which was designed to prevent any direct fire or shrapnel penetrating from the outside, the noise of the violence grew. He paused to pull the charging handle of his AR-15 'Commando' back to chamber a round, extending the retractable butt of the stock and flicking the selector switch to the rear – 'Auto' – as his eyes began to adjust to the dark outside.

In a stoop, he rounded the sandbags of the bunker into the trench and was out under the open sky. The sound of the fighting was intense now, much louder than from inside the bunker. To the left and right down the trench line into which the bunker opened Weaver could see South Korean soldiers blazing away down the hillside with M-16s and M-60 machine guns, their wide eyes lit in brief yellow strobes by the faint muzzle flashes from their modern weapons. Overhead, mortar-fired flares were popping brightly and then floating down on their little parachutes, casting a peculiar dim white light into the trench. Weaver was transfixed by the scene, watching as the darkness slowly retook the floor of the trench and rose up the opposite wall as the nearest flare descended.

Weaver was momentarily stunned into inaction by the force of a shock wave and sound from an artillery shell that detonated in the air above the trench line seventy meters away. Crouching lower in the trench, he saw the eyes of the South Korean rifleman to his right as the soldier also hunkered down against the earthen wall. He looked to his left and saw that the machine gun crew was heads down also, staring at him with panicked looks on faces slowly being eclipsed by darkness as the latest flare continued its descent.

Weaver slipped his rucksack from his shoulders and climbed up onto a firing position on the trench wall to look down the hill toward the DMZ. As he peered over the sandbags, the scene was just as he had imagined it but at the same time infinitely more terrifying to behold. Everywhere in the light from the flares, clusters of men clad in black were hurrying toward the lines of concertina wire carrying long logs by their handles. Scores of North Koreans behind them poured small-arms fire up the hill toward the South Koreans. Officers shouted and whistles blew in patterns and signals as orders were given in their shrill code. As the first group reached the barrier, they hurled their log forward onto the wire to press it down and then dropped to fire as the next log was humped along the path of the previous one – each farther up the hill. Men fell constantly on either side of the logs, but there were always enough to carry them forward that last distance to their objective and hurl them onto the wire and onto the occasional mine, which burst quickly, felling the North Koreans in the vicinity. It was brutally efficient, it was well drilled, and it was fast.

Weaver raised the cool plastic stock of his carbine to his cheek, lined up one clump of soldiers at the wire and squeezed off a short staccato burst. Recentering the rifle after the vicious recoil, he saw a pile of bodies on the wire where he had aimed. Before he could fire again, the pile grew as the South Korean soldiers on either side of him now poured lead down the hill. But other North Koreans had run up and were continuing the effort. Weaver fired again at the same spot, and more men fell.

When he had emptied his magazine, he backed down off the step at the firing position into the trench and hoisted his existence load onto his shoulders. *Time to get the hell outa Dodge and lie low*, he thought, his mind already settling upon a small hill with its jagged crags and outcroppings and thick vegetation that he had passed about half a mile behind the DMZ. *The better part of valor.* He looked down the trench line at the South Korean rifleman, who had ducked down into the trench and was watching him. He turned around to see that the M-60 crew was still firing, but keeping him in sight as well. *Where the hell is Pak anyway?* Weaver wondered angrily as he looked for the men's platoon leader, who must have been called to the Company Command Post.

He hesitated for a moment, halfway between the front and back walls of the trench. The rifleman continued to stare at him. *Why the hell didn't Pak buddy that son of a bitch up?* Weaver thought angrily, Pak having violated one of the principal rules of night infantry deployment: never leave men alone. 'Shit!' he said finally, slapping another magazine into his rifle and climbing back up to his firing position, this time keeping his load on his back.

Weaver ran through the second thirty-round magazine of his carbine in short bursts, seated his third magazine and resumed firing down the hill directly in front of his position. His carbine was an M-16 rifle with its barrel shortened from twenty to eleven inches. The shorter barrel severely reduced the muzzle velocity of the rounds and therefore their range, accuracy, and stopping power in favor of the carbine's light weight and compact design. It kicked out full-size NATO 5.56-mm rifle rounds, however, and several North Koreans fell with each squeeze of the trigger. The weapon was more than adequate for this job. A pistol would have downed them at that distance.

Weaver shifted from target to target in the rich environment, firing methodically until it was time to reload again. A full magazine now seated in his carbine, he hesitated. North Koreans were everywhere, at distances far closer now than the targets on a rifle range. There were just so many, and they were fully exposed to his fire. He brought the weapon back up to his cheek and began dropping more, his mind calming as he got used to combat and as the training – the long-drilled routines of placing targets on the front sight's post and squeezing the trigger – replaced the anxiety from before.

Just like King of the fucking Hill, Weaver thought. *I'm on the hill – I'm King, you bastards!*

But the North Koreans kept coming, and for the first time dirt began to kick up around his head and shoulders, forcing him to duck. After loading the fifth and next to last magazine into his carbine, he looked back up to see two groups of North Koreans almost simultaneously finish breaching the last strand of wire. Weaver aimed and let loose a burst at one of the two breaches just as a platoon-size unit rushed forward through the gap. Although their breach was narrow and several men stumbled to the ground in the burst, the majority made it through the choke point and quickly fanned out, continuing their rush up the hill.

Someone set off two Claymores, spraying hundreds of deadly pellets down the hill in an arc, killing dozens of black-clad North Koreans. Off in the distance to the southwest Weaver saw a line of helicopters – visible only in blackened outline because of the fires on the hill behind them – stream across the DMZ, heading south. He looked back down the hill. It was a simple formula now, he realized, rate of fire from the defenders versus speed of advance, and without the wire to slow them down, the North Koreans were closing the gap rapidly. It was a formula that would produce only one result, Weaver concluded with a start. This was not a feint or a probe. There were no intelligence officers in the darkness to the north registering the South Koreans' positions weapon-by-weapon from their muzzle flashes. They would not be bypassed. The breach would occur here. They were being overrun.

The chill sank into Weaver's bones as all the ramifications of his calculation became evident. He stared down the hill without focusing as his peripheral vision fed signs of movement up the hill from both sides of his position – the orange flashes and loud 'cracks' from each of their rifles now faintly distinct from the bursts of light and general roar of weapons all through the hills around him. Mechanically he flicked the selector switch to 'Semi' and began firing single rounds at individual targets as they rose to rush up the hill three or four steps at a time. Every second or third shot dropped another North Korean. Unlike before, however, taking action did not ease the involuntary clench that randomly seized his muscles or the churning of his bowels.

Weaver glanced nervously toward the M-60 to his left. To his horror he saw that North Koreans were pouring over the trench a hundred meters away and that the M-60 had fallen silent, its crew nowhere to be seen. Weaver turned to his right as bullets cut audibly through the night air by his head to see the soldier with the M-16 lying contorted in a twisted position at the bottom of the trench. Raising his carbine back to his cheek, he could see directly in front and out of the corners of his eyes numerous black clumps of men rushing up the slope toward the trench, only fifty meters in front of him now. Multiple breaches.

Weaver fired one more burst on full auto and dropped back down into the trench as a hail of bullets rained clumps of dirt down onto him and split the sandbags on the roof of the bunker behind him with a continuing drumbeat of heavy thumps.

Just as the outpouring of fire toward Weaver's small section of trench grew, the fighting elsewhere along the trench was dying down. The battle should have been reaching its peak as North Koreans stormed over the lip of the trenches, but the sounds of fighting were waning. He could suddenly hear the ringing in his ears from the firing of his carbine, like a whining tone through ears deadened as if by cotton plugs. 'Shit!' Weaver said as the realization of what was happening washed over him like the surf, its undertow pulling him and his heavy pack to the ground in the bottom of the trench with a faint jangle from his taped and well-placed equipment. *It's too late*, he thought in shock, looking up at the high front wall of the trench before him over which the North Koreans would pour any second now. *Goddammit – it's too fucking late*!

The artillery and automatic weapons fire was now being replaced by the much more ominous sound of single rifle cracks up and down the trench line. *Oh God, oh God, oh God* ran through Weaver's mind like a mantra, blotting out all other thoughts as his eyes flitted about the trench for some place to hide. A bright flash and jolt through his pants seat drew his attention to his left as he watched fire shoot out of the heavily sandbagged Command Post next in line down the trench. Black smoke billowed from its opening as he saw another flash of light over the hill behind it signal the same end for the next bunker. They were blowing the CPs – *big charges*, he thought, *satchels*.

What do I do? *What do I do*? he thought as his head spun and he forced himself to breathe. But his mind froze up, and the muscles and sinews of his body, highly conditioned and tested by relentless Special Forces training, sat on the ground waiting motionless for orders from the one organ that could never be fully prepared.

In those few seconds everything grew unreal. He was alone. Nothing came through to disturb the blankness that filled his brain, that blotted everything else out. The sound of sliding and of falling dirt and the sight of motion in Weaver's peripheral vision, however, drew his attention; the cold settled around him and he began to shiver. Pouring over the front edge of the trench on both sides of him were scores of North Koreans. Time slowed until it was almost frozen. The flares had ceased falling as the mortar crews packed up to flee less than a mile to the rear of the breakthrough, and Weaver watched in the darkness as the men to his left picked themselves up off the dirt floor of the trench. The first men to stand upright threw their rifles up onto the lip of the opposite wall and began clawing at the dirt, rising up and out of the trench to continue their advance. Weaver watched in horror as one by one they all followed suit, turning his head slowly as he sat with his back to the trench wall to see the men to his right – not fifteen meters away – doing the same.

In a few seconds they had all left and it was still again. Weaver was alone. He felt his mind thaw ever so slightly, sufficient to realize what had just happened. *First wave – keep on moving*, he thought. *Second wave . . .*

More bodies began to pour over the wall, and the icy dread coated him completely this time. He was shaking badly and his stomach muscles cramped from their clench. The taste of acid and steel nearly gagged him as he tried to force his dry mouth to swallow. The new men stayed on the floor of the trench. To his left Weaver saw the butt of a rifle rise up into the air, silhouetted for an instant against the still glowing fires that lit the night sky down the line of the trenches. He watched as the butt then followed the rest of the rifle to earth, thrust straight down in a line. The sound, like a burp, that followed completed the picture of a bayoneting, of the death of one of the fallen machine gunners. There was a brief, weak shout – a plea in a language that Weaver did not know but that was known to the attackers – as the bayoneting was repeated for the second man.

On hearing the man's plea – just the sound of the voice of another who found himself lying at the end of his life, like Weaver – a profound sense of resignation finally overcame the dread that had seized him just a few moments before when he had been counted among those still living. He had, in those few seconds, done what all but the very old never seem able to do. He had absorbed the fact of his own demise. He had accepted that his fate that warm summer evening would be death, here in this place – now. It was abrupt, and he had not until that very moment foreseen it, but it was done. It was a fact.

Almost as if it were a pointless detail, Weaver took a deep and ragged breath and pulled his now heavy rifle up to his shoulder. He took aim down the trench to his left at the forming squad of 'mop up' troops. He tried not to think, to hold back the tide of last thoughts that could do nothing more than torment him. Moving lethargically, his motions were not detected. The stability of his sitting position overcame the shaking of his hands. He pulled on the trigger, but he couldn't force himself to pull hard enough to release the carbine's sear and start the process of death, theirs and his own. Pictures – if it wasn't for the pictures that flashed before his closed eyelids . . .

Come on, Bernie, his conscious self urged, mouthing the words that stopped just short of being spoken out loud. *Just get it over with, man. Do it. Come on.*

Opening his eyes to ensure that his aim was true he saw the dark figures moving towards him down the trench. He filled his lungs to bursting with air. His skin crawled as he closed his eyes again and pulled the trigger all the way.

PART ONE

*Humanity has been compared . . . to a
sleeper who handles matches in his sleep
and wakes to find himself in flames.*

—H.G. WELLS
'The World Set Free'
1914

Chapter One

THE PENTAGON, OUTSIDE WASHINGTON, D.C.
June 11, 0430 GMT (2330 Local)

A single red light blinked on the desk phone's panel of twenty separate lines. It was not, General Andrew Thomas made sure, the President, the Pacific Command, or any of the other dedicated lines along the bottom row. It was just an ordinary outside line.

Thomas, chairman of the Joint Chiefs of Staff, rubbed his bleary eyes and returned to the logistics report from Eighth Army Command that lay in a puddle of light beneath his desk lamp. *Not the time for sleep*, Thomas thought, yawning. *I can sleep after the war.*

His eyes strayed up to the map table across the plush, seal-emblazoned carpeting of his office. The plastic overlay pressed onto the map of Korea, showing the latest North and South Korean troop dispositions. The light that shone indirectly on the table changed suddenly, and Thomas looked at the cabinet on the wall beside it to see 'NBC News Special Bulletin' splashed across the television screen. The scene switched to the White House Briefing Room for the President's address, and Thomas felt a sharp pain shoot through his jaw as he ground his teeth. He had just returned from the National Security Council meeting where he had received his orders, and the frustration and anger were still fresh.

'Dear God.' Thomas pulled a deep and ragged sigh and sat back in his padded, oversize chair, rubbing his temples and shutting his eyes. He felt a rising fear about what was coming and looked at the large wall map behind the table. The blue unit markers dotting Eastern Europe were barely visible on the map. Thomas shook his head. On his first tour at the Pentagon in the mid-1980s, the Reagan buildup had equipped them to fight two and a half wars at once — two major wars and one regional skirmish. By the time of the Gulf War, the Bush Administration had scaled back to a two-war capability. When he returned from his command of III Corps in southern Germany during the Clinton term, they had moved to a 'win-hold-win' policy — force levels designed to win wars in succession

rather than simultaneously. 'Win-lose-recover,' the planners called it
bitterly behind the politicos' backs.

He shook his head again; III Corps, V Corps, VII Corps – nearly all
of the regular army's heavy forces and four of her six heavy divisions
on the ground in Germany, Poland, and Slovakia and of no use to
him in Korea. It had been a purely political decision after the military
coup in Russia. The secret security agreements from the Bush era
with Poland and, at that time, Czechoslovakia had forced President
Livingston's hand – 'put up or shut up,' Secretary of State Moore,
more hawkish than any of the Joint Chiefs, had said. 'If you abrogate
those agreements in the face of a Russian redeployment to Byelarus,
there isn't a country in the world that will take us at our word when
we extend our security umbrella to them. Besides, all we're talking
about is a show of force.' *Force*, Thomas thought, *that we now need
somewhere else.*

And so now, what do they want? We told them. We told Congress in
the hearings what our capabilities would be at the current appropriations
levels. 'You heard the President,' the White House Chief of Staff Irv
Waller had said at the NSC meeting earlier. 'Find a way.'

The red light shone steadily; his secretary had picked up the line and
would get rid of the caller, probably some brass-balled reporter thinking,
'I'll just call the Pentagon and ask.' As he sat in the stillness of his office,
the familiar surroundings suddenly seemed alien, as if he was seeing
them for the first time. The glass-enclosed cases of mementos, the unit
flags with their campaign streamers, the framed commendations – they
seemed to be from a life he hadn't lived. It was the photographs from
the distant past that began the thread that ran through all the disparate
objects and linked them to the present. Grainy, sloppily taken photos
of grimy young men slouching under the weight of their own limbs –
back from 'the shit.' You took pictures when you came back because
you had survived, and you always took them in groups because that
was the way you wanted the memories to be – always together. He
felt a great sadness as he looked at the succession of photos that hung
on the wall, feeling each loss again as the group grew smaller. Thomas
had been too tired then to feel the pain.

The buzz of the intercom surprised him. He looked at the phone and
then poked the speaker button. 'I told you – no interruptions.'

'Sir, I'm sorry, sir, but . . . it's General Razov – on line one.'

'What?'

'General Razov . . . s-someone who says he's General Razov, sir,
is on line one.'

Thomas's eyes focused on the photo taken the year before. The
charisma of Razov – the dashing hero of the first Russo-Chinese War
who, at the unheard-of age of forty-six rose to command a Russian tank
army with his bold, slashing drives into the flanks of the Chinese attack

– shone brightly through the glass cover. And Thomas, graying and tired but jubilant over the younger man's string of stunning victories for which Thomas secretly, inwardly felt some measure of shared pride after near constant counsel during the forty days and nights of the war. 'Get the duty officer up here on the double,' he ordered, 'and trace the call.'

'Yes, sir.'

Thomas rested his finger atop the button on the telephone. The blinking light shone blood red through his fingernail. He rubbed the smooth plastic for a second and then pushed.

'Who the hell is this?' he asked loudly, anticipating the laughter of an old classmate from the Point with a poor sense of timing and humor.

'I am General Yuri Vladimirovich Razov, commander of Far Eastern Military District of Republic of Russia.' Thomas was stunned. 'Hello, Andr-rusha.' The faint white noise in the background hinted at the distance of the source.

'Yuri?'

'Yes, Andrushenka' came the response, again after a pause – a satellite transmission delay.

'What . . .?' Thomas began, but found himself at a loss.

'Andrew, I am calling you with very regrettable news,' the man said, his words slightly slurred as if by liquor, although Thomas knew that would not be the case.

He sounds exhausted, Thomas thought as he flicked a small switch on the side of his phone. A yellow light next to the word TAPING came on. 'Go ahead,' he said guardedly.

'We have taken our strategic rocket and ballistic missile submarine forces from 'Constant' to 'Increased' alert status. Your next satellite pass should confirm that. In addition, the Svobodnyy Missile Field in the Far East has gone all the way up to 'Maximum' alert.' Razov paused, and time seemed to stand still. 'In less than half an hour, my heavy artillery and rocket forces will strike fourteen tactical targets along our front in Occupied Northern China with nuclear weapons. We plan to lay open holes through which we will launch counterattacks intended to stabilize our lines. In order to avoid risking escalation, we will of course have to neutralize the Chinese strategic forces.'

'Yuri,' Thomas said as his mind reeled, 'in God's name you can't do this.' A shiver went up his chest as a box, long ago closed, opened suddenly to release its demons.

'We will do it, but not in God's name.'

'No' was all Thomas could think to say. 'No! Yuri, if the Chinese get a shot off . . .!'

'You know as well as I that the Chinese have only four operational T-4s capable of reaching our European populations. We will strike their T-3s, T-2s and T-1s plus their submarines and B-6 bomber bases, but once we knock out the T-4s they will be unable to threaten us strategically.'

'They could still get a shot off!'

'Their land-based missiles are all liquid fueled – nitrogen tetroxide as the oxidizer and unsymmetrical dimethylhydrazine as the fuel. You know what those liquids' corrosive effects do to the fuel tanks. Plus there are the evaporation rates. We have shared the intelligence, Andrusha, and I know your conclusions correspond to our own. Those missiles remain dry until prelaunch sequencing, and ever since we knocked their satellites down in the last war, they have had no technical means of monitoring our launches. Therefore, they won't have any warning until the reentry vehicles hit the upper atmosphere and ablation releases enough reflective material to return a radar signature. That would be no more than twenty to thirty seconds before detonation – not nearly enough time to fuel.'

'You can't do this, Yuri,' Thomas said, pressing his thumb into his ear as he sat hunched over his desk, staring off into space as thoughts began to fly like sparks through his mind, fears lit by the sparks beginning fires that consumed all other worries.

'Are you ready to hear the rest?' Razov asked, and Thomas pulled out a pencil and note pad. 'Our Strategic Rocket Forces will fire nineteen missiles of the type you have named SS-19, with the possibility of a small number more in a restrike within less than an hour's time. The missiles will deploy one hundred sixty-nine warheads.' Thomas wrote the numbers down. 'All will be fired exclusively from the Far Eastern Military District. None, I repeat, *none*, of these missiles will in any way threaten the United States or any of her allies.'

'The hell they won't, Yuri! This is *insane*! You *can't* do this!' Thomas noted the time on his watch and wrote that on his pad also. His secretary stuck his head in the door, his own phone to his ear. Thomas jabbed his finger at the mouthpiece of the telephone's handset, and his secretary rolled his finger in the air and pointed at his watch before returning to his desk.

Thomas had to stall. 'Listen to me, Yuri. I'm warning you, something will go wrong. Something *always* goes wrong! You know that! Your plans – they demand perfection. They're brittle. What if the Chinese have seen your ground troops maneuvering to hit spots on their line that make no sense, and they've put two and two together and gone to a higher alert status? What if there's a leak?'

'As usual,' Razov said with a hint of amusement, 'you sound like the prophet of doom. The Chinese are not on higher alert. We have confirmed that by technical means. And I can assure you, Andrew, that our plans are the most highly guarded secret in Russia today. We have an automated firing system, as you know, not launch crews as in your system. The only people who know of the plan are the principals of the Supreme High Command at STAVKA who authorized it, the two officers manning STAVKA's nuclear communicators, and my aide and two army commanders, who drew up the plan here in Khabarovsk. There is no way that they will get off a shot, Andrew. It is impossible.'

Thomas's secretary reappeared, and Thomas muted the telephone. 'They're tracing, sir, but it'll take—'

'Get the President on the line *now*! Emergency telephone conference! Then I want telephonic missile threat, missile warning system, and significant event conferences – in that order!' The secretary's eyes widened and he turned from the doorway to lunge for his desk. Thomas released the MUTE button. 'Yuri, nothing is impossible.' He closed his eyes and focused his attention on the phone, on the man at the other end. 'Do you remember the talks we had in the last war? You've got to have robust plans, plans that can withstand one, two, maybe three unanticipated things going horribly wrong and still work. Your plan falls apart if just one thing goes wrong, Yuri. If the Chinese find out . . .'

'I have told you. They will not find out.'

'Open discussions with them. Talk to them about a cease-fire. You'll have to give them back some of your security zone in Occupied China, but you'll do that one day anyway. Hell, threaten them with nuclear weapons if you have to, but Yuri, for the love of God, please don't play with fire. I'm warning you – you'll get burned.'

'The release orders have already been sent from the nuclear communicators,' Razov said. 'They were "Launch-at-Designated-Time" releases, Andrew. The launches are automatic from this point forward.'

Thomas gathered his strength to begin collecting from his desk the papers he would need. He heard a door burst open and the sound of running feet in the outer office. A colonel – the duty officer – and a major, his deputy, appeared at the door, both out of breath from their run. Thomas switched to the speakerphone and again pressed the MUTE button. 'Get down to the Tank,' Thomas ordered the two men in a flat voice, already emotionally drained from his worries. 'FLASH OVERRIDE. I'm declaring DEFCON 3 – all forces worldwide.'

'Andrew?' Razov said, and Thomas glanced at the phone, his finger still resting on the MUTE button. When he looked back up, the duty officer was standing ramrod straight. 'Get the senior duty controller at the Air Combat Command in Omaha. Have him scramble bomber and tanker crews to their aircraft and start their engines. Then get the ACC commander in chief and have him flush the bombers to their positive control points.'

'Andrew?' Razov said again.

'What Target Base, sir?' the duty officer asked.

Thomas felt a chill wash over him before he spoke the words. 'Strategic War Plan – Russia.'

The two officers looked stricken, and Thomas spoke hurriedly. 'I want a protective launch by all commands of their airborne command posts, and I also want all air base controllers to get everything they can up into the air. Have the navy surge the boomers to their firing stations . . . surge everything. Get 'em out to sea.'

He tried to remain composed in front of the officers but felt his heart racing as he spoke. 'I have the following alert order. Attack Condition Bravo. I repeat,' he said more slowly, enunciating each word and staring into the two men's eyes, 'Attack Condition Bravo.' The officers looked at each other and turned to run for the door of the outer office. 'And scramble the antisubmarine aircraft along the coasts. I want firing solutions on Russian boomers kept constant!' *Where the hell is the trace*? Thomas thought, swallowing to wet his drying throat and looking at his watch. He took his finger off the MUTE button. 'Yuri?'

'I must be going,' Razov said abruptly.

'Wait!' Thomas said, racking his brain for something to stall him. 'You said something about . . . You called me a "prophet."' Two military policemen with M-16s appeared in the door, and Thomas again muted the phone. 'Check with my secretary on the trace!'

One of the men disappeared as Thomas lifted his finger from the MUTE button. 'Are you still there?'

'Yes.'

'Do you remember the last time we talked about this plan, Yuri? About a plan to go nuclear with the Chinese?' Razov did not reply, but Thomas knew he remembered. 'It was in the last war. Things were at their bleakest. It was just before your counterattack, and you thought all was lost.'

'You were a prophet of doom then too, Andrew.'

'That's what you called me. I was up from Vladivostok on an inspection tour of our forward supply teams. Right there in your command post you and I discussed employing nuclear weapons to stop the Chinese, and you called me a prophet of doom when I warned you of the risks. Do you remember what you said to me? You quoted somebody.'

His secretary appeared at his door and rushed to his desk.

'Celano,' Razov said. 'I said you reminded me of something I had once read by Thomasso di Celano.'

Thomas read the message slip handed him by his secretary. 'Nippon Telephone & Telegraph ETS-V geosynchronous satellite. Uplink from Khabarovsk, Russia.'

Thomas rose to slip into the jacket held open for him by his secretary and then took the secure portable telephone handed to him. His secretary whispered, 'Conferences convened, sir.'

His mind raced with a dozen moves to be made, preoccupied now by the dozen orders urgently required. He was surprised to hear Razov's deep and thickly accented voice from the speaker.

'"Day of wrath! O day of mourning! See fulfilled the prophet's warning, heaven and earth in ashes burning!'" The soldiers in Thomas's office stared at the speakerphone in stunned silence. 'Good-bye, Andrusha. Good-bye.' The red light went black, and Thomas rushed toward the door.

THE JEAN LOUIS, WASHINGTON, D.C.
June 11, 0430 GMT (2330 Local)

'Greg!' Jane Lambert said as her husband walked up to the table. She rose on her tiptoes and pulled his head down with a cool hand on the back of his neck. He kissed her before turning to the other couple.

'I didn't think the President would let his national security adviser out for a dinner with friends on a night like this,' Pavel Filipov said, shaking Greg's hand warmly and nodding toward the television over the bar, the West Coast baseball game not yet interrupted for the President's address. Greg kissed Irina, Pavel's wife, on the cheek and then sat.

'Well, I can't stay long,' Greg said, grabbing Jane's hand under the table.

'I don't suppose we are still on for racquetball tomorrow?' Pavel asked.

Greg laughed as he took a large bite of bread. 'Not even close,' he said with his mouth full. 'Too bad too. I was looking forward to this new serve you've been developing in secret.'

'It drops dead in your backhand corner,' Pavel said, taking a sip of his wine.

'Bring it on. I'll just kick your butt again.'

Pavel scratched his eyelid with his middle finger, a gesture he had learned from Greg.

'G-r-r-r,' Jane said, making a fierce expression before laughing. 'It's called macho, Irina,' she said, flexing her thin arms and making muscles. 'Greg hasn't grown out of being a basketball star in college, and Pavel has a dose of the ex-jock too, I see.'

'Oh,' Irina said, shaking her head, 'it is not athletes. It is men. They are the same all over.' Greg rolled his eyes as Jane and Irina began to recount the most humiliating stories from their husbands' pasts.

As Pavel raised his napkin to his lips, Greg saw again the missing tip of his finger. *Frostbite*, he remembered as he did every time he saw it. *His index finger*. In the last Russo-Chinese War, Pavel's rifle company had run out of fuel on a hillside and had dug into the snow, fending off wave after wave of Chinese infantry for the next three days. The tip of his trigger finger, which he had left uncovered for too long against the cold, had been lost to frostbite. *The price of empire*, he thought.

Greg had studied military affairs, had years of experience with the

Defense Intelligence Agency, was a 'star' in the national security world – the new National Security Advisor at the unheard-of age of thirty-eight – but, being a civilian, he'd never experienced war. *The last war in China was just the winter before last,* he thought. Most Americans knew little of it, as the video was scarce, but Greg had researched it thoroughly. It had been one of his several claims to fame at DIA: calling for a Crisis Action Team well before the war's outbreak when all of his colleagues' attention had been on the Middle East and Southern Africa. It was inevitable, he had written, that the resurgent China, whose economy grew at double-digit rates, would be attracted to Siberian natural resources to the north, which were held increasingly tenuously by Russia, a declining European imperial power.

Pavel had been called back from Washington in the last Russo-Chinese War, but was sitting out this second round safely ensconced as military attaché at Russia's Washington embassy. *I wonder if he wishes he were there now, with his comrades*? Lambert thought. *With General Razov?*

'And so Greg tried to lift the car out of the mud with his bare hands. "It's only a fucking Fiat,"' Jane said in a mock, deep-voiced imitation as she regaled them with the distorted tale of their honeymoon. 'He could hardly walk for a week. We found a little inn in the middle of Nowheresville, France, and I propped him up in bed and we read *books*. He was *useless*. Completely useless,' she said, turning to Greg. 'I swear,' she continued, 'with so much testosterone running loose in this world, I don't know how it is that our two countries didn't get into a war all those years.'

In the silence that followed, Greg looked at Pavel, and then Pavel's eyes drifted to the television that hung over the bar. 'What is he going to say?'

Greg glanced at the screen. A special bulletin had interrupted the CBS broadcast. 'Pavel, can I . . . can we talk?'

'So you didn't come here to see your long lost wife?' Jane said. 'That explains it.'

Pavel and Greg were close friends, but it was not the first time that the friendship had been used for professional reasons. Always before, however, there had been a cooperative spirit in the games they played, as befitted the strange alliance their countries had forged during and after the first Russian war with China, in which the U.S. had provided substantial logistical assistance. Greg always asked the questions that Pavel wanted to answer, or vice versa, and each reported the 'contact' up the chain of command. 'Back channel' communications, they were called. Having become a part of such a channel himself quite by coincidence, Greg had come to realize how important those lines of communication were. But things had been strained since the military coup in Moscow in early spring and the U.S. deployment to Eastern

Europe in response that had so inflamed the Russian nationalists, and Greg had shied away from asking tough questions after the first flurry of activity, sensing Pavel's desire to avoid the subject.

'Sure,' Pavel said. 'Go ahead.'

Greg looked over at Jane and Irina, who sat there, expectant. 'Pavel, we have intelligence to indicate that there were high-level contacts over the last few days between the North Koreans and your Defense Ministry in Moscow.' Pavel's face remained blank. 'Any communications traffic,' Greg continued, supplying the source – technical means – in hopes of trading for more, 'might create an appearance of impropriety at a time when American lives are at risk.'

Pavel cleared his throat and said, 'As you know, Greg, we have regular relations with North Korea *and* utilize their road grid in the north for resupply of our forces in Occupied China.'

Nothing, Greg thought with a flash of anger. 'Did you have advance warning of the North Korean attack, Pavel? If you did, we're gonna want – the President is going to *expect* – some help, at least on the intelligence side.' Greg was irritated, and he broke the rules of the game by speaking so frankly. Pavel just arched his eyebrows. 'Come on, Pavel. I don't have time for this shit. I need something.'

Filipov took another sip of his wine, a furrow deepening between his brows. 'We have problems, Greg, of which you are only dimly aware. There are people in my country, people like General Zorin, who view things differently than you and I. They see U.S. troops in Eastern Europe and in the Sea of Japan and think it is a part of some vast Western conspiracy, a continuation of our countries' historical enmity.'

'Don't give me that horseshit about—' Greg stopped mid-sentence. He was too tired or too impatient to play the game, and he had almost made the mistake of hearing only what Pavel had said and not its meaning. *So it was Zorin who talked to the North Koreans*, Greg thought. *That makes sense. They're cut of the same cloth*. Pavel took another sip of his wine, the glass covering his mouth but the amusement evident in his eyes. *He loves the game*, Greg thought for the hundredth time.

'Well,' Greg said, 'I hope for both our countries' sakes that Zorin – these hard-line types – can be kept on the reservation.' Pavel said nothing, and Greg's patience again began to wear thin 'So . . . What? Are you saying that Razov needs the supply lines through North Korea so badly that he and Zorin agreed to let the North Koreans slip the leash and invade the South just five months short of reunification? Just after we completed withdrawal of our troops at the insistence of the North? That your old boss Razov is up to his eyeteeth with Zorin in this?'

Filipov didn't bite. It was Irina who blurted out the response. 'General Razov hates General Zorin!'

'Irisha,' Pavel said.

'But it's true! General Razov is friend of America. We could not have been victorious without America's aid in the last Chinese war, and Pavlik might not be here tonight if America would not have helped.' She was wilting under Pavel's gaze, knowing she should not have interrupted, so she just lowered her head and finished what she had to say. 'Zorin is all the time wandering off his reservations.'

Pavel leaned forward. 'Okay, I know you're busy. In answer to your question about' – he looked around, and continued in a whisper – 'about General Zorin, all I can say is steps are being taken.' He held up his hands as if to say, 'There!'

'Is STAVKA going to sack him?'

'The High Command,' Irina whispered to Jane, who nodded, and the two turned to listen.

Pavel again said nothing.

'Christ, Pavel, don't tell me there could be trouble in Moscow,' Greg said. 'That's the last thing we need right now, and you too, for that matter, with the way things are going in China.' All eyes were on Pavel, and Greg waited in silence for his response.

There was a chirp from the portable phone in Greg's jacket pocket. He pulled the phone out. 'Lambert.'

'White House switchboard, Mr Lambert,' the operator said. 'Please stand by.' Everybody watched as Greg listened to the faint tones and a pop over the phone. 'Please repeat,' the cool electronic woman's voice of the voiceprint identification system said, 'astrologer.'

'Astrologer.'

The waiter appeared behind Pavel. 'Colonel Filipov? Telephone, sir.'

'Precocious,' the computer said, not matching on the first try. 'Precocious,' Lambert said, enunciating the word carefully. 'Voice-print authenticated,' the computer said, and there was a click as Greg watched Pavel excuse himself. 'Please hold for Major Rogers,' the White House operator said. *Old Jolly Rogers*, Lambert thought, having already grown accustomed to his paranoid late-night calls about Iranian invasions of Saudi Arabia or Indo-Pakistani nuclear wars.

'Mr Lambert?'

'What is it, Larry?'

'Sir, we've gone to DEFCON 3, all forces worldwide. The Federal Emergency Management Agency is executing the Joint Emergency Evacuation Plan. You're a JEEP-1 cardholder, sir. Your point of departure is the White House. You'd better get a move on.'

Greg could no longer hear the buzz of conversations or the faint background clatter from the kitchen. 'What's going on?' he asked, his entire being focused on the faint hiss from the phone.

'Attack Condition Bravo, sir.' Greg heard the words, but the tingle along his scalp and the flood of disassociated thoughts prevented him from comprehending immediately. 'General Thomas has convened a missile threat conference. That's all I know.'

Greg stared out at the suddenly surreal room of late-night diners. Couples leaned over tables with hands intertwined and faces close. A crowd of apron-clad busboys at the bar waited for the President to appear on television for his address.

'What is it, sweetie?' Jane asked, looking at his face with concern.

'I'll be right there,' Greg mumbled, placing the phone in his pocket just as Pavel returned. Rather than taking his seat, Pavel leaned to whisper in Irina's ear. Greg saw Pavel's lips form the word *'Moskvu,'* and Irina knit her brows. *The accusative declension of the Russian word Moskva*, Greg silently translated, *meaning 'going to Moscow.'* 'Jane, can I . . . can I talk to you for a second?' She got up and followed Greg to the bar. Pavel and Irina watched, and Greg turned his back to them. Pavel's early training had been not with the army but with the KGB.

'Honey? Greg, what's . . .?'

'I want you to get in the car and head up to Leesburg. Better yet, call your parents and tell them you're going to meet them at the condo at Snowshoe.'

'What? Why?' She laughed nervously. 'What's going on?'

'I don't know,' he said as his mind raced. *North Korea? Zorin? The Russo-Chinese War? Something else?* 'They're evacuating the government, Jane.'

'They're doing what?' she gasped.

He pulled her to his chest and wrapped his arms around her, hugging her close. 'Oh, God, honey. There's . . . there's so much I want to say but . . . I've got to go. There's not much time. You understand?'

Jane was ashen, staring up at him and shaking her head. 'No. No, I don't understand at all!'

Greg had to go. The clock had started, and the timetables were skinny. 'Just get out of town. Don't stop for clothes, for food, for anything. Do you have gas in the car?' She stared at him without responding. 'Jane,' Greg said, taking her by the shoulders. She instantly wrapped herself in his arms. He hugged her, but softly said, 'Jane, is there gas in the Saab?' Her soft hair, just curled at the hair-dresser that afternoon, tickled his nose as she nodded, and he pressed his face through the curls to kiss her warm head. 'I have to go,' he said, gently prying her arms from around him. 'I love you,' he said, staring into her beautiful blue eyes before turning to leave. He said a hurried good-bye to Irina and Pavel and headed out of the restaurant. His driver quickly wheeled up to where he stood. 'The White House,' Greg said as he slammed the door. 'Use the light.'

Without asking any questions, the driver put the small red bubble light on the roof with a thud, its magnet holding it firmly in place, and he gunned the engine. The car growled to life, throwing Greg's head back and bouncing him as they rolled onto the street just as he reached for and at first try missed the buttons on his portable phone.

As the car's siren wailed from under its hood, Greg looked back to see Pavel jogging across the parking lot. At the door of the restaurant stood Jane and Irina. Jane was waving as she disappeared from his view, and after a moment he hit the autodial for the White House.

LOS ANGELES, CALIFORNIA
June 11, 0440 GMT (2040 Local)

'I can't see any way that the United States will enter the fighting,' the analyst on the CNN special report was saying. Melissa Chandler sat on the sofa in their family room, one ear on the television, the other on the sounds of David's footsteps upstairs. The network military pundit whom David had said earlier didn't sound as if he knew what he was talking about was inset in a box as the main picture showed the press milling about the White House Briefing Room, the podium at the front still empty. 'The North Koreans have advanced too far in too short a time. I'm afraid we're going to have to sit this one out and hope the South Korean Army can turn things around by itself, maybe with U.S. air support.'

Melissa's stomach hurt, and her back had begun to freeze up as she sat at an awkward angle holding her swollen belly. She slid farther up on the seat cushion to relieve the pain in her back, but the pressure of her womb on her bladder made her want to go to the bathroom again. The indigestion shot pains through her stomach. *The joys of pregnancy*, she thought, her hand rubbing the top of her taut abdomen.

'What about all of the troop movements that we've been hearing about over the last few hours and in the weeks and months leading up to yesterday's invasion?' the anchorman asked. He looked down at his notes. 'Carrier battle group sails from San Diego with partial crew. Marine Expeditionary Force training in the Sea of Japan. Marines depart Camp Pendleton. Two National Guard divisions activated. Two regular army divisions deployed to Germany. Fighter aircraft seen taking off from Yokota Air Base, Japan. Et cetera, et cetera. What do you make of all that?'

She heard David walking quickly across the floor in the bedroom.

'Just an abundance of caution,' the retired colonel, a former whistle-blower on the ill-fated hypersonic bomber, said from his little box on the screen. 'Rattle the sabers. But you see, that just proves my point. All of those forces are recallable. You send them out and call them back, the

essence of saber rattling. And the European forces don't have anything
to do with—'

'Excuse me,' the anchor cut in as the scene switched to a full-screen
view of the anchorman holding his earpiece close to his ear. 'We go now
to Bob Samuels at the White House.'

The scene shifted to a reporter standing in front of the familiar blue
backdrop from a different part of the Briefing Room. 'I can now tell
you that we were told, about an hour ago, to assemble in the White
House Briefing Room,' the reporter said, half turning around to take in
the room, 'for an announcement. About fifteen minutes ago, we were
told to expect an address by the President himself.'

In the background, a door off to the side of the podium opened, and
the President, followed by several military officers, entered.

The reporter continued in a hurried voice. 'I can also tell you that
I'm hearing – and this is unconfirmed – but what I am hearing is that
United States Air Force aircraft have, in the past hour, begun combat
operations against the invading North Koreans. That contrasts with the
earlier information, which was that the employment of U.S. aircraft was
exclusively for transportation of critical supplies to the South Koreans.
I have also been told that things are not going well for the South—'

'Ladies and gentlemen,' came a loud voice in the background, 'the
President of the United States.'

'David!' Melissa shouted. 'It's o-o-on!' A jab of pain shot through
her back, and she shifted position again.

'Let's listen now,' the reporter said in hushed tones as Melissa heard
David running across the floor upstairs.

President Livingston at the podium donned his reading glasses, pulled
several cards from his jacket pocket and glanced down at them before
facing the camera. 'My fellow Americans. I come to you tonight with the
gravest of news. Early yesterday morning, Washington time, elements
of the North Korean Army crossed the Demilitarized Zone into South
Korea in a massive invasion of that good friend and trusted ally. They
attacked without warning, and without provocation. Let me take this
opportunity to state, categorically, that we have no quarrel with the
people of North Korea, who are enslaved by the brutal policies of
their leadership, and that we remain open to discussion with the North
Koreans about ending the hostilities and returning to the preinvasion
borders. Repeated attempts, however, to contact the North Korean
leaders have all failed, and there are currently no further attempts
under way to initiate such contact.'

The camera zoomed in for a closer shot, and the President stared
right at it. Out of the corner of her eye Melissa caught sight of
David, his chest bare, entering from the darkened hallway carrying
his clothes. 'The position of this country, and of all the world leaders
with whom I have spoken, is clear. The invasion of South Korea will

not be tolerated, and North Korean troops must withdraw immediately and unconditionally.'

A man in a dark gray suit appeared next to the podium and distracted the President, breaking the drama of the moment. The President stepped back to read the message handed to him.

Melissa looked up at David. He already appeared different, Melissa thought. Not taller – he was six feet one – not more fit. She looked at his bare chest. He was trim but not skinny as he had been when they met, in good shape despite the toll that years of sitting at a desk practicing law took on a thirty-three-year-old. It was his dark hair, which he had gotten cut short, military-style, over lunch after listening to the morning news.

'What the hell's going on?' David asked from behind the sofa as the press in the room began to buzz with muted conversations at the unprecedented interruption. Melissa arched her neck to peer back at him. He was just back from a run, and his shoulders still glistened with perspiration despite his shower.

The President returned to the podium, his face creased with concern as he cleared his throat. He looked down at his notes, flipped through several cards and then said, simply, 'At the appropriate time, I will . . . I will be able to give you more information, but for now I'll turn it over to . . . to General Halcomb, here.'

David walked around the sofa and pulled one foot up to the sofa's arm, his leg covered by the mottled black, brown, and green of the camouflaged pants that Melissa had not seen for years. His eyes glued to the screen, David did not see her watching him as he laced his black boots.

The President left the podium, putting his glasses in his pocket, and followed the man who had interrupted him to the door of the Briefing Room amid a thunderous torrent of questions from the media.

'Mr President, Mr President, are U.S. forces engaged in combat right now?' 'Mr President, was it a mistake to withdraw U.S. ground troops before reunification?' 'Does the Russians' war with China have anything to do with the North Koreans' invasion?'

As the door closed behind the President, General Halcomb stepped up to the podium and raised his hand for quiet.

'I have no announcements,' the army general said after the room quieted, 'other than the following. "All leaves of U.S. military personnel are hereby canceled. All members of the 1st Infantry Division (Mech) are to report to Fort Riley, Kansas – immediately. All members of the 2nd Infantry Division – Fort Ord, California."' He looked up from his notebook. 'Unless I say otherwise, all orders mean immediately, by fastest available transport.' He looked back down. '"Fourth Infantry Division (Mech) – Fort Carson, Colorado. Seventh Infantry Division (Light) – Fort Lewis, Washington. Twenty-fourth Infantry Division

(Mech) – Fort Stewart, Georgia. Thirty-eighth Infantry Division (Army National Guard) – your Army Reserve Centers in Indiana.'"

The list went on for thirty minutes, but David was gone in ten.

RUSSIAN DEFENSE MINISTRY, MOSCOW
June 11, 0445 GMT (0645 Local)

'It's a complete mobilization,' the colonel said as he sat in front of the television screen with headphones on, having long since ceased the verbatim translation of the President's address and the military's call-up that followed.

Marshal Gribachov placed his telephone back into its cradle, and the other marshals of STAVKA – the Russian military's Supreme High Command – turned their attention from the television screen to the head of the long table. 'Our nuclear control orders have been received. General Razov reports that the weapons locks on the twenty-five ICBMs – nineteen in the first volley and six more in reserve – have been removed. Their status indicates "Ready" for "Launch at Designated Time."' He looked at the men before him. 'I have given him final authority to fire.'

'What about the Americans?' the commander of the RVSN, the Russian Strategic Rocket Forces, asked as he looked at the television screen.

'Razov called General Thomas. The Americans have been alerted.'

'Did you see the way they pulled President Livingston away in the middle of his speech?' the commander of the Western Strategic Direction asked. 'It makes me nervous. The Chinese watch CNN too, you know.'

'And so what?' the commander of the RVSN challenged. 'The President got pulled away by pressing matters related to the Korean War that they are about to enter, if they in fact intend to enter the fight.'

'They are going in,' Marshal Gribachov, commander of the Supreme High Command, said from his seat at the head of the table.

'And the missiles will be fired automatically?' the commander of the Western Strategic Direction asked.

'It's just a matter of time now,' Gribachov said.

'And may God have mercy on our souls,' the old marshal in charge of Naval Shipyards intoned.

There was a knock at the door and an aide entered, closing the heavy door behind him with a loud metallic pop of its latch. 'It is General Zorin, sir,' he said to Gribachov. 'He has arrived in response to your summons.'

'Oh,' the old marshal said with a sigh, and turned to the gathering with a questioning look. When no one objected, he said, 'We are through here. Send him in.'

The marshals had barely finished collecting and covering the papers spread out on the table detailing the supersecret launch plan when the door opened and in walked General Zorin, not alone as would have been more appropriate for the censure that was planned but with his entourage of aides. There were so many of them, as always, that several of the older men exchanged looks. One leaned over and whispered, 'Like an American prizefighter.'

Zorin eyed the fat men slumped in their padded chairs around the rosewood table as his aides began to mount charts and maps on the wall behind him.

'I thought it was we who had summoned you, General Zorin,' Marshal Gribachov rasped.

'I have come here to speak to you about the survival of our nation,' Zorin said in a low voice, his eyes slowly panning the long conference table to take in each of the men present in turn. 'The time has come to take action.' He was annoyed by the rustling noise of the paper maps behind him, which stole, he thought, some of the drama of the moment.

'To take what action, might I ask?' Gribachov said, settling back into his chair with a twinkle in his eye.

Zorin turned to the area maps as the aides were tacking them onto the corkboards on the conference room wall. Walking up to the largest of the maps, Zorin extracted a silver telescopic pointer from his jacket pocket and pulled it to full extension with a snap. He waited impatiently as an aide put the last tacks in the edge of a map that hung loosely and then stepped clear. Zorin slapped the pointer down sharply onto Poland, onto the blue boxes with unit markings hand drawn on the paper.

He turned to look at the marshals and picked up the pointer, slapping it down again with added force a little below its previous position.

The commander of the Black Sea Fleet cleared his throat and said, 'Are these your vacation plans or has Switzerland somehow offended our national pride?' Several of the marshals erupted in laughter, and Zorin looked back at the map and moved the pointer to its intended position in the Slovak Republic, to the other blue unit markers drawn there.

'No, Admiral,' Zorin replied. 'But I and thousands of other patriotic Russians are outraged at this government's reaction, or lack of reaction, to these American deployments!' Zorin saw the amusement drain from the men's faces at his outright insubordination. 'They have put troops right on the borders of our country! Two divisions, plus corps-level combat support and four tactical fighter wings! Over sixty thousand troops!'

Old Marshal Gribachov at the head of the table drew a deep breath
noisily into his lungs through his nose. 'I suppose by "our" borders you
mean the borders of Ukraine and Byelarus – "Greater Russia," as you
so artfully called it in that interview with the London *Times*.' Gribachov
shook his head and leaned forward to the table. 'You and we both know
what they are doing. The Poles and Slovaks pissed in their pants when
we declared martial law and redeployed into Byelarus, which seemed
to greatly amuse you at the time. Held a party at the Metropole, if
I am not mistaken, which was also reported in the Western press.
Your picture was even on the front page of the *Time* magazine issue
dedicated to what we had hoped would be a change in power that would
not be viewed as a threat to the West, and the article about you in that
shaded box was entitled what? "The Dark Horses." I never understood
what that meant?' Gribachov said, turning to look at the translator who
still sat hunched by the television.

There was a smattering of laughter around the table at the derision
evident in the voice of Gribachov, who knew exactly what the
expression meant, and then Gribachov continued. 'We went to great
lengths to reassure the West that we posed no threat, but you give
quotes to *Red Star* magazine that make you sound like the second
coming of Genghis Khan! And *you* view their action as provocative?
The Americans want nothing to do with Eastern Europe, that much is
clear from their absurdly public debates on policy, but the administration
was trapped.'

'That is just what they want you to think!' Zorin shouted, breaking
the silence with a jolt for effect. 'Don't you see what's happening?' He
slammed his hand down onto the conference table. Zorin abandoned the
numbers he had memorized and the computer projections displayed on
the charts and graphs behind him and pled from his heart, recounting
from memory the litany of indignities to the old men. 'Our borders have
been reduced to what they were *three hundred years* ago! We have all
sat here,' he continued, waving his arm to take in the marshals, his
seniors, 'listening to you disparage the pathetically weak bureaucrats in
Parliament and at the Kremlin who did nothing as the country spiraled
into disorder, cutting deals with the provinces just to hold Russia itself
together.'

'And so we have done something!' the commander of the Western
Strategic Direction said. 'We took power, kicked the bastards out onto
the street.'

'And then we ourselves do nothing!' Zorin exclaimed, feeling the
emotions flood in and his eyes almost fill with tears. He was exhausted
from weeks of sleepless nights in preparation for this big moment, and
he had to fight for control of himself. 'Do you not all remember the night
we spent in this very room listening to reports of the rapes and murders
of Russians – of families of our *own* men, even officers – as our troops

and fellow countrymen fled from Central Asia during the withdrawals? And when our men fired in self-defense, what did our government's "friends" in the West do? Sanctions!' Zorin shouted. 'The West gives our people free food and clothing and saps their will to work on the one hand, and then they *crush* our efforts at competition with sanctions on the other! Meanwhile their businessmen swarm over the carcass like hyenas to buy everything we have for a *fraction* of what it's worth! And the dollars they pay for the gold and diamonds and oil and everything else they take away from Russia barely cover the *interest* they charge on the *money* they have loaned us to buy *their goods*! Everything goes right back into *their* pockets! What we have is *theirs*, and what *they* have is theirs! Don't you see what they're *doing*?'

His aides, men his age and younger risen to the rank of major or colonel, listened with rapt attention, but the old men sat impassively. None of what he was saying registered on the members of STAVKA, but on he went, red-faced and determined to have his say at last.

'And the *Kazakhs*! When the Japanese launches began at Baykonyr, at the Cosmodrome that *we* built there, do they begin their profit-sharing payments as agreed? *No*! We suddenly owe them an "environmental clean-up charge"!' Zorin saw the commander in chief of the Southwestern Strategic Direction roll his eyes to his counterpart from the Air Defense Forces, amused by Zorin's tirade. 'Our soul,' Zorin shouted, 'our very soul is being auctioned off to foreigners. *Foreigners*! Our national treasures – the Tsarist antiquities in the Hermitage and the Kremlin's Oruzheynaya Palata, the French Impressionist artwork in the Pushkinskiy Museum . . .'

'Which we took from Hitler,' the commander of Construction Troops chortled, 'and he took from Paris!' He laughed at the humor of his comment, the laugh turning into a hacking cough through which Zorin waited, watching as the old man's meaty jowls began to glow crimson and he spat loudly into his handkerchief.

'It's a three-stage plan,' Zorin said, moving to the first table on the wall and slapping his pointer onto it in fine staff officer fashion. 'First, redeploy into Ukraine, the Baltic countries, and Kazakhstan.'

The marshals all spoke up at once.

'I thought first might be "defeat the Chinese"?' said the commander of Protivovozdushnaya Oborona Strany, or PVO-Strany, – the air defense force that is the Russian NORAD. 'Do you have a plan for that?'

'What?' Zorin asked theatrically and with genuine amusement. 'Your fair-haired General Razov hasn't been able to brush his little situation aside?'

'It's not a situation, it's a war,' Gribachov said with irritation that was growing evident, 'and it's not General Razov's war, it is Russia's war. Our war. One to which, I might add,' he said, pointing at Zorin's charts, 'we have committed the vast majority of the forces on which you undoubtedly count to implement your little Napoleonic scheme.'

'You all know there is a way to end the war with China,' Zorin said coldly. 'The plans have been circulating since the fighting last time, since Razov became Hero of the People with his little winter skirmish! We could end the war once and for all if we just summon the will to use all the weapons at our disposal. We could end the threat from China for a *hundred* years!' he shouted, again slamming the table with his hand. Several of the old men exchanged looks. *They know what I'm talking about*, Zorin thought in disgust, *but they're too weak even to spill Asian blood*.

After a long silence, Zorin said, 'Stage Two: demand the immediate withdrawal of all American troops from Eastern Europe.'

'And just why are they going to do that?' another marshal asked Zorin.

'Because we *will* them to,' Zorin said, leaning in a gap between two marshals out over the conference table. 'And because they are stretched too thin. Unless they intend to send their relatively unprepared reservists into war on the Korean peninsula,' Zorin said, nodding at the picture of the White House Briefing Room on television, 'they will have to extract their front line troops from Europe, won't they?'

There was silence from the officers, and Zorin's gaze finally settled on Marshal Gribachov, whose eyes drilled back into his own. 'Did you have something to do with General Pak's decision to invade South Korea?' Gribachov asked.

Zorin smiled, enjoying his transition from staff officer to actor on the world stage. 'It does put the Americans in a bind, doesn't it?'

'And when you retake Kazan, Dmitri the Terrible,' the commander of the Western Strategic Direction said to Zorin in a sudden burst of mockery, 'do you plan to build your own commemoration in Red Square or just rechristen St Basil's to mark the event?'

The insult and laughter that followed chilled Zorin to the bone, and time for him moved slowly now. He turned to Gribachov and got a disappointed shake of the old man's head. Suddenly, the beauty and grandeur of the wood-paneled room, with its plush Oriental rug, heroic works of art, and towering gold samovar seemed but an oasis amid the despair and poverty into which all else had fallen. And at the center of the oasis were these dozen old men, still growing fat on the fruits of their position, having grown too fat and too old to do anything to stem the tide of decline.

'You have tempted fate,' Gribachov said finally, 'first with the Americans, and now with us. You have played a high-risk game with the Americans, the results of which you do not fully understand, and in so doing have imperiled the very nation you sought to protect. And the game you have obviously played with us, General Zorin – it too has its risks.' He picked up the phone in front of him on the table. 'Send for Major Lubyanov,' he said, not waiting for Zorin's Stage Three. He replaced the receiver, smug in a confidence born of years of nearly supreme authority and power. Looking up at Zorin, he said, 'You are relieved of your duties. Return to your office and remain there until we call.'

Zorin's face betrayed nothing as he strode from the room. As the last of Zorin's aides shut the door, a loud popping sound from inside the heavy wood indicated that the latch had engaged, and now all was quiet.

Major Lubyanov, head of the STAVKA security detail, arrived with four soldiers in full combat gear and approached Zorin and his silent aides.

Lubyanov and his men stopped in front of Zorin, and for an instant a flicker of doubt passed through Zorin's mind. But Lubyanov said, 'They didn't go for it?' and Zorin relaxed. Of course his plans would work. He was a master at planning, and always had been. It had been his plans from right here in Moscow that had been used by Razov in the first border clashes with China last year that had earned Razov, junior to Zorin by many years, his fame and early promotions. Razov had ad-libbed, deviating slightly as the situation dictated, but it had nonetheless been Zorin's logistics schedules, tables of organization and equipment, and charts of every factor from petroleum-oil-lubricant consumption to unit morale that had won those first battles. The fact that fighting was raging on Chinese territory today and not Russian was due to those planning successes.

'Does everybody know what to do?' Zorin asked the officers gathered outside the conference room.

The men were silent, wavering.

'We – *we* would bring them the victory,' Zorin lashed out in muted tones at the hesitant group, jabbing a finger at the closed conference room door, 'and *they* would rise to the reviewing stand, waving their fat hands in the air and listening to the "U-u-r-r-a-a-hs!" of the troops. We showed them the way. It's as clear as the noses on their bloated faces! If we do nothing, it's over. We spend the rest of our careers' – he paused – 'no, *we* go to prison, and the army becomes a glorified border patrol – first at the Chinese border and then at the Urals – keeping the Asians out of Europe for the next few centuries until we're so inbred that *we're* the Asians!'

'We've always accepted it as our historical duty,' one aide said, seizing upon the higher goal, 'to hold the Asians off at the back door of Europe.'

'The only people prospering in Russia are the Ukrainians and the Georgians,' another aide said. 'The "Mafia."'

'And the Jews,' a third added.

'The old fools' decrepit minds are closed,' Zorin said. 'They just want to live out the remainder of their padded lives. But they could have *saved* our country! And now they feel they've seen the last of us. We've had our chance. We just had to wait our turn and then we too would be able to feed at the trough, but now we've thrown it all away. That's what they're thinking.'

Zorin watched carefully for the nodding heads and mentally segregated those loyal officers from the thoughtful ones who indicated nothing, not wanting to betray their reservations. They all knew the contingency plans if the marshals rejected the proposal. The contacts had already been made, with Major Lubyanov and his security detail, with communications and others. 'But this could be a blessing in disguise,' Zorin said. 'It's forced our hand.'

There was no more discussion. No words were spoken about the morality of their act. *After all*, Zorin thought, glancing one last time at the familiar door into the main STAVKA conference room, *the old men's hands are hardly clean. The same had been done on their orders before.*

They dispersed and moved quickly. Calls were made. The commander of the Taman Division, whose troops were already in their armored vehicles on the streets nearby, was called. A captain in the central communications facilities.

And, of course, the ordnance specialists.

General Zorin himself approached the two officers, one major and one captain, from the RVSN, the Russian Strategic Rocket Forces, as they sat in a small waiting area of the command facility. One was reading the Russian language version of *Der Zeitung*, the other rested his head on his hand, trying to nap while sitting. The two *chyorny chemodanchiki*, the 'little black suitcases' with their nuclear code books and communicators, rested at their feet.

'Major, I am General Zorin. I have been instructed to order you two to hand over your communicators.'

The men stared at Zorin, suddenly alert. 'I'm sorry, sir,' the senior officer said. 'We're not allowed to release them to anyone other than the relief officers, no matter who orders it.'

Zorin eyed them for a second, and then nodded, saying, 'You're entirely correct, Major,' and turned to leave. As he did, he reached into his tunic and retrieved his 9-mm silenced Makarov automatic. When Zorin turned back, the major was fumbling with his own shoulder holster and the captain was looking at him wide-eyed. The hollow explosion and jerk of the pistol in Zorin's hand surprised him, even though he had meant to pull the trigger. The thonk of the bullet's firing and distinct clacking of the slide blown back and then returned forward by its spring was loud but relatively low in pitch and would not pierce the insulated doors and walls of the STAVKA conference room.

A large black stain appeared around the single jagged tear in the breast pocket of the major's jacket as he slipped out of the chair and crumpled wide-eyed to the floor. His body's fall was impeded by his legs, which bent back under him at the knees.

Zorin turned to the captain, whose jaw was slack. The pistol jerked again as a terrific red splatter sprayed the wall behind the padded chair on which the captain sat, his face shattered by the bullet that struck squarely along the bridge of his nose. Zorin picked up the two black briefcases and walked to the door. Standing in the open doorway, he hesitated, forcing himself to turn around and look back at the first two people he had ever killed. It was curious how little the sight affected him. Neither the gore of the captain's head nor the open-eyed, vacant stare of the major had the effect he had expected. There was no shocking sense of the finality of the act he had just taken, just two lifeless forms sprawled across their chairs.

He closed the door, distracted – and somewhat disappointed – by the absence of any stronger emotions.

Frustrated by the communication problems, the commanders of the Ukrainian Strategic Direction and of Long-Range Aviation – generals in the Russian Army who had risen to the exalted honorary title of 'Marshal' – left the conference room and headed for their offices upstairs. As they got to the elevator of the secure inner sanctum in which they met, they saw two nervous soldiers in full combat gear instead of the usual dress uniform of STAVKA. The soldiers stepped in front of the elevator doors, blocking any access.

'Get the hell out of my way!' the commander of the Ukrainian Strategic Direction ordered.

One of the soldiers shouted, 'Starshi-*na-a-a*!' down the hallway – calling for the senior sergeant – but stood his ground in front of the elevator. '*Starshina-a-a*!' he shouted again, glancing nervously from the generals to the hallway behind them.

The old generals froze. They immediately sensed the danger of the situation – of the reaction of the soldiers to them, of the emptiness of the normally busy offices – which was so unlike that to which they were accustomed. The sound of brisk footsteps caused the old men to break their stares and turn to see the Starshina, a senior noncommissioned officer, walking toward them. 'If the generals would please return to the conference room, I have been instructed to inform you that there is an important communication awaiting you there.'

In the end, they returned at gunpoint, the faces in the conference room growing pale when they looked into the eyes of the returning generals and the muzzles of the rifles behind them. The two men sat and described what had happened in monotones. Some of the other officers grew irate and strode to the door, but it was now barred from the outside. Telephones were lifted from their cradles, but they were now completely dead – not even an apologetic operator promising to look into the problem.

Gribachov pounded the table. 'How could we have been so *stupid*!' he said, shaking his head in disbelief that he had relied on the one telephone call to security to ensure Zorin's arrest. *One little detail overlooked*, he thought. *How*? But he knew the answer. *Complacency*, he thought as two of the old marshals stood at the door attempting to hoist a plush leather chair into the air for use as a battering ram. *The power*, Gribachov thought. *I grew too comfortable with—*

In the next few hundredths of a second, the insulated subfloor of the conference room vaporized in the initial flash of heat from the 110 pounds of high explosives placed in the storage room below. The bomb had lost little of its potency despite its almost twenty-year wait on the shelf of the ordnance storage facility of what had been the Soviet Union's Komitet Gosudarstvennoy Bezopasnosty, the KGB. Designed to be buried in an air pocket under a paved street, the charge was molded into an arc and detonated in a burn calculated to direct its explosive force upward.

After the flash vaporized the insulation, the blast wave hit the cables, beams, hardwood flooring, and Oriental carpet of the conference room above with the force of a speeding freight train. The wood flooring shattered into tiny splinters and the steel reinforcement beams bent straight upward along the walls. The fragile flesh and bones of the old men were, together with the rug, chairs, and table, disintegrated by the force of the blast wave and the shredding of the wood splinters that the wave of pressure carried and then flash-burned to ash by the heat of the energy released in the explosion. All the contents of the room were carried up through the empty consoles in the communications room above and embedded into that room's concrete ceiling and walls.

The force of the bomb could be felt through the soles of the feet of the old babushkas sweeping the streets on their late-night shift throughout that area of Moscow. The women closest to the blast on the street outside the ministry stopped for a moment to look at each other and wait for something more. But there was nothing more. The underground command facility was now a tomb, the echoes in the enclosed spaces dying down quickly and giving way to the dark and the quiet more common at the cavelike depth of the hollowed space.

WASHINGTON, D.C.
June 11, 0445 GMT (2345 Local)

Greg Lambert's car raced through the dark streets of the capital as he listened to General Thomas brief the President in the threeway conference call, the alarm set off by the White House military switchboard blaring in the background of the President's phone.

'I've got it,' the President said. 'They just handed it to me. "White House Emergency Procedures Manual." I'll bring it with me. Now what's going to happen?'

'The E-4B will be ready at Andrews,' Thomas said. 'I'll meet you there, sir.'

'Will the Chinese hit the Russians back?' the President asked, and Lambert cringed as his driver barely slowed before heading through the red light at an intersection and then gunned the growling engine again.

'No, sir,' Thomas replied, the whine of his helicopter engine starting up in the background. 'Their generation time is too slow. They've probably squirreled away some tactical nukes somewhere, but they'd have a hard time delivering them through Russia's air defenses to anything other than purely tactical targets.'

'And DEFCON 3 – what exactly does that entail?' the President asked.

'Going from the normal DEFCON 5 to DEFCON 3 sets in motion a variety of things,' Thomas said, raising his voice over the engine noise until the helicopter door was slammed shut and the background noise diminished. 'Dispersion of forces, higher alert statuses, et cetera, for all forces other than the forces actually engaged in Korea, which are already on 1, and the strategic forces at Air Combat Command, which are on 2. It'll put shorter range nuclear weapons – the navy's cruise missiles and carrier-based nuclear-capable A-6s and F/A-18s – on Combat Alert Status along with the ground-launched cruise missiles and FB-111s and F-16s in Europe. I've also ordered the ACC bombers from ground alert into the air on Minimum Interval Takeoffs, twelve seconds in between. They'll stand by on airborne alert. In addition, Alternate Reconstitution Base teams, which set up air bases to receive ACC bombers after return, have been dispatched to their sites at civilian airports and various stretches of interstate highway around the country and in Europe. It also means emergency combat capability – maximum possible generation – out of the ICBMs, and subs to their firing stations.'

'Is it really necessary to evacuate like this?'

'Mr President, we're assuming Attack Condition Bravo, sufficient warning to evacuate full staffs. If it should turn out to be Alpha –

surprise destruction of peacetime headquarters – we'll be down to skeletal staffs at all branches of military and government.'

'But we're not even under attack. I don't see why – '

'Evacuation is automatic with DEFCON 3, sir,' Lambert interrupted. 'This has never happened before, Mr President, because we've never had anything like it. The Russians are going to launch ICBMs, missiles that are alternately aimed at this country, from silos in Siberia. They switched from the old single-target tapes years ago. Those missiles now have stored in their targeting banks cities and military facilities in the U.S. We won't get confirmation that their targets are in fact in China until those missiles complete their burns and roll over to the south – somewhere between six and eight minutes after launch. Until then, we have no way of knowing, other than General Razov's word, that they are heading to China. We have to play it safe. If those ICBMs are in fact coming this way in a coordinated attack, the SLBMs from Russian submarines in the Atlantic fired on a depressed trajectory would be just eight to ten minutes away from D.C.' The thought sickened him, and he mentally urged Jane on. 'There is the risk of a decapitation strike, sir.'

'Now wait a minute,' the President said. 'Is there any reason to expect that this is a Russian surprise attack, for God's sake?' He sounded exasperated, and he was clearly growing angry.

'Sir,' Lambert said, reiterating, 'the issue at a time like this is stability. Getting you airborne, sir, buys us time to stay ahead of things. We don't want any mistakes.'

'Shit,' the President said. 'I've got State ringing up foreign governments to tell them what's happening and what we're doing, and I'm already starting to get calls back. "Chancellor Gerhardt – holding, line two",' he said, obviously reading. '"Prime Minister Barrow." I've got to take some of these. What am I going to tell them? Who all are we evacuating?'

'JEEP, the Joint Emergency Evacuation Plan,' General Thomas said, 'calls for immediate evacuation by army and air force helicopter of forty-six JEEP-1 cardholders. They're mainly people in the line of presidential succession who're tracked by the Automated Central Locator System, but they're also key military leaders, Mr Lambert, and others, necessary to ensure continuity of government. Within four hours, two hundred forty-eight JEEP-2 cardholders – other senior officials, personnel in key posts at various agencies who happen to be on duty, and FEMA employees – will have been evacuated to ensure continuity of operations.'

'So how the hell are we going to run the government tomorrow morning?' the President asked as Lambert checked his wallet for his Federal Employee Emergency Identification Card. He found it just behind his racquetball club card. All it had was his name, picture, blood type, and the message, 'THE PERSON DESCRIBED ON THIS CARD HAS ESSENTIAL EMERGENCY DUTIES WITH THE FEDERAL GOVERNMENT. REQUEST FULL ASSISTANCE AND UNRESTRICTED MOVEMENT BE AFFORDED THE PERSON TO WHOM THIS CARD IS ISSUED.' Lambert turned the card over. Printed in large block letters was 'JEEP-1.'

'Well, sir,' Thomas said, 'in a couple of hours the Joint Air Transportation Service will start evacuating Category A Relocation Teams – skeleton staffs consisting of several dozen people from each department and key agency split into three teams, each going to a different location. By the end of the day, they'll have moved Category B Teams – people from the National Science Foundation, the FDIC, people like that. All Category C agency personnel, and all government personnel who aren't part of the relocation teams, should be getting 'Advanced Alert' phone calls from their superiors telling them to pack up and stand by. They in turn pass the alert to the next tier down on their organizational chart, and it goes on and on.'

'Where is everybody going?' President Livingston asked as Lambert saw the lights of the White House, its lawns brightly lit by floodlights, so stark in contrast to the other buildings mostly dark on this Sunday night.

'Well, the airborne evacuees,' General Thomas said, 'will just orbit. We'll send one E-4B with a presidential successor down to the Southern Hemisphere out over the mid-Atlantic, but the rest will remain over the continental United States. Everybody else goes to emergency relocation sites within the "Federal Arc" – within three hundred miles of D.C. – or to alternate command posts. You go to "Kneecap," the National Emergency Airborne Command Post, and the civilian government goes to Mount Weather or to the Alternate National Military Command Center at Raven Rock Mountain. And, I might add, there are several thousand state, county, and city blast-and-fallout-resistant emergency operations centers that were constructed to ensure continued local government. They're receiving the warning and should also be staffing up. I'm sorry, sir,' Thomas said, 'but I've got a call coming in from the Pacific Command. I'd better see what this is.'

'Okay, General Thomas. See you at Andrews. Greg, are you still there?'

'Yes, sir,' Lambert said as they pulled up to the White House gate.

'Okay. I'm going to take Barrow's and Gerhardt's calls. You get me Secretary Moore at State. I'm switching to this portable thing they're handing me and heading down to the South Lawn. I'll just be a second – you stay on the line with Moore.'

Instead of calling Jane on her car phone, as he had hoped to do, Lambert dialed the number of the White House switchboard. 'This is Greg Lambert. Get me the Secretary of State.'

'One moment, sir,' the operator said calmly, recognizing his voice and not wasting time with the new voice ID system that he knew the old ladies at the switchboard hated. Lambert's car pulled to a stop in the drive just by the South Lawn. Through the bushes he could see security personnel fanning out from the building.

'Greg?' the voice of Secretary Moore came from the speakerphone, the sound of a racing engine in the background.

'Bill, just a minute, the President wants to talk to you.'

'Helluva deal, hey, Greg?' the Secretary asked, but before Lambert could answer they heard 'Bill? Greg? Anyone there?'

'Yes, sir, Mr President,' Lambert said. 'We're both here.'

The bright landing lights of a helicopter descended with surprising speed to the lawn. It was not the dark green Marine One that normally carried the President, but a squat gray air force helicopter. 'Bill, listen to me. I want you to call the Chinese and tell them what's coming.'

'But sir . . .!' Lambert began.

'I will *not* be a party to this!' the President declared, and in the background Greg heard the voice of the director of the White House Military Office say, 'Mr President, Crown Helo has landed.'

'Look, Greg, we're pregnant with this, and I refuse to go down in history as tacitly endorsing the Russians' use of nuclear weapons by sitting on this information! Bill, you call Beijing directly and you warn them – right now! Where are you headed?'

'Raven Rock Mountain, sir,' Secretary Moore said.

'You call them,' President Livingston said just as Lambert noticed a large group of Secret Service agents emerge from the White House, 'then you report back to me when you get there.'

'Mr President!' Greg said, getting out of the car as he saw the President and First Lady head down the steps to the South Lawn. The helicopter's engines were deafening – the pilot kept the rotors turning at high speed. 'Sir!' Lambert shouted as he plugged one ear and began to trot across the lawn to meet the President at the helicopter door. 'We'd better think about whether – '

'What?' he heard faintly from the phone. 'I can't hear you!'

'Secretary Moore!' Lambert yelled as the branch of an unseen bush smacked his face. Lambert immediately stared down the barrel of an Uzi machine pistol; the red glow of a laser shone, he looked down to see, a tiny red dot of light on his chest. 'Secretary Moore!' Lambert shouted again, but as he looked up he saw the President at the door of the helicopter; his portable phone hung loosely in his hand as he spoke with the director of the White House Military Office.

'ID!' the agent with the Uzi snapped.

'Goddammit! It's Greg Lambert!' A flashlight flicked on from the right, and Lambert turned to face the glare of the bright light that shone in his face. 'It's okay! He's clear!' the second agent said, shutting off the light. Lambert immediately dashed for the helicopter.

At opposite sides of the lawn two pairs of Secret Service agents in dark suits stood, one of the men in each team with a slender tube, a Stinger missile, Lambert realized, mounted on his shoulder and pointing skyward. He hoped National Airport had gotten the word to divert their air traffic. On the ground at the door of the helicopter, three men in full combat gear knelt with rifles pointed out.

Lambert stooped under the rotor and dashed in the helicopter door, squeezing between the banks of electronic equipment in search of the President. Through the maze of crewmen seated in the aircraft jammed with gear he saw the Livingstons looking unsettled in their unfamiliar places, strapped into cramped bucket seats. The White House military aide – the air force officer carrying the nuclear code case known as the 'football' – was the last person to board, and the helicopter lifted off before the crew shut the door. Lambert and the military aide struggled to maintain their balance for the next minute or so as the helicopter maneuvered recklessly. Finally a crewman scrambled to shut the door and ushered Lambert to a lone fold-out seat. He strapped himself in, looking out the tiny porthole to see that they were flying at extremely low altitude. Lambert felt another steep bank just in time to see the brightly lit Washington Monument streak by his window. He leaned out to try to catch sight of the President down the narrow passageway to the rear of the helicopter, but a rack of equipment cut him from view. He even thought about trying to call the President from his portable phone, but he knew it would be too late. Secretary Moore would have already made his call.

The glowing Jefferson Memorial streaked by the small window, and Lambert felt faintly nauseous from the gyrations of the hurtling helicopter. The volume of the rotors was intense and vibrated through the metal wall at his back. The helicopter began a pattern of pitching first left, then right. *They're dodging imaginary antiaircraft missiles*! he realized. *Of course. Evasive maneuvering.* The helicopter's pilots who trained for this flight naturally prepared only for wartime conditions.

Lambert took a deep breath and tried to relax, settling back to watch the familiar sights streak by his small window. On one steep bank over the Potomac he saw the old buildings of Georgetown University, his alma mater, silhouetted against the city lights for an instant before they disappeared as the pilot threw the helicopter into another steep bank. *He's following the river*, Lambert guessed.

He was in his own private world, cut off from the others by the straps holding him to his seat and the noise filling the speeding aircraft. For the first time in days, he found himself idle. His mind wandered, and he let it drift.

Jane. Images of her floated before the dark and dimly reflective porthole like lilies in a pond. Though they were both now thirty-eight years old, Jane was almost unchanged from their days at Georgetown, her freshly scrubbed face still looking made up even when it wasn't. They were the kind of couple who gets greedily snatched up by the social circles of Washington – he, tall, blond, blue-eyed, a rising star; she, petite, auburn-haired, demure.

They had met their freshman year at Georgetown. He was at a shoot-around meeting his new teammates and coaches when a number of women had filed in for gymnastics tryouts. The girl on the end nearest him was Jane. He'd asked her to marry him their senior year, but she had refused. He had been accepted to Harvard Law School and had been drafted in the third round by the New Jersey Nets. Jane had replied she didn't think he was ready to make a decision like marriage with so much up in the air. He smiled, remembering. He had taken a wild guess that she was bluffing, insecure about his possible sports stardom, and wanted him to beg her, which he did. They were married in June.

His pre-NBA summer camp had been disheartening. A lowly seventh rounder at his position was the surprise star of the Nets' rookie review. Greg had declined the 'invitation' to try out in the fall. 'What would you think if I joined the army?' he had asked Jane on the plane to Maine after camp. She had laughed, not realizing he was serious.

Four years later, at age twenty-five, Greg had graduated Harvard with a law degree and a Masters in government. During the spring of his final year he had been approached by the CIA after a professor had anonymously recommended him. Greg had politely declined to interview for a job in Operations – for work in the field. He had asked, however, if there might be an opening in Intelligence. A few weeks later he had gotten a letter responding to his 'inquiry' about a position with the *Defense* Intelligence Agency. He had never even heard of it before.

And so they had returned to Washington. *Thirteen years ago*, he thought in amazement at how quickly time had passed. His first job at DIA had been excruciatingly boring – academic papers on the Soviet economy. His only excitement at work had come from his few trips to 'The Farm,' the CIA training facility in West Virginia. Every Friday the DIA had posted a list of weekend courses at The Farm that had open slots, and he had enrolled in the few that seemed somewhat exciting and dangerous.

Success at DIA had come quickly and unexpectedly. Having studied Russian at Georgetown's School of Foreign Service, he had been assigned the tedious job of compiling the increasingly dismal Soviet economic data from the late eighties. At the end of his reports, he had always thrown in unsolicited opinions about the Soviet Union. Unwittingly, he had chronicled the demise of the U.S.S.R.

In 1991 the intelligence community had still been reeling from its failure to predict Iraq's invasion of Kuwait the year before. As the Soviet Union's impending collapse became more and more apparent, his reports had been dusted off and he'd been trotted out as having predicted it years in advance. Quotes from his reports had been taken out of context. He had been put forward by the DIA to give testimony to the Senate Foreign Relations Committee. 'Insiders' at cocktail parties were abuzz with paraphrased 'predictions' he had supposedly made. He'd quickly become known as the guy who first 'called' the decline and fall of the U.S.S.R., and it was the call of the century. His fifteen minutes of fame.

Two months after the collapse, an engraved invitation had arrived. A private dinner with George and Barbara Bush. The conversation had turned to calls for a 'peace dividend' that were just beginning to circulate. The President had been concerned they would cut defense only to wake up one morning to find hard-liners at the other end of the hot line. He had been fishing for an opinion, for a call.

The wine had left Greg at ease, and his opinions had come freely. Jane had kicked him repeatedly under the table, but he had plunged into an area – strategic military affairs – for which he had no formal preparation. Russia was going to hell in a handbasket, he had opined. Their military would suffer right along with everything else. 'Just stay one step ahead of them, Mr President. Let them collapse faster than we reduce. Defer the cuts a little bit. Stay ahead of the game.'

'You seem sure of yourself, Greg,' Bush had said as he refilled Greg's wineglass.

'A peace dividend now is too fast, too soon,' he'd said, enamored of the position he had developed only moments before. 'I'd slow-play the cuts. Let the bottom drop out from under the Russians first.' Jane had kicked him so hard that the water glass on the table shook. Barbara Bush had laughed and then taken Jane on a tour of the White House while Greg looked over the preliminary force reduction plans in the Oval Office.

He had said the right things, and from that evening he'd been on the fast track. He had learned military affairs on the job. Even though administrations changed and the bureaucracy forgot why it was that he was a star, the lights on his career path had remained green. Greg was moved from one Crisis Action Team to another, spending more and more of his time in the White House – actually 100 feet beneath the White House, in the Situation Room.

When President-elect Livingston's transition team had requested a national security briefing, the DIA had sent Lambert. Two weeks later Jane's mother had telephoned. Greg's name and picture had been in *U.S. News & World Report* under a list of candidates for national security adviser in the new White House. He and Jane had run out in the rain to buy a copy. The issue, crumpled and fat from having been soaked, still sat in their nightstand. Jane had refused to throw it out. She never threw anything out; the closets were full of old cheerleader uniforms, basketball trophies, and her wedding dress, of course.

'You know we'll have to clean all this stuff out when we have a baby,' he'd said the weekend before last. From the look – the smile – on her face he had said the right thing. He had a knack for saying the right things. They had started trying for a baby that afternoon.

Greg closed his eyes as the helicopter now rose and fell over the dark country roads below. Jane was on one of them. He said a silent prayer, hoping the words he used were the right ones.

Chapter Two

FAR EAST ARMY COMMAND, KHABAROVSK, RUSSIA
June 11, 0450 GMT (1450 Local)

'Oh, it's Zorin all right!' Air Force General Mishin's voice came angrily over General Razov's speakerphone in the hardened wartime bunker deep under his headquarters building. 'His fingerprints are all over this, and the Taman Division – *your* people – are out of their barracks and taking up positions around the Kremlin.'

'Is that where Zorin is headed?' Razov asked. 'The Kremlin?'

'Well, of course!' Mishin yelled. 'The man believes all that hard-line messianic crap, and he's the Messiah!'

'I'll talk to the commander of the Taman Division,' Razov said. 'I know him well. Those men your people have seen are bound to be renegade units.'

'Whatever,' Mishin said. 'What do you want to do now? Do you want to consider postponing your strikes?'

'Absolutely impossible!' Razov said. 'The strategic weapons are all on automated launches at the designated times so that their phasing over targets will be timed correctly. Plus I've got an entire army group on the move right now toward holes in the Chinese lines that had damn well better be there when the lead echelon hits the line of departure. Those lead echelons are going to be close to ground zero as it is, in some cases less than a kilometer away. The timing is crucial.'

'You could just be a little less precise with your timing and use more weapons.'

'We don't have releases on more weapons, and Zorin has the damn nuclear communicators!'

'We could seize the silos and rewire the locks to bypass his communicators.'

'That would take time – maybe even days – and I can't wait. For God's sake, I've already told the Americans, who are busy, I'm sure, telling other NATO governments. Pretty soon, word is going to slip around to the Chinese. No! We've got to go as planned. We go now.'

'What about the Americans' alert orders? I still say we should follow our programs and send out our own alert orders in response.'

'General Thomas is only doing what I expected him to do,' Razov replied.

'But DEFCON 3! It bothers me, Yuri. I have to admit, it bothers me that we're not reacting.'

'You just worry about Zorin.'

'I'll take care of him,' the air force general responded. 'I'm assuming he'll set up shop like *Der Führer* down in the Deep-Underground Command Post, and I'm having my men cut off the Deep-Underground Subways to the Ramenki Facility near the university, and the Ex-Urban NCA and STAVKA facilities a hundred kilometers south of the city. We're also deploying troops at the exits at Vnukovo Airfield. That leaves only the connection here and the air vent and utility access shafts, all of which we'll have guarded.'

'Can you sever his unhardened communications?'

'We can cut everything but direct broadcast satellite and the deep-underground fiber optic emergency communications system – the nuclear command and control system wired into the two communicators. I hate to tip him off too soon, but we'll go ahead and start the process of cutting everything else. His logistics command has had a liaison officer right here at PVO-Strany who has been spying on us and surreptitiously telephoning Zorin on a dedicated line, and we might lay off him for a while to try to lull Zorin into a false sense of security.'

'Just don't let him sit on those nuclear communicators too long, for God's sake!' Razov said, hanging up.

In the silence that followed in the concrete-enclosed bunker, words of warning spoken in English crept into Razov's mind. '*Something will go wrong. Something always goes wrong*!' 'Murphy's Law,' General Thomas had called it. As the words echoed in Razov's head, the first twinge of anxiety rushed through his veins. Razov looked up at the duty officer. 'Get Zorin on the line.'

90TH STRATEGIC MISSILE WING, WARREN AFB, WYOMING
June 11, 0450 GMT (2150 Local)

As the Humvee slowed, Captain Chris Stuart awoke from his doze to see two air policemen with M-16s slung over their shoulders peering down into a silo. A single man with a blue hard hat protruded half out of the concrete mound into the brilliant lights of a trailer rolled up to the side of the silo's opening. The Humvee pulled to a stop just outside the open gate of the twelve-foot chain link fence, and the two technicians in the rear seat squeezed by Captain Scott Langford, Stuart's co-launch officer, and headed for the silo, donning their own hard hats in their vehicle's headlights.

'They got the blast door open on Number Eight,' Langford said, staring at the silo. 'Let's go take a look.'

'Oh, man,' Stuart said, wanting to get down to the center and resume his nap. 'We got an alert order. The shift begins in ten minutes.' *The 'graveyard' shift again*, Stuart thought as he yawned.

'We got time. Come on,' Langford said as he opened the door.

Stuart followed him out into the darkness and put on his 'pee-cutter' air force cap. They returned the salute of the air policeman – standing under the single light at the gate with his M-16 and attached grenade launcher slung over his shoulder – and entered the secure area around the hardened silo. Seeing the officers approach, the two air policemen at the silo opening walked down to the ground toward the gate, saluting as they passed.

The soles of Stuart's boots scuffed on the first of the concrete as the dirt gave way to the pad. Climbing the slope of the mound, he looked up to see that the single hydraulically operated blast door was opened about three feet and that a man hung in the gap by suspension gear hooked to the door itself. He was taking readings of the hydraulic fluids in the system that, in the event of a launch, would hurtle the door open down its internal tracks in a fraction of a second and fling from it any tons of debris that might have accumulated from a near miss. Langford stepped up onto the thick concrete-and-steel door itself. Stuart stayed on the pad to the side and eyed the man in between the door and the opposite wall, which was shaped to conform to the massive door's irregular features, with an involuntary sense of discomfort. *If the door were to close*, Stuart thought, and then shook off the revolting image that his mind manufactured as if solely to test his response.

'Take a look,' Langford said from on top as he peered down into the silo.

'Hey, be careful,' Stuart warned as he edged gingerly toward the opening, remembering the old Titan III missile in Arkansas that had blown and killed everyone around when someone dropped a wrench that penetrated its cellophane-thin fuselage and smashed into the liquid fuel tank.

As Stuart got closer, the silo chamber became visible through the opening and the internal floodlights shone on the cylindrical steel walls. He held onto the door and leaned, seeing the blunt, black nose of the MX missile just beneath the blast door. From a railing about a third of the way down the silo wall, an access bridge extended across the open space to the side of the fuselage, and several men were working on the massive missile. Shouts and the sound of activity drew Stuart's attention to several other crews working at various other points lower down the long jet-black body of the ICBM.

'What's going on?' he asked the sergeant suspended just inside the blast door.

'We were in the middle of the monthly go-over,' the man – Kline from the name stenciled on his breast pocket – replied in a twangy accent, carefully returning each tool to its assigned pouch. He was a senior NCO, Stuart noticed, his job not one entrusted to the young or the faint of heart. 'When the base went to DEFCON 2 they tol' us to close 'er up.'

The three warheads on that old Titan had blown right out of the silo, Stuart remembered. *There are ten warheads on the MX.* 'Let's go, Scott.'

Langford smiled and stood on one foot near the edge of the opening, extending his arms out to either side for balance.

'Fuck you, man,' Stuart said as he turned to walk down from the heavy mound of blast-hardened reinforced concrete. 'Come on.'

As Stuart walked through the darkness between the silo and the gate, a hand slapped his shoulder and he flinched, so slightly that Langford probably didn't notice. 'You're acting like those things are dangerous, sport!' Langford said. 'Don't you know that's the "Peacekeeper" – friend of small animals and schoolchildren alike.'

Stuart smiled, but didn't feel comfortable again until they were in the Humvee and headed to the launch center, several miles away.

DEEP-UNDERGROUND COMMAND POST, THE KREMLIN
June 11, 0455 GMT (0655 Local)

'All right!' Zorin shouted as the officers bombarded him with reports from all sides. The concrete-walled office would pass for Zorin's personal quarters until he solidified his control of the disparate commands. The junior officers stood quietly now in the stark light from bare overhead fixtures that made all the room's contents, material and human, appear harsh and hard-edged. 'Let's just all calm down here. Just calm down.' His voice shook, and he realized that he was exhausted. Two nights in a row with no sleep, and too much coffee to compensate.

'Leave me here,' Zorin said. 'No interruptions – I've got to think.' *Concentrate*! he ordered himself. The humiliation of the half dozen phone calls he had made to commanders of various field units in and around Moscow who all politely refused to comply had stung Zorin badly. He shook his head angrily just after his door was pulled closed.

Zorin stood up and walked over to the sink, the loaded H&K by his side. Even here, 300 meters under the Kremlin in the concrete-enclosed cavern designed for wartime command, Zorin did not feel safe. The mere effort of standing had renewed his painful headache, and, lost in thought, he tapped the medicine bottle to drop another painkiller into his palm. Not the aspirin with which he had started a couple of days ago, but a narcotic from the first aid kit.

Zorin swallowed the pill and looked up into the small mirror. *Oh, God, I need sleep*, he thought, staring at the red, baggy eyes and pale, haggard face. *The pill should take care of my head, but for the sleep?* he thought to himself silently. *Just fifteen minutes and I'll call them back. Fifteen minutes and I'll feel one hundred percent better*. He opened the cabinet doors to the side of the sink and pulled out a bottle of vodka, filling an oversize shot glass.

He turned the glass up, and the warm liquid drained down his throat, causing him to wince slightly as it burned the lining of his stomach. He quickly stuffed into his mouth a half-eaten piece of the hard black bread that sat next to the sink. With his first breath after the shot, his throat caught fire, but before his next breath the vodka had already begun its chemical reaction with the painkiller in his bloodstream, and the little aches and pains began to dull.

Zorin held his now unsettled stomach and walked over to the sofa, his mind growing comfortably blank as he lay the machine pistol on the floor and sank absentmindedly onto the soft cushions. *I'll just close my eyes and think*, Zorin decided and was about to lay his head on a folded wool blanket when he saw that he had not capped the vodka bottle and that the light from the sink would shine right into his eyes on the sofa.

What could the Americans be doing? he wondered as he padded over to the sink. The first communication from his liaison officer at PVO-Strany had reported the inexplicable American alert orders. The nagging concern activated his brain as if a switch had been thrown. His mind raced, lurching from one disjointed thought to a randomly proposed conclusion. By the time he reached the sink, he was cursing the thoughts that ricocheted through his head.

He picked up the bottle and cap and looked into the mirror from which stared the haggard face with the loose necktie twisted off-center. *One more to kill the jitters*, he thought as he poured and drank another large shot. He turned out the sink light and made his way by the bright corridor lights that shone under the crack in the door. He was deep in sleep when there was a knock at the door and it opened.

Zorin stared bleary-eyed at the profile of a man who stood in front of the brilliant light from the corridor. 'I told you no interruptions! What's your name?'

'Melnikov, sir.'

'Melnikov, if you value your career, you follow orders, do you understand? Now, what the hell do you want?'

The officer, in combat gear instead of staff dress uniform, said, 'It's General Razov, sir. He's on the telephone.'

Zorin's head pounded from his own shouting, and with it still burned a blinding red glare of anger. He rose slowly to a sitting position. 'You tell Razov to go to hell! I'm not in any mood to deal. Tell him, once he ceases his interference with my operations I'll talk to him.' The aide left him alone.

Zorin groped his way back to the sink in the dark, rubbing his eyes, which felt as if ice picks were jammed in them. He turned on the light and tried to open the bottle of pain pills, losing his patience and finally tearing at the top. *I've got a few tricks for you too, Razov*! he thought. *Planning, the finest of martial arts*! 'You think you'll just waltz right in here? Hah!' he said out loud as the pills flew out of the bottle and into the sink, aggravating him further. *But what next*? he thought. *What will they try next*? His mind fogged and drew a blank, and he jammed the heels of his hands into his eyes until they hurt. In his exhausted state his frustration level skyrocketed, and he slammed the wall by the sink.

Looking down into the sink through vision blurred from the vigorous rubbing Zorin saw that two of the pain pills were wet. He washed them both down with a shot of vodka before their capsules softened. Calming, he placed the bottle of amphetamines that the medic had provided beside the sink for when he rose and then gargled with mouthwash to rid himself of the reek. 'Got to keep up appearances!' he said out loud, turning off the light and finding his way back to the sofa.

No pain now, he thought, smiling as he lay down to plot his strategy. He was asleep in moments.

MARCH AIR FORCE BASE, RIVERSIDE, CALIFORNIA
June 11, 0500 GMT (2100 Local)

David Chandler pulled his Volvo into an empty parking space and turned the ignition off. He looked down at his car phone. 'No cellular or radio communications allowed on base, sir,' the air policeman had said, saluting David at the gate, forcing him to say his good-bye to Melissa too abruptly.

The quiet night air was split again with the crackling sound of jet engines. That had been the pattern ever since the interstate: a minute or so of quiet, and then a roar. David dipped his head, his hands still gripping the wheel, and looked up into the black night sky through the windshield to spot the departing aircraft. There, over that building, the streaking blue flame appeared as if shot out of thin air, the large body of the black four-engined aircraft sensed rather than seen as the few stars disappeared just before the exhaust flame passed.

He looked around him. He felt stuck, suspended between two worlds. The Volvo was an object from his other life, from the other side of the gulf that he could already feel forming between all that was before and whatever lay ahead. He had bought the car last year when Melissa and he had finally decided it was time to have a baby. In the back, the base to the as yet unused baby seat was buckled onto its seat belt, holding only his basketball in place. Chandler chuckled as he recalled the first time his golf buddies got a look at the car. 'What, do you have to *drive* women away or something?' they had roared with laughter. The 'babe magnet,' they called it.

Everything was quiet again. *How long will the car sit here*, he wondered as he fingered his wedding ring, the only piece of jewelry besides his watch that he had ever worn. The only time he'd ever even come close to taking the ring off his finger since his wedding day was once just out of idle curiosity, to see if it would slide past his second knuckle. It hadn't left his finger, stopping at the nail.

The ring slipped right off. It had to be done: regulations. He reached over, opened the glove compartment, and removed a tissue from a small packet, wrapping the ring in it and placing the package gently into the back of the glove compartment. He closed and locked the compartment's door.

I can't just leave it in the glove compartment, David thought. *They'll never find it*. He got a scrap of paper and a pen and was going to write, 'My ring is in the glove compartment.' *That's it*? he thought. *My ring is in the glove compartment and I loved you from the first moment I laid eyes on you until the very last breath passed from my lips*.

'My wedding ring is in the glove compartment. I love you. David,' he wrote. He left the note face down on the passenger seat.

The words still echoed through David's head even as his feet carried him to the door. 'Ma-a-jor Chandler,' the sergeant had said. 'U.S. Army Reserve. Here we go. Intelligence. Division Staff, 4th Infantry Division.' *Division Intelligence*, Chandler thought. *A staff position at Division Headquarters*. His mental picture of himself sitting at a desk was a bit of a letdown, but it was a relief too. *At least I know how to do that. Years of practice.* 'Flight 1451 – Presov, Slovakia. That'd be through that door.'

Chandler opened the door and entered a huge open hangar filled with soldiers.

'Hey!' a kid said, a private first class's single chevron and rocker pinned on his collar slightly askew. 'Oh, 'scuse me, sir,' he apologized, stiffening up, 'but everybody on this flight's s'posed ta pick up their personal weapons 'fore they process through. I think that means officers too – pro'bly.'

Chandler followed the general body language and nod of the kid to another line in the cavernous hangar. *'Please pick up your personal weapons before you board the plane,'* an imaginary flight attendant was saying in his head. The letdown he'd felt on learning of his presumably comfortable desk job moments earlier now gave way to renewed uncertainty.

At the front of the line, over the door into a steel cage that rose up from the floor of the hangar, Chandler saw the sign ARMORY. There were numerous steel cages all around the hangar, Chandler noticed, each with its own line. *'Ya'll have a good flight now, ya hear,'* Chandler's imaginary flight attendant was now saying, waving cheerily from the jetway as the plane's door was closed.

The guy who had been just ahead of Chandler at the processing desk and was now in this line turned slightly to acknowledge him. 'How'r ya doin', sir?' the man – a master sergeant, Chandler noted – asked.

'Well, okay, I guess,' Chandler said.

BARNES was the name stamped over the man's left breast pocket. The NCO laughed politely as Chandler picked up his suitcase to edge forward.

Chandler looked up at the cage they were approaching and caught sight instead of a man up ahead who was craning his neck to look back in line. The man saw him and nodded, disappearing as he leaned over to pick up his pack and then walking back down the line to Chandler as if they were acquainted.

'Sir! First Lieutenant Bailey, Stanley R., sir!' He was about Chandler's height but thinner, younger.

'How are you doing, Lieutenant,' Chandler said, reaching out to shake his hand before the line moved forward again. After Bailey said hello to Master Sergeant Barnes, an awkward silence descended on the little group.

'I guess we're all headed to Europe,' Bailey finally said, and Barnes and Chandler nodded.

'Slovakia,' Chandler said, and it was Barnes's and Bailey's turn to nod. Chandler noticed that the soldiers around them had grown quiet, their attention discreetly directed to the three men's conversation.

'What unit are you men with?' Chandler asked his companions.

'4th Infantry,' Bailey said. 'Scout Platoon – 1st of the 3rd. I was home on leave.'

Chandler looked at Barnes. 'Same for me. Batt Staff – 2/2.'

They looked at Chandler for a second before Bailey said, 'What about you, sir?'

'Oh. I'm, uh, I'm in the Reserves.' Chandler paused awkwardly before going on. 'I've been assigned to the 4th also. Division Intelligence.'

Bailey raised his eyebrows. Chandler didn't know what that meant. Was he impressed? Or was it one of the scorned staff jobs that soldiers from combat units despised?

They were getting close to the door of the armory-in-a-cage, and Chandler had begun noticing a variety of sounds from inside. There was a constant background noise from the cage – the clicking and jingling sounds of metal on metal, some sharp and light, others dull – that rose over the camouflaged backs of the soldiers ahead. And there was that steely smell. *Weapons*, Chandler thought.

'15813416 – Davis – 649–38–5831!' he heard called out. Rifle and soldier's serial numbers. The procedure was dimly familiar to him. Standard procedure at the rifle rack.

At the door to the cage, a counter with a soft, dented black top became visible. Behind it enlisted personnel rushed off and returned with 'personal weapons.' Most were the standard M-16A2 assault rifle, with its familiar squat, black plastic stock. Chandler felt the first tingle of excitement, and he tried to look as calm and businesslike as the others in line.

'Sixteen!' the first armory worker behind the counter shouted in a high-pitched voice. She was a small woman with short, straight brown hair. A soldier strode over to the rack, jerked a rifle out, and returned to the counter.

Chandler looked down the line that ran at a right angle through the cage along the counter. Some of the soldiers were obviously grenadiers. They got M-16s with an M-203 40-mm grenade launcher attached underneath the rifle's barrel. Others had SAWs, or Squad Automatic Weapons – the army's long-awaited successor to the World War II-era Browning Automatic Rifle. Out of the corner of his eye Chandler caught sight of a tall, broad-shouldered man farther down the line as he threw a 100-round belt of ammunition over his shoulder, the yellow brass standing out starkly against his camo blouse.

Ammunition! Chandler thought with alarm, never having seen ammo this close to weapons anyplace other than at the range. *Jesus*! he craned his neck to see that the man carried an M-60 machine gun. The ammunition on the belt was the old, and noticeably larger, 7.62mm NATO cartridges.

'MOS?' the woman at the counter asked. *Military Occupation Specialty*, Chandler translated.

'Nineteen,' Barnes said. *Infantry*, Chandler thought, trying to remember. *No, Armor*.

She immediately barked over her shoulder. 'Sixte-e-en!'

Chandler racked his brain for his own MOS. *What the hell's the officer's MOS for Intelligence? Thirty-five or something like that? I don't even know my own MOS!*

The woman turned back to face Chandler. 'What flavor, sir?' she asked.

'Pardon me?'

'Your personal weapon. What'd ya like?'

'Well, uh . . . what've you got?' *God, that sounds stupid*, Chandler thought.

The woman, a platoon sergeant, glanced back at the racks of weapons, and Chandler's eyes followed hers. He saw antitank missiles in cases on the floor. 'We've got it all,' she said, turning back, 'but I'd suggest an M-16. There're some nine millimeters back here but . . . I don't see how a pistol would do anybody much good.' She chuckled.

So I just order a weapon, Chandler thought. *'An M-60, a coupla Stingers, and throw in a case of Dragons. You can never be too careful.'*

'Oh, uh, that'd be fine,' Chandler said.

'What?'

'An M-16. I'll just take an M-16.'

'Sixteen!' she yelled, and Chandler stepped down the counter. *Now we're in business*, he thought. *Headed for Europe. Got an M-16 and my American Tourister luggage, and . . .*

'ID, sir,' a soldier said as he was handed an M-16 from behind.

After some fumbling and almost dropping his MasterCard, Chandler handed him his military ID. '16473980' he read off the rifle's stock, pausing to look at Chandler's ID. 'Chandler – 429-89-5463.'

'16473980 – Chandler – 429-89-5463!' repeated the scrivener of the great book of weapons at a desk behind the counter.

The soldier at the counter handed the rifle to Chandler. It was heavier than he remembered, and the rifle sagged in his hands as its weight was transferred. It seemed new – brand new. The stock was faintly oily, Chandler noted. *No, that wouldn't be. It's plastic. My hands . . . my hands are faintly oily*, he decided.

He moved on. The rifle was solid, tangible. Its hard grips and the power of the rounds it could unleash gave him confidence. He felt more like a soldier.

'Havin' fun, sir?' a young man with nerdy military-issue shatterproof glasses asked good-naturedly as he placed four 30-round magazines of ammunition on the counter. One hundred and twenty rounds of 5.56-mm ammunition, *to go with my M-16*, Chandler realized. *Maybe a thousand bucks' worth of brand-new assault rifle. Fires single shots or, with a quick flick of your right thumb, a burst of three rounds so quickly you couldn't repeat the sound with your tongue if you tried.* Chandler had tried, he remembered, after a fair number of drinks with some friends from work who were asking about disparate things military.

There was one more stop.

The words were spelled out in black on a yellow background. Easy to read, even in a panic. Three injectors stuck out of their pockets on the sides of the pouches lining the counter ahead, which were being picked up and carted off one by one. The pouches, Chandler knew, contained a gas mask and chemical-warfare suit. He picked one up and strapped it to his left shoulder, leaving the cage for the open air of the high-ceilinged

hangar. Whereas the rifle had calmed him down, given him a sense of
confidence, the chemical-warfare gear had the opposite effect. *You stick
– no, not stick – jam the injectors into your thigh*, Chandler's mind reeled
off as he headed toward an empty bench, *right into the skin and muscle
of the top of your thigh, straight through your clothes. All three of 'em,
one after the other. The tip is spring-loaded.*

Atropine. The word echoed in Chandler's mind. Atropine: nerve gas
antidote.

LOS ANGELES, CALIFORNIA
June 11, 0500 GMT (2100 Local)

Melissa Chandler stared transfixed at the television as she held her
overnight bag already packed for the hospital. The pain seized her
abdomen once again, but she concentrated on what they were saying
on CNN.

'I'm getting something here, Susan,' the reporter said from the
Washington, D.C., studio, reading a piece of paper. 'It appears that
there is activity around many of the principal government office buildings
here in Washington, and high government officials who have been
working long hours during what all have stated to be this critical
early phase of the Korean War have been coming and going – or more
correctly just going – in the past fifteen minutes or so. Helicopters can
be seen – '

The anchorwoman interrupted him. 'I'm getting something on this
end, excuse me, Doug.' She read the computer monitor off to the
side. 'It says here the Associated Press is reporting that the Federal
Emergency Management Agency has undertaken an evacuation of key
government officials from Washington and has sent word to the state
authorities advising them to do the same. The AP wire report says that
the President is already on his way from the White House to an unknown
destination.' The cramp shot pain once really hard, and Melissa winced.
'Doug, does this make any sense to you?'

'Well, Susan, it . . . it certainly sounds like the kind of evacuation
that's always been planned in the . . . in the event, and I hate to even
say the words . . . I'll just have to wait for a little more information.'

Oh, my God, Melissa thought and ran to the phone to call David.
'The Los Angeles cellular telephone user you are trying to call is either
unavailable or out of the Los Angeles cellular telephone area. Would you
please try your call again later.'

'Susan, I've just been handed a note that says an unnamed Congressional source – and I'm just reading what I was handed here – an
unnamed Congressional source confirms that a full-fledged emergency

evacuation of top government officials is currently taking place. This
. . . this is simply unprecedented. It's never happened before.'

'Could this indicate – and this of course would just be pure speculation
at this point – but could this indicate that some risk of . . . of nuclear
war is at least perceived by whomever . . . whomever ordered this
evacuation?'

'Well, Susan, that was obviously what I was alluding to earlier, but it's
really way too premature to even speculate about that right now. The
North Koreans do have nuclear weapons, but it is unthinkable, highly
unlikely, I would say, that they would ever use them against this country,
even if they could. And in all my talks with Defense Department officials,
not one has ever even expressed the least concern about that.'

Oh, my God, Melissa thought as she stood there with her bag, staring
at the television report. *What do I do*? It was just her. She was all
alone, and she had to make the decision by herself. The unsteady
picture now on television was of a black government car speeding
out of an underground parking lot with a police escort. *We're at war*,
she reasoned, *and they're evacuating Washington. And CNN is talking
about nuclear war.*

She laughed as she felt a wave of nausea, and in her shaky state tears
welled up in her eyes. *And I'm standing here in Los Angeles, California,
all by myself and going into labor!*

'We go now to our Fort Worth bureau,' the anchorwoman said.

A reporter stood in the glow of bright light against a chain link fence
and an otherwise black night. In the distance a nondescript building was
lit by a single spotlight. The man was unprepared and fumbled with his
earphone while speaking to someone off camera. After a few seconds he
straightened and said, 'Good evening. A few minutes ago – ' His report
was cut off by the roar of jet engines. The reporter half turned to look
over his shoulder. At the right edge of the picture there appeared four
brilliant streaks of blue, grouped in two sets of two, making their way
toward the center of the screen and away into the distance. The long
exhaust flames lifted slowly into the air as the camera zoomed unsteadily
in on the dark, nearly invisible aircraft.

The camera refocused on the reporter, who yelled over the receding
noise. 'Planes have been taking off here from Dyess Air Force Base a
few miles away from our CNN bureau for several minutes! We don't
know what's going on, we only just got here.'

'Do you know what kind of planes those are?' the anchorwoman
asked, her brow knitted.

'I'm not exactly sure,' the reporter said. 'It's very dark. Dyess is
home, however, to a great number of bombers, B-1 bombers, which
on any normal day you can see lined up wingtip to wingtip just over
this way.' He pointed into the darkness. A roar erupted again. 'Here
comes another one!'

Melissa had seen enough. She grabbed her bag and headed for the car.

ANDREWS AIR FORCE BASE, MARYLAND
June 11, 0500 GMT (0000 Local)

Crown Helo landed less than 100 feet from the E-4B, a huge 747, after the high-speed flight from the White House. As soon as Lambert and the President's entourage exited, the helicopter took off and headed away in the dark.

As they approached the plane, whose jet engines already whined at a loud volume, Lambert saw another group of men, in military uniform mostly but some in casual civilian clothes, climbing the stairs to the plane's door. Security troops in blue uniforms bloused into their combat boots and wearing black berets – air police, Lambert guessed – stood at intervals down the length of the aircraft, M-16 rifles at the ready and pointing out.

The President and First Lady began climbing the stairs, and Lambert and the White House military liaison with the nuclear codes and several Secret Service agents took to the steps behind him.

Lambert heard, 'Everybody on board!' from somewhere below, followed by the sound of running boots as the air police headed for the stairs. By the time Lambert got to the landing at the top, the first pair of men were in line behind him.

Lambert stepped into the aircraft past another armed air policeman and followed the President into the narrow corridor to the right.

'Welcome aboard, Mr President. My name is Brigadier General Sherman. I'm in charge of "Kneecap" operations.' The general shook the President's and then Lambert's hands. 'General Thomas is in conference right now, so let me give you a quick tour of everything here to get you oriented.' He led them down a narrow corridor to the cockpit through the line of air policemen who streamed aboard. The three-man crew was going over a checklist. 'There will be ninety-four of us on board this evening,' General Sherman continued. 'We've got three SAC flight crews, nine men and women, from the 55th Strategic Recon Wing out of Offut Air Force Base, Nebraska. They're the very best. Then we've got another eighteen aircraft crewmen in charge of food, repair, and maintenance.'

The aircraft began to move, and the President said to the flight crew taxiing the great aircraft in a cheerful, campaign voice, 'Don't you think you boys oughta open the shades?'

Lambert craned his neck to see into the cockpit. The windows were all covered with a thick, white shade. Mounted between the pilot and copilot, a glowing television screen showed the tarmac roll by in front of the plane.

'Those curtains are made of aluminized fabric, sir,' General Sherman replied. 'It's standard procedure.'

'You mean they're going to take off with the curtains drawn?' the First Lady asked.

'Yes, ma'am,' Sherman said. 'It's . . . it prevents, well, tissue dehydration and . . . and chlorioretinal burns if . . .' He didn't finish his sentence – he just smiled. 'It beats the system our tanker crewmen use. They use shaded goggles in daylight, but right now – at night when it's too dark to wear them – they put zinc oxide on their exposed skin and fly with an eye patch on to keep at least one eye, uh, unburned.'

There was an uncomfortable silence.

Leading the tour back down the hallway to the rear, Sherman said, 'In addition to the crew, we've got the sixteen armed air policemen you saw outside.'

'Why so many?' the First Lady asked. Some, Lambert had noticed, had grenade launchers mounted underneath their rifles, and others carried light machine guns.

'Well, ma'am, we really don't know just where we might have to land,' Sherman said, choosing his words carefully. 'I mean, what kind of security there will be there. This just gives us . . . widens our options.' After pausing to ensure that his response was satisfactory, General Sherman said, 'The aircraft has four thousand six hundred and twenty square feet of main deck divided into six areas. Immediately behind the cockpit here, in what would be first class, are your private quarters, Mr President.' The group peered into the cabin at bunk beds trimmed in gold.

Walking down the corridor, Sherman said, 'Next we've got your conference room,' and the group filed by the doorway. Lambert saw the Joint Chiefs – some in uniform, others in civilian clothes – seated about the rectangular table. There were telephones between every seat and at the head, which presumably was the President's seat, facing the display screen.

'Then, moving on back,' Sherman said, 'we have the briefing room.' They walked through an empty auditorium-style room with a couple of dozen seats facing a large screen and into a room filled with consoles, busy people working at each one. 'This is the battlestaff work area,' Sherman said to the President. 'We can monitor and update all of the information that is fed into the NORAD Command Center Processing and Display System, more commonly known as the "Big Board," to keep you informed of events around the world.'

Moving into another compartment, the general turned to an officer who was monitoring a computer console and asked, 'Is General Thomas still in conference?'

'Yes, sir,' the man said after checking the screen.

'And finally,' Sherman said, obviously extending his tour to stall for time, 'this is the communications control center.' As the plane, taxiing at high speed, turned and everyone stepped to one side to rebalance, the general said, 'When we get airborne, we'll play out a five-mile-long trailing wire antenna for very low frequency transmissions. The several-mile wavelength allows penetration directly through the earth to similarly equipped aircraft, ships, and ground installations. It's not perfect – the wave-formation time slows our rate of transmission significantly – but it gets through. Usually.'

General Sherman waited, getting only raised eyebrows from the First Lady, and then continued. 'For regular high-speed communications, which are subject to some interference under certain . . . in certain situations, we have a full range of high frequency transceivers. We also have a super high frequency system and satellite transceivers housed in a dorsal blister – that little bump on top of the aircraft just behind the big 'hump' of the 747. All our systems broadcast random information continuously to keep from alerting anyone to an increased pace of communications. When we want to talk to somebody, we just input the designated interrupt code and follow it with the message. We can basically talk to anybody you want – anywhere, anytime.'

'Too bad Jack's not here,' President Livingston said to his wife, referring to their son at Amherst. 'He'd eat this up.'

'Oh, uh, if you'd like to speak to your son or daughter, sir,' Sherman said, and then turned back to the officer at the console next to him. 'Where is the First Family now?'

The officer tapped at his keyboard for a second. 'A-3 is airborne on a Guard helo, sign Crown Three, and A-4 is' – he hesitated and tapped again – 'she's . . .' The man again hesitated as he read, and then he sat back and pointed at the screen for Sherman to read.

'Are you talking about Nancy?' the First Lady asked, stepping up to stare at the screen but without a glimmer of comprehension of the information displayed on it.

'Apparently ma'am, sir, your daughter does not want to, uh, participate in the evacuation. Secret Service agents are talking to her now, but . . .'

'Where are they being evacuated?' the President asked.

'Your son,' Sherman said as he ran his finger across a line on the screen and asked the console's operator, 'Alpha Lima 51, is that . . .?'

'Burlington, sir.'

'Your son is aboard an Air National Guard helicopter heading for the secure Presidential Emergency Facility outside Burlington, Vermont,' Sherman said, and squinted to read the screen again. 'Why the abort on A-4?' Sherman asked.

The console operator said, 'They missed the time line for Tahoe, sir.'

Sherman straightened up, stretching his back, and said, 'Your daughter was supposed to go from her home in San Francisco to the Presidential Emergency Facility in the northern Sierra Nevadas near Lake Tahoe, but because of the delay they've had to reroute her to Task Force 37 – to the U.S.S. *Enterprise* – as a temporary measure until . . . until further transportation is deemed appropriate.'

The President hesitated, and then he burst into hearty laughter. Lambert felt a smile creep onto his face. 'You're trying to take Nancy to an aircraft carrier?' he asked, and laughed again.

Lambert noticed, however, that the First Lady was not smiling. 'Is it necessary that she go?' she asked.

General Sherman shrugged, his mouth opening a full second before the words came out. 'It would make things simpler, ma'am.'

'Then let me speak to her,' the First Lady said without a hint of good humor. The President had grown somber, and Lambert wiped the smile off his face.

General Sherman sent an airman off with the First Lady to the President's cabin. He turned back to the group, and an awkward pause ensued. 'Oh,' Sherman said as if suddenly remembering, 'and if all our other communications systems fail, we've got meteor burst communications capabilities. Every few seconds, small meteors collide with the earth's atmosphere within line of sight of our aircraft. The friction causes ionization of the atoms making up the meteor and leaves a ten- to twenty-mile trail of free electrons at an altitude of fifty to seventy-five miles. An antenna monitors the sky for the trail, which dissipates after half a second, but in that time finds the trail with the correct angle from the source to the target and bursts a radio signal, which bounces down to a receiver at the target.'

Lambert could feel the aircraft taking off, and it felt strange that he, and everybody else, was just standing around during the roll-out instead of being strapped in.

'Good evening, Walter,' the Secretary of Defense said, walking up to the President and shaking his hand. 'Greg,' he said as they shook also. The group followed him up to the conference room.

'Good evening, sir,' General Thomas said as he and the other Chiefs – less Army Chief of Staff Halcomb, who had issued the televised call-up orders from the White House Briefing Room – stood around the conference table. 'We're finishing up a Commander's Availability Check. We're internetting all the major commands, tying everybody together over open links on different communications nets.'

The President sat at the head of the table as a scratchy voice on the speakerphone said, 'Island Sun Six is five by five.'

'That's the Ground Mobile Command Center with the Speaker of the House in it,' General Thomas translated.

'Scope Light is five by five,' said a different voice, distorted by transmission but clear.

'That's Atlantic Command,' Thomas said in a low voice.

'Silk Purse is five by five,' a voice with a still different quality of sound reported.

'European Command,' Thomas said. Both he and General Starnes, Chief of Staff of the Air Force, were making check marks on a preprinted sheet of paper.

'Blue Eagle is five by five.'

'Pacific Command,' Thomas said as Lambert took a seat by the President.

'Looking Glass is five by five.'

'That's ACC's twenty-four-hour-a-day alert aircraft on Doomsday Watch.'

The President, Lambert, Thomas, the Chiefs of the Air Force, Navy, and Marine Corps, and the Secretary of Defense sat around the table. The military aide with the football sat at the far end of the room against the wall with his bag in his lap.

'Cover All is five by five.'

'Okay. That's it,' Thomas said. 'Everybody's airborne or rolling. Oh, Cover All is CINCACC, the commander in chief of the Air Combat Command. We're Nightwatch. In addition to ACC's Looking Glass, we've gotten checks from ACC's two Post Attack Command and Control System auxiliary EC-135s, the three Airborne Launch Control Center aircraft that would fire our missiles if all the ground launch centers were destroyed, the navy's Atlantic and Pacific TACAMO aircraft for communicating with ballistic missile submarines, and the control aircraft for the fleet of tankers that'll keep everybody airborne.'

'In addition to the airborne commands,' General Starnes said, looking down and reading, 'we've gotten checks on NORAD in Cheyenne Mountain; the Alternate National Military Command Center at Raven Rock Mountain; the civilian authorities' alternate headquarters at Mount Weather; Congress's Greenbriar Facility in White Sulphur Springs, West Virginia; the White House Situation Room; the CIA Indications Office; the U.S. Intelligence Board National Indications Center; the U.N. Military Mission; the FEMA Alternate Warning Center in Olney, Maryland; the Civil Defense bunkers at Maynard, Massachusetts, and at Denton, Texas; the U.S. Coast Guard Operations Center; the FAA Executive Communications Control Center; and NATO Headquarters in Brussels. We've also touched base with the three RAPIER teams, which are 100-man staffs in eighteen-wheelers tearing ass out of Colorado Springs right now. They are NORAD and AFSPACECOM Rapid Emergency Reconstruction Teams that would provide early-warning attack assessment and postattack data reception and evaluation.'

The Secretary of Defense jumped in. 'We've also been contacted by the Federal Reserve System's Communications and Records Center in Culpeper, Virginia, which is downloading Federal Reserve account data onto optical disks as rapidly as possible. Plus we've gotten calls from the New York State Emergency Operating Center and Alternate Seat of Government in Albany, the Massachusetts State Bunker in Framingham, and the AT&T National Emergency Control Center under Netcong, New Jersey. They all want to know just what the hell's going on. Oh, and I ordered TREETOP II activated, and the Presidential Successor Emergency Support Plan is being implemented. That means your successors are being dispersed.'

'What do you mean, "dispersed"?' the President asked.

'Well, sir,' the Secretary of Defense said, 'let's see. The Vice President and Secretary of the Treasury are each airborne in separate E-4Bs. Secretary of State Moore is at Raven Rock. Then there are six Ground Mobile Command Centers, which are just ordinary looking eighteen-wheelers with a lead security team in a truck out on the highways. They're code-named Island Sun, and they carry the junior members of the line – the secretaries of HHS, HUD, Transportation, Education and Veterans Affairs – plus the Speaker of the House, who didn't want to be at Greenbriar, so we accommodated him.'

'That sounds like Bill,' the President laughed, having only half listened, it seemed to Lambert. 'He's claustrophobic, you know.' He turned to the air force steward who was filling his coffee cup and said, 'Cream and sugar, please.'

The Secretary of Defense continued. 'The President Pro Tempore of the Senate, the Attorney General, the secretaries of Interior and Labor, and the National Program Office's six extraconstitutional successors are en route to some of the eighty-four underground Presidential Emergency Facilities. The Secretary of Commerce was in Paris and is heading to NATO Headquarters. The Secretary of Agriculture is at Bethesda after his gallbladder surgery, and we have people standing by there to move him to Mount Weather where he can recuperate once the doctors say it's all right for him to travel. That gives us a check on all of your constitutional successors plus the NPO's six. Everybody has their emergency kits with war plans, regulations, systems instructions, fact sheets, et cetera.'

Brigadier General Sherman appeared in the doorway with a printout in his hand. 'Excuse me, but we just got this from CINCNORAD.' He looked down and read. 'Nineteen Russian ICBMs – believed Model SS-19 – and four shorter-range missiles of indeterminate model confirmed fired from Far East Russia. Am tracking, will confirm on rollover. Probable targets to south. Indications consistent with launch against People's Republic of China.'

He looked up, and as he did Lambert looked from face to face around the table. No one said a word. There was silence, calm, just the gentle whoosh of the air slipping by the giant aircraft and the faint whine of the engines on the wings.

FAR EAST ARMY COMMAND, KHABAROVSK
June 11, 0510 GMT (1510 Local)

'The commander of my heavy artillery and rocket forces reported that the tactical warheads were fired on time and all achieved acceptable detonations,' Razov said. 'I'm waiting now on the call from the RVSN about the Strategic Rocket Force's ICBMs'

'Finally something goes right,' Mishin said.

'Listen, I tried calling Zorin a while back . . .' Razov began.

'You did *what?*'

'It worries me. He has possession of those communicators, and he knows nothing about our plans to fire at the Chinese. I wanted to brief him on what was happening, but I've been unable to get through to him.'

'We've got assault troops moving into position around the Kremlin and we're cutting Zorin's communications to prevent any tactical warning of the assault,' Mishin said. 'I can stop my people and raise him on the special channels if you want. Or we can still go through his liaison officer.'

The duty officer came in and motioned to attract Razov's attention. When Razov looked up and arched his eyebrows, the man said, 'Far Eastern RVSN Command is on line three, General Razov.'

'There's my call on the ICBMs,' Razov said.

'What do you want to do about Zorin?'

Razov thought for a second as the red light blinked on his phone. 'Never mind. Finish cutting him off in there and proceed with the assault. I'll call to let you know about the ICBM firing.' Razov punched the button for line three on his phone. 'General Razov,' he said.

'This is General Makarin. We had faults showing on two missiles during prelaunch, but we worked around the problems. All of the missiles were fired in the correct phasing by the silos' automatic timers, and initial satellite yield data indicates detonations within acceptable ranges from all aim points.' Makarin then went on to discuss the reserve force.

Razov was distracted by the duty officer again at the door, this time waving a slip of paper to get his attention. 'I'm sorry, General Makarin. What did you say?' Razov waved the duty officer over.

'We'll have damage assessment in forty minutes on the 1550 local pass and will advise as to whether a restrike is necessary, which appears highly unlikely at this point.'

The duty officer leaned over and whispered into Razov's ear, 'PVO-Strany is on the line. General Mishin says it's urgent.'

I said I'd call! Razov thought angrily. 'Thank you, General Makarin. Keep me informed.'

The duty officer punched the blinking red light on Razov's telephone and the sound of the klaxon at the air defense headquarters blared from the speaker.

ABOARD NIGHTWATCH, OVER WESTERN MARYLAND
June 11, 0512 GMT (0012 Local)

'I thought you told me the Chinese couldn't fire their missiles in time! How could they have fired four?' the President demanded accusingly. Lambert's chin sank to his chest as the full weight of the disaster bore down on him.

'All of our intelligence,' General Thomas said, 'indicated that their liquid-fueled rockets required too much time to generate given the tactical warning times that they would have of inbound Russian ICBMs. Even if they were on higher alert because of the war, they wouldn't fuel those missile tanks.'

'Then what the hell happened?' the Secretary of Defense asked.

Thomas shook his head. 'The only thing it could be, Mr Secretary, is that somehow the Chinese got Indications and Warning. Maybe the Europeans – or the Japanese, more likely – screwed up big time and told them.' Thomas turned to the President. 'Indications and Warning is distinguished from tactical warning, which is actually detecting the incoming missiles. I&W is "forewarning of enemy actions or— "' Thomas stopped and stared at the shock registered on Livingston's face. The President's haunted eyes rose slowly to meet Lambert's.

DEEP-UNDERGROUND COMMAND POST, THE KREMLIN
June 11, 0515 GMT (0715 Local)

There was a knock on the door. Zorin awoke with a start, wet and chilled with sweat in his uniform. A wave of nausea washed over him instantly. There was another knock. 'What?' Zorin shouted. 'What is it?'

The door opened, the light causing daggers of pain to shoot into his head. Again it was the captain.

'I told you, you tell Razov I'll talk to him when I damn well please!'

'It's not General Razov, sir, it's American television.'

'What could the Americans possibly be doing?' Zorin asked out loud as an aide translated the CNN special report of B-1B bombers taking off from Dyess and Sawyer air force bases in Texas and Michigan. 'Why are they . . .?' His voice trailed off, the effort of speaking too great despite the lift he was feeling from the amphetamines he had taken to clear his head. The junior officers stood mutely around the long conference table. He would get no counsel from them. He had admitted no one of his age or rank to the inner circle.

Zorin looked down the table at the nuclear code cases and then turned to the captain who was translating the satellite television broadcast. 'And you say the government is evacuating Washington?' The translator nodded. 'And you're sure about the reports of American bombers?'

'That's what their television reported, sir.'

He looked at the two officers seated at the table. Their nuclear communicators sat darkly in front of them. Zorin stared at the two men, and they stared back. His body craved sleep, but he felt so jittery from the medicine he could not even force himself to sit. *What are they doing?* he thought again as he began to pace up and down the carpeted floor behind the nuclear communicators, like a nervous captain on the bridge of his ship. 'What could the Americans *possibly* be up to?' he mumbled, only afterward looking up at the staring faces of the men in the room and realizing that he had spoken the words aloud. He resumed his pacing, forcing the increasingly frantic thoughts and fears back into their cage with little energy left over for the effort of sorting through the puzzle.

The door burst open. The captain who had awakened him earlier but whose name he had forgotten said, 'General Zorin, you've got a call!' *Melnikov,* Zorin remembered.

Razov again. I'd forgotten. 'All right. Yes,' he said, walking to the console set up in the room by their signalmen. 'We'll get some answers now. Put General Razov on.'

'It's not General Razov, sir. It's PVO-Strany. Our liaison officer there. He said it was urgent.'

Zorin's eyes widened, and Melnikov pushed a button on the console. The piercing sound of the klaxon filled the room.

'What's going on there?' Zorin demanded as a tingle like electricity shot through his fragile nervous system.

'General Zorin! I don't have much time!' The muffled sound of men shouting and a high, grating whine like that of a drill that intermittently encountered dense obstructions could be heard in the background.

'They're trying to cut our communications! There is a missile attack under way, sir! The missiles are headed toward Moscow and will arrive—' The drilling sound groaned deeply and the line was cut with a screech.

'My God! What was that?' Zorin shouted.

His signals officer worked frantically at the communications panel until he finally said, 'This line is dead now too, sir.'

Zorin turned to stare at the two officers seated at the table. *Missiles. Missiles headed toward Moscow. An American evacuation. American bombers.* The prickly fingers of fear roamed his body as the realization hit home. 'They're crazy,' he mumbled. *How could they make such an insane mistake?* His breathing was rapid and shallow, and he grabbed onto the table as he felt light-headed. '*Goddamn* them!' He shook his head in utter disbelief and then clenched his teeth. Pain spread through his jaw as anger rose from deep within. His blood began to boil, and he had to force his voice to remain level as he stared down at the nuclear communicators.

'Activate those things.'

The two officers began opening the cases.

'Sir?' Captain Melnikov asked urgently. 'What're you doing?'

'We are under attack!' Zorin yelled, his anger finding a vent at the stupidity of the young officer. 'You heard it with your own ears!'

'But . . . but we don't know that,' the impudent junior officer replied. 'We don't know what's going on.'

General Zorin stared at the man in disbelief. Never before had he understood so clearly the innate superiority of staff officers over their cousins in the field. 'You saw the American television. They've already evacuated their government! Open them!' he shouted to the two men at the table.

'But . . . but why?' Melnikov whined.

'Because they see what's happening!' Zorin snapped, and in being forced to answer the man's question it all became clear. 'They somehow know of our seizure of power and that I have these code cases. They know of the fracturing of our command and control system that the seizure temporarily caused. It's their *window*!' he shouted, slamming his hand down on the table. 'They intend a decapitation strike – to kill us all here,' he said, straightening up to address the soldiers present in the room, 'and then destroy our strategic forces before command and control can be reconstituted.'

The men in the room all stared at Zorin, their faces registering the shock of what was happening, of what was about to happen to them all.

'But surely they know,' young Melnikov mumbled and then looked up at Zorin. 'Surely they know we will strike back somehow!'

'Would we?' Zorin asked, and left the question to hang in the air.

'After we are gone,' he said, looking at each of the chosen men, 'would "they" – those who have led us to this point – would they strike back with our few remaining nuclear forces against what would be overwhelming odds? Against an American nuclear arsenal that remains untouched?' Zorin shook his head slowly as the full gravity of what had happened weighed down on him. 'Would they have the will?' he mumbled.

The phone rang. Zorin and Melnikov jerked their heads to it, only to see that it was an intercom line. Zorin pressed the lit button. 'What is it?'

'General Zorin. There are . . . there are missiles! Missiles are rising up into the air all around the city!'

'Who is this?' Zorin asked.

'Lubyanov. On the roof of the Congress of People's Deputies!'

'Are they SA-10s?' Zorin asked.

'No, sir. I don't know what they are. They have yellow smoke trails, not white! There are more going up now, all over! They're going straight up into the sky to tremendous heights!'

'What are they?' Melnikov asked quietly.

'Antiballistic missiles,' Zorin replied in a stunned monotone as he grabbed the table with both hands.

'There was an enormous explosion in the sky!' Lubyanov screamed through the phone. 'A-a-a-ah! It's hot – it's hot on my skin! God!'

'Open the codebooks,' Zorin said, suddenly panicking that he had waited too long. The two officers each tore the sealed folders from the nuclear cases.

'*There's another!*' Lubyanov shouted. 'There's no sound, but it's a bright flash. You can't look at it directly! And it burns – like sunburn.'

'*Hurry!*' Zorin shouted.

'There was another one!' Lubyanov yelled over the phone. 'And another! They're all going off!' The tone of Lubyanov's voice attested to the awesomeness of the sight.

'The ABMs are nuclear tipped,' Zorin said to no one in particular as the code books were laid out on the conference table.

'Why is there no sound? No explosion?' Melnikov asked in a low voice, listening over the open intercom.

'They detonate in space, just outside the atmosphere.' Zorin's thoughts raced, his mind still casting about for some other explanation. 'Get Razov on the line!' he shouted at the communications officer. 'Or PVO-Strany, or Long-Range Aviation, or somebody! Try high-frequency radio.'

Zorin tried to edge past Melnikov to get to the codebooks.

'General, there has to be some mistake!' the young officer pleaded, seizing Zorin by the arm.

Zorin stared at the offending grip, saying nothing and pulling free.

Stepping behind the two men seated at the table, Zorin said quietly,

'Gentlemen – comrades – our country is under nuclear attack. I anticipate the worst at any moment, and I expect each of you to do your duty to the end.' Zorin paused, returning the anguished stares of the two officers, who had turned to look back at him. 'Now, what is the procedure?'

The officer immediately in front of him replied, 'You select an attack profile from the plan book, and we input the release codes into both devices simultaneously. The firing sequences are automatically sent from these communicators by hardened and encoded fiber optic and cellular links to a computer in the basement of the Defense Ministry. The two twelve-digit codes are fed into an algorithm and processed, and if the computer outputs a valid firing order, the computer launches the land-based missiles directly and sends preplanned instructions to the navy and manned bomber bases.' Zorin opened the thick black codebook.

'General Zorin,' Captain Melnikov said, 'I'm begging you – please wait until we have some sort of verification. This is insane! You cannot launch without some sort of verification of the attack!'

The first few pages of the book were general instructions. Zorin grabbed a thick group of pages and opened the book to near its middle. In large block letters at the top of the first page was 'ZM01349GZ771.' As the officer in front of the other device found the same page, and his own unique code, in his own book, Zorin read. 'Summary: Counterforce Strike Profile. Objective: Reduction of United States strategic nuclear force with minimal collateral damage. Primary Targets: ICBMs – Grand Forks, Malmstrom, Minot, and Warren AFBs; Bombers – Blytheville, Carswell, Dyess, Ellsworth, Fairchild, Grand Forks, Griffiss, Loring, March, McConnell, Minot, Sawyer, Whiteman, and Wurtsmith AFBs; Submarines – New London, Bremerton, and Kings Bay naval yards; and Command/Control – Cheyenne and Raven Rock mountains. Secondary Targets: EW System – Beale, Elmendorf, Falcon, Goodfellow, Kaena Point, McChord, Robins, Shemya Island, Thule, and Vandenberg AFBs and Otis ANGB; and Tactical Disruption – air and subsea bursts as specified below. City withholds specified below. BALLISTIC MISSILE SUBMARINES,' the boldface type said, 'see Special Release Orders specified below.'

'General Zorin,' the officer seated at the nearest communicator said to him in a low voice, nodding across the room.

When Zorin looked up, he saw Captain Melnikov, pistol raised. Lubyanov's shouts could be heard over the open intercom, coming to his receiver from a distance.

'General Zorin,' the scared Melnikov said uncertainly, 'please. Please!'

Lubyanov's shouts came closer to the phone and then he shouted 'General . . .!'

Everyone in the room jumped at the tearing screech of the telephone, followed almost immediately by the beginnings of a rumble that over the next few seconds rose to such a vibration that everyone grabbed onto tables and walls. The overhead lights went out, and a fraction of a second later the emergency lights recessed around the walls came on, leaving the room distinctly darker than before. Just as Zorin thought the vibrations would begin to tear the room apart, the rumbling began to subside slowly. Shouts could be heard from outside the conference room.

The door to the conference room burst open, and along the ceiling in the main room of the command center the faint haze of smoke could be seen drifting in, which lit with each spark of the electrical fires that snapped and popped furiously from the radios and other electronic gear outside. Army officers in full combat gear stood there staring at Captain Melnikov and Zorin, uncertain what to do.

A second jarring thud, and the rumbling that followed reverberated again through the room. There was a smaller explosion from down the hall and a flash of light, and the emergency lights went out completely. The glow from the two screens dimly lit the faces of the officers sitting erect and poised at the table, Zorin and Captain Melnikov standing behind them.

Beams from the flashlights of several soldiers began to dance around the room. Melnikov was spotlit in one, and, for an instant, Zorin saw a man at the door with rifle raised at the captain but with his eyes on Zorin. Zorin looked into the eyes of Melnikov and then at the soldier in the door and shook his head. As the emergency lights flickered back on, Zorin walked over to Melnikov and took the pistol from his hands, meeting no resistance.

Suddenly, a man came running into the room, his eyes wild as he shouted to Zorin. 'There was an explosion! A nuclear detonation! We saw it! It was just to the south of the city! There is . . . there is an enormous fireball rising up over the skyline!' The faces of the men standing in the doorway registered the same shock as the man who was speaking.

The lights and television set came back on after the loss of power, the army translator in front of the TV staring into the dark screen. Before the picture appeared, the American reporter could be heard speaking rapidly in English. It was now their only source of outside information – the satellite transmission received by their simple Kremlin dishes incapable of interruption or jamming and not having been burned up by the nuclear detonations' pulse – and everyone in the room seized upon the now glowing screen in the darkened underground room.

'There is some sort of nuclear alert under way,' the bespectacled Army translator began in a monotone inconsistent with the agitated sound of foreign reporter's voice or the force of the words spoken.

'CNN News has now received over a dozen reports from all across the country – bombers taking off from half a dozen bases, an aircraft carrier in Norfolk literally cutting her mooring lines and sailing with a third of her crew still on shore, evacuation of the federal government and activation of the first emergency centers at numerous state and local government levels. There has been no word from Civil Defense or FEMA yet as to what actions, if any, they would advise ordinary citizens to take, but on the line from Connecticut we have Simon Gardner, author of the book *Armageddon: It Could Still Happen.* Mr Gardner, are you there?'

'Yes, I can hear you.'

'Can you tell us, please, in as few words as possible, for obvious reasons, what it is that ordinary Americans sitting at home tonight might be able to do if the worst is true.' The Russian translation came a second or two after the English, and Zorin could hear the tremble, the edginess, in the newsman's voice.

'Sir,' they heard weakly over the intercom, 'we need medical assistance.' The words were forced out, forced in hisses through pain by Lubyanov on the roof. 'Most of my men are burned. All of their exposed skin – it's burned pretty badly.'

'Close that door and seal it!' Zorin said to the soldiers standing there. He looked at Captain Melnikov, who stood with his head bowed. Zorin turned to stare at the communicators for a moment before he could muster the energy required to speak – to issue the orders.

Chapter Three

GEOSYNCHRONOUS ORBIT, ABOVE THE INDIAN OCEAN
June 11, 0525 GMT (0525 Local)

Seven seconds after ignition of the SS-18's booster rocket and three seconds after its rocket nozzles emerged from its underground silo, the heat sensors of the 5,200-pound Block 14 satellite warmed sufficiently in the glow of thermal radiation from the exhaust plume to trigger a detection signal. Suspended at an altitude of 35,786 miles above the equator and spinning at the rate of seven rotations per minute, the satellite's sensors immediately calculated the intensity of the signal and the location on earth from which the signal originated.

The onboard computer began the process of comparing the detection information against a library containing temperature and location data on all previously detected launches. When a match was found two seconds later, the satellite transmitted a detection alert to earth. 'Missile Launch//Russian SS-18//Kartaly Missile Field Silo No. 42//0525:17:36Z.'

The first alarms sounded at the large Ground Processing Station at Nurungar, Australia, and the Simplified Station at Kapaun, Germany, both of which received the transmission directly from space. A laser on the satellite simultaneously pulsed the digitized information to the other two Block 14 satellites over South America and the central Pacific, which in turn beamed it down to trigger the alarm klaxons at Buckley Air National Guard Base in Colorado and in the six eighteen-wheel tractor-trailers roaming randomly amid the vast New Mexico desert from which the Air Force Space Defense Command operated its Mobile Ground Stations, the last defense against a surprise attack.

All of the ground stations simultaneously relayed the information to the command centers. Alarm after alarm shattered the quiet of the sealed war rooms and underground bunkers. At the National Military Command Center in the Pentagon, the 'Tank.' At the Alternate National Military Command Center buried deep inside Raven Rock Mountain on the Maryland-Pennsylvania border seventy miles north of Washington. At the blast-hardened three-acre ACC Command Post located on three subterranean floors at Offut Air Force Base outside Omaha, Nebraska. And in the fifteen spring-mounted steel buildings in the massive hollows of a great granite mountain, the NORAD Cheyenne Mountain Complex, in which the hearts of seventeen hundred people skipped a beat before they solemnly began the routines long rehearsed for their last minutes of life.

As the first signal reached NORAD outside Colorado Springs, Colorado, fifteen seconds after rocket motor ignition, the infrared sensors of the Block 14 satellite had begun processing four new heat signatures of similar intensity and location and buffered two dozen additional detections for which matches would be sought. The buffers would have data queued for processing for the next three minutes and forty-seven seconds, an eternity in computer time.

NORAD, CHEYENNE MOUNTAIN, COLORADO
June 11, 0525 GMT (2225 Local)

General Albert Wilson, commander in chief of the joint U.S.-Canadian North American Aerospace Defense Command, stood behind a Canadian officer at the Atomic Energy Detection System console in the area of the large room designated the Air Defense Operations Center. They were reviewing yield data on the Chinese missile detonations just south of Moscow that were inconsistent, satellite luminosity measurements differing from seismic reports. 'Those ABMs the Russians fired must at least have deflected the Chinese missiles or caused a malfunction,' the Canadian officer suggested. *Or the Chinese make shitty missiles*, Wilson thought. 'They just missed the southern suburbs of the city.'

The strident warning klaxon jarred Wilson. He looked across the frozen and silent personnel in the previously active room and saw the spinning red bubble light above the remote console of the complex's Missile Detection Center.

'I have an event!' the officer seated beneath the light shouted in surprise, spilling hot coffee from the Styrofoam cup on his fingers as he rushed to put the cup down. 'Probable SS-18 launch from Kartaly Missile Field!' he read from the monitor on his console, his fingers spinning the track ball to the side of his monitor and clicking the long cursor bar beneath.

My God! Wilson realized. *European Russia*! As he strode over to the Missile Detection Center, he looked up at the sixteen-foot-square screen of the Command Center Processing and Display System, or Big Board, covering the wall at the front of the room. A blinking red triangle had lit up on the map of western Russia.

'I have four more events!' the officer shouted, nearly jumping out of his seat. 'SS-18s out of Kartaly Missile Field!'

General Wilson put a hand gently but firmly on the shoulder board of the captain and looked at the small screen in front of the man. It was the familiar map of the Kartaly Missile Base, the blinking red triangles indicating the now empty silos. Along the bottom bar Wilson found the information he was looking for. TOT MISL – Total Missiles – was up to 8 and rising as the 'events' mounted. TTG – Time To Go before first detonation – read 00:29:37, the seconds ticking inexorably down.

Wilson turned to the man seated next to the captain. 'Take the DSP off "Auto-Detect" and run an error check.'

The captain in front of Wilson announced twenty-four new events, breaking them down by different missile fields all over European Russia, as the officer's hand flew back and forth along his track ball. Red triangles were popping onto the Big Board, the computer plotting the detections far ahead of the officer's ability to read them off.

This is not right, a voice in Wilson's head repeated over and over again. *They've already taken the Chinese strategic forces out.*

'Error check negative, sir,' the officer to Wilson's right said as he held Wilson's stare.

Another man ran up to Wilson from his station. 'ELINT reports post-launch telemetry transmissions verified.'

Wilson shouted over to the communications duty officer, 'Send an OPREP-3 PINNACLE NUCFLASH 4 to the National Command Authority on Nightwatch: SRV is "Valid," repeat System Report Verification is "Valid."' Wilson could see the man's Adam's apple bob and knew what he was thinking. *NUCFLASH 4 – detection of unidentified objects by missile-warning system creating risk of nuclear war.*

Wilson went up the stairs to the balcony overlooking the large open room, the Canadian and American airmen and officers making way. Stepping up to his desk that faced the room and the Big Board, Wilson picked up the white telephone receiver inset into the console and hit INTERCOM. 'This is CINCNORAD.' His voice boomed out across the large open space of the room and in the other buildings of the complex. 'I am declaring an Air Defense Emergency – Air Defense Warning Yellow, repeat, Air Defense Warning Yellow.' He picked up the 'red phone' and heard the Pentagon operator announcing, 'National Military Command Center,' as the phone reached his ear.

ABOARD NIGHTWATCH, OVER EASTERN MARYLAND
June 11, 0530 GMT (0030 Local)

The one knock on the door was barely distinguishable from the sound of it bursting open. An out-of-breath air force captain announced, 'CINCNORAD has declared "Lemon Juice"!'

Lambert saw General Thomas immediately lean forward in his chair and punch several buttons on the panel recessed into the conference table.

'What the hell does Lemon Juice mean?' the President asked.

'It means an attack by hostile aircraft and/or missiles is probable,' Lambert answered for the busy Thomas.

'Communications,' a woman said over the speakerphone.

'This is General Thomas. I want an air threat conference, a missile threat conference, and a space threat conference – simultaneously.'

'What the hell . . .?' the President began.

There was a long tone over the speakerphone, and then the woman said calmly, 'The conferences are convened, sir.' In the background, the sound of a rhythmic buzzer could be heard from one of the command centers.

'Al, what's the story?' Thomas asked the commander in chief of NORAD.

'DSP has thirty-six unconfirmed launches from western Russian fields,' Wilson replied. 'Early impact assessment is CONUS.'

Thomas's chin dropped to his chest and his eyes closed. Lambert's mind refused to admit the meaning of the words he had just heard, but he felt the shock of the news vicariously as its effects rippled down the table. Jaws dropped or wide eyes stared blankly into space as the stunned Joint Chiefs each absorbed the blow in his own way.

'What the hell's going on?' demanded the President, looking from one Chief to the next, all silent and ashen.

It was Lambert who translated. 'The Defense Support Program System has detected the infrared signatures of thirty-six missile launches from western Russia.' The words he spoke ignited a flame that began to burn slowly within Lambert. *The bastards*! his first thought as the news sank in. 'The probable points of impact are in the continental United States.'

'Forty-three now, sir,' a new voice said over the speakerphone. Lambert looked around the table at the faces of the military men and the Secretary of Defense. General Thomas returned his look, and with the tingle that ran down Lambert's spine there rose a resolve to do his job.

'But you said . . . you said "unconfirmed,"' the President managed in a voice so low he could have been talking to himself. 'Maybe there's a screwup somewhere.'

'I've got to go,' General Wilson said over the line and hung up.

'Wait!' the President shouted, but it was too late. The sounds of several lines disconnecting came over the speaker. 'Get that son of a bitch back on the line!'

'Mr President,' Thomas said, 'he's got a lot to do and not much time to do it in. We can answer your questions.' Lambert struggled against the state of shock into which he had fallen. Everything about the situation had an otherworldly quality to it, so much so that Lambert had to force the idea from his head that this was not real, that it was all just a vivid dream. 'We have a verification system based on the principle of dual-warning phenomenology, which means that we need warnings from two distinct types of warning systems before we declare an attack confirmed. We already have infrared detection, so we'll get radar confirmation in . . .' He looked at the captain, who lingered in the door, not wanting to leave. Wanting to know what was happening. 'When did CINCNORAD declare Lemon Juice?'

The man looked down at the flimsy piece of paper.

'Zero five two six fourteen Zulu,' the man said, his voice distant and distracted. The look on his face made Lambert shudder.

'That'll be all, Captain,' Thomas said, frowning. The captain left without closing the door. Lambert leaned over to give it a push as Thomas looked down at his watch. 'Assuming launch at zero five two four Zulu, we'll get first impact in about twenty-eight minutes unless they launch from subs near our shores, or have had cruise missiles in the air for some time now, or they use depressed trajectories on any of their ballistic missiles instead of lobbing them high in a typical flight profile. BMEWS – the Ballistic Missile Early Warning System of phased array radars across the north from Clear, Alaska, to Thule, Greenland, to Fylingdales in the U.K. – or Cobra Dane out of Shemya Island in the Aleutians should pick up the first postboost vehicle launched on a high trajectory any second now when it rises over the Arctic horizon.'

'Is there . . . is there any chance, any chance at all, that this is a false alarm?' the President asked, his hands raised and clasped in front of him as if in supplication.

General Thomas stared back at him. 'No, sir. We must have already gotten ELINT, electronic intelligence such as radio transmissions of telemetry on the missiles – which doesn't count as the second warning – from Diogenes Station in Sinop, Turkey, and Teufelsberg in Berlin that's consistent with massive launches from European fields, or General Wilson would've taken us down from Yellow by now. They're on the way, sir.'

'Check and make sure,' the President said, and Thomas turned to General Starnes, Air Force Chief of Staff, and nodded. Starnes picked up his telephone.

This is it, Lambert thought. *Oh, my God, this is it*! Jane's beautiful face flashed into his mind and he quickly did the calculation. She was on the Beltway nearing the Highway 193 exit. *In twenty-seven minutes*, he thought, *at sixty-five miles per hour, she'd be . . . about thirty miles away from D.C.* He heaved a sigh as if he had just witnessed her complete her escape. His skin tingled, and he felt drained emotionally. *Thirty miles*, he thought again. *That's far enough*. He caught himself almost speaking the last words. Nodding his head without realizing, Lambert's thoughts began an inventory of those next closest. *Mom and Dad*, he thought, *asleep in their beds on the thirty-second floor of their East 72nd Street apartment. New York*.

General Starnes placed the telephone's handset into its cradle. 'ELINT has twenty-eight high-frequency intercepts and counting. Spot Decrypt indicates high probability of telemetry.'

The Joint Chiefs stared at the President as if he had gotten his answer. President Livingston didn't ask for an explanation and seemed to deflate physically into a mere fraction of his former size and presence. 'Why?' the President asked faintly. 'Why?' Lambert felt a shiver run up his spine, and he crossed his arms to ward off the chill.

A stunned silence filled the room. Had the President at that moment shown decisive leadership, Lambert might have sunk into the noise of his scattered thoughts and taken a back seat to the men around him, all decades his senior. But when he saw the incredulity on the President's face, Lambert felt compelled to step to the fore and do his job as the President's national security adviser. He felt the adrenaline charge his system, and in an instant his mind cleared and Lambert felt – he saw – with a clarity not normally attained what was coming and what was required of him and of his boss. 'Mr President,' Lambert said, and everyone turned to him, 'we need to discuss an Air Combat Command alert order.'

'An alert order? An order to do what?'

Lambert's jaw hurt, and he forced himself to loosen its clench. He didn't hesitate – the apocalyptic vision born from years of study stood full-blown before his mind's eye, leaving only one rational course of action. 'An alert order to implement the Single Integrated Operational Plan, sir. To strike, and destroy, the remaining Russian nuclear forces.'

90TH STRATEGIC MISSILE WING, WARREN AFB, WYOMING
June 11, 0530 GMT (2230 Local)

Chris Stuart heard the heavy boom on closing of the Launch Control Center's concrete blast door, doubly reinforced with steel rods and coated with special polymers to dampen the electromagnetic pulse of a nuclear detonation. Access to the bottom of the elevator shaft was now sealed off. Double titanium blast doors had also closed off the top of the shaft. The physical links of the two men in the underground center to the aboveground Launch Control Facility and the three airmen stationed there were now severed.

Stuart looked over and watched while Scott Langford reached up and ran his index finger under the yellow ascot that he wore inside the collar of his blue blouse. The finality of the sound didn't seem to bother the man, who sat in his padded aircraft-style leather chair positioned twelve feet from and at a right angle to Stuart's chair.

The launch center, a one-piece steel capsule sunk 100 feet underneath the former cavalry post, was suspended from the roof of its cavern by four hydraulic jacks. Its interior ceiling was curved along the forty-one-foot length and twenty-six-foot width of the capsule.

The two men were on the second run through their prefiring checklists, confirming the correct positioning of every switch and the correct status of every indicator on their two identical consoles. Nine of the ten lights on Stuart's panel shone green. The tenth, missile number eight, which they had visited on their ride out to the Launch Control Center, shone red.

This is a drill. This is a drill. This is a drill, Stuart kept thinking, like a mantra, to keep himself calm. But the whole base had gone to DEFCON 2. He shook his head again and forced the thought to vanish. *I'll pick up a bottle of Scotch at the Ground Zero and have a whispered conversation about this with the other launch officers when my shift is up tomorrow.*

The buzzing of the 'red phone,' the Primary Alerting System connecting the Air Combat Command headquarters to its 152 missile launching centers, caused Stuart to freeze. A red light lit on the base of the phone.

Stuart looked at Langford, who was lifting his red phone off the cradle. As Stuart reached for his own phone, he could already hear in his head the cool voice of the computer from all the drills of training: 'Big Noise, Lemon Juice. Big Noise, Lemon Juice.'

The recorded message, repeating itself continually, was in the familiar cool woman's voice. 'Sea Plane, Lemon Juice. Sea Plane, Lemon Juice. Sea Plane, Lemon Juice.' The world stood still. It was as if the filter through which Stuart saw the world had suddenly changed and everything around him seemed alien, bathed in a stark new illumination. A tickling feeling spread over his scalp and trickled down his spine, and he shivered as he replaced the receiver in its cradle. He pushed the orange button off to the side of the phone, extinguishing, he knew, the one small light on the console at ACC Headquarters. One more person knew. He had been informed. He knew. '*Sea Plane*,' Stuart thought. '*This is not a drill.*'

'I have Air Defense Warning Yellow,' Langford said without turning around. 'Confirm.' It sounded to Stuart as if he were a mile away, but he responded as trained with, 'Air Defense Warning Yellow – confirmed.'

'I've still got number eight showing off line. Get on the horn and give 'em a shove,' Langford said, opening the black leather logbook of the Launch Control Center to record the event.

Stuart looked at the white radio telephone on his console for several seconds before he reached up to hit the button, ringing the telephone in the access tunnel of the number eight silo.

'Senior Master Sergeant Kline, here,' Stuart heard the tinny sound through the receiver. It was the twangy accent of the man they had seen earlier at the open blast door of the silo. *Kli-i-ine*, Stuart tried to mimic in his mind as he formed the name with his lips, flattening the *i* of the man's name as the sergeant had done himself.

'Sergeant Kline,' Stuart said, 'we've got a Yellow alert.' Stuart's own voice sounded distant, and he had to concentrate hard to remember the purpose of the call. 'How long before you can put number eight back up?'

'Jee-zus. What the hell's goin' on, sir?'

'I don't know.'

Stuart clearly heard a sigh over the line. 'Well, we could just deactivate the PENAID master control and patch 'er up.'

Stuart felt distracted as he blinked several times, Kli-i-ine's words looping back through his mind several times until he thought to process them. 'Do you, uh,' Stuart began, pausing to compose the rest of his question, 'do you have to take the whole PENAID package off?'

'Well . . . no, sir,' Kline said. 'The fault showed up in the chaff dispenser circuitry. We could get into the master control and – hell, we could just sear the circuits right off the board if ya think we should. All the penetration aids'll pro'bly show up as 'Non-Op' on the run-up, but the decoys and jammers'll be active. Hey, but we'd be messin' up a two thousand dollar circuit board.'

The logjam of Stuart's confused thoughts was suddenly broken by the realization. *It's a fuckin' test*, Stuart realized, *and Kline's in on it*! Stuart pinched his lips closed to mask his smile, knowing now what to do, his brain functioning smoothly again. 'How long would it take to sear the circuits off the board?'

'To get the assembly back in and closed,' Kline took a deep breath, 'oh, and then to reattach the comm umbilical – forty-five minutes. I don't know, maybe more.'

'That's too long, Sergeant,' Stuart said curtly, his lips curling up as he imagined how that would sound on the audio tapes they would review. *'Personnel Reliability Profile Tests,'* Stuart thought. They were always having to change things up since the first thing launch officers did was tell one another about the drills despite the stern warnings about secrecy.

'Well, sir,' Kline said, 'I guess we could go ahead and start reattachin' the umbilical now, but it'd violate safety procedures.' *Oh*, Stuart thought. *A good one. Safety versus combat capability.* 'You know,' Kline continued, 'if there's a surge when we slide the PENAID board back into the rack 'cause of the static electricity—'

'How long if you risk it?' Stuart asked. *'Logical problem solving,'* Stuart could see in his mind's eye as the PRP boys filled out his evaluation.

'Maybe thirty, twenty-five minutes.'

'Do it. It's on my authority,' Stuart said in a voice that he deepened for effect.

'Okay, sir,' Kline said. 'Oh, uh, sir . . . would ya mind keepin' me informed?'

'Sure,' Stuart said, hanging up with a smile. Stuart knew he had 'done good.' *Get the bird off the ground at all costs.*

'How long till number eight's back on line?' Langford asked.

The smile was still on Stuart's face. 'Kline said half an hour, minimum.'

Langford stared back at Stuart for a second but then went back to the checklist they had each been running through after the initial alert. Stuart picked up the laminated pages of the manual held together by three rings at the top and went to the beginning of the preceding page as was procedure if you were interrupted. *Bet Langford didn't think to do that*, Stuart thought smugly. *Score one for the Kid.*

As Stuart idly ran through the checklist, he glanced around the ceiling of the capsule for the camera that he'd heard they'd begun hiding for the 'Purps.' The row of lights in front of him shone from his console. *I bet the birds aren't even on our line*, he thought.

MARCH AIR FORCE BASE, RIVERSIDE, CALIFORNIA
June 11, 0530 GMT (2130 Local)

'Clear!' 'Clear!' 'Clear!' rang out, starting from the opposite end of the hangar and moving toward Chandler. At each shout, an airman raised his right arm straight up. The shouts grew closer.

'Clear!' the air force technical sergeant next to Chandler yelled, raising his own arm and then dropping it. The arms of the airmen down the line promptly fell also. As the sounds of roaring jet takeoffs from the runways outside still continued almost nonstop, the technical sergeant turned, walked over to a panel similar in appearance to a circuit breaker box, and pressed an oversize green button.

All at once the button lit up and a loud horn began repeatedly blasting out one short buzz after another. There was a loud mechanical click, and a deep rumble resonated throughout the hangar. The wall immediately in front of Chandler began to rise, moving slowly but at an even pace.

In a couple of seconds the whole scene on the tarmac became visible. In the artificial glare of lights whose sole purpose was to turn night into brilliant day there sat a fleet of eight aircraft over which frantically clambered dozens of air force personnel.

DELTA, AMERICAN, CONTINENTAL read the names along the gleaming white fuselages of their transports, their familiar colors and logos seeming terribly incongruous given their intended mission. A few cheers and 'all rights' rang up from the masses of men in the hangar. Chandler guessed that they, as he, had expected air force transports with webbed straps folded out from the wall.

The sights in the background, however, quickly squelched all conversations. A strategic bomber, a B-1B, roared down the runway, the blue flame streaking a hundred feet to the rear of its four engines as it rattled the night air with its awful noise. Many of the men covered their ears as the sound bordered on painful, and as the plane quickly receded into the distance and the technical sergeant shouted, 'What?' into the telephone on the wall next to him, another bomber turned out onto the runway. Just before its roaring engines lit up the night, Chandler heard the wail of a siren slowly rising and then falling.

'Yours is the Delta L-1011 at the far end of the first row, Major!' the technical sergeant shouted to Chandler over the roar, pointing at the aircraft.

'What the hell's going on?' Chandler shouted back.

The man stared back, his face a blank mask. 'Air raid' was all he said.

'Air raid?' Chandler shouted. '*Here*?'

The man just nodded his head, every bit as shocked as Chandler. 'You'd better get your men on that aircraft.'

Chandler looked out at the Delta jet. A large silver-haired man in a pilot's uniform stood on the landing atop the stairs, waving his arm toward the hangar furiously and throwing his head to one side in what must have been an angry shout. Master Sergeant Barnes and First Lieutenant Bailey looked over at him. Everyone was waiting. *Waiting on me*, Chandler realized.

He lifted the large camouflaged duffel bag heavily laden with gear that Barnes had obtained for him and turned for the first time to view the sea of faces staring at him from the column that had been formed behind him. 'Double t-i-ime, *ha-a-a-rch*!' he shouted, and then turned and began the slow run, laboring under the heavy load of equipment. Looking back out of the corner of his eyes after a few steps, he saw that the men and women were following.

UPPER ATMOSPHERE, NO. OF KARTALY MISSILE FIELD
June 11, 0533 GMT (0533 Local)

The 485,000-pound Russian SS-18 Model 4 was nearing the end of its boost phase, having risen to over 60 miles above the earth and the same distance to the north of its silo. At 121 feet in length and 10 feet in diameter, its throw-weight exceeded that of every other missile of war in the world. When its final stage shut off, the rocket booster motors would have given it nearly all of the impetus that it would need to carry it in the Minimum Energy Trajectory high over the polar ice cap to its target just east of Los Angeles, well within the 11,000-kilometer maximum range.

Just behind the warheads, the inertial guidance package's accelerometer was busy measuring the accelerations experienced by the spacecraft, converting those accelerations into estimates of distance traveled and speed. The onboard computer took the accelerometer's estimates and waited for the precise moment at which the momentum of the missile was perfectly matched to its point in space to allow for a ballistic trajectory onto the warheads' targets. The calculation was constantly changing as the position and velocity of the missile changed, but the computer easily handled the calculus. It was the accelerometer and the booster's engine on which all depended.

Assembled in a 'clean room,' the accelerometer was capable of causing hundreds of meters of variance of the actual from the designated ground zero if a single mote of dust was to foul the device. And the solid-fuel booster, chosen because of its nearly constant state of readiness, was not nearly as easily shut off at the end of the boost phase as the liquid spray of the older rockets. If its burn were one one-thousandth of a second too short or too long, the warheads would miss by 600 meters, a critical error when your targets were hardened missile silos and launch centers. This missile's target, however, was March Air Force Base, relatively soft and much larger, therefore more forgiving of slight errors.

Each of the components of the missile in the boost phase got only one chance. When the accelerometer's estimates caused the computer to shut off the booster, the missile went ballistic, becoming an artillery projectile on a long arc. The booster could not be restarted.

Shutoff came eight minutes and thirteen seconds into the burn. Shortly after the fire of the rocket motors died out, the bus carrying the Post-Boost Vehicle decoupled from the booster and the long quiet ride through space began. Separated in the darkness of space by thousands of meters, the other PBVs of the squadron raced toward their various targets. The squadron's missiles carried with them 120 thermonuclear

warheads, each fourteen times more powerful than the Hiroshima and
Nagasaki bombs put together. They were joined as they rose to pass
over the clean white Novaya Zemlya of far northern Russia by ten
other squadrons' missiles, all arcing soundlessly through space toward
the United States.

I–10 OUTSIDE MARCH AFB, RIVERSIDE, CALIFORNIA
June 11, 0534 GMT (2134 Local)

'This has been a news bulletin from ABC Radio. Stay tuned for news
as it happens here on your ABC Radio network. We return you now
to your regularly scheduled broadcast.' The pains had come and gone
again, but Melissa now felt as if she had to stop to go to the bathroom.
'We've got forty-five minutes of nonstop rock and roll coming up for you,
starting out with Led Zeppelin's "Whole Lotta Love", so stay tuned to
your classic rock station, the Z-e-e-e.'

'Looking for a quality used car but tired of all that hype . . .' Melissa
hit the SCAN button on the radio. As Mexican music burst forth, she
saw the sign for MARCH AFB NEXT EXIT up ahead. The radio's tuner
moved on, and as she passed the exit she readjusted the seat belt,
which had begun to press uncomfortably against her belly.

'No-no-no-no. That's where the caller is all wrong. President
Livingston doesn't have the backbone to stand up to a salesman
on the telephone much less lead this nation into war. No, the North
Koreans will make some promises and . . .'

Melissa drove past the massive air base, thinking how close she was
to David, to someone to help her through whatever was coming.

'. . . sources in Moscow say the bursts were just south of the
city. We go now to John McDonald, who is on the telephone now in
Moscow. John?' Melissa quickly stabbed at the radio to stop the tuner
from scanning on.

'Peter, the bursts lit up the early morning sky of the Moscow skyline
not fifteen minutes ago. I was asleep in bed when the first hit, and
narrowly avoided serious injury as the second, which was much closer
to where I am, shattered the windows of my apartment on Vokzalnaya
Ulitsa in the west-southwestern part of the city. When I went out onto
my balcony I could see three, repeat, three mushroom-shaped clouds,
all to the south and east of my vantage point, and many fires spreading
all around in that part of the city.'

'John,' the radio announcer interrupted, 'John, is there any doubt in
your mind that those blasts were nuclear explosions?'

'None, absolutely none whatsoever, Peter,' the clearly shaken
Moscow reporter said. 'I've pulled the phone as far as it will reach

and can see one of the mushroom clouds from here. Even though roughly fifteen minutes have passed, the cloud is still generally in the same shape as it was before. That should attest to its size. It literally reaches from the ground up into the heavens and blew a large, round hole in the cloud cover that has hung low over Moscow these past few days. The top of the cloud is just now beginning to show signs of drift on the winds; like the top of an anvil-shaped head of a major thundercloud it is being blown downwind, which by my roughest of initial estimates appears to be away, I repeat, away from downtown Moscow.'

'My God,' Melissa said, her skin crawling and eyes thickening with moisture.

'Do you have any idea, John, any idea at all what might be going on?'

'Oh my God oh my God,' Melissa repeated, the words barely squeaking out of her throat as panic set in.

'Really, no, Peter.'

The horn of a speeding Mercedes sedan blared past Melissa as it weaved at high speed first in front of her car and then back into the left lane through the growing traffic.

'As I said, I was awakened by the blast, and Moscow radio and television are both off the air. Of course, there is Russia's ongoing war with China, which is a nuclear power.'

A loud, high-pitched hum replaced the talk on the radio. It whined on and on and on. There was no explanation of what the tone was, no prerecorded qualifiers that it was only a test. None of that was necessary. It was a familiar tone. Melissa had grown up hearing it periodically, and no one needed to tell her what it meant. She lowered her foot to the floor, and her Mazda accelerated easily past 100 miles per hour, the engine noise drowned out by the sound of the Emergency Broadcast System's hum.

NORAD BMEWS CENTER, THULE, GREENLAND
June 11, 0538 GMT (0038 Local)

The first narrow fan of energy emitted by the huge radar transmitter skimmed across the horizon to the north in a straight line until it sliced through the sky high above the Arctic Circle in northern Russia. For a fraction of a second, it bathed in its beam of energy the slender cylinder rising through the last reaches of the earth's atmosphere. The packets of energy in the beam bounced off the missile's fuselage like tiny BBs.

Several of the tiny packets of energy bounced straight back and in an instant collided at widely separated points on the radar's football-field-size phased-array antenna. The energy collected by the antenna was minute, but it was enough to rise above the transient background energy noise that was automatically filtered out by digital computers in the radar's processing center. The antenna registered a return.

An instant later, the second fan of energy, whose elevation was only fractions of an arc-second separated from the lower first fan's, bathed the same missile at an altitude hundreds of meters above the point of the first fan's return.

The computers now had two points in space and a time interval in between. They calculated the position, direction, and velocity of the missile and projected the general area of its target. The entire process from transmission of energy to calculation of data was nearly instantaneous, and the information flashed onto the Big Boards at NORAD and the other three American national command centers and at the Canadian Defense Ministry in Ottawa, setting off another round of alarms and flashing lights.

ABOARD NIGHTWATCH, OVER MARYLAND
June 11, 0540 GMT (0040 Local)

'I still just don't know,' the President said. 'I just don't know.' He shook his head. 'Where exactly are the Russian missiles headed?'

'All TELINT, Telemetry Intelligence, can tell us at this point is these general areas,' General Starnes said, touching his pen with a click to the monitor recessed into the wall of the conference room. The monitor had a number of lines and symbols on it, some flashing and some in blue, green, and red. But Lambert could tell one thing: the general outline of the map was North America, and the general's pen was circling areas all over the United States.

'We've got a CINCNORAD "Highly Probable Assessment,"' Starnes continued, 'on the boost vehicles heading for the general areas of our missile bases, sub pens, bomber bases, and radar sites, plus command and control centers. That's a pattern called "counterforce," meaning they've gone after our ability to fight a nuclear war, not "countervalue," meaning populations, cities, and industrial base.'

'How many are there now?' the President asked, consumed, Lambert thought, by the desire to know that number. *He's asked that a hundred times!*

'We have,' Starnes said, reading the screen, 'two hundred and seventy confirmed by radar and almost a thousand unconfirmed. You've got to assume now they'll all be confirmed. Based on the tubes they've expended, they've shot five models – SS-17s, 18s, 19s, 24s, and 25s. The 17s are MIRVed with four warheads, the 19s with six, and the others with ten. All the multiple warheads are somewhere in the three- to four-hundred-kiloton yields. Some of the SS-18s, their Model 1s, however, are gonna have just one warhead – the big twenty-five-megaton mothers – we just don't know how many or which ones. They'd use 'em for deep digging, though, so I'd guess they're the ones targeted for our hardened command centers. Finally, if they fired any of their couple of dozen FOBS, Fractional Orbital Bombardment System weapons, that come up from over the South Pole instead of the North, we won't pick them up for a few minutes yet.'

'So what does all this mean?' the President asked. 'What's going to happen?' He was looking at the floor, and then at the wall, and then at the table. He fidgeted and never looked up at the eyes of the others in the room.

'Mr President,' Lambert said slowly, trying to break through whatever barriers prevented the President's understanding, 'somewhere around a thousand plus warheads are going to strike the U.S. with an aggregate yield of around six or seven hundred megatons.'

The silence in the room had a weight and presence of its own.

'When?' the President asked in a stricken voice as he stared down at the conference table.

'We've got twenty-five minutes to go, sir,' General Starnes said as he looked at the screen. 'We've got to send a nuclear control order at least three, preferably five or six, minutes before impact. After that, and the missiles may not have time to escape the blast effects.'

'How bad . . . how bad is it going to be?' President Livingston asked in a quivering voice.

Lambert watched the President as his head slowly disappeared behind the shield of his hands. General Thomas looked over at the Secretary of Defense.

'Well, as I said, sir,' Starnes answered, gesturing with his hands despite the fact that the President could not see them, 'CINCNORAD should be getting the PARCS – that's the Perimeter Acquisition Radar Attack Characterization System – he should be getting the PARCS data in shortly and he'll give us an assessment. But there won't be much time after that to react.'

Lambert swallowed, the dryness of his throat surprising. *It's so bad*, Lambert realized, *that Starnes can't even answer the question*.

'Sir,' the Secretary of Defense said, 'I have to tell you that I concur with Mr Lambert. I think it's time that you considered a nuclear control order. We clearly have tactical warning sufficient for you to release strategic nuclear weapons under the Congressional Nuclear War Powers Directive – Number 14 – that was passed by secret vote in 1972, and we are very shortly going to lose a substantial portion of our forces to that first wave of Russian missiles. We either fire them now, or . . . or they're gone, Mr President.'

The door opened and an airman, speaking to General Thomas, said, 'Sir, it's General Razov on line one.'

After a pause, the President said, 'How the hell did he know where we are?'

'He probably called the White House switchboard,' Thomas said as he leaned forward and rested his finger on the blinking button, pausing to ensure that all were quiet. 'General Razov?'

'General Thomas,' Razov began. 'There has been a tragic, tragic mistake, and my country is guilty of it. As you must know by now, missiles were fired at your country from certain land-based missile fields by a madman, a General Zorin, who had seized control of the nuclear codes. We had made every attempt possible to stop him and he will shortly be in our custody. But, obviously, we have failed in preventing this terrible atrocity, and in this we will forever be guilty in the eyes of humanity.'

'General Razov,' President Livingston said, suddenly animated, 'this is the President of the United States. Are you saying that this was a complete mistake?'

'Yes, sir,' Razov said, 'a mistake of terrible proportions but a mistake nonetheless.'

'And that means,' the President said, his eyes narrowing, 'that you will not fire *any* of the remaining weapons that you possess at this country, or take *any* other hostile actions against us of any kind?'

'Absolutely not, Mr President! We have no reason at all to harbor any hostility toward you, your people, or your nation. We are friends, allies. There will be no hostilities initiated by the armed forces of Russia from this moment forward.'

The President began to say something further, but Lambert stood and reached over to hit the MUTE button on the phone console. 'Mr President, I would advise you to terminate this communication right now.'

'Why?' the President asked. 'We can work this thing out. He said it was a mistake!'

'Mr President,' Lambert said in as even a voice as he could muster, allowing the words to provide the impetus, 'in twenty-two minutes, this nation will suffer the single worst loss of life in its history. There is only one rational response, and that is to retaliate massively, to destroy their remaining force before it can be generated and fired at us.'

'But . . . but you heard him,' the President said to the others around the table, clinging tenuously to his earlier position. 'It was a mistake. Greg, you above all others . . . You know these people. Do you think what Razov said is some sort of trick?'

'It doesn't matter *what* it was,' Lambert said. 'We're at war, whether by accident or by design.'

'General Thomas?' Razov said over the speakerphone. 'President Livingston?'

'We have twenty-one minutes,' Lambert said, stressing the words by speaking them slowly, 'to decide what to do, Mr President. We have work to do.'

Marine General Fuller spoke up. 'Mr President, Rome's burning, and we're screwin' around talkin' to this son of a bitch.'

'Sir,' the Secretary of Defense said, and all turned their attention to him. 'This attack is going to have a profound effect on our nation. You have to consider how it will appear, in the aftermath, if . . . if we were being talked out of retaliating while their attack was only minutes away from destroying the vast majority of our weapons on the ground.'

The President's eyes dropped to the table. 'You're all telling me I don't have a choice. I can't stop this thing.' Everyone watched as he took a deep breath and fell back into his chair, slumped lower now than before, his face ashen. He nodded at Lambert and waved his hand for Lambert to release the MUTE button.

'General Razov,' the President said in a tired, far-away voice. 'We expect to hold you to your pledge of no further aggression against our country. Good-bye.'

'Mr Presi—!' Razov shouted as Lambert cut the line.

There was a long silence, and then the Secretary of Defense said, 'Walter – it's time.'

'I don't know, I don't know,' the President said, his hands rubbing his scalp roughly and destroying the always neat order of his hair as he shook his head.

'Dammit, sir!' Starnes burst out. 'When we lose those ICBMs, we lose our ability to take out their ICBMs. Now, the sub-launched missiles are fine,' he said in the direction of the Chief of Naval Operations, 'but they're just not accurate or powerful enough, and there aren't enough of 'em, to do that job.'

Lambert took a deep breath and said, 'Sir, the possibility exists that after losing all of our ICBMs, our bomber bases, our air defense system, and our command centers, the Russians generate their remaining forces over the next few hours and fire again, this time at secondary and tertiary targets. Those targets would be everything we've got of strategic value, military *and* industrial. We'd lose not just millions dead, but tens of millions, maybe a hundred million, and we'd cease to exist as a functioning world military and economic power. Given that, sir, if a follow-on strike left their silos, I can assure you that the firing options we'd present to you for the submarines' missiles would not be remote Russian ICBM bases. It would truly be Doomsday, and the targets we'd recommend would start with the human populations of Moscow and St Petersburg.'

The President said nothing. He did nothing. 'Eighteen minutes, sir,' Starnes said quietly.

The President sat there motionless for a moment, and then, to everyone's amazement, rose from his chair and headed for the door. 'I'll be back in a few minutes,' he mumbled, and was gone.

The Joint Chiefs looked at each other, heads shaking.

General Starnes finally said, 'I've got tens of thousands of *my* men and *my* women sitting at their posts at ground zero waiting to *die*, and you and I *damn* well know where that son of a bitch is going. *Goddammit!*'

'Mr Secretary,' General Thomas said, 'if he's not back here in' – Thomas looked at his watch – 'two minutes, I'm going to ask you to poll the Cabinet and declare the President incompetent. That should give us just enough time . . .'

'General Thomas!' the Secretary of Defense said sharply. 'All of you! If I hear any more talk of that nature, I'll immediately relieve you of your commands!'

'Your quarters are right here, sir,' the Secret Service agent said, indicating a door on which a sign read NCA (KNOCK BEFORE ENTERING).

Walter Livingston opened the door and saw the First Lady resting on the lower bunk. She immediately swung her legs to the floor. He closed the door behind him and turned to face her.

'Walter?' she asked, and when he couldn't return her look she rose to her feet and walked over to embrace him. 'Darling, I've heard. I've heard.' She patted his back. 'I know about the Russian attack. A crewman told me.' Her hands stroked the back of his neck, and he dissolved into the arms of his wife, shaking his head. 'What?' she asked. 'Are you all right, Walter?' He couldn't answer. 'What is it?' When he said nothing, she ushered him to a seat at the cabin's small writing desk and stood behind him, rubbing his shoulders. 'Why don't you tell me what it is.'

With his eyes closed, the President shook his head. 'Walter,' she prodded, gently, gently.

'I've made a terrible, terrible mistake, Margaret. It's a mistake that is going to cost lives, millions of lives.' Her hands fell still for just a second, but in that second he knew that no matter how much support she or anyone else could lend him, he was all alone. It was he, and he alone, who had blundered. Her hands resumed their deep massage and she said, 'What happened?'

He turned and tugged her gently by the hand to sit on the bed so he could see her. 'I had Moore call the Chinese to warn them of the Russian attack.'

'And?'

'And that gave the Chinese the time to get a shot off at the Russians, which triggered their launch against us.'

She let out a sigh of relief, her hand resting on her chest as she relaxed. He realized just how tense he had made her. 'Walter, that's it? That's your great sin?'

He stared at her for a moment, feeling some relief in watching his wife's reaction despite the fact that she still didn't see the trouble coming. 'That's not why I'm here.' Margaret sat up straight and waited, as always. 'I've got to decide what to do, whether to retaliate. I don't have long, just a few minutes.'

Her eyes drifted off. 'Was their attack a mistake? Truly a mistake?'

'Probably. Yes.'

'And is it going to be . . .? How bad is it going to be?'

'Terrible. They're going to rain missiles down all over our bases.'

'But not the cities?'

'No, not yet.'

She again sat still, staring off into space. He looked at her, waiting as he'd always done. Despite what his detractors and the stand-up comics had regularly intimated, she never made the decisions for him. She didn't need to. They always agreed. She always came to the same conclusion that he knew in his heart to be the right one. He just needed to hear it. He needed one other person to be with him in making the big decisions, to help shoulder the weight of them. 'Do I shoot back, Margaret?' She looked up at him with a look of deep sympathy on her face, and his head drooped from the weight of her silent answer.

'Is he in there?' Lambert asked.

The Secret Service agent nodded.

Lambert knocked.

'Who is it?' came the muffled voice of the First Lady.

'Greg Lambert, ma'am.'

'Come in.'

Lambert opened the door, and the President and First Lady were sitting across a small desk from each other in the spartan quarters. 'Fourteen minutes, Mr President.'

The First Lady looked back over at her husband and patted him on the hand. 'It's time, dear,' she said.

'Are you sure? Is it the right thing to do?' the President asked.

'You know it is, Walter,' she said, leaning over to cup his cheek with her hand.

Lambert turned away, and the President joined him at the door for the walk to the conference room, the eyes of every airman they passed searching the President's haggard face. When they were almost to the conference room door, the President stopped and turned to Lambert.

The look in his eyes was that of a shattered man. *He's losing it*, Lambert thought. 'All my life, Greg, I dreamed of being President.' His face was pale and he looked sick. 'But I never dreamed . . .' He shook his head. 'It was never this way.'

General Thomas stepped out of the conference room and said, 'The CINCNORAD assessment is coming in, sir.'

The President turned and went into the conference room, Lambert following.

'We're all here, Al,' Thomas said in the direction of the speakerphone. 'Go ahead.' Thomas held up ten and then three fingers to the President – thirteen minutes – as General Wilson began to speak.

'Okay,' General Wilson said over the speaker. 'It's a classic "counter-force" attack, but with a piss-poor targeting plan. It's full of holes and phased all wrong. We've got roughly 70 warheads coming down on the 341st Strategic Missile Wing at Malmstrom, 230 on each of the 312th at Grand Forks and the 91st at Minot, and 270 on the 90th at Warren. Mr President, those'll put a whole lotta hurt on our Minutemen IIIs and MXs.'

'Where are those bases?' the President asked, composed again and sitting upright in his chair.

'Malmstrom's in Montana,' Starnes answered, 'Grand Forks and Minot are in North Dakota, and Warren is in Wyoming. Twelve minutes, sir,' he said as if to chastise the President for wasting time.

'Next, there's the ACC bomber/tanker bases,' General Wilson said. 'A dozen or so warheads are headed toward each of Blytheville in Arkansas, March in California, McConnell in Kansas, Loring in Maine, Sawyer and Wurtsmith in Michigan, Whiteman in Missouri, Griffis in upstate New York, Ellsworth in South Dakota, Carswell and Dyess in Texas, and Fairchild in Washington State. Those plus the warheads targeted at Grand Forks and Minot will hit all of our CONUS Bomb Wings and primary FB-111, B-1B, B-2, B-52G, and B-52H bases. Most of our aircraft are airborne now, but we'll have to operate out of alternate relocation and overseas bases, and we'll lose a lot of our support, maintenance, and rearmament capabilities.'

'Excuse me,' the military liaison officer, previously quiet as a church mouse, said at the opposite end of the table. 'Should I . . .?' he asked, putting both hands on the combination lock of the black leather satchel.

'Open it,' Thomas ordered as Wilson went on in the background.

'They also went for our boomer bases,' Wilson said as Lambert heard the sound of the zipper running down the case. 'Eight to ten were fired at each of New London, Connecticut; Bremerton, Washington; Kings Bay, Georgia; and Charleston, South Carolina. They left out Norfolk and San Diego, but they may be targeted from ballistic missile subs. They also went for our C³ – command, control, and communications.

Eight are targeted at Cheyenne Mountain in Colorado Springs, three at Raven Rock on the Pennsylvania-Maryland border, and two are headed for ACC headquarters at Offut. They didn't target D.C., Mount Weather, or Greenbriar, or something went wrong.'

'What about our early warning and air defense systems?' General Thomas asked.

'They sh-o-t,' Wilson said, casually stretching out the last word as if reading a grocery list, 'let's see, between one and five warheads each at Elmendorf and Shemya Island in Alaska, Beale and Vandenberg in California, Falcon in Colorado, Robins in Georgia, Kaena Point in Hawaii, Otis Air National Guard Base in Massachusetts, Goodfellow in Texas, and McChord in Washington State, plus the warheads that they already had for Griffiss in New York and two warheads for Thule, Greenland, the only target outside the U.S.'

'That may indicate an intention for a follow-on attack with bombers and sub-launched missiles,' Thomas said to the President, who listened impassively.

'I'm sorry, but TTG's eleven minutes,' General Wilson said over the speakerphone. 'I need to hurry. To finish up, there are twenty warheads in the 'Special' category. Three of 'em are up and down each of the coasts about a hundred miles out to sea, plus another south of Mississippi in the Gulf of Mexico. The others are a mystery. Some, I'm sure, will end up being high-altitude electro-magnetic pulse bursts, but the rest just look like flat-out misses that won't even fuse – I hope.'

'Al,' General Starnes said, 'this is Bill.'

'Hey, Billy,' Wilson's voice came over the speaker, the address oddly familiar in tone.

There was a brief pause during which Starnes's head dropped, and then rose again. 'What's the total count, Al?' Starnes asked.

'One thousand one hundred and twenty-two warheads in all,' Wilson said. 'One one two two,' he repeated.

'Thanks, Al,' the Secretary of Defense said, and the Joint Chiefs then all mouthed their thanks also. 'Overall, Mr President,' the Secretary continued, 'it's not a "strategic attack." It's not an attempt to reduce our general war-fighting capabilities or to eliminate our population. It's a "counterforce" strike like we thought, directed at our nuclear forces.'

'Any SLBMs or cruise missiles yet?' Admiral Dixon, Chief of Naval Operations, asked.

'Nope,' Wilson answered over the speaker. 'Nothing but the ICBMs Not even any bomber activity. I think that might explain the poor firing plot. They've left a lot of holes that presumably should've been – or are gonna be – filled by Backfires, submarine-launched ballistic missiles, and surface- and air-launched cruise missiles.'

'Ten minutes,' Thomas said.

'And they could be on the way,' the CNO said to the President. 'The seven warheads being shot into the water are clearly intended to "blue out" our sensors before exposing their boomers.'

'What the hell does that mean?' the President asked.

'The Russians keep most of their subs in a "bastion" defense,' Admiral Dixon explained, 'which are operational areas just off their ports at Kalina and Murmansk in the Kara Sea. They keep the bastions defended with combined arms naval and air units. They try to sneak out a few subs, however, to get them close to us and cut down the flight time. We've got tails on about two thirds of 'em and they'll never get a shot off on DEFCON 1, which we went to twenty minutes ago. As for the rest, we've got a few dozen P-3s and P-7s headed out to sea with a bellyful of torpedoes just waiting for us to give 'em coordinates, but those bursts are going to mean that we'll have to wait until their missiles break the surface before we get a solution.'

'Mr President,' Lambert interrupted, 'what are your orders?'

'Our tubes are flooded and ready to go,' the CNO said. 'I say we turn the bastards we got in our sights into scrap metal right now.'

'I've got to go,' General Wilson said, interrupting over the speakerphone.

The President spoke up. 'I'd like to know what's happening out there, General,' he said to the speakerphone. 'Give me a call as soon as you start getting reports.'

'I'm' – the hesitant voice came back over the speaker – 'I'm afraid this is probably it for me, Mr President. On behalf of my command and me, it's been an honor to have been at your service. Good luck to you all. See ya in hell, Billy.' The line clicked and went silent quickly, General Wilson clearly not wanting to force the men to respond.

Starnes was standing behind the military liaison officer, the general's normally erect frame slumped slightly. *They were friends*, it suddenly dawned on Lambert.

'Nine minutes, Mr President. It's time – right now,' General Thomas said, his jaw set firmly. 'They've got roughly two warheads targeted at each of our ICBM silos and launch centers. We've got to use those weapons now or they're gone.'

'I've already decided,' the President said, looking up from the table. There was a long pause before the President asked, 'What are my options?'

General Starnes quickly took the three black ring binders the military liaison officer had removed from the bag – the football – and placed them on the table between Lambert and the President.

'Do you have your code card, sir?' Thomas asked as Lambert read the books' covers: 'Procedures Manual for Emergency Broadcast System,' 'Presidential Emergency Facilities,' and the book whose importance dwarfed that of the others, 'Nuclear Control Orders – SIOP-6C.'

'There is one in here,' the military liaison officer said, rummaging around in the nearly empty bag.

'I've got mine,' the President said. He fished his wallet from his back pocket and pulled out a blue, red, and black plastic card, handing it to General Thomas. General Thomas peeled off the gold tape at the bottom and read 'Alpha Tango Five Seven Six Bravo.' The Chief of Staff of the Air Force repeated the code into the 'gold phone' of the Joint Chiefs of Staff Alerting Network. Over the gold phone's speaker, the CINCACC from his airborne command post and his doomed deputy commander standing on the balcony overlooking the half-football-field-size underground Air Combat Command Headquarters in Omaha could be heard passing the message along to their respective senior controllers.

At almost the same time, both men's voices came over the speakerphone saying, 'Authenticated!'

'Okay, Mr President,' General Starnes said, slowly opening the 'Black Book' with the nuclear options, all printed in red. 'We've got eight minutes,' he continued in a calm voice. 'You've just given nuclear weapons release authorization to all nuclear capable commands. We now need an Emergency Action Message, which will be the nuclear control order. Under Single Integrated Operational Plan 6C, you've got twelve nuclear execution messages divided into major attack options, selected attack options, limited attack options, and regional attack options. Each of the attack options is divided up into types of targets: counterforce, other military – including leadership – and economic. You've also got 'country withhold' options. There are about six thousand warheads programmed for use in SIOP, some of which would be held in reserve. It sounds like a lot, sir, but it's a whole helluva lot less than we used to have before the strategic reduction treaties.'

'What would you recommend?' the President asked.

'The major attack options,' Starnes said. 'Since they haven't targeted any of our larger cities or our economic infrastructure, I'd recommend retaliation in kind: counterforce. We should take out every nuclear weapon we can while withholding Russian cities.'

'Okay,' the President replied. 'Get rid of as many of their nuclear weapons as possible. That's the plan I want.' An airman stood beside the President with message slips in hand.

Starnes's hand jerked his telephone receiver off the hook, and he issued the orders.

'There are about five thousand warheads allocated to the major attack option – Russian counterforce strike,' Thomas said. 'Do you want to run over the target list, sir?'

'No, no. I'll leave that to you,' the President said, getting up and walking toward the door.

'What about the subs they've got out in open water, Mr President?'

Admiral Dixon shouted as the President stood in the doorway. The airman said, 'The prime ministers of Canada and Great Britain and the president of France are on the line, Mr President.'

'Sink them – sink them if you think you have to,' the President said, pausing a moment longer as if in confusion before taking the message slips and leaving.

The CNO grabbed his telephone to issue the orders. As Thomas and the Secretary of Defense picked up their own phones, Lambert watched the men's lips moving but couldn't hear their words. It all seemed like a dream, not the way a war was supposed to be fought. It was too rushed. Too panicked. Lambert looked over at Marine General Fuller, the only officer with nothing to do. Fuller's eyes were closed, and his lips were moving, mouthing words that only he and his Maker could hear.

UPPER ATMOSPHERE, OVER CENTRAL CALIFORNIA
June 11, 0549 GMT (0549 Local)

Falling from an altitude of 610 miles, the Post-Boost Vehicle was picking up speed rapidly. Just before the first wisps of atmosphere began to tug at the PBV, it reached its top speed of 12,160 miles per hour.

The inertial guidance system did its best to predict the PBV's actual position in space. Over the past few decades, highly refined geophysical measurements had been undertaken by Russian satellites to give the SS-18's instrument package precise information on the locations of the silo from which it was launched and the American air base at which it was aimed. The complex mathematical model of the earth's gravitational field had been refined over the years by teams of academics, and the model was programmed into the computer in the nose cone of the PBV. The precise positions of the moon and the sun had been predicted for decades into the future so that a launch at any moment in time during those decades would be able to factor in their ever changing gravitational effects.

The flight profile over the North Pole, however, had never actually been tested due to the inability to conduct over-the-Pole test flights. The gravitational field over the North Pole differed slightly from the gravity over the east-to-west test range from Kazakhstan to Siberia. A huge dome of dense molten nickel miles beneath the seafloor under the polar ice cap had created a gravitational anomaly that tugged the PBV downward slightly. The shot was low, as were many of the other shots from the missile's squadron that overflew the nickel dome.

The shroud eject motor in the PBV's nose jettisoned the cone, uncovering the missile's four-ton load of ten tightly packed warheads. At the precisely appointed moment the first warhead was ejected and the storable hypergolic liquid propellant fired briefly from the small fourth stage rocket in the tail of the PBV. A second warhead was released, and the rocket pivoted on its mount and fired again, vectoring the PBV in a slightly different direction and changing its momentum to target the third warhead 1,200 meters away from the second. The ballet continued for several seconds more through the thin upper atmosphere until the last of the warheads, coal-black cones with needle-sharp points, were flying free.

Like a mother protecting her young, the PBV began deployment of her penetration aids to cloak the ten warheads from the once planned but then canceled American ballistic missile defenses. Radar-reflective decoys were ejected and inflated to confuse nonexistent radars. A powerful electronic jammer switched on, blanketing the electromagnetic spectrum with noise to interfere with nonexistent radio-controlled interceptors. Canisters on both sides of the fuselage began to emit tiny strips of metallized glass fiber chaff in great spurts to lure nonexistent antiballistic missiles away from the warheads.

The atmosphere was thickening, and the PBV itself was beginning to suffer from the aerodynamic forces. The friction of the air against the PBV's nonaerodynamic shape heated its surfaces to ever higher temperatures. The airflow through the maze of brackets and wires began to buffet the craft, and it began a slow-motion yaw to the left. Wires were stripped out of the exposed areas. The computer heated to above its designed operating temperature and began to experience errors, automatically restarting itself over and over in a dying attempt to resume normal operation. The nonmetallic surfaces of the PBV began flaring, flashing brightly and then disappearing, as each substance reached its individual burning point. The metal itself began to glow.

Higher and higher the temperature climbed as the PBV's yaw became a tumble. The fuselage began to melt, the loosened liquid metal flying off the fuselage in a streak of fine white spray. The process accelerated. As the PBV tumbled, the temperature along each new leading edge shot up, melting away the metal and reducing the PBV's mass in fiery displays. Before the vehicle had completed one complete rotation, it had come apart into three pieces. Each of the three pieces in turn further melted and broke into more and smaller pieces. The spray of trailing liquids and gases from the metal components streaked downward toward the earth, trailing the larger remnants of the PBV like the tail of a comet. Many minutes later, remnants of the PBV, no piece larger than a marble, pelted the hills of central California, penetrating to embed a couple of meters under the dry western soil.

Chapter Four

90TH STRATEGIC MISSILE WING, WARREN AFB, WYOMING
June 11, 0553 GMT (2253 Local)

Stuart heard the warbling tone of the alarm. Although he had been expecting it, his head shot up to the rotating red beacon on the ceiling. The alarm and beacon could be set off, Stuart knew, only by an encrypted uplink sent automatically upon the lifting of the red phone from its cradle by an ACC senior controller. Or by the examiners sitting in their air-conditioned van, cables running into the Launch Control Facility above. His eyes fell to the red telephone on his console.

Langford yelled, 'EAM incoming!'

Stuart could feel his heart leap and his throat constrict as he lifted the red phone of the Primary Alerting System. Every pulse of the siren chilled him even though he knew it was just a game. The teletype in the corner began clattering. *An Emergency Action Message*, Stuart thought. *They're goin' all out.*

Stuart put the phone to his ear just in time to hear the voice of the senior controller say, 'November Echo Victor Two Four Bravo Niner Zulu Break Niner Golf Alpha Break Seven Lima Alpha Break Three Quebec Alpha.' The controller began to repeat the control code as Stuart copied it onto his notepad.

Stuart hung the telephone up and hit the ACKNOWLEDGE switch, extinguishing one of the two lights for their launch center on the senior controllers' panels, which were lit again on issuance of the new orders. He then pulled over his head the lanyard that hung from his neck and found the familiar flat metal key with a red grip. The electronically produced clattering sound from across the capsule indicated that Langford had opened the red safe at the base of his console.

I'm behind, I'm behind, Stuart thought. He jammed the key into the lock as Langford began reading, "November – Echo . . ." When Stuart opened his own red safe, its clattering sound, designed to prevent clandestine opening, joined that of Langford's safe. The world was filled with the sounds of a firing drill, just like in school.

Stuart pulled the sealed authenticator package from the safe and ripped it open. He dumped the metal board, ring binder, and round key out of the opaque plastic envelope as Langford continued his chant of numbers and letters. Picking up the felt marker from its holder, Stuart held the board up to his notes.

Suddenly, the alarm fell silent. 'Gentlemen,' a woman's voice said calmly but clearly over the center's loudspeaker, 'you have received an authorized launch instruction from the National Command Authority. Gentlemen, you have received an authorized launch instruction from the National Command Authority.' 'Betty,' as the recording was called, repeated the message four times.

'November!' Stuart said, writing the letter N in the first empty box of the board. Immediately above was the preprinted block letter N. 'Echo!' he said as he wrote E below the large black E above. 'Victor!' he said, repeating the procedure.

Langford yelled, 'I've got a valid EAM! Confirm!'

'Two!' Stuart said, writing and checking. 'Four!' he said. 'Bravo!' 'Niner!' 'Zulu!'

Stuart stared at the board on which all eight letters and numbers matched the preprinted authenticator letters and numbers. Stuart said, 'I confirm valid EAM!' and the first wispy shred of doubt about his earlier conclusion reached out to touch him, sending a chill down his back. He squirmed briefly in his chair. *They must have switched the sealed authenticator package with one especially for this test*, he decided. *They'd never send out the valid code.*

'EWO Checklist!' Langford ordered.

They began the Emergency War Order Checklist, activating the missile arming and firing circuits to the squadron's fifty missiles – if they were on line. Stuart knew that miles and miles away there were four other Launch Control Centers. *What are they doing?* he wondered. *Sitting there studying for their fucking MBAs*, he decided – the only way to get ahead in the Air Force. But the calm of his earlier rationalization, once doubted, would not return.

The first two launch centers whose officers turned the firing keys, Stuart knew – four men 'voting' for a launch – would send all of the squadron's forty-eight generated missiles up into space on their fiery treks. *If it's not a test*, Stuart thought.

'Command Data Buffer System clear!' Langford said.

'Clear,' Stuart replied, tensing in anticipation of the next item.

'Launch Option – Niner Golf,' Langford said.

'Niner Golf confirmed,' Stuart replied. *But why did I decide it was a test?* Stuart thought, trying to recall the reasoning.

'Dial it in,' Langford ordered.

Stuart punched '9 – G' into the option selector panel, his mind totally preoccupied with attempting to reconstruct the world in which everything was not as it seemed.

'Preparatory Launch Command – Alpha. Confirm!' Langford said.

'Preparatory Launch Command – Alpha!' Stuart replied. 'Confirmed.' *What if . . .?* Stuart thought. *Just what if this is for real? 'Alpha.' 'Auto Launch' when we turn the keys. No launch timer delay.*

The turmoil in Stuart's mind built as they then repeated the procedure for the other two launch commands – Seven Lima and Three Quebec – both also Auto Launch. Stuart glanced every so often over at Langford; his light blue blouse was now dark under his arms and around his neck.

'Enter Individual Launch Code!' Langford read off his checklist.

Stuart had to concentrate now to input his personal code, which he had memorized at the beginning of his watch and which was unknown to Langford, on the keypad at his console. It was a twelve digit Permissive Action Link. Once entered, the system was freed for terminal countdown to launch. 'Individual Launch Code entered,' Stuart said, his physical actions now ruled by rote memorization.

'Launch Enable on my command,' Langford said.

Stuart found the green key from the sealed authenticator package and flipped up the orange-striped key cover on the center of the console. A sticker read GENTLY just above the keyhole, and he inserted the key into the slot just hard enough to ensure that it was fully seated.

'Ready?' Langford asked.

A teletype began clattering again on the other side of the capsule. At almost the same time, a strident bell rang and two orange lights began flashing at the top of each of their consoles.

Somebody else has entered a 'Launch' order! Stuart realized. *If we turn the 'Launch' key, they fly*!

'*Are you ready*?' Langford screamed over all the noise, turned halfway around in his seat, sweat pouring down his red face.

Stuart bolted out of his chair for the ACC teletype along the commo wall.

'*Stuart*! Get back to your seat!' Langford yelled, turned fully around now, his hand on the chair's armrest three inches above his pistol holster.

Stuart ignored him. When he got to the ACC teletype, he saw the letters and digits of the EAM at the top of the piece of paper that protruded from the machine; the first transmission. He ejected several inches of the paper and tore it off, reading the second transmission quickly as he walked back to his chair.

FLASH REPORT
FROM: CINCACC//J3 NMCC WASHINGTON D.C.

TO: ALL ACC LAUNCH CREWS
AIG 9734
TOP SECRET
FJO//001//0547Z
1. SEA PLANE — APPLE JACK. RUSSIAN ICBM STRIKE IN PROG-
   RESS. EST. TOT 055512Z. 1,062 RVS CONFIRMED. TARGETS
   CONUS.
2. VALID EAM AND NCO BY NCA CONFIRMED. REPEAT. VALID
   EAM AND NCO BY NCA CONFIRMED.
3. GOOD SHOOTING.
RATHMAN
GEN, USAF
CINCACC

'What the hell does it say?' Langford shouted.
'It's . . . it's not a drill,' Stuart said, his voice coming out as an afterthought.
'What?' Langford shouted, cocking his head to hear better.
'Apple Jack,' Stuart said, staring at Langford. 'There's . . . there's an attack under way.'
In the instant before Langford spun his chair around, Stuart saw a furious flash of anger pass over and set in on his face, his teeth bared. 'Launch Enable on my command!' Langford yelled, his back to Stuart.
'We oughta call the controller,' Stuart said. In the back of his mind a voice was telling him, *You've really blown it now*! *A big fat 'Unsat' – no more missile duty for you.*
'Are you *ready*?' Langford screamed over the noise.
After a moment's hesitation, Stuart reached up, grasped his key firmly and said, 'Ready!'
'Mark!' Langford said.
Both men turned their keys. 'Enable switch is enabled!' Stuart said formally as he read from the checklist. 'At this time, the command is being transmitted to all missiles in the squadron!'
'Affirmative,' Langford said in a monotone. 'Wait for indications.'
Both men sat there in silence. They didn't have to wait long. A single bell, like a school bell, rang out briefly.
'Alarm Number Two!' Langford burst. 'Missiles have accepted command – I have Sorties Enabling!'
'Check!' Stuart said.
'Launch Execute on my command!' Langford said, his voice rising. 'Ready on my mark?'
Stuart picked the round key he had extracted from the sealed authenticator package up off the console. He flipped up the solid-red hinged metal flap covering the LAUNCH ENABLER keyhole. Carefully he inserted the key, again pressing gently, his hand shaking and his palm wet.

'Ready on my mark?' Langford repeated, and Stuart could see Langford look up at him in the oval mirror mounted atop his instrument console.

Stuart stared back for a second, but as Langford twisted in his chair, Stuart cut off the impending tirade by shouting, 'Ready! Ready!'

Langford was watching him now, and Stuart turned to look at Langford.

Stuart suddenly felt a faint but sustained vibration through the soles of his feet. Langford obviously did also because he looked up at the console. The alarm and flashing lights suddenly went out. When Stuart looked at his own console, he could see that the forty-eight small green lights were turning red across the panel in rapid and random succession.

'They've already fired. Somebody beat us to it,' Stuart said as the last of the green lights turned red. Of the five Launch Control Centers, the requisite two had already 'voted' for a launch and the missiles were already leaving their silos.

'Launch Execute on my command,' Langford repeated.

'What's the point?' Stuart asked. 'They're gone. Couldn't you feel it?'

'Complete the sequencing! *Ready on my mark*!' Langford yelled at the top of his voice, rattling Stuart with his outburst. 'Three, two, one – *mark*!'

Stuart turned the key one quarter to the right with an audible click, as Langford would be doing. 'Hold for five seconds,' Langford said even as Stuart silently counted. '*One one thousand – two one thousand – three one thousand – four one thousand – five one thousand*. Stuart let the key spring back to the neutral position. The final computer 'go-over' by the Launch Control Facility's Hewlett-Packard LC5400 mainframe, itself sheathed in titanium directly adjacent to their elevator shaft, would have taken almost a full minute after 'Launch Enable.' It then would issue a short blip of energy that opened the silo doors and fired the missiles.

'I show Key Turn is accomplished,' Langford said. The bell rang again. 'I've got Alarm Number Three. The command was received.'

Not that it mattered in their case. Stuart was certain he had already felt them fly. 'They were gone already, I'm tellin' ya.'

'You shouldn't have gone over to the teletype!' Langford snapped as he opened the big black logbook.

'What the hell are you *doing*?' Stuart snapped back, watching as Langford began to record the launch – to record the end of the world – in his book. When Langford slammed the book closed with a bang, Stuart jumped. Langford got up and walked over to Stuart's console, picking up the teletype and reading it.

Stuart jumped again when a phone buzzed. He picked up the white base telephone.

'Stuart,' he said.

'*What the hell's goin' on?*' the voice demanded.

Oh, my God! What've we done? Stuart panicked.

'Cap'n Stuart?' the voice said. It was Kline, Stuart realized.

'We . . . we got a valid EAM,' Stuart said simply.

'Where?' Kline asked. 'Where're they headed?'

'Don't know,' Stuart replied. 'Russia,' he amended.

'Jeezus Christ. Oh, Jeezus God Aw-mighty,' Kline said.

'Is that Kline?' Langford asked, anger dripping from his words.

'Yeah.'

'Ask him about eight.'

At first Stuart didn't understand what Langford was saying. Then his mind cleared, and he said, 'When will you have number eight up?'

Kline sighed. 'Oh, I don't know, Cap'n.' Away from the phone, Kline shouted, 'Hey! You guys close that plate and power up! Move it!' Then he asked more quietly into the phone, 'How much time we got, sir?'

Stuart said, 'I don't know, Sergeant.' He remembered the teletype and looked at his watch. He didn't bother with the answer.

'Well, we'll try,' Kline said. 'We'll do our best, sir.'

'Thanks, Sergeant.'

'Bye, Cap'n,' Kline said limply.

'Bye,' Stuart said, and the line clicked. He hung up reluctantly and slumped back against the leather chair. The phone rang again. It was the 'shed,' the Launch Control Facility one hundred feet above them. He hit the button to pick up the line. 'Stuart.'

'Cap'n Stuart, this is Airman Shackleford.'

'Come *on*, Shack!' someone shouted in the background over the sound of a Humvee revving its engine.

'Request permission to . . . to get the hell outa here, sir!'

'Permission granted.'

'Good luck, sir,' Shackleford blurted before hanging up.

Stuart turned to Langford as he replaced the receiver. 'I . . . I gave the guys up top permission to bail out.'

There was dead silence now as time passed. Stuart heard a metallic clacking sound from Langford's direction. He looked over to see Langford resting his head against the back of the chair.

Stuart reached down and grabbed the seat restraints, pressed out of the way into the folds of the chair. After fishing the belts out, dirty with crumbs and hair from the crevices, he inserted his arms through the harness and pulled the crotch strap up between his legs, pushing the three-way locking mechanism together with loud clacks.

The straps were tight, and he reached down to make certain that his right hand could reach the 9-mm Beretta automatic at his side. He undid the flap on the top of the holster. The air force had told them the weapons were for the security of the Launch Control Center. Popular press had it that they were in case the other launch officer went berserk. But strapped into chairs in a metal capsule one hundred feet below ground zero waiting for the enemy's missiles to strike, the launch officers knew what they were really for.

NORAD, CHEYENNE MOUNTAIN, COLORADO
June 11, 0554 GMT (2254 Local)

General Wilson completed his walk around, shaking the hands of the men and women in the main room. Very few of them were busy now. The only ones still working at the frantic pace of a few minutes earlier were those trying to outload data from the complex's many computers. He left those people alone to do their jobs and went back up to his office.

From behind the glass wall he looked down at the milling men and women below. A lot of good-byes. Handshakes, mostly, a few hugs. Several men sat at their consoles, their heads bowed in prayer or thought. Several others were not dealing with it well, and small crowds gathered around the disturbances in attempts to help them through it.

Al Wilson pulled the cord to shut the blinds covering the glass wall, walked over to his desk and sat. Picking up the picture of his wife and kids and pulling the photo out of the glass frame, he touched the fresh-scrubbed faces of the boys – now older but it didn't matter. And his wife . . . his wife. He looked at the phone. They would be asleep. He resisted the selfish temptation to listen to the groggy voice of his wife, to have her wake the boys, deciding to let her sleep in their dream house in the hills a couple of miles from the complex entrance. Too close. Way, way too close. It would be better if they were asleep.

Wilson knew by heart now all the particulars of the attack. If he had wanted, he could have predicted the headlines in the papers the next day and imagined what the war damage would be at almost every target on the Big Board. His mind was a blank, however. His world – everything he knew, everyone he loved – was coming to an end.

Wilson unbuttoned two buttons on the center of his blouse and placed the cool photograph against his chest, rebuttoning the blouse and holding the picture in place with his crossed arms. It slowly warmed to his body temperature, and he could no longer feel it. But the image stayed in his mind – the fresh-faced boys, his wife glowing with pride.

The only sound was the ticking of the clock on his desk. Al Wilson closed his eyes, focusing on the photograph. Remembering the day it was taken. *Our Father, who art in heaven, hallowed be thy name . . .*

ABOARD NIGHTWATCH, OVER MARYLAND
June 11, 0555 GMT (0055 Local)

The President, Secretary of Defense, and Joint Chiefs stood in the battlestaff work area around Lambert, waiting. The passageways on either end of the area were filled with off-duty personnel. Lambert listened as General Starnes explained to the President what everybody's job was. Lambert, who was feeling ill and considered excusing himself to go to the bathroom, listened distractedly.

'One ERCS is up, sir,' an officer said in a somber, almost reverent tone from a nearby bank of consoles.

'The Emergency Rocket Communications System,' Starnes explained, although the President didn't seem to care. 'We've got ten old Minutemen II ICBMs at Whiteman Air Force Base in Missouri that had their warheads replaced with a communications satellite. We injected a prerecorded launch order into the radio package of one of 'em and fired it into low earth orbit. It'll broadcast for about thirty minutes to all our bombers and the navy's TACAMO aircraft.'

'TACAMO?' the President asked out of the blue. Lambert clenched his teeth and looked away, a shot of anger flaring at the annoying behavior of his boss. *Now he's asking stupid questions like there's gonna be a quiz at the end of the fucking war*, Lambert thought.

'TACAMO stands for Take Charge and Move Out,' Admiral Dixon answered. 'They're E-6A aircraft airborne over the Atlantic and Pacific. They'll pass the nuclear control orders along to any subs that didn't receive shore-based extremely low frequency transmissions.'

'And you said bombers?' the President asked.

General Starnes hesitated. 'Uh, yes, sir. We and the navy have got about a thousand aircraft en route to Russia now, mainly ACC bombers from the U.S. and navy strike aircraft off Pacific and Norwegian Sea carrier battle groups, but some Quick Reaction Alert aircraft from USAFE in Europe.'

'A-a-a-h-h!' Lambert heard screams as several men and women clawed at their headsets and pulled them off their ears. Immediately, muted alarms and beeps began sounding from various consoles.

A colonel standing behind a group of three consoles on the next row said, 'We've got blackout, sir,' to Brigadier General Sherman.

General Thomas said, almost whispering, 'There's been a burst.'

Everyone and everything fell silent, as if time missed a beat.

'FLASH OPREP-3 PINNACLE – NUDET!' a woman sitting at a console in front of them shouted. 'NDDS reports detection. Coordinates: longitude 88 degrees, 47 minutes, 17 seconds West. Latitude 43 degrees, 29 minutes, 36 seconds North. Altitude: 575,000 feet.'

The President looked tiredly at General Thomas, waiting for the translation.

'The Nuclear Detonation Detection System just reported a nuclear detonation at 575,000 feet – where?' Thomas asked, turning to General Starnes.

'Over Wisconsin. Milwaukee, more or less,' the air force general replied.

'I thought you said they weren't targeting cities!' the President exclaimed.

'Mr President,' General Thomas said, 'at that altitude – over 100 miles – there'll be almost no effect on Milwaukee other than the EMP effects.'

'Unless you stare straight at it,' General Starnes amended.

'FLASH OPREP-3 PINNACLE NUDET,' the woman said again. 'NDDS reports detection. Coordinates—'

'You can dispense with the coordinates, Lieutenant,' General Starnes said. 'Just the altitude and common map locations.'

'Altitude 560,000 feet, approximate ground zero' – she looked at the map on the screen of the officer to her right – 'northwest Colorado between Boulder and Salt Lake City.'

'Why are they blowing up so high?' the President asked with what sounded like a glimmer of hope in his voice.

'They're intended to create EMP, sir,' Starnes replied in a monotone as he waited with his eyes fixed on the female lieutenant's screen. 'Electromagnetic pulse. At those altitudes, most of the energy of the blast is released as gamma radiation, which causes secondary reactions in the atmosphere that release electrons and photoelectrons. Wave guides like antennas, cabling, power lines, grounding systems, and even sewer pipes focus the energy and create high-voltage surges. Solid-state circuitry, which is about ten million times more vulnerable than the older vacuum tube technologies, gets burned out by the power spikes. The armed forces harden most of their critical circuitry – surge protectors and dampeners – to defeat EMP, but those two bursts just burned up some large portion of the country's civilian electronics. We don't have any way of knowing just how much.'

'Damn bonanza for the Japanese,' General Fuller muttered, and several of the senior officers shot him a disapproving glance. Fuller pursed his lips and frowned, but fell quiet.

'FLASH OPREP-3 PINNACLE NUDET,' the woman said. Everyone turned back to her and waited. She looked over at another screen and then said, 'Multiple nuclear detonations – indeterminate number – Warren Air Force Base. Altitude: near ground level.'

Before anyone could say anything, she said, 'FLASH OPREP-3 PINNACLE,' and then paused, the words stuck in her mouth as she listened. 'NUDET! Three . . . five detonations . . . indeterminate number of detonations at Minot Air Force Base. Altitude . . . altitudes all near ground level!'

General Sherman put his hands on her shoulders and leaned over to say something to her in a quiet voice.

'FLASH OPREP-3 PINNACLE NUDET! the officer next to her yelled. 'Nuclear detonation . . .'

The battlestaff work area was filled suddenly with calls from eight different work stations at once: '. . . Multiple detonations . . .'

'FLASH OPREP-3 PINNACLE NUDET,' the female officer said, calmer now, and several other officers began repeating the same words.

'Grand Forks Air Force Base. Near ground level.'

'FLASH OPREP-3 PINNACLE NUDET. Multiple detonations . . .'

'. . . Air burst – altitude 5,000 feet – Sawyer Air Force Base.'

'FLASH OPREP-3 PINNACLE NUDET. Nuclear detonations – indeterminate number – Wurtsmith Air Force Base. Altitude: 7,000 feet.'

Lambert ran to the bathroom, clamping his hand over his mouth as his stomach heaved.

MARCH AIR FORCE BASE, RIVERSIDE, CALIFORNIA
June 11, 0555 GMT (2155 Local)

The SS-18's warhead streaked downward like a meteor past 125,000 feet, its blunt rounded bottom leading the way. The needle nose was pointed away from the direction of flight, scientists having learned in the early days of space flight that ablation – the process by which the heat-resistant ceramic surface of the warhead's exterior slowly vaporized in the friction of reentry – occurred much less rapidly along a blunt surface than along a pointed one.

The arming system, which had completed prearming before the missile left its silo, was now beginning the final arming sequence. Accelerometers integrated into the Environmental Sensing Device had measured the stresses of launch, the minutes of weightlessness after the three boosters' burns were completed, and then the deceleration through the reentry phase. All matched the tiny computer's expectations. An outside pressure switch in the ESD had sensed the near vacuum of low earth orbit as and when expected, and now detected the growing weight of the atmosphere.

All appeared normal, and the final locks were released. The computer sent a brief pulse of electricity down a circuit running to the warhead's fusing system, and the warhead was armed. The fusing system now began a steady signal to the firing system to charge its battery with sufficient energy to power the detonators when the time came.

Two altimeters began estimating the warhead's altitude. The first measured air pressure through a tiny hole on the warhead's side. The other was a more sophisticated radar unit in the base. The computer checked both against the inertial guidance system's estimate. When the three altimeters simultaneously registered an altitude of 80,000 feet above mean sea level, the fusing system directed a test signal to the firing system. The firing system in turn sent a low energy signal to the dozens of firing circuits connected to detonators embedded in high explosives deep inside the warhead. The circuits all returned a positive test signal. All was ready. The firing system waited on the fusing system, and the fusing system waited on the three altimeters. All waited for the onrushing ground.

The large hangar was alive with activity, NCOs shouting to the thousand-odd troops who remained awaiting transport. They were checking one another's chemical protective gear or just beginning to make small shelters for themselves out of packs and bags, most crammed against the walls as they curled up on the cold concrete floor.

'Keep your eyes closed!' the base commander yelled, standing there in shirtsleeves, his hands on his hips as he bellowed out his commands. 'Open your mouths and jam your fingers in your ears!'

He looked at his watch. *Not long now*, he thought. *Just gotta get 'em through these last coupla minutes*. He looked out on the mass of soldiers who were growing still in their positions. They were all huddled together, he noticed, none off by him- or herself. No loners, not at a time like this. He felt the urge to join them, to crawl into the piles of arms and legs and lie down with them. There was a strange emotion welling inside his chest, and he swallowed hard as his eyes watered. He swallowed again as he walked down the line of soldiers along one wall. 'Hug your knees to your chest! Put your face in your knees!'

The SS-18's warhead had been targeted to detonate at 4,500 feet above ground level directly over the air base, but the trajectory had been misshapen by the Arctic nickel dome and it plummeted toward the ground several hundred yards off to the side of one of March Air Force Base's runways. When the warhead reached 4,500 feet above ground level at the airfield, the final electrical impulse was delivered by the warhead's fusing system to its firing system. The dozens of firing circuits were opened, and the current stored in the now charged battery flowed into the detonators, which popped with not much more energy than a powerful firecracker.

As the warhead passed 4,497 feet above ground level, the high explosives in which the detonators were embedded ignited in the heat of the small explosions and began an extremely fast burn. The rate of advance of the explosives' reaction zone was so great as to exceed the velocity of sound in the unreacted material, the rate of deflagration so great as to be known to nonscientists as an explosion.

As the warhead fell another two feet, the shell of high explosives completed its burn. If it had been possible to take a snapshot of the exterior of the warhead at that moment, nothing unusual would have been noticed, as the explosives were shaped in such a way as to direct their energy inward. The wave of wasted backblast had not built up pressure on the outer walls sufficient to warp the warhead's shape. The pressure wave, however, inside the 'pit' – the shell of explosives surrounding the warhead's core – flew toward the exact center of the sphere at supersonic speeds. The wall of pressure pushed in front of it the uranium 235 around which the explosives had been wrapped.

With every inch of the warhead's descent, the compression of the uranium 235 inward continued. As the gaps between the atoms of compressing U-235 were reduced, the 235 neutrons released from the 'explosions' of the inherently unstable and 'decaying' uranium atoms began to strike other atoms. More atoms began to burst, sending still more subatomic shrapnel outward to hit or miss its neighbors randomly. Fission had begun, and the laws of statistics defined the process. The more dense the compacting U-235 became, the lower the chance that the neutrons would fly through the gaps and out of the warhead without causing damage to their neighbors.

At an altitude of 4,494 feet, the core of U-235 reached critical mass. From that moment forward, no further compression of the core was needed. Each time an atom of U-235 disintegrated now, more than one of the surrounding atoms of U-235 was, on average, being broken apart.

The rate of radioactive decay began doubling, and then doubling again and again as the subatomic matter shattered atoms and sent still more matter flying outward. The growth was exponential. It was a chain reaction.

With each atom's disintegration, a tiny amount of electromagnetic energy was released. The amount of energy released is measured by temperature, and before the warhead had streaked through the air another foot, the temperature created by the fission reaction had climbed to 1 million degrees at the very core of the warhead. Now, the real explosion began.

The fission or 'atomic' explosion had merely been a detonator of its own, creating the heat to ignite a 'thermonuclear' reaction. Everywhere the lick of million-degree heat found two atoms of ever present hydrogen, the two atoms' nuclei fused into one atom of the heavier element helium. Since the total energy confined within two hydrogen atoms slightly exceeds the energy of one helium atom, the difference is released on fusion in the form of still more energy. These brief pulses of energy were powerful, their wavelengths the shortest measured along the electromagnetic spectrum. They were gamma rays, and the temperature of the gamma rays released in the fission reaction paled in comparison to the temperature of the thermonuclear burn.

The thermonuclear burn wave expanded outward from the warhead's core at tremendous speed, riding the crest of a 20-million-degree wave of gamma rays. The burn wave slammed into the only barrier between it and the still undisturbed shell of the black warhead: a blanket of uranium 238 called the 'tamper,' which was wrapped around the warhead's 'pit.' The tamper absorbed and greatly reduced the gamma rays burning outward from the pit, reducing the 'prompt radiation' produced by the newer model, relatively 'clean' Russian warhead. As the temperature in the tamper rose, however, the U-238, normally stable, began to decay, and a new fission reaction began.

The third and final phase of the 'fission-fusion-fission' weapon began as the tamper exploded, the last stage more than doubling the explosive force of the warhead.

The world of March Air Force Base's commander alit in an intensely white flash as the heat vaporized the aluminum upper walls and roof of the hangar. He felt the sensation of heat on his exposed neck, which immediately grew to searing pain as if a hot iron had touched him there. His eyes jammed shut against the intensifying glare.

An expanding sphere of plasma, atoms of gas in the atmosphere around the artificial sun violently 'ionized' as they were stripped of their electron shells, pushed the un-ionized air around it outward at a tremendous rate. The border of the shock wave was as clearly defined as the sphere of a soap bubble as the wave propagated outward in all directions, slamming first into the ground directly beneath it. The ground itself rippled under the blow like the surface of a still pond into which a stone had been thrown. Liquefaction of the soil occurred, the solid earth behaving like a liquid before settling moments later.

Outward the seismic ripple radiated, the speed of its travel through the dense earth exceeding the speed of the wave through the air. A longitudinal compression wave, the 'P' or primary wave, combined with the shearing transverse and bucking surface waves in the earth to shatter the concrete blocks of an electrical substation feeding power to the runway lights.

Before the unmelted blocks on the far side of the small building could fall to the ground, however, the atmospheric blast wave, a wall of compressed air, surged across the earth and obliterated any trace of the structure above foundation level.

The fireball that formed outside of the plasma sphere began to rise into the air above ground zero at a rate of hundreds of feet per second. Initially sharply defined by the luminous shock front, the fireball now was deteriorating into a ragged ball as it ignited and burned the air itself all along the radiation front.

On ground level, powerful winds – the 'dynamic pressure' of the blast – spread outward, forming a base surge moving behind the blast wave at 290 miles per hour.

The ground bucked up under the base commander twice in rapid succession, the first breaking both ankles and leaving him unsupported in midair and the second striking upward at the soles of his feet and shattering the tibia and fibula of both shins. The first pulse was the direct shock and the second the echo off the base rock lying 160 feet beneath the earth's surface. At the same moment the blast wave swept over him, instantly shooting the pressure of the air to over twenty pounds per square inch, and his eardrums burst with a pain like ice picks jammed into his ears. He had time to scream as the howling gale erupted full blown and the pressure continued to rise. He was swept off his wobbly stance, and he clawed at the air for an anchor.

As the fireball floated upward through the air about one mile from the hangar, it peeked over the low concrete-block walls ringing the hangar and shone its radiant energy directly onto the exposed skin of the base commander, which instantly rose to several hundred degrees Centigrade. Over and over he tumbled, his hands and face flash burning and every blow of his body on the concrete floor causing damage that was quickly growing sufficiently traumatic as to be fatal, his world a spinning blur of darkness and silence. Pain erupted from every corner of his body as melting strips of aluminum and small pieces of concrete blasted off the hangar's walls tore into him like buckshot.

Most damaging of all, however, was the crushing weight of the atmosphere. As the pressure exceeded thirty pounds per square inch, his lungs were emptied of air and his organs began to burst and hemorrhage in a rapid progression toward death. He mercifully lost consciousness before the radiant heat of the fireball, now shining directly onto his body, raised the temperature of first his skin and then the bone and tissue that composed his body above their burning points, reduced much of him to the elements. Before the blast wave had swept him across the hangar floor to the far wall, little remained of the man.

Just as quickly as the base surge had washed outward across the surface, the afterwinds reversed direction and scoured back across the earth toward ground zero. The concrete blocks forming the base of the hangar's wall, which had stubbornly stood against the explosion, gave way to the implosion that followed seconds later as the nuclear fireball gulped oxygen to sustain its flames. The afterwinds sucked inward by the updrafts associated with the rising fireball fed a brief but fierce firestorm around ground zero. Flammable materials that were heated above the burning point had been starved for oxygen as the main burn of the explosion fed itself, but now they were flooded with oxygen and flared. Grass and wood burst into flame and were sucked up into the air as ash. They never reached the fireball of the airburst, however, and therefore fell back to earth without being irradiated.

Almost no 'fallout' was released to contaminate the earth from the relatively clean airburst, but the effective yield of the SS-18's warhead was right at the 550 kilotons at which it was rated, substantially the same as the yields of the eight other warheads that burst high in the air over March Air Force Base within the next thirty-five seconds, extinguishing all life within a radius of nine miles of the base.

I–10, TWENTY-FIVE MILES EAST OF MARCH AFB
June 11, 0555 GMT (2155 Local)

The eerie drone of the Emergency Broadcast System had grown familiar over the car radio. Melissa Chandler kept looking into the rearview mirror at the air base where David said his flight would depart, which was also in the general direction of downtown Los Angeles. Was he gone already? And if so, where? Was he still there, close, and she had just passed him in the night?

After the station to which she had been tuned went off the air, she had scanned the radio dial for other stations but, where moments earlier there had been the usual plethora of stations in the Valley, now there were none, just the EBS hum. She was driving with one white-knuckled hand on the wheel to weave in and out among the swelling traffic on the highway. She settled into the middle lane at eighty miles per hour, slow compared to the Porsches and Mercedes from L.A. that blazed by in the left lane, and cringed as the reckless idiots raced up from behind, swerving around and then cutting back in front of her in their desperate flight from the city. She had to watch all sides of the car and press her one free hand to the small of her aching back. It had gotten so bad she seriously considered stopping to go to the bathroom on the side of the road, but still dared not risk it.

The radio suddenly went quiet save for popping sounds like those preceding an old phonograph record – and then a woman's voice: 'Attention all news agencies. Attention all news agencies. This is the Federal Emergency Management Agency National Warning Center. Emergency. Emergency. An Attack Warning has been declared. Repeat. An Attack Warning has been declared.'

The radio fell silent, and Melissa began to shiver uncontrollably. She jumped when the EBS hum returned. *That's it?* she thought angrily, and began to cry, but forced herself to stop by grinding her teeth painfully. She had to keep her eyes clear for the road.

'David, David, David,' she whispered nervously, then thought, *Why am I having to do this alone?* 'Nobody we *know* is in the Reserves!' she said out loud. 'You said you'd quit!' *You promised. If you had kept your promise* . . .

Her heart leapt as a huge truck raced up close behind her, then static burst from the car's stereo speakers. She looked in terror into the rearview mirror, expecting to see the impending collision with the oncoming headlamps, and the light forced her to jam her eyes shut. She slapped at the mirror to deflect its glare from her face and looked out the passenger window. It was as if the sun had risen, the overpass under which she had passed casting a shadow across the highway several hundred feet in front of her car.

But it was not like daylight at all. The color was all wrong. And the landscaped grounds of the office park to her right were bathed in chalky white light, shaded darkly on one side and brightly lit on the other. The sky was pitch-black, but the patchy clouds shone luminescent. The light flared again, and then again, each time a light with the intensity of a strobe. The intense light of each new glare faded slowly. She counted nine altogether. Nine strobes, nine suns.

As the light began to dim, she waited for the end. On and on she drove, night enveloping the highway and its travelers once more. The lights high above the parking lot of the shopping center she passed flickered back on, their automatic switches fooled briefly by the man-made dawn. She looked back through the rearview mirror several more times and saw nothing now but a glow over the horizon and a strange reddish tint to the clouds above, as if they were on fire. She was tempted to join the many drivers who had pulled over to the side of the road and were gazing back toward the city, back toward March Air Force Base, but decided against it.

There had not been any sound other than the scratching of the static on the radio now emitting its steady hum again. No sound, no wind, no fire. Nothing. Just nine small suns, lit up on the earth.

Melissa looked down at the speedometer – *105 miles per hour* – and eased off the accelerator. She worried briefly about David, her questions about him and his whereabouts ever more critical now. Suddenly she realized that her feet were drenched and cold. Her water had broken, and a whole new dimension to her problems arose. There was another sharp jab of pain to her midsection. Her mind cleared, and she began to look now for an exit, for a town, any town. Back and forth her eyes went from the exit signs to the night sky in front and to the sides, looking for a hospital, looking up at the stars and waiting for one to move, to explode.

OVER BANNING, 15 MILES EAST OF MARCH AFB
June 11, 0555 GMT (2155 Local)

The small windows of the Delta jet alit with brilliant light that bathed the first class cabin and all its passengers with a glow so white it washed out all the other colors. Soldiers slapped and clawed at the shades, which came down one by one, returning the cabin to its semidarkness just as David Chandler heard a hissing sound from the cockpit in front that sounded like a rattlesnake but was punctuated by snapping noises: the uncontrolled discharge of electricity. He leaned out into the aisle and saw the light from the sparks flashing underneath the cockpit door just as it burst open and a whooshing sound accompanied the sight of a man shooting long bursts of white powder onto the sparks from the instrument console just inside the door. Acrid tendrils of smoke reached Chandler's nose and made his eyes water like smelling salts.

The plane began to buffet steadily and with growing intensity. As the shaking and vibrations rapidly grew, the Delta flight crewman fighting the fire in front fell to the floor onto the flat of his back, shooting one long uncontrolled burst of powder into the air down the aisle into the cabin, dousing several of the soldiers seated there. Chandler's insides grew unsettled as the seat belt and seat transmitted the vibrations into his body. A buzzer sounded loudly from the cockpit, its insistent tone matching the intensity of the pilot and copilot, whose hands could be seen through the smoke locked on their respective control wheels. The aircraft itself began to groan, and all of the sudden it felt as if they had driven off a cliff. They were dropping.

Chandler felt his heart skip as the jet nosed over and the descent grew more and more rapid. The turbulence increased and a whine just like in the movies began to grow. The sensation of falling nearly lifted his limbs into the air as blood rushed to his head sickeningly. Through his popping ears he could hear the plane's engines roaring now at what must have been maximum power, but it no longer seemed enough to keep the plane airborne. Oxygen masks dropped from the overhead compartments, and Chandler released his painful grip on the armrests long enough to put his on, thankful for the fresh air it dispensed.

Slowly, ever so slowly, Chandler felt the pressure increase on the seat of his pants as the plane pulled out of its descent, returning with another rush of Gs, this one downward, to straight and level flight. Almost as quickly as it had begun, the noise and turbulence ended, and all was quiet again. All, that is, except the storm of thoughts that raged in his head. It was only then that he realized how terrified he had been, and he let go of the armrests and straightened his cramping fingers.

NORAD, CHEYENNE MOUNTAIN, COLORADO
June 11, 0555 GMT (2255 Local)

The penetrator from the first warhead struck the loose accumulation of soil at the base of the mountain. Traveling at 17,000 miles per hour and hardened for penetration, it burrowed to a depth of almost 100 meters before the trailing warhead caught up with it and detonated.

The blast wave from the twenty-five megaton warhead threw the entire NORAD complex three feet to one side, knocking all the personnel who were standing to the floor in a heap. Ankles were broken as feet slid from their shoes. Bodies were bruised and cut. One man died and three were seriously injured as their heads and necks struck sharp edges of tables or railings. The vibrations immediately caused nausea for the seventeen hundred American and Canadian airmen, shaking their bodies as they lay on the metal floor and rattling the screams that erupted from their chests. The crashing sounds of glass and clanging sounds of metal panels falling from twisted consoles were almost lost against the tremendous rumble of the intense, man-made earthquake. The noise was so great that General Wilson was spared from hearing the screams of his men and women as he rose up from beneath the overturned chair.

Six seconds after the first detonation, the second penetrator and warhead streaked down toward the ground. The tremendous updraft from the first explosion caused both to glance off the top of the granite mountain and tumble. The unusual stresses on the fusing system resulted in a fuse abort, and the warhead skittered along the side of the mountain until it embedded itself into an outcropping, spewing its poisonous nuclear materials down the mountainside below.

The third penetrator and warhead followed three seconds behind, crashing squarely into the side of the mountain. The tremendous speed of the dense penetrator melted the granite and dug over twenty meters into the mountain before the warhead following it into the hole exploded.

The shock waves threw the buildings of the underground complex completely off their spring supports and caused the structural failure of several. Hundreds of the huge metal bolts in the cavern's ceiling were sheared in two, and a 400-ton slab of granite was cleaved from the ceiling of the chamber along a preexisting fault and fell to crush one of the complex's buildings and part of a second. The emergency lights of the complex failed now, as hundreds died in a darkness lit only by the exploding sparks of freely discharging power lines. The high frequency vibration of the chamber's atmosphere was perceived by the human ears as an earsplitting screech. Wilson involuntarily clamped his hands over the pain in his ears.

The fourth penetrator/warhead package also struck the mountain squarely after a respite of only four seconds. The heat of the warhead's detonation vaporized a cavity inside the mountain that opened into the entrance tunnel leading down to the complex at a point inside the blast doors. The expanding gases of the vaporized granite shot down the channel and into the main chamber of the complex. The wave of superheated gases created a blast wall that surged through the chamber at five times the speed of sound. Everything in its path was obliterated by a blast force inside the enclosed chamber more powerful than any force ever before created by man. In an instant the cavern was pressurized to over 1 million pounds per square inch, far in excess of the thirty PSI that the human body can tolerate. The effect was the instantaneous death by burning and crushing of all life in the complex, mammal and bacteria alike.

Only after seeking out every nook and cranny of the main chamber and tunnel did the blast wave from the nuclear fire that still burned deep inside the mountain's granite press back against the two main blast doors at the tunnel entrance with its full force. First one and then the other door burst outward, flying out of the tunnel into the inferno outside on the crest of a 10,000-degree jet of gas. The sixty-ton doors tumbled end over end and landed in great crashes several hundred meters down the mountainside. Just as they came to rest, the first of the remaining four incoming warheads detonated, their wasted energy further reducing the jagged crag that had been Cheyenne Mountain.

90TH STRATEGIC MISSILE WING, WARREN AFB, WYOMING
June 11, 0556 GMT (2256 Local)

Stuart felt the sickening jolt of the first of the warheads through his back and the soles of his feet. An alarm went off as the low-level Doppler Ground Radar network surrounding the Launch Control Facility at the surface detected motion in the Outer Security Zone. As the rumbling began, the lights went out and were replaced by the red emergency lights from the center's batteries. The security alarm ceased sounding abruptly as the console went dead.

Jolt after jolt punctuated the nearly constant vibration that Stuart felt through every point of his chair. Some jolts were strong, others brief and distant.

Stuart's eyes were closed, and he mentally estimated the distance of each detonation. *Six hundred feet*, he thought. *The center was hardened to two hundred PSI. Two hundred PSI* – a sharp jolt caused Stuart to jump, and he began to quiver – *two hundred PSI*, he concentrated, *means it can take . . . it can take five hundred . . . five hundred kilotons at six hundred feet. Or, it could . . . it could take a direct hit by a thirty-five-kiloton warhead.* Stuart tried to fill his mind with conscious thought as he rode out the storm, fending off the involuntary thoughts that raged like barbarians outside the walls erected to protect his sanity.

A strong jolt wrenched his stomach and chest, and he cringed against what was coming. The screech of ripping metal started what he thought would be the end. There was a crash, but the end did not come. *Close,* Stuart thought as he grew strangely detached, loosing his imagination to speculate how much more powerful the blast that would kill them would be. Another even stronger jolt passed through the center and his constantly shaken body. The center groaned, but no more sounds of metallic ripping could be heard. Stuart felt the sweat pour down his face and realized it had grown hot in their underground capsule.

Sparks lit the center from behind Stuart's head.

'Electrical fire!' Langford yelled, barely audible above the rumble, as he unhooked his chair restraints and ran out of sight behind Stuart.

Stuart unhooked himself as the reek of noxious smoke filled his nostrils. He stood up just in time to be thrown to his knees by another shock, his legs just moving from beneath him despite their solid traction a moment before. He could feel the gradual settling motions of the capsule's suspension system as it completed the dampening of the latest blast wave.

His knees hurt as he looked up to see Langford sitting on the floor squirting powder in great bursts from the extinguisher into the electrical panel by the access tunnel. The fire was dying down, so Stuart climbed back up into his chair, coughing, and strapped himself in again.

Another shock wave hit the center, and Stuart heard a clatter.

'Shit!' Langford shouted, picking the fire extinguisher and himself up off the floor and getting to his chair. Several more waves rumbled through the center, but none was as strong as the earlier ones. A few seconds after the last jolt, all fell quiet. The center rocked slowly on its suspension until all was still, all was dark save the blinking red light on the emergency power console.

ABOARD NIGHTWATCH, OVER MARYLAND
June 11, 0605 GMT (0105 Local)

'What we're trying to say, Mr President,' Lambert said, 'is that the Russians have not yet targeted our population centers. In fact, their targetiers have very deftly avoided striking any target, no matter how valuable, which is located in a place of high population density. San Diego Naval Base, for instance.'

'But their submarines haven't fired yet,' Admiral Dixon said. 'They're going to be the force that is targeted at our cities, sir, because their accuracy sucks. The bulk of their fleet is in the Kara Sea defended in their "Bastion." They can make good subs, but our antisub boys are better and so they fall back on defense. They deploy all these subs, you see,' the admiral said, holding his hands slightly apart in the air, 'in the Kara Sea north of Murmansk and Polyarnyy. Then, while the subs lay low and quiet, their conventional surface and submarine forces, and massive numbers of land-based air force aircraft, defend that area.'

'So you're saying we can't sink these submarines in this Bastion?' the President asked.

'You give me a month or so to marshal enough assets and we'll sink 'em, Mr President. It'll be one bloody hell of a battle, though. We'll lose some ships, even a carrier, maybe.'

The President's head drooped. 'The point is, sir,' General Thomas said, 'that those submarines' missiles are not as accurate as their ICBMs. The longer they stay underwater, the more outdated their positioning systems grow. Consequently, they need big targets, where missing by a few hundred meters won't matter much.' The President looked up at him. 'They're aimed at our cities, sir. The hammer is cocked, and you can damn sure bet after the punishing we're giving them that the safety's off.'

'What do we do?' the President asked.

'That's a political question, sir,' Thomas said, and the Secretary of Defense nodded. A long silence followed.

'That should about conclude this trans-attack assessment conference, Mr President,' the Secretary said. 'We'll have another in about half an hour to assess our missile strikes and all of the new damage reports from the Russian attack on us. Meanwhile, if you don't mind, sir, we've got some work to do and this would probably be the best place for us to do it.'

The President stood almost immediately and said, 'I'll be on the phone to . . . to London and our other allies. And to the Congressional leadership.'

As soon as he left, General Thomas asked, 'Okay. How the hell did the Chinese get that shot off?'

General Starnes shook his head and said, 'I just can't imagine, Andy. There must've been a leak or an intercept. They could've intercepted Razov's call to you, but' – shaking his head again – 'that sure seems beyond their technical capabilities.'

'The President ordered Secretary Moore to tell them.'

All heads turned to look at Lambert, and he felt his throat constrict, but he swallowed and continued. 'While he was on the way to Crown Helo, on his portable phone.' Lambert looked down at the table. 'I tried . . .' he opened his mouth to say, but he couldn't bring himself to tell them how he had tried to stop him but failed. How it wasn't his fault.

When he looked up, the faces of the others gathered there registered various emotions, really varying degrees of the same emotion. 'Jee-sus H. Christ!' Fuller said, burying his face in his hands and shaking his head. 'That stupid fucking ignorant bastard! That stupid, *stu*-pid *bastard*!'

Lambert was shocked at Fuller's disrespect for the President and waited for the reprimand. Instead, however, Thomas looked over at the Secretary of Defense. 'Sir, I recommend that we start keeping the Vice President informed of events more closely.'

The Secretary thought about it for a moment and then nodded slowly. 'And Greg,' the Secretary of Defense said, turning to him, 'if I were you I think I'd put everything down about that conversation that I could remember before it, you know, fades.' He stared back at Lambert, but the others avoided Lambert's eyes. 'You understand?'

Lambert nodded. *A C.Y.A. memo,* he thought, and shook his head. *Missiles are raining down, Jane is fleeing for her life, and I'm going to write a memo.* It sickened him. Everything is always C.Y.A. War, peace, government life is the same. He shook his head again, thinking, *C.Y.A. – Cover Your Ass.*

FAR EAST ARMY COMMAND, KHABAROVSK
June 11, 0620 GMT (1620 Local)

General Razov stood with his staff on the roof of the building above his command bunker, insistent on watching the nuclear attack on his country from this vantage. The Svobodnyy Missile Field was almost 400 kilometers away, however, and in the twilight of early evening he didn't expect much of a show. The officers who stood there wore a mix of uniforms and were in various states of appearance. Crisp, clean, bright-eyed officers in dress uniforms from the warm beds of Khabarovsk and dirty, reeking men whose camouflaged battle dress and dull stares only hinted of the distant life in the field from which they had just been summoned.

'There!'

Razov followed the direction of the pointed finger and could then clearly see to the northwest that the sky along the horizon was growing brighter. It was as if a second sun were setting, the new one slightly behind the old.

It's beautiful, Razov found himself thinking before purging himself of the awful thought. The men watched in silence as the thin clouds grew red in the artificial sunset over the horizon. The glare of detonation after detonation popped silently like slow-motion flashbulbs seemingly all at the exact same point on the earth. When the last of the glow dimmed, Razov turned to leave.

Another glow silently lit the horizon to the south. Razov froze, and his entourage stopped around him. Against the much darker background of the sky to the south there glowed a now clearly recognizable nuclear fire.

'What the hell is that?' one of the officers behind Razov asked.

'It's gotta be Vladivostok,' another answered, his voice sounding disbelief.

A bright flash burst the night sky open to their left, to the east this time and closer.

'My God!' one of the officers said, his voice low but his tone strident.

'What's going on?' another asked.

'That's close,' someone said as they watched the glow grow much brighter than the others, the wall surrounding the roof casting a steep and dim shadow. 'Must be Sakhalin.'

'But what's happening? What are the Americans doing?' the first officer repeated, voicing the question that echoed through Razov's own mind.

OVER FLAGSTAFF, ARIZONA
June 11, 0625 GMT (2325 Local)

Chandler heard the bong and saw the FASTEN YOUR SEAT BELT sign turn dark. 'Uh, ladies and gentlemen,' he heard over the PA system, the first announcement since the fires other than emergency instructions to the flight attendants, 'we're gonna let you go off oxygen. You can just stick the masks back up in the overhead compartments. If you need them again, though, if the fumes are still too much for you, we'll leave the oxygen turned on and you can just get the masks back down.'

Chandler took his mask off, unbuckled his seat belt, and stood. It had been half an hour since the rapid descent, and his muscles ached from the tension of sitting.

When Chandler turned to face the cabin, most of the men and women looked at him expectantly. Several of the soldiers coughed a couple of times and held the masks to draw oxygen every few breaths. He could smell the burned plastic in the air, but it didn't bother him. When he looked down, his eyes met those of Barnes, who sat across the aisle from him.

'I think I'll go find out what happened,' Chandler said, and Barnes nodded in agreement.

He went up to the cockpit door and knocked. The door opened a couple of inches, and Chandler saw the flight engineer eyeing him. 'It's a passenger,' the man said.

'Go away, passenger!' Chandler heard boomed from the cockpit.

The flight engineer turned and shrugged in apology, closing the door. Chandler's anger rose immediately and he pounded on the door. The door opened wide and the flight engineer waved Chandler in.

'Dammit, we got an airplane to fly!' the pilot said without turning around. 'What the *hell* do you want?'

Chandler looked at the massive bank of avionics to his left, charred black, he could see, in the places not coated with white fire extinguisher foam. Racks of components had been pulled out, leaving holes through which more foam had obviously been sprayed. The flight engineer's left hand was wrapped in a bandage, and a first aid kit sat on his small desk, which was otherwise covered with a map and drawing tools.

'What the hell happened?' Chandler asked.

'What kinda way is that to start a conversation?' the pilot said. 'Aren't you gonna interduce yerself?'

'I'm Major David Chandler, U.S. Army Reserve.'

'Cap'n Golding,' he said, 'Delta Airlines. This here is my copilot, Mr Frazier.' The man waved with one hand as his other carefully clicked through the radio frequencies, headphones hugging his ears. 'And that back there is Gator, the flight engineer and dead reckoner extraordinaire.'

'I got some city lights down there,' the copilot said. 'Two o'clock, about ten miles.'

'Flagsta-a-aff,' Gator said, placing a mark and a time on his map and using his ruler to draw a line with his pencil connecting it to the previous mark.

'What's going on?'

'Gator's playin' connect the dots,' Captain Golding said. 'We lost all our navigation aids. Did you ever see Jimmy Stewart in *The Spirit of St Louis*? *Damn* good movie!'

'You mean you're flying this thing by finding lights in the dark and matching them up to a *map*?'

'Well, we got a compass and a watch,' Gator said, holding his wristwatch up for Chandler to see, 'and the printout of wind speed and direction from when we filed our flight plan. There won't be many more lights out west, here, but we'll muddle along.'

'What happened?'

In the silence that followed, the only sound that he heard was the slow click – click – click of the copilot's search across the radio spectrum. In their reluctance to respond to his question Chandler had his answer.

'That air raid back at March . . . was it . . .?

'I'm afraid so, son,' the pilot said in a voice that was surprisingly gentle for so gruff a man.

'Russians?' Chandler asked, incredulous.

''Parently so.'

He shook his head. '*Why?* What in God's name happened? I mean . . . right out of the blue like that and all?' He could not believe it. There must have been some mistake, some huge, monumental mistake.

'It don't make much sense to us, either,' the pilot said slowly.

'Did they hit L.A.?' Chandler could feel his heart pounding, and his head grew light.

'I don't know.'

He was in shock. He wanted to cry, but he suddenly had to fight the inexplicable urge to laugh. His lips curled up at the edges and he said, 'I can't believe it.' He had to know more. The need to know rapidly consumed him. 'Can't you radio anybody? LAX? Find out?'

'Nope,' Captain Golding said. 'Either our transceiver's fried or the regional control centers are all gone or the FAA just shut 'em down so as not to give homing beacons to any Russian bombers or whatever that may be pokin' around up here somewhere.' Golding looked to the front and out to the sides as if to search for Russian aircraft.

'Shouldn't you land?' Chandler said. 'I mean' – he looked at the burnt equipment – 'Jesus Christ! You can't fly like this.'

'I'd rather take my chances up here, personally,' Golding said.

'So where are we going?'

'The last we heard outa L.A. before the Regional there went off the air was that the Russians had attacked and that we should head somewhere safe. There was a whole bunch of us on the air – everybody who got flushed outa March – and we were all askin' where the hell is safe. The guy didn't know, but his supervisor came on and said Gander, Newfoundland. He told us they didn't know what was goin' on, but said we should head to Gander, Newfoundland. Musta repeated it ten different times to other charters like us, which are about all that's flyin' since they activated the Civilian Reserve Air Fleet yesterday after the Ko-rean invasion.'

'So that's where we're headed?' Chandler asked, incredulous. 'Newfoundland?'

'That's where they told me to go. I just work here.'

'Yeah, but . . . Newfoundland?'

'Major,' Golding began in an irritated voice, and then turned for the first time. He had a white patch, a bandage, over one eye. He looked at Chandler for a second with his unbandaged eye and then turned to look back out the windshield. 'Major, I don't know what's goin' on. I don't know which airport is still operational, which airport may be gone, which airport may be the next target, which one may be two feet thick in fallout. I just don't know nothin'. We passed a coupla other flights headin' in the opposite direction, but they were as ignorant as we are. Frazier here's tryin' to find some civilian radio stations so we can get more info, but until then I'm goin' to Gander 'cause they told me to, and 'cause it sounds safe. Who the hell would wanta blow up a place like Gander, for Christ's sake?'

'What happened to your eye?' Chandler asked.

'Oh, nothin',' Golding said, scratching at the itchy tape around it. 'We had our backs to March, fifteen miles out. We counted nine detonations. It was bright as shit. We had a full-blown stall, you know, when those winds caught up with us from behind. Took the lift right off the wings. Dropped our airspeed to damn near zero for a few seconds while the blast wave rushed by, and we fell like a stone. *And* we had a fire. *And* our night vision was completely screwed up by the flash.'

Chandler realized for the first time that these guys must be a good crew. *Fifteen miles from nine nuclear detonations*, he thought for a moment before the pictures of home, of Melissa sitting in their family room . . . He jammed his eyes shut and tried to force the thoughts from his mind. *Later*, he thought. *Not now*. When he opened his eyes he had to grab onto the flight engineer's desk.

'You all right?' the crewman asked, almost whispering.

Chandler nodded. He looked back at Golding as a wave of nausea swept over him, and he willed himself to ignore it. He took a deep breath of air filled with the smell of burnt plastic. 'So why the patch?'

The copilot looked at Golding and then back around at Chandler. 'In case it happens again,' he said. 'So he'll still have one eye left.' The copilot's head suddenly jerked to look at his hand on the radio. 'Got something!' Golding and Gator quickly looked at the frequency and rolled their own tuners to the same number. Chandler watched as the flight engineer pressed his headset closer to his ears.

'What?' Chandler asked, and Gator held up his hand to silence him. 'What is it?'

Gator opened a drawer and handed Chandler a headset, plugging it into a jack just behind the pilot's chair as Chandler put the headphones on. There was nothing but a hiss, and Chandler reached out to roll the volume dial by the jack all the way up and pressed the headphones tightly to his head.

'. . . the blackest of nights in human history . . .' The signal faded out, but the voice had been unmistakable: President Livingston. '. . . can cry, we can grieve, but now is not the time for revenge. I have been assured,' the President said as the signal rose, 'that the Russian attack was an accident, an accident caused by a tragic chain of events as the Russians' war with the Chinese entered a nuclear phase.' The signal was slowly beginning to fade again, and Chandler again pressed the headphones painfully to his ears to chase it. 'At this very moment, as our armed forces are taking appropriate retaliatory measures, to you, the great and generous American people, I have this to say. I believe that the attack was a mistake. The Russians will pay dearly for that mistake, as have we, but we are not at war with Russia, and . . . to discuss a cessation . . . bless the United States of America. Good night.'

Chandler and the others were silent. Chandler removed the headphones and leaned in emotional exhaustion against the bulkhead behind him. He looked around at the cockpit door and said, 'Somebody ought to tell the others.'

Golding lifted the microphone from the dash and instead of raising it to his mouth held it over his shoulder to Chandler.

'Push to talk' was all he said.

PART TWO

O God! O God! that it were possible
To undo things done; to call back yesterday
That Time could turn up his swift sandy glass,
To untell the days, and to redeem these hours.

—THOMAS HEYWOOD
A Woman Killed with Kindness
Act 4, scene 6

Chapter Five

ABOARD NIGHTWATCH, OVER MARYLAND
June 11, 0630 GMT (0130 Local)

'No, sir.' The tinny voice came over the speakerphone, the constant whine of engines evident in the background. 'I can see where I-80 and I-25 come into . . . where they came into Cheyenne, but . . . the junction itself is gone.'

'Are there fires?' General Starnes asked.

'Not really. There's smoke, but everything on the ground is all burned out already, it looks like,' he said, obviously fighting the growing quiver in his voice. 'The light's' – he cleared his voice – 'the light's still pretty dim, but I've got the belly lens on high, and all I can see is rubble. Charred rubble.'

Several heads turned to look at each other. Lambert had thought he had heard something in the pilot's voice earlier, but now it was clear. Lambert felt his eyes begin to droop. It was early morning Washington time, and he had had only a couple of hours' sleep the night before. He caught his sagging chin with a jerk of his head that woke him with a start. The headache, the fatigue – it was something more than just ordinary sleepiness. It was tension. Hours of unrelenting tension. It took its toll.

'Sorry, sir.' The voice returned, weaker now. 'There's still a lot of haze . . . but the . . . the cloud's moved on off to the southeast, maybe eight or nine miles already, over Orchard Valley. Everything in Cheyenne is . . .'

Lambert and the others waited a second for the pilot to finish his statement, but he never did. A sound – just the hint of a sound, really – was again emitted over the speaker. Lambert was already familiar enough with the system from listening to the earlier reports to know that the pilot's microphone was activated by sound, any sound.

'Is he sick?' the President asked in a voice too low to be picked up by the speakerphone. 'Radiation?'

General Starnes shook his head. 'He knows what he's doing,' he said in a similarly low voice. 'Our TR-1A pilots practice it all the time. He'd

never go near the cloud.' Then, lifting his voice, Starnes said, 'Major
. . . uh, where're you based, son?'

'Warren, sir,' the distant voice said, calmer now.

The President mouthed the question 'There?' as he pointed down.
Starnes nodded.

I wonder how many times he's looked for his house? Lambert thought,
shaking his head as he thought about the faceless pilot. *How does he do
it?* Lambert wondered. *How do you go on?* Lambert knew his wife was
safe – Washington had been spared – but this man?

'Where are you headed, Major?' General Starnes asked, the tone of
professionalism breaking the spell.

After an audible sigh, the pilot said, 'I gotta take a drink over Baffin
Island and then shoot some spotlight imagery of Thule. Then it's
another sip and on to do some standoff strips of Magnitogorsk with
the SLAR.'

'Side Looking Airborne Radar,' Starnes translated in a low voice
for the President. 'The Advanced Synthetic Aperture Radar System
– ASARS-2 – will give us some strikingly clear images. Just like a
black-and-white photo, only in any weather, day or night.' He then
spoke loudly into the microphone. 'You've got a long day ahead of you,
Major,' Starnes said. 'Good luck to you.'

'Thank you, sir,' the pilot said. 'Sir?'

'Yes?' Starnes replied.

'Make 'em pay, sir. Make 'em pay.'

Lambert felt a chill tingle his spine.

OUTSIDE KHABAROVSK, RUSSIA
June 11, 1030 GMT (2030 Local)

'They're coming,' General Mishin reported to General Razov from
PVO-Strany's Alternate Wartime Facility over the speaker on the
BTR-80's radio. 'PKO's antisatellite and PRO's antiballistic missiles
are still operational, but Radio-Technical Forces reports loss of all of
their long-range radars. Every time one of our IL-76s turns on its radar
they sprint a flight of F-111s or F-14s in to knock it down. The navy
keeps putting up Ka-25s to patch in holes, but helicopters are sitting
ducks. We're working on establishing our mobile ground-based radars
into some sort of cohesive grid, but it's going to take time.'

'So we don't know what's going on?' Razov asked.

'Well, we get snapshots. It looks like they've got everything in their
arsenal headed in – B-52Hs, B-1Bs, FB-111s, cruise missiles from
standoff aircraft, plus their air defense suppression packages, tankers,
everything. We can only assume that the B-2s are out there somewhere

too, maybe even F-117s, but they're 'stealth' weapons so we can't see them. There are even A-6 strikes under way from their carriers off the coast of Korea and F-16s from some of their NATO forces in Europe, plus cruise missiles from submarines and surface ships.'

'Are you saying that we're unable to put up any meaningful air defense?'

'General Razov,' Mishin said slowly, 'we've had every single air defense facility of any significance hit with nuclear warheads. Every single one. We're now operating out of civilian airports. As long as the Americans can run offensive operations out of the U.S. unhampered, we're going to be rocked back on our heels.'

'What are you suggesting?' Razov asked, knowing full well the position of the air force.

'We have to take the fight to them. Hit back. At least their carrier battle groups and NATO facilities.'

'General, need I remind you who started this war?' Razov said, mustering a stern edge to his voice despite the depression into which he had sunk. 'You're just going to have to do your best. Reestablish air superiority over the perimeter first, then we'll worry about force projection.'

'Perhaps, General Razov,' Mishin's response again came slowly over the radio, 'I haven't been clear enough about how grave the air situation is. By our last count, they've put up seventeen AWACS aircraft to direct their traffic spread from the Kola Peninsula up over the Laptev Sea and down as far south as the Cherskiy Ranges.'

'Do you mean they have AWACS orbiting over Russian territory?' Razov asked, astonished.

The roof hatch on the BTR opened, and Razov's aide dropped into the vehicle, clearly desiring to get Razov's attention. Razov held his hand up to silence the officer.

'There's one airborne just a few hundred kilometers north of your position right now,' the air force general replied, 'complete with tankers and fighters. We've lost everything other than purely local air supremacy over the civilian airports from which our fighters are operating, and even that might not last. If we don't strike back, General, we need to consider conserving our air resources.'

'Conserving them for what?' Razov asked.

'For what might,' he said, again slowly, 'be coming next.'

Razov thought for the first time about the possibility that this might not cool off immediately after the Americans exacted their terrible revenge. 'What about Zorin?' Razov asked.

'We have the poor bastard,' Mishin said in disgust. 'I'm of half a mind to put a bullet in his head myself.' They went on to discuss the successful consolidation of their commands under the newly constituted STAVKA. Razov would serve as commander of the Supreme High Command.

After signing off, Razov's aide said, 'Sir, we have to move again. The wind has shifted.'

Razov turned to his aide and said, 'Get me transportation to Moscow. I can't manage things from here.'

PALM SPRINGS, CALIFORNIA
June 11, 1030 GMT (0230 Local)

'I want an epidural!' Melissa banged her head back down against the pillow. 'It hurts!'

'You're having a baby. It's supposed to hurt,' the nurse said calmly.

Melissa was crying and gasping for breath. 'I want my epidu-u-u-ural!' she screamed again.

'Mrs Chandler, the anesthesiologists are all busy right now.'

'Get one,' Melissa whimpered, pleading as the next contraction built. 'P-please, get o-o-*one*!'

She hardly heard the woman's explanation about why they were busy, about how she was sure Melissa understood. The pain was all she could understand, and it was excruciating.

Melissa awoke, and the first thing she saw was her baby, lying in a diaper far too big for it, with a gold heart taped onto its bare back. She blinked her eyes to clear the tears that welled up immediately, and the picture was just the same. The red glow over the now clean baby's skin grew in intensity, and Melissa looked up to see the electric lamp like the food warmers at a fast-food restaurant light up for a few seconds and then grow dim again.

She sniffed and rolled painfully over onto her back. At the foot of her bed, half obscured by a cloth partition that had been wheeled into place, a woman rolled from side to side in her bed moaning softly as a man in blue jeans held a wet cloth to her head. Squeezed in beside her bed to her left, another woman lay elevated with a newborn at her breast.

The woman smiled at Melissa and whispered, 'Pretty baby,' nodding at Melissa's before pulling her chin in to look down at her own, who had lost her nipple. '*It's a boy*,' the nurse had said, Melissa remembered, and she looked over at the tiny thing in his bed, his splotchy red back slowly rising and falling as he slept deeply.

There were noises outside the door, some louder, others muffled and indistinct. 'I need whole blood!' someone yelled from just outside. 'Two pints – stat!'

Melissa turned to the breast-feeding woman. 'What's going on?' she whispered.

The woman, who had been smiling and murmured baby talk to her child as she used the fingers of her free hand to feed him the nipple again, looked up at Melissa as if she had just startled her with an angry shout, and then returned to her baby, smiling and cooing as if there had been no interruption. Melissa pulled the thin sheet off her legs. She could feel the pain from the incision between her legs, and on her shins in huge block letters was written, she guessed, some sort of patient ID in black marker ink.

There was a long, wailing moan of a shout from the corridor outside, followed by, 'Jane-et! Janet! Help me get this one back down!'

With the greatest of effort and pain Melissa slid to the floor and walked slowly past the bed of the woman in labor.

She opened the door to a world of bright light, of swirling action as nurses and doctors and orderlies ran from patient to patient and wheeled gurneys through the thick maze of stretchers. People lay on the crowded floor of the hallway holding gauze over parts of their exposed bodies, the uncovered parts of many burned and ugly. Others in various states of nonhospital garb – some hurt themselves – milled about the more seriously wounded, helping or holding hands and weeping. Bloody and burned clothes littered the floor of the corridor where they had been tossed after being cut from injured bodies. A person – man or woman, Melissa couldn't tell – on the stretcher nearest Melissa let out a long moan through bandages that obscured his or her face completely. He or she lay there, all alone and moaning, abandoned.

'I'm sorry,' she heard as a hand pushed her out into the hallway. She turned to see the husband from inside her room closing the door, an apologetic look on his face.

Left standing in the hallway, Melissa grabbed a nurse who was walking briskly by in bloody scrubs, sweaty hair matted to her forehead. 'I want to check out,' Melissa said. 'I'm Melissa Chandler, and I want to check out and I want to take my baby with me.'

'Okay,' the nurse snapped. 'Go,' she said as she tried to pull free.

'Who do I see about the bill?' Melissa asked, holding onto the woman's sleeve by twisting her fingers into it.

'*Bill?*' the woman shouted with a look of disbelief on her face, jerking her sleeve painfully through Melissa's fingers and rushing on. The faceless person on the stretcher next to her moaned again, an inhuman sound.

ABOARD NIGHTWATCH, OVER MARYLAND
June 11, 1100 GMT (0600 Local)

Over the soft background *whoosh* of jet flight, which had the odd effect of making Lambert drowsy, General Starnes said, 'Our CAOSOP reports –

the twelve different reports generated under the Coordination of Atomic Operations Standing Operating Procedures – indicate that the Phase II strikes from Quick Reaction Alert aircraft are going well.' He spoke in a voice raised loud enough to make sure that he was heard by Vice President Costanzo over the speakerphone. 'We've taken minimal losses – two A-6s, an FB-111, and a B-52 – and we're well into the strikes. Of course, the aircraft still have to exit, but the Russians are loading up on the inbound approaches and are less concerned with egress.'

'What have we hit?' the President asked, sounding numb.

Starnes looked down at his report. 'Mainly with missiles, we've hit the sub bases at Petropavlovsk, Vladivostok, Ponoy, Murmansk, Polyarnyy, Pechenga, Dikson Ostrov, Kaliningrad, Matochin Shar, and Arkhangelsk. We hit Vladivostok and Murmansk with conventional weapons to limit civilian damage, although we also used two low-yield nuclear torpedoes at Vladivostok. We're using attack subs to root out the subsea tunnels off their piers one by one and will drag the deep fjords where they may be lying low. We have a 99.7 percent destroyed on the ICBM fields at Yedrovo, Kartaly, Kostroma, Teykovo, Yoshkar Ola, Perm, Tatishchevo, Dombarovskiy, Imeni Gostello, Aleysk, Uzhur, Gladkaya, Drovyanaya, Olovyannaya, and Svobodnyy. The Kozelsk shot fell short, and we're going after it with B-1Bs. We've also knocked out the bomber bases at Shimanaovsk, Gusinoozersk, Irkutsk, Pskov, Perm, Michurinsk, Prikumsk, Novaya Kazanka, and Monchegorsk. Some of their Backfires, Bisons, Bears, and Badger/Blinders and their tankers are airborne, presumably armed with nuclear weapons, but we're taking them down everywhere we can or waiting for 'em to land so that we can locate and hit their relocation bases when and as they put down. Finally, we've taken out about twenty early-warning sites and are going after Yuzhno-Sakhalinsk with carrier-based A-6s from the *Carl Vinson*.'

Lambert looked at the President, who seemed not to be listening. 'What about their C³ capabilities?' Lambert asked.

'We left a lot of it alone,' Starnes replied, looking at the President in the hopes that he would hear. 'They've got pretty good communications, and their command and control should be intact. Nothing around Moscow, PVO-Strany included, has been touched.'

'What about our own air defenses?' Lambert asked on mention of PVO-Strany, the Russian NORAD.

'Well, I see why Al said it was a piss-poor firing plot,' Starnes said. 'We've got all our satellites intact. On the ground we've got Fylingdales left from the BMEWS line; the old DEW and Pine Tree lines to the north; the four Pave Paws SLBM systems to the east, west, and south; and the new Over-the-Horizon Backscatter systems watching the Atlantic and Pacific for bombers and cruise missiles. If we lose those, we could still patch our experimental tracking station in New Boston, New Hampshire; and the navy's space surveillance radars at Gila River, Arizona, Lake Kickapoo, Texas, and Jordan Lake, California, together with the FAA's radars, some Aegis Cruisers off the East and West coasts, and a couple of squadrons of AWACS. We could go another round with the bastards.'

'How are we working around our C^3 damage?' the Secretary of Defense asked.

'Everything is patched into the headquarters of the 23rd NORAD Region at Tyndall Air Force Base in Florida,' Starnes answered, 'which is a fully capable NORAD Back-Up Facility. If we lose Tyndall, we've got the headquarters of the Canadian NORAD Region at Canadian Forces Base in North Bay, Ontario, and then the four regional operations control rooms of the Joint Surveillance System. After them, there are seven AWACS that can control national air defense.'

'And you can stop any Russian bombers?' the President asked.

'There's not much we can do about standoff cruise missiles,' Starnes said, 'but if the bastards come in to drop iron we'll rough 'em up. We've issued a NOTAM – Notice to Airmen – informing civil aviation that we've extended the Air Defense Intercept Zone to two hundred miles and we'll fire on radar intercept if flight plans aren't cleared five hours in advance. ADACC – the Air Defense Air Combat Command – has put up combat air patrols out of their twenty-six alert facilities. They've got five air divisions, a total of ninety F-15Cs, and the Air National Guard is adding nine more air divisions or one hundred sixty-two F-15Cs and older F-4s and F-106s. Add to those Canada's fifty-four CF-18 Hornets and Air Combat Command's augmentation forces of F-15Cs, and we'll attrit the hell out of 'em unless they coordinate a whole lot better than in the first strike.'

'What about the submarines?' Vice President Costanzo asked over the speakerphone. 'Any missile firings yet out of the Bastion?'

Admiral Dixon, the Chief of Naval Operations, said, 'No strategic missiles, no, Mr Vice President. They've fired a few surface-to-surface nonnuclear missiles at our antisubmarine units in the area, and we've taken some hits from those and from two separate torpedo engagements. The U.S.S. *Talbot*, a Brooke-class frigate, and the U.S.S. *Dahlgren*, a Coontz-class destroyer, were damaged, and we have an initial report of several dozen killed and wounded. It's uncertain whether the *Talbot* will make it, but the *Dahlgren* is making her own way and can put back to sea without dry dock.'

'What are the reports on Russian sub kills?' Thomas asked.

'Twenty-one boomers confirmed killed, one afloat and on fire, and six probables,' the CNO read through glasses at the end of his nose. 'If the six are all kills, then we've pretty much cleaned up the blue water firing stations – maybe a stray sub or two lying low. They haven't interfered with the SONUS system of listening devices along the bottom of the ocean and we just made one ID along our GIUK line, the Greenland-Iceland-United Kingdom choke-point. That one's a goner, so that pretty much leaves us with just the Bastion to worry about.'

'Tell your boys good work,' General Thomas said.

'And, I should report, good work by the Royal Navy,' Admiral Dixon said. 'Five of those kills are theirs. And the Canadian Defense Forces are responsible for two contacts leading to kills.'

'What about our other allies?' the President asked Lambert.

Lambert arched his eyebrows and looked at the Secretary of Defense, who said, 'We're encountering some . . . difficulties with the Germans. We had a couple of damaged aircraft, an FB-111 and a B-1B, come in for emergency landings at German Air Force fields that are alternate recovery sites under NATO war plans. The German controllers refused permission to land.'

'What the hell happened?' President Livingston asked.

'They went ahead and put down. Rather than begin repairs of the aircraft, at least to get them back to the U.K. where we can turn them around and put them back in service, the Germans' initial position is that the aircraft are impounded for unauthorized landings.'

'And the pilots?'

'They're being held at the air bases. One is being treated in a military hospital for radiation wounds received in action. I have to tell you, Mr President,' Lambert said shaking his head, 'that as far as our defense establishment is concerned this constitutes a breach of the NATO Treaty obligations by the Germans. In fact, the Germans and several other NATO countries have begun mobilizations, but the units assigned to the American NATO commanders in Brussels have quite pointedly not responded to alert orders sent out to prepare them for deployment. They are presumably awaiting some sort of political decision, but that's not the way it's supposed to work. There's no decision. A NATO member was attacked, and all other member nations are required to treat that attack as an attack on their own countries.'

'We'll have to keep an eye on the situation,' the President said. 'I'll make a few calls.'

Just then an air force captain entered the conference room. He obviously had intended only to whisper into General Starnes' ear, but the natural break in the briefing left only him to fill the void. 'The Glass Eye Report is coming in, sir,' he said to the group.

'We'd better get FEMA on the line,' General Thomas said, picking up the telephone and asking for a conference with FEMA officials at Mount Weather.

'What's a Glass Eye Report?' the President asked.

The telephone chirped as Thomas began to reply. Thomas punched a button and said, 'Yes?'

'Jack Sims, the emergency director of FEMA, is on the line, sir,' the now familiar voice of the female communications officer said.

'Mr Sims,' Thomas said, speaking more loudly.

'Uh, yes . . .'

A terrible screech cut off the rest of his sentence.

'Oh, my God, not again!' the President gasped, jumping out of his seat, a look of horror in his eyes.

Over the phone in the background the Vice President's voice could be heard shouting, 'Close that door!' The phone fell silent, and then the Vice President said, 'Sorry. Must've gotten some feedback or something. Jack's right next to me and our doors are open. It should be fine now.'

Everyone waited for the President, who slowly settled back into his chair, looking down at the table in front of him.

'Mr Sims,' General Thomas said, eyeing the President, 'we just got your report and the President was asking for an explanation.'

'Oh, Mr President,' they heard from the speakerphone, 'this is Jack Sims. You were asking about, what, the Civil Situation Report?'

The President gave General Thomas a lost look. 'No,' General Thomas said, 'the Glass Eye Report.'

'Oh, yes, uh, I'm sorry,' Sims said. 'We're working on so many reports. Our computers' resource data catalog has millions of items of data – every grain silo, bank, hospital, television station, retail store, mine, cave, et cetera, and over two million buildings and their fallout-protective characteristics – all broken down by sixty-five thousand geographical subdivisions. Every one has a vulnerability number associated with it and its exact longitude and latitude. Our READY program will—'

'Excuse me, Mr Sims,' Thomas said, 'but the President was asking about the Glass Eye Report.'

'Yes – yes,' Sims said over the speakerphone. 'The fallout is preliminarily estimated by our radiological defense officers. At noon and midnight every day, one hundred thirty-four National Weather Service weather stations – well, now it's one hundred eleven – release balloons and take other meteorological measurements and feed the data into our computers.'

An air force sergeant brought a stack of papers in and handed them to the captain, who distributed them.

'Are we doing reconnaissance over Russia too?' the President asked.

'We have the Strategic Reconnaissance Plan,' Starnes said, 'which is a part of SIOP. That's what that major we were talking to over Cheyenne earlier was operating under.'

Lambert looked down at his copy of the report. The first thing that jumped out at him was the map. Circles dotted the map of the country like a pox, each one a target. Next, and most ominously, huge sweeping tails swung out of some of the holes, lashing out at the countryside beneath.

'The map shows the targets,' Starnes said, 'and the estimated casualties from the direct effects and fallout.'

'Right over Norfolk,' Admiral Dixon said, shaking his head. 'We've still got San Diego untouched, Mr President, but this fallout on Norfolk is gonna wreak havoc on our Atlantic operations.'

'The damage is really remarkably light,' Sims said. 'Of course, it's terrible at the target sites, and the fallout is bad, but if this thing had happened ten or twenty years ago back before the reductions and when most of the weapons were older "dirty" models that—'

'My God,' the President said. 'How . . . how accurate are these figures?' He was clearly in a state of shock. He looked like a trapped animal, his eyes darting and wild, unable to focus.

'For any given target area, Mr President,' Sims answered, 'the direct-effects numbers could be off by as much as fifty percent. The fallout numbers are even more uncertain, maybe seventy-five percent. But for the aggregate casualties, it's going to be pretty close, maybe plus or minus fifteen or twenty percent. We'll get better data when we get reports from local Civil Defense Weapons Effects Reporting Stations. There's one for every hundred square miles in rural areas and every nine in urban areas.'

The huge tail sweeping down the coast from Pennsylvania caught Lambert's eye. *Right over D.C.*, he thought. *That one goes right over D.C.!* As everyone looked over the report, the first giving any estimates of damage, Lambert tried to imagine what was happening in his neighborhood, in the homes of his friends and acquaintances. *Death*, he realized. *Dying and death. Everybody. The doorman at my building. My maid and her family. My secretary and her husband and kids.* Lambert jammed his eyes shut, the concept too much for him. But the pictures would not go away. *They're alive now, but they will die. They're already dead, for all intents and purposes. What are they doing?* he wondered. *Do they know? Are they busy, stuffing wet towels under doors and wearing bandannas around their mouths and noses to keep from ingesting the particles? Or are they just sitting there, too depressed to move as they wait to die?*

'So you're saying that – what?' the President flipped pages until he found what he was looking for. 'Something between four and a half and seven million people just *died?*'

Everyone in the room looked at the President, and the speakerphone grew silent. *He's cracking up*, Lambert thought, resuming his close attention to the fallout pattern over the map of the Virginia-West Virginia border.

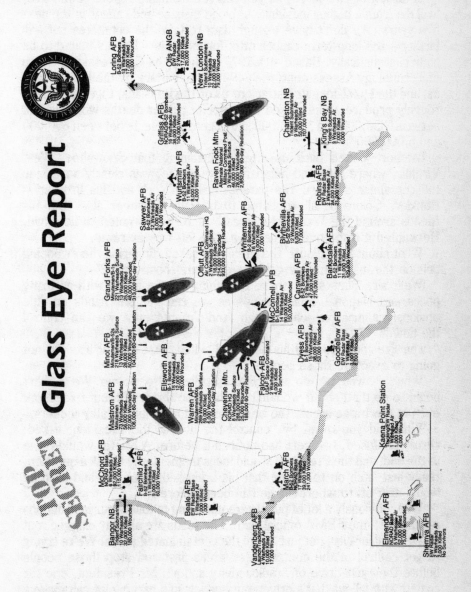

'Well, that's the right number including fallout deaths, which are measured out to sixty days,' Sims said.

'Mr Sims,' Lambert said, his eyes on the stricken Livingston. 'What about the long-term casualties?'

'A million or two more, as you can see from the report,' Sims said, 'will die from a higher incidence of blood disease and cancer in the next five years. We don't have enough data to take the estimates out any farther – the long-term cancer rate, for example – but it's bound to be higher, statistically. Based on a 1979 study by the Congressional Office of Technology Assessment, the 649-megaton attack by the Russians on us, and the 1,092-megaton attack by us on the Russians, together should roughly produce an increased incidence of cancer deaths worldwide of between 350,000 and 3,500,000 and of genetic defects between 600,000 and 6,000,000.'

Lambert looked back up after determining that Snowshoe, West Virginia, where Jane and her parents would be, was clearly not inside the contaminated area. His parents in New York and his brother in Boulder, Colorado, all appeared to be out of danger also. But his friends around the Washington area . . . He just wanted to lie down. He wanted it to be over. The fatigue he felt was extreme.

'What about the fallout?' the President asked, fingering the swooping tails on the map. 'Are we going to evacuate those areas?'

'Well, sir,' Sims said, 'we're cordoning off the areas with as many police and National Guard troops as we can get our hands on. It's obviously a massive job, though, and I'm not sure we can control the flow.'

The President cocked his head and asked, 'Are you or are you not going to evacuate those people?'

'Why . . . well, n-n-no, sir,' Sims stuttered. 'No, no, no. We couldn't begin to do that, and it wouldn't be the wise thing. Without exception, even in the fringe areas, the best thing is for people to stay indoors.'

'What did you mean by "control the flow"?' the President asked, clearly confused. Lambert had noticed it before. A briefer would come to the end, and the President would focus momentarily to ask a question, really just latch on to words that his brain had recorded, and then he would drift off to wherever he had been before.

'Well, obviously a lot of people are not going to follow our instructions to stay put,' the FEMA official said. 'The roads are already clogged, out of every major city, not just out of the contaminated areas. We're trying to get control of the contaminated areas first and stop those people before they just drive off, radioactivity and all. Mr President, one car coated with fallout that's driven out and left in a parking lot can make a whole lotta people sick. We're just trying to isolate the contamination; that's the plan.'

'So what will you do?' the President asked, more focused this time.

'Stop these people at the edge of the contaminated areas and do what with them?'

'Well, we'll quarantine them,' Sims said, 'long enough to confiscate their property and wash 'em off. We're setting up displaced persons camps to house and treat them. It's all set out in our plans, Mr President.'

The President just stared off into space, not saying or doing anything.

General Thomas, who had been watching the President's distracted stare, said, 'Thank you, Mr Sims. We'll get back to you later.'

'Oh,' Sims said, 'while I've got you, Mr President, we've got some paperwork that we need you to sign. We need a national emergency declaration so that the CEFR, the Code of Emergency Federal Regulations, becomes effective. Otherwise, what we're doing is . . . well, technically it's illegal.'

'Okay,' the President said. 'Fax whatever you need. Do we have a fax machine on board?'

General Starnes nodded and said, 'Yes, sir.'

'Excuse me, sir,' Sims said, 'but you've already got it. It's in the football.'

The military liaison officer who had sat silently at the end of the table with the football, his duty now done, suddenly sprang to life and rummaged through his case until he found some papers in a side pocket. He brought them down to the President.

'There's a document in blank in there,' the FEMA man said, 'that declares a national emergency.'

The President looked distractedly at the papers and then shoved them across the table to Lambert, who began to look for the paper that Sims was continuing to describe.

'Have you found it?' Sims asked over the speaker.

'This is Greg Lambert,' Lambert said to stall while he continued his search. 'There's a – it says "Declaration of War" at the top, and it says "The United States of America hereby declares war on" – and then there's a blank.'

Sims said, 'No, no,' and went on to describe the document.

Lambert interrupted, 'Got it. "Declaration of National Emergency." It has a blank for the areas and a blank for the date.'

'Mr President, I'd say "All fifty states plus the District of Columbia" and put in, let's see, I guess today's date,' Sims said.

Lambert looked at the President, who nodded, and then printed the information as neatly as possible in the blanks. When he had finished, the President signed it and said, 'Okay. It's done.' Sims thanked him and asked for a copy before he hung up.

As Lambert collected the small pile of forms – one for succession after

incapacitation of the National Command Authority, one for the appoint-
ment of new Cabinet officers, others for various similar emergencies –
he saw again the first form that he had come upon. He picked up the
single sheet of paper and held it in front of him delicately with both
hands as he reread it.

The President stood to leave, but Lambert looked over at the
Secretary of Defense across the table and then said, 'Mr President.'
President Livingston stopped where he stood at the head of the table,
looking at Lambert and waiting. 'On a different subject, sir, it occurs
to me that you ought to consider calling Congress back into Special
Session.'

The President looked at the Secretary of Defense, and then down
at the piece of paper in Lambert's hands. The military men remained
silent, aloof. This was a matter for the civilians – a political question.

ABOARD B-1B, 125 MILES SOUTH OF MOSCOW
June 11, 1100 GMT (1300 Local)

'SRAM fuel cell warmers?' the copilot asked.

'On,' the bombardier-navigator, or Offensive Weapons Officer,
replied.

'Position data dump?'

'Indicates complete.'

'Front bay doors?'

'Setting to open.' Captain Edgar Solomon, the B-1B's Defensive
Weapons Officer, felt the drag of the opening doors on the extremely
aerodynamic B-1B and the jarring thud through his feet as they locked.
After over an hour of low-level flight had alternately washed blood away
from his head and flushed it full as the giant bomber's terrain-following
flight system hugged the earth on the HARD setting, Solomon was
physically exhausted and relieved to reach the first weapons release
point. Down the list the other crewmen went. In his mind, Solomon
could see the plastic-covered sheet of paper with the questions and
correct responses. He could see in his mind's eye that they were on
the last page.

'Front bay door indicator?'

'Indicator light is green.'

The second rumbling and thud that Solomon felt, all normal and
expected, was the lowering of the rotary missile launcher to its
firing position. At seventy-five miles from the mobile radar facility,
which guarded the inbound approaches to Kozelsk Missile Field – the
target of the B-1Bs that followed several hundred miles behind – the
rotary launcher would fire one AGM-69A Short-Range Attack Missile,

or SRAM, and then rotate one eighth of a revolution to prepare to fire a second at a stretch of the main highway between Moscow and Orel that was being used as an interceptor base. Streaking off at Mach 3, the SRAMs would be on target in two and a half minutes, detonating their Mark 12A 350-kiloton warheads and knocking out their targets with kilotonnage to spare. After that, the rotary launcher would retract into the bomb bay and the doors would close, 'slicking up' the B-1B for the flight to its third target, a nuclear weapons plant in western Russia that was on their way home.

Home, Solomon thought. *If we make it, if it even exists.* After the third target, the B-1B would have five SRAMs left on the first rotary launcher and another sixteen in the two weapons bays behind the first in case ACC called in any new targets of opportunity. Solomon focused again on his job: monitoring the electromagnetic spectrum for hints that they had been painted by Russian radar. Once detected, he would pull out the B-1B's enormous bag of expensive tricks and go to work, lighting up the Russian radar screens with snow or dozens of bombers all headed in the same direction or two bombers whose paths diverged slowly – one phantom, one real.

'SRAM Run – Nuclear,' the copilot said.

Solomon's skin tingled as he heard the words he had never thought he would hear. He saw the boldfaced heading in his mind. All the words beneath it were in stark red letters, so completely unlike the businesslike black of the other checklists that filled the ordinary routine of their jobs.

'SRAM Inhibit Switch?' the copilot asked.

'Off,' Solomon's rear seatmate replied.

'Special Weapons Lock Indicators?'

'Indicate unlocked.'

'Release Circuits Disconnect?'

'Connected – light on.'

'SRAM Release Indicator Circuit?'

'Select – light dim.'

'Master SRAM Control Switch?'

'On,' the Offensive Weapons Officer's voice broke, and he cleared his throat. 'Light on,' he said rapidly, and then there was a pause.

'All right, girls,' a new voice – the pilot – said. 'It's time to break things and hurt people. Let 'er rip.'

'Bombs away' were the OWO's only words, and with the words he released hell incarnate.

ABOARD NIGHTWATCH, OVER CENTRAL NEBRASKA
June 11, 2145 GMT (1545 Local)

'Nex-s,' President Livingston continued, the hands under his chin distorting his speech. Lambert surreptitiously looked at his watch. The President had come to expect Lambert's attendance at all his meetings, even meetings on 'housekeeping' such as this that took Lambert from the more pressing responsibilities of his role as national security adviser.

'Health and Human Services, sir,' the voice came over the speakerphone. 'We're charged with the sanitary disposition of the dead. Plan D, which will be approved by the Executive Order, authorizes the omission of embalming, the use of caskets, lying in state, and individual religious ceremonies.'

'N'kay,' the President said, his chin weighing heavily on his hands and his elbows on the conference table.

'I'm sorry, Mr President,' the man said, 'but I wasn't through. Because it's June, bodies will be buried on the later of the fourth day following death or the date of recovery. The bodies will be laid out in lots by date of death – 10,000 per 5.5 acres – for public viewing and identification. Three-person identification teams will sift through personal effects, document identifiable features, take Polaroids, et cetera. They should each be able to handle about ten bodies an hour. Ultimate disposal will be in mechanically dug continuous trenches – side-by-side if equipment digs a wide enough trench, otherwise head-to-toe.'

There was silence. The President finally asked, 'Am I supposed to approve that or something?' He looked at Lambert aghast.

'Yes, sir,' the man from HHS said over the phone.

'Okay,' Livingston said. 'I approve.'

'Uh, Housing and Urban Development, sir,' the next voice said. 'We're providing emergency housing to displaced persons and dehoused workers in essential industries. Rents will be set at prevailing prewar comparables but will be suspended if a failure to pay is beyond the control of the occupant. Initially, housing would be in requisitioned tents, hastily constructed barracks, or privately owned homes whose owners have disappeared. If the homeowners show up, the tenants will have thirty days to vacate. Housing standards will be relaxed to allow units without windows as long as they are covered with paper, board, plastic, or similar material. We'll inspect for radioactive contaminants, obviously, and we'll also inspect the electrical wiring even if there is no electrical service because—'

'Okay, okay,' the President said. 'I approve. Who's next.'

'Department of Agriculture, sir,' a woman said. 'Our main crop losses will be our corn crop in the Midwest, which will suffer organic damage because of the radioactivity. If the attack had just been in August, the crop could have been salvaged, but the young plants won't be able to survive. Moving on, we propose to direct that all contaminated milk be processed into cheese, which could be stored for a few months until radioactive decay rendered it safe for human consumption. In addition, Plan D would declare effective five Defense Food Orders to provide for rationing and emergency distribution. They're designed to maintain a twenty-five-hundred-calorie-per-day diet, which is two-thirds the prewar American average. The National Emergency Maximum Food Distribution Allowance under Defense Food Order Number Two would limit weekly sales to three pounds of boneless meat or four with bone or thirty-six eggs or eight and one-quarter pounds of potatoes or three pounds of dry peas or—'

'Jee-sus Christ!' the President exploded. 'I don't have time to get bogged down in all that detail. I approve. Let's get on with this. Who's next?'

'The Postal Service, sir,' a very timid voice said. 'The Postmaster General's Standby Emergency Actions as published in the "Postal Service Emergency Planning Manual" direct the burning of all stamps to prevent them from falling into enemy hands, the—'

'Wait!' the President yelled. 'Don't burn the damn stamps, for Christ's sake! Jee-sus!'

'Y-yes, yes, sir,' the man said. 'How about first class mail deliveries only?'

'Fine,' the President replied. 'Next.'

'Oh – oh,' the Postal Service representative said. 'What about a halt on all money orders payable in Russia, Ukraine, or Byelarus?'

The President took a deep breath and said in a calm voice, 'That's okay too.'

There was a pause, and Lambert could hear some papers rustling over the speaker. 'I guess, well,' the man said, 'there's just authorization to print up Forms 809, which are emergency change-of-address cards, safety notification cards, well . . . that kind of stuff.'

'It's approved,' the President said. 'But don't burn anything. Everybody listen. Don't burn any money, or break any mint plates, or do anything stupid. Now, I know you are all being asked to assume responsibilities that are a little greater than you're used to, but just use your common sense, don't just do whatever your manuals say. Now, who's next?' the President asked, his hands pressed palm down on the table in preparation to leave the conference room and doubtless get some sleep before the military grabbed him for another briefing.

'I'm the director of the General Services Administration's Relocation Team B,' the speaker said. 'There's one agency that wasn't discussed, the Cultural Heritage Emergency Preparedness Group, which we oversee. It's charged with preserving the nation's museums, libraries, archives, monuments, et cetera. We have a problem. Several years ago, we contracted with the Underground Vault & Storage Company in Hutchinson, Kansas, to store the fifty most culturally valuable paintings in the country in the Carey Salt Mine. When the paintings started showing up on military flights, it turned out that the company had gone bankrupt, and—'

'Just deal with it, will you?' the President said, standing.

'Can I use one of those Orders of Taking someone was talking about earlier to requisition mine space?' the man asked. 'The mine's operator said we'd have to get approval from the bankruptcy court, and I'm worried about some of the oils. They're out in the weather, and—'

'Look! I don't care!' the President yelled. 'Get the military to seize the damn mine, or piss on the fucking paintings. Whatever! Who gives a shit? Meeting adjourned.' With that, he turned to leave.

'But, sir!' the man from GSA said. Lambert winced as the President turned to face the speakerphone.

'Whoever the hell you are,' the President yelled, 'if you say one more word you're out of a job!'

'But the National Archives, Mr President,' the man burst out. 'When the war started, the duty officer at the Pentagon telephoned the guard's office at the Smithsonian. As per the rules, the guard went to the main display room and turned a key to fire four explosive charges destroying the hydraulic shuttle mechanism over the main vault.'

'What the *hell* is your point?' the President growled, his teeth grinding and his hands, knuckles white, grasping the back of his leather chair.

'The vault weighs fifty-five tons,' he said. 'We'll need special heavy equipment and personnel to get down to it. Military engineers, we were thinking.'

'Oh, for God's sake!' the President shouted, turning for the door. 'I don't have time for this!'

'But, Mr President!' the man shouted. 'The Declaration of Independence! The Constitution!'

The President stopped dead in his tracks at the door and after a few moments slowly turned. 'What do you need?' he asked quietly, returning to his seat.

PALM SPRINGS, CALIFORNIA
June 11, 2145 GMT (1345 Local)

Melissa had towels stuffed under the door to the hotel room, and had filled the bathtub with water. They said there was no radio-activity, but she was taking no chances. She didn't trust tap water anymore. She didn't trust anything or anyone. She was on her own.

The single room was already a mess, and a sign at the front desk on check-in had said there would be no maid service. Matthew was falling asleep at her breast as Melissa watched the weatherman for NBC.

'There are rainstorms forecast for eastern Colorado and western Kansas. We remind you again that rain through the nuclear cloud is very, *very* dangerous. If you are in one of the areas experiencing fallout that we went over earlier and it begins to rain, you are to take shelter immediately. The concentrations of radiation that rain will bring down are many tens of times greater than ordinary fallout. The rain literally washes the air clean of the tiny particles that carry the radioactivity – or that are radioactive themselves, I guess. After a rain, avoid puddles or runoff or places where puddles or runoff might have been. Even a couple of dozen feet or so away from the radioactive debris and it's relatively safe, but the low-lying areas where the rainwater will carry the fallout and concentrate it are particularly dangerous.'

'Thank you,' the anchorman said. 'We go now to Jim Luciano at the Greenbriar resort in White Sulphur Springs, West Virginia, underneath which Congress is now meeting in its secret underground bunker code-named Casper. Jim?' The still picture of a resort appeared on the screen.

'Congress is still trying to gather a quorum to meet in Special Session. The Senate is just a couple of Senators short of the fifty necessary, but apparently the House is far short of its quorum requirements. Already, however, the House and the Senate have convened an extraordinary joint committee, the Ad Hoc Committee to Investigate the Nuclear War, to begin looking into the causes of the war. It will also recommend certain actions to the two chambers – including whether to declare war on Russia, NBC News has been told – once quorums are obtained.'

A chill shot through Melissa. *David*! she thought. *Where are you*?

After the report on Congress was over, the picture switched to the NBC studio. 'Some of our local affiliates have conducted a random sample of man-on-the-street interviews around the country,' the anchorman said, 'and here are our unscientific results.'

The images shifted to a middle-age man with a big mustache, and the text along the bottom said 'Atlanta.' 'I think we oughta turn those mother' – the electronic tone masked the man's next word – 'into a' – another tone – 'crematorium.'

The next person, a woman from Los Angeles, said, 'I saw the flashes from Riverside. It was just a-awful what happened to those people. We ought to do something about this nuclear situation so that it just doesn't happen ever again.'

The off-camera reporter asked, 'Do you think we should declare war on Russia?'

'Oh, no,' she said. 'I don't want a war. It's already been so terrible. I just think we should make the Russians get rid of all their nuclear weapons.'

Next, a handsome young unshaven man from Chicago wearing a Northwestern T-shirt said, 'We're goin' down to sign up right now.' He turned, and the camera panned the group of several men and two women, all of college age. 'We gotta get in there and finish the Russians off!' the boy said. 'Just wipe 'em out!' a girl in the background said. '*Yeah*!' a third student shouted, and they all began a chant of 'U-S-A! U-S-A! U-S-A!'

Melissa looked down to see that the baby was fully asleep, his lips sucking now into thin air. She held him tight, using his little body's warmth against the cold air and trying not to let her sobs wake him.

ABOARD NIGHTWATCH, OVER SOUTHERN IDAHO
June 11, 2300 GMT (1600 Local)

'But it was an accident!' the President shouted even though the speakerphone was directly in front of his chair.

'But, but, but,' the Minority Leader of the Senate broke in. 'But nothing! The Russians attacked our country, the country that *we* were elected to protect, in an unprovoked and massive nuclear attack that killed millions of people. Radioactivity covers half my state *right now*! And those bastards' submarines in this . . . this Bastion threaten our very *survival* as a nation!'

'Bob—' the President began, but was cut off.

'Goddammit!' the Minority Leader continued. 'It's time to shit or get off the pot! We don't have to declare war; we're already in the middle of one!'

'Bob,' the President finally succeeded in getting in, 'you should have been briefed already on what our response has been. *Hell*, Bob, we're putting it to the Russians even as we speak, nuclear weapons and all! What more would you have me do?'

The voices of several people erupted over the phone at once. 'Nuclear disarmament! Nu-nu-*nu*-clear disarmament!'

'Do you think the Russians are just going to lay down their nuclear weapons?' the President shouted.

'Mr President, Mr President!' Lambert recognized the voice of the President's Chief of Staff, Irving Waller, who was with the Vice President at Mount Weather. 'I'm sorry, but might I have a word with you on your private line for a second?'

The electronic gathering of Congressional leadership and the Cabinet on the secure conference call exploded into a cacophony of views as the

President nodded at the air force technician who ran the show. The noise of the conference call was replaced with the calmer sounds of two people's voices, the Chief of Staff and the Vice President.

'Are you there?' the President asked.

'Yes,' the two men said in unison.

'Okay, Mr President,' Waller said. 'Here's the story. This thing is getting away from us and we've got to move. We've got to get out in front. The people out there are gonna go crazy – I can feel it. They're gonna demand blood. I mean that literally.'

'Look. Now's not the time to start thinking opinion polls and reelection.'

'Mr President,' the White House Chief of Staff said, almost beside himself, 'I'm not talking about your *popularity*, I'm talking about your *survival*! One flinch, one twitch, and this bandwagon is gonna roll right over you! Right now, you've got to be the brave leader, out in front, leading the charge. No more 'time for healing' bullshit. I'm afraid the healing is going to have to wait. This thing has turned, and it's turned bad – you've got to trust me on this one. And you've got to get your face on television. I don't care what your military people say, you've got to go on the air and talk to the people. Who listens to radio anymore? CNN carried the radio address with a picture of a 747 flying over the map, and then shots inside Air Force One of your quarters and of the lounge bar, for Christ's sake! Made it look like a damn party plane!'

'There is no television broadcasting capability from up here,' the President said. 'The Vice President is going to address the nation from Mount Weather.'

'Fine and dandy, just fine and dandy. But you better get in front of the cameras yourself. Good God, Walter, we're talking major damage control here!'

The President drew in a deep breath, letting it out with the word, 'O-k-a-a-y. Let's get back on the line with the others,' he said, looking up at the technician.

The speaker exploded to life.

'You tell that . . .' the Minority Leader of the Senate was shouting, being interrupted by, 'You can't just . . .' from his counterpart the Majority Leader. 'You tell that to the fifty percent of my constituency that survives the radioactivity!'

'That's enough!' the President shouted, to the surprise of Lambert. 'I've made my decision. We will entreat the Russians for a cease-fire, and begin negotiations with them for a mutual and more stringently monitored reduction in our remaining arsenals of nuclear weapons.'

Several people shouted angrily at once, one of whom was the White House Chief of Staff, but the loud repetition of 'Mr President! Mr President!' by the Minority Leader finally got him the floor. The silence that followed seemed to crackle with electricity. 'Mr President,' he said more quietly, 'I am going to put before the Senate a resolution declaring war on Russia and directing the President of the United States to prosecute that war until he can certify to Congress that all their nuclear weapons have been turned over to the International Atomic Energy Agency or have been destroyed.' There was a long pause. 'Will you, as commander in chief, implement such a declaration of war if passed by both houses?'

Lambert looked over at the President. He stared down at the table, his hands covering his mouth and nose. He dropped his hands. 'I will not.'

The telephone was silent, even the majority leadership from the President's own party.

'In that case, Mr President,' the Minority Leader said, 'as cochairman of the Committee to Investigate the Nuclear War, I hereby subpoena Mr Gregory Lambert to testify before our committee at Greenbriar two days from now at nine A.M.'

President Livingston looked over at Lambert, and Lambert, a charge running through his nervous system like a jolt of electricity, forced himself to meet his gaze.

'What on earth for?' the President asked.

'To determine the exact sequence of events that led to the nuclear attack on the United States,' the Speaker of the House said gently. 'I'm sorry, Walter, but more specifically to determine how it is that the Chinese got their missiles off, which led to the Russians' firing at us.'

'But, but . . .' the President stammered.

'As your friend, Walter,' the Speaker said, 'I'd advise you not to comment at this time until you've had the opportunity to confer with White House counsel.'

DEEP-UNDERGROUND COMMAND POST, THE KREMLIN
June 11, 2345 GMT (0145 Local)

'Is there any evidence at all that the Americans are slackening the pace of their sorties?' General Razov asked the officers in the room, still faintly smoky from the fighting that had preceded Zorin's arrest.

Air Force General Mishin shook his head. 'There are three hundred and fifty plus radar contacts inbound right now, and the last nuclear detonation report was ten minutes ago.'

General Karyakin, the new commander of the Strategic Rocket Forces, slammed his hand down on the conference table. 'How much of this do you plan on taking?' he shouted, turning then to look at each of the twenty or so senior officers gathered for the first full meeting of the new STAVKA. 'All right, a mistake was made! Zorin has been arrested and is in custody. I'm sure he will be executed, after a proper trial, et cetera. And still the Americans come at us! I for one have had enough!'

'And what do you propose?' Razov asked.

Karyakin stared back at Razov, finally saying, 'We still have the submarines in the Kara Bastion.'

'And you would like to do what with them?' the commander of Military Production asked in an incredulous voice. 'Fire at the American cities?'

'They plan on reducing us to a Third World nation. President Livingston lied to us! He's just buying time for another wave of attacks.'

'There will be no missile firings from the Bastion,' Razov said. 'I intend to issue the recall orders.'

There was silence, and from the averted gaze of several of his closest friends Razov sensed a lack of support. 'We have less than an hour and a half,' he said. 'Exactly twenty hours after firing – at zero seven two four hours Moscow time – all of the submarines in the Bastion will have the aerials on their periscope masts up for five minutes. It's risky to do even that, so those aerials won't be up for one second longer. Admiral Verkhovensky informs me that they will also take air samples and check for ordinary civilian radio and television broadcasts. The air samples will show inordinately high levels of radioactivity, and the radio and television stations for which they are looking will be off the air. If there is no recall during that five-minute window, the nuclear control orders Zorin issued will send those submarines to deep station. There will be no recall option then. As I understand it,' Razov said, looking at the commander of the Northern Fleet, 'the only communications they would accept after the window passes would be a firing order, and they would remain on station until their stores ran so low that they were forced to return to port.'

'Which the Americans have destroyed,' the naval commander groused.

'But,' Razov said, pausing to look at each of the officers for effect, 'but, after having each received valid control orders, then conducted their independent tests to confirm the occurrence of a nuclear exchange, *then* not received a recall at the twenty-hour mark and gone to deep station, those submarines' hammers will be cocked. It is a "fail-deadly" nuclear control policy. If – *if* they are attacked, if any *one* of the submarines' commanders determines that an attack on his vessel is under way, he is under standing orders to fire his missiles according to the preprogrammed firing plan initiated by Zorin's nuclear control orders. In addition, if any submarine fires its missiles, it will also broadcast an encrypted acoustic control code that will be detected by the seafloor sensors that lace the Kara Sea and relayed by cable to all the other sensors, which will themselves rebroadcast the acoustic control code directing all the other submarines in the Bastion to fire. Is that correct, Admiral?'

The naval officer nodded his head. 'And,' the Admiral said, looking off into the distance, seeing the picture in his head, 'the underwater sound of a launch to the other subs in the Bastion would be unmistakable. Even if the Americans disabled the seafloor relay system, the submarines would still launch. They would all blow ballast and fire on the sounds of any of them firing, especially if the sounds of an attack – torpedo splashes or detonations, depth charges, et cetera – were the obvious explanation for the launch.'

The tragedy of it came through in the sound of the older man's voice, in the physical effect the image of it had on his frame, posture, and visage.

Razov again gauged the faces of the men at the table. He was the acknowledged senior officer there, all clearly understood: commander of the Supreme High Command. But matters of this importance were a collective decision. *They're with me*, Razov decided.

'But the Americans are a peace-loving people,' General Karyakin said suddenly in a high and sarcastic voice, his hands held up in mock confusion as he addressed the group. 'That's why we are not responding to their continued attacks on us. They'll stop incinerating our people when it seems the decent thing to do!' His hands slammed down on the table. 'And if the war is not over, are we to take our only remaining deterrent out of service? If the Americans keep up their attacks, the submarines wouldn't even make it back to port! *Or*' – he paused, holding his index finger up into the air and looking from face to face – 'or, do we leave them in the Bastion, where we can defend them with our conventional air and naval forces? They're our last, great remaining national asset. I vote for their safekeeping!'

The chiefs of the various branches of service represented around the table nodded at the proposed 'compromise,' and Razov sensed his consensus slipping away. 'Is there any other way we can remove their firing authorization at a later date?' Air Force General Mishin asked Admiral Verkhovensky.

Razov scrutinized the admiral and then Karyakin, the two officers who commanded the nation's strategic nuclear arsenal. The admiral shook his head. Neither man appeared guarded or conspiratorial, and Razov himself relaxed. Neither man seemed to know what Razov knew – neither knew of his 'ace in the hole,' as General Thomas would have called it. 'Those submarines are on a war footing. Their commanders have each received valid launch orders with a built-in hold. None of them would have any direct evidence of the attack – detonation flashes, et cetera – but from the moment they opened their sealed war orders for Zorin's firing plan, they knew that those same orders included the firing of the entire land-based nuclear arsenal

of the RVSN at the United States. And they would also know what
would happen next. Their homes, their families . . . The planners who
programmed the targeting options did not want to risk, in a protracted
nuclear engagement, the potential that the Americans might issue false
recall orders to the submarine fleet and then pick them off when they
blew their ballasts. The submarines' computers will not even alert the
crews that a message arrived unless the computers get either a recall
at precisely twenty hours after receipt of the initial firing order or a
valid preprogrammed nuclear firing order.'

'And we have no other means of communicating with the submarines?'
Razov asked.

'They're at war, General, and will be for the next nine to twelve
months, depending upon each boat's current provisioning. They are
under orders to accept no communications. And even if they turned
their extremely low frequency receivers back on, I have complete
confidence that every last one of them would reject as an American
artifice any recall orders received after the twenty-hour window has
passed.'

'I propose,' General Karyakin said in a loud voice, leaning forward,
'that we allow the submarines to remain on station. All those in favor?'
he asked abruptly, raising his hand.

As hands slowly rose around the table and Razov saw that he had
lost, he raised his own hand. *Better to stay with the majority*, he decided.
Choose your fights carefully and hang onto your 'ace in the hole.' He
noticed the stare of Filipov from the wall next to the door, and lowered
his hand a little more quickly than the others.

'Very well,' Razov said, turning the briefing book to the next item
on the agenda.

'What are the preprogrammed targets?' Razov heard, and he looked
up to see to his great surprise that the speaker had been Filipov. The
generals and admirals craned their necks or turned to see just who it
was along the back walls of the conference room.

'What?' the commander of the Northern Fleet asked.

'What are the submarines' preprogrammed targets, sir?' Filipov
repeated. 'If they perceive that they are under attack and fire their
missiles on their own under the fail-deadly policy, what targets were
programmed by Zorin's nuclear control orders?'

There was an awkward silence as Razov stared at his haggard aide,
worrying at the sight of him and at his unprecedented interruption.

General Mishin cleared his throat and said, 'Oh, uh, gentlemen, this
is Colonel Filipov. You might remember him as General Razov's aide
from the last war.' Several of the old men nodded.

'What are the submarines' preprogrammed targets, sir?' Filipov said
again, amazingly calmly to Razov's relief and surprise.

Admiral Verkhovensky turned to stare at Filipov, and then looked down at his hands, his mouth hanging open for a moment before answering. 'Well,' he began, never lifting his eyes. 'Apparently, Admiral Grubov had raised the alert status of the submarine fleet to "Increased" before the Chinese strikes, before he and the other members of STAVKA were murdered by Zorin. When Zorin's control orders were issued, all of the submarines not already on station were flushed. Right now, the Kara Bastion contains 22 ballistic-missile submarines of various classes.' He paused, his thoughts straying before he refocused and went on, a deep solemnity to his voice. 'They have 416 SLBMs with 3,760 warheads. They are redundantly targeted.' His voice seemed to sink deeper with his frame the further he went. '"Overtargeting" – we assume not all platforms, maybe less than a quarter, would actually survive American antisubmarine efforts and fire.'

He looked up, not at Filipov but at Razov. 'The targets for 1,610 warheads, under the firing plan selected by Zorin, are the 536 U.S. military installations worldwide that remain unhit. The balance – 2,150 warheads – are targeted at the 304 largest American cities.'

Chapter Six

ABOARD NIGHTWATCH, OVER EASTERN OREGON
June 12, 0000 GMT (1600 Local)

'We're eighteen hours into SIOP-6C, sir,' General Thomas said as Lambert and the Joint Chiefs sat around the conference table. 'We have four hundred and forty sorties over Russia at this moment, thirty-six of which have nuclear weapons locks removed. Most should achieve a release, but some won't make target and others will abort because of weather minimums or mechanical problems or safe separation violations determined to exist by the controllers, or some other reason.'

The President sat erect. He was showered and clean-shaven, and although he couldn't have had much sleep, Lambert thought that he looked refreshed, invigorated. Lambert told himself it was time for him to do the same. He felt grungy in the suit he had worn for over thirty hours straight, and it affected his disposition.

'All right,' the President said, his voice firm and sure, 'here are your orders.' He looked at the gathering of generals and the admiral one at a time, and then spoke slowly as several put pens to notepads. 'You are to cease all combat operations against the Russians immediately. Nuclear, conventional, whatever. No incursions into Russian airspace, no provocative action of any kind anywhere in the world.' There was silence. 'It's over, gentlemen. This was is over.'

A silence descended over the room until Air Force General Starnes squirmed in his seat and cleared his throat. 'Do you mean, as of right now, sir? Effective immediately? 'Cause we got all those people over Russia right now, and . . .' He concluded just by shaking his head.

'I mean, gentlemen, that all authority previously granted by me for the conduct of offensive military operations against the armed forces of Russia is hereby revoked. The – war – is – over. It's that simple.'

Lambert's eyes followed those of the military officers to the Secretary of Defense, who sat with hands clasped before him and eyes downcast. Lambert raised a hand to rub the back of his neck and caught the eye of General Thomas across the table from him. 'I'm afraid it might not be quite that simple, Walter,' the Secretary said. He heaved a deep sigh before looking at President Livingston. 'Those air force and navy crews over Russia right now not only have to fight their way in, they've gotta fight their way out too.'

'Then just call off all future incursions into Russian airspace,' the President interrupted, still sounding confident.

'Some of the air defense suppression missions that are supposed to help them get out haven't penetrated Russian airspace yet,' the Secretary said.

'Then I'll permit only *those* missions to violate Russian airspace, but you call off all others.'

The Secretary was obviously highly uncomfortable, and his hands grabbed his face and pulled the skin back, covering his tired, bloodshot eyes for a moment before he went on. 'That's not the hard part, sir. The hard part is this. We've got thousands upon thousands of units large and small spread all across the globe facing off against the Russians at this very moment. From the four tactical fighter wings in Eastern Europe whose combat air patrols are in near constant contact with Russian fighters, to attack submarines on both sides who are maneuvering, I guarantee you, this very moment for shots deep underwater in the Arctic, Western Pacific, and Indian Oceans and Norwegian, Mediterranean, and Barents Seas. And there are ground troops, sir, in Eastern Europe that are awfully close to Russian forces, awfully close.'

'I hear what you are saying,' the President said, staring straight back at his Secretary, and then looking at the military men and continuing, 'but I am commander in chief of the armed forces of the United States, and if I say the war is over, then the war is over.' He looked back at the Secretary. 'Of course, our units have, as they've always had, the right to take action in self-defense. But nothing more. Is that absolutely clear?' he asked the table in a louder than normal voice.

As the men gathered there nodded or mumbled their affirmations, Lambert marveled at the President's transformation. He seemed to have gathered himself, and with it, gained strength. Lambert knew him to be a man who all his life had abhorred war, and it made sense that he would go to war reluctantly but seek peace with resolve. The President glanced at Lambert by his side and winked, the briefest of smiles betraying a spark of life that had returned to the man.

'Sir,' General Thomas said, 'just to make clear what exactly the rules of engagement are, may I pose a series of scenarios to you, and you respond with whether or not our forces may fire in "self-defense"?'

'I think that's an excellent idea, General,' the President said, nodding once and rocking back in his chair to listen.

General Thomas hesitated, the faint whoosh of air slipping by the jet filling the silence, and then began in deadly earnest. 'The sonarman in the combat information center of an aircraft carrier in the Indian Ocean reports a contact inside the defensive perimeter of the battle group and within range of the carrier with rocket-assisted torpedoes. May the carrier captain fire at the contact?'

The President sighed and looked off, refocusing on Thomas a moment later and saying, 'Yes, he may,' in an authoritative tone.

As the Chief of Naval Operations began to write on his legal pad, Thomas said, 'The radar operator on an AWACS over the Sea of Japan reports a large contact at low altitude and high speed inbound for Japan. The senior controller vectors a pair of F-15Cs for a closer look. The F-15's long-range cameras identify the contact as two Russian nuclear-capable Su-27 attack aircraft. An AWACS radarman plots an intercept and informs the senior controller that, based on the Su-27s' speed, range, and heading, and the F-15s' fuel status, there is only one intercept point between the Russian planes' present position and potential weapons release points against our bases in Japan. May the senior controller vector the intercept?'

'I see what you're doing here, General Thomas,' the President said, and Lambert searched his voice for any trace of animosity but found none. 'But let me tell you what I'm trying to do. I'm trying to prevent World War Three, a war that nobody, not the Russians and certainly not we, wanted or had any reason whatsoever *for*.'

'We got about six million dead or dyin' reasons now,' Marine General Fuller muttered, but the President ignored him.

'Now, I understand your need for rules, and I'll work with you in the drafting of a rule that says reasonable force may be exercised if a commander in good faith determines, after due inquiry and upon consultation, that some preventative action may be necessary, including even the preemptive use of deadly force, or some such language. But all of your hypotheticals, General, are designed to get me to authorize the use of force, and in order to stop this thing, gentlemen,' he said as he looked at the group, 'I'm warning you right now – somebody, somewhere, is going to have to absorb some blows and take some losses.'

The Secretary of Defense spoke up. 'Uh, Walter, the scenarios Andy was just sketching were from reports that came in just before this briefing. The F-15s shot down both Su-27s, but the carrier captain held his fire. It seems there was a British submarine somewhere in the vicinity that was unaccounted for according to the preliminary inquiry. A Russian sub hit one of his auxiliaries. She's afire, and there was heavy loss of life.'

'The captain in question has been relieved of his command,' Admiral Dixon said.

'All right,' the President said. 'You draft the rules with enough latitude for our forces to defend themselves, and I'll review them.' General Thomas nodded.

The President turned to Lambert. 'Now, Greg, I think it's time to call the Russians. Can you get General Razov on the line?'

As shocked as anyone in the conference room by the sudden request, Lambert nevertheless recovered quickly and picked up the phone in front of him. As the Joint Chiefs continued their briefing of the President in lowered voices, Lambert went through a series of Russian military operators. The Russians all reacted with surprise, presumably hearing the thick American accent he had always been told he had when he spoke Russian. Suddenly, Lambert heard, 'Hello?' in a voice he'd known for years.

'Filipov? Pavel, is that you?' Lambert asked in amazement, and the briefing stopped as the men around the table looked his way.

'It's me, Greg,' Pavel said after a momentary transmission delay.

'Is, uh, General Razov there?' Lambert asked, feeling the stares of the men around the table.

'Just one minute,' Filipov said, his monotone voice responding in kind to Lambert's own formality.

Greg cupped his hand over the phone. 'Either Filipov has flown to Khabarovsk, or Razov has flown to Moscow,' he whispered. 'My guess is the latter.'

'Razov,' the hoarse voice came over the phone.

'*Sekundochky, pozhal'sta*' – one second, please – Lambert said. He hit the speakerphone button. The taping light came on automatically. Lambert nodded at the President.

'General Razov?'

'Mr President.' From the looks Lambert saw exchanged, the barely civil tone of Razov's voice struck everyone in the room.

Undeterred, the President said, 'I've called you to talk peace.'

The burst of air into Razov's mouthpiece that crackled out of the table's speaker could only have been the bitter beginnings of a chuckle. 'Peace? You wish to discuss peace?' Razov had twice spat the word 'peace' from his mouth. In the background, muted reports could be heard from many voices in a hectic and confused scene. 'And even now your nuclear weapons continue to rain down on my country. Let me tell you this, Mr President. I have held my fire, as I promised, and have employed not one nuclear weapon after the initial accident, but I am under strong, very strong pressure here from my colleagues to resume the war with all means available.'

'That will most certainly not be necessary,' President Livingston said, sliding up to the front of his chair. 'I have just ordered all units of this country's armed forces to cease and desist from further offensive operations against your country except as required by their temporary tactical situation. You have my word, General, that this war is over.'

'*Yaderniy vzryv!*' Lambert heard shouted in the background. 'Nuclear detonation,' Lambert translated in a quiet voice for those in the room.

General Starnes read from his computer printout. 'Saratov Domestic Airport,' he said in a low voice, and made a notation on the computer paper after looking at his watch.

'Mr President, it goes against every fiber of my body to trust you after the attack that you are conducting against my country and my people. As a Russian, as a patriot like yourself, I feel an outrage at the senseless destruction that your gross overreaction has wrought upon the innocent. General Zorin's orders were issued by mistake. Yours, sir, are quite intentional.' General Fuller snorted, looking angrily from face to face around the table.

'I have given you my word that the war is over,' the President said. 'May I have yours?'

There was a long pause. 'If what you say is true, if your forces are in fact withdrawn from the field and assume a nonthreatening posture, then I will give the forces of the Republic of Russia similar orders to stand down. As I stated, Mr President, and as I pledged to you in our last conversation, we have not conducted, and will not conduct, if you keep your pledge, further hostile action against your country.'

An air force sergeant came into the room carrying a handful of papers. 'All right, then,' the President said, and Lambert motioned the uncertain man over and took the papers, 'let us plan to talk again in, say, twelve hours' time. By then our good faith should be evident.'

The air force sergeant leaned down to whisper to Lambert. 'We picked up a local broadcast station from Seattle. The Vice President's speech is in a couple of minutes, sir.'

'Patch it in here, if you can,' Lambert whispered back.

A pop over the speakerphone indicated Razov's undiplomatically abrupt disconnection of the line. 'Well, what do you think?' the President asked. Lambert looked through the papers. They were a telecopy from Mount Weather. He looked at the second page. 'Draft of address by Vice President Costanzo,' the heading said.

'Excuse me, sir,' Lambert interrupted just as the single screen in the room lit and the lights were dimmed slightly. 'They've just picked up the signal for a television station that will broadcast the Vice President's speech, and this draft of it just came in.' He handed the fax to the President.

As the television signal wavered and was tuned almost constantly to achieve a barely acceptable signal, which showed an empty podium with two American flags standing in the background, the Secretary of Defense asked, 'What's he going to say?'

Putting on his reading glasses and turning to the first page of the speech, the President said, 'He's going to tell everybody not to worry, that the government is still functioning, that . . .' The President grew silent, and Lambert and the others looked from the screen to see the

President rise slowly to his feet as he read with a look of astonishment on his face. 'Oh, my God,' he said.

'Ladies and gentlemen,' the voice of an off-screen announcer came from the speaker amid hissing static as Paul Costanzo took the podium, 'the Vice President of the United States.'

PALM SPRINGS, CALIFORNIA
June 12, 0015 GMT (1615 Local)

'This perfidy, this unparalleled evil, this sin of biblical proportions will not go unpunished!' The drama in the Vice President's voice gripped Melissa Chandler, her attention focused on the hotel room's television. 'The men and women of our armed forces stand ready to take up their arms and go forth, seeking justice from those who have committed this crime! They stand ready to lay down their lives for the cause of peace, that the scourge of nuclear weapons might never again blight our planet! But if, God forbid, the gates of hell are ever again opened to loose the flame of nuclear war upon mankind, I for one say: let it not be *our* bowed and bloody but unbroken nation that is blackened or *our* people whose lives are lost!'

There were no crowds, no applause, but Melissa could feel the tingle as the words achieved their intended effect. 'Let me quote a great man who led this nation through its last great trial. Many years before assuming the highest office in the land, Abraham Lincoln had this to say about the fortitude and capacity of our nation: "At what point shall we expect the danger? By what means shall we fortify against it? Shall we expect some transatlantic military giant, to step the Ocean, and crush us at a blow? *Never!* All the armies of Europe, Asia and Africa combined, with all the treasure of the earth . . . could not by force, take a drink from the Ohio, or make a track on the Blue Ridge, in a trial of a thousand years . . . If destruction be our lot, we must ourselves be its author and finisher. As a nation of freemen, we must live through all time, or die by suicide."

'Last night was a night of infamy, but the days to come shall be days of glory, and this nation of free men and women will prevail and, by prevailing, rid the world of the Russian menace once and for all. This nation, our great United States of America, *shall* live through all time. We *shall* meet our enemy on the field of battle, and we *shall* prevail! Every generation has its great cause. Join me in this one. Take up the banner, rise to fight our enemy as one nation, and no force in the world can stop us! Good night, my fellow Americans, and God bless the United States of America, and the success of her armed forces!'

As the scene faded and the camera focused on the crossed American flags behind the now empty podium, Melissa's eyes filled with tears. She sat on the bed by her sleeping baby, steeling herself to deal with the war that was sure to come, the war that her husband, if he was still alive, would have to fight but that she would have to endure.

GANDER AIRPORT, NEWFOUNDLAND
June 12, 0030 GMT (2030 Local)

After returning from the open-air mess, David Chandler sat in the crushed grass of the low hills by the tarmac and unzipped his heavy camouflage bag. He still ached from the unpleasant attempt at sleep on the ground the night before and from the day of hard work unloading supplies, digging latrines, and other jobs involving manual labor in which he had joined his men but to which he was unaccustomed. Inside his bag, however, was the still unexplored world of goods acquired for him by Master Sergeant Barnes, and he wanted to get through it before dark.

On top lay a field jacket, gloves, sleeping bag, flashlight, knife – a bayonet actually. He could not imagine the situation in which you would ever attach it to a rifle like the M-16. Most likely, if you crossed rifles with the M-16 in hand-to-hand fighting, its plastic stock would crack, and if the crack were in the butt, the spring that dampened the rifle's ferocious recoil would catch. The result: probably a radical dislocation of your shoulder the next time you pulled the trigger. *Thank you, U.S. Army*, he thought sarcastically as he pulled out more of the goodies. Miscellaneous stuff: a poncho, water purification tablets, first aid kit. Barnes must have been the best customer the quartermaster at March Air Force Base had.

March Air Force Base, he thought, sitting and looking out at the men and women who dotted the low hills around him, brushing their teeth or shaving, seemingly much more comfortable than he with life on the land. It was gone, March Air Force Base, and all who had been there. *Melissa*, he thought, and shook his head, chasing away the thoughts. She was fine. She would be at home right now, and her friend Lisa or her parents or somebody would be staying with her as she waited to deliver their baby. *She's fine*, he repeated to himself. *She's fine*.

Chandler pulled out the webbing. He had tried to tell Barnes gently that he didn't think he needed the full load the others carried. 'Well, uh – I'm gonna be on staff, ya know?' Chandler had said. Stifling a grin, he pieced the pistol belt and padded braces together. *Playing dress-up*, he thought, *just to satisfy the army's idea of what a soldier should look like.*

He put on the belt and braces – his ALICE, or All-purpose Lightweight

Individual Carrying Equipment system – and searched on. Canteen, pouch with compass, two ammo pouches for the four thirty-round magazines. Chandler mounted those, together with the folding shovel – an 'entrenching tool' – with its own holder, the bayonet in its scabbard, and the first aid kit onto his ALICE. They were all standard – what the army calls a 'fighting load' – but Chandler felt strange with all of it hanging from him as he stood up for the first time. *Gotta keep up appearances for the locals*, he thought as he saw the chow line and the old ladies from Gander who had volunteered to come out to help the stranded American soldiers.

He returned to the big bag and pulled out an empty field pack. It carries the 'existence load,' Chandler recalled, mouthing the words as he continued his private tutorial in the relative seclusion that his status as major seemed to buy, the enlisted men and women feeling more comfortable steering clear of him. *The existence load would go on over your* ALICE *– carry extra ammo, water, rations, clothing, sleeping bag, et cetera.* Chandler noted that Barnes had gotten him the 'medium,' his one concession to the staff officer. *Hell of a thing to call a pack that weighs fifty pounds loaded*, he thought. He knew, however, that it was twenty pounds lighter than the infantrymen's 'large.'

He slipped it off and sat, peering back into the verdant world of new belongings still inside the camo bag. There was a helmet. He had felt increasingly naked without one as the day wore on – the sight of a bare head growing rare as the sergeants whipped the privates and corporals into some sort of order and the gear more and more appearing in their proper places on the soldiers' bodies. He lifted the helmet out. Standard new issue, covered with the ubiquitous camouflage cloth, the new shape Kevlar helmet that sweeps low over the ears and around the back of the skull. He adjusted the liner inside to fit and left it on his head to continue his search through the bag.

Chandler had thought the brown cardboard box of MREs that he saw next was the last of it. Almost lost at one end of the green bag, however, was a large, flat object. *What the hell's that?* he wondered. He tugged on it, then reached in with both hands and pulled it out. *Body armor – a flak jacket.* Melissa had specifically asked him about it on the car phone before he got to March. *Would I get a 'bulletproof vest'?* He hadn't known. 'Probably,' he had amended after the silence from her end of the line grew. 'I want you to get one,' she had concluded, but he really had not known whether they would be issued.

Body armor. Melissa had thought it almost magical in its protective powers. Chandler had not told her of its limitations. It could stop a pistol bullet, probably. Break a rib, knock you down and the wind out of you, but not kill you. The problem was, nobody carried pistols anymore. Military body armor was intended to prevent wounds due to shrapnel, whose irregular, nonaerodynamic shape limited its velocity and penetrability. But not a high-powered rifle bullet of a modern assault rifle or machine gun. No way, not even close. Instead, it would flatten and distort the bullet's jacket on penetration, slowing it from thousands of feet per second to hundreds, transforming energy from potential into kinetic and discharging the force released into your body. That, he recalled from school, was a bad thing. Force equals mass times velocity squared. *The velocity's the trick*, Chandler thought. *And not only would the bullet knock the holy shit out of you, it would enter dirty, its shape smashed or even shattered or splintered.*

No, Chandler decided, if you were going to be hit by a rifle or machine gun bullet, better not to wear the armor. Better to just get it over with – in and on through – with as little disturbance to the projectile and therefore as narrow a 'trauma channel' as possible. Maybe it would keep spinning, not tumble, and go through soft low-priority tissue like muscles and fat, and not hit organs or a bone and ricochet around inside. That way it would exit with all of its speed – its potential energy – intact to waste on something else. Somehow it made him feel better to think of such perils. If he were the one in danger – if he, not she, were the one at risk – then all was right with his world, and he could concentrate on his own problems. Like what to do with the two hundred odd men and women from his flight.

Chandler put all of his new gear on and then stood and took a little half jump, the various metal parts of his load sounding like a symphony of clacks and jingles. It felt awkward and odd, but he was satisfied that the pack stayed in place pretty well.

Master Sergeant Barnes appeared out of nowhere and asked for Chandler's canteen. He took it and left, he said, to fill it to the cap from the Gander fire department's tank truck, which was providing their water. To prevent noisy sloshing, he had indicated by shaking the half-empty canteen. While he was gone, Chandler put the body armor on and it fit well. He readjusted his ALICE and put it on and donned his helmet to adjust the chin strap. He felt Barnes replacing the now full canteen onto his belt and turned to see the man peeling some dark green tape off a roll with his thumbnail. 'Just a sec, sir,' he said, beginning a process that involved fifteen minutes and a half dozen little jumps in the air after each of which Barnes attempted to reduce the noise emanating from Chandler's equipment. Half the roll of tape later, Barnes ended up taking the pack from Chandler to 'sorta rearrange things a little.'

'You tryin' to turn me into a Ninja, Master Sergeant Barnes?' Chandler laughed, relieving himself of the heavy load of equipment. Barnes just smiled.

At the very bottom of the nearly empty bag Chandler noticed the final items Barnes had included. Chandler pulled the first book from the bag. 'FM 19–21 – U.S. Army Armor Operations.' He looked over at Barnes,

who appeared not to be paying him any attention. Chandler picked up
the stack of manuals and a flashlight and set off to find a quiet place.

ABOARD NIGHTWATCH, OVER EASTERN OREGON
June 12, 0045 GMT (1645 Local)

'*Goddammit*, Paul!' the President shouted over the speakerphone at
the Vice President, beside himself with anger. He rose from his
seat and leaned out over the conference table. 'What in God's name
possessed you to give a speech like that? How dare you not clear it
with me first!'

'Walter, we've gotta talk.'

'You're damn right we gotta talk! I'm coming down there to Mount
Weather right now! And in the meantime you just dig yourself a hole
and crawl in it! No press contact, no public statements, no contacts
with any branches of any government, foreign or domestic –'

'Walter,' the Vice President said, but the President snapped, 'I'm not
through yet!'

'May I ask who is in the room with you?' the Vice President said, and
the President for the first time hesitated. 'Just Greg Lambert,' he said,
'and the military aide,' he added, barely glancing at the stone-faced air
force major who sat hugging the football at the end of the table.

'May we speak in private?' Paul Costanzo asked, and Lambert and
the major rose to leave. 'Greg, you should stay.'

Lambert sank back down, bewildered by the Vice President's
suggestion. When the door closed, President Livingston demanded
angrily, 'What is it?'

'Walter, I told you before, when we spoke, that I didn't agree with
your policy of appeasement of the Russians.'

'*Appeasement*!' Livingston shouted. 'What appeasement? This thing
was a mistake! We're not talking Neville Chamberlain here. There was
no confrontation, no animosity, before the thing happened.'

'But there is now,' the Vice President said. 'There is plenty now.
The issues have changed.'

'Now we're talking issues!' Livingston shouted. 'Okay! What issues?
What are you proposing?'

'The same thing we talked about before.'

'Disarmament?' the President shouted. 'You expect me to demand
Russian nuclear disarmament after we just dropped five *thousand*
nuclear warheads on them in response to their mistake? You weren't
a party to the last conversation we had with General Razov, but let me
tell you, he was in no mood to hear terms.'

'That's another thing. I think you should include me more in your discussions about the situation – military briefings, discussions with foreign leaders, that sort of thing.'

'You *do*, do you?' Livingston said, a look of angry disbelief on his face. A grin broke out as he shook his head.

'And so do the Speaker, and Jim Bailey,' the Vice President said softly, the latter referring to the chairman of the Democratic National Committee. 'And by the way, Mr Lambert, the Speaker wanted me to remind you that your testimony is requested tomorrow at nine a.m. at their underground facility at Greenbriar in West Virginia.'

Lambert's first thought was *West Virginia*. Jane was at Snowshoe. He would see her tomorrow. His heart leapt and spirits soared.

Livingston sank into his seat. The grin was gone. He nodded his head, looking over at Lambert. 'So that's what this is all about. I get it. You've gone around behind my back.'

'They all just happened to be here, Walter, and we talked.'

'I want you incommunicado, from this moment forward.'

'I don't think that'll do, Walter,' the Vice President said, again softly.

The President took a deep breath as his anger grew to proportions that Lambert had never before witnessed. 'Then I want your fucking resignation.'

There was a long pause, and finally the Vice President said, 'I don't think that'll do, either.'

Livingston raised his index finger in the air and poked the button to disconnect the line with a hard jab. His finger fell next on another button on the console. 'Put this thing on the ground! I'm going to Mount Weather!'

PHILADELPHIA INTERNATIONAL AIRPORT
June 12, 0600 GMT (0100 Local)

Lambert descended the stairs of the E-4B. When he got to the bottom, he looked at the identical plane sitting one hundred yards away with its engines idling. The President and First Lady, however, were just disappearing through the door of a helicopter. Close on their heels was the White House legal counsel, who had met the President on the tarmac. He was already talking to the President in his rapid-fire style.

Before Lambert got into the ubiquitous black government car, the helicopter lifted off, rushing the President to Mount Weather for his showdown with the Vice President. Lambert turned to his escort, a Congressional aide.

'I need to make a call,' Lambert said.

'You can make it from the car,' the aide suggested.

As the car sped off, the aide handed Lambert the mobile phone and Lambert dialed the number of the condo at Snowshoe.

'Jane Lambert, please,' Greg said to the switchboard operator who answered, the anxiety pumping adrenaline into his system.

'I'm sorry, sir, but there is no Jane Lambert – L-A-M-B-E-R-T – staying with us,' the operator said.

Greg felt a slight chill. 'Well, is there anybody by the name of Collins? She might be with her parents.'

After a pause, the operator said, 'No, sir, I'm sorry. We have no Collins, either.'

'Maybe – are you booked up solid?' Greg asked, finding peace with that explanation.

'Yes, sir,' the operator said. 'Everybody from – well, the refugees.'

Greg nodded – their condo was rented out and they had to find some other place – but then thought to ask, 'When did you fill up?'

'Oh, a couple of hours ago, I guess,' the operator answered.

Lambert held the phone to his ear. *They should have been there within an hour or so after my call*, Lambert thought.

'Sir?' the operator said.

'Oh, uh, thank you,' Lambert said, swallowing the dryness from his throat.

'Good luck, sir,' the woman said, a sad kindness in her voice.

Lambert looked over at the aide on the seat next to him, but the young man turned away to gaze out the dark window.

With terrible trepidation, Lambert phoned his and Jane's apartment. To Lambert's surprise, the telephone rang. His heart froze into a block of ice as he feared it would be picked up. On the third ring, the answering machine came on and he relaxed. Greg quickly punched in their personal access code. Putting the phone back up to his ear, he heard the familiar computerized voice say, 'Number of messages received – three.'

His nerves were taut now. Lambert listened to the first tone. 'Honey, if Pavel calls,' Jane said – from the background noise she was clearly in her speeding Saab, to Greg's great relief – 'don't forget to tell him Irina's with me. Bye.'

He tried to remain calm as the beep over the phone sounded again. 'Greg,' Jane said, and he grew sick at the sound of her voice. She was frightened. 'The engine started smoking, and then it just stopped.' He felt the physical effect that the blow of her words had. In the background, Greg could hear the hum of the Emergency Broadcast System. He closed his eyes; the sound of the recording was his world now.

'Tell him about the radio,' Greg heard Irina say. Irina's voice shook.

'The . . . the radio stations went off the air. I'm scared, Greg. Oh, I'm so, so scared.' The quiver in her voice was audible. 'I'm gonna hang up now. Mom and Dad may be trying to call. They're coming to get me. Bye,' she said, not seeming to want to hang up. 'Bye-bye, darling.'

Greg listened as there was another click. His mouth was dry and his breathing was difficult against the weight forming on his chest. The third beep, the final one. He heard Jane's voice as if from the pit of his own private hell. 'Greg,' and a cough. 'Oh, honey, what's happening?' Jane barely managed before the coughing overcame her. Greg heard Irina vomiting in the background.

PALM SPRINGS, CALIFORNIA
June 12, 1400 GMT (0600 Local)

'I got a call from my sister,' the gray-haired woman in line next to Melissa was saying, pressing a tissue to her nose. 'She's in Kansas, just sitting in her house.'

'Oh, that's awful,' Melissa said as they inched forward. 'Isn't there anything they can do?'

'No. Everybody's in the same boat. The telephone lines work, so at least they're not alone. She's at the old home place. It's farming country there, you know. Everything is just normal. She's got electricity, and cable TV, and water. But she's dying, she says, she can feel it. The local TV stations say her part of the county got one hundred of whatever it is, radiation.' The tears began to flow. She was so old, and her skin was so white and dry, that Melissa found herself surprised at the volume of tears that rolled down her cheeks.

'Doesn't she have a basement or something?' Melissa asked, hoisting little Matthew higher up onto her aching shoulder, shifting his weight uncomfortably in her weakened state.

'She's got a storm cellar. That part gets cyclones. I told her to get on down in it, but she was asleep when the damn Russians dropped the bombs and didn't hear about it till the next morning on TV. By then, they were saying, the radiation was already all over the place. If you hadn't stuffed rags under the doors and some such, then it was too late. It was inside the house, and the cellar, and everything, like the old dust storms. Breathed it right into your lungs too, Edith said.' She was shaking her head. 'I always said she shoulda come out here with me after Frank – he was her husband, you know – after he passed.'

'Can she get out at all?' Melissa asked. 'Even for a quick trip to get some food?'

The woman shook her head. 'Can't rightly keep food down anymore, Edith says, so she doesn't even try. Never was much of an eater, always slim as a reed. We're twins, you know,' she said, smiling up through her thick eyeglasses. 'Prettiest girls in the county, they used to say.' Her eyes drifted down the line in which they stood. 'There are too many people here. I think I'll just come back later.'

'But we're almost there,' Melissa said, nodding at the door just ahead. 'There may not be any food later on.'

'I can get food somewhere. I've got a vegetable garden in my backyard. If I have to, I can go ahead and harvest early.'

'Are you sure, ma'am?' Melissa said, reaching out to touch the frail, bony shoulder of the sweet old woman.

'Thank you, darlin'. I think I'll head on back and give Edith a ring. She hung up on me before, sayin' it must be costing a fortune. The more I think about it, I think how silly that is. Who cares how much it costs? But, you know, old ways die hard.' She was off.

Melissa couldn't have felt much worse as she inched forward to the glass door. A large poster was taped to the window beside it. BY ORDER OF U.S. GOV'T, ONLY PERISHABLES WILL BE SOLD UNTIL JUNE 16TH. That much she knew, the word having filtered back down the line half an hour earlier. Her eyes, however, focused on the other large print, this written in bold letters across the front page of the *Los Angeles Times* held by the security guard, who read intently as the crowd filed by in a surprisingly calm fashion. Melissa could barely take her eyes off the paper, looking away just briefly as a man let her go in front of him at the door but being drawn back to reread the banner headlines, which took up nearly one third of the front page. She shook her head, the words still unreal, repeating them soundlessly over and over in her head. '*WORLD WAR III – WORLD WAR III.*'

CONGRESSIONAL FACILITY, WEST VIRGINIA
June 12, 1400 GMT (0900 Local)

'State your full name, please,' the Majority Leader began.

'Gregory Philip Lambert.'

'And your position.'

'Special Assistant to the President for National Security.'

'Now, Mr Lambert,' the Majority Leader said as he looked at his notes, 'I understand . . . I've heard about your loss, and so I'll be brief. On the night of June eleventh, were you in telephone contact with President Livingston?'

'Yes,' Lambert said, unfazed by the glare of the lights for Congressional film cameras as he sat numbly before the committee.

'I'm sorry, sir,' the Majority Leader asked softly. 'Could you speak a little more directly into the microphones.'

Lambert leaned forward into the small bundle of microphones. 'Yes,' Lambert repeated with no inflection in his voice.

The Majority Leader glanced out of the corner of his eye at his Republican colleague, and then said, 'I'm sorry, Mr Lambert, but we've got to ask you these questions. Did the President have you get the late Secretary Moore on the telephone that night of June eleventh?'

'Yes.'

'And what did President Livingston say to Secretary Moore?'

'I am not at liberty to discuss the matter,' Lambert said in a monotone, all emotion long drained from him, 'on the ground that it might compromise the national security of the United States during the pendency of a defense emergency.' He had recited the sentence three times over the telephone during his one-hour preparation with White House counsel that had preceded the closed-session hearing.

Lambert was focused on the green cloth that covered the Congressmen's dais, his mind a fog when he realized that the Majority Leader was saying something to him.

'Can you repeat your question?' Lambert asked.

'It wasn't a question, it was a statement. You have been asked a direct question during a properly convened hearing of a committee of both houses of Congress. The session is behind closed doors, and everything you say will be held in strictest confidence. Now, I will ask you the question again. What did President Livingston say to Secretary Moore?'

'I am not at liberty to discuss the matter on the ground that it might compromise the national security of the United States during the pendency of a defense emergency.'

'You realize, don't you, sir,' a Republican Congressman said, 'that you are subject to the penalty of criminal contempt.'

Lambert nodded, and the senior Congressmen conferred behind the chairman. Finally, the chairman said, 'Mr Lambert, we are going to dismiss you pending recall after a resolution of the legal issues involved. You are instructed to remain available for recall on short notice.'

Outside the hearing room, Lambert ran into General Thomas.

'Hello, Greg,' the general said, motioning Lambert over to the side. 'They called me down here for a briefing on the war, or conflict, or whatever we're supposed to call it.'

Lambert gave the general a slight nod.

General Thomas put his hand on Lambert's shoulder. 'Greg,' he said in a compassionate voice, 'I'm sorry – I just heard.' Lambert nodded again. The two were silent for a moment before Thomas said, 'Is there anything I can do to help?'

'I need to find her,' Lambert said, suddenly very agitated by the possibility. He looked at Thomas.

'It's pretty hot down there, Greg.'

'There are people working inside the contaminated zone,' Greg protested.

'In shifts, flown in and out quickly in protective gear.'

Lambert looked up at General Thomas. Thomas stared back for a moment, straight into Lambert's eyes, and then nodded, saying, 'See Colonel Rutherford. He'll arrange it.'

'Thank you,' Greg said, his head heavy, his eyes dropping again to look at the floor.

'Greg,' General Thomas continued, his voice a little sterner this time, 'you can grieve, if the worst is true, but you can't blame yourself. You had a job to do that took you away from home like millions of other men and women, and—'

'She drove a Saab,' Greg said, his lower lip quivering like a child's. 'She kept telling me that . . . that the engine temperature light came on. I was working such long hours that I put off taking it into the shop. She never would, because she was timid about car repairs, things like that.' He swallowed back the tears, batting his eyes and looking up and off into space. 'She . . . uh . . . called our answering machine on her car phone. The engine had overheated on the way to the mountains. She was already sick,' he said, breaking into tears. General Thomas wrapped both arms around the taller man, his own eyes watering as they hugged.

THE PENTAGON, OUTSIDE WASHINGTON, D.C.
June 12, 2200 GMT (1700 Local)

The crates were heavy. Lambert's back hurt after the first one, and the sticky feeling he had felt since putting on the chemical-biological-radiological gear – charcoal-impregnated outer garments and gas mask – had turned into a drenching sweat.

As he and the army helicopter crewman hefted the last of the heavy crates to the similarly dressed men who had dashed out the door of the Pentagon into the interior courtyard's helipad, the crewman turned to the cockpit and gave the thumbs up to the pilot.

The military had insisted on dropping off the supplies to the staff of the Tank, the sealed war room on the third floor of the Pentagon, before proceeding with the 'secondary mission.' Now, however, they were Lambert's, and it was a race against time. The swirling downdraft of the rotor blades had coated them all in fallout radiating thirty roentgens per hour. A cumulative dose of two hundred roentgens killed some humans, and six hundred would kill almost anybody. The clock would continue to run until they got back to the decontamination site outside Dundalk, Maryland.

As they climbed to a thousand feet over the still city, Lambert noticed the army crewman in back watching him. He'd heard the crew's bitching when they received their orders, but was pressing on despite the feeling of guilt their complaints had raised.

'Shut up, man!' the helicopter's pilot had said. 'He's some fuckin' White House bigwig.'

Nothing moved on the ground below. The crewman, a Specialist 4th Class, was leaning out the open side door of the helicopter into the wind, brushing his uniform with his free hand in an attempt to decontaminate himself as much as possible. Lambert noticed that he began and ended by brushing his crotch.

Lambert looked down at his own dark green suit. He could see nothing on it, and he cared so little that he did nothing, just sat and peered down at the green Virginia countryside as it rolled by.

They followed Highway 193, which itself roughly followed the Potomac upstream. The Potomac and many other rivers and streams were emptying radioactivity into the Atlantic at an alarming rate. The Europeans were panicking, sending ships of their navies not to fight the Russians but to track the contamination in the Gulf Stream up the East Coast to forewarn of its passage across the north Atlantic to Europe. The Canadians had halted fishing in the great banks off Nova Scotia, and the Europeans were incensed that some U.S. weapons detonated in Russia caused fallout in their countries. Hundreds of thousands, even millions, outside the U.S. and Russia might perish from increased rates of cancer.

They're worried about their fish and milk products, Lambert thought, *and the Spec 4 here is brushing fallout off his pants*. He shook his head. *Fuck them. Fuck everything.*

The helicopter began to drop. The copilot turned back to Lambert and pointed down with her finger. Lambert looked out the window, and after several seconds he picked out the highway.

There were cars everywhere. They looked so normal, as if they were idling in rush-hour traffic. Many were pulled off to the side but most were right on the road. Lambert suddenly noticed that most, almost all, had dim headlights shining despite the fact that it was after five o'clock in the afternoon. *They died in the night*, he realized.

Looking at all the cars on the road below, he grew disheartened. *We'll never find her car in all that*, he thought. The helicopter was lower but sped on by the traffic jam, which Lambert saw was caused by a major accident.

Lambert had not been able to look at each of the cars as they flashed by, and he got up and walked forward to the cockpit.

'You're going too fast!' Lambert yelled to make himself heard through his mask and the hood of the copilot and over the noise of the engine.

'We're not there yet!' the woman yelled back, looking down at her map and then up ahead out through the windshield. 'There!' she said, pointing ahead to the junction of a road with the highway with exaggerated jabs of her index finger.

Lambert turned his head slightly to rid the lens of his gas mask of the glare, and he saw it as plain as day. Jane's car, right where her message had said it would be.

The silver Saab was all by itself on the side of the road, the hood raised. The headlights were off. The copilot pointed and the pilot nodded as he picked out the car, and Lambert's pulse began to speed.

Oh, God, he thought. He never really believed they would find her car. Deep down, he had thought that she would mysteriously just not be there. The thing he hadn't come to grips with was the fact that he might really find her. *Oh, my God*, he thought in sudden panic.

The helicopter was very low now, and the white dust it kicked up as it made its last bank to land facing the car was, Lambert realized, ash – fallout.

As soon as the skids touched down, the Spec 4 shouted, 'Come on!' and Lambert followed him, jumping the few feet to the ground. The world around them seemed strange and alien. From the confines of the gear Lambert wore, it felt to him as if he were on another planet. As he followed the Spec 4 up to the car, the only sounds he could hear were the *thock-thock-thock* of the helicopter's rotors and the sound of his own breathing through the mask's filter. It reminded him of scuba diving – he was in a place where man was never meant to be . . . self-contained . . . alone.

'It's empty!' the Spec 4 yelled, having wiped the windows clear with his gloved hand. Greg looked in the two cleared windows. There was no sign of Jane or Irina.

'Let's go!' the enlisted man yelled as he took off back to the helicopter. Lambert turned to follow, breaking into a trot as the crewman turned to wave him on. Lambert looked all around the car to the sides of the road. There was no one.

As soon as he was aboard, the helicopter took off. The crewman sat next to Lambert panting, but Lambert forced himself up to the cockpit.

'Head on down 193 toward Leesburg a little way!' Lambert yelled.

The copilot and pilot looked at each other, and the copilot pointed at her watch, worn outside her gear. Lambert grabbed her arm and looked at the watch.

'We've got time!' he shouted. 'Let's go a little farther!'

'Fifteen minutes!' the woman said, and the pilot headed on.

'Look for a black Mercedes – big car!' Lambert yelled. Jane had said that she was waiting for her parents, but she was afraid they would be too late. *She was so afraid*, he thought, and the emotions engulfed him for a moment, but he forced them down again. There would be time later.

The Spec 4 stuck his head into the space to Lambert's left.

'What the hell's goin' *on*?' he yelled.

'We're looking for a Mercedes!' the pilot said.

'*Shit*!' the Spec 4 whined, slamming his hand on the bulkhead behind the pilot's back and returning, Lambert noticed, to the open door to brush his crotch some more.

The cars, now few and far between, slid by on the road below. Most were on the side of the road as if blown off by some powerful wind. It was like a scene after an ice storm, but it was summertime. Lambert tried not to think about what was inside the cars.

'There!' the copilot shouted, pointing up ahead at a car that was off the side of the road at an odd angle and pointing the wrong way. 'Is that it?' she asked.

'I can't tell!' Lambert said. 'Let's check it out!'

'If we land one more time,' the pilot said, 'that's it! We're headed back!'

Lambert looked at the car. The color didn't look quite right; it looked brown, not black, under its coat of dust, but the model was right and there were no cars in sight up ahead.

'Okay!' he shouted. 'Check it out!'

The helicopter landed in the same way as before, and Lambert and the Spec 4 began their dash. Even before Lambert made it to the car he knew that it was Jane's parents'.

Lambert swallowed as he got to the window. The Spec 4 was peering through it, having cleared a small spot and shielded his eyes against the glare. He stood up looking at Lambert and stepped back. Greg's heart raced and he felt faint. He bent to look in.

Slumped over to her right was Jane's mother. Jane's father had slid all the way off the passenger seat to the floor, his back arched awkwardly over the front edge of the seat and his head and shoulders suspended in air.

Jane's mother never drove, Lambert thought. *Dad must have been sick*. He had to force the breaths into his lungs as he stepped over to the rear window and brushed at it with his glove, the first swipe leaving four streaks where his fingertips had passed through the fine, powderlike ash. With the flat of his hand he wiped a large circle clear. Irina sat on the floorboard with her head on crossed arms on the seat cushion. Jane lay across the back seat, their little girl asleep on a long car trip.

OUTSIDE DUNDALK, MARYLAND
June 12, 2230 GMT (1730 Local)

The blast of hot water almost knocked Lambert over. He stood on the concrete just outside the drive-through that had once cleaned cars but now cleaned people. Through the droplets on the lens of his gas mask he watched the world rotate as he slowly turned, arms in the air, the jet of liquid digging into his body and leaving in its path a warm, itchy feeling from its force.

Into view came the washer, himself wearing protective clothing. Then the others from their flight being sprayed in front of their own stalls. Then the dikes of black wet dirt, scraped up, he assumed, by the bulldozer that sat off to the side of the decontamination facility. Then he saw the pool of water and the streams from the sprays that trickled down to add to the pool – yellow-and-black RADIOACTIVE signs stuck into the earthen dam that contained the dangerous shallow pond.

Before he had completed the revolution, the spray quit pummeling him as the washer turned to the cement surface around him, pushing with small walls of water the dirt Lambert had tracked in.

The soldier yelled, 'Over there!' and motioned with the nozzle of his sprayer before flexing his fingers from the unnatural strain of the sprayer's recoil. In the background their helicopter was being scrubbed with large brushes mounted on the end of poles by other protectively clad troops. The helicopter, Lambert noticed, had its own much larger dike system, and a fire truck was parked next to it, the hoses lying on the ground ready for the rinse cycle.

At the edge of the dike, a soldier wearing only a mask and gloves held a long wand in one hand with a wire running to the box held in his other. He ran the wand slowly down Lambert's front and then said, 'Turn around!' Lambert watched as the rest of the helicopter crew walked toward him.

'You're clean!' the man said, and Lambert turned and awkwardly stepped over the dike. Rather than reach out to hold his arm, the man with the Geiger counter stepped back.

'You can take your mask off outside that rope and put your gear in the pile,' he said, indicating the mound of wet, dark green protective clothing that lay just inside a thin rope stretched between orange cones. 'Gloves last,' the man said in parting.

Lambert walked over to the pile and took off his suit. When the mask came off and the cool, fresh air caressed his face and filled his lungs, the world suddenly seemed normal again. The sounds of the sprays and of shouts from up ahead where soldiers were unloading crates from a truck near the makeshift helipad attracted Lambert's attention in a way that they never would have before. A fresh crew in protective gear awaited decontamination and loading of their helicopter as mechanics gingerly carried the engine's air filter to the dike at the end of an oversize pair of metal tongs. A slight breeze, cool against his hair matted with sweat, brushed along the back of his neck.

'Excuse me!' a man in camouflaged military uniform said from the other side of a truck several yards to his left, waving Lambert toward him.

Painted on the hard panel of the truck was a red cross on a square white background. The man whom Lambert approached had a clipboard. He looked out of place in military garb with his gray hair and protruding paunch.

As Lambert rounded the truck, he saw a woman in powder blue hospital scrubs and a white smock. The man turned back to Lambert and without saying a word unclipped the thin tube, like a pen, from the breast pocket of Lambert's button-down dress shirt. Lambert had forgotten about the dosimeter that he wore.

'Whew!' the man said, holding the tube up to the light. 'You are?' he asked, handing the dosimeter to the woman and holding up the clipboard.

'Lambert. Greg Lambert.'

Making a note on the board, he said, 'Oh, yes, of course, Mr Lambert,' looking up at him in recognition. 'I'm Dr Gray, Major – Army Reserve. And this is Samantha James,' he said indicating the woman. 'She's my nurse from the hospital in Baltimore. I thought she could help.'

The copilot walked up from behind, and Lambert turned to nod at her.

'I'll be with you in a minute,' the doctor said. 'Mr Lambert, you've just received a lifetime dose of radiation. Seventeen RADs – Radiation Absorbed Doses. Based on the data from the sarcophagus workers at Chernobyl, it's not dangerous, statistically speaking, but it's more than three times the annual dose permitted for U.S. nuclear power workers. Any more and you could have complications. Do you understand?'

Lambert nodded.

'Now, you're over fifteen RADs, so I'm going to have to report you to the health authorities,' the doctor continued, 'and they'll keep track of it for their own purposes, which includes triage, but you won't be denied any medical treatment at this level. If another eighteen RADs are reported, you'll be denied medical treatment of any sort by law until the emergency's over. Now. You take these pills – they block thyroid concentration of anything you might have ingested – and you should be okay.'

'What about – we brought my wife and her parents back with us. And a friend.'

'Bring them over. I'll take a look at 'em.'

'They're dead,' Lambert said simply.

'Oh. I'm sorry,' the doctor said. 'And they're contaminated?'

Lambert nodded.

'Graves Registration is over there. But they won't let you see them. They've probably already buried them,' the doctor said, indicating the general area of the dikes and the yellow-and-black RADIOACTIVE signs. 'But they will take their names and register them, take care of all the paperwork.'

Lambert turned to go and saw the rest of the crew. They stood there mute and looking at him.

'Thank you,' he said to them, and walked off hanging his head.

Lambert felt someone grab his arm. He looked up to see the Spec 4, a handsome young black kid with closely cut hair who could not have been more than nineteen. 'Hey, sir, it'll be okay.'

Lambert knew the soldier was wrong, but thanked him and walked over to the roped-off area. He looked at the pools of radioactive suds and water trapped inside the dikes. *I'm sorry, Jane. Oh, God, I'm sorry.* The words were hollow. They meant nothing and did no good.

THE KREMLIN, MOSCOW
June 12, 2345 GMT (0145 Local)

'You all know that I think this is madness,' Razov said, barely managing to control his temper as he addressed the full meeting of STAVKA through clenched teeth. 'Everything we have done to this point in time can be explained away as Zorin's mistake. *This*,' Razov said, tossing the folder with the proposed operational plans onto the table after a momentary loss of his temper, 'this is our doing.'

'What good has it been,' General Karyakin asked, shrugging, 'proving our innocence to the Americans? Perhaps you haven't been keeping up with your reading.' He looked down the table at the others, at the swing votes from the air force and navy. He picked up the slips of paper that had been handed each of the STAVKA members over the hours of debate they were now completing. '"ORACLE,"' he read, looking up at the head of GRU, the chief intelligence directorate of STAVKA. 'Who's that?'

'It's a composite of human sources located across the United States,' the man answered. 'Embassy and consular officials, visiting students and businessmen, trade representatives, third-country nationals.'

'Well, ORACLE reports,' Karyakin continued, putting on his reading glasses, '"U.S. mobilization continuing. Civilian airports at Denver, Dallas, Houston, Salt Lake City, St Louis, Chicago, Atlanta, Philadelphia, and New York being used as staging points for departures to Far East and Europe. Civilian air traffic at a standstill as all available transport activated for military use. Naval transports continue loading at New Orleans, Galveston, San Diego, Seattle, Philadelphia, and Jacksonville.'"

He picked up the next report, looking down his nose as he read. 'This one is also a GRU report. "Satellite imagery indicates American V Corps units in Nürnberg, Germany, and elements of 1st Armored Division in Erlangen, Germany, engaging in road deployment. Initial indications are objectives east."' He looked up – 'To the *east*' – and picked up a third report. 'American 4th Mechanized Infantry Division in Presov, Slovakia, reported on full-combat-alert status. One brigade deploying to field along Ukraine border. Second brigade estimated forty percent combat strength, intentions unknown.' That comes from our liaison to the Ukrainian Army Command in Kiev.'

As he picked up another slip of paper, Razov said, 'We've all read the reports, General.'

'Then what the hell is the debate about?' Karyakin shouted as he lifted the heavy stack of paper in front of him. '*You* may not *want* to be, and *Livingston* may *profess* not to be, but we're still at war, General Razov!' He pulled a slip of paper out of the stack at random. 'Alternate Air Defense Commander, Polyarnyy: "Suspected American Air Force TR-1 strategic reconnaissance aircraft made four incursions into Russian airspace between 0024 and 0059, Moscow time. Request permission to pursue into Finnish and/or Norwegian airspace." Permission denied!' he said, glaring at Razov. 'Pacific Fleet Command, Vladivostok: "Three American P-3 anti-submarine warfare aircraft made six torpedo attack runs at position within primary firing station of Pacific Fleet ballistic missile submarines. Believe contact is with surviving submarine. Request permission to intercept two U.S. Navy antisubmarine helicopters inbound from Aleutian Islands." Permission denied!'

'That's enough!' Razov shouted as Karyakin pulled another report from the stack. Razov looked down the table at the thoughtful faces of Russia's senior military officers. Many, he noted, were holding or looking down at their own stacks of reports. Many of the reports, Razov knew from having read each one as they were handed to him, were frantic calls for support in spots around the globe where the war had been rekindled by a chance meeting, or an over-anxious commander, mainly on the U.S. side.

The door opened noiselessly, and three men began their now familiar walk around the table, laying another report in front of each of the senior officers. As Razov raised the report he was handed, he saw Filipov enter through the open door behind them and walk to the empty seat immediately behind Razov. The report read:

BLACK SEA FLEET COMMAND. KIROV-CLASS CRUISER *SAK-HAROV* TASKED TO SHADOW U.S. NAVY SIXTH FLEET CARRIER

BATTLE GROUP OFF COAST OF ISRAEL IN EASTERN MEDITERRA-
NEAN COLLIDED WITH PERRY-CLASS FRIGATE, HULL NUMBER
432, FORTY-SIX KILOMETERS WEST-SOUTHWEST OF U.S.S.
THEODORE ROOSEVELT. AFTER SAKHAROV RESUMED PRIOR
COURSE, U.S. FRIGATE INITIATED HOSTILE MANEUVERS DESPITE
EXTENSIVE DAMAGE TO PORT HULL AT WATER LINE. TWO RADIO
WARNINGS ISSUED BY COMMANDER OF SAKHAROV – FIRST AT
0132 LOCAL TIME, SECOND AT 0134. U.S. SHIP MAINTAINED
COLLISION BEARING AND SPEED, AND WHEN U.S. FRIGATE
CLOSED TO RANGE OF FOUR HUNDRED METERS AT 0137, CAPTAIN
OF SAKHAROV FIRED TWO SURFACE-TO-SURFACE MISSILES AT
FRIGATE. ONE MISSILE DETONATED, AND ONE FAILED TO
FUSE. FRIGATE'S SUPERSTRUCTURE IS AFIRE, AND SHIP IS
LISTING TO PORT. SAKHAROV'S AIR COMBAT CENTER REPORTS
FOUR AIRCRAFT, BELIEVED MODEL F/A-18 ATTACK AIRCRAFT,
LAUNCHED FROM DECK OF THEODORE ROOSEVELT AT 0141 AND
CURRENTLY INBOUND TO SAKHAROV'S POSITION. CAPTAIN
REQUESTS PERMISSION TO FIRE AT THEODORE ROOSEVELT.
[PERMISSION DENIED.] CAPTAIN REQUESTS PERMISSION TO
FIRE AT INBOUND AIRCRAFT. [PERMISSION GRANTED.] CAPTAIN
REQUESTS PERMISSION TO LAUNCH TORPEDOES AT UNKNOWN
SONAR CONTACT FOUR THOUSAND METERS ASTERN. [PERMIS-
SION DENIED.]

As Razov finished reading the half-page flimsy, another report was
handed to him. 'First Officer, Kirov-class cruiser *Sakharov*, requests
search and rescue, position one-one-six kilometers west-southwest of
Haifa, Israel. [Communication terminated. Black Sea Fleet Command
unable to raise *Sakharov*.]'

'We've got some exposure here, Yuri,' Air Force General Mishin said,
'from a purely military standpoint. We hadn't made up for our losses in
the first Chinese war last year and were straining our resources to the
limit in the new fighting. We've got everything in the Far East. We're
. . . we're exposed, dangerously exposed, in the West. In Europe.'

'And let's not forget the damage from the nuclear exchange,' Admiral
Verkhovensky said, both swing votes now on Karyakin's side. 'The
Americans went after a much broader target set than we did. As I
understand it, our supply system is completely frozen up. It has been
in shambles for years now, and we had stripped everything in the West
clean to send it to the Far East during the Chinese war, but now I'm told
that we can't even reestablish our rail grid for internal shipments because
of the radioactivity and blast damage. Nobody has the slightest idea
where to start working around all the problems, filling in all the gaps.'

'Exposure, Yuri,' Mishin said. 'We can't just sit back and watch it
happen.'

Razov took a deep breath and looked up. 'All right. If we're going to do this, we'd better do it right.' *And we will do it at my command and on my authority*, he thought turning to Admiral Verkhovensky. 'The army will give you one airborne division: the alert division, the 104th Guards at Krasnodar. That will make the 105th at Omsk the new alert division,' he said, speaking rapidly as he turned to the Army's Airborne Forces commander, the most junior officer present. 'The 104th will seize Reykjavik and Hafnarfjordhur in the south' – he spun on Verkhovensky – 'and your marines will land east of Husasik and move west to capture the cities along Iceland's northern coast, all as per the General Operational Plan.' He pointed at Air Force General Mishin. 'You give them every AN-22 and IL-76 you've got for transport, and you put at least three wings of air superiority and two of attack aircraft into Reykjavik the second that airport's secure. They have permission to fire on any U.S. naval or air forces that come within range, and they have express orders to knock down any flight headed east across the northern Atlantic, including regularly scheduled commercial flights after a one-time-only four-hour warning advisory.'

He spun to point at the commander of the Western Strategic Direction before anyone could comment. 'You are to deploy into Ukraine to take up defensive positions opposite the American 4th Infantry Division. Any Ukrainian Army resistance is to be met with force, but I will personally call President Belachuk to warn him that any such resistance will be deemed to be an act of war. I will then contact Far East Army Command and order a halt to the counterattack into northern China.'

'But we're rolling over the little yellow bastards . . .!' the old commander of Construction Troops began.

'The Far East Army Command,' Razov interrupted, 'will be ordered to redeploy all available forces to strategically defensible positions. That means,' Razov said, pausing to ensure the full attention of his audience, 'to refuse the sea around and to the north of Vladivostok.' He watched the chilling effect of his words quiet the officers who moments before were on the edge of their seats wanting to speak. 'They will also be informed to expect to conduct operations from this point forward on existing stocks and on anything captured from the Chinese. I want all war materials produced,' he ordered the director of Military Production, 'redirected to our European stocks.'

It was a wrenching, radical change in policy, and the implications underlying it were clearly expressed on the sullen, contemplative faces of the senior officers. They were all silent now. Razov had one last hope: that the realities of the situation had finally sunk in on them. 'Are we sure we're ready for this?' he asked in a low, measured tone. At just that moment, the double doors opened and in walked another set of message slips. His question would not now be answered. The spell was broken, and the die was cast.

The meeting broke up quickly, and Razov arranged his papers, intending to stay behind and use the conference room to read the reports on which he was getting behind. He avoided eye contact with the departing officers, easily mustering a concerned and preoccupied look on his face to ward off the notorious talkers who might dawdle and waste minutes of his valuable time. When the last of the officers and their staff had left, he turned to see that Filipov was still there. Filipov looked like death itself.

'Pavel, have you, uh, heard anything from Irina?' asked Razov.

Pavel looked off into the corner of the empty room, his face growing even more set in a mask of worry and pain. 'No.'

Razov had seen the GRU's radiological reports for Washington, D.C. They were dying there. 'Pavel,' Razov said, waiting an inordinately long time for his aide's head to swivel to return Razov's gaze, 'have you tried making contact with her? Is there anybody there you could call who might know where she is? What about your friend, this man Lambert? You could use military channels.'

Pavel stared with eyes focusing ever more intently on empty space across the room. The bags under his eyes, like his mood, were dark. He shook his head, and then shook it again. 'I have no friends in America.'

PART THREE

After the great destructions,
Everyone will prove that he was innocent.

—GÜNTER EICH
Think of This
1955

Chapter Seven

SPECIAL FACILITY, MOUNT WEATHER, VIRGINIA
June 13, 0600 GMT (0100 Local)

The plain black government car followed the twists and turns of County Route 601 past Berryville, Virginia. Lambert sat in back by himself, looking out through his reflection into the dark, remembering. The trees floated past his window like ghosts, and all that Jane had been, all the things about her that he had loved, came back to him one by one. The tears flowed silently, unseen.

Just past Heart Trouble Lane, the driver slowed at a flashing yellow light and a ten-miles-per-hour sign. Around the next bend in the empty road Lambert saw a gate opening into a ten-foot-high chain-link fence topped with six strands of barbed wire. Half a dozen men, some soldiers clad in full battle dress, others in uniforms and hats like those of county sheriffs – all with M-16s – stood around the gate. They came up to the car and checked the IDs of both men carefully, shining the flashlight in Lambert's hastily wiped face for nearly a minute before admitting the car.

Inside the compound, they passed manicured lawns and a dozen or so white cinder block buildings, many bristling with antennas and microwave relay stations. The helipads were all full, and crews and soldiers armed with rifles milled about beside the aircraft. A small control tower stood amid the fleet of choppers, dim light emanating from the panes of angled glass. The car pulled into a parking lot, and the driver slipped into an empty visitors space. It was pitch-dark when Lambert got out. The night was still.

'This way, sir,' the driver said, ushering him toward a concrete ramp angling down from the edge of the parking lot. The ramp descended into a massive cut in the earth, and the concrete wall dimly visible at the bottom looked like a dam erected to hold back the dirt. In the center of the wall was a round tunnel. More guards checked their IDs at a gate at the top of the ramp. One picked up a telephone and said, 'Mr Lambert is here.' They motioned him down alone. He heard the sound of his shoes scuffing the pavement as he looked up into the blackness of space overhead. The stars shone brightly on the warm summer night. Slowly his view of the night sky was eclipsed by the massive edifice before him.

'This way, Mr Lambert,' a voice said when he reached the dark tunnel entrance. A red light was switched on to illuminate the massive blast door – like the door of a bank vault but large enough to close off a tunnel down which ran a two-lane road – which was slightly ajar. Lambert followed the man clad in a blue jumpsuit into the well-lit shaft. The road descended into the rough-hewn stone of the solid mountain, its gentle curve defying any estimate as to its length, as to the depth to which it descended. The man pinned a badge to the pocket of Lambert's jacket before they boarded a four-seat electric cart for the ride down into the bowels of the earth.

'Have you ever been to Mount Weather, sir?' the man asked cheerily. He was wearing the seal of the Federal Emergency Management Agency on the left breast of his coveralls.

Lambert shook his head.

As the electric motor wound up to full whine for the ride downhill, his guide said, 'Blasted it right outa the greenstone back in the fifties. Used to be an experimental drilling location for the Bureau of Mines. They wanted to try out their drill bits on the hardest rock they could find.' Lambert looked at the raw stone walls, patched in some places with concrete and punctured by an occasional bolt of some sort. His ears popped, and he felt the chill of the increasing depth.

'We got a power chamber with diesel generators, refrigerators for food storage, a cafeteria, a hospital, radio and TV studios, everything. There are about a thousand people down here now.' Lambert felt the man's gaze shift to him. 'They say we could take one, we could take one right on the chin, and it still wouldn't blast through that greenstone. Greenstone is some tough rock. You see that door we came through up top?'

Lambert nodded as he cleared his ears once again. The slight breeze caused him to cross his arms and hug them to his body.

'One hint of a flash and down comes the "Guillotine Gate." It's five feet thick and twenty feet across. Solid steel. Drops straight down.'

The cart pulled out into a slightly larger opening as the roadway leveled off. The floor of the opening was flat and paved, roads leading off in two directions. It was the rough stone walls that reminded you that you were in a cavern. Lambert cleared his ears one last time as they turned a corner and stopped in front of a one-story building nestled into a side tunnel cut out of the stone. Lambert and his escort got out of the cart just as another cart rushed by, this one with two officers, one man and one woman, whom Lambert recognized from years at the Defense Intelligence Agency. One nodded, the other gave a halfhearted salute.

'So,' the FEMA employee said, 'you know, you don't need to worry or anything.' Lambert looked at him without saying a word. 'You know. They say it could take a hit. Straight on – a bull's-eye – and we'd be fine down here.' The man stared straight into Lambert's eyes, and Lambert focused on him, remembering that he was there. 'I mean, not like what happened at Cheyenne Mountain.'

Lambert nodded and turned to enter the building.

It was busy inside. The building appeared to consist of one long room that was a warren of partitioned offices, and Lambert wandered aimlessly back through the maze taking in the hectic pace. It was the stuff of most offices. Telephone calls, men or women in front of computers, a coffee bar with people seated on the counter-top shooting the bull.

'Hello, sir,' a woman said as she squeezed past. Lambert could not recall her name.

In an open space toward the center of the large main room were row after row of folding metal chairs facing a large bulletin board on which were posted a variety of maps of different sizes, various lists, and some computer printouts, displayed seemingly in random order.

'Evening, Mr Lambert,' a young man in air force uniform – a lieutenant – said as he skirted the area.

Lambert walked over to the message board. One map showed the latest radiological levels of various sites around the country. Another showed the levels of radiation being carried by streams or dropping straight into the Atlantic to be swept north along the coast by the Gulf Stream. A multipage report was pinned with thumbtacks along the top. It listed various emergency facilities around the country still operational, with telephone numbers and contact persons. 'The White House' jumped out at him. Underneath he saw 'Situation Room' and a telephone number. 'Rogers, Lawrence, Maj., USAF' was the contact person. The only other number listed was 'Main Switchboard,' but handwritten alongside was, 'Went off line 2015 EST – 6/11.' *Over nineteen hours after the attack*, Lambert thought.

Lambert pictured the gray-haired women at the switchboard, whom he had visited many times to inquire as to the whereabouts of various high officials. They usually had better information than the Central Locater Service, and they were conveniently situated right there in the White House. Their jobs were important. *They sat there till they died*, he realized.

'Oh, there you are, sir.' Lambert turned to see one of the junior aides on the staff of the National Security Council. He walked up to Lambert and stood there awkwardly before saying, 'I'm sorry. We heard. We're all so sorry.' He shook his head.

'What's that?' Lambert asked, nodding at the papers the man held in his hand.

'Oh,' he said, clearly relieved as was Lambert to get on with business. 'It's a report on foreign governments' responses to our proposal to threaten use of nuclear weapons against North Korea to force their withdrawal across the DMZ.'

Lambert knit his brow, and the man said, 'I guess you missed that. Well, while you were . . . earlier today, the President authorized the use of tactical nuclear weapons against the North Koreans.'

'You're kidding.'

He made a face mimicking Lambert's surprise and shook his head. 'We'll warn them first. Then a high-altitude demonstration burst over Pyongyang. Anyway, these are summaries of the responses from some back-channel security establishment contacts we've been making to allied governments.'

'Why us? Why not State?'

'State's non-op. They're a shambles. Secretary Moore was killed at Raven Rock, you know, and half of their under and assistant secretaries are still unaccounted for. They haven't gotten their shit together yet, so we made the calls ourselves.'

'All right,' Lambert said, 'I'll read it and brief the President. Where is he?'

'Who's he in there with?' Lambert asked the President's appointments secretary.

'White House counsel,' she said, eyeing Lambert as if that information held particular import for him.

'I need to speak to him.'

'He asked not to be interrupted.' She opened up the thick appointments book. 'I'll see if I can get you in at around – '

'Now.' Lambert looked at the woman, always one of the most powerful figures in the White House. 'I need to see him now.'

She picked up the phone and said, 'Mr President, Mr Lambert is here to see you.' After a moment, she said, with an icy expression, 'You may go right in.'

The President opened the door before Lambert got to it. 'Greg,' he said, placing his hands on Lambert's shoulders. They stood there like that for a moment in the doorway, the President much too close for Lambert to feel comfortable. 'I cannot tell you how deeply grieved Margaret and I are about your loss. Jane was a special woman, special to us all. We will really miss her.'

Every word, every single word, that the President spoke struck Lambert in a way the President had not intended. He wanted no one to speak of Jane. Only *he* knew her. Only *he* felt her passing. Everyone else was simply an intruder in his private life.

Lambert stepped out of the President's grasp and walked into his office. 'I've come here to tell you that I am resigning as national security adviser.' His back was to Livingston, and the President could not get a read on his face.

Seated at the opposite side of a conference table taking Greg in with quiet interest was the President's lawyer, his pen poised but motionless over the yellow pad as he watched the scene.

'I can't do it,' Lambert said. The words were easy. They took no effort. He needed sleep, he realized. He felt that if only he could close his eyes he could sleep for days.

'Greg, is it' – Livingston looked at his lawyer, who stared back at him with a face registering intense concern – 'is it for political reasons?'

'No!' Lambert blurted out, and out of the corner of his eye Livingston saw his lawyer relax slightly. 'I just don't know if . . . I don't know if I can get up in the morning and shave and put my suit on, much less serve as national security adviser at a time like this.'

Livingston heard the emotional strain evident in his voice. Lambert sounded exhausted. Livingston reached out and rested his hand on Lambert's shoulder.

'I need you, Greg. Things are very touchy right now. The situation with the Russians hangs in the balance. As much as I try, I can't seem to separate us, our two countries' armed forces. It's like we're in some giant clench, all over the globe, and for one of us to let go is a risk that's too great to take. You have contacts with the Russians. That man, Filipov, is now General Razov's aide. You know him, and he knows you. The Russians may trust you, and I need trust right now more than anything else in the world. I need you, Greg.'

Lambert sighed deeply. There was a brisk knock on the still open door behind him, and then Colonel Rutherford, General Thomas's aide, said, 'We've had another contact in the Barents Sea, Mr President.'

'Oh, Lord. Did we lose anybody?'

'No, sir. But one of our attack submarines sank a Russian sub. It wasn't a boomer, just another hunter-killer.'

'You tell them to clear out of there. Break it off.'

'There's also been another incident in Poland. Two helicopters of unidentified origin penetrated Polish airspace. An F-16 downed them. The wreckage is clearly on Polish territory, and although the ID isn't positive since we haven't gotten to the crash site, the Polish government has already protested to the Russians and is trying to get the incident on the agenda at the U.N. Security Council meeting.'

'Is that all?'

'Yes, sir. We do have a body count on that auxiliary that got torpedoed out of the Port of New Orleans. It's not good. Tentatively, it's about four hundred dead, with only about a hundred survivors. The press is asking us for that number. Can we give it to them?'

'Oh, shit,' the President said, shaking his head and looking at Lambert. 'You know, we could lose a whole task force in the Norwegian Sea and it wouldn't merit two lines on the evening news these days, but some jake-leg camera crew in a traffic helicopter out of New Orleans gets dramatic pictures of a sinking supply ship and it's the lead story.' He shook his head again and turned to Rutherford. 'Stall them with those numbers a little longer. Tell them they're too preliminary – no, no. Tell them we've got to contact the families first.'

When the door closed behind Rutherford, the White House counsel was the first to speak. 'Mr Lambert, you'll be happy to know that the Supreme Court has ruled in your favor on your refusal to testify before the Committee to Investigate the Nuclear War.'

'Oh, yes,' the President said. 'The Justices are all down here in Mount Weather. They only took four hours after oral arguments to publish their decision. We asked them to rule that there was a national security privilege against your testimony. They upheld your refusal to testify, but not on those Constitutional grounds. They held the committee not to have been properly constituted under House rules. The House didn't have a quorum, it seems, when they purportedly established the ad hoc committee, and so that action was invalid.'

'You know, Greg,' the White House counsel said, 'if I can call you that. It would be a really bad time for the President if you were to, you know, bail out on him like this. It would look bad, you understand?'

There was another knock on the door, and General Thomas stepped in. He glanced briefly at the President and then faced Lambert. Thomas looked exhausted, and his stare was hard.

'Mr Lambert, you and I have been subpoenaed to testify before the Armed Forces Committee in closed session at Congress's special facility at zero nine hundred hours tomorrow. They want a report on the continued fighting between Russia and the United States. You'll need to prepare briefing notes, and you've got a lot of catching up to do. I recommend that you come with me and attend the Joint Chiefs' briefing, and then participate in this afternoon's full NSC meeting.'

'That son of a bitch Costanzo is behind this,' the President said glancing at his lawyer and then turning to Lambert to explain. 'When I got here, he'd already hightailed it over to the Congressional Facility. Now he's using Congress's subpoena powers to get the military briefings that I cut him out of.' The President looked at his counsel and then at General Thomas. 'Fuck him. I'm going with you to Greenbriar. Unannounced, this time!'

PALM SPRINGS, CALIFORNIA
June 13, 0830 GMT (0030 Local)

The baby was tossing and turning among the pillows lying next to Melissa in a drawer from the room's armoire. His sleep was fitful, and he cried most of the time he was awake. Melissa's milk had never come in, either

her nerves or poor diet ruining her chance at nursing her child. Getting out of bed, she padded over to the vanity in the bathroom where she kept the remainder of her meager cache from the day's forage: two eggs and some droopy lettuce.

She broke open the eggs and drank them from a glass, stuffing a leaf of lettuce into her mouth. She gagged. Her eyes jammed shut and she thought, *Three days. The ban will be lifted in three days.* Her chest bucked, and she began to sob. The government had banned the sale of all food other than perishables for five days after the attack in order, the store manager at the last of the six stores she had tried had explained, to prevent inflation. She had offered him a thousand dollars for a few cans of soup, but he had refused.

The attack was two days ago. *Four more days and I can go home,* she thought. *Tomorrow I get my gas ration book. Three days and I can buy some food and enough gas to get home.*

Sniffling as she sat weakly back down on the bed, she resolved to watch one more hour of news and then try again to sleep.

She groped for the remote in the darkness and hit the now familiar POWER button. The sound came on immediately, and the room lit in the growing brightness from the screen. As always, the channel was reset to the advertisement for the pay-per-view offerings of the hotel. She changed to CNN.

'Well, at least we may finally be in for some good news,' the anchorwoman said. 'What effect do you think the administration's threat to use nuclear weapons against North Korea will have in the short term? Will the fighting stop immediately, or will it drag on for a little while?'

'There's no way to know, really,' some man said. 'We can't even be sure that the North Koreans will actually stop fighting.'

'But surely they wouldn't risk nuclear attack by the United States,' the anchorwoman said. 'That would be suicide.'

'Oh, I'm not disagreeing with you,' the analyst said, 'but this is still a liberal Democratic administration, and they are negotiating with the Russians despite having the Russians, who had been badly weakened by the war with China, on the ropes militarily. All I'm saying is that the North Koreans might just decide to roll the dice.'

'A-all right,' the anchorwoman said as she shook her head in disbelief and turned to face a different camera. 'We go now to Philadelphia for the latest domestic political developments. Bob?'

'Yes, Christine,' the man said. A map of the eastern U.S., marking Philadelphia, the nation's temporary capital, with a star, appeared on the screen.

'We apologize to our viewers, but we still haven't solved our video transmission difficulties,' Christine said. 'Bob, as day breaks in West Virginia, what's in store at the underground Congressional Facility today?'

'A lot,' Bob answered, the quality of the audio poor. 'First off, the Ad Hoc Joint Committee to Investigate the Nuclear War will continue its deliberations despite being held improperly convened by White House legal maneuvering designed to defeat a subpoena of top White House aide Gregory Lambert, the President's national security adviser. Then Under Secretary Anderson, the acting Secretary of State who is just returning from a quick mini-tour of NATO capitals where he got rather chilly receptions in Berlin and Paris, will be called to testify before the Senate Foreign Relations Committee about President Livingston's relatively ineffective marshaling of allied support. The real fireworks, however, will begin tomorrow morning when the Armed Services Committee begins its briefings on the continuing hostilities with Russia.'

'Any word on when the debate on the proposal for a Declaration of War might get kicked off?'

'Well, it's difficult to say. All bets appear off. Some are saying that it could begin as early as today, but if precedent is any guide I expect it'll be sometime next week before the Joint Session will take up the Republican resolution, signed by all but four of the Republican Congressmen present, to declare war on Russia and to destroy through military action all of their remaining nuclear arsenal. The Democrats are preparing their own resolution to declare war on Russia, without the approval of President Livingston but with, we are told, the backing of the Democratic party apparatus and the Vice President, that will be debated if the vote on the Republicans' proposal is defeated or tabled.'

'Bob,' the anchorwoman said as the reporter continued talking. 'Bob. Let me interrupt you for a second to say that we're showing some new videotape that just arrived from Warner Robins, Georgia, site of the former Robins Air Force Base, without editing. Viewers are warned that some of the footage may be graphic and disturbing.'

The warning came too late. Close-ups on the next shot showed a large group of burn victims lying under an open three-cornered tent of an army medical unit.

'O-h-h,' Melissa moaned, shaking her head and averting her eyes from the television.

'Is the Republican measure expected to pass?'

'Again, it's difficult to say. The President is opposed to it, but what cannot be known is how many of the Democrats will stay with the President and how many will jump the aisle and vote for the first proposal to come before the Joint Session – the Republicans' – under intense pressure from their constituencies. Of course the President is the commander in chief, and he would still have to give the orders to the military to actually fight.'

'Well, whatever happens needs to happen soon,' the anchorwoman said. 'We seem to be in some kind of limbo, with low-intensity but still deadly combat flaring up spontaneously every few hours around the periphery of both countries and, in fact, all around the globe.'

When Melissa saw out of the corner of her eyes that the tape had ended she looked back at the picture of the CNN studios in Atlanta.

'While the President circled the nation high above it all in his luxury 747, the Russian attack, by all appearances, has galvanized the American people like no other event in modern history. It's beginning to look like the Alamo, the bombing of the U.S.S. *Maine*, the sinking of the *Lusitania*, and Pearl Harbor all wrapped into one. In the latest CNN/Gallup Poll,' she said, and the poll's graphics replaced the picture on the screen, 'an astonishing ninety-three percent of the people polled favor a Declaration of War against Russia, with a margin of error of plus or minus five percent.'

As the story ran on, Melissa's eyes glazed over in the flickering light of the television. After several minutes, Melissa said quietly, 'Come home, David. Come home.'

SPECIAL FACILITY, MOUNT WEATHER, VIRGINIA
June 13, 1700 GMT (1200 Local)

'We've had over three hundred engagements reported since the President declared a cease-fire,' said Colonel Rutherford, General Thomas's aide, as he stood before the National Security Council. Lambert, the senior civilian adviser there given the absence of the Secretary of Defense, who was in Philadelphia trying to organize the massive bureaucracy that is the Defense Department, sat at the side of the President at the head of the table. 'The contacts have tapered off noticeably, but with the Russian naval and ground force movements that we are monitoring the situation across most of Eurasia remains tense.'

Maps bathed Rutherford in their projected light. The old Mount Weather facility used front-projection technology – a slide show, basically – and as Rutherford stepped out of one projector's light he revealed a map of Eastern Europe covered with unit markers. The Russian 2nd Guards Army had deployed into Byelarus and the 9th Army had deployed into the Baltics after the Russian military coup in March, which had ended the long battle between reformers and hard-liners. The U.S. divisions counterdeployed into Poland and Slovakia over the last three months in response just across the thin, imaginary line of the border separating those countries. And now, most ominously, the Russian 8th Guards Army had just been detected deploying into Ukraine. The deployment was marked by a thick, menacing arrow.

'Of particular concern are Russian moves in these two areas,'

Rutherford continued, his pointer first indicating Eastern Europe. 'A few hours ago, the 8th Guards Army began deployment into Ukraine, apparently with the Ukrainians' consent.'

'Yeah,' General Fuller said in a whisper still loud enough to draw a pause from Rutherford. 'I'm sure the Ukrainians were fuckin' thrilled about it.'

After the smattering of laughter died down, Rutherford continued. 'The 8th Guards, which is one of Russia's better armies, comes from forces allocated to its Western Strategic Direction and is under operational command of the Moscow Military District's Independent Army Group. It currently fields the 22nd Tank Division and four motorized rifle divisions – the 9th and 16th Guards and the 47th and 60th – in addition to its army-level forces. There is no indication yet that the group commander is also sending the 4th Artillery Division, which he holds in reserve east of Kursk, Russia, into Ukraine with the 8th Guards Army.'

'The 22nd Tank and 16th Guards are good units,' Army General Halcomb interrupted, 'but the other rifle divisions are pretty much paper tigers at this point. They were stripped bare of serviceable equipment and practically all of their full-strength battalions for the Chinese war. DIA puts them at under fifty percent effectiveness, and I'd be surprised, quite frankly, if they were in good enough repair to make the Slovakian border.'

'I thought you said that it was one of Russia's better armies?' the President asked.

'It is, sir,' Halcomb said, staring back at him.

After a pause, Rutherford, one of the military's better briefers, Lambert knew, resumed. 'Those deployments, combined with the fourteen separate Russian air-to-ground attacks reported by the 1st Cav in Poland, have resulted in our issuance of action orders to VII Armored Corps in Krakow to prepare for engagement.'

'I issued orders to disengage!' the President shouted from the semidarkness, slamming his hand down at the disobedience.

General Thomas turned quickly to address the President. 'The action orders to VII Corps are just precautionary, Mr President.'

'Sir,' Army Chief of Staff Halcomb said, 'you can see the predicament my people are in just by looking at the map. The VII Corps commander is staring at a Russian combined-arms army barreling down on units he's got sitting in barracks with their heavy weapons still in pre-positioning warehouses or on rail sidings back in Germany. He's practically livid, sir. Now, the Russians may be having their problems, but if those forces don't stop at the border, our people are looking at first contact with at least twenty and maybe thirty or forty thousand Russian troops in under forty-eight hours. If we issue preparatory action orders right now, sir, the 4th Infantry Division in Slovakia could field one brigade reinforced with a few miscellaneous units – about six thousand men.'

There was a long silence during which the President's chair creaked and he snorted an angry huff. 'All right! Tell him he can go ahead and deploy, but only to *defensive* positions.'

After a moment's silence, Rutherford resumed the briefing. 'The other troublesome spot is in the Barents Sea. We were moving a carrier battle group, Task Group 20.3 with the carrier *United States*, up from the Norwegian Sea to stand ready to go into the Kara Sea Bastion if necessary. Satellite photos, however, indicate activity in the port of Arkhangelsk – not the sub pens which we struck with nuclear weapons but the conventional port – consistent with a staging operation for a Russian amphibious assault force. If that force puts to sea, it is the unanimous recommendation of the Joint Chiefs to intercept it off the coast of Norway to prevent any potential for a landing in Norway or Iceland.'

'You leave those ships alone,' the President said. 'The Russians are just doing the same thing we are: posturing.' The President was tired, and his frustration at being unable to disengage forces from the fighting surfaced at every meeting now. 'Everybody just sit tight; no itchy trigger fingers. How many times do I have to say this? The longer we let things cool off, the better the chance we can keep this from getting out of control.'

'Sir,' Thomas said, 'if we let the Russians land that force astride our supply lines to Europe—'

'You will do *nothing*,' the President said, his resolve strengthening. 'Don't you see? You're thinking in terms of "losing Iceland." I'm trying to avoid World War III! Now, which of those two outcomes do you think I should weigh more heavily in my decision-making?' The President turned to take in the Joint Chiefs. 'Which?' Nobody responded. 'Okay, let's get on with this. What was that you were telling me, Greg, about possible use of biological-warfare weapons?'

'We had a report, sir,' Lambert said, 'from our emergency airbase in Guam that a "Sniffer" – an air sampler – had detected suspected biologicals in the air shortly after a single Russian submarine-launched cruise missile mined their runway with scatterable munitions. Now it would be atypical for a mine delivery system to include a special weapons subsystem like chemicals or biologicals, but the report was' – Lambert looked down to read – '"Suspected Biological Agent – Indeterminate Nature."'

'It would make sense that they'd use 'em on a place like Guam, sir,' Air Force General Starnes said. 'It would isolate the risk of the infection spreading. That way you'd only knock out our base and the civilian population of that island but not have it spread uncontrolled across whole continents.'

The President looked horrified. 'Look, are those Sniffer things accurate?' the President asked, turning to Lambert. Lambert shrugged. 'You don't buy the report, do you, Greg?'

'No, sir,' Lambert said, looking at General Starnes. 'The Pacific Command has a team on the ground in Guam right now doing a more sophisticated analysis, but I think they just hadn't turned the Sniffer on in so long, or that it was tested so infrequently, or that it works so poorly, that it just went off as soon as they powered it up.'

'Well, when did they turn it on?' the President asked General Starnes. 'Did it go off like Greg said the second they turned it on?'

'I don't know, sir,' Starnes replied.

'Could you find out for us, please?' the President suggested, and Starnes snatched his telephone from its cradle. 'Okay,' the President said, leaning back in his chair and locking his interlaced fingers on top of his head, 'both Razov and I have issued orders for all units to stand down, but we have had over three hundred engagements in, what, the last forty-odd hours. "Friction," I think you called it. *Plus* you think the Russians are getting ready to invade Norway or Iceland, and have *already* attacked us with germ weapons. I hate to even ask, but what's next on the agenda?'

'Deployments,' Thomas said, his voice and manner indicating a greater significance than the otherwise innocuous word would deserve. Thomas sat up and rested his elbows on the table, lifting the deployment plan that Lambert had read and reread several dozen times. 'I've spoken with the Secretary of Defense in Philadelphia and with Mr Lambert,' Thomas said, nodding at Greg. 'Our considered advice to you, sir, is that we begin the general deployment of troops called for by our contingency plans in the event, God forbid, of war with Russia.'

'Now, wait a minute,' the President said. 'I've already agreed to sign Congress's mobilization order. That means the Russians are going to be watching while the Selective Service Administration calls up every single able-bodied boy aged eighteen and nineteen, and holds a lottery to call up thirty-five percent of the young women of similar age and fitness. Now I know we're going to spin the call-up so that it looks like a massive community service effort to "Rebuild America," but every one of those teenagers, as I understand it, is first going to be sweating their butts off on some rifle range in Georgia or wherever. If we start deploying troops consistent with plans we have for fighting a war with Russia, don't you think that'll be a red flag to the Kremlin? Wouldn't the Russians consider the two together somewhat threatening,' he asked in a sarcastic tone, 'especially given the noise coming out of Congress and our own Vice President?'

'Well, sir,' Thomas replied, 'if our most optimistic assessments of the intentions of the Russians in deploying troops into Ukraine and staging at Arkhangelsk are correct, then we would be doing nothing more than responding in kind. But if they plan on fighting . . .'

After a few moments of silence, the President leaned forward and sighed. 'What are the plans? Just the broad brush picture. Get me a copy of the details to read later.'

Thomas looked down at the tables and figures on the sheets he held and drew a deep breath. 'Okay, sir. If you'll turn to tab Nine-A in your briefing book and look at the table on the first page entitled, "Summary USA, USMC, and USAF Deployments."'

A rustle of paper followed as the lights came up and everyone turned to tab Nine-A. The page to which the tab was attached said, 'General War Plan – Russia.'

'If all of our efforts to avoid war fail, sir,' Thomas said, 'we would need the six corps and the other independent ground units from the army, basically the entire Marine Corps, and sixteen tactical fighter wings from the air force – all as shown on the table – in order to implement the current version of our General War Plan. The effort just to deploy them would be tremendous, but we already had a lot of it under way – activation of the Civilian Reserve Air Fleet, mobilization of the Military Sealift Command Reserve units, et cetera – in the buildup prior to the North Korean invasion. And of course, sir, we had already completed substantial deployments to Eastern Europe in response to our treaty obligations.'

'Could we win that war with these forces?' the President asked, the tug of curiosity demanding that the question be posed, however reluctantly. He looked at Lambert.

'The Russian military,' Lambert said, 'like most of the country, was in a shambles even before our nuclear counterattack. Add to that, sir, the two ruinous wars against the Chinese to which they currently have deployed the bulk of their armed forces.' Lambert shook his head. 'I'd rather be coaching our team than theirs, sir.'

Livingston looked around the table at the stony faces of the military men. *Are they looks of confidence*, he wondered, *or grim resolution to give it a go, if necessary?* History would forget these men's names if the wrong decision was made. But not his. 'Greg,' he said, turning to his young aide, 'you say you'd rather coach our team, but do you mean it? After all, the Russians would be the home team, not to abuse the metaphor.'

'It's an odd situation, sir. Yes, we have farther to go, longer supply routes. But ours are, for the most part, unimpeded by war damage from the nuclear exchange, and most of it, at least until you get into Eastern Europe, is over a sea-road-rail grid developed to Western standards. The Russians, in contrast, had a piss-poor transportation network to start with. Ninety-two percent of their roads are unpaved. There are only six all-weather roads stretching across the west from Moscow to

Europe, and the best of them is twenty-four feet wide. Ninety-eight percent of their freight moves by rail, and now the rail lines are chock full of holes and cut up with fallout patterns. We're basically dealing right now with a Russian military that's a bunch of parts, not any kind of cohesive whole. Plus, since the fall of the Soviet Union, they've suffered pilferage, poor maintenance, declines in morale and discipline and cannibalization of units for piecemeal dispatch to the Far East, in addition to their enormous losses in the two wars there. The Russians quite simply are not able to mount operations on anything like the scale of the Soviet military of the eighties.'

'They never were that good,' Marine General Fuller growled in a low voice, and everyone turned to him. 'Their equipment is shit. Back in the Gulf War, the Iraqis had this little problem with their T-72 tanks. Seems their turrets just sorta popped right off from the kinetic energy of a hit. Don't do too damn much good to have nice thick armor or bolt-on reactive plates if the turret comes off on ya.'

Is mine the only voice of caution here? Livingston wondered with a sinking feeling. His eyes drifted back down to the deployment table. *God, God, God*, he thought as he contemplated the course of action he had entered the room privately committed to taking. He looked up at Lambert, at the blue eyes from which burned the bright light of intellect. *But judgment?* he thought. *Does he have judgment?*

'Okay,' the President said. 'I approve the deployments.' Everyone sat around the table in silence. 'I approve all deployments,' the President said, leaning forward and speaking in a measured voice as if meant to be quoted, 'that are consistent with preparation – *preparation* – for the possibility of continued hostilities with Russia.' He looked from eye to eye around the table. 'I want you gentlemen to understand that my standing orders are still to do everything possible to disengage, and I will study the details of this deployment carefully after this meeting to determine for myself, with Mr Lambert's help, whether any safe minimum separations appear to be violated or whether any of the deployments appear to me to so provoke the Russians as to be counterproductive. But if neither is the case, then you may – in fact I insist that you must – go ahead with all your deployments.'

The Joint Chiefs were, Lambert knew, as unprepared for this response as he was. They had spent hours justifying their plans with mock arguments, junior officers playing 'DA' – 'devil's advocate,' he was told officially, 'Democratic appeaser,' they let on conspiratorially, worse he imagined when he was not in the room. As a result, they had made numerous revisions to modify the plans precisely so that the President would not find them overly provocative. However, their contingencies had not included, Lambert knew, a lay-down by the President.

'Perhaps, sir,' Lambert began, hesitantly, 'you might inform us of the reasons why you so readily agree to the deployment plans so that we might all more accurately interpret the orders in light of the spirit in which they were intended.'

Marine General Fuller and the President, an unlikely pair, both laughed suddenly, and Lambert felt his face redden. 'Old lawyering habits die hard, hey, Greg?' the President said as Fuller cracked his own joke to Admiral Dixon in a whisper that Lambert could not pick up. 'Just kidding, Greg. It's a good idea, if I understand it correctly,' Livingston said smiling, and then he paused to think for a second. 'My number one reason for approving the deployments is that, if we really do lose control of things, I'll be damned if this country isn't in the best possible position to win a war that I, as commander in chief, can put it. But I must tell you that my other motivation in approving this,' he said, tapping the first page of over 100 pages that followed, the 'summary' of a plan whose details were far too long for any one book, 'is to press home the point with Razov and his buddies on the Russian general staff that if they want to mess around with us, they're gonna get burned. With that as our "stick," I hope to launch a new round of initiatives when State gets back up and operational. These deployments should put us in position to extract at least some concessions from the Russians on weapons levels before we both begin a new arms race to rebuild our now depleted nuclear arsenals.'

The President looked around the table to ensure his answer was satisfactory.

Just then the phone rang in front of General Starnes, and he picked it up. After listening for a moment while everyone waited, as always, in tense anticipation of what the call, any call, might foretell, Starnes said, 'All right, take everybody back off MOPP Level Four and send out an advisory to all commands retracting our prior assessment and warning order.' He listened for a moment longer and said, 'Just do it!' and hung up. Starnes looked up at the President. 'The air samplers on Guam were turned on only after the cruise missile attack, and they immediately sounded their alarms. The PACOM CBR team has conducted their initial tests, and the preliminary judgment is bee pollen.'

There was silence until the President finally repeated, 'Bee pollen? You mean bees, as in *b-z-z-z*? Bee pollen?'

'Yessir,' Starnes said, as forceful in retraction as he had been in assertion of his position. 'Bee pollen triggered the alarms. The air's thick with it, apparently.'

The President's mood darkened noticeably, angered, Lambert presumed, by the near overreaction based on bad information. 'All right, now what I want to know is,' the President asked, holding up the briefing book, 'will these deployments put us in position to fulfill our treaty obligations in defending Eastern Europe? And what the hell is this "Far Eastern Front" that all these marines are allocated to? Cut to the chase, General Thomas. If the Russians moving into Ukraine don't stop at the Polish and Slovak borders and I take your muzzle off, can we hold them?'

Thomas hesitated, trying to decide, Lambert realized, where to start. It was then that it dawned on Lambert how unprepared his boss, elected, as had been his recent predecessors, solely on his domestic affairs agenda, was for the rapidly evolving concepts of national strategic thinking. That was his own fault, Lambert realized. He was the President's national security adviser.

'If we go to war, Mr President,' Lambert blurted out, jumping in before Thomas could respond, 'all of the plans are to fight to win and win quickly. The cost to the nation would be billions – *billions* – of dollars every . . . single . . . *day.*'

'Greg,' the President said in irritation at the nonresponsive lecture of his relatively new young aide, 'you know too much. I have a simple question, and I want a simple answer. What are the ultimate military objectives of all these plans I'm approving?'

'Have you ever heard of the Lehman Doctrine, sir?' The President shook his head. 'Ronald Reagan's Secretary of the Navy, John Lehman, was an A-6 strike pilot in the navy reserve. During his tenure, the Navy Department formulated a plan to take the war deep into Siberia from the Pacific, striking at Russia itself where their forces were weakest – from the east – as a penalty for encroachment in Western Europe. It was highly classified, and it was called the Lehman Doctrine.'

That was too much for the President. 'If you don't get to the point, Greg, I'll get a national security adviser who knows how to give me a straight answer when I ask for one!'

Lambert began his answer in a low voice. 'Our current plan is called Operation Avenging Sword,' he said, and he felt the eyes of the Joint Chiefs on him now. 'If war with Russia comes, the objective in the Far East, Mr President, would be to sever the Trans-Siberian Railroad by air strikes, force a landing of marines and army troops on the Pacific coast of Russia, engage and neutralize the Russian Far East Army Command, and seize the Russian Pacific Fleet's home port of Vladivostok. That would effectively contest control of all of Siberia east of a line running from the Kara Sea in the north to Tomsk and Novosibirsk in the south, or approximately one half the landmass of Russia.'

The President stared at Lambert, thinking his aide had lost his mind. He looked around the table and nervously loosed a burst of air as a smile of disbelief spread across his face. The smile was short-lived, however, as he inventoried the grim faces of the men present. 'My God, you're serious, aren't you?'

His gaze ended on Lambert, who completed the lesson with the capper.

'And the objective of the forces deployed into Poland and Slovakia, the "Eastern European Front" with their three armored corps, three armored cavalry regiments, six armored and mechanized infantry divisions, and twelve of the twenty tactical fighter wings of the Air Combat Command plus all the allied troops we can muster, sir – the largest concentration of firepower in the history of the world – would be to drive into and through Byelarus and Ukraine, engage and destroy in the field the army of Russia, and capture the Russian capital, Moscow, all before the first snows of winter.'

GANDER AIRPORT, NEWFOUNDLAND
June 14, 1000 GMT (0600 Local)

'The tank is the weapon of decision on the modern battlefield,' David Chandler read in the beam of his flashlight. 'The individual soldier in a tank unit must be indoctrinated with the spirit of the offensive. His thinking must be geared to the speed and violence of mobile warfare. He is trained to operate deep in hostile territory. He must regard the presence of the enemy to his front, flanks, and rear as a condition to be expected. He must develop a spirit of daring that will ensure effective engagement of the enemy.'

The manual went on and on and on. Chandler was in his element: cramming for the big exam. *I know this stuff*, he thought, reassured as it all came back to him. Cross-attachment of units, mixing and matching of armor and infantry. Sections on mortars, artillery, tactical air support, ground surveillance radar. For the second night in a row he hadn't been able to sleep on the ground like all the snoring men spread over the low hills around – the same problem he'd had since Boy Scouts – and he relished the opportunity to quietly calm his self-doubts with a foray into the arcane and only dimly familiar science of warfare.

Hidden down at number six of nine neat things about tanks he read, 'Rapidly exploit effects of mass destruction weapons.' *Probably works like a charm*, he thought. *Wipe out an area along the enemy's front line with nukes or chemicals or biologicals and then pour through it into his rear, safe and sound buttoned up in your thick-skinned, overpressured vehicles*. It was a trick that the Russians surely knew too, he realized.

Small-unit tactics. *Always just remember*, he thought, *fire and maneuver. Advancing by bounds*. Alternate. One unit leap-frogging another. Or successive, always the same unit in front, with the unit behind assuming the front unit's old position.

Dominant terrain. Cover and concealment, the former meaning protection from fire, the latter, from observation. Avoid being near conspicuous landmarks like the tops of hills, places where the Russians would shell and bomb. Chandler wondered whether the telltale antennas and command vehicles of Division Headquarters would attract Russian shells and bombs, remembering from Armor School with a momentary chill the rain of fire they had been told Russian 'radio-electronic' troops could be expected to direct on any such targets. *I wonder if they're still as good as the training officers said back in the old Soviet days?* Chandler returned his attention to the manual.

Tank armament. Fire distribution. Helpful hints: 'When attacking unprotected infantry, attack with the maximum possible speed and violence, and disruption may occur.' *'Disruption,'* Chandler thought, shaking his head at the understatement. *You need euphemisms. Panic, desperation, collapse, and inevitable death – let's refer to that as 'disruption.'*

Chandler yawned and lay his head down, holding the book up and repositioning the flashlight. Reconnaissance and security. Offensive operations. Exploitation and pursuit. Defensive operations. As tired as he was, he forced himself to keep reading. *Better to not think about home, about Melissa.*

The mere recollection of her name soured his mood, and he found concentration on the manuals no longer possible. He crawled out of his sleeping bag, itching from three days of living on the land without a bath, his muscles aching from the field march on which he had led his 'command' the day before, his bones aching from his unsuccessful attempts to sleep on the hard ground. He threw his pack and webbing onto his shoulders, grabbed his rifle and flak jacket and headed off toward the terminal. Once out of sight, he put his full combat load on, taking time to get the straps adjusted so the heavy load felt right. He had led his men on a ten-mile march around the marshes and grass the day before, but they had left a guard with their heavy gear and taken only their rifles and a light load. His sore legs protested now under the seventy-odd pounds, and he was surprised that his breathing picked up and he broke into a sweat on the cool morning after walking just a short distance.

He had not yet had the opportunity to get accustomed to the heft and feel of his pack and webbing, and his hesitation at becoming grist for the bored regular-army types' ridicule mill with his comical full dress rehearsal made this predawn hour the best time for his excursion.

He carefully skirted the other troop areas, not only because he felt like a joke from the Orvis catalog, but because they may have posted armed guards. All was quiet, however, and the darkness of the night cloaked him in the desired anonymity.

As he approached the only lights within sight at the airport terminal building he heard a heavy, rhythmic beat that was growing louder. From around the side of the terminal, the front of a large formation of men appeared. They were running in step and clapping their hands each time their left boot fell with a hollow thud on the tarmac's concrete, the cumulative sound of the two hundred feet pounding the ground in unison creating a muted thunder. There were so many, and they were so synchronized, it was an awe-some sight.

As they ran past, Chandler heard a deep, gravelly voice yell, 'Compa-*ny-y-y*,' followed by the repeated, 'Plat*o-o-o-n*' from several voices, 'single time – *ha-a-arch!*' Pulling even with Chandler, they slowed to a regular cadence and then were halted and given a 'left face' by the deep-voiced leader, their boots again sounding in perfect unison.

'Listen up, Alpha Company!' a new voice shouted. 'You got thirty minutes to clean yer weapons, take a shit, and be back here with full loads for an equipment check and field exercises! Dismiss the men, First Sergeant!'

There was a pause, and then the deep voice from before once again rocked the night. This time, the first sergeant's words were repeated from the chests of over a hundred men shouting in unison.

'I recognize that I volunteered as a *Ranger*!'

'I RECOGNIZE THAT I VOLUNTEERED AS A RANGER!'

'I accept the fact that as a *Ranger* . . .'

'I ACCEPT THE FACT THAT AS A RANGER . . .'

'. . . my country expects *me* . . .'

'. . . MY COUNTRY EXPECTS ME . . .'

'. . . to move further . . .'

'. . . FURTHER . . .'

'. . . *faster* . . .'

'. . . FASTER . . .'

'. . . and fight *harder* . . .'

'. . . HARDER . . .'

'. . . *than any other soldier in the world*!'

'RANGERS-LEAD-THE-WAY! RAN-ger! *RAN*-ger! *RAN*-ger! A-A-A-A-R-R-R!' the men ended in a guttural growl.

Chandler stepped back into the shadows to let the soldiers pass.

CONGRESSIONAL FACILITY, WEST VIRGINIA
June 14, 1400 GMT (0900 Local)

The elevator down to the Senate chambers was crowded despite its considerable size. In it were the President, the Joint Chiefs, Lambert, two staffers from the NSC, and the ubiquitous Secret Service agents, whose security detail was nearly triple its prewar size.

The doors opened, revealing a large group of people gathered to meet them, complete with minicams and press photographers. The President led the group out into the open semicircle formed by the crowd as flashes erupted on a dozen cameras. The Secret Service agents quickly moved to the front, forming a cordon between the still uncertain situation and their charge. As Lambert sorted out the scene he began to pick faces out of the crowd through the camera lights. Network news anchormen, House and Senate leadership, rank and file members, and in the center stood Vice President Costanzo.

'What's the meaning of this?' President Livingston asked.

One of the men whom Lambert had not noticed before suddenly stepped out in front of the group. As the camera lights turned to illuminate the man, Lambert's eyes were relieved of the glare and he instantly recognized the sergeant at arms. Behind him were four men who wore the uniform of the Capitol Hill police.

'By order of the House of Representatives,' the sergeant at arms shouted as he read from the note card in the palm of his hand, 'voting in Special Session on this day, Gregory Philip Lambert is hereby called to give testimony before said body and any committees thereof duly constituted under the rules of said house! There being due cause to expect said witness to resist this call, be it resolved that the sergeant at arms is hereby authorized and directed to take said Gregory Lambert, Special Assistant to the President for National Security, into protective custody on penalty of criminal contempt in the event of resistance!'

The sergeant at arms lowered his card and leveled his eyes on Lambert. 'There he is,' he said to the police officer next to him, pointing at Lambert, 'the tall blond man in the gray pinstripe suit.' The bright lights from the television cameras bathed Lambert in their warm glow.

The police moved toward Lambert, but the Secret Service agents closed ranks, blocking their path. The senior agent turned to look at the President.

'Now, just wait a minute!' the President said, and the cameras and lights turned now to him. 'Mr Lambert came here voluntarily to brief the Armed Services Committee on national security matters. This is an outrage!'

'Stand aside,' the sergeant at arms said to the Secret Service agents, and Lambert could see the agents, shoulder-to-shoulder, stagger backward slightly against a push by the Capital Hill policemen. An agent in the second rank pulled an Uzi from the holster against the flat of his back and pointed it straight into the air with his elbow cocked.

There was a gasp from the crowd and the senior agent turned again and said, 'Mr President!' in an almost pleading voice.

Lambert edged forward and around the Joint Chiefs until he was in the open. The television lights were blinding, and the tussle between agents and police ceased. The sergeant at arms walked over to Lambert. 'Will you come with me voluntarily, sir?'

Lambert nodded.

'Just one minute!' White House counsel said, pushing through the crowd. 'This man has not been properly served with a subpoena, and we have a Supreme Court decision holding unconstitutional the earlier subpoena of the Committee to Investigate the Nuclear War. This action is both unlawful and unconstitutional. The Committee to Investigate the Nuclear War is not properly constituted!'

'We're not calling him to testify before that committee,' the Speaker of the House said from the front edge of the crowd. 'I'm sorry, Walter. Mr Lambert is being called to testify before the Judiciary Committee.'

'The Judiciary Committee?' the President asked, confusion spreading across his face.

The Speaker nodded his head. 'There has been a resolution on the floor, Walter, a resolution calling for your impeachment. I'm sorry. There's nothing I can do. Would you come with us, Mr Lambert.'

The White House counsel stepped up beside Lambert and said in a low voice, 'Don't say a word. I'm coming with you. We'll file another petition with the district court. Just sit tight.' As Lambert, accompanied by the sergeant at arms, and the White House counsel followed the Speaker, Lambert glanced back once to see the President, staring into the crowd. He followed his eyes to the Vice President, who turned to disappear into the growing sea of boisterous Congressmen and staffers who had jammed the underground facility's lobby to witness the spectacle.

'Mr Lambert cannot answer that question,' White House counsel said, 'as it is privileged for reasons of national security.'

'Did the President instruct Secretary Moore,' the chairman of the Judiciary Committee asked, 'to contact the Chinese prior to his evacuation from the White House?'

'Mr Lambert cannot answer that question,' Lambert's counsel said, 'as it is privileged for reasons of national security.'

'Is there any person other than yourself, the President, the late Secretary Moore, and the operators on the White House switchboard, also deceased, who might have any information pertinent to the question of whether President Livingston spoke with Secretary Moore after the evacuation was begun?'

'Mr Lambert cannot answer that question, as it is privileged for reasons of national security.'

The senior Congressman sighed deeply and drew back to gather the Congressmen on either side of him for a discussion. They in turn talked to the Congressmen to their side, and the word spread down the table to either side as the chairman cleared his throat and said, 'We are not, Mr Lambert, going to hold you in contempt and arrest you. We understand that your refusal is on advice of counsel and at the direction of the White House, and we further understand that your job is vitally important during these dangerous times. We will await a resolution of this by the courts, but make no mistake about it, sir, you will testify before this Congress. Let the record show that this closed session of the Judiciary Committee of the House of Representatives is now adjourned. There will be a fifteen-minute recess. Mr Lambert, you are free to go.'

Lambert entered the conference room not knowing what he would find. The television droned on at low volume in the background, and in the room sat the Joint Chiefs of Staff, their aides, and Lambert's own aides. All looked at him with keen interest as he entered.

'Did you spill yer guts?' General Fuller asked as Lambert took one of the empty seats at the table among the generals and admiral. 'Hot pokers up yer butt, bamboo under yer nails, that sorta thing?'

Lambert shook his head. 'White House counsel is petitioning the federal district court again, and it'll probably go all the way back up to the Supreme Court, maybe even by tomorrow. The chairman of the Judiciary Committee said he'd wait until they rule.'

'Fuckin' lawyers,' Fuller said, and then, 'Oh, 'scuse me,' to Lambert.

The group's attention gravitated back toward the television on which was now shown Lambert's just-completed departure from the hearing room through a throng of reporters and photographers hurling questions at him, which he ignored.

'. . . clearly upset at the loss of his wife, whose body, Congressional sources say, Mr Lambert found during a resupply mission into contaminated Washington. One can only imagine what effect that might have had on Mr Lambert's decision not to testify at this hearing.' The video shifted to a picture of the Vice President and his Secret Service detail and staff making their way down one of the facility's underground corridors. 'We go now to live pictures of Vice President Costanzo, who is emerging from his historic meeting with President Livingston.' One of the reporters met the oncoming Vice President with a microphone in his hand. 'Mr Vice President, what were you just discussing with President Livingston?'

The picture shook as the entire crew – CBS according to the logo that had just appeared on the lower corner of the screen – followed the Vice President. The reporter was shoved away by a Secret Service agent. 'We covered certain political issues that I'm not at liberty to discuss.'

The reporter was losing ground to the fast-walking Vice President, but the camera stayed alongside. 'Where are you going now, sir?'

'To a military briefing with the National Security Council,' the Vice President said over his shoulder as he turned the corner just down the hall from the conference room in which Lambert and the others sat, and Capitol Hill police stopped the press at a cordon.

'Shit,' General Fuller said. 'Why don't we just invite the press on in. Or better yet, why don't we just fax Razov our plans?'

'The President is, I'm hearing,' the reporter said, now standing in the light of the camera and pressing his earphone to his ear, 'departing the Congressional Facility, presumably to head back to his own supersecret facility at Mount Weather, eight miles from Berryville, Virginia.'

'Jeezus Christ!' Fuller said. 'Can I go shoot that fucker for treason?' There was laughter from most around the table, but Lambert could feel the depression swirling round and round in his brain as the words of the reporter about Jane's death broke the levee he had erected in his mind. He felt as if he were swimming in the depression, and it was warm and inviting.

The door burst open and the Vice President walked briskly in. 'Gentlemen,' he said as everyone rose. He walked quickly to the head of the table and placed his briefcase on top as he sat. Taking several reports and a notepad from the briefcase he said, 'Turn that thing off,' nodding his head at the television. 'Now' – he closed the briefcase and put it on the floor – 'I want you to tell me where it is that the Russians have weak spots, and what we've got that can hurt them.'

Lambert knew what the prepared text of the briefing said, and the military men looked at one another in a quandary. Lambert spoke up first. 'Mr Vice President, the President's orders are to begin deployment of our principal combat formations while, at the same time, disengaging from contact with the Russians. Much of these men's efforts, much of what they came prepared to say today, revolve around those two directives.'

The Vice President nodded. He then stood and began to pace behind his chair at the head of the table. 'I have just met with the President. We are at a political impasse. This nation appears at this moment to be heading toward the greatest constitutional crisis since the Civil War.' The Vice President was not looking at his audience as he spoke, too busy composing his speech, constructing his arguments. He looked instead at his hands, which he clasped in front of him. 'I have been informed by the leadership of both houses, both minority *and* majority, that Congress will vote upon and approve a resolution declaring war on the Russian Republic within twenty-four hours.'

Lambert could almost feel his heart thumping in his chest, which felt as if it was wrapped too tightly around it. He had to remind himself to breathe as he looked at the Joint Chiefs, each of whom displayed varying degrees of dismay. 'The President has given notice that he intends to exercise his discretion as commander in chief to refuse to prosecute that war.'

'Now,' Costanzo said, pivoting crisply at one side of the room and pacing in the opposite direction, 'I'm sensitive to your extreme disinclination to involve yourself in any way in political matters, and certainly in constitutional matters of this magnitude. But I'm sorry to say that this is one from which you cannot be insulated. This is a national crisis in the making, and as Americans, you are, each and every one of you, involved in its resolution. Depending upon how this situation resolves itself, we either will be at war with Russia within the next few days or weeks or we will not be. If we *are* at war, I need not tell you gentlemen how much needs to be done to achieve victory on the battlefield. If we *are* at war, gentlemen, you have a lot to do, and I am recommending to you that, from this moment forward, you prepare yourselves and your commands by whatever means necessary to prosecute that war.'

The Vice President stood now with his hands on the back of his chair, which formed a podium of sorts for the speech to come. 'Have any of you seen the Harris Poll done by telephone yesterday? Ninety-four percent – *ninety-four* percent – of the American population supports a continuation of hostilities against the Russians until the threat of their nuclear weapons has been removed. *Ninety-four percent!*'

Lambert wanted to interrupt – to ask, 'Removed how?' – but he kept silent.

'There are demonstrations taking place all across the country demanding that action be taken. The faxes and telegrams are running over twelve hundred to one in favor of war. As the elected representatives of the people, gentlemen, the Congress is going to declare that war. As the Vice President of the United States, also elected directly by the people, I am going to support that declaration.'

'We have no choice,' General Thomas interrupted, the frustration, the anguish, over what was happening evident in his voice, 'no choice whatsoever,' he continued, looking at the other Chiefs, 'but to follow the lawful orders of the commander in chief.'

The Vice President held up his finger, his eyebrows arched. 'The *lawful* orders. The lawful orders.'

'We *cannot* be asked to involve ourselves in legal hairsplitting!' Thomas said, the show of anger uncharacteristic in the normally staid general. 'I am greatly troubled, Mr Vice President, by the way even this meeting might appear were the substance of our discussion to become public. That appearance, it seems to me, sir, comes dangerously close to what might be construed to be discussions of an extra-constitutional coup, and if it continues on along these lines much farther I am afraid that I will have to absent myself *and* promptly inform the President of what has taken place.'

The Vice President still stood behind his 'podium,' but he was slumped over it, his arms draping over the seat back to hang lazily in front. 'I am afraid you are correct, General Thomas, in your description of the situation as a coup.' Lambert felt a chill run down his spine, and the heads of the aides who sat or stood away from the table turned to one another to stare with jaws dropping as the Joint Chiefs focused on the Vice President. 'But it will not be *extra*-constitutional. It will be entirely by the book, so to speak. It will be constitutional. The Congress will, of course, petition the Supreme Court for a writ demanding that the President prosecute the war, but no one imagines that route to be very promising.'

'And so you intend to impeach President Livingston,' Lambert asked, 'and then prosecute Congress's Declaration of War?'

Everyone looked at the Vice President. 'In a word,' he said anticlimactically, 'yes.'

Chapter Eight

THE KREMLIN, MOSCOW
June 16, 0750 GMT (0950 Local)

The assembled generals listened politely as the briefing droned on.

'One week basic skills and physical conditioning,' read General Abramov, former commander of the Far East Command's 24th Guards Army now reluctantly returned to Europe to assume command of the new Provisional Troops that were being raised. More significantly, he was an artfully engineered addition to General Razov's 'camp' in STAVKA. Abramov went on with the training schedule for the citizens militia, the 'Provisionals.' 'Basic firearms, insignia recognition, hygiene . . .'

A young captain walked into the room and headed for Razov, who listened to the training regimen for the Provisionals with dismay. *Construction troops – that's all they'll be good for, if that,* he thought. The captain leaned over to whisper in Razov's ear. 'They're getting ready to vote, sir.'

'Second week: small unit tactics, arm and hand signals—'

'Excuse me, General Abramov,' Razov said, 'but the American Congress is getting ready to vote.'

The aide turned on the television at the far end of the conference table. Half a world away, the latest prime-time American political drama was unfolding in the underground Congressional bunker, and the world, as always, was watching.

Before the tube warmed up, it was obvious that the vote was already under way. One of the older generals who didn't speak English asked what they were saying. General Razov said, for the benefit of all, that they were voting out loud, and that 'aye' meant the same as 'yes.'

'Cole?' a man called, and a distant 'Aye' was heard. 'Cole votes Aye. Collins?'

'Aye.'

'Collins votes Aye. Cooper?'

By now, the television had warmed up, and the CNN count was 138 for and 9 against.

'Chto znachit "for"?' the old general asked.

'"For" *znachit golos* "Aye" *ili* "Yes." "Against" *znachit* "No" – *protiv*,' Razov explained.

'*Bozhe moi*,' the old man said laughing, putting his hand to his cheek. 'How many ways can you say it – either yes or no?'

Several others laughed, but most watched the spectacle in silence. The old general was enjoying the program, turning to rib Razov good-naturedly. 'And this is the system you wanted to copy, Yuri?'

Razov smiled politely. The old man was his mentor, the only one who spoke to him *na ti* – in the familiar – among the officers gathered there.

The old man's enjoyment diminished as the picture shifted to scenes obviously shot earlier in the day from several cities across the United States. While still maintaining the audio from the roll call and with the graphics of the vote count printed at the bottom of the screen, CNN showed the enormous crowds of demonstrators that had gathered in city after city.

The silence at the conference table grew thick as the images streamed in. Angry crowds pumping fists in the air, teeth bared. In Denver an effigy, a figure in a ghoulish mask wearing a military hat with a placard saying 'Russia' hanging from its neck, held aloft by a noose dangling from a pole and set afire; the crowd stomped it to pieces. A sign in the window of a burned-out deli named Noviy Mir in Brighton Beach, New York, that read AMERICAN OWNED. A sign held aloft by a grim-faced grandmotherly woman in Seattle that showed the picture of a young girl looking out from behind blond curls that read JESSICA, AGE 3, KILLED BY RUSSIANS. A shot from a helicopter showing a line, four or five abreast, of young men and women in Los Angeles that circled a huge city block. Standing on the street behind police cordons was an even larger crowd of people cheering wildly and continuously. Children were held aloft by parents, and the crowd waved signs and flags. As the camera zoomed in unsteadily on the building at the front of the line, the sign over the door said US ARMY RECRUITMENT DEPOT. When the camera settled, a smaller handwritten poster taped to the wall at the side of the main door came into focus. It read IT'S TIME TO SETTLE THE SCORE, a line Razov knew to be from a recently popular American superhero movie.

As the outcome of the vote became apparent and many of the generals looked away, clearly discomfited by the scenes, conversations switched to the practical.

'So what's going to happen now?' Air Force General Mishin asked.

'I don't know,' Razov said, shaking his head. 'This is more confusing than if they kept everything secret.'

'This is ridiculous,' another general said, his hand held out palm up in the direction of the television. 'First we're at war by mistake. Then we're not at war but still getting attacked. Then we're at war, but not getting attacked. Then we're not at war again, but they're deploying as if we are. And now this!'

'We've got to start taking more active measures to defend ourselves,' Admiral Verkhovensky said.

'I agree,' said the new commander of the Ukrainian Strategic Direction. 'Regardless of what they say, regardless of their political charades,' he continued, also looking at the television on which was shown the cramped concrete chamber in which the vote in favor was growing to overwhelming proportions, 'the fact is militarily simple. They have an army corps with two divisions on our western borders with another corps moving down the roads through eastern Germany and already into western Poland and the Czech Republic. We've had contact all up and down the line with them already. A battery of their multiple rocket launchers put over fifty rockets with cluster munitions onto one of my tank battalions in road formation as they pulled up on line. The devastation was almost complete: three vehicles left operational out of over a hundred.'

'They saw a battalion heading toward their lines less than four kilometers from the border,' Razov said, too tired to argue forcefully a position with which he no longer fully agreed.

'On *our* side of the border!'

'In Byelarus,' Abramov said calmly, 'not Russia.'

'The point is,' Admiral Verkhovensky said, 'that they're preparing for war. In a few weeks, they'll have three army corps in Europe and an entire marine expeditionary force in the Sea of Japan.'

'Which is committed to Korea,' Razov said. 'I have a firm pledge from General Park that he will continue the attack into the South.'

'In the face of the Americans' nuclear threat?' Verkhovensky practically shouted. 'Our forces in the Far East are having a hard time just holding the Chinese at bay! What could we possibly ask them to do if . . .?' He did not complete his question.

'You don't honestly believe the Americans will use nuclear weapons in Korea?' Mishin asked, the humor of it written across his face.

'I believe the point is,' Karyakin supplied with a smile, 'that we have to begin to prepare for what is looking like the inevitable.'

'We *are* preparing,' Razov said. 'We're raising General Abramov's Provisionals.'

The commander of the Ukrainian Strategic Direction said with as much tact as he could muster, 'With all due respect to General Abramov, I think everyone here knows the risks involved should we come to blows with the Americans. If we allow them to stage one of their huge set-piece operations – a massively supplied, totally orchestrated multicorps extravaganza, which is the only thing they have ever been able to do right in the entire military history of their country – then we could well be looking at another "Barbarossa."

'What are you suggesting?' Razov asked. 'The submarines in the Bastion again?'

'No!' the army general said. 'But we can't get caught flat-footed! We've got to start attriting their forces before they stage. We've got to start using our own forces before we degrade. Everyone here knows the equation! We've run model after model! They ship forces to Europe over open seas and through open skies. They disembark at seaports and airports and travel down highways and railways that are first class and were untouched in the nuclear exchange. Every week that goes by, their forces on the Continent grow stronger. But every week that goes by, our forces grow weaker as we have yet to even reestablish uncontaminated lines of communication to the troops in the field. Their supplies and readiness levels are already falling as a result.'

'But can the Americans sustain their forces over supply lines that stretch and stretch and stretch?' the old general in charge of Construction asked.

'This is not 1812,' Air Force General Mishin said, 'or even 1941. Both Napoleon and Hitler depended primarily on the same method of transportation: horses! Good God! How can we possibly rely on beating the Americans by relying on shortcomings in their *logistics*! That's a martial art that they practically *invented*!'

'What a landslide,' the anchorman on television said. 'I guess you could say the American people have spoken here today. Four hundred and sixty-one in favor, twenty-eight opposed. It's been quite a historic day, hasn't it?'

The commentator, a former senior member of the Senate, shook his head and said, 'What a dramatic way to end what is surely the most historic single day in the history of Congress. I'm just . . . I'm just stunned by how rapidly Congress has moved on this.'

'Well, they're clearly galvanized by the polls,' a Washington political analyst said. 'Over ninety-seven percent of the American people now believe that major concessions should have been extracted from the Russians before President Livingston called a cease-fire. Over eighty percent believe the Russians have shown such a level of irresponsibility that we should demand their complete nuclear disarmament *forever*.'

'Well, regardless,' the anchorman said as the camera focused in on his face, 'what exactly the outcome of today's historic session will be remains in doubt. What has happened in this rapidly developing story, however, is this. This afternoon, at four fifty-five Eastern Daylight Time, Congress, sitting in special Joint Session, declared war on the Republic of Russia, the first declaration of war issued by this country since December 9th, 1941. The President responded immediately, declaring in a widely criticized national television address from Mount Weather within fifteen minutes of the vote that, as commander in chief, he would not prosecute that war. He had, sources tell CNN, just gotten off the phone with the Kremlin and assured them the same. And now, by our clock, minutes before three a.m. on this June sixteenth, just over five days after the Russian warheads rained down on our country, the first successful impeachment of the President of the United States in the House of Representatives since the 1868 impeachment of President Andrew Johnson. Now, it's on to the Senate, where the President will be tried and, if convicted, removed from office.'

SPECIAL FACILITY, MOUNT WEATHER, VIRGINIA
June 16, 2200 GMT (1700 Local)

Lambert could hear the muffled explosions and ripping automatic weapons fire even through the thick door to the main conference room in the otherwise quiet underground facility. He opened the door, and it took a moment for his eyes to adjust to the darkness as he slipped into the room.

Identical scenes of combat played on the screens covering the walls as Lambert skirted the backs of the chairs at the table looking for a seat in the crowded room – late because of the crisis action meeting he had called on the Russian troop deployments toward the Pacific coast from the now cooling Russo-Chinese War. There were no seats at the table, but a woman seated along the wall that Lambert vaguely recognized as a junior member of the U.N. mission in New York jumped up. 'Take this seat, sir,' the woman whispered, and Lambert sat behind the director of the CIA as the woman moved to the standing-room-only end of the conference table behind the acting Secretary of State.

Lambert settled in to watch the jerky footage of fighting. The three letters ITN – International Television News – were printed in the lower right-hand corner of the four new rear-projection screens just built into the walls of the facility's briefing room, and a date and time stamp a couple of hours old was superimposed along the bottom of the picture. The raw video, Lambert assumed, must have been intercepted from satellite transmissions sent back by the network for editing, and it was not very informative, mainly just tracer rounds streaking back and forth through the dark hills of Korea interrupted occasionally by a brief burst of light. In the dimly lit room, however, the stunning clarity of the high-definition video displays and the gut-shaking audio of the room's new surround-sound processors that pumped twenty-four-inch subwoofers under the table were dramatic, apparently even for the military men, who had seen the real thing. Cups filled with coffee rattled against saucers on the table with each burst of an explosion's sound wave to reach the cameraman, whose camera shook when hit by the shock.

Suddenly, the scene went to a colorful pattern of vertical bars, and the speakers fell deathly silent. The test pattern was quickly replaced with an aerial shot in bright daylight. The horizon above the dark and distant landscape was hazy, the sky above fading quickly from purple to black, and the earth below distant and featureless. The sides of the screen were boxed, and data were crammed into the margins of the blue frame. Superimposed on the picture itself in the corner were the white digits of a clock, numbers flying by as the hundredths of a second rolled off.

'That's from a TR-1 just off the coast of North Korea,' General Starnes said into the stillness of the packed and stuffy room. 'Roughly in the center of the picture on the ground should be the capital, Pyongyang.'

'It's kind of hard to pick anything out of that picture,' the President said as Lambert saw the count on the clock roll past 1:00:00 and start heading down. *One minute*, he thought. *Just in time.*

'Oh, you'll see it, sir,' Starnes said.

'Greg, are you here?' the President called out in the semi-darkness.

'Yes, sir!'

'Are we ready to go with the cable giving them the ultimatum?'

'Yes, sir. It's drafted and will go to the North Korean delegation to the U.N. as soon as we confirm the success of the mission.'

'What did we decide on as the second target if the North Koreans don't agree to the cease-fire and withdrawal?' the head of the National Security Agency asked.

'Wonsan harbor,' General Thomas replied.

'Whew. There'll be some civilian casualties.'

'The South Koreans insisted,' the President answered. 'Last night it seems the North Korean troops ran wild through Tongduchon just south of the DMZ. It began as just looting – VCRs, clothes, Western things – but it got wilder and wilder and they began raping and murdering the population. Reports are that we're talking thousands, maybe tens of thousands of civilians murdered. The North Koreans are shooting their own men today trying to restore order, but . . .'

The President fell silent as the clock's counter fell under forty seconds. All eyes were glued to the screen.

'What kind of weapon are we using?' the director of the CIA asked.

'SRAM from a B-1B,' Starnes replied. 'Three hundred and seventeen kiloton.'

'But you're sure nobody's going to be hurt?' the President asked.

'Only if they look at the fireball, sir. Otherwise, they shouldn't get much more than a tan.'

'We were going to use a sub-launched Tomahawk,' Admiral Dixon said, 'but it's a sea-skimmer. We couldn't get up to the hundred-thousand-foot altitude set as the mission's minimum.'

'A little bit more of a demonstration than we wanted, eh?' Irv Waller joked – sounding filled with nervous energy – but drew no reply.

Twenty seconds. The sky was so placid, Lambert thought as the clarity of the screen's image, so much more striking in daylight than the pictures of night fighting had been, drew him into their grasp. 'What's the altitude of your TR-1, Bill?' General Thomas asked.

Starnes squinted at the tiny numbers embedded in the box around the picture and said, 'Seventy-four thousand.'

The sky high above was pitch black. Ten seconds, Lambert saw. Nine, eight, seven, six, five, four, three, two, one. A single point of white light pierced the purple that divided earth from space. The light expanded at a brisk rate, quickly forming a perfect white sphere of ever increasing proportions high in the sky directly over the North Korean capital. Although its rate of expansion slowed, the orb of light still grew at unimaginable speed, opening a clean hole in the high, thin layer of clouds above which it had burst.

The camera jerked as the cameraman in the cockpit of the reconnaissance plane zoomed in, the orb now filling the screen and showing the first faint tinges of yellow all about its otherwise pristine surface. They all watched as the yellow turned deeper and darker in color, showing the first signs of swirls and patterns like that seen in the violent displays from the surface of the sun. The orb suddenly slipped from view as the camera wobbled – first black space and then dark earth with a tiny white coastline separating it from the blue sea below. The camera's wobble continued for a moment longer before it settled and reacquired the now dissipating sphere.

'Shock wave,' was all General Starnes said to explain, and Lambert realized that it was the aircraft, not the camera, which was firmly mounted in the cockpit, that had been doing the rocking – the blast wave sending it from wingtip to wingtip.

'Can we get any audio?' the President asked.

'Well, from the pilot, yes, sir,' Starnes replied, nodding at the technician who stood in the corner of the room.

A moment later there burst into the room a distorted electronic whine of a woman's highly agitated voice saying, 'That was one helluva ride, Sierra Foxtrot! Ho-o-ly-Moley! Lost two thousand feet.'

'Don't worry about it, Indigo Six,' the far clearer voice of another woman said. 'You're all by your lonesome up there. You're not going to run into anybody.'

'The fireball appears to be breaking up now,' the pilot said.

'I've got video, five by five,' her controller replied. 'Are you ready to tango?'

'Ready as I'm ever gonna be,' the pilot responded, her voice much calmer now. 'I'm gonna put the hand-held in the twelve o'clock brackets now.'

The camera jerked and showed brief glimpses of the inside of the cockpit and then the helmeted head of the pilot, twisting around to fill half of the picture with the black lenses of her flight helmet and her black oxygen mask. After one final jerk of the camera and then some twisting of the pilot's gloved hands on either side as she obviously fastened screws, the pilot straightened in her seat. The camera now displayed a view of the top of the cockpit's dashboard as it pointed straight out the front windshield.

'How's the picture?' the pilot asked.

'Hey, it's a Kodak moment,' the flight controller replied. 'You're clear to go.'

'Executing a ninety,' the pilot said, and the plane banked. The image was so stunningly clear in the room, which had just the day before been upgraded to Pentagon and Situation Room standards of high-definition TV and surround sound, that Lambert felt himself grabbing for the arms of his chair as the angled horizon cut across the TR-1's windshield. When the plane righted itself, the windshield was filled with the now ragged but still enormous ball of smoke, the center of which quite clearly still burned in a glowing red ball.

'I'm heading in, feet dry, speed five six zero knots and climbing.' The whine of the engines were much louder and could now be heard clearly in the background.

'What the hell is she doing?' the President asked in a concerned voice.

'Air samples and an image strip over ground zero,' Starnes replied matter-of-factly.

'She looks like she's headed right at it,' the President said, agitated by the prospect of approaching the inferno, agitated as was Lambert by being taken along as the picture of the sphere grew larger.

'Well, sir, that's just what she's doing,' the air force general replied. 'She's gonna go right through the heart of it.'

'You've gotta be kidding!' the President exclaimed as Lambert looked at the flames, which were growing darker and more diffuse. 'Look, put a stop to this. Dial that woman up right now!'

'Sir,' Starnes replied as the door opened and the light from the corridor outside briefly lit the room, 'they've got this thing timed. It'll be okay by the time she gets to it. She's in more danger from SAMs than from that fireball, although we've got air defense suppression going in under her: two flights of Wild Weasels, one on each coast, ready to hose the North Koreans down if they try to paint her on her transverse of the peninsula.'

'What about radiation?'

'She'll be through there so quick it won't be any worse than an X-ray. We haven't had any opportunities like this with our own weapons' bursts since we stopped aboveground testing forty years ago.'

The President was staring at the awesome sight of the rapidly growing ball of thinning smoke, his mouth open in dread as he held the message handed to him by the navy lieutenant who still stood behind him. The sight of the man entering their little cocoon of sights and sounds broke through Lambert's almost hypnotic attraction to the show and he said, 'Sir, do you want me to send the cable to the North Koreans now?'

The President was reading the message slip in the thin beam of light shone on it from the penlight of the lieutenant behind him. 'No,' he said, breaking the spell of the others in the room as heads turned to look his way. 'The North Korean ambassador to the U.N. has contacted our delegation and is seeking a cease-fire. No terms were discussed, but I think we oughta hit them with our laundry list.'

'That was quick,' the head of the NSA chuckled.

'That's the beauty of modern science,' Marine General Fuller rasped with a chuckle, as all eyes were attracted back to the picture on the screen. 'Better living through physics.' The first wispy layers of smoke shot by the windshield of the aircraft before the pilot and all in the room were plunged into the darkness – the heart of the inferno – only to burst just as quickly back out into the bright daylight beyond. The windshield now filled again with the beautiful summer day. The deep blue sea of the opposite shore was faintly visible in the distance ahead.

'Sierra Foxtrot, this is Indigo Six,' the pilot said, her voice calmer by far than Lambert felt he could have mustered at that moment. 'All done. I'm through clean.'

'Congrats, Indigo Six. You bagged your first burst. I'll have the boys at Yokota waiting with a spray can and stencil to paint this one on when you get back.'

'Just get me home, Sierra Foxtrot. Just get me home.'

'Roger that, Indigo Six. Come to heading of one zero seven. Maintain present course and altitude. Over.'

JUNCTION OF I–10 AND HIGHWAY 91, SAN BERNARDINO, CALIFORNIA
June 17, 1700 GMT (0900 Local)

'This is ABC Radio,' Melissa heard over the car stereo as she sped down the freeway, and on reflex she reached and turned up the volume. 'It's official. North Korea announced today that it will pull back to its former positions along the Thirty-eighth Parallel and immediately cease all hostilities. This follows yesterday's detonation of a nuclear-tipped missile in the sky high above the North Korean capital of Pyongyang by U.S. Air Force bombers. No word yet as to what other terms have been agreed upon, but administration sources tell ABC News that the U.S. will insist upon a monitored dismantling of North Korean nuclear weapons facilities and a cap on both the size and deployment of

North Korea's conventional forces. The reunification of North and South previously scheduled for the fall, however, appears to be on hold.'

Melissa applied the brakes as the taillights of the traffic ahead signaled another jam. 'In domestic news, a spokesman for the Internal Revenue Service in Philadelphia has just confirmed the imposition of a fifteen percent national sales tax to be levied by the Livingston Administration under federal emergency rules. The new tax, which would go into effect on July first, will be used initially to refinance the massive eighty-billion-dollar short-term note offering that is scheduled for next week to cover initial costs of both emergency federal disaster aid for the war sites and burgeoning military expenditures as the Defense Department has begun to purchase massive quantities of fuel and other supplies ranging from boots to bullets.'

Melissa pulled the car up to the bumper of a truck in line ahead of her and began to inch forward toward the bottleneck.

She rolled the window down and could see that there was a roadblock ahead, the lights of the police cars flashing at the junction of I-10 and another highway. 'In other news. "We are not at war." So says the President in a photo opportunity from his underground bunker in Virginia. The Russians, however, appear to think otherwise. Sources inside the Defense Department tell ABC News that the massive invasion force of Russian marines that yesterday had a run-in with Norway's navy is now in the Norwegian Sea, having passed within miles of U.S. Navy ships heading in the opposite direction toward the Barents Sea just outside the infamous Bastion of Russian ballistic missile submarines in the Kara Sea. The U.S. ships were, unnamed sources in the Defense Department report, under strict orders to avoid contact with the Russians – unlike the Norwegian Navy, which twice exchanged fire with Russian ships screening the flotilla of amphibious landing ships, both times involving surface-to-surface missiles that sank two Norwegian and three Russian ships and left one Russian ship ablaze.'

The car inched forward, and Matthew began to stir in his seat. *He's getting hungry*, Melissa thought. *I've got to find some more formula somewhere*. 'Meanwhile, more clashes on the ground in Eastern Europe, this time in Slovakia as Russian forces take up positions, apparently with at least the tacit approval of the Ukrainian government, just across the Ukrainian border from U.S. Army combat troops. We go now to Allison Tinsley, who is in Slovakia with U.S. troops along the Ukrainian border.'

'During the early morning hours here,' the woman said over a telephone hookup, 'just before dawn, a U.S. patrol of five M-3 Bradley armored scout vehicles from the 4th Infantry Division using low-light sights spotted a patrol in force of a dozen Russian armored vehicles fording a small stream over three miles inside the Slovakian border. Brigadier General Simmons, commander of the one brigade of the 4th which is currently operational, said in a briefing just concluded that he determined the Russian forces posed a threat to Czech troops recently deployed into neighboring Slovakia and ordered the U.S. scout vehicles to open fire with their TOW antitank missiles and 25-mm cannon. In a brief but fierce firefight, one U.S. M-3 and seven Russian armored vehicles were destroyed, resulting in three American dead and two wounded . . .'

As the news report moved on to the preparations for the Senate impeachment trial, Melissa drew closer to the roadblock. Highway patrolmen wearing gas masks were stopping to speak to the drivers before waving them through. Patrol cars with lights flashing and more permanent bright orange barrels walled off the exit ramps for Highway 91 South, which led, as the signs reminded, to Riverside. *To David*, flashed fleetingly through her mind before she banished the impossible thought.

A loud knock on the window startled her, and she looked out into the reptilian eyes of a black gas mask. The patrolman motioned with his fingers for her to lower the window, and she rolled it down.

'Where are you headed?' he said, his voice muffled and distorted by the mask.

'L.A.,' she said. 'I live there.' She saw him look at Matthew, who was so little that she felt he still belonged safe and sound floating in her womb. 'Is it okay?' Melissa asked. 'Up ahead, I mean?'

'Well, all the exits are closed between here and I-15 about fourteen miles ahead,' he said, his chest bucking with the exertion of making himself heard. 'You got enough gas to make it?'

Melissa looked down to see that she still had a quarter of a tank. 'I think so.' Just then she noticed the dust rising ahead as cars were crossing the median to turn around and head back the other way down I-10. 'Is it safe?'

'Yes, ma'am, but we're recommending that you maintain a speed of at least seventy-five along this stretch, and no stopping or slowing down to "rubberneck" any of the war damage. You should also close off your outside vents and turn off your AC. There'll be some fire trucks on the other side to hose your car down,' he said, and she saw the fire trucks to the side of the Highway 91 overpass doing the same for the eastbound traffic, 'and you'll be told to ride with your fan on full and windows down to blow everything out, but the levels aren't bad.'

He rose to move on to the next car. 'Hey, wait!' Melissa said, leaning out the window as the man walked back. 'You mean there's radiation up there?'

'Not much, ma'am,' he said from behind his mask. 'Those bombs over Riverside blew up high in the air. They didn't pick up dirt from the ground to make any fallout. They say it's safe. Just follow the instructions and you'll be okay.' He moved on, and Melissa rolled the window up as she inched forward. She pushed up on the other window buttons to ensure that all were closed tight and inched forward again. Melissa found the vent slide on the dashboard – or what she thought was the vent slide, at least – and closed it. She turned off the air conditioning, and looked up to see that there were only two cars ahead of her now. Her car was sandwiched in the middle lane.

The patrolmen looked down and waved the front rank on. The three cars accelerated away, and Melissa inched ahead. Watching the departing cars, the patrolmen waited a few seconds and then motioned the cars just in front of her to go. They too accelerated, their rank quickly growing staggered as the truck picked up speed more slowly than the two cars. Melissa was next. She looked at the long, straight stretch of highway ahead down which the three vehicles quickly receded. When they passed the Highway 91 overpass, the patrolmen waved and Melissa stepped on the accelerator.

Her Mazda accelerated smoothly, and Melissa leapt out in front of the two older-model cars on either side of her. She slid quickly by the junction and, on passing, felt as if she was now in alien territory. She kept her foot on the gas as she passed seventy-five miles per hour and settled on ninety. She overtook the truck ahead and began a leisurely weave through the thin traffic as they passed the completely abandoned landscape.

The downed television antenna at a roadside gas station was the first sign of damage, and she drove on for several miles thinking that was all she would see of the great destruction.

Rising over a small hill she saw the blackened grass and brush and the bowed trees of the valley ahead. The windows of a coffee shop and motel were black and empty, jagged glass jutting into the openings and doors of many of the motel rooms flung wide open. It got worse ahead, as overturned trailers in a small campground and blackened, roofless houses attested to the force of the winds that had preceded the fires. She had to force herself to watch the road as cars slowed and she concentrated on keeping her car's speed up passing the first of the cars and trucks, windowless and sometimes overturned, along the shoulder of the road.

As the car crested another gentle rise, Melissa took her foot off the accelerator and felt the car decelerate slowly, her eyes fixed on the sight ahead. An old blue-green bus lay on its side in the median, sleeping bags, camping gear, clothing, and other articles strewn wildly all about. AFRICAN METHODIST EPISCOPAL SCHOOL was printed on the back of the bus, and a small wooden cross made of sticks was planted at an angle in the soil between the two lanes.

THE KREMLIN, MOSCOW
June 18, 0600 GMT (0800 Local)

Filipov opened the door to the conference room and was surprised to hear English being spoken. The speaker, a paunchy, balding man in his late forties, was answering questions as he stood in front of the full STAVKA meeting.

'Have you seen the actual Articles of Impeachment?' he asked, rummaging through his beat-up briefcase. 'I . . . I have a copy of them somewhere.' The interpreter's translation came nearly simultaneously.

Filipov went over to Razov and handed him the final plans for the Iceland invasion. 'Who is this?' he whispered.

'Some American law professor who was at Moscow University on an exchange program,' Razov said. 'He was more than happy to give us a briefing about "impeachment,"' he said, using the English word.

'He's a fucking pacifist,' Admiral Verkhovensky whispered, leaning across. 'Practically kissed me on the mouth when they brought him in.'

'Ah! Here it is,' the professor said, and then he cleared his throat. Most of the military officers waited on the interpreter's translation, but Filipov, Razov, and a few others mostly in their 'camp' eschewed the Russian, listening to the English.

'"Articles of Impeachment. Resolved, that Walter N. Livingston, President of the United States, is impeached for treason and other high crimes and misdemeanors, and that the following articles of impeachment be exhibited to the Senate."' He looked up. 'You see, a resolution is brought by a Congressman, investigated by the Judiciary Committee, and then voted on by the House. If a majority passes, as they did, the matter is referred to the Senate for trial. There are several articles, but the key one is Article II.'

He looked down and again cleared his throat. '"Article II. In his conduct of the office of President of the United States, Walter N. Livingston, in violation of his constitutional oath faithfully to execute the office of President of the United States and, to the best of his ability, preserve, protect, and defend the Constitution of the United States from its enemies, and in violation of his constitutional duty to take care that the laws be faithfully executed, has prevented, obstructed, and impeded and does prevent, obstruct and impede the prosecution of war against enemies of the United States duly and properly declared by the Congress of the United States in that, on June 16th of this year, he did direct the Joint Chiefs of Staff of this nation's armed forces to refrain from prosecution of offensive military action against the armed forces of the Republic of Russia."'

He looked up. 'It goes on with the other articles that relate to a variety of things such as informing the Chinese of the impending attack, and then concludes with, "In all of this, Walter N. Livingston has acted in a manner contrary to his position of trust as President and subversive of constitutional government, to the great prejudice of the cause of law and to the manifest injury to the people of the United States and to the nation's security. Wherefore, Walter N. Livingston, by such conduct, warrants impeachment and trial, and removal from office.'"

'And so the American word impeachment does not mean removal from office?' one of the officers asked.

After translation, the American lawyer said, 'No. Impeachment really just means indictment – the bringing of a charge. The President is going to be tried in a court of sorts with the full Senate acting as jury and the Chief Justice of the Supreme Court presiding. In order to remove the President from office, two-thirds of the Senators present must vote to convict.'

'And are these articles proper reasons to convict Livingston?'

After the delay, the professor said, 'It's impossible to say. Impeachment is, at its heart, a purely political process. Former President Gerald Ford once said, "An impeachable offense is whatever a majority of the House of Representatives considers it to be," and Nixon's Attorney General said, "You don't need facts to impeach a President, just votes." It's been established that it's not necessary to have committed a crime, but just what's impeachable and what's not is anybody's guess.'

'Thank you, Professor,' Razov spoke up, picking the invasion plans for Iceland off the table, and then nodded at the captain who stood against the wall behind the professor.

'I . . . I wanted to say a couple of words about . . .' The captain allowed him just enough time to put his papers in his briefcase, but not enough time to close it. He stumbled toward the door holding the briefcase closed with the captain's firm grip on his elbow. 'On behalf of all Americans, and the Committee for Nonviolence of the Union of Tenured Educators,' he said as the door was opened and he arched his head over his shoulder, this text obviously prepared, 'let me say that the American people want no part of this war. We are against all war. We want alternative dispute resolution mechanisms to be—' The door closed in his face.

Many of the officers had smiles of amusement on their faces, and Strategic Rocket Forces' General Karyakin said, 'And that was a specimen of the nation of which we are frightened?'

Laughter broke out all across the room.

'What do you think, Colonel Filipov?' Admiral Verkhovensky asked smiling, jarring Filipov's wandering attention back to the room, back from his imaginary search for Irina. 'You are our "expert" on America. Is this man an example of what we are up against?' There was still more laughter.

'No,' Filipov said loudly enough to be heard over the laughter, louder than he intended, as much to his own surprise as to the surprise of the senior officers whose humor he had interrupted. They had not expected an answer, but now they all looked with fading smiles at the young colonel, waiting. 'I just mean, I know what most of you think of Americans.' Filipov looked at the faces of the senior officers who stared back at him, waiting for him to make a point. 'You think they're lazy, greedy hedonists who suckle on the carcass of a country into which they had the good fortune to be born.' There were smiles from some. 'In normal times that operating assumption suffices, but these are not normal times.'

Filipov felt Razov's hand on his forearm but chose to ignore it. He had long chafed at the comfortable ignorance of his superiors about America. At last he had been asked his opinion, and at a juncture at which the truth about the American character was critical. 'Americans are a strange people. On an individual level, they are for the most part generous and kind. But as a people they send their armed forces off to faraway places to kill and maim and destroy with remarkable indifference *when* they believe they are right, when they believe the war is just. When they believe they're in the right, they muster their force with all their energy and deliver blows that crush entire *peoples*. This kind nation, that vast "silent" majority of gentle and fair people, will destroy *everything* that comes before it with the self-righteous zeal of a crusading army *if* they think the cause is just!'

Razov sat back and watched Filipov, as did everyone else in the room, as he leaned out over the polished wood of the conference table that he only rarely had approached before.

'I've studied America for most of my life, I lived there for years, and I have never witnessed anything like what I am seeing reported in their press. The nuclear exchange was a cathartic experience for both our nations, but for the Americans . . .! Nothing like this has happened to them since their Civil War ended in 1865! They have forgotten what war is like, and instead of concluding what most of the world has the misfortune of recalling from all too recent experience – that war, any war, is a human disaster of unparalleled magnitude – the Americans are choosing instead to attribute their civilian dead to villainies, to atrocities, to *us*! To *you*, to *me*, to *Russians*, as if we somehow broke the rules of war and the norms of behavior. They are *demonizing* us, haven't you *seen*? That man, that professor you just had in here, he doesn't represent what's happening. He doesn't see what's coming. But I do. And it *is* coming, like a tidal wave it's coming.' The room fell silent, all eyes on Filipov.

'This time, they believe the cause is just. This time, that silent majority of Americans believes it is right.'

GANDER AIRPORT, NEWFOUNDLAND
June 18, 2300 GMT (1900 Local)

The soft ground felt good, delicious. David Chandler's field manual dropped several times before he finally laid it down. Pictures of tank battles – cartoonlike drawings from the manual – ran through his head. Tanks in column, rolling out to line formation as if in some video game. Re-forming into a column to squeeze between two obstacles. Formation after formation. Terrain rolling by on the map. Always moving forward, just as they wanted. Leaping over each other like frogs, each tank landing in front of the next. Hopping, dancing to the music.

The music woke him, and he opened his eyes. He had fallen asleep while reading. A heavy, rhythmic beat broke the silence from just over the hill. It was odd to him how quickly he had grown used to the sounds of the outdoors, to the rushing wind, the sounds of soldiers talking or shouting near and far with no walls to break the passage of the noise. But the sounds of music had grown odd. He got up and grabbed his rifle. With ammunition so abundant, and the Russians, by latest rumor, somewhere out in the Atlantic, standing orders required all soldiers to carry their personal weapons everywhere and at all times. He cradled his now familiar M-16 rifle in the crook of his arm and walked out toward the center of his company area, closer to the music.

The clustering of the men and women into their respective squads had cleared small open areas through which one could navigate. The clusters reminded Chandler of living cells, each soldier a part of the organism. When he was near the middle of the company area, it was as if he were inside a living beast, multicellular and alive with activity.

He found the psychological dynamic that had taken place, the bonding of virtually randomly selected men and women into cohesive squads and platoons, very interesting, and he enjoyed walking through the troops. He stopped to talk occasionally but mainly enjoyed the anonymity that his frequent walk-throughs bred.

Rising to the crest of the low hill he saw that a commotion centered around a 'boom box.' *Someone on that air force transport that landed earlier*, Chandler thought, *must have brought batteries*. The particularly boisterous troops were active and vocal, feeling good that afternoon, Chandler guessed, after taking their first shower since their arrival in Newfoundland, in the new portable showers the plane had unloaded. *Or excited*, he thought with a rush of nervousness himself, that the phone system would be put back on line and they would each be allowed a call. Chandler wandered down to where one of the soldiers loaded a new CD. Rap music with a thudding bass. 'Can't touch this . . .'

The scene reminded him of old documentaries. Music. Soldiers on their feet, dancing by themselves, everyone getting into it. The feeling was infectious, intoxicating. Neighboring groups joined in as the music was turned up. It was a good sound.

'*Hammer time!*' High fives. Soul handshakes. The pictures. The pictures from Vietnam had been different. These men were about half and half, black and white, and the high fives were for the guy next to you, white or black. Unlike the society from which the men came, there were no racial lines here. They were not integrated as much as fused. '*Hammer time!*' They all knew which lyrics to sing out – black and white, men and women. They were comfortable with their little social rituals, with the society of the cell.

The song ended, and the self-appointed DJ hit a button, delaying the start of the music until he had found the song he wanted and then holding the CD player high in the air. When the next song burst forth, the men and women all jumped to their feet, singing, rapping along, shouting the lyrics at the top of their lungs. The music's beat was felt as much as heard. Rhythmic. '*Yo-sweet-ness, is-for-weakness! Yo-sweet-ness, is-for-weak-me-e-en!*'

The energy levels were up. Very soon now, their hands will be filled. Maybe a heavy machine gun ready to rattle out rounds from the cupola of a vehicle or a minigun swiveling in the door of a helicopter. *Would there be a beat in their minds then? In the sounds of their weapons?* If there was, Chandler knew, it would be this beat. This would be the music of their war. They were getting ready, and he pitied the poor bastards who would stare down the open ends of these men's gun barrels, for even though the soldiers were solidly middle class, products of suburbia, their music was born in the mean streets of a violent country. It brooked no compromise, no mercy. The men in their gunsights would die in great numbers.

SPECIAL FACILITY, MOUNT WEATHER, VIRGINIA
June 19, 2200 GMT (1700 Local)

Lambert walked up to the long desk that sat atop the slightly elevated platform to stand in front of the nine robed Justices, and turned to wait for the White House counsel, Solicitor General, and Special Counsel to the Judiciary Committee to leave the chamber, closing the door behind them.

'Mr Lambert,' Chief Justice Rehnquist said, 'this courtroom has now been cleared of everyone but this Court and you. We have taken this unusual step in consideration of the fact that you are, yourself, a licensed attorney and have agreed for purposes of giving this testimony that you will represent yourself pro se. Are we correct in this understanding?'

'Yes, Your Honor.'

'Congratulations. You are now certified to practice law before the highest court in the land. We'll worry about the commemorative certificate later.'

A couple of the Associate Justices chuckled, and Lambert forced a smile as he shifted from one foot to the other.

'Would the witness be more comfortable sitting?' Justice Scalia asked.

'Uh, no, sir,' Lambert said. 'I'm fine.'

'Very well,' Justice Rehnquist said, looking down at his notes. 'You understand, of course, that you are still under oath?'

'Yes, sir, Your Honor.'

'Now, Mr Lambert, each of the members of this Court has reviewed the brief filed by your counsel, the White House counsel, and the amicus curiae brief filed by the Solicitor General on behalf of the United States, on the one hand, and the brief of the Special Counsel to the Judiciary Committee and the amicus curiae briefs filed by several other persons and groups including a most thorough job by the People for the American Way.' He held up a stack of paper that had to be at least four inches thick and looked at the other Justices, who seemed amused. The Chief Justice then looked down at Lambert, removing his eyeglasses and dangling them in the air with one hand. 'We are, as of our conference immediately preceding this hearing, of differing opinions as to the state of the law on the privilege you have claimed. It was decided, however, that one fact that was material to the decision of a majority of the Justices and therefore potentially dispositive of the issue raised was not contained in the record passed up to us from the circuit court, and due to the expedited nature of the proceedings which we have undertaken, we have decided not to remand the matter to the district court, which is, as you know, the primary finder of fact in our legal system. I am now going to ask you to supply that fact, in camera,' he said, holding his hands up to indicate the empty chamber, 'and I expect you to comply with my request.'

The Chief Justice looked down at his notes, and then back up at Lambert. 'Did President Livingston tell Secretary Moore during his evacuation from the White House to inform representatives of the government of the People's Republic of China of the impending Russian nuclear attack?'

'Yes, sir,' Lambert said without hesitation. 'Yes, sir, he did.'

'And do you have any reason to believe that Secretary Moore did not in fact notify the Chinese as directed by the President?'

'No, sir, I do not.'

Justice Rehnquist looked to either side, and when none of the other Justices spoke up, the Chief Justice surprised Lambert with, 'Thank you, Mr Lambert. We have no further questions at this time.'

Lambert entered the small office outside the Supreme Court's chamber. President Livingston sat on the cheap vinyl couch, his closest advisers crowded around him. All eyes turned to Lambert.

He tried to decide what to say. He felt like Brutus as he slowly walked up to face the President through the suddenly quiet group. Staring at Walter Livingston, a decent man on whom had been heaped every imaginable burden of office and on whom was hung the responsibility for the millions who had perished, Lambert tried to think of a way to soften the latest blow.

He opened his mouth to explain how the proceeding had progressed after they had cleared the chamber. He said simply, 'I told them about your instructions to Secretary Moore.'

Livingston nodded as if in acknowledgment of a minor point and reached out to briefly squeeze Lambert's forearm. The man had already shouldered so heavy a burden these past weeks, Lambert realized, that his news was of little consequence.

'Is the testimony really that critical?' the President's press secretary asked.

'Our people at Greenbriar say we're hovering right there on the edge,' Irv Waller said, unusually circumspect. 'They finally identified Senator Albritton's body. His plane had an electrical fire when the pulse from one of the Russians' warheads fried its circuits, and it went down over Missouri. With Senator Shavers dead in the Colorado Springs attack, that reduces the Senate membership to ninety-eight. Two thirds of the ninety-eight is sixty-six to convict. But Barney Clark was in Bethesda Naval Hospital in ICU for a heart lung. They couldn't move him until yesterday, and Bethesda got a heavy dusting of fallout from the Raven Rock blast. The navy shuttled volunteers through the hospital every few hours for the people like Barney whom they couldn't move. Can you imagine?' Waller shook his head, truly lost in his own story, and Lambert wondered at this side of the man, who had always struck him as an unrelenting jerk.

'Jesus, we're that close?' the press secretary asked, and the President hung his head.

Lambert, standing in front of his boss and staring, said, 'Mr President—'

The door burst open. 'They're back,' one of the junior staffers reported from the doorway.

The President stood, straightened his jacket and tie, and clapped Lambert lightly on the arm. He nodded and winked, a half-grin turning up one corner of his mouth but passing without registering in his eyes. He led the small procession out. Like Judas, Greg had received Livingston's forgiveness.

'Mr Lambert, would you please stand?' Chief Justice Rehnquist said, and Lambert and White House counsel rose. 'Mr Lambert, the Court has reached a decision. I will let Justice Ginsburg render it for the majority.'

Justice Ginsburg sat forward and said, 'Mr Lambert, all members of this Court, both in the majority and dissenting, have found that a privilege exists for matters highly sensitive to the national security of this country during a time of national emergency. By a majority of seven to two, however, this Court has found neither precedents in prior case law nor reasoning as expressed in the briefing of the matters before this Court persuasive of the position that such privilege is absolute. In reaching its decision, therefore, a majority of seven of the Justices found that the interests of the executive branch in preserving the security of our nation's secrets by invoking a privilege against testimony on grounds of national security must be weighed against the interests of the Senate in conducting a trial of the President of the United States following impeachment by the House of Representatives. In weighing such competing interests, a majority of seven is of the opinion that, under the facts as presented to this Court in the instant matter, the interests of the orderly and fair conduct of the Senate's trial of the President prevail. Accordingly, this Court instructs Gregory Philip Lambert, Special Assistant to the President for National Security, to answer all questions put to him by the United States Senate in open hearing on the subject of whether President Livingston instructed the late Secretary Moore to contact the government of the People's Republic of China on the night of June eleventh of this year.'

'The dissent will issue no opinion,' the Chief Justice announced. 'This Court is adjourned.' The gavel came down, and everyone rose as the Justices filed out.

LOS ANGELES, CALIFORNIA
June 20, 0000 GMT (1600 Local)

Melissa Chandler lay baby Matthew in his crib. Carefully lowering his head to the mattress so as not to jar him awake as she had done twice before, her mouth hung open and her face contorted with the effort of concentration.

The phone rang loudly through the open door. She grimaced and quickly covered Matthew with the blanket, rushing on tiptoes to the door and pulling it quietly closed. She heaved a deep sigh of relief as she trudged down the hall, of half a mind to unplug the phone so as not to have to talk to this cousin or that aunt. *The phone companies must be raking it in these days*, she thought as she closed the bedroom door. *Nuclear war is even better for business than Mother's Day.*

'Hel-l-o-o-o,' she said, slumping and resting her head onto the earpiece for the long conversation to come.

'Melissa?'

Her entire world shifted its focus onto the faint hiss coming out of the telephone. She held her breath to pick up every sound, and she could feel her heart beating against her chest. 'D-David?' She reached up and pressed her fingers to her lips as her eyes watered instantly.

'Oh, God, thank God,' he said, his voice breaking.

She sank into the chair and broke out laughing, tears flooding her eyes. She tried to cry and laugh at the same time, managing only the words, 'Are you all right?' which were mangled by the effort required.

'Yeah – yeah,' he said, laughter breaking through a voice that was thick with his own quiet tears.

Melissa dissolved into sobs, her chest bucking so that she was unable to talk.

'How about you?' David asked.

She tried, but she just could not get the words to come out.

'Melissa? What?'

'No-o-o!' she finally said. 'We're *fi-i-ine*!'

There was nothing but the hiss of the line for several long seconds. 'We?' David finally asked.

Melissa forced the words out. 'We had a baby.' The sobs seized her for a moment, but then she said, 'He's perfect. Don't worry. He's beautiful.'

'A boy,' David said, his voice far away and the connection poor. 'Matthew?'

'Yes,' she sniffed, 'Matthew.'

'Hah!' he laughed. 'A baby!' She grinned on hearing his excitement at the news she had been bursting with desire to share with him. She didn't know where he was, but in the background she heard him laughing and shouting, 'It's a boy! I had a boy!' There was laughter, male voices. 'And everybody's fine?' he asked. 'Everybody? Our parents, everybody?'

'Yes. Nobody was hurt.'

'Unbelievable. I mean, that's unbelievable. Matthew,' he said, sniffing and then laughing again. 'Matthew!'

'He's healthy as a horse!' she said, a grin breaking through. 'Eight pounds, four ounces. He's red and pimply looking. He's so ugly he's cute.' He asked, and she told him about the delivery. Finally, she asked, 'Where are *you*?'

'Uhm' – his laughter came to an abrupt halt – 'well, I'm not supposed to say.'

'Oh, come on. You're joking.'

'No. You know, they don't want us to give that stuff out.'

'Do you think . . . is there any chance you're coming home?'

There was a long pause. 'I don't know.'

'Are you near any of the fighting?'

'What fighting?'

Melissa thought for a second. *Where on earth could he be that he*

couldn't find out what was happening? 'Well, they're calling it the
Phony War, like in Europe before the Blitzkrieg in 1940. But every
hour there's a special bulletin about some flare-up somewhere. Mainly
in Eastern Europe, but sometimes it'll be, like, the Mediterranean or
the Indian Ocean or off Hawaii. And there's this big Russian invasion
force near Iceland that nobody knows where it's going.'

Melissa waited for David to respond, but he was quiet. She tried hard
to come up with a question, some code, to ask him his whereabouts
that wouldn't lead to the same frustrating response, but before she could
speak he said, 'Honey, I don't have much time. Just five minutes total.
Can you tell me what the hell is going on?'

He's not in this country, she guessed, *or he'd know more. But where*?
'What do you mean? With the war zones? The White House calls them
"disaster sites," but everybody else – the news media, the Congress
– calls them the war zones. And you know about the Declaration
of War?'

'Yes.'

'Oh, and the impeachment trial in the Senate!'

'What about the Russian amphibious force?'

'The what?' Melissa asked.

'The Russian invasion force, off Iceland.'

Iceland! she thought. *What in God's name is he doing there*? 'It's . . .'
she began, suddenly wishing she had paid more attention to that story,
'they don't know where it's going, or if it's going anywhere. At first
they thought it might be headed toward Norway and the Norwegians
even shot at them, but then it kept going and is in the Norwegian Sea
and so they think' – she paused to swallow – 'they think it may be headed
toward Iceland.' A shot of fear trickled down her spine like ice water.

'And the navy is just going to let it go?' David asked, his voice
rising.

'Oh, I don't know, David.' He sounded so concerned that she began
to cry again. 'David, where are you?' she demanded, needing to know
something, anything, to arm herself for battle with the demons that
tormented her when she was alone. Surely the fears were unfounded.
He was in the reserves, not the real army. He put his uniform on and
went to meetings once a month, and then sat in an air-conditioned office
in Atlanta and pushed papers a couple of weeks every year!

'Are they going to impeach the President?' David asked, ignoring the
question.

Melissa shut her eyes, descending into melancholy as the tears
drained slowly from her, seeing the days and weeks stretch out before
her during which the fears, the demons, would run unchecked and wreak
havoc on her already fragile moods.

'Honey? Are they going to impeach President Livingston?'

With her eyes still closed, she said, 'I don't know,' in a monotone.

'The trial starts tomorrow. They say it'll be short, maybe only one day.'

'Honey, it's time. I've got to go.'

She realized suddenly that she had done all the talking, that he had asked all the questions. She had to have something, something to get her through the ordeal to come. 'David, oh, David, can't you tell me something? Anything *at all*?'

There was a pause. 'I love you, and I love Matthew,' and then the line was disconnected before she could answer.

90TH STRATEGIC MISSILE WING, WARREN AFB, WYOMING
June 23, 1100 GMT (0400 Local)

Chris Stuart poked at the shrimp Creole and chocolate pudding from the emergency rations as he reclined against the wall by the main ventilation duct. Sitting in the darkness and watching the wobbly light signal Langford's return from the escape tunnel, he breathed deeply the warm air that flowed gently from the metal grate – not fresh, but not the thick, stale air that hung heavy in the launch center toward the end of the ventilation system's down time.

The light now steadied, and Stuart could see it flash into the room and then appear at the doorway. He stood up and took the flashlight and Geiger counter from Langford. Waving the wand and light over Langford's protective garments, Stuart heard only an occasional tick of detection.

'You're clean,' he said, and Langford began to remove the gear. 'What's it like?'

Langford removed his hood and gas mask in one swipe and huffed a heavy sigh. 'Gets hot up at about the fifth or sixth rung from the top. Must be cookin' out there.'

'What about the escape hatch?' Stuart asked, too drained to sound as anxious as he felt about the answer.

'It was dogged tight, but I got it to turn,' Langford said. After a moment of quiet, Langford said, 'I vote we go for it.'

'You said it was still hot. Hell, it's less than two weeks. We'd be fried before we could get off the base.' Langford didn't respond. 'Look, we can hold out here for another month, I figure. By that time, the levels should be way down. Let's just keep our cool, use our heads.'

In the darkness, Stuart heard Langford's stomach churn with a violent liquid sound. Langford said, 'Oh, man,' with a tinge of pain and then, 'I gotta go.' He took the flashlight and ran off to the head, vomiting, as occasionally happened, from the stench after emptying his cramping bowels.

Stuart settled back in at the vent in the pitch darkness for the remaining few minutes before they turned the system off to conserve batteries. As always, he quietly rubbed the smooth, cool metal of his Beretta, his only sure way out.

SPECIAL FACILITY, MOUNT WEATHER, VIRGINIA
June 23, 1100 GMT (0600 Local)

Lambert knocked on the door to the President's quarters.

'Come in!' he heard, and he opened the door to hear the laughter of the President's son and to see the broad grin of the President.

'Oh, Greg!' President Livingston said, wiping his lips and getting up from the small table.

'I don't want to disturb you, sir,' he said, eyeing the First Lady and their two children, Nancy and Jack, who must have arrived during the night.

'No, nonsense,' he said walking around the table to greet him. 'Thanks for coming.'

The First Lady appeared right behind him. She paused just briefly with a look of deep sadness on her face and then reached out to embrace him. Lambert was at first uncomfortable, but when he felt her hand patting the back of his shoulders and heard her saying how sorry she was, he relaxed until she finally drew back, her cool hand cupping his cheek for one final look of compassion.

'Thank you,' he mumbled, his social graces failing him as he stood there confused. She had briefly broken through the barrier he had erected, and he didn't know how to act.

'Come with me for a minute, would you, Greg?' the President said, turning to lead him by the breakfast table and into his bedroom. As Greg passed the two children – Jack, the neatly groomed college student and their daughter Nancy, pretty but with hair shorn short on one side and flowing long on the other, multiple earrings running up one ear – they stared back at him with guarded interest. He nodded, but they didn't reciprocate.

I'm the guy who's going to testify against him, he thought. *I'm the enemy*.

The President closed the door to the bedroom behind him. 'Have a seat,' he said, motioning Lambert to the room's one chair while he sat on the unmade bed.

He hunched over immediately, resting his elbows on his knees and running his hands all the way up over his head to the back of his neck as he looked at the floor. He had changed completely, Lambert realized, once the door had been closed.

'I wonder what he's doing right now?' the President asked.

'Who, sir?' Lambert replied, his voice assuming the low and measured tone of the President's own. It was the tone of voice one used in the middle of the night when all were asleep. Or at a funeral.

'Razov. I wonder what he is doing right now? Does he have a place like this?' The President and then Lambert looked at the bare walls of the small room. Although you couldn't see the heavy stone just on the other side, the low ceilings and always inadequate lighting were an ever present reminder of the great weight that pressed in all around you.

'The Kremlin has a deep-underground command post, yes, sir.'

The President nodded as if he appreciated Lambert's help and then sighed deeply. 'Greg, here's the deal. Come this time tomorrow or the day after, I may be heading home to New York a private citizen.'

'Sir, they have no case. You haven't done anything—'

President Livingston held up his hand, and Lambert fell quiet. 'We'll just wait and see. But I called you in here in case the worst happens.' The President sat up and stretched his back, sitting more erect than before with his hands on the tops of his thighs. 'If I am convicted, and the Vice President accedes to the Presidency, there will be war. Are we ready for that war?'

Lambert opened his mouth to speak, hesitating as he turned the question over in his mind. Finally, he said, 'It'll be . . . we'll take casualties. The Russians are already probing across the European borders with regularity, as you know. They know where we are, and they'll be ready. And their subs have begun taking potshots at the Seventh Fleet in the Western Pacific, so they're wise to us there. They've picked up the pace, but it's nothing like what we'll get if the balloon really does go up.'

'And that balloon will go up the moment it becomes obvious that the impeachment vote will carry two-thirds of the Senate,' the President said, his eyes straying off into the distance. 'That's why I – and Vice President Costanzo – have discussed it with the Senate leadership, and they have agreed that a straw vote will be taken in secret prior to the real vote. If the results of the straw vote indicate that I will be impeached, there will be a four-hour delay before the real vote is taken.' He looked now at Lambert with total concentration. 'Four hours, do you understand?'

Lambert nodded.

'Get together with General Thomas. I'd do it myself, but my "handlers" say that I'm not supposed to show any sign of weakness. I'm supposed to be totally confident that I will win.'

'Do you think you will?' Lambert asked.

The President glanced once at the door and said, 'No, of course not.'

He ground his jaws as he stared off into space and said, 'It could be close, but the numbers haven't been there for days now.' He heaved a deep sigh and looked up. 'That's why I told my lawyers not to fight for more time by petitioning the Supreme Court at every twist and turn. The Senate leadership is right. We need to be done with this, and to move on.'

A long silence fell over them then, and after a respectful pause Lambert slowly rose to leave.

'One other thing, Greg,' the President said without looking up, and Lambert sank back into his chair. 'If I do lose, and we go to war . . .'

Lambert waited, but the President did not complete the sentence. 'Yes, sir?'

The President's stared off into space again. 'I'm just afraid.'

Lambert licked his lips and asked in as soft a voice as he could muster. 'Of what, sir?'

The President's gaze returned once again to Lambert, who sat directly in front of him. 'Those missiles – the submarines in the Bastion.'

Lambert struggled with his personal rationalization as to why he wasn't worried about that, why nobody screamed out the alarm. Finally, he shrugged. 'General Razov would have nothing to gain by firing those missiles at us. We'd just fire our submarines' missiles at his country; he knows that.'

'I didn't say anything about Razov firing those missiles. This whole thing was an accident. Who's to say it won't happen again, only this time it's the real thing, the one from everybody's worst nightmares?'

Lambert had no answer, and the President rubbed the palms of his hands on his pants legs. 'Well, anyway, what I wanted to say to you was that I want you to do what you can. I know Costanzo has said he would keep you and the rest of the national security team around if . . . if it happens, and I quite intentionally wanted to burden you with that fear, Greg, with the fear that I've borne ever since I first heard the word Bastion on the night this all started – because I trust you. You're an honorable man.' Livingston looked down and shook his head. 'Bastion – the word itself, I don't know, it just sounds . . . medieval, like the dark ages we came from.'

Lambert was at a loss. He knew the President needed someone to help share his burdens, but all he could think to say was, 'All we can do, sir, is pray.'

'To whom?' President Livingston asked, looking up at Lambert as if he had touched upon something of importance, something troubling. 'Pray to whom, Greg? I can't help feeling that all the gods are dead. All the gods are dead except the gods of Armageddon.'

Chapter Nine

CONGRESSIONAL FACILITY, WEST VIRGINIA
June 24, 1700 GMT (1200 Local)

'Hear ye, hear ye!' the sergeant at arms read as he looked down his nose through his reading glasses at the three-by-five card. 'The trial upon the Articles of Impeachment of Walter N. Livingston, President of the United States of America, shall now come to order! The Right Honorable William H. Rehnquist, Chief Justice of the Supreme Court, presiding.'

Lambert watched as the Chief Justice gaveled the trial to order from his bench hastily erected where the large underground chamber's speaker's podium had been. 'Will the sergeant at arms please read the Articles of Impeachment.'

As the man read the now familiar charges, Lambert's eyes strayed across the room. The Senators – the jury – were crammed into their seats, three at each desk meant for one to make room for the 'gallery' filled with Congressmen, the press, ambassadors from several dozen nations, and other luminaries who had trekked down to the subterranean facility for the historic proceeding. Down in front were counsels' tables. The House 'managers,' six Congressmen chosen to prosecute the charges contained in the Articles of Impeachment approved by the House of Representatives – three Democrats and three Republicans – sat at the table on the right with their constitutional scholars and lawyers. The President's men – the Attorney General, who had resigned that morning to lead the defense, and several other defense lawyers – sat at the table on the left.

Lambert sat in the front row on the far left, along with General Thomas and numerous other potential witnesses, including even the Secret Service agents who had accompanied the President on the night of the nuclear attack. Lambert had been told, however, that few of the witnesses could be expected to be called to testify. The facts were not in dispute, and the normal evidentiary procedures of a court trial were not strictly applicable.

The sergeant at arms completed his reading and took his seat below the Chief Justice's bench. 'Let it be shown,' Justice Rehnquist said, 'that the Senate has received these Articles of Impeachment and that the Chief Justice of the Supreme Court was so informed. Let it also be shown that the Senate duly served a summons on the President of the United States, Walter N. Livingston, reciting the Articles of Impeachment and requesting an answer to the charges. The President has chosen not to appear at this trial in person, but be it noted that he has answered and is represented by counsel.'

The former Attorney General stood and nodded at the Chief Justice, and the cameras turned to him and then back to the bench. Lambert knew the President, his family at his side at Mount Weather, would be watching now as Chief Justice Rehnquist rummaged through the papers on his desk.

'Would the Senators present please stand and raise your right hands?'

There was the sound of movement and scraping chairs as ninety-seven Senators rose. The ninety-eighth, Senator Clark, lay gravely ill of radiation sickness as of the latest report. Lambert looked up at the men and women, rising up in the auditorium-style chamber to his right to stand with right hands raised.

'Do you solemnly swear to well and faithfully discharge your duties as Senators of the United States and to do impartial justice in the proceeding that will follow?'

'I do,' was heard from the many voices nearly all at once.

'Please be seated.' Again the sounds disrupted the quiet but then quickly died down. 'Because a state of war exists between our country and the Republic of Russia' – a man in blue jeans with a minicam ran quickly to stand right in front of Lambert and General Thomas, the red light on his camera blinking on – 'many of the rules of this body governing the conduct of an impeachment trial have, out of a desire to expedite the proceeding and resolve the issues raised, been suspended by previous vote of the Senate.'

'And I object, Your Honor, to such suspension. The President is entitled to due process under the law, and—'

'The Supreme Court has already ruled on your petition and held eight to one that the rule-making power of the Senate is, subject to the few procedures and rights expressly set out in the Constitution, absolute. And let me take this opportunity to make this point clear to you and to all who watch this proceeding, both within this chamber and outside it. This is not a trial under the criminal laws of the United States. It is a trial under the Constitution. The rules of evidence and of procedure in a criminal trial, and the rights of an individual accused of a crime in this country, do not therefore come into play. The President, were he to be convicted by the Senate in this trial, would then become fully subject to the criminal laws of these United States, but this proceeding will have no precedential value whatsoever as to any such matter. It is a trial to determine *not* whether the President has violated any laws, but whether the nature of the charges brought against him by the House of Representatives in the Articles of Impeachment warrant, in the opinion of two-thirds of the Senators present, his removal from office.'

The Chief Justice went on to read the rules. All rules of procedure and evidence were what the Chief Justice said they were, although the full Senate could, by vote, overrule him. Senators could submit questions to be asked by the Chief Justice, who could also ask questions in his own discretion. There would be no debate by Senators during the trial, but shortly before a vote was taken there would be a closed-door session, with public and press barred, during which Senators could debate subject to a fifteen-minute time limit to prevent filibusters.

Lambert forced himself not to look at General Thomas. It was then, during the closed session, that the straw poll would be taken. It was then, if two-thirds of the Senators voted against the President, that the war would begin. Lambert's mind reeled with the facts and figures and plans that were being made ready.

The trial began, but Lambert's mind drifted to the details of the job that had seeped into every single second of his existence these last couple of weeks. His eye roamed the battlefields far and wide, seeing the death and great destruction that even now was being stored up like a spring slowly coiled to maximum tension, a spring that would be loosed by the vote of the sixty-six men and women seated around that underground chamber.

LOS ANGELES, CALIFORNIA
June 24, 2200 GMT (1400 Local)

'No, Mom, I'm not picking him up too much,' Melissa said, rolling her eyes as she held Matthew and watched the trial on television, the phone pressed to her ear.

'I always thought you'd be one who holds the baby 'round the clock,' her mother said with an annoying laugh delivered, in her mother's mind, Melissa knew, to disguise and soften the criticism. Melissa ground her teeth. 'I know I've told you this before, but if you hold him too much he'll be spoiled. Sometimes it's best just to let him cry. No child has ever had anything bad go wrong from just crying, for goodness sakes.'

Melissa had quit concentrating on the phone, watching instead as the camera focused on the tall blond man, a deeply sad look writ all across his face, seated among the generals in the front row of the Senate chamber.

'I just wish the airlines were running so your father and I could come out there and take care of that poor child.'

'Mom,' Melissa said, fumbling with the remote, 'I want to see what's going on in the trial.'

'What?'

'On television. The trial.'

'Oh, that.' She laughed. 'You do keep his diapers clean, don't you?'

'Mom, I'll call you later,' Melissa said, as she demuted the television.

'The decision cleared the way for Gregory Lambert, national security adviser, to testify before the Senate in what will surely be the most dramatic testimony of the trial,' the low voice of ABC's legal commentator said as the camera shifted back to the Chief Justice.

'. . . rash that can be just awful, you mark my words, Missy. Are you listening to me, darling?'

'Bye-bye, Mom.' Melissa hung up, knowing that she would have to pay for the act later.

The Chief Justice said, 'On motion from Senator Stern, duly seconded and resolved, this chair calls to the stand Mr Gregory Philip Lambert.'

CONGRESSIONAL FACILITY, WEST VIRGINIA
June 24, 2200 GMT (1700 Local)

'Now,' the Congressman, one of the 'managers' from the House whose job it was to prosecute the President, said as he looked at his notes, 'you have testified that on the night of June eleventh you were working late at the White House.'

'Yes,' Lambert said, trying to remain unfazed by the glare of the television cameras and the huge bundle of microphones in front of him with network letters and station call signs of various sorts written on them.

'What is your position?'

'I am the Special Assistant to the President for National Security.'

'Now, Mr Lambert, you have testified that the President telephoned the late Secretary Moore on the night of June eleventh. What did President Livingston say to Secretary Moore?'

'He told the Secretary to inform the Chinese of the impending nuclear attack on their country by the Russians.' Lambert heard the rush of gasps and muted conversations and saw out of the corners of his eyes some reporters at the side of the room dash out through the doors.

Chief Justice Rehnquist hammered his gavel down three times and said, in a loud voice, 'There will be order in this chamber or I'll have it cleared!'

When the noise died down, the Congressman said, 'Can you recall any of the exact words that the President used when he directed the

Secretary of State to forewarn the Chinese of the impending Russian attack?'

'He said "I'll not be a party to this," or something like that,' Lambert said.

'"I will not be a party to this"?' the manager repeated slowly, half-turning to the 'jury' of Senators as if this were the county courthouse. Lambert nodded. 'And what did Secretary Moore say, if anything?'

Lambert thought for a second, then said, 'Nothing.'

'Did he object? Tell the President that what he was doing was ill advised?'

Lambert thought about that night again. Jane had still been alive then. Swallowing, he said, 'It sounded like Secretary Moore began to object, but the President cut him off.'

'He cut him off.' The manager shook his head at the dastardly behavior of the President. 'How did the President cut him off? What words did he use?'

'I don't remember. He just told him to do it,' Lambert said.

'"Just do it"?' the Congressman repeated.

'Something like that.'

'No questions asked?' he said as he swept his hand up into the air, turning from Lambert to walk toward the gallery. 'No discussion? No consultation with military experts with whom he could easily have been in contact to discuss the *ramifications* of such a *monumentally* significant blunder?'

'No,' Lambert said to the Congressman's back.

'Did *you* try to stop the President, Mr Lambert? Did you say anything?'

'Yes.'

'And what was the President's response?'

'He couldn't hear me. We were on the White House lawn. The noise of the helicopter that had landed to take us to Andrews – Crown Helo, it's called – made continuation of our telephone call over the portable phone impossible.' The thought tormented him for the hundredth time. He could have saved her, if only he had stopped the President.

'And you tried, but he couldn't hear you?' She was alive, unharmed, as healthy as a person could be, flushed with a summer tan from the tennis lessons she worked so hard on to give them a sport they could play together. Together, for the rest of their lives, that was the way it was supposed to be. 'Because of the noise of a helicopter?' Her eyes were blue, but when she wore her green sundress they turned green. She was magic. 'Mr Lambert?'

'Uh, I . . . I called out over the portable phone' – his mind was wandering, and he didn't fight too hard to keep it focused – 'and I ran across the lawn, but when I got to the helicopter they took off immediately.' *Why did you let this happen, God? How could you do this?* 'I could barely make it to a seat. The ride was . . . wild – very low.' *Like the helicopter ride to find Jane's lifeless body.* He had carried her body in his arms. It had been different. She felt heavier than he remembered, different because every time before she had wrapped her arms around his neck, made it easier, made herself lighter. She was magic.

'Mr Lambert,' the Congressman asked in a kindly voice, 'I only have one other question for you. You were on board the President's Airborne Command Post during the nuclear attack together with the Joint Chiefs of Staff, were you not?'

'Yes.'

'And did this topic come up?'

'Yes. The Joint Chiefs were speculating as to how it was that the Chinese fired their missiles, and I told them of the conversation that the President had with Secretary Moore.' Out of the corner of his eye, he saw Colonel Rutherford, General Thomas's aide, whispering in Thomas's ear.

'And what was their reaction?'

'They were surprised – shocked, I guess you'd say.'

'And why do you suppose that was?'

'Because it was that forewarning that allowed the Chinese time to generate their missiles, and it was the Chinese missile attack on the Russians that prompted the Russians to mistakenly fire at us.'

A rush of voices rose up from the crowd now and filled the chamber.

'I have no other questions,' the Congressman said and returned to his table.

'Mr Dodson?' the Chief Justice said, and the old gentleman who was President Livingston's long-time lawyer rose, buttoning his jacket.

'I have only one question, Your Honor.' He looked at Lambert. 'What, sir, is your opinion of President Livingston?'

There were a few muted whispers around the chamber at that question, and Lambert searched his brain for an answer. After a long pause during which the lawyer waited patiently, Lambert said, 'I think President Livingston is the most decent man I have ever met.' He began to say something about Livingston the President, but he stopped short, closing his mouth instead and falling silent.

Dodson nodded. 'No further questions, Your Honor,' he said as he unbuttoned his jacket and sat.

'You are dismissed, Mr Lambert,' the Chief Justice said.

Lambert walked back to his seat in a daze, the memories of her so fresh he felt he could reach out and touch her. Thomas was chopping an outstretched palm with the heel of his hand as he spoke rapidly and angrily to Rutherford. Rutherford nodded and started to leave, but Thomas grabbed his arm and said something more to which the colonel nodded again and then strode briskly for the side door, breaking into a run once he was through the door and into the hallway.

As the House managers called their next witness, Lambert sat, looking over at Thomas, whose knitted brow betrayed deep concern. Thomas put his hand on Lambert's forearm, and Lambert leaned to meet Thomas halfway between their chairs.

'The Russians are landing on Iceland,' Thomas whispered. Lambert looked up at his face, at his grinding jaw, just as Thomas's head jerked in silent curse. 'Just sailed right up and put troops ashore.' He was shaking his head. 'They've got airborne troops coming down all over Reykjavik. They'll have aircraft operating out of there in a few hours.' His head jerked again, but this time Lambert heard an audible 'Shit!'

It was a military disaster, Lambert knew, but it was something more. He looked back up at the Senators. The vote was only hours away. With word that Iceland was going to fall with hardly a fight after the newspapers and television had trumpeted the risk for days, there would be hell to pay. And it would be Livingston who would pay it.

GANDER AIRPORT, NEWFOUNDLAND
June 25, 0200 GMT (2200 Local)

There were soldiers and airmen everywhere, engineers laying metal gratelike sections of tarmac off to the side of the concrete for additional parking areas, bladders of fuel and pallets of equipment rolling down the brightly lit rear ramps of giant C-5A and C-17 transports, tent cities going up with astonishing rapidity, fighter-bombers roaring off in pairs with flames shooting out the rear. Iceland was, he had heard, close to falling to Russian paratroopers and marines. The battle was on, but the routine established by Chandler and his men and women over the last two weeks was unchanged. Nobody knew who they were or what was going to happen to them.

'Jackpot!' 'Ho-o-o, man!' 'Lordy, lordy!' Chandler slowly approached the commotion as he wandered down the corridor. A small clump of soldiers stood among the much larger group that lay on their bags all along the windowless stretch of concourse. They were laughing good-naturedly and punching the shoulder of a man – a boy, really, who looked to Chandler to still be in his teens – around whom they formed a semicircle as he gathered his gear. As the tall, skinny boy left to follow a private to a door, Chandler surmised that he had finally gotten his orders and was off. *Lucky bastard*!

Through the open door to which the boy was led, Chandler saw another group of soldiers kneeling in the harsh, artificial light of the tarmac, their gear resting around them, and he stopped to stare. All were on their knees, facing in the same direction. An arm extended down, cut off from its body by the doorframe. The arm wafted gracefully down to the mouth of the soldier nearest the door, his face black with greasepaint. The soldier stuck his tongue out and drew the small wafer into his mouth, bowing his head to pray. The arm with no body made the sign of a cross and rested for a second on the stubble of the man's head, palm down.

The boy in the doorway put his cap on as he exited. Chandler's last sight of him was as he clamped his hand on his cap to keep from losing it in the backblast of jet engines.

You wouldn't want to lose a cap like that, Chandler thought. *It takes a year of training to win a Green Beret.*

He wandered on down the concourse, his mind blurring as he came to a glass-walled section. As the dim rays of the setting sun bathed the tarmac in faint light, he saw Special Forces troops filing up the rear ramp of a transport, even their strong backs bowed under the weight of their weapons, existence loads, and parachutes. Chandler felt the goose bumps rise on his chest and arms as he imagined where they were headed, what lay in store for them upon their arrival.

'You lookin' for somebody, Major?' a man with a gravelly voice standing unnoticed off to Chandler's right asked.

'Well . . .' Chandler started to say 'Top' when he saw the man was a first sergeant, the highest ranking NCO in a company-size field unit, but stopped, uncomfortable with the word. 'I'm trying to find out when my men and I get out of here. We've been stuck in Gander for two weeks.'

'You pro'bly oughta ask the flyboys at the operations center downtown,' Top said, pulling up on his pistol belt from which hung a 9-mm Beretta.

Chandler smiled and shook his head. He'd been wandering around for hours, ever since the transports started flooding the airport during the afternoon. *Sure*, he thought, *that makes sense. The army is at the airport, and the air force is in the town.* 'What's going on with Iceland?'

'Oh,' Top said, rocking from heel to toe, 'our fearless leader gave it to the Russians, and now he wants us to go get it back. Sort of an Indian giver.' Chandler could sense the first Sergeant's ease in speaking to him, to a major. He had noticed before a stiffness of manner when he had spoken to most army enlisted men and women, but Top's world was spent giving orders to sergeants on the one side and reports to officers on the other. He was the liaison between the two worlds of the enlisted and the commissioned, and he was comfortable in both.

Despite being anxious to move on, Chandler politely asked the first sergeant when he was off. He got a bigger reaction than he'd bargained for.

'Oh! Well, ya see, Major,' Top spat the words out bitterly, a smile on his lips but not in his eyes, 'this is as far as I *go*.' He grew agitated, rocking and straightening his belt again. 'I'm too *valuable*, ya see,' he said, nodding his head at Chandler, his lips pulled thin over his teeth. 'It's only World War Fuckin' *Three*! They're *savin'* me, ya see, sir,' the first sergeant continued. 'Couldn't *risk* it – need *me* here!' He waved his arm ceremoniously over the hangar, which was filled with soldiers lying lazily on the floor with nothing to do. Chandler looked back at Top. The man was furious. His eyes, however, scanned the hangar. His head jerked as his eyes picked up a target – two o'clock, moving, twenty meters.

'*Hey you! Soldier!*' Chandler jumped involuntarily on the first word, like at the sound of a door slamming unexpectedly. '*Yeah you,*' Top continued, '*you sad-sack piece o' shit!*'

Chandler's reaction paled in comparison to that of the lounging enlisted men. For a radius of about fifty meters every eye was now on Top. Arms once draped over the faces of soundly sleeping soldiers flew up, and heads were raised. Conversations were halted, and soldiers froze in their tracks. The alarm was general – but just long enough to see that the object of Top's salutation was someone else. Then there was only mild interest, a perverse sense of enjoyment. '*There but for the Grace of God . . .*' Chandler thought.

"Scuse me a second, sir,' Top said, politely. 'Just tryin' to get these little boys ready, ya know, for what's comin'.' Chandler nodded.

Top never again raised that awesome voice, that force erupting from deep in his barrel chest born of a career of exercise. He didn't need it. The soldier – at rigid attention, almost visibly quivering – was jellified by the mere whispers of the first sergeant, whispers projected at the private from close range.

The older man exhibited that tendency of NCOs, perfected by drill instructors, to invade a soldier's space. His behavior was, in fact, quite reminiscent of a DI, which was seldom encountered once you joined a unit. *A crash course in discipline*, Chandler thought as he watched. *Exhibition games are over. It's time for the regular season.*

Top never appeared to be on the verge of raising his hand to strike the poor soul, but flinches and small jars shook the soldier's body as if blows were landed. Contrary to popular impression among the civilian population, Chandler knew, one of the surest ways to find your career in the military ended – and possibly a new one begun in the stockade – was to strike a subordinate. But the threat of physical suffering at the hands of the vastly more accomplished NCO was always there just beneath the surface. The persona of the senior NCO, no matter what their physical stature or age, could be summed up with the words they almost never had to use: 'Don't fuck with me.'

The private's was the only voice you could hear. 'Yes, First Sergeant!' 'Yes, First Sergeant!' Never 'Sir' – only officers were 'Sir.' You didn't insult an NCO more than once in your military life with that mistake. And not 'Sergeant' either. Sergeants were 'buck sergeants' – three chevrons forming inverted Vs, and only three. Upon promotion, you get rockers underneath the chevrons and a new title, and neither were to be taken from you by the sloppy terminology of some mere private. One rocker: staff sergeant. Two: platoon sergeant. Three: master sergeant. And three with a diamond in the middle: 'Top.'

'Yes, First Sergeant!' the private, ever correct, barked crisply. Chandler watched as Top roamed the contours of the boy's face and head. At an altitude of about one inch, the teacher was instructing the pupil in the errors of his ways. His nose to the boy's nose, then descending off that prominence and onto the plain of the private's cheek in order for Top to turn his ear to hear the wimpy answer, shouted at the top of the private's lungs – 'Yes, First Sergeant!' Top finally returned to Chandler.

'Sorry about that, sir,' Top said, shaking his head as he watched the soldier depart. Chandler had detected nothing wrong in the first place, but the first sergeant seemed to think the boy was irredeemable. The private, Chandler noted, no longer headed in his prior direction but dropped instead against the wall to rest after a short distance. *Mission, whatever it'd been, aborted.*

'Well,' Chandler said, 'I think I'll be off,' and turned to go.

'Sir.' Chandler stopped and looked back at the older man. Top wore a troubled look on his face as he removed his helmet and swiped a hand over the gray stubble on his tanned head. Looking at Chandler and squinting as he replaced the helmet, he said, 'You got kids, sir?'

Chandler froze at the unexpected question. 'I've got a son.' It was the first time in his life he'd ever uttered those words.

The first sergeant scanned the row of men who lay resting on their gear and said, 'Good. I don't much care for officers that ain't got no sons.' Top's eyes drilled back into Chandler, the intensity of the look so great as to cause Chandler to avert his gaze. In so doing, he looked down at the men lying closest to him. Big, sweaty, dirty men. All of them sons, somebody's sons. Above the men, the near total darkness of the now empty tarmac made a mirror of the window, and in the darkened glass Chandler saw his image reflected.

Standing there, the features of his face indistinct in the dim reflection, Chandler saw a man in mottled green, brown, and black camouflage fatigues and combat boots, wearing his helmet and fighting load, an M-16 slung over his shoulder.

Pretty good impersonation, Chandler thought. *Even fooled Top.*

CONGRESSIONAL FACILITY, WEST VIRGINIA
June 25, 0300 GMT (2200 Local)

Henry Dodson, the President's lawyer, rose to address the Senate. He had a kindly smile, like that of an old man whom the years had mellowed. His slight stoop, short silver hair, and bow tie dated him to an age long gone. His blue eyes, however, hinted that the torch of life still burned brightly within him.

With a smile he bowed slightly to the Chief Justice and then turned to the Senators. 'You hold the world in your hands.' The only sound Lambert heard was the whirring of the movie camera not three feet from his head. 'It is yours to dispose of as you wish. Will there be war? Peace? Nuclear oblivion? Is this a time for healing, or the end of the world? Those are the great questions that spin in your head. It's enough to make a man dizzy with the weight of it. But, luckily enough, it's not the question before you today.

'This is a trial of one man, Walter Nathaniel Livingston, President of the United States of America, and there are only two facts, when you boil it all down, that are of any significance whatsoever. President Livingston was informed of a dastardly attack by the Russians against China, a nuclear surprise attack that would certainly bring about massive death and destruction in that most populous nation. From that moment forward he had two choices: remain silent, thereby tacitly becoming a party to a great and tragic villainy, or refuse to subject himself, and with him this nation, to that indignity. To live *up* to the ideals of this peace-loving country, and forewarn a fellow member of the family of nations of the coming storm of fire and death.' He stopped and looked up, adding almost perfunctorily, 'He chose the latter, and that, ladies and gentlemen, is fact number one.

'We all know what happened next. The Russians fired at the Chinese, the Chinese returned fire, and an obscure Russian general in Moscow who had, unbeknownst to the rest of the world, only just seized control of their nuclear arsenal mistakenly fired a massive volley of warheads at *our* homeland in an attack that, although *horrific*, was nonetheless mistaken.

'Tempers run hot, white hot, after such disasters. You cannot blame anyone for a flood. You cannot rail against anyone but perhaps a deity for a hurricane, or an earthquake, or a tornado. But we Americans have a *President*, a real flesh-and-blood man, to blame for all that has happened. We were *attacked!*' he shouted. 'A *thousand* nuclear weapons rained down on us! And it's *his* fault! *His!* *The President's!* Walter Nathaniel Livingston!'

The old lawyer took in the whole of the room now, with one slow sweep of his shaking head, his lips pursed. 'That anger, that pressure, built up, and slowly but surely it found a vent. Demonstrations. Burnings and lootings of stores whose owners had Russian names. The ransacking of impounded Russian freighters. A Declaration of *War*,' he said eyeing the Senate, 'the ultimate vent to *all* of our anger!'

He dropped now to a low tone, exhausted, it seemed, by his one-man battle. 'This may well be the last voice you hear on the subject of peace for quite a while. What lies between my words tonight and that next counsel whose voice will rise from the charred landscape like a fresh green sprout to say, "Enough"? Death, more death, and, unless we are all *very*, very lucky, possibly the end of the world. For you see, this war that everyone seems to want is not about issues, about establishing who is right in the surest way we as a species have developed – by imposition of justice by the conqueror over the conquered. This war of yours is about *punishment*, pure and simple.

'But the Russians *have* paid, haven't they? They have paid, and now, ladies and gentlemen, here, today, it is time for the death and destruction to stop. And what if it doesn't? What if the war goes on? They too have suffered the hammering blows from the sky. Do you imagine that the Russians are inclined to bow to our demands that they lie down at our feet and lick our *boots*? That is *madness – absurd*! And, ladies and gentlemen, it is dangerous.

'President Walter Livingston knows what lies ahead if war be our path. We will call upon our men and women to fight and die for what cause? We press home our attack, and if, God forbid, we are successful, it can have but *one* result! If we roll over their country, slaying all who rise up in its defense, scorching the earth that shakes under the treads of our mighty war machines, swooping down from the skies like great birds of some long-ago nightmare, what is it that awaits us? Is it glorious victory? A parade, with the head of General Razov on a stick at the lead?'

He shook his head slowly. 'If their patriots are anything like our own – and I fear, ladies and gentlemen of the Senate, that they are – then you and I both know what the last act of this tragedy will be. As our conquering troops close in, at the moment of our greatest triumph, the groping hand of that dying Russian patriot will bravely seize upon that last remaining instrument of war at his disposal, and in that spasm of death will *unleash* the Four Horsemen of the Apocalypse, and the fires of hell will consume us all.

'Walter Livingston knows this. Walter Livingston is all that stands between us and that end. Leave him there, in the office to which he was elected. Let him go down in history as the greatest coward, the most infamous villain, that this nation has ever known, but leave him there in his office – to save us. To save our nation, to save our world, from destruction.'

U.S.S. NASSAU, SEA OF JAPAN
June 25, 0300 GMT (1300 Local)

'. . . six, seven, eight, nine, *ten*! Yeah, buddy! Stu-u-u-d! Tol' ya you could do it.'

Marine Lance Corporal Terrence Monk spun his leg up and over the bench on which he had been pressing 220 pounds. The sounds of clacking iron weights and grunting men with spotters and squadmates urging them on filled the large open compartment of the amphibious assault ship.

'Shi-i-i-t, man!' Mouth shouted. 'Ain't *nobody* gonna touch T Man but Bone. You up for it, Bone?'

Monk got up off the bench, sweat pouring from every pore in his body, drenching his red USMC T-shirt until it looked black. The ship's exercise room was humid, its special air conditioning precisely matching the norms of temperature and humidity for June on the Far East Pacific coast as part of the acclimatization system.

The hulking Oklahoma boy they called Bone – short for 'Bone Crusher' Crenshaw – stepped up to Monk and stood menacingly in his face before lying down on the bench. The other members of First Squad added beat-up black five-pound weights to each end of the bar and fastened them on.

'Spot me,' Bone said to the men over him, who grinned, enjoying the masochistic end to their twice daily workout.

Two of the men hoisted the heavy bar off the rack. 'You got it?' a tall gangling man named Stick asked. Bone nodded, not wasting on the effort of speaking the heavy puffs of breath that he was storing.

His arms buckled and the bar came down. Slowly he pushed it back up. 'One!' the men counted off. Down and up. 'Two!'

Monk watched without joining the others in the count as Bone slowly approached the requisite minimum to score the victory. His mind wandered as the sounds of other Marines' shouts and profanity echoed through the enclosed space. '*Ten*! You done it, Bone man!' Mouth shouted.

But Bone wasn't through. With the greatest of efforts, his face red and the veins at his temples bulging, Bone lowered the weights one more time.

'Whoa! Shit, man! Bone ain't through, unh-uh!' Mouth said in his annoyingly hyperactive manner. Bone's press back up was labored and slow. At one point about halfway, the bar ceased rising and the spotters moved to grab it, but Bone let a burst of air out in a loud growl and drew another breath, resuming his effort. The bar rose.

'*Eleven*!' the group yelled as the spotters moved the bar back onto the rack. Bone stood up, his face beet red and sweat dripping off his jaw, and

faced Monk, Bone towering over the much more compact man. Standing
close, Bone stared at him for a moment and then brushed by, heading
for the showers.

Monk and the rest of the men of his rifle squad gathered their towels
and followed.

'You men sweat all that bad shit out?' boomed from off to the group's
left, emanating from a barrel-chested man. The small group of marines
snapped to rigid attention. Being the senior man, Monk cautiously
turned his head to face the lieutenant colonel, who stood there with
sweat glowing amid the gray stubble on his head, his PT or 'Physical
Training' gear dark with perspiration.

'Yes, *sir*!' Monk replied, barking out the 'sir' in proper form.

'Excellent, excellent,' the lieutenant colonel said, "cause this is the
last PT we're gonna get for a while. You men carry on.'

They continued tentatively on to the showers, not talking until they
were some distance from the officer. One of the new arrivals to the
squad, which had been brought up to full strength only after the Russian
nuclear attack, ran up from behind and said, 'Hey! Hey, guys! I heard
we got an all-hands call down on the well deck at twenty-one hundred.
This may be it!'

'Say?' Mouth whined. 'Who the fuck are you, man? What the fuck do
you know? We was jus' rappin' with the colonel, and I know my man
woulda tol' me if—'

'Where'd you hear that?' Monk interrupted.

'Some guys over in Headquarters Company say the CO was up all
night last night goin' over things.'

'That don't mean nothin', shitface,' Mouth said. 'Pro'bly in there
whackin' off.'

'Yeah, well, Armed Forces Radio outa Japan said the Senate is gettin'
ready to vote. They said all personnel who aren't on medical leave
should return to base and that if they impeach the President that we're
at war.'

'They said that on AFR?' Mouth asked, the pitch of his skeptical voice
stuck at the highest level possible.

'Well . . . the stuff about the vote, and about everybody getting back
on base.'

The opinions as to whether they would see action or whether the
Russians would back down flooded out of the older men, those in their
early twenties who had been in the Corps for a couple of years now.
Monk's thoughts and his gaze drifted. Off at one end of the large exercise
room unnoticed by the majority of its occupants, Monk saw a detail of
sailors quietly breaking down the exercise equipment and stowing it
along a bulkhead. A second detail was bolting metal frames in pairs
into brackets on the deck, each upright about six feet from its mate.
As they reached the showers, Monk stopped to watch the 'Squids.'

The frames were going up in rows, and each pair had a rod sticking up above it with four hooks protruding from the rod. Hooks for IV bags, frames for litters to be placed on them. Monk's eyes followed the regular pattern of brackets along the deck. They ran the full length of the huge compartment.

GANDER, NEWFOUNDLAND
June 25, 0500 GMT (0100 Local)

'Can you at least tell me where the bathroom is?' Chandler asked.

The air force lieutenant looked up, black bags underneath his red eyes. 'Men's locker room,' he said.

Chandler was fed up with the effort of trying to find something out about his predicament and needed to get back to his people, but this was obviously the right place, and he would try a few more desks before he gave up.

Squeaking across the floor of the basketball court-turned-operations center – its hardwood surface coated with condensation presumably caused by the ice rink that lay under it – Chandler entered the locker room. The conversations inside were mainly just random chatter, centering around the national sport of American males: 'shit-giving.'

As Chandler entered one of the stalls, his heart leapt when he saw a newspaper at his feet. It was opened to the middle and fat from having gotten wet and then dried. He picked it up and searched for the first page of the section. The New York Times! Chandler realized with a surge of anticipation as he saw the page, splattered with heavy black headlines.

It was a gold mine of information. One after another the headlines rocked Chandler, his jaw dropping with each revelation. The world was exploding with change. WILL PRESIDENT LIVINGSTON DISSOLVE NATO? the large type of one headline read, and underneath, two different stories in two columns: U.S. CONSIDERS NEW PACT WITH BRITISH, OTHERS and FRANCE AND GERMANY REFUSE TO SUPPORT U.S.

Chandler quickly scanned the first article. 'Secretary of State Anderson last night began negotiation of a new "Treaty on Euro-American Military Security" with his counterparts from the United Kingdom, Italy, Canada, Poland, the Czech and Slovak Republics, Hungary, Iceland, Greece and Turkey. "TEAMS" would, if approved by the newly combative Congress (see story on p. 17), establish a political and military alliance among the signatories that could replace NATO upon its collapse, which appears imminent.'

'President Authorizes Full Mobilization,' another major headline read; DRAFT TO BE UNIVERSAL FOR MALES, the smaller line beneath it read.

'Despite the controversy with Congress, the President signed an order authorizing the Selective Service Administration to begin the call-up of all males and of up to thirty-five percent of all females, between the ages of eighteen and twenty. Administration spokesmen went to great lengths to assure the Russian government that the influx of personnel, which could ultimately swell the ranks of the armed forces with up to 2,750,000 men and 500,000 women, was by no means intended to be perceived as a threat of continued hostilities. Senior members of the Livingston Administration also asserted that the inductions would be staged over many months and perhaps years, and that after basic training, recruits would not necessarily be posted to combat units but might instead be used to rebuild war-damaged sites in the U.S. Despite those assertions, however, defense analysts around the world are viewing the announcement of a major call-up as another of a series of signs coming out of Washington in past days that the inception of general hostilities is viewed as imminent.'

In the middle of the page, a grainy photo's caption read 'U.S.S. *Fife* limps into Yokohama. Dozens feared perished. Japanese gather at docks to protest ship's presence.' Chandler studied the photo of the wounded ship. It was small – a destroyer – and it was listing. Smoke billowed out of a black tear in its side, streaming back only slightly toward the stern as water was sprayed onto its superstructure by a fireboat. *What blows had she absorbed?* Chandler wondered.

It was then Chandler noticed that the banter had died down in the locker room. He heard a few people greeting a recent entrant. After the greetings, the room fell virtually silent again but for the sound of running water.

'I mean, there wa'n't a thing you could do,' someone said. 'Not one fuckin' thing, man.'

'Thanks.'

Chandler looked back at the front page. A small blurb announced a permanent suspension of the baseball season.

From a new, tentative voice, Chandler heard, 'What was it like?'

In the pause that followed, Chandler looked down at the lower left-hand side of the newspaper's front page. Two articles were set inside a dark border: the day's editions of some special series on the nuclear war. 'The Death of Great Falls, Montana' and '"All I Saw Was the Flash,"' a quote from some guy in Rome, New York. Chandler found nothing about March Air Force Base.

It was the silence that drew Chandler's attention. The room was full of people, and the silence was deafening.

'We were all over the place. Shit was flying off the racks. A coupla guys who were headin' back from the shitter – they went flyin' too, right straight through the air like they was in space or somethin'.'

'How'd they get ya?' the first questioner asked gently.

'A recon flight of Foxbats tryin' to sneak in all the way 'round from the south of Iceland, and along we come, fat, dumb, and happy. We was droppin' Special Forces types out on some old lava fields outside Reykjavik and soon as we went feet dry . . . I had my 'chute on 'cause I was workin' the jump when we started a hard roll. Cap'n Ames musta laid into it with everything he had. A full, wing-over port roll in a fuckin' C-141. You could feel it in your legs, they kinda started bucklin' – and all hell was breakin' loose. I called the flight engineer, and he said, 'Bandits, bandits!' and then, 'They got us. Oh, shit, man, they got us.' You could hear buzzers and tones in the cockpit – stall warning, radar threat, everything.'

He paused again, this time for a while. He took a deep, ragged breath. 'It was sorta . . . sorta sick'nin', you know, from the Gs. He stood us' – probably some hand gestures, Chandler guessed – 'I mean, almost up on the tail. It wa'n't more'n . . .' He paused, choking on the words.

Chandler – and probably the rest of his audience – hung there, suspended in the air on the huge transport plane. Seconds passed. The missile would have hit by now. Chandler could almost hear the boom. *How loud?* Chandler wondered. *What could it have possibly been like?*

'The tail – it just plain blew off. I sorta twisted around to look back. There just weren't nothin' back there. You could look right out at the ground. And *shit*.' The man struggled to continue. Again there was a pause, but then he continued, his voice strained. 'Everything was just flyin' *out*, and . . .'

'Hey, it'll be okay, man,' somebody said.

'. . . so I just up and jumped,' the storyteller said with a loud, ragged sigh. 'I popped the service door and jumped. We was still goin' up, but everything was creakin' and groanin' and the wind was howlin'. I thought about callin' the cockpit, to let 'em know what was happenin', and' – he struggled again – 'but, shit, ya know, the plane was . . . ya know, it was' – his voice faltered again, quaking as he forced himself to finish – 'spinnin' sideways like – you never felt anything like that before – and . . . shit!' Chandler sat there, his head bowed, the only noise the beating of his heart. From the sounds of it, the storyteller was older, some sort of crew chief, maybe. Those were *his* men, and he'd bailed out on them. There was no question among his audience that he'd done the right thing. He knew that but wasn't interested and got no comfort from others saying so. There would be no death of the monster that now haunted his soul. *Those were* his *men, and he'd bailed out on them.*

LOS ANGELES, CALIFORNIA
June 25, 0800 GMT (0000 Local)

'What do you think's going to happen?' Lisa, Melissa's best friend, asked over the phone as Melissa sat on the sofa, the room lit only by the flickering light of the TV as she gave Matthew his midnight feeding.

'I don't know. They'll impeach him, I guess.' Melissa was practically whispering, but even so she could not hear the commentary that droned on at low volume from her television in the background. She didn't need to. It blasted loud and clear from Lisa's television. One of the last single friends of Melissa and David, Lisa was unencumbered by sleeping infants.

'But they've been in there a long time,' Lisa said. 'Who knows? Maybe there's hope yet?'

Melissa held the phone to her ear with her shoulder as she sat Matthew up to burp him. After much work with a breast pump and a free check at a woman's clinic for radioactivity, which would be concentrated in breast milk, she had finally begun breastfeeding. 'I thought you hated Livingston.'

'Well, I do. I mean, shit, who doesn't? But, if impeaching him means we go straight to war . . . I mean, you know, with your situation. With David being God knows where.'

Matthew let loose a loud burp and immediately began to squirm. Melissa quickly attached him to the other nipple.

'What was that?' Lisa asked.

'Matthew burped.'

'Oh. Wait! Look.'

Melissa looked at the shaking pictures of the cameras as the reporters ran down the now familiar underground corridor of Congress's Greenbriar bunker. Over the telephone she could hear the sound from Lisa's television.

'General Thomas! Mr Lambert!' the reporter was yelling, his voice shaking with each step as the camera approached the elevator banks. 'Does this mean there's been a decision?' another reporter asked. 'Are you leaving the facility?' a third yelled.

Melissa looked into the faces of the two men who glanced just briefly at the camera before getting on the elevator. They said nothing, their faces stern masks of silence. As the elevator doors shut, a Congressional staffer stepped into the picture from the other side of the cordon restraining the photographers and held out his arms to ask the press to move back.

'Are General Thomas and Mr Lambert leaving the facility?' a reporter shouted.

'No, no,' the man said. 'The Senate has been in its closed session

debate now for quite some time. Mr Lambert and the general are just
heading to a conference room for a quick check of the world situation,
that's all.'

'How much longer?' several reporters shouted at once. 'Hours?
Days?' one concluded.

'It'll be some hours yet,' the Congressional staffer said, turning
to leave.

'What are you gonna do?' Lisa asked.

'What do you mean?'

'I mean, if they impeach him.'

'I still don't understand. What am I supposed to do?'

'I mean, are you going to stick around town?'

'I just got home,' Melissa said, upset at what Lisa was implying.

'I know but . . . if we really go to war.'

'You didn't even leave when the nuclear attack hit us.'

'I was sound asleep. I didn't even know what was going on until the
next morning.'

'That's my point. Why evacuate now? You didn't even know it
happened last time until you read about it in the paper.'

'My windows shook,' Lisa said, recounting her brush with death. 'And
when I got out of bed, the water in the pool was rocking back and forth
like an earthquake, I swear to God.'

'And you went back to sleep,' Melissa said. 'I told you what it was
like living in that hotel room. I'm staying right here.'

Lisa fell silent as they saw the scene switch to Europe, where it was
already a bright Sunday morning. Melissa stared intently at the pictures
of soldiers, looking for David's face. The scene was like that of some
disaster – a train derailment, or a massive car pileup. Small groups of
medics tended to men whose bodies were littered all across a road and
into a field. 'Eastern Poland' appeared at the bottom of the screen.

'Joni and Tom are leaving,' Lisa said. 'They're packing everything up
in the Range Rover and leaving tomorrow.'

'What about you?'

Lisa didn't answer at once. The scenes on television switched just
then to a displaced persons camp on the edge of a war zone. A nurse,
wearing full protective gear and gas mask, was adjusting the valve on a
drip by a cot on which lay a radiation victim. It was hard to say how old
the man was. His hair was mostly gone, and there were red blotches
and open sores all over his pale hands and face. The story was about the
dwindling stocks of opiates for radiation hospices, and the Food and Drug
Administration's consideration of approval of drugs for euthanasia, to be
used at the discretion of two concurring physicians and the patient.

'Why don't you come with me?' Lisa said. 'We could pack up
tomorrow, the three of us!'

'I'm not going anywhere, Lisa,' Melissa said, dejected.

'I don't want to leave without you.'

'My parents are on the way. They'll get a flight out here one of these days.'

'M, are you sure?'

Melissa felt a sinking feeling spread. 'David might call.' Lisa sighed. 'When are you leaving?'

'I don't know. As soon as they impeach ole Wally, I guess.'

'Will you call before you go?' Melissa asked, tears flooding her eyes.

'Of course I'll call! It may be in the middle of the night, though.'

'I leave the phone on these days,' Melissa said, laughing. Lisa laughed also. Some people slept with radios and TVs on in order to get some warning. Unplugging the telephone was an absurd concept. Melissa looked down at Matthew. He was sound asleep, his mouth open an inch away from her nipple.

When Melissa hung up, she took Matthew upstairs and put him in the daybed beside her bed and lay down to sleep. After tossing and turning in the quiet room, the only noise the gentle whistle of Matthew's breath, she got up and turned the bedroom television on. It was her only link, and she would leave it on now around the clock.

CONGRESSIONAL FACILITY, WEST VIRGINIA
June 25, 0800 GMT (0300 Local)

'I want those flights vectored inbound right now,' Thomas said. 'I don't give a damn about German flight controllers. Use our own controllers to keep 'em clear and get them airborne, now!'

'Commandant's office,' the marine said over the phone that Lambert held.

'This is Greg Lambert. Let me speak to General Fuller.'

'Just a moment, sir,' he heard, and General Thomas said into his phone, 'How many and when?' As he listened to the response, he mouthed the word 'Damn!' and then looked over at Lambert, covering the phone's mouthpiece with his hand. 'The Russians just came across the Slovak border – spoiling attack.'

'With ground forces?' Lambert asked as Thomas nodded but redirected his attention to the phone. 'Hell, yes, he's got authority to counterdeploy. Yes, he can cross the border. It's go – go, go, go! Execute Operation Avenging Sword.'

'Hel-lo, Greg,' General Fuller drawled, his deep voice dripping the syllables off his tongue.

'General Fuller, the straw vote is in. It's not even close: eighty-six to nine, with two undecided. The Vice President has given the go-ahead.'

Lambert heard Thomas standing next to him uncharacteristically losing his cool. 'Sink the thing! You got free-fire rules everywhere except the Kara Sea Bastion!'

'General Fuller, execute Operation Avenging Sword.'

'O-o-okey-dokey.' The line clicked, and Lambert stared at the phone for a second before looking at the next number on his list: the U.S. Space Command, whose specially modified F-15s would begin knocking down Russia's satellites one by one.

'Shouldn't you call the President?' Thomas asked as he dialed his next number.

Lambert hesitated. *What an awful call*, he thought, but he knew he should make it. He dialed Mount Weather. 'This is Greg Lambert. Get me President Livingston, please.' There was a brief pause before a ringing tone. Livingston picked the phone up himself on the second ring.

'Mr President, it's Greg Lambert.' There was an awkward pause.

'It's all right, Greg. Thanks for calling.'

'I'm sorry, sir.'

'It's started already, hasn't it?'

The war, Lambert knew he meant. 'Yes, sir, it has.'

'You remember our talk, Greg. You just remember our talk. I'm counting on you being my voice, my conscience, in all those meetings that are coming. I'm counting on you, Greg.'

'*To save the world*,' he left unspoken, and Lambert came very close to objecting to the absurdity of the obligation. 'I'll do what I can, Mr President.'

'It's just Walter, Greg,' the President said. 'Walter Livingston.'

PART FOUR

Cry 'Havoc,' and let slip the dogs of war.

—WILLIAM SHAKESPEARE
Julius Caesar
Act 3, scene 1, line 273

Chapter Ten

OVER THE BALTIC SEA, WEST OF KRONSTADT, RUSSIA
June 11, 1000 GMT (1200 Local)

'Viper Two, stay on me,' Captain Patrick O'Brian heard through his left ear. He glanced over in the direction of the sound to see through the pouring rain the dark form of the F-15E Strike Eagle that was his leader.

'Two,' O'Brian said simply in reply, maintaining his concentration on the gray surface of the ocean one twitch of his stick arm beneath his massive strike aircraft. With the thumb of his left hand on the throttle he flicked the speedbrake open and then back closed to bleed twenty knots off his airspeed, which he replaced with a little throttle after he had fallen into position slightly behind his flight leader.

'Twenty,' O'Brian heard through the speakers of his helmet from behind, much clearer than the artificially produced 'coke-bottle' sound of incoming calls. The aircraft's communications bay vectored sound, whether communications or threat warnings, to his ears from the direction in space of the source no matter which way his head was turned, making distant sources seem far away. The clear sound from behind O'Brian was his Wizzo – the Weapons Officer in the rear seat – counting down the miles to target.

The canopy in front of O'Brian lit up with a new set of symbols and data.

'Ball's on target,' First Lieutenant Ramirez said from behind.

O'Brian saw the bright box he was looking for off to the left on the flat screen of the HUD, the Head Up Display. The HUD was invisible against the canopy, and the symbols on it were focused on infinity so that only when you looked through them and off into the distance did they become clear.

A line streaked from the center of the display to the center of the box, indicating the course adjustment he needed to make. The box was the bomb release point through which he must fly the aircraft, and it was growing larger, closer.

Ramirez, bent over at the waist with his head buried in 'the feed bag,' the padded screen right in front of his chest where O'Brian's stick was, had acquired the landmarks demarking their route of ingress visually despite the lack of visibility over the storm-tossed ocean. The Pave Tack FLIR, or Forward-Looking Infra Red imager, produced a high resolution thermal image of the shoreline ahead, and Ramirez had simply rolled the trackball to move the cross hairs onto the landmark and then punched the bar beneath it to lock it on. The computer then calculated the position of the target relative to the landmark and generated the release point on O'Brian's display. O'Brian watched the computer's slight adjustments of the box's position and size as the Pave Tack's laser read the line-of-sight range to the landmark – the hypotenuse of the triangle – and the altimeter told the computer the triangle's base. The computer then came up with the critical third leg: the range along the ground to the landmark and, from there, to the target. With that range, together with readings of acceleration from the gyros of the aircraft's inertial navigation system and airspeed from the Pitot tube, the computer would release the bombs with incredible precision. All O'Brian had to do was fly through the box.

'Viper Two, come left twelve,' the voice of his flight leader said into O'Brian's left ear from just ahead.

'Two copy,' O'Brian said curtly as he rolled his stick gently to the left and applied slight pressure to the left rudder pedal to complete the coordinated turn. When the heading readout on the HUD ticked down from 272 degrees to 260 degrees he reversed stick and rudder to return to straight and level flight. O'Brian saw that the line danced only slightly off the center point in the box after the turn. As long as the end of the line stayed inside the box, the bombs could be released on target by the computer's jinking of the flight controls. *This is it*, O'Brian thought. *Viper One's found it too*.

With only the minute movement of his right arm and left leg in manipulating the flight controls during the turn, O'Brian had felt the extreme tightness of his muscles. Two hours in the cockpit and thirty minutes at extremely low-level flight were having their effect. *Shit!* he thought. *Don't cramp now*.

He wanted to stretch, to roll his shoulders and limber his arms and legs, but at only 150 feet above water in bad weather and about the same distance beneath the first fans of radar energy reaching out to find them, it would mean almost certain death for the two of them. The thought did nothing to ease the tension in his muscles. O'Brian glanced down at the airspeed indicator on the HUD. It read 512 knots. At 150 feet the two massive aircraft would be leaving a wake in the water behind them. He swallowed the stricture that had swelled in his throat.

O'Brian had to fight against his natural inclination to 'white knuckle' the controls, focusing on easing his grip to allow blood and therefore oxygen to the muscles of his extremities. He remembered well the exercise that the flight surgeon had put his jet school class through: gripping a broom handle tightly for a couple of minutes during his lecture on flight endurance. His hand had shaken as if palsied from oxygen starvation when he held it up afterward.

'Fifteen,' Ramirez said.

Off to the right out of the corner of his eye O'Brian could see a bright flame, then a second, and then half a dozen more light up the dark gray sky, piercing the rain and fog that completely obscured all lines separating sky and ocean and land. 'HARMs on the way,' he said for the benefit of Ramirez, who remained head down.

O'Brian stole a short glance to the right but could no longer see the eight tiny points of light streaking off toward land. The 809-pound AGM-88A High-Speed Anti-Radiation Missiles, HARMs, were tracking on the radar transmitters of the Russian air defense system, which would be shutting themselves off any second now. But it would be too late. The HARMs would track on the last known point of radiation and come smashing in at tremendous speed, blasting the transmitters out of existence. The transmitters that were left off until after the first wave of missiles and then turned on would be attacked by the aircraft that had fired the HARMs – F-16s configured as advanced 'Wild Weasels.'

First in, last out, the Wild Weasels would douse all high-frequency radiation emitters more powerful than a microwave oven at close range with M61A-1 Vulcan 20-mm cannon. With a rate of fire of 100 explosive cannon shells per second, the rotating six-barreled Vulcan sounded like a buzz saw, and the target would be consumed quickly in the eruption of hundreds of tiny explosions.

'Twelve,' Ramirez said as the flashes of HARM explosions began to appear along what must be the shoreline ahead.

O'Brian was surprised that the next breath came into his lungs raggedly. *You're nervous, Patty,* he thought, and took a deep breath. *Get your shit together, sports fan.*

'Leopard Flight, bogeys – two o'clock – Angels six!' The faint but clear call from above O'Brian's head announced the expected arrival of the Russian interceptors, interceptors whose sole target would be O'Brian's flight of eight F-15Es.

'Combat spread. Switches hot. Tallyho!' came the distant voice of their top cover's commander.

'One's hot.'

'Two's hot.'

'I've got right!'

'Eleven,' Ramirez said, the tension coming through loud and clear in his voice. *He's listening too,* O'Brian thought.

'Sweet tone. Firing one,' a fighter pilot above said over the humming sound of a radar lock on his missile's prey. O'Brian could hear the familiar whoosh of the missile's rocket igniting in the background as the last words were spoken.

O'Brian checked his own load of air-to-air missiles: two short-range infrared-seeking Sidewinders and two medium-range radar-guided Sparrows. In looking down he suddenly remembered: *Instrument check! Shit!* He dropped his eyes from the canopy in the precisely prescribed pattern for the last precombat check, which he was late in starting at less than eleven miles to target. Down to his instruments and then back up to ensure the aircraft was straight and level and then back down, one instrument at a time. *Engine temp: right's still runnin' hot but okay. Back up – straight and level.*

'Splash one!' the distant sound of jubilation could be heard from above.

'Ten miles,' Ramirez said.

Ten miles! Jesus, where was I? Fuel: fuel's green. Eyes up . . . CHRIST! O'Brian's heart stopped as he saw the readout from his radar altimeter on the HUD: *85 feet!*

O'Brian eased the aircraft up with the slightest back pressure on the stick to rejoin the flight leader, who had missed his nearly fatal transgression while doing his own check, O'Brian figured. He made a special point to concentrate on the altimeter, watching it bounce between 148 and 152 feet. His heart was pounding and he could feel each beat tap the carotid artery of his neck against his flight suit. *Eighty-five feet!* he thought – the lowest he had ever been in bad weather. *Jesus!*

'Break! Break!' he heard from high above.

'Nine,' Ramirez said, his voice coming loudly by comparison. 'I'm going hot,' the distant voice said. O'Brian saw a picture of his aircraft's eighteen conventional bombs show up on the HUD and read 'Armed – Fuse Alt. 0.' *Surface burst,* O'Brian thought.

O'Brian concentrated hard to keep the edges of the line inside the box while keeping the blurred outline of his flight leader's aircraft in the corner of his eye. He could feel sweat begin to flood out of all his pores, cold and uncomfortable.

'Pull! Pull! Burners!'

'Eight miles,' Ramirez counted down, the surprise of the loud voice causing O'Brian to flinch.

O'Brian abandoned his instrument check after the scare of allowing the nose to settle. *I screwed up. I waited too long to get started with it,* he thought, having gotten wrapped up in the sounds of the battle above.

'Splash two. Got another one!'

'Stay with me, Viper Two,' the flight leader said from above and to the left. O'Brian pressed forward on the throttle almost imperceptibly with his left hand and banked again to the left, moving closer to the other Strike Eagle before recentering in the box.

'Seven miles,' Ramirez said, his voice an octave higher than usual. *Ramirez is nervous, tight*, O'Brian thought, knowing that Ramirez watched what O'Brian could not yet see: the rugged shoreline toward which they rushed, his face pressed against the padded blinders surrounding his imaging screen.

O'Brian heard the faint wisp of a tone from in front of his aircraft, wavering in and out, getting stronger each time it came back.

'Watch for SAMs,' O'Brian's lead said as they got within range of the enemy surface-to-air missiles.

The skin of their aircraft was being 'painted' by the first weak pulses of energy from the transmitter of a radar system that must just have been turned on. One good return to the radar's receiver and the brilliant flame of a missile's exhaust would be seen ahead. The missile would quickly turn level with the water and hurtle straight at O'Brian's plane, its flight time just a few seconds at their tremendous closing speeds. The proximity detonator would put a fog of shrapnel in front of their speeding aircraft that would shred them as they flew through it. O'Brian put the line back in the box.

'Six miles,' Ramirez said. 'You see that power line off to the right?'

O'Brian glanced down at his own FLIR screen. Ramirez had it on maximum magnification, and the black-and-white picture of the shoreline was strikingly clear. 'Got it,' O'Brian said as he looked up into the dark sky ahead. He concentrated on memorizing the location in the real world of the cold black metal towers and power lines dimly visible on the screen. *No quicker way to die than to plow into those*. As he looked at the shore, they burst out of the squall line and the ocean and horizon and flight leader all became clear. The low clouds streaked by the top of O'Brian's canopy.

'Triple A,' O'Brian's lead said.

O'Brian could see now the antiaircraft artillery bursting in golden plumes of death beneath and inside the clouds ahead. *'The Golden BB,'* he said to himself, marveling at his first sight ever of the heavy Russian gun defenses.

Suddenly, O'Brian felt death's cold grip reaching out for them, waiting for them ahead. From the ocean below – at twenty feet the F-15's jet air intakes would gulp water right up from the surface. From the lead aircraft thirty feet away from O'Brian's Plexiglas canopy – one light tap against his horizontal stabilizer and both aircraft would begin the rapid and inexorable process of midair disintegration. From the blazing fireworks ahead, the ragged metal chunks filling the air right in the middle of the release box on the HUD. From the fat radar-guided missiles that sat on their rails waiting, their arrival presaged by the threat warning hums in O'Brian's ears. From the small heat-seeking missiles that came at you with no warning – you had to see them to survive. From the power lines and hills and even birds scared to flight by the passage of the two F-15s just ahead whose red-hot exhausts O'Brian could barely see.

'Uh, five . . . five miles,' Ramirez said. He sounded as if he was nauseous. *This isn't the way it's supposed to be*, O'Brian thought, the chill growing from his chest to grip his entire body as his confidence waned.

'Leopard One, check your six, check your six!' O'Brian heard from the 'furball,' the multiaircraft dogfight, high above.

And from enemy interceptors, O'Brian remembered.

'Where is he?' came distantly over the headphones, panic-stricken.

'On your six, on your six! Two miles back!'

'I don't have him! I can't see him!'

'He's right on you! I'm goin' guns! Break right!'

'Four miles. Pass the stick.'

'He's still on me, Two! Shoot him, shoot him! He's got *lock*!'

'Pass the stick, O'Brian!' Ramirez yelled. 'Three point five miles!'

O'Brian tore himself from the sounds of the battle above and felt the top of the stick with his thumb, jabbing the auto release switch forward. Control over the aircraft for the terminal bombing phase had now been transferred to the onboard computer. 'Passed – sorry,' O'Brian said as he felt the stick begin to make slight corrections on its own. He kept his hands lightly on the stick as all pilots did to override if necessary.

The line was centered now in the growing box. *Right down the pipe*, O'Brian thought, trying to calm himself as he watched for the bright flash of a missile ahead, reminding himself with a start not to break left into the flight leader if one was spotted.

'Three miles,' Ramirez said, continuing his mantra.

'He fired, he fired!' Despite the distance, the voice of the fighter pilot was loud, shouted at a high pitch.

'*Ho-ly . . . Je-sus*!' the prey's voice came from above, the breath pressed out of the pilot's lungs as the Gs of his violent maneuvering crushed his diaphragm.

'Eject! Get outa there! *Get outa there, Rod*!'

'Two miles,' Ramirez said. 'Weapons hot. Here we go!'

There was a short burst of static from above, a ghost of a sound that in O'Brian's mind was a scream of agony. 'Aw, God. Oh, Jesus,' a voice said from on high. 'A-a-h,' and then a pause. 'Ah, Rimfire, this is Leopard Two,' the voice said. 'Leopard One is . . . he's down, repeat, Leopard One is down.'

'One mile,' Ramirez said.

'You need C-SAR?' a voice asked from a great distance and behind O'Brian's head, offering Combat Search and Rescue forces to fight their way in for the downed pilot.

'Ah, negative, negative. He . . . uh . . . he didn't get out.'

O'Brian saw the eruption of bright orange explosions ahead as the bombs of the two lead aircraft struck. Suddenly, the stick jerked back and O'Brian was pressed momentarily into his seat as his aircraft rose, his visibility dropping to near zero as his canopy was enshrouded in clouds. A second surge skyward could be felt even though the stick remained steady.

'Bombs away!' Ramirez cried, and the HUD shifted automatically to its air-to-air readout.

O'Brian seized control of the stick and followed his lead in a steep bank to the left and descent toward the deck, breaking out of the clouds and therefore not able to follow as the stick of eighteen Mark 83 thousand-pound general purpose bombs flew up almost a thousand feet into the clouds and then began to settle back down to earth. The computer had lobbed the bombs skyward with a jerk up of the aircraft's nose in order to spare the strike plane the danger of flying straight over their target. As the F-15s continued their wide turn back out to the safety of the sea, the bombs plunged down toward the busy wharves of Kronstadt Naval Base.

O'Brian was inland almost even with his target and half a mile to the north when the first of the bombs began to rain down. In the next second and a half, the eighteen bombs, which had been released milliseconds apart to place them in a long line, began impacting. The first bomb fell into the water thirty yards short of a line of missile patrol boats tied up to the wharf. The blast wave created by the 445 pounds of Tritonal explosive would have sunk the nearest boat by crushing its hull with a pressure wave had not the next bomb struck it squarely amidships, blowing its bow and stern ten feet into the air. The severed ends sunk immediately to the sandy bottom.

All the remaining bombs struck with an awesome tearing sound along the shore in a steep angle to the waterline. Each of the blasts threw over four thousand cubic feet of concrete and soil high into the air as it made a crater eighteen feet deep and twenty-five feet wide. The Russian dockworkers who had flung themselves to the ground when the two lead aircrafts' bombs began impacting some four hundred yards up the wharf were bounced into the air as the shock wave snapped through the earth. Many died from the trauma of the jolt, equivalent to being struck in the chest by a falling log, and others died from collapsed lungs as the blasts' overpressure washed over them. The dockworkers who were still running for cover, however, suffered worst of all. Almost everyone standing within six hundred feet of a blast died as the bomb casings disintegrated by design and the irregularly shaped shrapnel – some pieces large, others small – ripped through their bodies at hundreds of feet per second.

The eight F-15Es' 144 bombs fell on the docks in sixteen seconds of hell, and one of Russia's greatest naval bases was knocked out of action for weeks to come.

During the conflagration O'Brian was struggling to stay close to Viper One. As he watched the glowing exhaust of the lead's twin afterburning turbofans, O'Brian suddenly saw bright dots pouring out of the tail of his partner – six to a group.

'SAM! SAM! SAM!' the flight leader's voice cried from just ahead.

As the lead F-15 suddenly broke steeply to the left, O'Brian expected to see the small heat-seeking missile fly straight up its tailpipe. By the time O'Brian thumbed his own flare-dispenser button and banked right, his fate was sealed. The shoulder-fired SA-7 surface-to-air missile that was locked onto his superhot exhaust was successfully decoyed by the even hotter flares that O'Brian ejected from his aircraft's tail, but it detonated only eight feet behind the F-15. The flash lit the instrument panel in front of O'Brian in a strobe of stark white light, and the sphere of steel rods expanding from the small missile's warhead riddled the rear of the aircraft. Nine lights – some clustered in the row of engine indicators, others widely dispersed – switched instantly from green to bright red, bypassing the early warning yellow as the ragged skin of the torn fuselage caused the aircraft to buffet. Three distinct tones blared into O'Brian's ears, warbling, buzzing, and bonging insistently. But over all those sounds, the instantly triggered woman's voice was all he heard: 'Eject.'

In rapid succession, the supercombustible JP-4 jet fuel spewed out of a ruptured fuel line directly onto the engine of the fighter-bomber, igniting in midair from the engine's radiant heat even before making contact. 'Eject,' the calm voice of the woman repeated as O'Brian jerked his left hand from the throttle for the eject handle, jamming his eyes shut. 'Ejec . . .' the cool voice of the computer began, but the fire leapt in the wink of an eye back through the source of the leak, following the maze of fuel lines up into the honeycombed wing tanks of the aircraft.

God was merciful. O'Brian and Ramirez never felt a thing.

DEEP-UNDERGROUND COMMAND POST, THE KREMLIN
June 25, 1200 GMT (1400 Local)

Filipov saw that Razov had given up on conducting a formal STAVKA meeting as the senior officers were now almost constantly on the phone to their various commands. The vote on the American C-SPAN was still ongoing.

'Ukrainian Air Defense reports significant contact inbound north of Lvov. Probable FB-111s, low altitude, high speed, heading zero seven seven degrees.'

The captain who had read the report ran out to tear another off the teletype, and a waiting junior naval officer read, "'Subsea sensors in Gulf of Finland report contact, probable American hunter-killer submarine, headed east fourteen kilometers north of Tallinn. Fast missile patrol boats have put out from Kronstadt to intercept.'"

By the time he had finished, there were two others in line behind him waiting to speak to the senior officers, most of whom were in animated conversations over the telephone and heard nothing. But Filipov, and Razov in front of him, listened. Without a field command, Razov's job as commander in chief of the Supreme High Command was the big picture, and Filipov was Razov's aide.

'Commander of 103rd Motorized Rifle Division reports leading elements reaching third objective ten kilometers east of Michalovce, Slovakia. Resistance on the ground is reported to be light, but air interdiction efforts are intensifying. Requests permission for extension of timetable for fourth objective, which is Michalovce itself.'

'Request denied,' snapped the commander of the Ukrainian Strategic Direction, which would soon be renamed the Ukrainian Front, taking his ear just briefly away from the phone before returning to it and saying, 'Continue.'

'That was a good idea of yours, General Razov,' General Karyakin said as he lounged in his chair next to Razov, the Strategic Rocket Forces officer also having very little to do. 'A spoiling attack against their forces in eastern Slovakia, good idea.' He nodded at the vote tallies on television, which were mounting quickly in favor of impeachment. 'The Americans don't seem to be waiting, so why should we?'

'Commander of Iceland Landing Force reports contact with main elements of American 82nd Airborne Division. He has ordered his men to temporarily assume a tactical defense and requests information as to when next resupply convoy or airdrop will arrive.'

Razov looked at Admiral Verkhovensky, who despite having phones pressed to each ear had obviously heard the report. Verkhovensky looked at Razov and shook his head.

'Tell the commander,' Razov said, raising his voice over the noise, 'to assume both the tactical and the strategic defensive. Tell him that we are unable at this time . . . that we are unable to resupply him.'

The aide looked at Razov for just a moment longer than normal, then nodded curtly and turned to leave. When Verkhovensky hung one of the two phones up, Razov said, 'What about the Kara Bastion?'

Several of the senior commanders' heads turned at that question. Verkhovensky shook his head and cupped the mouthpiece. 'They're building in the Barents Sea west of Novaya Zemlya – have one carrier battle group on station and another on the way – but they seem to be making no attempts to penetrate.'

'They're probably just cutting off Iceland from our northern ports,' the commander of Construction Troops said.

'That is an awful lot of naval power for the interdiction role,' Verkhovensky said, but then got pulled back onto the phone. 'No! I want everything we've got pulled back into the Sea of Japan. Everything!' He listened. 'Yes, that includes the Petrozavodsk battle group.' He listened again. 'Then we give up the Kurils and they fight their way through the Soya Strait! Everything comes back to the Sea of Japan!'

'Two more votes, sir,' Filipov said, keeping one eye on the screen as he stepped forward from the wall to whisper in Razov's ear.

Razov looked at the screen. Sixty-four in favor of impeachment, three opposed.

'All right!' Razov said in a loud voice, the American Senate's vote a foregone conclusion now. 'Everybody back to their wartime command posts. Next STAVKA meeting in sixteen hours.'

Almost all of the commanders and their aides were up at once, and a bottleneck built at the door. The noise in the room began to die down as the men, now switching to cellular telephones, filed out.

'Si-i-ixty,' Karyakin said, holding his hand pointed up in the shape of a pistol as he watched the television, 'six!' He pointed his hand down at the television screen just as the number rolled up, squeezing the trigger. 'That does it. We're at war.'

Razov looked at the man, who, Filipov thought, seemed almost pleased with the outcome. Karyakin and the commanders of Construction Troops and Military Production stood and headed for the door.

'Oh, I don't know if you noticed,' Karyakin said, casually picking at the fingernail of his bent finger with his thumb as he turned from the doorway, 'but we have completed decontamination of forty-nine intact silos and are beginning reloading tonight.' He looked up at Razov. 'They should be on line and ready to fly within the week. Just thought you'd like to know,' he said smiling, and left.

'Close the door, Pavel,' Razov said to Filipov. When the door was shut, they were alone. 'I've got a job for you.' When Filipov looked up at Razov's face, there was a momentary period during which Filipov felt the general's scrutiny. Filipov focused his concentration, as was so difficult to do these days.

'You saw the newspaper digests from the USA/Canada Bureau about the death of your friend Lambert's wife,' Razov said, and Filipov nodded. 'But you still have no word of Irina?'

Filipov shook his head again. He had gotten the full articles and poured over every word of the sketchy details – sneaking away from his official duties with deepening guilt at doing so – but still there was no word of Irina's having been with Jane. Which meant she was where? In Washington? Lying dead, unidentified, in one of those mass viewing areas or already bulldozed into a trench? In a fallout shelter? She had asked once as they had a snack in the cafeteria of the National Gallery, Filipov remembered, what the yellow and black sign in the basement meant. Fallout shelter! He had told her the sign meant fallout shelter! It was like a drowning man thrown a life preserver.

'Pavel,' Razov said in a low voice, and Filipov remembered where he was and focused on the general. 'This is a matter of vital importance. The fate of our nation, of ours and of the United States, may well ride on the outcome of your mission.'

Filipov nodded.

'I want you to go to America.'

'Yes, sir!' Filipov blurted.

'I'm telling you this in here because it's the only room I'm absolutely certain is not bugged. I want you to go to America under cover of a search for your wife, meet with this Lambert, and inform him of the fail-deadly firing orders of our submarines in the Kara Sea Bastion.'

Filipov stared back at Razov in silence. 'Do you understand,' Razov said as Filipov felt the intense, unblinking stare of the man's gray eyes, 'the profound and urgent importance of communicating to the Americans what would happen if they carried their attacks into the Kara Sea?'

The chill sank in on Filipov, and he nodded.

'You understand also,' Razov said, 'that you are not doing this at the behest of STAVKA, or of any officer other than myself?' Filipov nodded. 'And you understand further that discussion with the Americans of the nuclear war orders of our remaining submarine forces would quite probably be considered by some to be treason during time of war?' Filipov nodded again. 'And you know the punishment for that crime?'

Filipov stared back at Razov, and then nodded a final time, having waited a respectable period to feign consideration of Razov's request, as Razov appeared to desire, but thinking the entire time, *Irina, Irina*.

CONGRESSIONAL FACILITY, WEST VIRGINIA
June 25, 1600 GMT (1100 Local)

'Please repeat after me,' Chief Justice Rehnquist said as Costanzo raised his right hand and placed his left on the family Bible held by his wife. Lambert stood, as did everyone else in the packed Senate chamber. 'I, Paul Stephen Costanzo . . .'

'I, Paul Stephen Costanzo,' he said, repeating the oath, 'do solemnly swear . . . that I will faithfully execute . . . the office of President of the United States . . . and will, to the best of my ability . . . preserve, protect, and defend . . . the Constitution of the United States of America.'

'Congratulations, Mr President,' the Chief Justice said, shaking Costanzo's hand, and the enclosed chamber exploded in a standing ovation that went on for several minutes.

Lambert and Thomas walked to the side door of the packed chamber to watch from there. Lambert felt the eye of the television lens stray onto him and Thomas frequently during the long ovation, and he tried not to let his impatience show. Finally, the new President took to the podium.

'My fellow Americans,' Costanzo repeated several times until the crowd fell quiet, 'my fellow Americans, I will keep my remarks brief. As I assume the great office of President, I do so knowing our country to be scarred and blackened with great wounds. Several millions of our countrymen lie dead, and millions of others bless us with their presence only for the moment, and will soon be gone, having come to a tragic and terrible end due to a force that no one can see, or taste, or smell, or feel.'

Lambert dropped his head, but as he did he saw the red light on the minicam stuck into his face. He was being shown to the nation, he knew, by some network news director as the poster boy of grieving relatives, and he ground his jaw and stared sternly at the podium.

'I do not enter this humbling office at a time of peace, but to the great misfortune of all I enter it at a time of war. It is not a war of our own choosing, for we are a peace-loving people. But once roused, once the blood of our young patriots is committed to a great cause, this mighty land of ours shall surely enter the fray no matter how great the cost, how great the sacrifice. And let me assure you, my fellow Americans, this nation shall also just as surely prevail.'

Again there was a rousing ovation, just as ardent from both sides of the aisle.

'All Americans,' Costanzo began, trying to force the Joint Session of Congress to quiet, 'all Americans . . . all Americans remember December seventh as the day on which the Japanese attacked Pearl Harbor. Our President, Franklin Delano Roosevelt, said then that day will live in infamy for all time. But how much more infamous a day was June eleventh? I will leave it for historians to decide, but for all of us who lived through it, it was truly a day of infamy. Tomorrow, however, will be a day of victory, for early this morning I and former President Livingston jointly authorized the armed forces of this country to initiate Operation Avenging Sword. I will have more to say about the war effort in the near future, but suffice it to say that we shall take the war to the Russians, we shall prosecute that war with the utmost zeal, conviction, and resolve, and our guns will not fall silent until our forces have achieved victory on the field of battle!' The roar of cheers exploded from the standing men and women. 'May God bless the United States of

America,' he shouted into the roar, 'and the success of her armed forces!'

The shouting and cheering were deafening inside the cramped enclosure.

When the President, followed by Lambert and General Thomas, burst into the conference room, the scene was hectic, unlike what Lambert had expected. 'Jesus Christ, how the hell . . .'

'President's on deck!' one of the navy aides said, and stood, as did Admiral Dixon. The rest of the Chiefs, whose torsos were projected onto three screens along the walls of the room beside those of the secretaries of State and Defense and the directors of the CIA and NSA, all fell quiet.

Costanzo strode straight to the head of the table and said, 'Be seated, gentlemen – and lady,' he said, nodding at one of Lambert's aides. When he himself had sunk into his seat, his hands clasped in front of him on the table, he said, 'How goes the war?'

'Uh, I'm afraid we've got a situation on our hands here, sir,' Air Force General Starnes said from one of the screens.

'And just what situation is that, General, exactly?'

'Well, sir, it seems that Russian Backfire bombers of their Long-Range Aviation forces, which are large, supersonic aircraft similar to our B-1Bs, are in the process of raiding certain of our facilities – naval facilities, mainly, but also fuel storage and some power generation. They're nuclear-capable bombers, but they're using them to deliver conventional ordnance.'

'Well, General,' Costanzo said as he looked at Starnes on the projection screen, shrugging and spreading his hands to show his lack of surprise, 'this is a war.' He hesitated, and then said, 'Wait, did you say they're raiding our power generation facilities?'

'Yes, sir. They hit us pretty quick and hard, but we've got interceptors in fast pursuit. We'll either knock down most of 'em or we'll run 'em outa fuel before—'

'Wait a minute!' Costanzo interrupted. 'Where did they attack? Where were these facilities?'

Starnes looked down at the paper in front of him. 'San Diego Naval Shipyard; a Chevron fuel tank farm in New Jersey just across the river from New York; and civilian power stations, both hydrocarbon and nuclear, supplying New York, Boston, Philadelphia, Seattle, San Francisco, and Los Angeles.'

LOS ANGELES, CALIFORNIA
June 25, 1600 GMT (0800 Local)

'Channel Four interrupts this network broadcast to bring you a special bulletin.'

Melissa stared bleary-eyed at the television with Matthew lying propped up on her bare thighs.

The scene changed to a harried local newsman, who was holding his earphone to his ear and shouting, 'What?' off to the side of the camera. He turned back and said, 'Channel Four just received word that the FAA has issued a Notice to Airmen warning all civilian flights away from LAX and Orange County airport. The word we received just moments ago from the tower at LAX was that civilian radars at the FAA Regional Air Control Center had picked up . . .'

There was a deep rumble, and the clock on the mantelpiece shook. Melissa waited frozen in time for the bright light that would precede the breaking of glass, the fires, the winds that would end it all.

'I don't know if you could hear that!' the reporter shouted. 'A very, very loud explosion or series of explosions. We could hear it right here in our studios.'

Another series of crumping sounds rattled the windowpanes of Melissa's family room.

'There! There it is again! Another one, louder than before.'

Melissa put Matthew on her shoulder and ran to the back door. The deck was on the side of the hill, offering a partial view of the brown air over downtown Los Angeles.

'The Los Angeles Fire Department is advising everyone to stay in their homes,' Melissa heard through the open door as she walked to the wood railing and looked out in the distance at the black smoke that rose over the hills to her left.

'The possibility of broken glass or downed power—' There was a loud string of booms over the hills that seemed to shake the very air around her, and she saw just briefly a red ball of flame rise up and then cool to a boiling cloud of black smoke. In the flicker of an eye she saw two large black aircraft sweep through the hills below her, banking steeply and disappearing behind her neighbor's house on the right. Her heart stopped as their engines' scream tore across the back of the house, rattling the windows and causing Matthew to jerk and then begin crying, his little body rigid with the effort.

She went back inside, fighting a quiver that vibrated her body and made her mouth dry. 'There, there, Matthew,' she said patting his back as the man-made thunder of the jet engines quickly receded and she got a bottle of breast milk out of the refrigerator. The picture of the black jets, impossibly big as they streaked by her at eye level not a quarter of a mile away, played over and over in her head.

Matthew was screaming at the top of his lungs. 'There, there,' she kept repeating as she put the bottle in the microwave. She closed the door and tapped in the time. The buttons didn't beep. She walked around to look at the television. It was dark. The whole house was dark.

GANDER AIRPORT, NEWFOUNDLAND
June 25, 1600 GMT (1200 Local)

They crossed the tarmac to the Delta L-1011 and began to board. As David Chandler, Lieutenant Bailey, and Master Sergeant Barnes reached the top of the stairs, a flight attendant in a gray Delta uniform dress turned and said, 'Welcome aboard.'

Chandler nodded, surprised to see the woman.

'I'm Rebecca Healy, and this is Jennifer Sims.'

'David Chandler,' he said, shaking hands and introducing Barnes and Bailey. Chandler had thought for a second that maybe this was the same jet they had flown in on, but these were not the same flight attendants as before.

'Why don't you gentlemen make yourselves comfortable in first class,' Rebecca said. 'The flight engineer said we've got a weight and balance problem and need to move some passengers up to the front.' She turned to Jennifer. 'You want to ask if we have anyone holding our frequent flyer card?'

Jennifer started for the PA system before Rebecca had the chance to laugh at her own joke. She reached out and lightly grabbed Jennifer's arm. 'No, no, just kidding. The major will get some people up here. About a dozen ought to do it,' she said, turning to Chandler, 'give or take a few. The flight engineer will figure it exactly.'

'Lieutenant Bailey, why don't you get all our officers and senior NCOs up here.' Bailey took off toward the rear of the plane, taking one last look at Jennifer. She noticed and smiled at him, causing Bailey to nearly collide with the wall of the coat closet.

Chandler stood in the open doorway looking down at the terminal building and beyond, to the west. *Farther away*, he thought. *I'm going farther away*.

About an hour into the flight, Chandler unbuckled his seat belt, walked up to the cockpit door, and knocked.

The door opened a crack, and Chandler saw a quick smile crease the face of Gator, the flight engineer from the flight that had dropped them on Newfoundland, and then the door closed in his face.

'This joke of yours is wearing thin, Golding!' Chandler said through the closed door. 'Open up!'

'Can't!' Golding said. 'FAA regulations! You might have a gun! Might hijack us someplace dangerous!' Chandler could hear the snickers from the cockpit, and as he raised a closed fist the door opened.

'How'd you enjoy sunny Newfoundland, plowboy?'

Chandler looked at the rack of electronic components just inside the door that had been charred and burned before but now looked brand new. 'How the hell did I end up drawing you guys again?'

'Luck o' the fuckin' Irish, Major,' Golding said. 'We've been flyin' convoys. When they pulled the eight planes they routed to Gander back to Newark, we just sorta stuck together. Gator there's got this homo-sexual thing goin' on with one of the American Airlines copilots, so . . .'

'With all due respect, Cap'n,' Gator said, 'fuck you.'

'Ya see, there he goes again with his sexual harassment.'

'So you've been to Europe?' Chandler asked, and they fell silent. 'What's going on?'

'Can't tell you,' Golding said. 'It's a secret. You might be a Russkie spy.'

'Dammit, Golding,' Chandler said, 'answer my question. Newfoundland is not exactly the hub of the telecommunications industry. I don't know what's going on. Have you seen any fighting?'

'Well, no,' Golding said in a mocking voice as he rubbed his chin, 'no, we haven't. But now that you mention it, huh – don't that seem kinda strange, fellas, that we haven't seen anything untoward, this bein' World War Three an' all?'

'I'm serious, Golding.'

'And I'm serious when I tell ya that we're not supposed to talk about anything.'

'And you're going to follow that rule? You, Captain Golding, are going to let them gag you?'

Golding sat there in silent thought for a second, and then said, 'Whaddaya think, fellas? Should we tell him?'

The other two seemed indifferent, and Chandler just waited.

'Well, let's see.' Golding fell quiet, and the silence hung over the copilot and flight engineer as well, both of whom seemed to drift back in time as their eyes lost their focus. 'We flew into Frankfurt two days ago right after a Russian cruise missile attack on the airport. It was like a scene from Dante's *Inferno*. We came in at night, and there were fires blazin' all around. The signal from the air traffic controller was weak, like the guy was holdin' a walkie-talkie or somethin', and he didn't know shit. No wind, no barometric pressure so we could set our altimeters, nothin'. He just said "Come on down."'

Golding glanced over at Frazier, the copilot. 'Damn near hit a chopper comin' straight up off the deck like a bat outa hell. There weren't any runway lights, but there were crews out there workin' – patchin' up holes – so we dragged the runway once, you know, to see if it looked okay. We flew by at about a hundred feet so that's what we set our altimeter at – didn't worry about mean sea level. Gator stuck his head up here an' found a wind sock. Here we are in a three-hundred-and-fifty-thousand-pound hundred-million-dollar airplane with two hundred and fifty people in back draggin' a runway at a hundred feet like we were drivin' a Cessna.

'Anyway,' Golding continued after shaking his head in disgust, 'we did a short-field landing on the good end of the runway and taxied on up pretty as you please. It was a madhouse,' he intoned slowly as if seeing it before his eyes again as he spoke. 'We thought we'd have to inflate the damn slides to get the people out. They were real gung-ho types, yellin' shit out and slappin' hands like they were gonna start killin' Russkies at the baggage claim. They were hangin' from the door, droppin' down with a big hoop an' holler and then cussin' up a storm when they broke their damn ankles on the concrete. Eventually, the ground service shows up and we start deplanin' the smarter ones down the stairs. Not one minute too soon, 'cause the whole time we were starin' right out, not more'n two hundred feet away, at a 747 and what looked to be a '67 lyin' there in big fat pieces all burnt to a crisp.'

All Chandler could think was, *Were they empty, or were they full*? 'And this was Frankfurt?' Chandler asked. 'Two days ago? But the war didn't start till today.'

'Well,' Golding said, 'that's sort of a definitional thing, you know, and it looks like the Russkies were on a different page than we were 'cause they been tearin' new assholes outa airfields all up and down Germany and England.

'Anyway,' he continued, after a pause, 'there was a whole huge crowd of people off to the edge of the tarmac. When we first got there, you couldn't really see 'em – they were out in the dark – but you could hear 'em. And they could see us, 'cause by the time we started deplanin', they were pushin' forward. Women and children. The MPs were strung out tryin' to hold 'em back, gettin' a little rough, but there really weren't enough of 'em. When the last of the soldiers was off, they just broke. Stormed right on up. It was awful. These were *Americans*, you understand, some Brits – vacationers mostly. The MPs just sorta disappeared, and the civilians kept comin'. Not fightin' or anything, but not givin' a shit about pushin' real hard. The kids were screamin' bloody murder.' Golding's voice trailed off as he shook his head.

'I don't know what they'd been seein',' he said with a huge sigh, 'but they were wild-eyed – it was scary. The seats filled up in no time. We were at the door, sayin', 'No, no, we're full, we can't take anybody else.'

They just put their heads down – the adults – avoidin' eye contact and pushed on in like they didn't hear. Finally even the aisles were all filled up and the people on the stairs couldn't fit on. I think they would've kept on tryin', though, if it hadn't a been for another jet landin'. It was like you drew a line through the crowd – those inside the door stayed put, everybody on the other side was off to the races.

'So we were closin' the door when a soldier came runnin' up. I thought maybe he had a message or somethin'. Next thing I know and I'm starin' down the barrel of a fuckin' M-16. He says, "Hold on, just hold on" and looks off and says, "Come on, babe, it's okay", and up comes a woman with a baby. I started to tell him that we were full, but he was pretty hyper, you know. Must've been AWOL. So I just went with the flow.

'The thing was,' Golding's voice faltered just for a second, 'well, they said good-bye. And she sorta, sorta' – the words caught in his throat – 'begged him to go too, and he says, "Oh, baby, ya know I can't," and he kisses 'em, her and the baby. The little girl was still in her jammies. Musta been in a big hurry. Then he was off, ran clear outa sight, off into the dark.'

'How'd you take off with all those people?' Chandler asked.

'Well, the baggage compartment was empty, plus we were light on fuel, almost too light. We'd used up a bunch 'cause we were afraid to turn off the engines – might not've gotten a generator to turn 'em back over. But ole Gator here crunched the numbers and said we could pro'bly do it, so we taxied way out into the grass so we could get a runnin' start on the short runway and off we went. Scattered them German engineers workin' on that runway perty good, but we were off the ground with, oh, twenty or thirty feet to spare. She flew like a pregnant whale.'

'The weight was all too far forward, ya see,' the copilot explained. 'Just barely made Heathrow. Fuel was shit.'

'I don't get it,' Chandler said. 'Why were they all so hot to get outa Germany? I mean, it's not like the States were much safer.'

The copilot and Gator both looked at Golding, who shifted uncomfortably in his leather seat. 'Look,' Golding continued. 'They tol' us not to talk about *any* of this shit, not one bit. But they *especially* tol' us not to talk about what I'm gonna tell you now, so don't you go blabbin' it around, 'cause they're *damned* serious about it, okay?' He paused. 'You know all those civilians we brought out? Well, we bring 'em back to England, and that's as far as they get. Quarantined. Now, that's all I know. You tell me, Mr U-S Army, what the hell does that tell you? Huh?'

Biological warfare, that's what it told Chandler. *My God*, he thought, understanding immediately the reason for all the secrecy. *How many would get on this plane if they knew or suspected*? he wondered. Getting killed or maimed by bullets or high explosives was one thing, but germ warfare . . .

'We're quarantined too, technically,' Golding said. 'They detox the airplane on the ground in England, bomb it in this sealed-up hangar. They quarantine us physically when we fly back into the States. These bastards look like they're dressed up to go to the *moon* when they bring us our food. Hell, Major, welcome to the World of the Damned. You're one of *us* now.'

Jesus, Chandler thought. *But they've gotta be mistaken.* 'Has anybody gotten sick?'

'Nope,' the copilot answered. 'Not that I've heard.'

'Maybe they've got some sorta timed-release bug,' Golding said. 'Or maybe it just screws up your sex drive.'

'Then it ain't worth a shit,' Gator cracked.

They all laughed. *Gallows humor*, Chandler thought. They had obviously had lots of time to talk it over, to put pet theories in play. They had also had time to adjust. He put the worry aside for the moment.

When he returned to his seat, Rebecca was walking down the aisle serving.

'Care for some coffee, Major?'

'No, thanks,' he said as his face contorted in a big yawn. He was tired, and he decided he ought to sleep.

'Are you doing okay?' she asked. 'I mean' – she glanced at the cockpit – 'I saw you talking.' *'I know what you know,' she means*, Chandler thought. *'I'm one of the Damned too.'*

'Yeah,' he said. 'I'm okay, thanks.'

'You sure you still want to go through with this?' she said and laughed.

Chandler grinned and shook his head. 'Sounds like it's a bit late to change my mind. But you – you and the rest of the crew? I don't get it. What are you doing here?'

'Well, when they requisitioned the aircraft, they posted a notice at the supervisors' offices at DFW that asked for volunteers. It was before the war, and . . . well, we just wanted to help out. You know.'

Chandler knew, but it still seemed special somehow.

Bailey's overly loud laugh caught Chandler's attention. Both he and Rebecca looked back at the galley. Chandler couldn't see Jennifer, but it was clear that Bailey was talking to her, compiling the make-work report on the food service plan that Chandler had devised to get the overzealous young lieutenant out of his hair. Bailey lifted his eyes only rarely from the piece of paper on which he was writing.

'What about her?' Chandler asked. He had noticed Rebecca spending a lot of time showing Jennifer the ropes. 'This looks like her first flight over.'

'This is her first flight anywhere, at least after she got through school.'

'And she knows about . . . the war, but she volunteered?'

Rebecca shrugged. 'She's just a good kid.'

Through the open doors to the rear cabin behind Bailey, Chandler saw the bright, energetic faces of the young enlisted troops, kids in their teens and very early twenties. While the older officers and NCOs in front mostly took the opportunity to sleep, the noise from the back of the plane was more or less constant. They were pumped up, their eager faces animated as they knelt on seat cushions and ducked just before bags of peanuts flew over their seat backs. They acted like they were on the school bus headed for the big game, as many must have been just a year or two before, maybe less.

Rebecca hadn't said it. She probably hadn't even thought it, Chandler realized as he settled back in his chair. But *he* thought it. *Every one of them is a good kid. Every one you lose is a good kid.*

He turned on his reading light and pulled out his now dog-eared manuals. When Rebecca returned down the aisle, he said, 'Cream and sugar, please.'

SPECIAL FACILITY, MOUNT WEATHER, VIRGINIA
June 25, 1700 GMT (1200 Local)

'What are you telling me?' Lambert asked into the telephone receiver he held to his right ear, pacing behind his chair and desperate to go to the bathroom.

'I'm saying they launched three regimental-size spoiling attacks against the 4th Infantry in Slovakia out of Ukraine,' the man from V Corps Headquarters in Prague said over the poor connection. 'They came over—'

'Just a second,' Lambert interrupted, pulling the mouthpiece of the other phone on his left ear up to speak. 'V Corps is saying the Russians launched three spoiling attacks along the Ukrainian border into the line held by the 4th.'

'Marvelous!' the Brit said from the TEAMS Forward Headquarters in London. 'Just bloody marvelous! With what size force were the attacks made?'

'Regiments,' Lambert said, and then heard the man from Prague say, 'Those were only the lead elements of what are probably at least two divisions of motorized rifle troops,' which Lambert repeated in the awkward, low-tech teleconference.

In Lambert's office waiting on him were three sets of people, all looking harried and anxious. 'What does that do to our step-off time?' Arthur, the liaison officer in London, asked.

'What's the timetable now?' Lambert asked the U.S. Army officer in Prague as he motioned for the waiting naval officer to hand over her report. 'We're saying a twenty-four- to thirty-six-hour delay until they can pocket the troops with Czech and Slovak forces and then get back up onto the line.'

'There are three reports,' the woman whispered to Lambert. 'There was a missile attack on marine transports by Russian landbased attack aircraft – that's this one,' she said, pulling the report on bottom out and holding it in front of him. 'One supply ship was hit, and her magazine went off, killing all hands.'

Lambert nodded and held up his hand. 'V Corps says there'll be a twenty-four- to thirty-six-hour delay, Arty.'

'"Arthur,"' the British officer said testily. 'And that puts us into a bit of a mess now, doesn't it?'

'This one,' the woman continued in a low tone, pointing to the report on top, 'is on the 509th Combat Team's airdrop onto the banks of the Bosporus in Turkey. Their drop zone was attacked by Spetsnaz shortly after landing. Sixth Fleet thinks they landed right on top of a Russian attempt to mine the strait.'

'Mr Lambert, are you there?' the British officer asked indignantly.

'Yes.'

'You do realize the gravity of the problem, do you not?'

'The third report is on another torpedo attack on a transport in the Gulf of Mexico – this one just off Galveston, Texas. We had debris from the last P-3 run and had listed a kill in the vicinity as confirmed, but either there were *two* Russian subs out there or we missed on the earlier run. Regardless, it's diesel-electric, not nuclear, or we would have heard it, and we sank their sub tender off the coast of Cuba, so it shouldn't be long before—'

'Your VII Corps out of Poland is ahead of schedule,' Arthur said, just as the officer from V Corps on the other phone asked, 'Do you still need me, sir?'

'Yes,' Lambert said as the British officer continued. 'If that Northern Prong continues much farther to the east, its right flank will be exposed since the Southern Prong attack out of Slovakia is now a nonstarter – is that what I am hearing from CINCEUR?'

Lambert put the two phones to his chest, trying not to hop like a child on one foot as his bladder felt like bursting from the gallons of coffee he had consumed, and said to the naval officer, 'Put them on my desk. I'll read them later.'

As she left, the Finnish general and his aide, both clad in civilian clothes for the clandestine visit, stood and claimed their right next in line ahead of the Selected Service Administration official with draft registration figures, who had been waiting for two hours now, continually preempted.

'What is the President's thinking on this matter?' Arthur asked. 'Are we going to slow the advance of the Northern Prong, or stop it altogether, pending the Southern Prong's assumption of the offensive, or are we to continue the Northern Prong's advance without support of a parallel column? That is the question *du jour*.'

Lambert's secretary appeared and said, 'General Thomas has convened another missile threat conference – line seven,' announcing the fifth such alert in the nine hours since the war began.

'Jesus!' Lambert said, more irritated than concerned. 'What is it this time?' he asked his secretary, who kept her ear to her phone, the cord pulled to maximum extension as she stood in the doorway.

With her hand cupped over the mouthpiece she said, 'Sounds like CINCNORAD thinks it's just another gas pipeline explosion after one of our air attacks that the satellite reported as a mobile ballistic missile launch. They're running it down but want you on line just in case.'

Just behind her appeared former President Livingston and his family.

'We've just had an air raid warning go off here!' the officer from V Corps Headquarters said. 'Everybody is putting chemical protective gear on and going to the shelter. I'd like to at least get my mask out, if that's all right with you, Mr Lambert?'

Mr and Mrs Livingston waved good-bye as Lambert listened to the strident wail of a siren over the phone and said, 'Go ahead and go to shelter,' intending to hang up and run after the former President for a proper send-off.

His secretary reappeared behind the departing family and jabbed her finger at the phone, making a face before she said, 'No, General Thomas, he's right here, I swear.' She made another face, her finger pointed at her telephone as she stared at Lambert.

Thomas let the President go, hanging up on the angry British liaison officer, then going to the missile threat conference, then running to the bathroom at risk of an international incident on the eve of the secret admission of the Finns to the TEAMS alliance.

U.S.S. NASSAU, SEA OF JAPAN
June 25, 1900 GMT (0500 Local)

Mouth held his two fists out to Monk as they stood outside the hulking LVTP-7A1 amphibious assault vehicle, or 'Amtrac.' 'Gonna do it, gonna kick some ass.'

Monk tapped lightly down with his own fists.

'You said *that* right,' Cool J said. 'Gonna pop our cherries ta-*day*!' and held his fists out for the tap to Monk and Mouth.

Monk looked over at the spectacle of Bone, who was making the rounds bumping helmets like a linebacker after a good play.

Thonk he heard as Bone butted heads with the new guy, who waited a respectable time before pulling the helmet up off his face. Seeing the red mark across the bridge of the guy's nose in the dim light of the well deck, Monk wiggled his jaw to ensure that his chin strap was secure.

'Say, Bone,' Mouth said. 'You got so much greasepaint on your face you look like a bruthah.'

Cool J laughed, and Monk had to smile. They all had greasepaint on, but Bone had gone around to everybody that he could corner and asked them for their opinion about his camo job. The result, naturally, was a face covered thick with his squadmates' helpful 'finishing touches' of black, green, and brown that looked gray in the red-lit well deck and made him look more like a circus clown than a marine.

Bone butted Mouth's head especially hard, and Mouth said, 'Shit,' quietly, looking at Bone out of the sides of his eyes in anger.

As Mouth was taking his helmet off to replace it on his head properly, Bone stepped up to Monk, pausing to look down at him. Their squadmates all watched Bone slowly bend over and lightly tap the front brims of their helmets, keeping his eyes fixed on Monk's the entire time.

Monk understood, and nodded his head slightly up and down.

'Shit, man,' Mouth said, putting his helmet back on his head. 'Why don't you jus' give T Man the tongue, Bone?'

Bone shot Mouth a look and Mouth rocked back, holding up his hands in retraction.

'Well deck's almost flooded,' the new guy said, and the men of First Squad all peered out between their Amtrac and Second Squad's next to it. Sure enough, black water lapped up almost to the tracks of the front Amtrac, two rows ahead of their own. The ship's pumps were shifting ballast to the rear, pressing the ramp at the end of the well deck down into the water.

Far back in the recesses of the ship, Monk could hear the heavy machinery start the conveyor belt that rolled supplies forward to the well deck from the ship's hold. All morning cargo elevators had rumbled through the vessel, and the angled ramps that honeycombed the *Nassau* had been jammed with traffic. Just in front of the conveyor belt, at the end of the well deck away from the opening, the eleven monorail cars on their overhead tracks could be seen lowering supplies from the ceiling into the nooks and crannies of two of the big LCUs, Landing Craft Utility, each carrying two M-1A1 main battle tanks and thirty tons of fuel and supplies.

In front of the LCUs were the two LCACs – Landing Craft Air Cushion. Each of the two hydrofoils would dash onto the beach at forty knots to insert four eight-wheeled LAV-25 Light Armored Vehicles, each of them with a 25-mm Bushmaster automatic cannon and coaxial 7.62-mm machine gun, crew of three and six combat-ready marines. Finally, in the very front were eight Amtracs like Monk's, with thirty-two more Amtracs in the follow-on. This would be a full, battalion-size landing. An opposed landing, they had been told in the briefing.

After us, Monk thought to ward off the slight chill he felt in his blood, *there'll be two more LCUs and a coupla big LCMs to bring in supplies. That's just from our ship. Then there's the* Iwo Jima, *the* Tripoli, *and the* Portland. *That's another three thousand marines*, he thought. *We should be okay. And they say there's another landing team on up the coast, maybe four thousand more troops*. He swallowed, and there was a thick lump in his throat.

The whine of a helicopter's jet turbines as they lifted it off the flight deck broke through the open end of the ship over the constant din of the working sailors. The sound of the choppers was sometimes accompanied by a brief glimpse of the helicopters' lights – of either a string of CH-53E Super Stallion transports ferrying assault troops several miles inland or an occasional AH-1 Super Cobra gunship, rearmed and refueled and wheeling like a fighter plane back into the battle on shore that had begun over an hour ago. Many of the ship's two thousand marines were already in the shit, Monk knew. The first of the eight AV-8B Harrier jump jets should soon be returning also, landing vertically like a helicopter on the *Nassau*'s flat, aircraft-carrier-style deck atop a cushion of air blasted downward by the vectored exhaust of its jet engines. They would be back in action to support the main landing.

'All hands, all hands,' the PA system boomed, and men threw their cigarettes to the deck, one landing just under the no smoking sign, Monk noticed. 'Now hear this.' There was a rattle over the speakers as the microphone was handed off.

'1st Battalion, 3rd Marines,' came the voice of the battalion commander, 'you men are about to have the rare opportunity to make history! Many years from now, they will write about this battle! What they will say is up to you! You know what's expected! You know what to do! And by doing your jobs, you will join that long line of men who call themselves . . . Marines! "We few, we happy few, we band of brothers, for he today that sheds his blood with me shall be my brother." *Semper fidelis!*'

Over a thousand men in the hollow well deck exploded into their boot camp '*A-a-r-r-u-u-g-g-a-a-h*,' followed by their deep guttural barks, body slams and punches, and Monk felt the tingly rush of excitement caused by the release of adrenaline. It washed all over his body like the rush he felt during the kickoff of a football game. He grunted and growled in the cacophony of male sounds and slammed his shoulders hard up against his squadmates. He felt it. He was ready. He even wanted it, needing to release the energy and tension.

Some guy from Second Squad whom Monk barely recognized under the greasepaint said, 'Fuckin' dead, cold meat, man,' holding his fists up and barking. 'Fuckin' *killin'* time!'

Monk hammered fists with the guy, setting his jaw and nodding while boiling inside. The marine moved on. 'Gonna fuck 'em up, man,' he said to Cool J, hammering with Cool J and then Mouth. 'Gonna fuck 'em up *real* bad,' Cool J responded.

Mouth said, 'No pris'ners, home boy!' Mouth then turned to the neighboring Second Squad, each of the two squads standing behind their own Amtrac. They were archenemies normally and opponents in brawl after brawl on the sports field, but when Mouth shouted, 'Kill 'em *a-a-a-l-l!*' the shout brought forth the animal sounds of '*A-a-r-r-u-u-g-g-a-a-h!*' from their rivals in which Monk and his squadmates now joined, whipped up by the ritual. The deep u-u sounds of the shout, more of a bark from deep in the men's diaphragms than a voice, rippled throughout the cavernous deck as the thousand marines all suddenly joined in. The barks could not, however, drown out the commands boomed from the more accomplished lungs of the gunnery sergeants.

'*Mount up!*' they yelled from various parts of the deck, and the men began scrambling through the open rear doors of their armored assault craft.

Chapter Eleven

THREE HUNDRED MILES SOUTH OF ICELAND
June 25, 1900 GMT (1500 Local)

When Bailey was finally off on his next errand, Chandler fished out of his pack the manual he'd been waiting impatiently to read. He noticed that Barnes eyed the book's cover, 'NBC Handbook,' then caught Chandler's eye.

'*NBC*,' Chandler thought. Letters that strike fear into soldiers' hearts. '*Nuclear-Biological-Chemical*.' Chandler opened the manual and read.

'Biological agents are microorganisms that are used to cause disease among personnel, animals, or plants. They are capable of covering extensive areas with minimum munitions expenditure because of the small quantities of biological agent required for an effective dose. CB agents are generally released as aerosols that are carried over the target area by the prevailing winds.'

He'd heard it all before in lectures, but had not paid it much attention. The stuff had been around in the last world war but hadn't been used.

'Nerve agents produce their effect by blockage of the normal muscle relaxation that takes place as a result of a chemical process at the nerve-muscle juncture. Because of constriction of the muscles involved in respiration, death usually results through respiratory failure.' Chandler looked over at his gear. The atropine injectors were visible on the side of the pouch. It would help slow the action of a nerve agent, maybe even save you. *Maybe*.

Difficult to detect, Chandler read. Colorless, odorless, tasteless. Effectiveness dependent on meteorological and terrain conditions – temperature, wind, humidity, terrain contours, etc. Best usage – '*best*' Chandler thought, shaking his head – is at night, against unprotected troops in hollows formed by terrain into which the heavier-than-air gas would settle. *Insecticide. Killing by insecticide. And it would be best at night, of course; evaporation is limited then. It also happens to be when troops are frightened and alone – in the dark.*

Nerve gas penetrates through the skin. A tiny vapor droplet – one single, invisible droplet on your arm, or hand, or face – and you're dead. Maybe a minute or two, maybe you don't even know anything is wrong for almost an hour, depending on which of the two principal concoctions is used: 'GB' or 'VX.' But sooner or later, pinpointing of the pupils, flushed skin, sweating, tightness of the chest, dimness of vision, and then, the first tremors. Chandler put the book down.

Please God, don't let me see this, Chandler thought. Bailey came back to his seat from the forward galley, stopping in the aisle to acknowledge something that Jennifer was saying, and smiling. Chandler quickly dived back into the manual, less to avoid having to talk to Bailey in particular and more to avoid talking to anyone at that moment. Bailey obliged, content to take his seat and gaze at the bulkhead ahead, smiling to himself.

Bailey's new notepad was, Chandler observed out of the corner of his eye, faintly pink in color. Up at the top, buried amid swirling green vines and red flowers, was the letterhead of 'Jennifer M. Sims' with her Dallas address beneath.

Just a coincidence that her address and phone number are on the piece of paper she gave him, Chandler thought with amusement. Bailey folded up the blank piece of paper and put it in his pack, ending the move just as Jennifer appeared and poured Bailey some orange juice, a broad smile on her pretty face. Bailey smiled back, but couldn't hold his eyes on hers for long. *Bailey thinks he just pulled a fast one*, Chandler realized, shaking his head ever so slightly. *Melissa was right. Women eat men for breakfast when it comes to shit like this*.

He looked back down at his book. 'Blister Agents.' Chandler pressed on, reading as rapidly as possible. Warning signs of an attack: shells hitting with no explosion.

Protective gear, whose usage is prescribed by the MOPP level – Mission Oriented Protective Posture – each with its own number, one through four. The suits were hot and you couldn't wear them for long. *Ours, at least, are 'breathable,'* Chandler thought – charcoal filtered and more comfortable than the Russians' rubber outfits. The charcoal in the Americans', however, would get saturated and you would have to get a new suit.

Overpressured vehicles that keep the harmful vapors out, decontamination, first aid, reporting and area-marking procedures, even how to read the signs that the unnamed enemy – 'The Threat' – would post delimiting contaminated areas, interestingly always shown as being in the Russian language.

When Chandler had finished the manual, he was agitated and stood up, looking around for something to do. He felt drawn to the cockpit, and knocked on the door. The door opened just wide enough for Gator to see him. 'It's the Major.'

'Go away,' Golding said, and in his agitated mood Chandler prepared to meet Golding's repartee with a sharp remark. He hesitated, however. The pilot and copilot were staring intently out of the cockpit, both of Golding's hands on the wheel and the left hand of Frazier, the copilot, on the throttle. 'Go away, Major,' Golding said. 'I'm not kidding.' He was tense, intent on his job.

'Come left,' Frazier said, dipping his head and looking up out of the windshield on the sunny day. Golding turned the wheel slightly to the left. 'Okay, okay!' Frazier said, throttling back with the most delicate of movements as his gaze remained fixed on the sky above. Golding was steering left and right and Frazier was adding or reducing power.

The flight engineer did not seem particularly busy by comparison, and Chandler asked in a hushed tone, 'What're they doing?'

'We're in formation with the other six aircraft,' Gator said, and Chandler bent down to look out the windshield.

The massive forms of two wide-bodied airliners filled the sky just a few hundred feet above. 'Jesus Christ!' he said as he stared at the undulating formation, every plane rising or falling in slow motion in its position relative to the others.

'Shut the fuck up, okay?' Golding said, sweat coating his forehead and brow.

'Why this close?'

'Only gives 'em one radar signature,' Gator said. 'It's a mother of a return, but their Intell guys can't sit down there and count us as we fly by Iceland.' 'Orlando,' Chandler read on the flight engineer's nameplate. *Orlando – 'Gator' – Florida. Or was it 'Gator' as in 'Navigator'?* Chandler wondered.

'We just went solo,' Gator said. 'No more fighter escort. The Tomcats are headed home.'

The first beep sounded from a small device crudely taped on the dash just below the windshield. When the series of tones quickened to a constant, rapid beat, Golding said, 'Turn that thing off.'

Frazier reached over, and the device fell silent, a red light blinking in place of the tones.

'What's that?'

'Up fifty,' Golding ordered, and Frazier's hand moved the throttle forward a millimeter, the engines sounding only slightly higher in pitch.

'Is that . . .?' Chandler looked down at Gator, who stared sullenly, unmoving, at the map of the trackless blue ocean at the very top of which, Chandler saw, was the island of Iceland. 'Is that a radar detector, like for your car?'

'Yeah,' Gator said, not looking up. 'We're lit up like a Halloween pumpkin.'

He didn't appear overly concerned, but Chandler felt a rising tide of fear as he watched Gator slump dejectedly in his chair. *Resignation,*

Chandler thought, *but to what*? He looked up at the rapidly pulsing red light on the simple car radar detector.

'What happens if we get jumped?' Chandler asked, his voice kept low in the tense cockpit.

'We die,' Golding said.

'No, really,' Chandler asked, but Golding said nothing more.

'The most recent orders are to ditch,' Gator elaborated. 'It worked for a Federal Express jet – picked up fourteen survivors.'

'Out of how many?' Chandler asked, and Gator shrugged. 'Glad it's a proven method,' Chandler mumbled.

The men in the cockpit were quiet, still, but with every glance at the radar detector's flashing red light Chandler grew more agitated. 'You mean you just put the nose down and fly into the fucking *ocean*?'

'You keep your gear retracted,' Golding answered, 'and settle down right over the top of a wave – down the backside into the trough. It's a crapshoot. If you hit the uphill side of one of them forty-foot North Atlantic swells you might as well fly into the wall of the Grand Canyon.'

'They're callin' this the Iceland Triangle,' Gator said, ''cause the Russians know just where—'

'Shut up!' Golding ordered, followed quickly by, 'Acknowledged, Niner One. Navaho Six Five Seven Two Seven breaking low. Good luck. Out.' Chandler suddenly felt light on his feet as the plane's nose dropped and he grabbed onto the bulkhead, the background noise in the aircraft rising with the increasing speed.

'Gator, we got bandits – small contact – bearing two niner one, angels one point five at seventy-two miles,' Golding said, his voice an even monotone. Gator scrambled to jot down the information. 'They got the heaters on, nine hun'erd and fifty knots. We're bustin' formation; we drew the deck. I'm takin' her to five hundred, maybe lower – you give me a course.'

Chandler watched in the strangely calm cockpit as Gator's pencil flew in straight lines on the map to connect dots he had just drawn. As the whine of the descent increased in pitch, Gator held up an odd-shaped clear plastic card like a ruler. He made marks and punched numbers on a keypad built into his instrument console. 'Second point?' he asked while his pencil still flew.

Golding said, 'Last was bearing two eight niner at seventy.'

Gator repeated his marks and calculations and sat back saying, 'Come left to zero one seven.'

'Say again?' Golding said.

'Zero one seven!' Gator snapped, and Golding began his bank left. Chandler felt the weight on his legs and his ears pop.

'Uh, Gator,' Frazier said. 'Zero one seven is, like, north, right at Iceland.'

Gator, with his maps spread out in front of him, tossed his plastic ruler down and snapped, 'North! No shit – really?' He huffed and stretched his neck. 'It's the fastest way outa the interception envelope, *if* they hold course a minute or two more on afterburner.'

Golding reached forward and tapped a button on the dash, which illuminated to say SEAT BELTS. He picked up the microphone. 'Flight attendants prepare for ditching,' he said in a low voice, obviously intentionally mumbling so the passengers might not hear what he said, and panic. *Little good that'll do*, Chandler thought as he stared down at the gray ocean, white spray whipped off the caps of swells and sliding by at the ever lower belly of the Delta jet.

'Five hundred,' the copilot announced, but Golding kept going down.

'Looks like the wind is bearin' about two eight zero,' Golding said. 'Whaddaya think, Fraze?'

The copilot peeked up over the dash at the white caps. 'That's about right,' he said as he sank back. 'Four hundred.' His voice was calm, but his face reflected dimly in the windshield showed agonizing worry. 'Three hundred.' The water below slid by at remarkable speed. 'Two fifty, Larr'.' Golding leveled the aircraft.

'I got . . . I got the E-2!' Frazier shouted. 'Sounds like . . . they're vectorin' Tomcats!'

'Where the hell'd they come from?' Golding asked.

'It's Tango Charlie Six,' Frazier said, glancing over at his seatmate.

'Could they have gotten a drink?' Golding asked softly, not taking his eyes from the windshield.

'No way,' Frazier said in the quietness that followed. 'They had to be on burners all the way from . . . Missiles away!'

'But they were "Bingo Fuel,"' Gator said, looking at the two pilots, who said nothing.

There was another silence, and Chandler asked, 'What the hell is "Bingo Fuel?"' in a near whisper, transfixed by the drama but not understanding it.

'It means,' Golding said slowly, 'they had just enough fuel to make it back to the *Eisenhower* when they left station earlier.'

'Splash one!' Frazier shouted. 'Splash two! They got 'em!' Then he grew quiet again. There was no sustained jubilation.

'I don't understand,' Chandler said. 'I thought you said we didn't have escorts anymore.'

'What VHF are they monitoring?' Golding asked Frazier.

'One two two point five,' Frazier replied, and Golding turned a knob on his armrest.

'Tango Charlie Six, this is Navaho Six Five Seven Two Seven. You read me, over?'

After a pause, Golding said, 'Thanks a lot, boys. You pulled our fat asses outa that fire.'

After another brief pause, Golding and Frazier both laughed. 'Sorry, ma'am,' Golding said. 'Thank you too.' They listened again. 'Well,' Golding said, 'I just wanted to say . . . thanks. Thanks and . . . and good luck.'

The Delta pilots listened again for a long time. 'Roger. Copy. I'll do that. Navaho Two Seven out.'

Chandler heard Golding take a long, deep breath. After another brief radio communication he told Gator to plot a new course, and they slowly banked and rose higher and higher into the sky. The red light on the radar detector no longer blinked.

After a minute or so in silence, Frazier said softly, 'They just punched.' Chandler could see in the slightly mirrored windshield Golding's one unpatched eye close for a couple of seconds.

'So the navy'll go pick 'em up, right?' Chandler said. 'They'll send a search and rescue helicopter. I mean, they know where they are.'

'No,' Golding said slowly and quietly. 'They won't. The Russians' land-based aircraft own the skies around Iceland right now. The navy can't get close enough to launch a helicopter.'

'So – what?' Chandler said, looking out onto the unbroken expanse of the North Atlantic. 'They can't just leave 'em there.'

'Those four people are dead, Major,' Golding snapped, staring back at Chandler in the reflective windshield as if it was suddenly important that Chandler understood the point. 'Oh, you can still talk to 'em if you want. We can patch you into the radio they carry in their survival pack, assumin' they didn't crack their heads open on the canopy or break their necks in the dynamic pressure of the wind, and their 'chutes didn't fail to deploy. Yeah, if everything's okay, they can start clawin' their way out from under the nylon through all the pesky little streamers an' straps any minute now. You ever see a big sheet of wet nylon spread out on the surface of water? May be tough with the swell and all, a little disoriented under the water, to find your way back up for that gulp of air and to—'

'That's enough, Larr',' Frazier said quietly.

The silence hung over the cockpit, and after a few moments, Chandler said, 'I'll get outa your way.'

'Wait a minute,' Golding said. 'The pilot of one of those 14s tol' me to tell your men somethin'' – he reached up and punched the SEAT BELT button and it went dark – 'but I'm gonna tell you and then I want you to go back there and tell your men what he said.'

Chandler stood at the door waiting, dreading.

'He said to "send those bastards to hell so's he could get his hands on 'em," I believe were his exact words, and' – Golding's voice broke momentarily – 'and tell 'em his wife's name was Sandy, Sandy from Norfolk.'

U.S.S. NASSAU, SEA OF JAPAN
June 25, 2000 GMT (0600 Local)

In the quiet before the engine started, the marines could still hear the sailors who lined the railing high above the well deck. Grimy and sweaty from their work, they had cheered and whistled, thumbs up and pumping fists in the air, in a display of support never before witnessed. Two men held a large American flag over the railing.

For the benefit of the fourteen men of their First Squad and the four-man company mortar team seated along the walls of the Amtrac, Mouth said loudly, 'Fuckin' Squids gotta get some *female* ass for a change. They startin' to like *us!*' The men all burst out laughing, even Bone.

The Amtrac's ramp suddenly began rising, slowly snuffing out the natural light of the new dawn from the open end of the ship. The whine of the electric motor shut off, and all fell quiet. Ignition of the engine followed, its noise drowning out all but shouts, and Monk felt its tremendous vibration through his back, which rested on the welded aluminum armor.

He twisted to adjust his webbing and reposition his bayonet, accidently bumping into Smalls, the new guy, in the cramped space.

'Sorry,' the kid said to Monk, who nodded back at him in forgiveness. Smalls's voice had quivered, and Monk was surprised to feel his own breath catch in his lungs. He forced his lungs to fill with air, taking a deep breath to blow out the strictures.

Looking forward, Monk saw Gunny peer out of the vehicle commander's vision blocks. Wearing the oversize Vehicle Crewman's Helmet, Gunny reached up and held the boom mike that crossed in front of his mouth closer, saying something. The Amtrac lurched forward. The ride had begun, and Monk braced himself for the debarkation.

After a few small starts and stops, the Amtrac's driver put the pedal down, and the hulking Amtrac surged forward, throwing the two rows of men along the bench seats toward their neighbor to the rear. Picking up speed in its race down the deck, the huge vehicle tilted forward just as the men had straightened themselves up and they were all thrown to the front.

Monk felt the sickening fall of the huge chunk of armor into the ocean, and it chilled him as always. The oversize Amtracs were cavernous as armored vehicles went, with three times the personnel load of the army's Bradleys. The purpose of all that size was the displacement of enough water to make them buoyant, but at thirty tons their buoyancy seemed counterintuitive.

Monk could hear the rush of water all around the hull as the Amtrac began to swim. The gray early morning light that filtered through the vision blocks of the driver, commander, and gunner all confirmed once again that the Amtrac floated.

The marines in back were quiet. Something was missing. Normally, there was pushing and accusations as their bodies were slammed together in the debarkation and a cheer from one of the rednecks in their squad as they dropped into the sea. But they were all silent this time. Monk felt the adrenaline wearing off and a faint chill setting into his bones.

He lay his head back against the hull, the helmet gently passing the vibration from the engine into his scalp like a massage. He took another deep breath that ended with a yawn. He didn't feel tired despite not sleeping at all after the missile attack the night before. The vibrations felt good, all the way down his tense neck. He closed his eyes, suddenly feeling exhausted. The loud noise of the engine and the smooth whoosh of the water jets that propelled the Amtrac soothed Monk and allowed him to rest. It would be over an hour before they were all formed up for the run in to the beach.

Monk's mind drifted, as always returning to calm himself before sleep to the cabin that his family rented up on Mullet Lake each summer for a week. His father had loved fishing, and his enjoyment of it had infected the entire family. But the part Monk had loved most was at night when it got cold and they had to build a fire in the rough cabin's single room and curl up in sleeping bags, telling stories and talking.

As he rested, the fond memories of wrestling with his brothers in the thick quilts and of listening to his father's stories slowly began to turn on him. Creeping around outside the cabin in the night like the wolf that he always feared from his brothers' tales, he tried at first to shut it out, to rest peacefully, to blank his mind for its calming effect. But he remembered looking at the windows long after the rest were asleep, expecting to see the wolf's glowing red eyes.

Monk looked around. Most of the men lining the hull appeared to be asleep. He lay his head back with a thonk and closed his eyes again, but still sleep would not come. What was it that crept up on his cozy place, stealing his rest like a thief? He decided to confront the thought, still lurking in the shadowy recesses of his mind.

Monk opened the door and let it in. Stepping out of the shadows, 'the Beast' revealed itself to Monk. He was wide awake now. His eyes remained closed, but his mind sped up. His throat felt thick as the chill returned with a vengeance. Monk tried to force down the shakes with slow, deep breaths. But the physical reaction to confrontation of the Beast was too much, and he slammed the door of the cabin closed against it. Let it lurk out there in the dark a little longer. There was no way to win the confrontation, nothing to be gained by thinking about the beach.

Something else, Monk thought. *Football. Offense or defense? Coach*

*said I'd be best as a DB – I'd get more playin' time – but to carry the
ball, that'd be somethin'!*

'It'll be an opposed landing,' the battalion commander had said late the
night before on the well deck. It was something in the lieutenant colonel's
voice . . . Everyone had heard it. The men all looked at each other and
had their confirmation in the eyes of their buddies. Marine infantrymen
trained for opposed landings, but marine officers trained to avoid them.
The battalion commander's tone had been almost apologetic, and the
words – 'I want to thank all you men for the honor and the privilege,'
et cetera, et cetera . . . The door to the cabin burst wide open, and in
rushed the Beast, all drools and snarls and menace.

Shit! Monk thought, pissed off that his stomach began to churn,
making him want to go to the bathroom. Although his eyes were closed,
his blood surged through his veins and his bowels turned like after a
bellyful of the chief's coffee. *What a time to have to go*, he thought.

'*Goddammit*!' the voice exploded right in front of Monk.

Monk's eyes, along with all the other men's, shot wide open.

'Is that your gear, Lance Corporal?' Gunny shouted right at Monk's
face.

'Yes, Gunnery Sergeant!'

'Then *stow* it, Goddammit!'

'Aye aye, Gunnery Sergeant!' Monk replied, bending over to shove
his field pack the four extra inches that it would move underneath
his seat.

Gunny continued toward the rear of the Amtrac to a ripple of heels
that jammed back into their gear. Next to the rear ramp, which glistened
with condensation as the metal cooled in the water, he knelt down and
began a quiet conversation with their squad leader, Sergeant Simmons.
Simmons sat next to the ramp and would lead them out. Monk cursed
his luck at having drawn Gunnery Sergeant Dirks's Amtrac. *It would've
been better if it was the LT*, Monk thought. At the same time, however,
he felt strangely relieved by Gunny's presence. *Ain't nobody who can
kill him*, Monk thought. *Mean motherfucker*.

'You think it's gonna be bad?' Mouth asked just loud enough to be
heard over the engine noise.

Monk noticed Cool J., who somehow had gotten separated in the
seating from his two friends by the new guy Smalls, lean out to listen
to his answer. The new guy pressed his helmet back against the hull
to allow Cool J. to see.

Back came the Beast, and Monk couldn't answer. Instead, he just
closed his eyes and allowed the tug of fatigue to pull him toward sleep,
away from the reality of the moment. '*It'll be an opposed landing*.' The
words echoed through his head. *An opposed landing*, he thought, *on the
coast of Russia*. He was wide awake again.

SPECIAL FACILITY, MOUNT WEATHER, VIRGINIA
June 25, 2000 GMT (1500 Local)

'One!' President Costanzo said into the speakerphone that connected him to the Free World's leaders. 'The North Atlantic Treaty states that, in the event of an attack upon one member nation, all other members shall treat that attack as an attack upon their nations. On June eleventh, the strategic nuclear forces of the Republic of Russia struck the continental United States with a massive and unprovoked nuclear attack, but the governments of the member nations Germany, France, Norway, Denmark, the Netherlands, and Belgium have chosen to reject their obligations under the treaty. Therefore, the United States of America hereby abrogates the North Atlantic Treaty as it relates to the defense by the United States of any of those nations.'

Costanzo looked around the table at the combined meeting of the Joint Chiefs and his Cabinet – some new, others from Livingston's old Cabinet – as voices erupted from the speakerphone. 'Two! The armed forces of the United States will continue to use their bases wherever located without impediment by the governments of the host countries and all transportation facilities previously dedicated for use by NATO during time of war. *If* – he raised his voice – 'if there is any interference in *any* way with the prosecution of our war effort by *any* of our *former* allies, those allies will have more to fear than just Russian weapons!'

The president of France intoned in French, with the English translation coming a second later like a bad dubbing of a B-grade movie, the obvious outrage in the man's voice being translated in a monotone, 'Mr President, you cannot, you will not use European territory to conduct hostilities without the consent of the European Community. The day when you could sit in Washington and—'

'*Any* attempt,' Costanzo interrupted, 'to interfere with our operations will be deemed an act of war.' The room and the telephone grew quiet. 'And furthermore, if I am informed by my field commanders that any further maneuvers by your and Chancellor Gerhardt's EuroCorps outside our bases are deemed to be hostile, I will order immediate air interdiction by the Air Combat Command. Let me make myself clear on this point, ladies and gentlemen. When you breached the North Atlantic Treaty, you ceased being an ally of the United States of America. Your betrayal of us in time of dire need puts you on the cusp of becoming our enemies. If you try to stop us, we'll take you down one by one or all together.'

Thomas leaned over from Lambert's right and General Fuller met him halfway from Lambert's left. 'What was it you called him?' Thomas whispered. '"California enviroweenie"?'

Fuller shrugged and shook his head in befuddlement. 'Man's a politician. It don't take a weatherman to know which way the wind's blowin',' Fuller said in an ironic twist of the lyric from the two men's Vietnam days. 'Mount Weatherman,' Fuller completed.

When the President was finished, he disconnected the line just as the French president's bluster began. Placing his hands down on the table, he said, 'Now, let's see what the Brits think of the performance.'

The question was answered as soon as the technician switched lines. Their laughter had obviously been stifled for too long.

ABOARD LVTP-7, SEA OF JAPAN
June 25, 2100 GMT (0700 Local)

Sergeant Simmons squatted in front of Monk and the three men around him. 'You exit right!' Simmons shouted. 'Monk, you take your fire team to the far left! Get on up to the treeline, chop-chop! Make contact with Third Platoon, which should be to your left, and then we move on in, all three platoons abreast! Whatever you do, don't take cover behind the Amtrac! The driver's gonna back on off the beach to pick up the second wave, so clear out! Okay?'

Monk nodded, and Sergeant Simmons waited until he had gotten confirmation from Mouth, Cool J., and the new guy. It was Monk's fire team, but they all had to know what to do, just in case. Simmons moved on down to the next fire team.

Bong! reverberated throughout the hollow shell of the Amtrac. The men jumped as the strange slamming sound pierced the hull. Monk looked at Mouth, who stared back waiting.

Bong! They all jumped again. The sound, more a sustained deep whine than anything else, seemed otherworldly.

'What the fuck is that, man?' Mouth shouted. 'Sounds like a motherfuckin' ray gun or somethin'!'

All of the sudden, the Amtrac echoed with a string of the sounds, random but continuous.

'Shit, man!' Mouth screamed. 'What the hell *is* that? Hey! Cheese-breath!' Mouth yelled, and the Amtrac's gunner lowered his head out of the cupola to look back at Mouth. 'What the hell is that?' Mouth practically screamed as the sounds grew louder.

'Shut *up*!' Gunny shouted, turning to face Mouth. 'It's artillery! Now *can* it!' Both he and the gunner resumed a vigil at their fighting posts.

Monk's mouth went dry. Those were shells landing in the water, a sound they had never heard in training. Monk looked up at the huge flat ceiling of the thinly armored Amtrac. He pictured the incoming shell – *right through the roof like an old-style beer opener*, Monk thought. *Blow up in here, down below the waterline. It'd be over so quick you probably wouldn't even know what had happened.*

'Shit!' Mouth yelled, jostling Monk as he could not keep still. The sounds were unbearably loud now. 'We're drivin' right into a wall of that shit, man!'

Monk glanced up at Gunny, expecting him to ream Mouth, but Gunny was braced in his position peering out ahead.

Louder and louder, closer they drew. Finally, the men in the Amtrac jumped with every single blast, each so loud it sounded like a hit. The bongs did not sound like explosions – more like the inside of a metal trash can with somebody banging on it from outside. Monk could feel them through the armored hull against his back.

Slowly the sound of the blasts began to recede. Although still loud, they were growing more distant with each passing explosion. And they seemed to be letting up some too.

'I bet the navy's pounding 'em right now!' the new kid said.

Monk pictured the artillery emplacements, themselves suffering a rain of death like that they had attempted to inflict, their wrecked guns smoldering in the dug-in positions.

'Missiles!' Cheesebreath shouted from the crew deck in front.

Mouth rolled his head and his eyes at the same time. 'Oh, man! This is fuckin' ridiculous!'

'Stay cool, man,' Monk said more calmly than he felt.

But Mouth couldn't sit still; rolling his head and huffing and squirming in his seat, he began to bitch in a constant chatter.

The gunner in the Amtrac's new upgunned weapons station opened up with the M-279, its machine-gun-like spitting of twelve 40-mm grenades per second breaking the relative quiet of the Amtrac with a staccato burst. Another rip from the gun fired a half dozen or so bullet-shaped grenades at the shore, their velocity so low that the Russians should actually see them in flight. Obviously spotting individual targets on the beach, the gunner then switched to the rattling M-2 .50-caliber heavy machine gun, pouring out the thick bullets until shifting back to the grenade launcher in a more or less constant process of killing.

'The navy's firin' smoke! Switch to thermal!' Gunny yelled.

Time seemed to slide by. It could have been minutes, or it could have been seconds – Monk could not tell which. Mouth was silent now. Monk glanced over at him to see if anything was wrong, but Mouth just looked down at the deck. Monk looked down also, and when he did he could feel it. The beginning of the surge.

Monk looked at the other men. Several appeared ill in spite of the relatively calm seas. Right next to him Monk saw the new guy, his mouth wide open and head tilted back, his chin resting on the raised front sight of his M-16. Monk backhanded the kid's leg, and when he looked over Monk gave him a brief nod of his head. The kid smiled and licked his lips, looking around to see if anyone else cared to acknowledge his existence.

There was no bravado now, just men dealing with the Beast.

'Get your gear on!' Gunny yelled from in front.

Bumping and jostling accompanied the command as all of the men began moving at once. Monk realized just how difficult sitting there still and quiet had been, and it felt good to have a purpose and take action.

After Monk's field pack was securely placed on his back, he sat awkwardly on the front edge of the bench. He felt a chill, and his breath was ragged. Breathing did not seem at all natural anymore.

They were close, seeming to stop their forward progress as the surf washed back out to sea and then to rush forward with the next wave. *Three, maybe four more surges and we're on dry ground*, Monk thought as his senses monitored the ever more pronounced effects on the Amtrac of the currents near shore.

'Lock and *lo-o-oad*!' Gunny yelled, turning all the way around to face the eighteen marines in the back of the Amtrac, checking each out with his eyes like a mother before her kids headed for the school bus on a cold winter day. 'Safe your weapons!' he yelled. 'Unsafe 'em on the beach! Semiauto. This ain't the army!'

The sound of clicks and clacks, of metal on metal, filled Monk's ears as he pulled a twenty-round magazine out of his ammo pouch. Tapping the magazine on his helmet with loud thwacks to ensure that it was fully loaded and that the cartridges' bases were flush against the wall, he slid the magazine into the rifle's guide, slapping the end to hear the click as it seated. He then pointed the rifle toward the ceiling and pulled the charging handle fully back. Watching as the brass cartridge on top of the stack in the magazine appeared in the open bolt, he slid the charging handle forward. The bolt grabbed the top round and slid it into the chamber.

Monk felt for the selector switch with his thumb. It was all the way forward on safe, but he looked to make certain. Above the trigger housing was written SEMI, the real marine's setting. The drill instructors had pounded marksmanship into the recruits – making single shots count – in this day and age of full auto. They'd always preached that it was because real soldiers exercise fire discipline, as distinguished from the army where you just close your eyes when a twig snaps and spray everything and then call in artillery and air strikes. But Monk had always suspected that the real reason for marines' fire discipline was that their supply lines ran out to sea, and the navy couldn't wait to find an excuse to pull their ships out to the safety of 'blue water' – away from the shore and the stupid jarheads who clung to the beachhead by their fingernails. Monk knew, as each marine was implicitly taught, that you carried what you needed on your back, and that was all the support you could expect.

'Don't waste ammo,' Monk said to the new kid, but loud enough for Mouth and Cool J to hear. He then felt another surge, and just as the Amtrac began to pull back away from the beach in the heavy surf its tracks found bottom, grinding against the rocks. The driver transitioned the Amtrac's drive train to its treads with a groan, and the vehicle lurched and roared up onto dry land to full height, its tracks clawing into the rocks on the shore. That's when the highpitched pings began to sound off the aluminum frontal armor. Monk's mind reluctantly admitted what they must be, yet another sound they had never heard in training. The Amtrac was able to withstand 7.62-mm fire and shrapnel, and Monk prayed for nothing heavier to come their way.

It suddenly seemed unreal. It wasn't happening. He wasn't where he thought he was. There was no war. There was nobody trying to kill him. He'd never have to leave his seat in the Amtrac.

The grenade launcher let loose what had to be an entire box of ammo, the gunner bowed over behind his weapon like a B-17 gunner in the old movies, slewing the gun from left to right.

Gunny pulled the trigger on the pistol grip that extended down from the ceiling next to his position, firing two dozen smoke grenades to the front of the vehicle roughly along the arc that the Amtrac's gunner was devastating. The ramp in back cracked open and the man-made crackling of small-arms fire and rips from machine guns and automatic grenade launchers made the roar of nature's surf seem trifling by comparison.

They also masked the crashing sounds that smashed through the Amtrac. 'A-A-A-A-H-H!' one of the mortarmen screamed as he clawed at his pack and sank to his knees across from Monk. Another heavy-caliber round came crashing in, and smoke began to fill the compartment around the stooped and ducking marines.

The sound of shouting, a steady yell that was taught each marine from the earliest days, announced that the ramp had lowered sufficiently to exit. The strangled end to one marine's shout from outside presaged something else.

Monk stood and followed the two files of men past the wounded mortarman, each step an effort of utmost will. His voice joined the chorus as he trotted to the end of the bench, shouting to block out the reality of his feet touching the angled ramp and then the beach itself. Shouting at the top of his lungs, he turned into the confused crackle of gunfire. He was outside in the gray morning air, with nothing between him and the raging storm of fire from the smoky woods ahead. He was on the beach. His mouth dried, and his shout fell off. He broke into a labored run under the heavy pack to follow the receding forms of the marines through the smoke toward the faintly visible trees. His boots slipped on the smooth wet rocks.

ZING Monk heard over the general roar of guns and explosions.

ZING . . . ZING-ZING-ZING. He stooped to drop to the rocks but he tripped and fell instead.

Landing hard, he grunted heavily and grimaced at the pain that racked his body from a dozen places at once. He began to pat himself frantically for a wound, but the pains faded quickly. He felt a hand grab his pant leg from behind.

Monk looked through the drifting smoke to see Cool J., a corpsman straddling his chest trying frantically to patch Cool J.'s neck as the blood spurted all the way up to the medic's face. The corpsman spit the blood away from his lips in a stringy spray and held the bandage pouch up to his teeth with one hand as his other hand pinched the artery in Cool J.'s neck closed. The corpsman's arms were coated and dripping dark blood, and Monk heard the screams of others whom he saw twisting under the weight of their packs, many with water washing onto their feet with each wave.

Cool J. twisted the fabric of Monk's trousers and opened his mouth to say something, his eyes glassy and panic-stricken. Monk reached out to squeeze his arm as the corpsman fumbled in all the gore and another spurt shot up from his patient's neck.

A crushing shock thudded through Monk's body with a blast of heat and he felt the wind knocked from his lungs. A loud whining sound blared in his ears as he clawed at the pain, and then the world seemed to crash down around him.

Crushed to the ground by the thin upper branches of a fallen tree, Monk felt another huge thud, this one followed by bucketfuls of water that rained down. *Heavy artillery!* he realized through the dizziness and confusion. *That must be heavy artillery!* The Russians were beginning to pound the beach.

He looked through the green leaves and saw the corpsman, frozen with his hands just below Cool J.'s breastbone in mid-press of his CPR, staring ahead in shock. Monk rose up to see through the branches of the shattered tree the wreckage that had been marines strewn all about the beach and into the woods in the thinning smoke.

He felt as much as heard the heavy shells thudding sporadically up and down the beach. He sensed motion and turned in time to see the corpsman rushing forward with his medical kit and rifle.

'Hey!' Monk yelled, scrambling over to Cool J. to continue the lifesaving CPR.

Cool J. was dead. It was clear on first sight.

'*Come on!*' rang out above the now totally surreal sounds of battle, coming to Monk through aching ears that were closed to most sound. '*First and Second squads – get your asses moving!*'

It was Gunny. Monk saw him picking men off their stomachs and throwing them bodily toward the Russian positions. He kicked one man who didn't move, then kicked another who got up like a startled animal and ran for the fighting. One by one Gunny picked his way through, leaving the dead in their places, cursing and kicking the living to send them off to join the dead.

With one last look at Cool J. and a squeeze of his arm, Monk got to his feet to run forward toward Gunny. *'Goddammit, Lance Corporal!'* Gunny yelled. 'You get with the sixty and move 'em on! Keep headin' inland! Don't stop!'

'Aye aye, Gunny!' Monk yelled on instinct, his entire body quivering as he ran toward the roar of guns. His feet fell on the earth in great plops, his body jarred and twisted with each uncertain step. He forced himself forward against the air-splitting sound of bullets flying by his body – random but deadly – blocking everything else out but the motion of his legs as he squinted and grimaced in anticipation of any one of the dozens of bullets tearing a wound open in his body.

Great crashing sounds and red-hot fire erupted in the woods around him every few seconds. With each explosion Monk cringed in expectation of great pain but felt only the jabbing at his ears and the burning on his exposed arms and neck. Death was everywhere, shot out, shredding trees and humans indiscriminately and peppering the ground with large droplets of hot steel rain. And in between, the woods were alive with streaking bullets. Leaves shook. Bark splintered off trees. The closer ones made their brief presence known with a cutting or buzzing sound as they missed by feet or inches in the randomness of life and death in war.

Human remains littered the landscape. A piece here, a bit of equipment with something still attached there. *One man or two?* the question Monk's mind would involuntarily pose as he stepped high into the air over this human pulp or that man's smoldering torso. Monk's mind refused to admit the true nature of what lay at his feet, focusing instead with great effort on avoiding the soiling of his boots with the wretched mess.

His breath came in shallow pants now, not winded from his run but ragged from near hysteria. The Beast, cold and slimy, had slithered into the cabin, into his sleeping bag, right up his spine. It embraced his chest tightly, and Monk had trouble breathing.

Stick! Monk thought on seeing his shipmate, his heart speeding as his running legs slowed. 'Oh, man, shit!' He ran on. He ran from the legless, tattered body of his squadmate. It was too horrible, not because Stick's wounds differed from the others that had come before, but because of the paper-white face that lay undisturbed atop the wreckage, so clearly identifying the owner of the various parts. Monk tried to escape, to escape from Stick, from the long legs of the tall skinny boy. *Z-z-z-zip, zip, zip* – bullets flew by him at incredible speed on all sides. Sounds came from his chest as he ran, freeing themselves through his throat and mouth and betraying for all to see the collapse of his reason. But there was no one to see but the dead and the horribly wounded who writhed almost blind with pain. The sounds vibrated at Monk's lower lip, which quivered uncontrollably and modulated the stream of sound.

The trees and bodies rushed by – American and, now, the first Russians. *Tattoo – you too, man*? Monk's rational mind asked as he kept running. '*Ah!*' the air came from his lungs as he took an awkward step and smashed through a low limb to avoid Sergeant Simmons, his squad leader, draped over a fighting hole next to two dead Russians. The back half of Simmons's helmetless head was a shiny red, uneven mess.

Monk ducked every time he heard the buzzing sounds splitting the air beside him – far too late to do any good as the bullets passed even before you knew they were there.

The fighting was loud now, closer, and Monk's hearing was returning slowly as the shelling died down. The intensity of the spitting sound of bullets splintering through the trees increased, and Monk zigged one way and then zagged the other as he had done while running the Confidence Course at Parris Island, bent over at the waist and propelling himself toward the familiar sounds of firing from marine weapons. Toward the living.

Bursting straight through thick brush and into a small clearing, Monk saw an M-60 rattling out its rounds, its muzzle partially lost in the shimmer of heat rising above it as it spit short streams of bullets. Monk threw himself down next to the two prone men who manned the gun.

It was Bone and the new kid.

'Reload,' the kid yelled as the last of the belt chinged through the machine gun's chamber.

'Monk! All right, man!' Bone yelled. 'Cover us while we change barrels!'

Monk had to look down to see that he still carried his rifle. He raised it to his shoulder without thinking, flicked the selector by feel to SEMI, and looked down its black length, his right eye settling behind the round rear sight. His gaze blurred and he had to continually refocus his efforts to find a suitable target. Out of the corner of his eye, Monk could see Smalls, thick mittens on his hands, unscrewing the superhot barrel of the M-60 and then sticking the new barrel on.

Blinking and forcing himself to look down the rifle into the woods ahead, Monk saw a bush shake for an instant and then grow still. Casually he aimed the rifle in its direction. At the same instant that Monk rested the top of the bush on the center blade of the M-16's front sight, a man rose straight up. Monk's immediate reaction was panic that he had almost shot the man, who began to run away, dropping his rifle and pumping his arms furiously.

It was an easy shot: at less than eighty meters the man ran straight away, not dodging and weaving as taught. Centering the sight between his shoulder blades, Monk squeezed the trigger and the rifle bucked once.

As the brief blur from the heat of the blast dissipated, Monk could see the man falling forward, his back arched and his blond hair suddenly visible as his helmet flew off.

The Russian disappeared to the ground, and Monk felt a punch land on his arm.

'*Shot*, man!' Bone yelled, holding the flat of his palm up for a high five.

I didn't mean to shoot the guy, Monk thought to himself. The Russian National Guard unit that faced them began to crumble, the woods in front filled with running men. Bone's M-60 opened up again, reaping its harvest in great swaths as it and other unseen guns cut down the fleeing men.

Fuck it! Monk thought as he began to jerk the trigger of his M-16 roughly, missing most of his targets because of the poor form but seeing some men fall just from the statistics of war. He never fired more than once at a man; if he missed he reaimed at another as they climbed the bare hill opposite the beachhead a couple of hundred meters away. It was only fair, he figured, since he didn't have it in for any one of them in particular.

When the last of the targets had fallen before reaching the crest of the hill, Bone and the kid reloaded their machine gun and Bone said, 'We better hook back up with the rest of the guys. Where do you think they are?'

Monk dropped his rifle and lowered his head into the crooks of his arms. He jammed his eyes shut so hard he heard a rushing sound in his ears.

'Hey, T Man,' Bone said, 'what's wrong? You *hit*?'

Monk shook his head, and as Bone persisted in trying to talk to him and gently pull his arms away from his face, Smalls went back to look for their squad leader. Monk kept his head buried in his arms and tried to sleep, tried desperately to forget everything and never remember again.

PRESOV, SLOVAKIA
June 26, 1000 GMT (1100 Local)

Chandler felt a trickle of excitement run down his spine as he looked out the window. After eighteen hours on the plane, almost half of it on the ground at bombed-out Stuttgart airport awaiting a new shipment of fuel straight from air force trucks, they were moments away from leaving the aircraft for good. The plane was very low now, a few hundred feet

off the ground. Golding or Frazier was working the throttle all the time
– up a little, then down and back up all the way to a roar.

The plane burst out over the airport environs and the engine was cut
to idle. Below, the standard high chain link fence and cleared, grassy,
tabletop surface streamed by. About a hundred yards inside the high
fence there was concertina wire, coils of barbed wire running in constant
strands parallel to the main fence. Behind the wire, the green grass was
scarred with angry gashes of dark brown and black – slit trenches and
sand-bagged bunkers filled with the heads of Slovak security forces
helmeted in steel. The jet engines whirred to life once again, the pitch
of their sound rising quickly, dramatically, and finally roaring, then being
throttled back to a low whine.

Runway streamed by underneath. A line of craters stitched across
the grass at a steep angle to the runway; the scars of the bombs that
had found the concrete were being tended to by engineers who flashed
underneath Chandler's window ducking and holding their ears. The plane
was flying level over the damaged portion.

Suddenly the engines were cut completely again. The plane sank like a
stone, thudding hard on the runway and bouncing back up again, settling
back down agonizingly slowly. Chandler's pulse began to race. His new
life was about to begin.

As the plane bounced briefly again off the concrete, eating up runway
at a prodigious rate, Chandler noticed that they were awfully close
to the edge. The wing extended far out over the blue lights and
grass. A final squeal of the tires and jarring shake were followed by
a ferocious roar from the engines' reverse thrust that, in combination
with what had to be maximum application of the brakes, threw
Chandler forward hard against the seat belt of the vibrating airplane.
Crashing sounds were heard from the galley and a deeper bump
from elsewhere behind as loose objects shifted with the force of
the deceleration. The aircraft creaked and the brakes moaned, a
fact registered more through the soles of David's feet than with
his ears.

'Please gather your belongings and prepare to exit through the front
galley doors,' Rebecca said with a rapidity sounding almost urgent. 'You
may leave your seats, but please brace yourselves for any sudden turns
or stops.'

Everyone was up. Chandler took one last look out to see the still
speeding plane's turn reveal a long, battered shell of a building, its
face pockmarked with holes and its windows gone. The walls above
the windows were blackened from the fires that had completed the
building's destruction.

A stairway was waiting on the tarmac and, as they came to a hard
stop, throwing the standing soldiers forward a step, the stairway was
rolled up to the plane.

Chandler got up. The whine of the engines came loudly through the open door of the galley.

The cockpit door burst open.

'Everybody off, right now!' Golding shouted. 'Chandler, there should be an Air Mobility Command Combat Control Team down there somewhere.'

Chandler felt the baggage doors underneath the plane jar open. Barnes dashed out the door followed by a stream of men and women.

Chandler turned back to Golding. 'What the hell's the deal?'

'Gotta get outa here right now,' Golding said. 'There's a flight of bogeys bearin' down. I'd get your men as far away from this airfield as possible.'

It was then that Chandler noticed the wail of a siren through the open door of the plane. *Air raid*! Chandler jostled his way to the door and stepped out onto the small landing of the stairs. Barnes was down beneath, directing men to the mound of camouflaged gear that was growing on the concrete as Slovak soldiers tossed everything from the plane's open belly.

'*Barnes*!' Chandler yelled. 'There's an air raid on the way! Get the men to pick up a load, anybody's load, and head 'em off the tarmac to some cover!'

'*Sir*!' Barnes acknowledged, turning to relay the order. Soldiers were pouring down the stairs.

Chandler thought, *Air raid*, and then yelled, '*Barnes*! MOPP Level Four!' Full chemical protective gear. Who knew what was loaded on the attacking aircraft?

Chandler headed to his seat for his gear. Bailey stood in the rear of the line exiting first class. When Chandler got to his seat, he noticed through the open door that the cockpit crew was completing their preflight check. He retrieved his chemical gear and rifle from the overhead compartment.

'Major!' It was Golding, twisting around in his seat, already strapped in.

Chandler stepped into the cockpit, expecting more of Golding's shit.

'I just wanted to say – good luck, son.' He extended his right hand up over his seat back, which Chandler shook, along with Frazier's and Gator's.

'Good luck to you,' Chandler said. 'By the way, that was the shittiest landing I've ever seen. You almost missed the runway.'

'I did miss the runway,' Golding said. 'That was the taxiway we landed on. Runway's got a coupla potholes in it – near as bad as a New York City street.'

Chandler snorted and ran for the door.

As he got there, Jennifer kissed Bailey on the cheek. *Wars have a way of speeding up romances*, Chandler thought. Bailey leapt for the door to follow the last soldiers down, two women who had sat near Chandler's bench way back in the hangar at March Air Force Base.

'Good luck!' Rebecca yelled as she slammed the door behind them.

The engines of the L-1011 were loud. On the runway, another jet could be heard taking off, no fuel being spared as the loud roar came almost as a crackle of sound. Chandler ran to pick up the few remaining bags and packs lying on the concrete. The baggage doors were already closed, and the Slovak soldiers rolled the stairway back just far enough to clear the plane's wing before taking off toward the bombed-out building at a dead run.

As Chandler passed under the wing, Golding increased the throttle and a burst of hot exhaust just about blew Chandler off his feet. There was a tremendous noise, like a ragged tear, as the engine revved up to higher power. Chandler dropped everything, going down on one knee, to hold his fingers to his ears. Bailey and the two women did the same. When the plane turned, the noise and pain abated and Chandler urged everyone to keep moving, his words muted by the ringing in his ears and drowned out by the still loud jet engines. The air was foul with the smell of exhaust.

There were no bags remaining to be carried off, so Chandler led the little group in pursuit of the line of troops trailing off into the grass at the side of the tarmac, the invisible clock against which they raced ticking on.

From the opposite side of the airfield, Chandler heard first one and then several explosions – more like loud pops – followed immediately by a loud and continuous whoosh. He looked over his shoulder as he ran and saw missiles riding a half dozen white plumes of smoke up from the ground in an arc that flattened parallel with the earth and headed off, away from the airport.

'Faster!' Chandler yelled. *We've gotta get our chemical gear on*! he thought, suddenly in a near panic. As they reached the grass, a man in a gas mask, hood, and heavy protective suit waved at them with his gloved hand. When they reached him, Chandler saw that there was a dry drainage ditch and that in it lay his troops. He slid down into the ditch, dropping his rifle and tearing into the pouch containing his chemical protective gear. The others did the same. No one said a word except for one of the women, who urged herself on as she mouthed the instructions on use of the gear one article at a time.

Mask, Chandler thought to himself, working frantically. *Fold hood away, press against face, exhale. Cover air intake with hand. Inhale*. The gas mask sucked down against his face as it should. *Seal's good*. He pulled out the suit and climbed in, zipping it up and pulling the hood down over his shoulders. *Gloves on. Overshoes on. Done!*

The man who had waved them over checked Chandler quickly, straightening some pieces of the suit's material and hood, and then moved on to the other late arrivals. It was Barnes, of course, Chandler realised.

Chandler lay down just in time. Barnes and the others dropped a fraction of a second later, but safely. There had been no warning, just a hint of sound, a high-pitched whine increasing in intensity.

Two planes, wingtip to wingtip, had overflown the center of the airfield at incredible speed. Chandler had not followed them with his eyes. He had only gotten a snapshot through the lens of his mask and they were gone. They had come from the direction in which the missiles had departed, and in their wake a stupendous wall of sound broke down upon him and continued as a roar for some time, but there were no explosions. Chandler's heartbeat felt irregular and unnatural as he lay there, waiting.

He looked out onto the airfield, and saw to his horror the Delta jet turning only now onto the taxiway-turned-runway. And up above, spinning slowly toward the ground in an unalterable trajectory, was a string of bombs, clearly visible.

Time seemed to stand still. The Delta jet, turning, turning, would never make it. The bombs, on whose tails four air brakes like slowly turning propellers had spread out, forming a cross, arced down to their target. They came from high above at a steep angle, having been lobbed by the Russian jets seeking to escape the danger of the explosions.

Sitting squarely on the bombs' target, the Delta jet was just a bonus, a stroke of luck. Good luck for the enemy, bad for Golding, Frazier, Gator, Rebecca, and Jennifer, the Good Kid. Chandler forced himself to watch the final act.

CR-R-R-UMP, CR-R-R-UMP, CR-R-R-UMP, CR-R-R-UMP, CR-R-R-UMP, CR-R-R-UMP. Chandler's head dropped involuntarily. The shock waves battered the fabric of his suit like puffs from a child's air rifle and shook the ground as the earth transmitted the blows to his body. His ears suffered an assault of sound unlike any he had ever thought possible. The sound itself distorted to a long crackle as it exceeded the decibel level that his ears could tolerate along all audible frequencies; the pain was excruciating.

Chandler forced himself to look up as the crackle became a snarl of echoes and was surprised by the momentary wobble of his head. The dizziness passed and he saw a nearly solid wall of jet black geysers rising from the center of the airfield and smoking debris beginning to rain down onto the concrete, some bouncing, others splatting. He stared at the sight for a long second or two, waiting for the horror to unfold. All at once, the nose of the Delta jet appeared on the right side of the wall of smoke, followed by its long body and finally the tail. The jet was picking up speed despite numerous ragged pockmarks along its smooth white fuselage.

From the same direction as the first fighter-bombers, another enemy aircraft screamed by. Again a string of bombs trailed, three like the six before them. But the Delta jet was clear of the bombs' target this time, far down the runway and gaining takeoff speed.

Chandler covered his ears, trying to save whatever hearing he had left. He hadn't heard the L-1011's engines through the ringing in his ears even though he knew they must be at full power. Again he felt the thuds through the ground and the shock waves against his body, but the sound of the bombs' explosions was muffled by his hands and the reduced acuity of his damaged ears. From the location of the explosions, which fell in a line short of the black clouds still lingering from the first bombs, Chandler guessed that the taxi-way-turned-runway was now destroyed also.

Golding's jet lifted slowly off the ground and headed away. Chandler just lay there. He could hear himself breathing and his heart beating, but his ears were ringing so loudly that it drowned out all sounds. The faint ache felt like an itch punctuated every so often by the surprise of a sharp jab of pain at which he winced. He felt completely insulated from his surroundings by the suit and mask, cut off, sealed off, from the world he had left a few moments before. Chandler could hear a distant siren sounding the steady tone that was universal for 'all clear.'

Barnes removed his mask and hood.

'Musta been runway-cratering bombs,' Barnes said looking at the receding Delta jet.

Chandler removed his mask and looked back at the smoky airfield, nodding his head in understanding. That would explain the survival of the L-1011. The bombs were designed with a delayed-action fuse so that they would burrow deep into the ground to dig up a large crater. Consequently, they blew all their energy upward in a steep inverted cone. Had those been ordinary high-explosive bombs bursting on impact or, worse yet, in the air twenty or thirty feet above ground, the Delta jet would have been destroyed by the blast effects alone.

Crews of engineers hustled their equipment from the bombed-out building over toward the impact zone. They stopped about a hundred yards away.

Barnes stood there, looking at Chandler and waiting for something. 'Take 'em down off MOPP Four, Master Sergeant.'

Barnes held up his mask and waved it in the air. Everyone began removing their gear.

'*Stow it all back in your pouches!*' he yelled.

'Looks like they're scared of something,' a soldier said as she watched the engineers, who appeared to be doing nothing while maintaining their distance, many lying on the ground.

'They're waitin' to see if there were any delayed-fuse bombs, or if any of 'em scattered any landmine submunitions around the craters,' a staff sergeant explained. 'Them holes cost the Russians a lotta money to make. They package a bunch of shit to keep engineers from fixin' 'em too easy.'

'You want me to form everybody up, sir?' Barnes asked. 'Sort out the gear while we send out a couple of NCOs to find out where the Combat Control Team is?'

'Yeah,' Chandler said. 'Good idea.'

Chandler saw that Bailey had finished repacking his chemical gear and was kneeling on the ground in front of it. He appeared lost deep in thought, staring off at the black smudge on the horizon that was the exhaust of the departed Delta jet.

'Lieutenant Bailey,' Chandler said.

'Yes . . . yes, sir?' He snapped out of his reverie.

'Uh – Lieutenant,' Chandler said as he looked around. He looked over at the fence beyond their ditch. It was unguarded. 'Why don't you, uh, determine what the local security situation is – make sure we've got a defensible position until somebody shows up here to process us.'

Bailey looked over at the chain link fence and said, 'Yes, sir!' *A combat mission, his first*! Chandler thought, stifling a smile as he watched Bailey instantly come alive. *My first too.* 'Should we load our rifles, sir?' Bailey asked.

'Uhm, sure, I guess so,' Chandler said. 'Just don't chamber a round and keep the safety on.' Bailey carefully, almost reverently, pulled a magazine out of his pouch and slid it into his M-16. Then, grabbing a couple of soldiers, he rose to the opposite side of the ditch and looked around.

Chandler turned to see the two NCOs that Barnes had dispatched jogging off with their rifles in different directions while out of the charred terminal building soldiers emerged in no particular order. They and Chandler's NCO approached and shook hands – a soul shake, with a dramatic flourish. Chandler's NCO talked to them for a second, then pointed in Chandler's direction and pressed on. The men began to walk slowly toward the edge of the tarmac by the ditch. They were soldiers from a flight just like theirs, Chandler surmised.

Chandler looked around again, seeking out something to do, but Barnes was organizing the sorting of the troops' gear. He scanned the horizon in all directions but could not see anyone around to meet them.

Nothing out on the runway except the Slovak engineers. *Maybe we should ask them*, he thought. Nobody else near the building, or out on the empty grass field between the tarmac and the fence. Nobody but Bailey and his two men, spread out in good military fashion.

That's odd, Chandler thought. *There were security troops placed at regular intervals when we came in. Why would they leave this area totally undefended?*

The answer came to him, not slowly, but instantaneously fully formed and complete. '*Bailey*! *Fre-e-e-eze*!' Chandler screamed at the top of his lungs. Two of the men froze, but the man on the far left turned, taking another step.

The explosion almost cracked Chandler's sanity. He watched in horror as the man was blown fifteen feet into the air, a lifeless rag doll. Slowly, the main portion of his body turned in the air and plopped gracelessly back onto the ground, spilling its once precious contents onto the grass all around. Bailey and the other man had both been blown or dived to the ground and lay there, not moving except to raise their heads to see the destruction the landmine had wrought.

The sound of the explosion echoed through the stillness off the surrounding buildings. Chandler's victim lay on the ground in a shapeless heap. He had in an instant simply been destroyed. There was no other word for it, looking at his body lying strewn about the green field. Not 'Killed in Action,' KIA, but DIA, 'Destroyed in Action.' And not just his body, but his universe, his life, all that he had been, lost forever as if in the flick of a switch.

I read all those manuals, Chandler thought with a helpless, sinking feeling. *I'm as prepared as I could get, and still* . . . This was not training. This was the real thing, and it had taken less than ten minutes to confirm Chandler's worst fears. *I don't know what the fuck I'm doing*!

Chapter Twelve

Lambert watched General Thomas walk up to the podium and waited as a hundred conversations fell silent nearly at once. Thomas turned and nodded, and two aides pulled back a curtain covering a huge map of Central Europe on the wall behind him. Gasps and whispers rose from the second-tier officials of the U.S. and allied governments, and Thomas pulled a telescopic silver pointer to its full extension.

'Good morning, ladies and gentlemen,' Thomas said to the gathering in the large auditorium-style cafeteria of the underground facility. Seated around and behind Lambert on the first two rows were the President and his Cabinet, the leadership of Congress, and the Justices of the Supreme Court. The rest of the room was filled with over two hundred diplomats and officials from the governments of TEAMS, America's new allies from the Treaty on Euro-American Military Security.

'We will begin with the European Theater,' Thomas said in a loud voice that easily carried over the occasional cough or scraping chair. 'There are two prongs to the attack from the west. The Northern Prong from Poland and the Southern Prong from Slovakia. To the European Theater the United States has deployed or will deploy three armored corps, each with an armored cavalry regiment and Special Forces Group, and a total of six heavy divisions, almost two thirds of the U.S. Army's heavy forces. In addition to U.S. troops, the coalition will field the two divisions of I British Corps, three divisions and two Alpine brigades from Italy, and thirteen divisions or division equivalents from Poland, Slovakia, and the Czech Republic. The objective of the attacks in the European Theater . . . is Moscow.'

There was an eruption of cheers from the audience, surprising, Lambert noted, General Thomas but pleasing President Costanzo immensely. The President turned to grin broadly at the crowd, many of whom were on their feet and clapping wildly. When the cheering died down, Thomas raised his voice over the now buzzing conversations from the stirred mass of people.

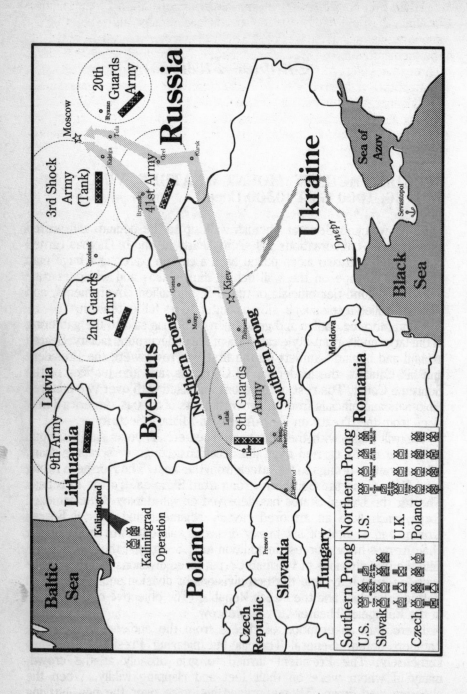

'While I do not generally intend to discuss operational results in this briefing, I would like to relate to you anecdotally the results of the supporting attack made by Polish armored and mechanized divisions into the semiautonomous Russian republic of Kaliningrad along the Baltic. Three hours after the Polish troops crossed the border and shortly after first contact with forces of the Russian garrison there, the government of Kaliningrad petitioned the TEAMS coalition for membership.'

The audience roared with laughter and applause. The humor was infectious, and Lambert could tell from Thomas's face that he too enjoyed the moment.

'Moving on now to the Mediterranean Theater, units of the TEAMS alliance have seized the Bosporus and secured access to the Black Sea for ships of the U.S. Sixth Fleet and the Italian Navy. Their objective will be to destroy the Russian Black Sea Fleet and begin a campaign of carrier air strikes against Russian petroleum production in the Caucasus.' This time the applause was more obligatory than the first spontaneous outburst. It died down quickly.

'In the North Atlantic, our Icelandic Campaign is proceeding apace. U.S. Army forces have now been joined by a brigade group from Canada and are rapidly reducing the Russian invasion forces.' Before Thomas moved on, there was a smattering of applause for what Lambert knew to be a bloody battle between light infantry – Russian, American, and Canadian – whose heaviest weapons were usually hand-carried mortars and whose killing was close-in. 'Finally, in the Barents Sea north of Scandinavia, U.S., British, and Canadian naval forces continue to deny the Russian Navy access to the Atlantic from Murmansk and Arkhangelsk.' He made no mention of the Kara Sea Bastion.

Thomas walked now over to the map of the Pacific coast of Russia. 'In the Far Eastern Theater, the objective of the U.S. Marines and Army is to secure the Russian naval facility at Vladivostok and their rather sizable stocks of nuclear weapons there and to fix in place the substantial Russian ground forces previously committed to the Russo-Chinese War. By severing the Trans-Siberian Railroad here and here' – his pointer indicated two points along the southern edges of Siberia deep inside Russia – 'we hope to split Russia in two and thereby tie down two thirds of the Russian Army in the Far East and prevent their strategic redeployment to oppose our advance in Europe.'

When the applause died down, General Thomas looked up and hesitated. Lambert turned to see an army major walking up the center aisle with half-sheets of paper Lambert recognized as FLASH reports straight off the printer. Turning to look at the rear of the cafeteria, Lambert saw the aide's electric car parked just outside the open door on the subterranean street.

Everyone stirred as the pause lengthened. The major strode up to the platform, whispered in Thomas's ear, and then handed Thomas three

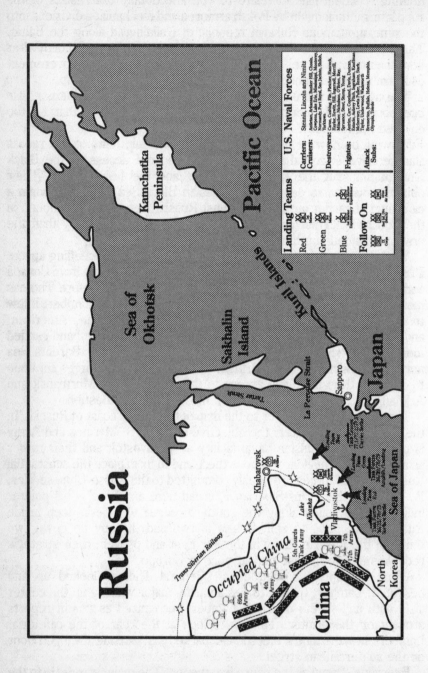

slips of paper. Thomas read the first and then glanced at the other messages as the murmur of voices in the room grew louder still. He then motioned with his finger for the Chief of Naval Operations to come up to the podium and made a beeline for the President. As the major left the podium, he stopped and handed Lambert a sealed envelope. Lambert saw the stamps of the Swiss Embassy in Moscow and of the U.S. Embassy in Zurich. A large 'Eyes Only' stamp appeared just under the embassy stamps bearing Lambert's name. He opened it.

It was a terse message from the Swiss Embassy. 'Colonel Pavel Filipov of the Army of Russia requests to meet with Mr Gregory Lambert of the United States government at his earliest convenience. Col. Filipov will arrive in Philadelphia by KLM Airlines flight from Amsterdam at nine hundred hours tomorrow Philadelphia time in civilian clothes. Utmost discretion is urged.'

The CNO cleared his throat and said, 'I'll give you just a summary now, and save the details for later.'

Lambert saw Thomas engaged in a muted conversation with the President, who grabbed one of the messages from his hand with a look of anger on his face. Lambert got out of his chair and crossed the aisle to tell them about Filipov's request, dropping on one knee next to the stooped Thomas and seated President.

'Those bastards,' Costanzo said as he read, and Thomas handed Lambert one of the other reports. 'It's a FLASH OVERRIDE,' Thomas said as Lambert raised the report to read.

CIC: JGAA//
TOP SECRET//
CHEMREP/001//
PLATG/4378N/0372W/094712Z//
CASLTY/22//
DEATHS/5//
4TH MECH REPORTS FROG MISSILE ATTACK ON ARTILLERY BATT AT 0447Z/CASUALTIES OCCURRED DESPITE USE OF MASKS/DEATHS OCCURRED WITHIN MINUTES/SYMPTS INCL TIGHTNESS OF CHEST /INITIAL SITREP IS PERSISTENT NERVE AGENT/ID BY FIELD DETECTION KIT IS GB PROBABLE/5 KIA/17 WIA/GROSS AREA DECONTAMINATION DELAYED IN ANTICIPATION OF FURTHER ATTACKS/CIVILIAN CASUALTIES PROBABLE//
END//

'Nerve gas?' Costanzo asked.

In the background, Thomas could hear the admiral going over the details of the Sixth Fleet's forced entry into the Black Sea.

'Yes, sir,' Thomas said. 'Three separate attacks. All the reports are the same.'

The President's eyes were focused far away. Without rising from his reverie, the President asked, 'How soon can we be ready to retaliate in kind?'

Thomas's chin dropped to his chest, his mood darkening. 'Well, sir, the Germans would go crazy if they knew we were transporting even binary weapons through their country. We could airlift a few shells in directly from the States and they could be employed within about twelve hours, but only on a limited basis. The only way to employ large numbers of the weapons would be to ship them by sea from the States and go straight into the Polish ports on the Baltic, and that would be a month or two off.'

'I don't want to use the stuff in dribs and drabs,' Costanzo said. 'Give it top priority on the bills of lading for the Sealift Command and plan a massive delivery when enough is on hand.' After a pause he asked, 'Is something wrong?'

Thomas hesitated before continuing. 'Sir, it's just that the Russians will be around after this war is over, and we're going to have to live with whatever feelings they have toward us.'

'It was their decision to escalate to chemical weapons!' the President said angrily. 'I have not established as this administration's policy, as some have advised, the wholesale destruction of the Russian state and its people. But I will not fight with one hand tied behind my back.'

'But, Mr President, chemical weapons – nerve gas and blistering agents – are of little military effectiveness against the Russian Army. They're well equipped to fight a chemical war. It'll just fan the flames of—'

'Then use it against the Provisional Troops the Russians are conscripting,' Costanzo said, and looked Thomas in the eye for some time. 'Do they have protective gear?' he finally asked.

Thomas stared back at the President. 'No, sir.'

'Then gas *them*,' the President said, turning his attention to shake the hand of the Finnish ambassador, smiling broadly at the representative of the newest and most secret member of the TEAMS alliance.

PRESOV, SLOVAKIA
June 26, 1400 GMT (1500 Local)

The Humvee sped right up to Chandler, the tires screeching as it stopped. Doors flew open on both sides.

'Who's in charge here?' a captain asked.

Chandler looked over at the colonel who had walked up with the mob from the burned-out building. An awkward silence descended until the captain noticed the soldier's body, which the Slovak engineers had retrieved, and the charred hole in the field. Looking at Chandler and then the colonel, the captain said to the latter, 'Are you in charge here, Colonel?'

'I didn't have *anything* to do with this mess,' he said.

Chandler stepped forward to face the man. 'My name is Major David Chandler. Those are my men out there,' he said, indicating the troops in the grass. 'I've had one casualty.' The captain looked back at the body of the dead man.

Having shifted from one foot to the other impatiently, the colonel finally said, 'When the hell were you planning on getting here? We've been waiting around for almost an hour! No wonder V Corps is so screwed up down here! We never planned on incompetents running the operation!'

The captain's eyes settled tiredly on the colonel for a moment. 'And these are your men?' he asked him, looking at the mob.

The colonel smirked and shook his head. 'Look, Captain, I know what you're trying to do here. No, I take no responsibility for those men. We came over on the same flight – that's all.'

The captain called back to the Humvee for an ambulance, then turned back to Chandler. 'What happened?'

'I sent them out to secure the perimeter,' Chandler said simply.

Barnes interrupted. 'Pardon me, sir,' he said to the captain. Chandler turned to see Barnes's jaw bulging as he ground his teeth. 'Why the hell was that minefield not marked?'

'I don't know, Master Sergeant,' the captain answered quietly.

'Goddammit!' Barnes exploded as he looked away, causing Chandler to flinch involuntarily. 'I've got one dead trooper and not a single sign posted anywhere down the length of the tarmac! Shit! What kind of—?' Barnes bit off the last with great effort.

Turning to speak alternately to Barnes and Chandler, the captain said, 'They mined this area yesterday morning after six men had their throats cut by Spetsnaz while on sentry duty, and then a hundred and forty men and women who had just deplaned like you were killed or wounded in an attack on their staging area. We've lost a lot of people, but I'm sorry about what happened.'

He was a reasonable man, Chandler realized, exhausted to the point of resignation to the loss of life. His eyes were red and his eyelids puffy. And there was a ring along the edge of his face and under his chin. The red indentation fit the size and shape of the standard-issue gas mask.

'We'll take care of the body, sir,' the captain said. 'What's the man's name?'

Chandler didn't know, he realized suddenly, he hadn't even asked. The colonel huffed a big sigh, his patience wearing thin, and again eyed the sky in the direction of the earlier raid.

'The dead man's name, sir. What was it?'

'I don't know,' Chandler said.

The captain nodded. 'Okay, we'll get it later. Right now we have to get your people processed.'

With the mention of the word 'processed,' the colonel said in an arrogant voice, 'My name is Lieutenant Colonel Mitchell. I want immediate transport to V Corps Forward Headquarters.'

The captain pulled out a spiral notebook and a pen. 'What's your command or MOS, sir?' he asked, but without waiting for the answer yelled, 'Rodriguez! Take care of the enlisted personnel.' He turned back to the lieutenant colonel.

'What the hell difference does that make!' the man shouted. 'Civil Affairs! Now, what kind of transportation do you have?'

'Sir,' the captain began patiently, 'the processing back Stateside is totally screwed up, so we've been ordered to disregard assigned billets and fill certain high-need postings unless the individual is an officer and is already posted to a unit command or has a specialty in a listed field. Since you . . . since neither one of those things applies to you, sir, I need to ask to see your orders, please.'

'Listen to me, you little *f-f-uck*,' the colonel said through clenched teeth. 'I am a lieutenant colonel in the United States Army! I was specially assigned to V Corps *Headquarters* by General Atkins himself! Do you know who he is?'

'No, sir.'

'No, of course you don't. 'He is the deputy liaison officer to the House Armed Services Committee, and I am here on his *express* orders! So I don't give a flying fuck what piddly-assed list you and your staff have generated! *You*' – poking the captain's chest with fingers again – 'get me to V Corps Forward!'

The captain then did something unexpected: he ignored the colonel. 'Major, how about you? What's your post?'

Chandler started to answer, but Mitchell beat him to it. 'How *dare* you! I'll have your bars for this. Your career in the army is *over – finished*!'

'Choppers headed in!' one of the soldiers shouted from the Humvee, a radio handset to his ear under his helmet, and the captain glanced over his shoulder at the man before responding to the colonel. 'V Corps Forward Headquarters,' he said with a sudden liveliness in his eyes, 'is in a bit of shit right now. We're havin' some trouble gettin' stuff through to 'em – supplies and things like that – but I've got some favors owed me. Are you airborne qualified?' he asked, raising his notepad. 'I can check the board and see when our next air defense suppression mission goes in.'

Mitchell fell into a quiet but obviously surly mood.

'Fourth Infantry Division,' Chandler said after a pause during which the two men stared at each other. 'Division Intelligence.' *Am I a protected species?* Chandler wondered as he waited for the captain to scan his list. In the background Rodriguez was yelling, '*Armored and Armored Cav on my left, Infantry on my right, everybody else just back on up!*'

'May I see your orders, sir?' the captain asked Chandler.

Chandler handed them over along with his ORB, his Officer Record Brief, and his military biography, which he had brought along for delivery to his commanding officer. After a few moments' study, the captain said, 'Armor School. You had any Armor postings, sir?'

A job interview, Chandler thought, *on a bombed-out runway on the border of Ukraine. For a job for which I'm not qualified. Just ask what's left of the man lying under the poncho for references*, Chandler thought, but then said, 'One, straight out of O.C.S.' The captain fumbled with Chandler's orders to find it. *Then on to law school on the special deal I wrangled from the recruiters desperate back then to make their quotas.*

The captain was obviously rereading Chandler's résumé, some of it out loud. '"Intelligence Analysts School,"' he said. '"Armor School at Knox – 3 of 136."' Finally the captain said, 'Very impressive, sir. If you'd step over there' – he pointed to a small group being counted off – 'they'll take care of you.' Chandler saw that Barnes and Bailey were already standing at the group's fringe.

Chandler put his orders back into his pocket and walked off in a daze as the colonel resumed his tirade. The chop of helicopter rotors could be heard, growing louder as the aircraft approached. The sound grew until the first of a long line of twin-rotor CH-47 Chinook transports meandered out from around the burned-out building and nosed up to decelerate.

Passing the enlisted men's 'processing' area, the soldier named Rodriguez was listening impatiently to the protests of a small group of Chandler's men who apparently were objecting to being split up.

'No, you dumb motherfuckers!' Rodriguez shouted to the four protesting men, to be heard over the helicopters. '*You*'re goin' to the main corps staging area. *He*'s goin' straight to the FEBA.'

As Chandler passed, the lone man whom Rodriguez had singled out, a medic with a red cross on his armband, was shaking hands with his friends and picking up his gear.

'Just follow the major there!' Rodriguez yelled at the medic from behind Chandler.

'*To the FEBA*,' Chandler thought. *The Forward Edge of the Battle Area*. From around the main line of Chinooks swung a different helicopter, a Blackhawk, apparently not a part of the large formation of transports. The helicopter landed just ahead, and Chandler's group, including Bailey and Barnes, was directed to it at a run by an NCO. In the door, a gunner swiveled a six-barreled mini-gun up safely away from the troops on the ground. He then jumped to the concrete and lay down on his back to peer up at the bottom of the fuselage. He wiggled the ragged metal that hung loose and pulled it back to peer inside. The side of the helicopter was pockmarked with holes.

Chandler and his guide turned one last corner and went down some sandbagged steps guarded by two sentries, rifles at the ready. There was a machine gun across the open space of a small square in the town dug in behind still more sandbags. Everywhere there were burned-out vehicles, military and civilian, and blackened buildings with holes of all sizes punched into them.

Half buried into the ground, the door that the private opened unveiled the hectic pace that Chandler had anticipated. As he walked in he sensed that he was in his new home. Maps on tables and easels. Radio operators, seated, chattering into their communications nets with officers pacing behind their backs while they transcribed messages on small laptop computers. Men and women rushing to and fro carrying pieces of paper, the currency of all office jobs.

One man in this room was the brigade commander – only one. It was on his shoulders that the onus fell. As Chandler followed the private, who had dropped his gear by the door, it became clear who that man was.

Standing with one foot propped up on the seat of a wooden chair was a large man with short hair almost completely gray.

'I don't give a shit *what* you do with them,' the brigade commander was saying. 'I'm just warning you: if any reporters set foot in this CP, I'll have them arrested and you shot. You read me?'

The man to whom the colonel spoke, about half the size of the towering brigade commander, shook his balding head. He lifted his glasses up with his fingers so that he could rub his eyes, and in that position said, 'Colonel, I understand what you're saying, but . . . this is not something that anybody has any choice about. The orders came in from—'

'*I know who they're from, you little shit*! *I can read*! Look, just keep 'em away from me, you got that?'

The balding man guessed wrong. 'I'm just trying to do my job, Colonel, just like everybody—'

'*Get outa here*! I don't have time for this shit!'

The motion in the room had paused as people watched the scene. The colonel turned his attention to Chandler. The other two men left, looking at each other out of the corners of their eyes as they headed for the door.

Chandler snapped to attention. 'Major David Chandler, reporting for duty, sir.'

The colonel looked him over briefly. 'At ease, Major.' They shook hands. 'Colonel Harkness' were the only words of greeting that he spoke. 'Lemme see your orders,' he slurred. He paused only briefly at the posting page and went straight to the résumé. After a quick read and a nod, he rolled the orders and biography up and held them in one hand like a baton. Chandler assumed that they were his now.

'Here's what I want you to do,' Harkness said. 'You know what's going on here, Major?'

'No, sir.'

'We were supposed to go on the offensive yesterday and be about forty miles east of here well into Ukraine, but a few hours before our attack was to begin the Russians launched a spoiling attack that caught us in the middle of staging – all strung out in road formation. It was a mess. We've been trying to recover ever since, and most of the fighting has been taking place on *this* side of the border back in *Slovakia*, not on the Ukrainian side. Right now I don't know who it is that's surrounding who, but the situation is stabilized. I'm now getting orders to begin the advance and let the Czechs and Slovaks finish the Russians off. Not a very damn auspicious beginning, and certainly not the way those Command and General Staff College studs at corps had it all planned out.'

Harkness stopped suddenly and looked around. 'Got your personal equipment?' he asked.

'Yes, sir.'

'Good, good.' Harkness was tired. His face was old close up, although at the rank of colonel and in command of a brigade he had to have been in his mid-forties. His eyes were red and puffy from lack of sleep. The softness of his voice when he made the last remark and his concern over Chandler's personal needs indicated that, in quieter times, he probably was a good man to work for.

'Okay,' Harkness resumed. 'You're going to assume command of the now forming 2nd of the 415th Armor.'

Harkness shuffled through papers on his desk as Chandler fell dumbstruck. He had to dissect the sentence completely before the meaning truly sunk in. '*Command*' – *battalion Commander*, he thought. *Not staff officer – commander*. And the job for a lieutenant colonel at least six years, maybe ten, his senior. The colonel looked up. Chandler felt his mouth hanging open and closed it. He swallowed to wet his throat and licked his parched lips. Harkness stood straight up and stared now directly at Chandler, waiting. *Where do I begin*? Chandler thought. *Is now the time to tell him*? *Is he the one I have to tell*?

'Major, what part of my order did you not understand?' Harkness said finally, his tone low and measured.

'I'm . . . I'm sorry, sir,' Chandler said. 'It's just – I specialize in Intell. I was supposed to be assigned to 4th Mech – to Division Staff.'

'But you have had Armor training?' Harkness asked, and Chandler sensed that pressure was building behind the dam of Harkness's patience.

'Well, yes, sir . . . but I mean' – Chandler cleared his throat and tried to regroup – 'I've been to Armor School, but . . . but it was a while ago. And I haven't held a field command since, well . . .'

The dam was nearly full now, Chandler realized. Harkness rubbed his head, his hand passing over the short hair, and he looked away from Chandler while he bit his lower lip. Finally he turned back and said in a voice that surprised Chandler with how even it was, 'Listen, Major. I don't need a staff officer here. I need a battalion commander, because I need a battalion, you understand? We're patching the 2/415 together out of the division staging area. We lost the entire battalion's personnel at some nuked air base back in the States, and I'm taking all individuals with armor training and plugging them in to raise a battalion. Now, let's start this thing over. *You*,' he said pointing, 'are going to command *my* battalion for *me*. I'd do it myself, but I've got two or three other things to take care of,' he said, waving his hand in a broad sweep around the room. 'Okay?'

Chandler said nothing.

'Okay. Sergeant Estavez!' Harkness yelled. 'Take the major down to the rail yard. Your men should be there – some of 'em, at least. We'll get you up to a full complement in the next coupla days. You've got ten days to get them rolling.'

It was Chandler's turn to grow angry. 'Do . . . do you mean, sir, that you want me to take a group of people, throw them together into units with every specialty filled, break equipment off of railcars, load everybody up with the right combat loads, and roll an armored battalion into combat in *ten days*?'

Chandler's anger had grown as he realized the absurdity of the proposition. *Get somebody else to lead those men to slaughter*, he thought.

Harkness just stared at Chandler, his jaw set. 'The men are from cannibalized platoon-size units, for the most part,' Harkness replied. 'They've been thrown together back at some screwed-up processing centers in the States and they're missing some billets, but they're regular army. And the equipment is prepositioned top-of-the-line stuff from NATO stocks in Germany, ready to roll with combat loads. Plus, a good number of the men have had several days of work on the stuff with some pretty good NCOs bustin' their tails. It should all be broken out and serviceable. You should even have time for an exercise or two, although I can't give you too much fuel right now and you've gotta assume constant air and special operations threats.'

'Sir, even assuming that we have all the right specialties here, and all the right equipment, and everything falls into place just right, *how* could we be expected—'

'*Expected*!' The dam burst. The motion in the room stopped again. 'Ex-*pec*-ted! You want to know what's *expected*? You don't like it that I only gave you *ten days*? I've only got two battalions in the field right now, and I don't know whether I can even hold *this* position for ten days! But they want me to head on off to *Russia*!' His arm shot up, pointing, Chandler assumed, east.

'Expected? I'll tell you what's expected. At zero nine thirty this morning I got handed one of those little sheets of paper over there,' he said, pointing to a pile to which the radio operator sitting next to it added, 'and it said that a company of MPs that I'd sent up to the line' – he had to stop, choking with anger – 'had been overrun on the reverse slope of a hill. They'd been trying to get to the top, but the Russians got there first. And that little message wasn't the last one either. Oh, no! They went on and on. You see, the first wave that overran 'em didn't stop to kill 'em all. They didn't have time. They just shot every one of 'em they could as they drove on by. So, what do the MPs do? They go on up to the top of the fucking hill like I ordered and *they dig in, Goddammit! They dig in!*'

He was right in Chandler's face, yelling with foul coffee breath.

'So, along about mid-morning, I get another of those little pieces of paper,' Harkness continued. '*Another* echelon had overrun 'em, shooting 'em up again. They were just calling to let us know. Just to let us know and to ask *where the fuck was the help they'd been screaming for while they dug for their lives!*' He paused to look down at the clutter of his desk as he rubbed a hand across the back of his neck. Chandler felt the eyes of the others in the still room burning holes in his back. 'They never stood a chance. They were trucked up there on buses. The third wave killed 'em all. Every last one of 'em. Dead, prisoner, I don't even know, 'cause once they quit handing me those *fucking* pieces of paper, I don't know *anything*! They're just gone! A whole company' – he looked up at Chandler, wild-eyed, menacing – 'every last one of 'em *women*! Goddamned *women* left after we'd stripped about five MP companies of all the males for infantrymen!' He paused, his gaze dropping again, then said quietly, 'Those women were on foot, Major. You'll have tanks.'

PHILADELPHIA, PENNSYLVANIA
June 27, 1500 GMT (1000 Local)

The driver had taken the nondescript car off the main roads to try to avoid the enormous traffic jam that had developed. Filipov looked out the window on the gray day at the slums of the underprivileged, mostly black. Irina would have been upset. He tried to avoid showing her things like this. He tried to make her love America.

From where Filipov sat nearly parked in the traffic, he could not see what lay ahead. A sign at the intersection in front of the car indicated that Veterans Stadium lay in that direction, and Filipov wondered whether the American baseball season was resuming already. People streamed by the car on both sides of the street and headed up the hill away from the river. A family, their young child on her daddy's shoulders. The incongruous picture of three laughing boys, wearing counterculture clothes but carrying small American flags. An elderly couple, somber and quiet, ambling their way slowly up the sidewalk.

'What's the delay?' Filipov asked the FBI agent in the seat in front of him.

The man was pointing to the empty lane on their left and saying, 'Just pull out around this shit,' to the driver. He then turned to face Filipov. 'Just a little rally. Thought you'd like to take a look.' There was no disrespect in his voice. There was also nothing friendly about it either. The agent rolled down his window. The electric whine was almost immediately drowned out by the full-throated roar of a crowd cheering in the distance.

The driver twisted in his seat to look over his shoulder and then pulled out into the empty lane for opposing traffic, accelerating boldly up the hill. Just before he got to the turn that was his goal, a policeman stepped out into the street and held both hands out for him to stop.

'Shit!' the driver said, rolling down his window. Filipov looked out onto the backs of the crowd stretching across the closed street ahead just as there was another roar. American flags, large and small, were being waved above the sea of heads. The crowd itself was, Filipov noticed, a cross-section of Middle America, mostly families with some groups of young gathered together and rowdy, all facing the speaker standing somewhere in the direction of the giant stadium in the distance.

'A-a-ll right!' the cop said. 'Just whaddaya think yer doin'?'

The driver pulled out his badge and said, 'FBI.'

Filipov opened the door and stood up on the floorboard as he leaned out of the car. 'Hey!' the agent in the front seat shouted and opened his own door, one hand grabbing the butt of the pistol he wore under his armpit. The other agent was out also, his pistol drawn and resting on the roof of the car pointing straight at Filipov. The policeman stood there confused by the commotion and staring at Filipov, whose own attention turned to the crowd that from his elevated vantage was now in full view.

The speaker was so distorted that all Filipov could tell was that some man was shouting with great volume and energy. There were large, homemade banners held aloft by dozens in the center of the crowd. There was smoke and a flame as a dummy burned on the end of a pole held up in the air. Everywhere there were flags. Another great cheer rose up and with it ten thousand, a hundred thousand pumping fists in one long, continuous shout that slowly grew organized.

'U-S-A! U-S-A! U-S-A!' the orderly crowd shouted as if at an Olympic event. The crowd covered the great distance all the way to the stadium, repeating the chant over and over. The speaker was finished, and Filipov now realized that he was not standing in front of the stadium, he was in the stadium itself, and the stadium was filled to capacity.

CIA SAFE HOUSE, HARRISBURG, PENNSYLVANIA
June 27, 1700 GMT (1200 Local)

'My name is James Anderson, Central Intelligence Agency. This is Colonel Petry, Defense Intelligence Agency. And of course you know Mr Lambert with the White House. Why don't we all have a seat?' Anderson suggested, ushering Filipov to the sofa so that he would face Camera 1, the only color camera in the old house.

The place was dusty and had smelled of disuse when Lambert and the agents had arrived there an hour earlier. They had spent most of their time frantically pulling sheets off furniture, even sending one of the three agents in the camera room out to the Safeway to get new light bulbs for the darkened parlor. *Not getting too much use for these places*, Lambert thought bitterly, *now that we're such good friends with the Russians*.

Filipov stood waiting until Anderson placed him in the correct seat, Filipov's eyes continually drawn back to Lambert. 'Greg, I don't know what I can say,' Filipov had said when greeted at the door, waiting afterward through the awkward silence for a reply that did not come. 'I'm so sorry about Jane' were the only other words spoken.

After they all were seated, Lambert looked up at Filipov, and Filipov stared back at him, concern etched deep into his face. Filipov cocked his head as if to ask Lambert what was wrong. He gave up and looked at the other two intelligence officers before looking back at Lambert. 'Thank you for agreeing to this meeting,' Filipov began formally.

Anderson and Petry sat there like stones, clearly there to listen, not talk.

'I have come here on a matter of great importance,' Filipov continued. 'It is also of such great sensitivity that the most extreme discretion is required, on your part as well as our own.' Filipov swallowed and licked his lips, and Lambert wondered whether he should offer him a drink but took his cue from the two operatives with him and sat still.

'First, let me tell you that I come here at the direction of General Razov. Secondly, let me tell you also that none of the other members of STAVKA know of this visit. That is the reason why this visit must remain discreet. The other members of STAVKA would object to my telling you what I am about to tell you.'

Out of the corner of his eye Lambert saw Anderson and Petry glance at each other. Lambert concentrated on Pavel, whose eyes remained fixed on Anderson for quite some time before looking over at Lambert.

The silence hung over the room.

Filipov's eyes fell to the floor as his palms came to rest on his knees, his stiff arms conveying the discomfort that he obviously felt. 'As you doubtless know, the ballistic missile submarine force of our country's navy remains largely intact and is currently defended from your forces in a bastion located in the Kara Sea.' He looked up at Lambert, and Lambert gave him the slightest of nods. 'As you also are aware, those submarines did not fire their missiles in the exchange on June eleventh.' Again Lambert nodded. Filipov opened his mouth as he looked back down at the floor, struggling with the words.

Finally he said in a rush, 'There is one other thing of which you are probably not aware, however.' He now looked straight up at Lambert. 'The submarines' nuclear control orders employ a doctrine most commonly called "fail deadly." Under those fail-deadly orders, the commanders received at the time of the exchange *both* targeting coordinates and release orders. The release orders are conditioned upon satisfaction of one of two criteria. They will fire if they receive a valid launch order from the nuclear communicators possessed by STAVKA, *or* they will fire if any of those boats' commanders believes that he is under attack. In the latter case, the launches would be against the targets whose coordinates were part of the original firing orders Zorin selected. Those targets include U.S. military bases worldwide . . . and the three hundred and four largest cities in the United States.'

The silence was so complete that Lambert's subconscious mind tried to fill it with sounds – a deep rumble just beyond audible range, a whoosh from the street outside that did not quite materialize.

'Well,' Filipov said, slapping his palms on his thighs and rubbing before he stood, 'I think that I'd better be going now.'

Anderson and Petry again looked at each other, and then rose, uncertainly, to their feet. Lambert stood also.

'Just one question,' Lambert said.

'I am sorry. I am not at liberty to answer any questions, nor would I be so inclined if I were.'

Filipov's English was always impeccable, but the answer he had just given was stilted. Not a moment's hesitation. Not a single search for a word. Rehearsed.

'Pavel,' Lambert said, 'can you recall those submarines?'

'I'm sorry, Greg. I'm not at liberty to discuss control orders further.'

'We are engaged in a war, Pavel. If what you're telling us is true, and those submarines are "cocked and locked," then one mistake, one stray weapon or inadvertent contact . . .'

'And "that's the ball game,"' Filipov said, as Lambert stared at him.

Lambert saw that Petry was about to say something, but Anderson jumped in and held out his hand. 'Thank you very much, Pavel Sergeevich.' They shook hands.

They ushered Filipov to the front door. Anderson nodded at Lambert as they all waited for Petry to open the door, which he did not do, and Lambert said, 'Might I have a word with you in private, Pavel?'

'Yes,' Filipov said, immediately jumping at the chance and following Lambert into an anteroom. Lambert pulled the pocket doors closed on the two men outside, consciously avoiding a glance at the side table under which one of the room's microphones was placed.

'Where is Irina?' Filipov blurted out immediately. 'I've phoned everywhere and I can't find her.'

Lambert felt the great weight again pressing down on him. 'What?' Filipov asked, his face paling before Lambert's eyes.

'I have to ask you this first, Pavel. Please forgive me.' It was distasteful to make him wait, but he had to do his job. 'Back there in the parlor – what you told us – is it true? I absolutely have to know, Pavel. Would those submarines fire on their own authority if attacked?'

'Yes,' Filipov said, but then quickly asked, 'Where is she?'

Lambert looked at Filipov, his face, his posture, everything about him a pathetic jumble of nerves. He knew he should press on, that Pavel would not be of much use after he was told, but he couldn't. It was too much. 'She's dead, Pavel. I'm sorry. She's dead.'

SPECIAL FACILITY, MOUNT WEATHER, VIRGINIA
June 27, 2100 GMT (1600 Local)

'The release orders are conditioned upon satisfaction of one of two criteria,' Filipov said. Lambert was on edge. Pavel's own agitation was contagious. It reminded Lambert of the old Cold War defection scenes, CIA safe house, senior Russian officer . . . 'They will fire if they receive a valid launch order from the nuclear communicators possessed by STAVKA, *or* they will fire if any of those boats' commanders believes that he is under attack. In the latter case, the launches would be against the targets whose coordinates were part of the original firing orders Zorin selected. Those targets include U.S. military bases worldwide . . . and the three hundred and four largest cities in the United States.'

The image on the screen froze with Filipov's eyelids drooping in an odd manner.

The lights came up.

'Jee-zus Christ!' the acting Secretary of State exclaimed. Lambert had expected the reaction to the tape. 'Is this guy for real?' he asked Lambert, who stood next to the President at the head of the conference table.

'He's a colonel in the Russian Army. He's just returned from STAVKA Headquarters in Moscow where he is aide-de-camp to General Razov. He was previously military attaché at their embassy in Washington.'

'And you know him well?' the President asked.

'For five years, sir. He was' – Lambert paused – 'he was my best friend. Still is, I guess.'

The President looked at Lambert. 'Well, then, was he telling the truth?'

Lambert hesitated. 'Yes, sir, I think he was – at least what he thinks is the truth.'

There was silence in the room for a moment, and then the President said, 'Okay,' turning to the table. 'Let's assume those subs may fire at their commanders' discretion.'

'I don't buy it,' the director of the CIA said suddenly. 'It's just a gut feeling, sir. Doesn't sound "Russian" to me, too de-centralized, too much discretion given to individual commanders. They'd want everything controlled by the center.' He shook his head. 'I say he's bluffing.'

'There is a question about the probable verity of this man Filipov's communication,' Bill Weinberg, the former MIT mathematics professor who headed the National Security Agency, said. 'We've run our own fail-deadly options through batteries of scenarios. The failure rate was always far too high. If given enough time, somebody fired on false reads no matter how detailed the criteria and how onerous the procedures. We call it an "unstable" system – one in which the probability of a mistaken firing is low but constant. The result is that the risk of the system's breaking down, of an accidental firing, at any given time isn't high, but when looked at over months and months it becomes not just a possibility but more likely than not. When you factor in the human element, the self-destructive, self-abusive tendencies of the decision-makers when subjected to the tension of a wartime footing on a submarine lying low in that Bastion – the air and water growing steadily more stale, the food going from fresh to emergency rations, the lights low to conserve energy, the noise discipline, the worries about home – I would argue that you've got a steadily increasing risk of system breakdown over time. The system, *if* it is their system, is growing more and more brittle with every passing moment.'

The short, rotund man paused to take a bite of Danish, left over from their morning briefing, and wash it down with coffee. Lambert considered getting a pastry from the tray as his stomach growled; instead he just returned to his chair. He didn't care much about food, he just wanted sleep, painless sleep. If only he could shut his office door, curl up on his couch, and gain a brief respite from the agonizing storm of emotions that took considerable energy to suppress.

'So if they're lying, what do you think is going on?' the President asked.

'Well, that's easy,' the NSA chief said, licking his fingers. 'Regardless of whether what they're saying is true, one thing is clear. They're saying, "Don't touch those subs." That makes perfect sense under any set of facts. Those submarines are the great equalizer. Measuring our conventional forces alone against theirs, it's a fair fight, but a fight with only one possible outcome.'

'All right,' the President said. 'But you haven't said what you think. Could the Russians have that fail-deadly system in place?'

The NSA chief shrugged and said, 'Sure, it's possible.' He looked up at the President. 'I don't believe it, though. NSA agrees with CIA's assessment.' He turned then to his aide and said, 'Could you get me one of those jelly-filled ones, please?'

NORTH OF PARTIZANSK, RUSSIA
June 28, 2200 GMT (0800 Local)

'All right!' Monk shouted, his words drowned out by yet another immense concussion from the Russian artillery some distance away down the line of their battalion. 'Here we go again. Dig . . .!' Monk yelled hoarsely as he rose, his last word catching in his dry throat and forcing him to cough. His voice was giving out after three days of shouting and fighting and almost no sleep. Monk grabbed his men to push them to their positions up and down the line through the man-made fog from the Russian artillery's smoke rounds.

They all dropped their packs and pulled out their entrenching tools. Monk tightened the flimsy metal shovel's blade at a ninety-degree angle from the shaft and began to spade the soft earth at his feet, his raw hands and lower back painfully sore from the dozen or so holes he had dug since the landing.

All of the burrowing men around Monk were quiet except Mouth. 'I cain't take this *shit* no more, man,' Mouth said as he chopped at the ground, the blows of his shovel distorting the sound of every third word. 'Fuckin' root!' he cursed, chopping down frantically at the obstacle before pulling it up with both hands and resuming his dig. 'I just cain't *take* this no more. *No* more, man. This is *it.*'

'Shut up, Mouth,' Monk snapped as he heard Gunny begin to issue orders from down the line. 'Pile the dirt to your front!' Gunny yelled and Monk cursed his stupidity under his breath. He turned to point his butt at the approaching Russians and scrape the dark brown earth into a pile in front of what would be his sole protection from all manner of deadly things.

'Hold your fire until you hear me open up!' Gunny ordered from his position, which should be the junction between Monk's First and the new Second Squad, their platoon's new half-strength order of battle. 'Field packs . . . in front of your fighting hole!' Gunny's voice caught mid-sentence as he himself spaded the ground.

Come on, come on, come on, Monk thought, his anxiety growing with each thick slice at the earth, using every ounce of strength that he had to add inches to his hole and percentage points to his probability of survival. He knew that every slice of earth scraped out counted, and involuntary grunts began to escape from his lungs as he dug, ignoring the pain now.

'Grenadiers, load shot,' Gunny continued. 'Fire the grenade on your first shot and then your rifle; don't take the time to reload grenades! Riflemen, single shots! Automatic weapons, squeeze 'em off – don't waste ammo!' Monk's indentation was growing into a hole now. *Just a couple of more minutes*, Monk thought as he dug on. *Deeper, deeper, deeper.*

'Everybody down – pass it along,' Mouth said from the ground next to Monk. Everybody between Mouth and Gunny was lying flat on the ground, bringing weapons up onto their packs. Gunny was pressing the palm of one hand emphatically down to the ground, his other hand holding the radio handset up under his helmet.

'Get down!' Monk hissed to Bone and Smalls next to him in their two-man hole as he dropped into his own nine-inch-deep depression. 'Pass it on!'

The smoke was thinning. *They fired their smoke too early*, Monk thought as he scanned the woods through the sights of his M-249, a Belgian-made Squad Automatic Weapon, or SAW. Monk, like most of the other men, was now humping more firepower than they normally carried, having discarded their M-16s for the heavier weaponry of fallen marines.

Monk checked to ensure that the 200-round box magazine of 5.56-mm ammo was full and properly seated and then grasped the long bolt handle and slid it all the way back, hearing the clack of the spring locking. Monk pushed the bolt back forward to chamber

the first round and lock the breech. From there on, he was on auto
– *rock 'n' roll*, Bone called it.

Searching the woods ahead for the figures who would pour out of
the smoke toward him, Monk saw nothing but trees. Several times he
trained his M-249 on a tree, picturing in his mind's eye the slow and
deliberate pace of a point man. The sound of shells passing over their
heads split the air above, these originating from behind their lines. Even
though they were fired by the good guys, Monk lowered his cheek into
the dirt. Once the shells left their tubes they killed indiscriminately.

A frantic rip of pops like loud firecrackers tore through the woods
from the direction of the oncoming Russians. With each artillery shell
that passed over, another string of seventy pops sounded.

Cluster munitions, Monk thought. Tiny silver disks, antipersonnel
bomblets with the explosive power of hand grenades, released from
the back of the artillery shells into the air over the Russians' heads.
He could only imagine what the men underneath were going through.

Monk looked over at Bone and saw Bone's cheek pressed to the
stock of his M-60. Smalls was lying to his left, a fresh 100-round belt
of 7.62-mm ammo held in the air with his two hands above and in front
of his head.

Monk felt his adrenaline begin to pump despite his fatigue, creating
a strange, unpleasant feeling: a profound need to rest accompanied by
a jittery need to act. His head, which now ached constantly from lack of
sleep and food and from the noise and stress of combat, began to throb
with astonishing intensity just behind Monk's eyes, timed, it seemed,
with each pulse of his heart. He rubbed his eyes with the fingers of
his trigger hand and then squeezed his right arm against his side to
stamp out the cold trickle of sweat that ran across his chest from his
armpit.

Come on, Monk thought as he scanned the hazy recesses of the
woods ahead. *Get here already*. He pressed his cheek to the cool plastic
stock of the SAW and elevated the weapon's butt until the front sight
settled onto the rear, and both pointed out into the trees.

Some low limbs shook and then flew out of a running man's way
deep in the woods to Monk's left. The man wasn't just running – he
was fleeing, Monk realized, as he swiveled his weapon in the man's
direction. No weapon in his hand. No helmet on his head. His face –
even from that distance it was clear that he was panic-stricken. And he
was yelling 'Peso-darenda!' or something like that.

Monk now saw more men running, these with rifles and helmets. As
the first man approached their line, Monk thought Gunny was waiting
too long. Nearer and nearer he ran.

Monk looked back down the length of his weapon, putting the front
sight on the chest of one of the Russians approaching in the distance.
There were twenty or thirty soldiers visible now as they jogged forward

at a slight crouch, and he could hear an urgent but hushed command spat out in Russian. Monk squeezed the trigger, but not quite far enough to loose a round. He, and everyone else, waited for Gunny.

Out of the corner of his eye, Monk watched the fleeing man near their line, running straight at Gunny. As the man raced the last few yards to the slight rise, still babbling away in Russian, Monk refined his aim on the man nearest his front sight. 'Plees-I-surrenda-a-h,' Monk heard as the sound of a single shot set off an eruption of noise from Monk's left and right. Monk's weapon bucked without him even consciously realizing that he had added pressure to the trigger, and the hammering recoil of the half a dozen bullets shot pain into the hollow of his shoulder, long bruised from days of similar abuse.

Monk slewed the weapon from right to left as his eyes filled with moisture. *Fuck it*! he thought to clear his eyes, to clear his mind. First one and then several Russian soldiers fell backward and forward and spun this way and that. *Just fuck it, man*! he thought with a vicious burst from his SAW.

At close range it was possible to witness the bullets' effects. Everywhere parts of men were cleaved away from or punched out of their bodies by the impact and tumble of the projectiles, their hard copper jackets wrapped around lead bodies that in turn encased steel penetrator darts. All was scientifically engineered to kill homo sapiens, the crowning achievement of centuries of work.

The entire platoon was firing with abandon, and the noise was astounding. Mouth, who now began to squeeze off rounds from his M-16, had momentarily frozen after watching the carnage produced by his 40-mm grenade launcher. A canister of shot – shotgun style – had severed an arm at the shoulder from one man and the head from another directly behind him. Monk fired methodically at the fewer and fewer targets remaining available, a sneer set on his face and his jaw clenched. *Just fuck everybody and every Goddamn thing*! he raged as his weapon bucked. Many times as he trained the SAW on his target he saw it splay its arms out and tumble to the ground, killed before he could fire.

Monk slowed his fire down to cool the weapon, picking his shots at the mostly crawling survivors. He aimed intently at each evidence of life – a muzzle flash, grass, weeds or leaves blown around by a rifle's gases, or the writhing in pain or crawling forward of a body, so difficult to tell which.

The smoky trails of several rifle grenades fired toward the marines' line all at once caused Monk to lower his head. Instead of high explosives, however, the grenades contained smoke and his view of the killing ground clouded.

Dirt spattered Monk's face as randomly fired rounds thumped into the soil in front. He stuck his head down in the hole, and dirt was spit up onto him again.

'Hold your fire!' Gunny yelled through the cotton of Monk's ears. Monk could not see anything of the killing ground ahead as the smoke rounds continued to come streaking in.

'Listen up!' Gunny shouted. 'Riflemen, aimed fire only – three round bursts!' Monk again ducked as the only sound of firing was up ahead from the Russians and from other units engaged on their flanks. The Russians' thick but undisciplined fire was snapping through branches and splintering off bark all around.

'Grenadiers, load shot and hold fire!' Gunny continued. 'Automatic weapons, grazing fire – forty-five-degree angles! Stake 'em out!'

Monk looked around and found two dry sticks. Exposed as he knelt in his hole, he jammed one stick into the dirt in front of his pack to the right, and another to the left as the familiar *z-z-z-zings* split the air all around him. Relieved to lie back down in the relative safety of his shallow hole, he leveled the SAW so that it would 'graze' along parallel with the ground; he lined the barrel up with the rightmost stick, pointing blindly into the smoke.

Cra-a-a-a-a-ack erupted with a stream of five bullets, fired in one third of a second. His rifle beat into his sore shoulder. He moved the rifle slightly to the left and again squeezed the trigger.

Out of a thin spot of smoke to Monk's left he saw the back of a Russian creeping up toward the line. He was beyond Monk's left stick so he kept to his pattern of fire, now slewing back to the right. As the man rose up to toss a grenade, he froze on his knees, his legs preventing him from tumbling backward after being shot through with rifle fire. The grenade that he had raised to toss went off behind him, illuminating his human form in profile before shredding it to pieces in the storm of fire that engulfed his body.

Monk caught sight of an object bounding along the ground toward him at the very last second, bouncing straight toward his hole and smoking.

He threw his head down. *W-H-A-A-A-N-N-N-G!*

He tumbled over and over and over through pain that gripped his head in a vise. When the spinning didn't stop, Monk tried to decide whether he was lying on his stomach, back or side. *Lying,* he realized, *on my back – no, no, my stomach.* The pain that Monk felt now, from his ears across his forehead and at his eyes, made his earlier headache seem trifling in comparison. He had no idea how long he had lain there but all was silent, the fighting over. He tried to lift his head to look around despite the intense wave of pain the movement caused, but a rush of nausea caused him to retch immediately in great heaves right where he lay. As the heaves became dry and less forceful, he lay still in utter exhaustion.

I gotta open my eyes, Monk thought as he braced himself. Lying still, he forced his eyes open and saw Mouth, spent shells flying out of the

ejector of his M-16 at a frantic pace. Behind him, Gunny was pulling
grenade after grenade from the platoon's resupply pouch and throwing
them football-style. They were close. They were coming to kill him!

Monk mustered all his strength and looked up. He could see figures
running through the thinning smoke toward him.

The mouths of the grimacing Russian soldiers were wide with
shouts as they charged, bright orange flames blazing from guns
fired from their hips. The clatter of noise from the raging battle
was overwhelmed, however, by the whooshing throb of his pulse
in his ears, pounding his head with pain. Monk winced and closed
his eyes as another stab of pain pierced his ears like ice picks. With
each jab of pain, however, the volume of the fighting worked its way
through.

Monk reached for his M-16, surprised to find it was a SAW, and
pulled it up onto the pack. Pain shot into his shoulder as he seated it
against his skin. *We're being overrun*! he realized when all at once he
saw the huge number of men rushing at them. Monk felt the jarring
blow of a grenade from behind and between Mouth and him, the jets
of fire and sprays of dark earth mere feet away as he took aim. Debris
showered down onto him.

Monk fired point-blank at the nearest Russians, squeezing his finger
full back and holding it, knocking down first one, then two, then three
Russians as easily as he knocked down the two flimsy sticks on either
side of his weapon's barrel. He sprayed back and forth and back
again. Fifteen, ten meters in front they fell in swaths as his SAW
pummeled the hollow of his shoulder, the pain there an incessant
sickly-sweet itch.

It didn't matter. Nothing mattered. Monk watched their faces explode
in pink mist and chests spurt fountains of frothy orange blood. He
watched the thudding impact of his bullets stand stooped men straight
up or send helmets strapped securely to men's chins off heads creased
with deep red gashes.

He ran out of ammo and dropped down to release the empty box
quickly, his breath coming in pants and his larynx emitting random
sounds through his clenched teeth as he feverishly worked to slap
another magazine heavy with bullets into its place, counting down
the strides that separated the approaching Russians from his hole.
Searing pain shot through his hand as he grasped the barrel of the
burning-hot gun.

Half rolling back onto his stomach to fire, all he saw was a running
man. He jerked himself up to the sitting position, bringing the weapon
up with him. The Russian's assault rifle was leveled at his chest but
he didn't fire as he fumbled with a new magazine on the dead run.
His stubby black bayonet was at Monk's eye level, five, four, three
strides away.

Monk pulled the trigger back for one brief jerk, 'stitching' the man, as they taught, from crotch to head. Before his face exploded in a puff of red, Monk caught a glimpse not of pain or terror, but of astonishment. The force of the four rounds had stopped him dead in full stride.

A sudden blow, like a sledgehammer to his side, knocked the breath out of Monk, and he fell onto his pack and then slid his body down behind it.

Monk felt another set of heavy thuds through the earth, and his ears popped like on an airplane, instantly admitting the roar of battle all around. He looked up into the trees above him and tried desperately to draw air into his lungs. Movement out of the corner of his eye caused him to twist around and see Mouth, digging his heels into the dirt and pushing himself away from his hole on his back as he fired his rifle in bursts between his knees, indescribable terror writ over his face.

Without thinking and in searing pain from his ribs Monk rolled over onto his knees again and raised the SAW, the trigger pulled full back. The hot breath of a rifle fired on full auto brushed by his cheek as he killed its owner, who fell draped over the top of Monk's pack. He went on spraying bullets in all directions into the mass of attacking Russians. In front he saw two men – Monk squeezed and they died. Over to the right, straight down the line – squeeze and die. 'You basta-a-ards!' Monk yelled.

'*Sappers in*! *Sappers in*!' Gunny yelled distantly over the hum in his ears. Monk didn't heed the call to get down, the call that signaled all friendlies to hug the earth and fire all around at anything above ground level. Monk was killing from his knees; his gun was rocking.

He laid waste until another 200 rounds were gone, and he dropped to load a magazine into the SAW, which stank from the smoke rising from its barrel. The woods ahead exploded with grenades. Still the Russians came.

His breathing was labored and painful now as he grew dizzy. He raised the weapon to his right hip and sprayed. Through the painful chimes sounding in his ears Monk heard the distinct string of cracks from the SAW that sounded in time with the vibrations he felt in his hands and at his side. Monk screamed from the pain of the left side of his chest, the sound inhuman, like the cry of some animal, but lost in the noise and confusion of the killing.

A man rose, running slowly forward with a limp and firing his rifle from his hip. *Splat*! Monk's mind added as his burst swung across the man's midsection and he split apart, spilling the contents of his abdomen as his legs continued to carry him forward.

Pull! *Pull*! *Pull*! Monk yelled in his head and each time the weapon bucked, each time men fell dead. Monk's helmet slammed down on his nose, pain and a white splash of light shooting across his face. Reaching up to raise the brim of his helmet, Monk felt a trickle of blood onto his upper lip.

'You can't kill *me-e-e-e*!' Monk thought or yelled as he sprayed one long burst from his SAW.

They kept coming. *Gonna kill 'em all*! Monk barely noticed the pain of his jaw's firm clench. *One on the right – squeeze – dead*! *To the left – rifle jammed – bang*! *Hah*! 'You bastard, you're *dead*!' *Straight ahead*! *Come on, you fucking – Z-Z-Z-I-P*! *Hah*! 'Meat!'

Monk raised the SAW to his shoulder to blast the Russians who crawled away. With each pull of the trigger he yelled it. 'I got the rhythm!' he said to himself or out loud. 'The killin' rhythm – MOTHER-FUCK-ERS!' Squeeze the trigger – drop – '*dead*!' Monk shouted over and over again. When nobody crawled, Monk's rage built rapidly from lack of release. *Where are you, you bastards*! *Come on*! *Come an' get it*! His fury blinding now, he rose to his feet and fired at the squirmers. When nobody squirmed, he fired into the green shapes of the dead. It did no good. He got no release. His breath came in shallow pants, and he hated everything. His head jerked, but he could find nothing in the thinning smoke, nothing to kill. Grinding his bared teeth so hard that the pain shot through his face, he jammed his eyes shut and yelled, holding the trigger down and spraying the smoky woods from right to left until the gun ceased bucking.

Monk felt a hand jerk him around and a foot placed behind his trip him to the ground, pain again shooting through the ribs on the left side of his chest. '*Cease fire*!' Gunny yelled as he knelt and shook Monk by his webbing. 'It's over! It's over, Goddammit!'

His nostrils filled with the smell of burned gunpowder and he could hear now the crackle rising from the length of his SAW's white-hot barrel. He slackened the pull on his cramping trigger finger, which was jammed full back on the empty weapon.

'Hm! Hm! Hm!' came the mewls from Monk's chest as he fought back the tears that welled up in his eyes. Gunny moved on, checking the other men.

Monk gazed down the smoky line of marines. Mouth lay with his face almost flat in the dirt, mouth open and eyes jammed shut, crying. Marines rose slowly from their fighting holes exhausted, not from the physical strain of the battle but from the mental, the emotional. As after every such firefight, tears streaked down grimy faces in dirty streams as men sat on the edge of their holes in a daze. Monk's attention was drawn again to the floor of the woods around and in front of their line. There were bodies everywhere, as far as the eye could see through the light haze that remained.

Above the brush Monk could see elbows and shoulders and heads marking the fallen. The air was still thick with the acrid smell of smoke from the guns. By tomorrow it would be thick with a different odor.

Chapter Thirteen

PRESOV, SLOVAKIA
June 30, 1300 GMT (1400 Local)

Chandler and Barnes walked down the rows of M-1A1 main battle tanks
parked barrel to barrel under camouflage netting.

'Who ordered these tanks parked so close together?' Chandler
asked.

'Cap'n Loomis, Sir,' Barnes replied, referring to the battalion's
executive officer, second in command. 'The men are working in teams
instead of by tank crew. One team'll brush the barrels. Another'll lube
the road wheels. We gotta take the tracks clean off 'cause they been
in storage – ain't been lubed in a while. Wouldn't git ten clicks.'

'Yeah, well, I'm just worried about the placement,' Chandler said
looking up into the hazy summer sky through the small holes in the
netting.

'It goes quicker this way, but you're right, sir, it's a risk.' Barnes
stopped. 'Here she is.'

Chandler looked at the hulking dark green vehicle. Squat – the turret
barely as high as the top of his helmet – the huge, low-slung tank spread
wider and longer than the old M-60, its predecessor with which he was
familiar from a decade before. Chandler felt Barnes's eyes on him.

'Get these tanks spread out, Master Sergeant. Stagger 'em, at least
thirty meters separation. Individual netting for each tank.'

'Yes, sir,' Barnes replied, leaving Chandler alone.

Chandler walked up to the vehicle, rubbing his hand down the finely
grained armor – the ceramic-metallic honeycomb so different from the
smooth metal of the older models. He found a step loop by the front
fender and climbed up onto the deck, grabbing onto the thick barrel of
the 120-mm main gun. He would have to remember not to do that after
firing: even one shot would heat the barrel so hot that his hand would
fry to the bone.

Standing up under the spreaders of the camo netting he could see
men crawling all over the metal monsters up and down the line. And
this was only one of his four companies, fourteen of his fifty-eight

tanks. It seemed an insurmountable force, unstoppable to the Russians, uncontrollable to Chandler. How was he going to keep it together in the heat of battle, keep one company from running wild or getting left behind or shooting up friendly troops? He looked down at the massive flat deck to his tank's turret and wished he could content himself with fighting just this one vehicle. He knew he could handle that, given time to master it.

He climbed up onto the turret behind the huge .50-caliber M-2 heavy machine gun, the 'Ma Deuce.' The thumb-size bullets it spit out would pound through the cylinder block of a heavy truck engine at two miles. Everyone thought the sole purpose of a tank was the main gun, but it was the five-foot-long black machine gun in front of the commander's hatch that the infantry feared.

'Sixty-six is ready to roll, sir!' shouted the slender enlisted man from the ground at the next tank over. He sweated at a large clawlike crowbar with which he was attempting to lever together the treads of the neighboring tank to insert the pin that held the last link together. He handed the job off to another soldier and walked up to the side of the tank, wiping his hands and then stopping to salute. 'Spec 4 Jefferson, sir. I'm your loader.'

Chandler returned his salute. 'She looks like she's in fine shape.'

'Yes, sir. She's good to go.'

'Hey' – they heard a grunting shout – 'could you . . .?'

Jefferson looked back at the man who strained unsuccessfully at the bar and then up at Chandler. 'We gonna kick some mother-fuckin' ass with this baby, sir,' he said, lovingly patting the armored fender, 'if you don't mind me sayin'.' He waved a sloppy salute before returning to his tread. From down the line, Chandler saw sparks from a welding torch flying out onto the churned-up brown dirt and green grass, huge ruts torn into the soft soil with every move of the tanks' treads. The activity level was high. Everybody was working, but there was still so much to be done.

In human chains men hoisted the heavy rounds of the main gun up to others. Thick black hoses snaked up onto the rear decks for fueling, tiny orange flags sunk into the ground around the curling hoses to ward off potentially disastrous accidents by inattentive drivers.

Chandler's eyes wandered across the rolling hills outside the netting. About a quarter of a mile away he could see his next stop: the brigade supply point. The army logistics people had solved the problem of the wider-gauged rails in Eastern Europe, a relic of strategic planning intentionally engineered by the Soviets, by simply leasing up practically all of the aging rolling stock in the former Warsaw Pact countries. The result was what had become known as the 'Rotterdam Corridor,' a supply chain from the U.S. through Rotterdam – the old NATO-designated port of entry that had been reluctantly left open by the former allies – that fed a rail grid across Germany to the east. At every rail siding for miles around there grew mounds of wooden or cardboard crates with black stenciling in cryptic English letters and numbers.

Chandler shook his head. When they had first designated the supply point at which he looked a few days before, they had chosen a spot next to a copse of trees so that the camo netting would form a natural extension of the dark greenery to the inattentive enemy eye. Looking at it now he chuckled. The mound of crates had grown to a mountain, only haphazardly covered by netting. And the logistics people had lost control. It was easier, he had been told by one brigade supply officer, to special-order something from the States than to look through the stacks of crates that forklifts and cranes built with every train's arrival. It would be weeks, the exhausted man had said, before they even got the crates already on hand open to see what was inside, and more crates arrived every day.

He looked back down at his tank. The open commander's and loader's hatches beckoned. Chandler swung his feet up onto the turret and down into the black hole. Probing for a foothold, he held himself up over the opening with hands on either side of the hatch. Finally he found the commander's seat and stood there for a moment. Lying just below him the thick tube of the main gun pointed the way – low, straight, powerful. Jefferson and the others had hand-painted 'Suck on this' on the base of the barrel. Chandler's machine gun sat swiveled to the right side of his hatch, the loader's smaller M-60 7.62-mm machine gun swiveled symmetrically to his side of the turret on Chandler's left. Chandler dropped down into the vehicle.

He didn't get far. Halfway in his equipment jammed painfully into his kidneys as his canteen and M-16 ammo pouches and miscellaneous gear got stuck on the hatch. *Shit*! he thought, quickly checking the men around his tank. A team labored as they ran the thick brush back out of the barrel across from him, stripped to the waist and too hot and too tired to notice. Chandler took his belt off and sank on in, sitting in darkness with the heavy pistol belt in his hand. It was hot, dark, and quiet. The cabin was roomier than it looked from outside. He had no idea how to turn the crew compartment's lights on, so he removed his flashlight from his belt.

The huge breech of the main gun dominated the center of the cabin to his left and below him as he sat high in the commander's perch. There was very little else lining the antiseptic white walls of the compartment. He found the gunner's position below and in front of his own, the padded sights and gun controls a duplicate of the set just in front of him. He put the flashlight back onto his belt and in the dim light filtering through the netting and hatch above he lightly grasped the joystick that would turn the turret and raise, lower, and fire the main gun. He pressed his face against the sight's pads as he sat on his seat just under the hatch.

The screen was dark, but the pad fit snugly around his eyes just over his nose.

A screech, the sound filling his armored cocoon, tore past the open hatch overhead, and he sat there in the dark, his heart skipping a beat. The jet engines were gone in an instant as the camo netting above his hatch gently rose and fell in the wash of air they trailed. In the quiet, Chandler heard shouts and then *pop-pop-pop-pop-pop-pop* in a rapid-fire chain. A second later he heard the harsh horn of the chemical weapons detector.

'Gas-gas-gas!' someone shouted and Chandler took one deep breath and began to fumble with the bag containing his mask and suit. He raced against a silent count as he held his breath, banging his elbows and knees and head onto the compartment's walls as he struggled into his gear. This time he won, shivering in cold dread as he climbed awkwardly back out of the hatch, his breath hissing inside his mask and its 'no-fog' lenses fogging immediately. A small clump of hooded men gathered in what, through the fogging lenses, looked like a writhing green mound just below the abandoned rammer still jutting from the tank barrel opposite Chandler's. Climbing out onto the turret, Chandler saw their charcoal-suit-covered arms and backs jerking with frantic effort, atropine injectors being stabbed down into the object of their attention from all sides. Chandler caught a glimpse of the soldier over whom they struggled: wearing only his mask, the man's bare torso was pasty white and he convulsed with jerks and spasms that seemed machinelike, inhuman.

LOS ANGELES, CALIFORNIA
June 30, 1700 GMT (0900 Local)

'POSTWAR VCR!' the sign read, and Melissa wheeled Matthew, crumpled down in the umbrella stroller sound asleep, over to the window of the electronics store at the Galleria. SHIPMENT WAS IN-BOUND FROM JAPAN, NO EMP DAMAGE, ABSOLUTELY GUARANTEED!

'TWO THOUSAND DOLLARS,' she read out loud, incredulous. BUY ANY TV – GET A GAS MASK FOR FREE! another sign read. A shiver ran down her spine. The news reports were sketchy – the government wasn't talking – but the news media's speculation was running wild. *What's the world coming to?* she thought as she looked down at her sleeping newborn. Melissa had hoped the trip out would help her, but she felt no better.

She walked on. The mall was nearly deserted, and very few stores were open. She passed an accessories store, the smell of fine leather wafting out into the air-conditioned walkway of the second level. 'You looking for work?' the proprietor asked, walking out around the counter holding a rag with which she had been dusting.

Melissa smiled and shook her head. 'No, thank you.'

'Oh,' the woman said, huffing and looking down at Matthew, smiling sadly. She shook her head and looked around the empty mall. 'I just don't know how much longer I can stay open.'

'Why? What do you mean?'

'Well, with all these new regulations – federal taxes, state taxes, city taxes . . . I normally do the books and the banking, and now changing over to the new taxes is a full-time job but I can't ever get out of the store.'

Melissa noticed the HELP WANTED sign posted in her window. 'Why?'

'Because everybody skipped out on me. One girl came to work two days after the war – the nuclear attack – because it was a Friday, pay day, but none of the others even called in.' She hung her head and shrugged. 'It's not exactly like business has been booming though.'

Melissa looked down the row of stores ahead, metal gates closed across their glass fronts. One, an Oriental rug store, had a ONE DAY ONLY GOING OUT OF BUSINESS SALE! banner pasted diagonally across the plate glass window. The now closed store appeared to be full of rugs still. 'Where is everybody?' Melissa asked. 'I thought it would be packed on a Sunday.'

'They've headed for the hills. Weekends are the worst. It seems like everybody who has a car just packs up and heads out of town.'

'Why?'

The woman chuckled. 'Because of the Russians,' she said as if the question made no sense. 'You know, in case it happens on a weekend, they won't be in the city.'

'In case what . . .?' Melissa began to ask, but stopped when she realized the answer.

'You haven't gotten out much, have you, dear?'

'No. I've watched TV almost nonstop. Mainly just the national news, though. My husband is in the army somewhere.'

'Oh, dear,' the shop owner said, putting her hand on Melissa's arm and looking down at their child. 'I guess there are more important things to worry about. I'm sorry for being so self-centered.'

Melissa shook her head and smiled, looking into the store at a handbag.

'You see something you like?'

'Yes,' she said, wheeling Matthew in and walking up to the display. Louis Vuitton. She felt guilty even contemplating it, but this was her first treat since the war, the first time she had gotten up, dressed, put makeup on, and gone out just for entertainment.

'That's a lovely purse,' the shopkeeper said. 'They're very popular.

Or were, anyway.' She handed Melissa the bag. Melissa looked up at
the woman, and behind her at the empty Galleria. She had hoped to see
and be with people. The woman was the only person she had met.

'I'll take it.'

'Oh, wonderful,' she said, rounding the counter to the cash register
as Melissa fumbled with her wallet. Melissa put a credit card on the glass
counter, and the woman looked up but did not reach for it. She filled her
lungs with air to speak, but faltered, finally saying, 'Oh, I'm sorry.' She
shook her head. 'No credit cards,' she said and smiled meekly, pointing
at another sign in the window. 'I really should put that where you can see
it better, but I thought everybody knew.' Melissa pulled the gold card
back awkwardly. 'You see, it's not me, dear. So many of the banks that
were issuing those things have been closed, plus the computers that
do the authorizations work so slowly now they're almost impossible to
use. Plus my bank told me no credit cards.'

Melissa smiled and nodded, putting away the card. 'Well, I'm sorry.
I don't have that much cash.'

'Of course not.' The woman smiled a kindly, pitying smile at Melissa
and her baby.

'I've got a job,' Melissa said. 'I mean, I'm on maternity leave, but I'm
a lawyer with a downtown firm. And so is my husband, although he's
on vacation pay for another couple of weeks and then goes, you know,
unpaid.'

The woman smiled and walked around to take a closer look at
Matthew. 'Well, you've got a beautiful baby. Is it a boy?'

'Yes. Matthew.'

'If you're on maternity leave, and you don't have to be in L.A., if you
don't mind my asking, what are you doing here?'

'I . . . I live here.'

'Well, sure, but . . .' She glanced down at Matthew and then back
up at Melissa. She smiled. 'Of course.'

Melissa turned to go, her mind a fog of confused thoughts. Everybody
else has fled. What should she do? Go back on the road like before? It
had been so difficult.

'Excuse me,' the woman said from behind, and when Melissa turned
she saw the shopkeeper removing the security tag on the handbag.
'Why don't you take this?'

'Oh, no,' Melissa said, shaking her head as the woman held the bag
out to her. 'I couldn't.'

'Oh, go ahead.'

'But I couldn't!'

'Why not? I don't know who I'm kidding. The only way this war is
going to end soon is if we blow each other up, and if it doesn't end by
next week I'll miss my lease payment. They shut you down at twelve
oh one these days – come in and change the locks in the middle of the

night. Anyway, either way, I figure this handbag is a goner.' She laughed nervously, and hung the bag on the stroller handle.

'Thank you,' Melissa said, and she rolled Matthew on out.

'Take care of that little one,' the woman called. 'He's our future.' Melissa smiled as she watched the woman return lovingly to her dusting of the bags and belts that hung in the empty little store.

90TH STRATEGIC MISSILE WING, WARREN AFB, WYOMING
June 30, 2200 GMT (1400 Local)

Stuart lay on the cot in pitch darkness, drawing the heavy, stale air into his lungs without feeling refreshed by the effort. Langford coughed for the millionth time from his cot on the opposite end of the capsule as far as possible from Stuart's. The cough annoyed Stuart immensely nevertheless, and he sat up intending to yell for him to shut up. Grinding his teeth he managed to hold it in.

Langford coughed again, a wracking, tortured cough that went on for almost a full minute. With his first breath, Langford said, 'Sorry,' and then coughed again.

I can't take it anymore, Stuart thought. *Not for one more day. Not for one more hour*. He spun his bare feet to the floor. He and Langford were stripped down to their underwear but still they sweat almost nonstop in the stifling atmosphere. He would put his uniform and protective gear on, and he would get out of this tomb.

'I'm leaving,' Stuart said into the darkness. He waited, but there was no answer. 'I really mean it this time.'

'Go on, then! Go!'

Stuart angrily switched his flashlight on and in the fading, dim beam searched the confines of what had been the communications section of the capsule for his clothing. The light was weak, and he knew they were running low on batteries. He flicked the light off, and tossed it in the darkness from memory onto the cot, collapsing down beside it onto the hard but slightly cooler metal floor and running his hands through his filthy, sweat-soaked hair, grown too long and feeling unnatural.

'Hang in there, buddy,' Langford said, the last words strained as he barely completed the short sentence before coughing. 'We can do this. We can make it. Just stick to the plan. We've' – he coughed again – 'we've been down here three weeks. We're halfway there.'

Halfway, Stuart thought. *Just three more weeks. Just three more weeks*. He rose and lay back down on the cot, which was wet and slightly cool. *Where were we? 'T' – we were in the 'Ts'. At this rate* . . . He stopped to do the math. They should be somewhere in the P-Q-R-S range on the second run through the alphabet when they ran out of food and battery power, and therefore air. *Three weeks*.

T, he thought. 'Triathlon,' he said out loud.

After a moment Langford said, 'Temperature.'

'Texture,' Stuart replied.

'Tuxedo,' Stuart heard Langford say as he coughed again. Stuart's mind wandered back to the same subject as always. To the quote from somewhere long ago that had meant nothing to him at all. 'Tuxedo,' Langford repeated. 'Your turn.' When Stuart didn't answer, Langford fell silent and left him alone.

The quote from some long-ago class or book rang through his head and captured his attention completely. He had never understood it before; it had meant nothing to him, and he'd just stored it away. But now he understood. The quote spoke to him with the clarity of a truth discovered by experience.

Langford coughed again, a long, dry cough whose bodily purpose Stuart could not fathom. '*Hell is a very small place*,' Stuart thought again. '*Hell is a very small place*.'

SPECIAL FACILITY, MOUNT WEATHER, VIRGINIA
July 2, 1300 GMT (0800 Local)

'Where the hell are the SIGINT reports for Northern Europe?' Lambert yelled through his open door, clasping his palm over the telephone's mouthpiece and hoping his secretary was there.

'They're on your desk,' she said, rushing in and waving a new batch of stapled papers in front of him before placing them with a theatrical motion on the center of his desk. He tilted his head and sighed in exasperation. 'I swear I put that fax right there,' she said, continuing her defense as she walked past him to return to her desk.

'Wait, what's that?' Lambert asked, nodding at the newest additions to the pile of paper covering the blotter pad on his cold metal desk.

She turned, still peevish after his charge that she had lost a fax, and picked up one of the sheaves of paper. 'The Turks want to open another front into Russia from the south and are asking for immediate arms purchase credits. The Greeks have protested. You will also find an addendum from State, which opines that the Armenians are prepared to join the war on the Russian side if the Turks come their way.' She threw it down and picked up another. 'Several German opposition groups have scheduled a sit-in to block road grids across Germany from Rotterdam to protest the war. Eighth Army commanders have requested permission to employ military policemen to clear the demonstrators if German federal police don't keep the roads open.' She threw the report down.

'Have you considered maybe taking a nap?' Lambert suggested, but before she could answer he heard the tinny voice through the phone say, 'Mr Lambert, would you be so kind as to either speak to me now or ring later.'

'Oh, I'm sorry, Arty,' Lambert said.

'It's Arthur,' the British military liaison said from his London office as Lambert watched two junior air force officers appear at his door. Lambert motioned for them to enter. 'MI5 has already determined from its own signals intelligence that . . .'

The air force officers handed him a computer printout filled with row after row and column after column of numbers and symbols, some of them completely unrecognizable. The heading read 'Spectrographic Analyses of Air Samples.'

'. . . and if you take what the Germans and French have been saying at the U.N. as any evidence of their current intentions, we believe that you must assume the worst.'

'What worst, Arty? What are you talking about?' Lambert cupped the receiver and whispered to the officers, 'What are these, Martian love poems?'

'I'm talking about the French and Germans actively interfering with our operations by cutting off utilities to our bases, gradually restricting use of their road grids . . .'

'We've got a second report of probable biologicals, this one from Okinawa,' the air force captain in front of him said.

When one of Lambert's aides came in and held up a thick stack of paper that could only be the President's morning briefing package – several oversize maps pressed under his free arm – Lambert looked at his watch. *Jesus*, he thought, realizing that he was supposed to give the briefing in thirty minutes. 'Okay, Arthur, here's what I'll do,' he said into the phone as he motioned for his aide to put the report on his desk. 'I'll have the President get Gerhardt on the line and lay it out for him one more time, but look, I thought the Foreign Secretary and the Secretary of State got together and allocated responsibility for relations with the whole European Community to you guys over there.'

'Well, that's quite a job now, isn't it?' Arthur said as Lambert looked at the aide taking down the last unit position maps, now eight hours old, from his wall and putting the new maps up. He squinted to see the finely drawn lines, but even across the room he could see that the Southern Prong of the European attack out of Slovakia still couldn't seem to get going. 'Shit,' he cursed under his breath.

'That seems to be an extremely versatile word for you, Gregory.'

'What? Oh, never mind. It was something else. Look, I'll get to it later on.'

'And if that is too late? If the Germans begin stopping our convoys?'

'Then we blow the holy *shit* out of 'em!'

'Oh, well, of course. How silly of me.'

The air force captain dangled the air sample report from the fingers of both hands and wiggled it in front of Lambert to attract his attention. Behind him entered Lambert's secretary, who rounded his desk and began to rummage through the paper that covered it.

'I'll call you later, Arthur.'

'Sir, we've got to do something about these biological attacks,' the air force officer said as Lambert hung up and pushed by him to walk over to the newly hung maps. 'General Starnes said that any response to the suspected attacks was a purely political decision, and we thought, you know, since you seemed to be on our side and all . . .' The Northern Prong out of Poland was way ahead of schedule, but from the small circles and longer oblongs drawn in pockets all over eastern Slovakia, the Russians' 'spoiling attack,' begun hours before Operation Avenging Sword, had lived up to its name. Judging by the map, there was no Southern Prong to speak of, more like a Southern Bulge arcing the wrong way back into Slovakia.

'Aha!' his secretary declared, pulling a soiled piece of paper from his wastebasket, oily stains forming blotches all over the fax. 'Absolutely covered in butter and cheese from that Danish you had for breakfast!'

'Are you ready for a run-through?' his aide asked, taking his watch off his wrist to time the presentation.

'What does it say?' Lambert asked, turning as an afterthought to make sure his secretary knew he was talking to her.

She cleared her throat. 'It is from the Department of State. It says, "The Ukrainian Parliament voted this morning at 9:12 a.m. Kiev time to abrogate their mutual security treaty with the Republic of Russia and to declare a unilateral cease-fire against all troops of the Western coalition effective as of 11:00 a.m. Kiev time (0900 hours Greenwich Mean Time). Terms were as discussed – paren – a halt on allied attacks in and around Kiev, Odessa, D-ne-pro-petrovsk," she pronounced with difficulty, "and Donetsk, retention of strategic nuclear arsenal, return of Black Sea Fleet to port, etc. – close paren. U.N. delegation is awaiting word within the hour from Minsk on Byelorussian decision, but expects similar accord and cease-fire."'

The President's Chief of Staff appeared, leaning against Lambert's doorframe, stuffing a bagel into his mouth and holding a paper plate under it to catch the crumbs.

'Sir, the air samples,' the air force officer behind him said.

'Has anybody gotten sick yet?'

'Not yet, sir, but they might not for some time still.'

'Come back when somebody gets sick,' Lambert said, disappointing the two junior men, who clearly thought they were onto something big, but keeping his eyes on the smiling Chief of Staff in the doorway.

'Can I have a sec, Greg?' Sol Rosen asked.

'That's about all the time I've got, Sol,' Greg said, waving at the office full of paper and people.

'I meant alone.'

Lambert looked at the others. They filed out past Rosen, who entered the office and closed the door behind him.

'What can I do for you?' Lambert asked the powerful man, Costanzo's right hand.

'Well, I'm glad you asked that. I want to ask you for a favor.'

'Okay,' Lambert shrugged, 'shoot.'

'You know July fourth is a very important day for Paul – politically, I mean?'

'You mean the "photo op from hell"?' Lambert said, and Rosen laughed.

'He called it that, but he also appreciates the importance of it. Since Livingston never broke out of the grasp first of his military handlers and then of his legal counsel, this'll be the first visit to the disaster sites by a President. It's also the coming-out party for the U.S. government, emerging from the bunkers and moving into our temporary offices in Philadelphia on the Fourth of July. It's big, symbolically, and it'll be a big morale booster for the public. We've had a real problem, you've heard I'm sure, with absenteeism at the workplace. People are shying away from the big cities. They're spooked. Plus, the editorialists are having a field day with us running things out of here. Have you seen the political cartoonists' most recent efforts?'

'I don't have much time for cartoons, Sol,' Lambert said, feeling the ache from the sleepless nights and resentful that his time was being spent so trivially.

The smile left Rosen's face. 'I think it would be a good thing if you accompanied the President on his tour.'

Lambert made a face. 'You're kidding!' Rosen stared back blankly. 'You *are* kidding, right?'

'Greg, you may not care much for the political side of things, but don't make the mistake of underestimating its importance. Look at where that got Livingston.' Rosen held up his hand as Lambert tried to interrupt. 'I'm talking morale here, also, Greg. The public's morale. The latest polls' – his hand shot up again as if to ward off Lambert's objection – 'and I know you like to pretend you're one of the military boys in these things, but you're not. You're on the political side of government, Greg, not the military. Regardless, the polls are significant militarily, and they already show a weakening of support for the war with all the nerve gas and biological warfare rumors and fears about the Bastion. Support's back down in the eighty percent range.'

'Jesus, Sol, eighty percent is—'

'Less than ninety percent, which is what it was when the war began.' He tossed his plate and napkin into Lambert's trash can. 'Look, I'm not

asking you to stump the country to sell war bonds, just that you come
out of this molehill and be seen with the President. One day!'

'But why me?' Lambert asked. 'There must be dozens of people running around here with one tenth the number of things on their plate.'

'Well,' Rosen sighed, 'to lay it all out for you, you've got high
favorables.'

'I've got what?'

'High favorables,' Rosen said. 'The public's image of you – it's highly
favorable.'

'Since when does the public even know who the hell I am?'

'Right!' Rosen said, smiling broadly again but then looking back at
Lambert quizzically. After a moment or two of studying Lambert's
expression, Rosen said, 'You really are out of it, aren't you? You're
big *news*, son. You have been ever since you averted what was almost
a "bloody shoot-out for constitutional control of the country" on national
television in the lobby of the Congressional Facility at Greenbriar.'

Lambert began shaking his head, the whole concept seeming ridiculous to him. More people, strangers in his government and those of his
allies, seemed to know him and treat him with greater deference than
before, but he had just assumed that to be because of his heightened
importance during the war. But Rosen was right, Lambert realized,
about one thing: he had been out of it since the nuclear attack and
didn't know what was going on aboveground. He was curious. 'Come
on, Greg. Surely you must know how it's being played?' His voice was
low, playfully conspiratorial. 'You're a bright guy. You've been in the
business for a while.'

Lambert resented the implication that he was somehow cultivating
his public image, and he glared back at Rosen.

'You really don't know, do you?' Rosen sat back. 'Well, I'll be damned.
Paul was right,' he said, shaking his head. 'Okay, let me lay it out for
you. And I mean no disrespect, but this is what your press boils down
to.' He held up one hand as if he were placing block letters in the air
in front of Lambert. '"Former jock."' He looked down at Lambert.
'Basketball, right?' Lambert nodded, and Rosen's hands went back
up in the air. '"Former basketball player turned Harvard scholar."'
Risen to become national security adviser at, what, thirty-eight?
Tries desperately to stop President Livingston from foolish act that
leads to the war in which his wife perishes. Not caring about risk, he
delivers supplies into radioactive capital on off chance of finding her and,
tragically, he does. Despite being distraught, young aide doesn't bow to
pressure, thinks of country first, and bravely testifies to end nation's
constitutional crisis.'

'Are you finished?' Lambert asked, barely managing to hide his
disgust.

Rosen sighed. 'Come on, Greg,' he said apologetically. 'I'm sorry if

I offended you. But I'm just doing my job. And my job is to cut through the bullshit.'

Greg laughed and looked up at the ceiling.

'You think that's funny? You think that I'm nothing *but* bullshit? Well, you're right. I live in bullshit. I wade knee-deep through it every waking hour. But you know the scary thing? So does the President, son, so does the President. You think everything is crisp and neat and clean like your morning briefings – just the truth, the whole truth, and nothing but the truth. But I'm here to tell you that ninety percent of what the President hears on any given day is bullshit. "The tax credit for steel plant expansion will lower the per unit cost of the navy's new ships significantly, Mr President," only come to find out new ships are mostly made of aluminum, not steel. "There were some minor bidding irregularities in mining leases for that lot, but it's nothing that should raise any eyebrows," and then the sweetheart deals in the Bureau of Land Management's "Coppergate" blow up in our faces. "There has been price gouging, war profiteering in our materials costs and we've got to put a federal cap on magnesium prices," only to find out from the magnesium mining companies after issuing the price controls that the fabricators who gave us those figures are making a two hundred and thirty per cent profit that makes us look like dupes, at best, or criminal co-conspirators at worst.'

'So what are you saying, Sol? I've got to go give a briefing.'

'I'm saying, cutting through all the bullshit, that you're a big tall good-looking guy with strong favorables! Did you know you were the number one choice among the crackpots and retirees who wrote in to replace Secretary Moore over at the State Department? And the Democratic National Committee flagged you when your name kept coming up unsolicited in focus groups the DNC put together to float Paul's new Cabinet nominees before sending them to the Senate.' Rosen stared intently at Lambert now. 'I want you to go on that tour with the President, stick by his side like a leech. Figure out where every camera is and position yourself so that you show up right behind or to the side, but never in front, of the President. Speak up if the President calls you to the mike – I don't care what you say. Just be there, Greg.'

Lambert huffed and tried to think of a way out.

'Greg, I want this,' Rosen said. 'I want this, and so does the President.'

OVER CHARLESTON, SOUTH CAROLINA
July 4, 1800 GMT (1300 Local)

The blackened, twisted wreckage of the city slid by underneath the

Coast Guard helicopter as President Costanzo and Lambert, both strapped tightly into their seats, facing each other on either side of the large open side door, stared down in horror. Every tree was blackened, every house was burned and broken, the highways and major streets were jammed with cars charred deep brown on the side facing the naval shipyard but brightly painted their various colors on the sheltered side.

'And you say people made it out of there?' the President shouted over the noise.

The helmeted crew chief nodded in exaggerated motion as the minicam, held high by the standing cameraman, pointed down to take the whole picture in: the President asking questions, shaking his head, pointing at particularly devastated churches or schools for Lambert to look at, all the while the blackened landscape streaming by.

'*Three thirty at the latest*' was all that kept running through Lambert's mind. '*When do you have to make the network feed for the evening news?*' Rosen had asked before they boarded – before they cut a visit to a burn unit from the itinerary so that the reporter from the television pool could make his deadline. '*No loss,*' Rosen had said to the President's advance man. '*The pictures wouldn't have been worth a shit. Nobody wants to see that at dinnertime.*'

The helicopter heeled over and headed inland, and Lambert watched as the trees became greener, the occasional house stood with only windows broken, and the roads were clear. Passing a set of roadblocks clearly visible along several twisting roads into the town, life suddenly appeared. The trees were all bent over away from the sea as if by some great hurricane, but in open spaces passed one after the other by the speeding helicopter Lambert saw large groups of people living like squatters in a variety of army and Red Cross tents or in lean-tos and other crude shelters. Lambert wondered why they hadn't gone farther away, instead of just to the other side of the barricades. *There isn't anything left*, he thought. *Why stay*? But he knew the answer. This was home – not the house in which they lived, but the place.

The helicopter settled slowly toward the earth, sinking to a large, open area on the edge of one of the camps. The President took the opportunity as the cameraman changed batteries to look at the three-by-five cards he had taken from his jacket pocket, flipping them one after the other in a rapid review. He waved Rosen over and held up a card, shouting, 'How do you pronounce this guy's name?'

'Ree-show!' Rosen replied.

'And he's, what, the new mayor?'

'County Clerk!' Rosen yelled, and the President nodded. 'He's a Democrat!'

The helicopter settled in, and Lambert looked at his watch. *Jesus, I've got so much to do*, he thought testily.

'Let's go, Greg,' the President said slapping his leg as the whine from the rotors began to die down.

Lambert followed the President out, Rosen giving way so that Lambert would be right behind Costanzo. There was polite applause for the warm-up speaker by the people gathered to greet the President, but Lambert also saw a sprinkling of signs at the fringes of the crowd on which were scrawled FOOD, SHELTER, CLOTHING, MEDICINE! and AMERICA FIRST!

They walked toward a small platform on which stood a row of chairs and, in front, a podium. As the helicopter's engines fell silent, Lambert heard the speaker's rousing voice, the Southern accent deep.

'. . . because we are *all* citizens of the *U*-nited States, the ger-*reatest* nation on the face of the earth!' There was applause and a couple of cheers, but Lambert thought the large crowd to be surprisingly dispirited – nothing like the roars he had heard during his earlier forays into Presidential campaigns as a volunteer.

The President noticed it too. 'Thank God the election isn't *this* November,' he turned and said with a smile to Lambert and Rosen as they approached the edge of the podium. They all waited for the local politician's introduction.

'And now, without further ado,' he said, and there was a sprinkling of applause and some laughter, 'the *Pres*-ident of the *U*-nited States, Mr Paul Co-stan-zo!' As the audience applauded, a band struck up and Lambert looked across the platform to see what looked to be a high school band, very few of its small number wearing any semblance of their uniform – many, in fact, standing there with no instrument at all – as they croaked out a truly wretched rendition of 'Hail to the Chief.'

Lambert sat beside the 'master of ceremonies,' a grinning, cherubic man so brimming with enthusiasm that he resumed his applause, joining the rhythmic clapping that was slowly developing in the crowd of several thousand.

The President spoke. There was intermittent applause, and Lambert dutifully joined in. But he heard nothing, his mind in a daze. Finally, the man next to him rose during one of the extended periods of applause and joined the President at the podium.

'Thank you, Mr President,' the South Carolinian said, 'for those most gracious words.' The man turned and looked back, straight at Lambert.

'Now, I wonder if we might be able to coax a word or two from your Mr Lambert?' the cherub said, half turning to look at Lambert as the cheers rose up again. *Shit*! Lambert thought as he glanced at the President, who motioned him to the podium with a wave of his hand. He instantly felt the heat of a full-blown blush assault his face, and as County Clerk Ree-show stood back from the podium applauding as fast as his pudgy hands could manage, Lambert rose and walked up to the microphone, which he had to raise so that it didn't press into the middle of his chest. The cameraman already had the camera on his shoulder and back to his eye, and the red light was blazing. The roving cameraman did not focus in on any narrow band of the crowd this time, but had walked back all the way to the stage itself and panned the full width of the still cheering throng.

Lambert just stood there, letting the crowd's cheers die in their own time. The President and the MC took their seats behind him. As the crowd grew quiet, Lambert felt himself all alone at the podium. In front of him were the faces of thousands of people, many of them dirty and etched with deep lines that he imagined must be the result of a loss, of grief. It touched a chord, a common experience, a shared feeling.

'I have never been to Charleston before,' he began, his voice coming back to him through the speakers much louder than he expected. 'I have probably never met any of you before. I'm not a politician. I've never run for or been elected to any office in my life.'

He swallowed the lump that was forming in his throat as the words he was about to speak formed in his head. 'Until the night of June eleventh, I was, like all of you, just going about my life, living it from day to day without . . . without appreciating just what it was that I had.' Even his sigh was audible over the speakers. 'Unlike some of you, however' – he felt his eyes water, and he fought against the tears – 'I had the distinct privilege of saying good-bye to my wife. I was able to put my arms around her, to kiss her, and to say "I love you" one last time. I had that privilege because of my job, of course, because I was informed of the emergency while at dinner with her. But I have, I must tell you,' he said, air coming into his lungs raggedly, 'I have felt some guilt about that. I felt that guilt because I know that many people, many of you, did not have that opportunity. Maybe it was your spouse at work on the night shift, or your parents away in another part of town, or your children, God forbid, asleep in their beds while you were away. Maybe your last words with your spouse were in argument, or your last act a scolding of your child, or maybe you had forgotten to call your parents for too long.'

Lambert looked up to see men and women hugging, lonely figures sobbing into hands clasped over their mouths and faces, all staring up at him in rapt attention.

'But you see, we all have our private agonies. We all have our crosses to bear. I keep telling myself – every time I awaken and I look over at the cot in my windowless underground office to see that my wife is not there beside me, as she was in my dreams – I keep telling myself that it will pass, that I will get over it if I just fill my days and nights with more work, more activity, more meetings and phone calls and reports. But the cruel truth is, it will not pass. I have lost someone who is – was – so clearly more precious than I ever knew during the time that I had her.

'I know, standing here today after having seen what happened to your city, that each of you understands that loss, and I take a special strength from knowing that. I only hope that you can take strength from hearing these words, from knowing that, in tens of millions of hearts and tens of millions of souls in every part of this country and across the sea in the country of our enemy, there are others out there who struggle day and night with the same burden. I only hope that you take strength from hearing that you are not alone – you are not alone. Thank you.'

Lambert stepped away from the podium to dead silence. His head was hung and he saw only the shoes of the people seated behind him as they rose. He looked up to see the arms of President Costanzo reach out to give him a gentle bear hug as the first tentative applause rose up from the crowd. The clerk and the other men and women from Charleston on the podium gathered around, and hands patted him on the shoulders, a woman touching his head softly.

And the applause grew. It grew, and grew, and grew to a crescendo. No shouts could be heard, no breaks piercing the steady torrent of claps, and Lambert turned to look at the people of Charleston with a heartfelt relief that he truly was not alone as he had so long felt among the hundreds of people with whom he had worked, none of whom, it seemed, had lost a loved one. He had not realized how much had built up in him in the weeks since finding Jane, and he had forced his feelings into a bottle, had fled from the few brave souls who felt comfortable enough in quieter moments to ask him how he felt.

'You okay, Greg?' the President asked as he faced him only inches away.

'Yes. Yes, sir.'

Costanzo nodded, and loosed Greg from his clench.

'It was an honor and a privilege, Mr Lambert,' Clerk Reeshow said, shaking his hand. Next came an old lady, whose cool hand reached up to cup his face as she said, 'Dear boy,' shaking her head. He saw on her dress above a carnation four red hearts, tiny stickers that people had taken to wearing. Four deaths in her family.

The President had already left the podium to work the crowd from within his cordon of wary Secret Service agents as the local dignitaries shook his hand one by one, each with words of thanks and sympathy. Sol Rosen suddenly appeared between Lambert and the next local to say, 'Thank you, folks,' and guide Lambert with a strong grip on his elbow to join up with the President, who was at the front edge of the crowd meeting a group of men and women wearing dirty white lab coats.

As Rosen thrust Lambert to the President's side, putting him in position for the camera to take in the scene, Lambert heard President Costanzo saying, 'And I would like to take this opportunity to say, to the people of France, that it is groups like your Medicins Sans Frontiers that show that the true depth of feeling between our two peoples remains great and unchanged despite the differences expressed between our two governments.'

Lambert saw the big grin as Costanzo pumped the hand of the lithe, bespectacled woman – a doctor, Lambert presumed – who was trying to say something in a voice that barely carried over the noise and commotion that surrounded the President.

'What?' he said, leaning closer to the woman.

'We have a team, Mr President, in Grodno,' she shouted up toward his ear on tiptoes, her thick French accent making understanding even more difficult, 'that cannot get supplies through your forces, which surround the city!'

'Well, fine! Fine!' the President said, moving on deeper into the crowd to shake the hands thrust over heads at him. Lambert could not tell whether Costanzo had heard the woman.

'Can I help?' he asked, and she repeated her statement. 'Who do we talk to get this straightened out?' Lambert asked. 'Do you have a telephone number and a name?'

'Yes, yes!' she said excitedly, and she pulled out a pad and pen and wrote the name and number down, carefully reading them out in case he had trouble reading her handwriting. Before she could hand the slip of paper to him, Lambert felt a strong tug at his arm, pulling him off in the wake of the President. He pulled his arm forcefully from the grasp of the Chief of Staff, who glared at him and nodded in the direction of the President, in the direction of the cameras.

Lambert took the slip from the woman, who wrapped both of her hands around his with a touch that seemed to him to be the first human contact he could recall since he pulled himself from Jane's arms in the restaurant.

SOUTH OF ARSENYEV, RUSSIA
July 5, 2100 GMT (0700 Local)

'Sergeant Monk?'

The pain flooded in. He opened his eyes. It was so bright that he could only look down at his body, curled and twisted in the small hole, instead of up at the voice and into the sunlight.

Oh, man, Monk thought. His head pounded and his rib, broken by a bullet glancing off his body armor, ached with each breath. As he stirred, every muscle screamed, and his legs, arms, neck, and especially his back hardly moved from the stiffness. Squinting and looking along the slope of the hill, he could see the other heads and shoulders protruding up from their fighting holes as he arched his back.

'O-o-o-w,' Monk said tiredly and looked up at the five men. 'Who the hell're you?' he asked, the steely taste in his mouth adding to his general misery.

'We were told to report to you, Sergeant,' said the man in front, a kid really.

Monk looked them up and down. Fresh uniforms, all their equipment neatly hung in all the right places on their bodies, M-16s and SAWs all at the ready.

Monk closed his dry eyes and rubbed his temples. *It's daylight*, he thought. 'What time is it?' Monk asked.

'Thirteen zero two hours, Sergeant.'

Monk struggled to get up, groaning and cursing with every new pain. When he got to his feet, the group stiffened. Their eyes, Monk noted, darted here and there but mainly up to his face and then away sheepishly.

'Who are you?' Monk asked the talkative one, a private first class. They were all privates or PFCs, Monk noted.

'They told us we were in your squad.' Monk looked at the hillside around his hole. Nothing but black bloodstains and a few scraps of equipment remained of the Russians, whose bodies had obviously been removed from the slope in the night.

'Hey!' one of the new guys said with a grin, picking up a Russian Army helmet as if he'd found a souvenir of great value. 'Don't touch anything, shithead,' Monk said, not knowing his name. 'You'll go home with hooks stickin' out your arms.'

Monk led the small group to the top of the hill where they found the first line of fighting holes from which the marines had withdrawn. Monk said, 'Be careful up here. There's mines all over this forward slope.' The men froze where they stood, a step or two behind Monk. Russian helmets were everywhere, and in them were Russian soldiers lying twisted and splayed all along the ground down the hill and into the flats below. Fat black birds walked the earth around them, not yet straying close to their unripened prey. The few vehicles they had brought with them still smoldered in the distance. The last leg of their journey of life had been on foot.

As the marines behind him pointed and whispered in muted tones at the sights and scenes of the battlefield, Monk spotted his first fighting hole, littered with empty brass cartridges. He remembered. Flashes from the Russians' muzzles as they fired on the run. Muzzle flashes from Monk's own SAW lighting patches of the ground in front of his hole, spoiling his night vision. Black shapes moving in the dark, not betraying their positions by firing but suddenly illuminated for killing in the phosphorous fires from grenades rolled down among them.

'Mornin', Sergeant Monk!' Gunnery Sergeant Dirks said. 'Enjoy yer beauty rest?'

The new guys laughed until Dirks glanced their way. Monk reached up and ran his hand around the various cuts and stitches that crisscrossed his face, the result of shattered glass at a window some days before, and only then got the joke.

From out of the woods behind the ridge came the deep rumble of armor. Monk's heart skipped a beat until he saw that they were Army M-109s – self-propelled 155-mm howitzers. Atop each one of the eight lumbering guns a man in an oversize Combat Vehicle Crewman's helmet and sunglasses stood at the .50-caliber machine gun raised high in front of his hatch. As the vehicles pulled to a stop at the base of the ridge about forty meters away and the rear doors opened, three ammunition handlers emerged from each gun. The section leader roamed around the guns giving orders for the fire mission, but inside the gunner and driver remained at their posts, ready to 'shoot and scoot' before the first sign of Russian fire being returned.

'I s'pose that's the end of our boys' naps,' Gunny said to Monk, who snorted a laughing response as they watched the guns begin to elevate and slew, the last of their movements minute.

The stunning BOOM of the first M-109 firing its shell at a target almost twenty thousand yards away caused even Gunny to flinch. Just one gun fired, but the barrels of all eight pointed in the same direction. In the distance, one gun from the other section of eight in the army's battery let loose a single round.

'Gunny!' his RTO yelled from his fighting hole. 'CO's on the horn!' Gunny walked down the hill to his hole.

'What's that stink?' one of the cherries asked.

The day was growing warm, and Monk smelled the faint odor in the breeze for the first time. The new guys were all sniffing the air like a herd alerted to some danger. They looked around. The smell of death and decay was everywhere.

'You'll get used to it,' Monk said.

The eight M-109s fired in volley all at once, and the new men slapped their hands over their virgin ears. Monk felt only a faint itching from his own tortured eardrums, then saw the men of his squad stir in their holes below. '*Shi-i-t!*' he heard Mouth whine.

'You guys come over from the States?' Monk asked.

'Yes, Sergeant,' one answered. 'Pendleton.'

'How bad is it – back home?'

'Oh, man. It's the radioactivity now.' Bone, Mouth, Smalls, and some of the other guys rose from their holes, slowly heading up and the hill and looking groggy from their sleep.

Monk let the barrage from the M-109s finish up, the shots becoming more scattered as the gun crews operated the weapons at different speeds.

'You know anything about Detroit?' Monk asked.

'They hit a coupla places in Michigan,' one said, 'but Detroit looked okay. They got these maps, like weather maps, they put up on TV all the time that shows the fallout an' stuff. Hell, ya know that Weather Channel they got on cable's like the most popular channel on TV. I don't think Detroit got any of the shit, though.'

'Na-a-aw,' another said. 'I gotta cousin up there. It's okay.'

'What about Tulsa?' Bone asked. The guns erupted.

None of them seemed to know. Finally one said, 'There was some shit comin' down from Kansas and . . . and from Colorado. Goin' southeast. Ain't that where Oklahoma is?'

'You're damn *right* it is!' Bone said, growing wild-eyed and reaching up to twist the scraped skin of his forearm in sudden agitation. Monk kept his eyes on Bone: *he's dangerous now*, Monk realized. Bone began to interrogate each of the cherries in turn, grabbing their webbing with both hands and not letting go until he had extracted all information pertinent to Oklahoma.

Bone shoved the last of them back roughly and said, 'Mo-ther-fuck-er!' His eyes were wide now and the cords in his forearms tensed as he balled his fists. Monk was relieved to see that the cherries picked up on the danger, like a herd sensing the presence of a predator. They shifted on their feet and shied away as another round of shots blasted out of the howitzers below. These shots were separated widely enough for the other men to get in snippets of conversation – questions and answers, really.

'Memphis?'

'Don't know' – *BOOM*! – 'pro'bly okay.'

'Columbus – Ohio?'

BOOM! 'It's okay. Ohio's okay.'

BOOM!

'Kansas City, Missouri?'

BOOM!

'What about Kansas City?' Smalls asked again.

Nobody said a word. Bone stepped up to the closest man and grabbed his body armor. The man's face showed defiance and he grabbed Bone's wrists saying, 'Hey! Let go'a me!' but he did nothing about it.

'Tell the man about Kansas City, fuckhead,' Bone said in a low voice.

'It's . . . They got fallout! A whole thick dose of the shit, okay! Now let me go! Come on!'

Bone let him go, and everybody remained silent for a few seconds. Smalls looked stricken, and his upper lip peeled back over his teeth and began to quiver. It took a second for Monk to realize that he was beginning to cry. Bone went over to him and said, 'Hey, man,' and then nothing, his usual gift for words failing him.

Monk walked over to Smalls, and he and Mouth both rested their hands on his shoulder momentarily. But it was Bone who swung into action. 'Look, man,' he said, grabbing Smalls by his shoulders. 'We're gonna tear these bastards up. You an' me – on the sixty. Ain't gonna be nobody left when we get through here, man. Shit, some'a that shit landed in Oklahoma, man. Don't nobody mess with Oklahoma. Gonna take a little walk in the woods, just you an' me an' the sixty. Gonna find ourselves some Russians, man, gonna clean up them woods.'

As others walked up to ask about their homes, the army guns began to move. It occurred to Monk that Russian counterbattery fire might be incoming, but the holes were close enough so he didn't issue a warning to the marines on the ridge. He listened for the sound of splitting air overhead that would presage the Russian shells' arrival as he looked down at the gory display on the slope and valley below. Off in the distance to the north lay trees as far as the eye could see. Looking at those woods, some almost certainly filled with Russian soldiers, evoked a shudder. *Bad shit happens in woods*, Monk thought.

Chapter Fourteen

UZHGOROD, UKRAINE
July 6, 0800 GMT (0900 Local)

Chandler put his bulky Combat Vehicle Crewman's helmet on, plugged in the commo cables and hit the Intercom. Pressing the PUSH-TO-TALK button in the remote box at the tank commander's position in the hatch, he asked, 'Driver, you read me?'

'Five by five, sir,' came the tinny response.

'Gunner?'

'Five by, sir.'

'Loader?'

'Sir!'

Chandler heard the electric whine of the turret motor as the gunner raised and lowered the main gun and then slewed the turret left and right and back to the center. From his hatch Chandler could see Barnes walking from vehicle to vehicle to make sure they didn't take another wrong turn. *Five hours behind schedule*, Chandler thought as he flicked on his feeds to the two radios. One radio was tuned to the brigade net above him and fed into his left earphone. The other radio was on his own battalion net below him and fed into his right earphone. Both were silent. He nodded at Specialist 4th Class Jefferson, his loader who sat in his hatch next to him, and told him that he was back on net, relieving him of his monitoring duties.

Bailey, his battalion's Scout Platoon leader, and his six M-3 Bradley Armored Fighting Vehicles sat poised at the head of his battalion's re-forming column, their 25-mm cannon angled out forty-five degrees to the side in proper alternating fashion. The vehicle commanders, Bailey included, protruded from hatches atop their vehicles' turrets warily eyeing the crowd that had gathered along the side of the street ahead.

Despite the fact that Ukraine and Byelarus had declared themselves noncombatants and withdrawn their forces from the field, the crowd made Chandler nervous. The last briefing at brigade had said that a five-thousand-man U.S. Special Forces Group organized into hundreds

of 'A' Teams had been dropped behind Russian lines in eastern Ukraine
in the early hours of the war. The PSYOPS people of the Green Berets
– Psychological Operations forces – were organizing very effective
resistance, they had been told, among the anti-Russian Ukrainians
living to the east. There was no reason, Chandler reasoned, that the
Russian Spetsnaz could not do the same in the western Ukraine among
the millions of ethnic Russians who had intermixed with the Ukrainians
in the days of the old Soviet Union.

He decided to load the .50-caliber heavy machine gun in front of his
hatch. Safety in fire position. Pull back charging handle on right, opening
chamber. Safety in 'safe' position. Open ammo box cover and remove
ammo belt. Raise feed tray on top of gun, place belt in chamber, feeling
for first round.

The .50 caliber bullets felt huge, heavy. Once the lead round was
seated nicely in the open chamber, he placed the safety on fire and
eased the charging handle forward, moving a bullet into the chamber
and closing the bolt. There was a heavy, clacking sound as the
mechanism worked smoothly. He closed the gun's feed tray and the
ammo box cover, and the machine gun was ready to fire. One hundred
armor-piercing rounds, ten per second, spewing out the end of the
ninety-pound gun. It could knock down a helicopter at a mile, Chandler
knew, if you could hit it.

He safed the gun. Jefferson was arming his smaller M-60 machine
gun in front of his hatch on the left, and Chandler could hear the gunner
from inside the tank taking his cue and loading the coax, the machine
gun mounted to fire parallel with the main gun. Chandler and the gunner
could fire their two machine guns while 'buttoned up' inside the tank with
Chandler's M-2 locked to its ring mount.

'Juliet Lima One, this is Sierra Alpha One, do you read me, over?'
Chandler heard through his right ear.

Chandler rolled his eyes. Bailey, playing with the radio again.

Chandler hit the PUSH-TO-TALK button on his CVC helmet, waiting a
fraction of a second as the whirring fan of the radio activated and the
radio powered up. 'Sierra Alpha One, this is Juliet Lima One, I read
you, over.'

'Radio check.'

'Loud and clear,' Chandler said as briskly as possible to get off the
radio. He looked up at Bailey and noticed that the battalion was bunched
up behind Bailey's Bradleys. He knew he could risk the column formation
this far behind friendly lines and with general air superiority, but the
vehicles were still too close. Chandler keyed the radio and said, 'Sierra
Alpha One, move forward three hundred, over.'

'Say again, over.'

'I say again, move forward three hundred, over.'

'Wilco, out.'

Beside Chandler's tank he caught sight of Master Sergeant Barnes. Barnes shouted, 'Ready to try it again, sir?'

'All right!' Chandler replied. 'Let's do it!' He raised his right arm, circled it in the air, and pumped his fist down three times. Chandler radioed Bailey – the only unit commander in front of him, who might not, therefore, have seen his arm and hand signals or had it passed along to him – and ordered him to proceed slowly.

From behind, the vehicles' engines began to turn over, the growl filling the hard canyons of the city street with a solid, deep rumble, only to settle into the loud whine of the tanks' turbines. *I hope we don't have any dead batteries like at the rail yard*, Chandler thought. Slaving off the helpless hulks had been embarrassing. The supply troops on the railways had gotten a good laugh at the dashing tankers as their tanks maneuvered awkwardly to run cables across to their cousins' dead batteries. From then on, Chandler had randomly asked tank commanders on stops how long since he last ran his engine to recharge. Twenty minutes every two hours, that was the rule in combat.

What's next? he wondered, sighing deeply and shaking his head. He winced when he remembered his latest mistake, forgetting the night before to ensure that the company commanders put out OP/LPs, Observation Posts/Listening Posts. *Mistakes now are counted in lives*, he thought.

He looked around. His tank was parked on the curb, or what used to be the old stone curb before his treads crushed it to chips and dust. The engines of the tanks on the street strained, and the procession began. First came Alpha Company – fourteen M-1A1 Abrams Main Battle Tanks like the one atop which Chandler sat, their 120-mm smooth-bore turret-stabilized main guns slewed alternately from left to right in fashion similar to the much smaller guns on Bailey's M-3s. Each had the new millimeter-wave IFF (Identify Friend or Foe) transceivers that automatically alerted lazing gunners that they had an American tank in their sights, and strips of dully refractive tape in inverted Vs on the rear and sides like hunters' vests, intended to be seen and therefore not shot by those units without the IFF electronics. *More worried about friendly fire than Russian fire*, Chandler thought. *That's a good sign*.

The vehicles rolled by, their commanders and loaders sitting at perches with their torsos and heads extending from their hatches. Chandler returned the salute of the Alpha Company commander as his tank passed, and the commander of the next tank, having seen his CO, saluted also. Thus began the parade: each vehicle passing in review, each vehicle's commander saluting. It quickly grew stylized, the crewmen at attention in their hatches, turning their torsos in unison 'eyes left' and saluting on whispered command with a snap of their arms. Chandler felt like an idiot, terribly self-conscious each time he saluted but forced to salute with a flourish to acknowledge the men's formality. As the civilians watched the procession from the doors and windows of the buildings, however, he began to feel exposed. Chandler made a mental note to give to Barnes, who was his acting command sergeant major: no more saluting in the field. No sense giving the Russians a target – the commanding officer.

Next came Delta Company, his battalion's only infantry. Having 'traded' a tank company with one of the brigade's infantry battalions for one of its infantry companies, the two battalions became, in army parlance, 'task forces' – no longer battalions of pure armor or infantry. 'Battalion-strength task forces' – Chandler's being Task Force 2/415 Armor. Lieutenant Colonel Honig, the commander of the infantry battalion, now commanded Task Force 3/415 Infantry.

The infantry's M-2 Bradleys streamed by. Chandler tried to break the parade-like 'pass in review' by intentionally not returning the salute of the first vehicle's commander, but when the second vehicle's crew saluted, he relented. On they came. Larger than armor companies' sixty-two men, the 111 officers and men of the infantry company rode in thirteen M-2 Bradleys. Nine of the Bradleys held infantry squads of nine men each, and the other four held the three platoon and the one company headquarters sections.

The Bradleys bristled with weapons. In addition to the stabilized M-242 25-mm chain gun and M-240C 7.62-mm co-axial machine gun fired from the small turret atop the Bradley, Chandler saw that the crews had raised the twin TOW-2 antitank missile launchers on the left of the turret into their firing positions. Then, protruding like bristles from a porcupine, two on each side and two from the rear of the Bradley, were six ball-jointed M-231 5.56-mm assault rifles that the infantrymen could pivot and fire from inside the Bradley on the move. Atop three of the thirteen Bradleys, the gunners held FIM-92A shoulder-fired Stinger antiaircraft missiles at the ready. Finally, Chandler knew, added to all of that were the hidden contents of each of the vehicles that would be taken with the men when dismounting: an M-60 machine gun, a SAW, two 40-mm grenade launchers, four M-16s, a Dragon antitank missile launcher, and two smaller AT-4 antitank missiles.

When the last of the Bradleys passed, the fourteen sixty-ton M-1A1 tanks of Bravo Company followed, dwarfing, Chandler noticed, the smaller Bradleys.

Then came the 331 men of Headquarters Company, itself more than twice the size of an entire Russian tank battalion, riding in a variety of vehicles including special command, ambulance, recovery and maintenance variants of M-113 armored personnel carriers and Bradleys, tankers filled with fuel, two-and-a-half-ton supply trucks – 'deuce and a quarters' they were called – and Humvees. The thirty men and six M-3 Bradleys of Bailey's scout platoon, which were up at the head of the column, were a part of the Headquarters Company, as were the six 4.2-inch self-propelled heavy mortars that paraded by – Chandler's personal 'artillery.'

Finally came Charlie Company: fourteen more M-1A1 tanks, the last three of which had their guns slewed to the rear – to the left, right, and straight back – covering their tails.

As the last of the vehicles passed, through Chandler's mind flashed the fleeting image of the legendary Jason, as told by a B-grade movie he had watched as a child. Monsters in skeletal form had arisen from the ground where their bones had been strewn. In this instance, the monsters had been disgorged from flatbed railcars and were made of steel. Ten days ago they had sat inert, in packing crates and under tarpaulins, but now they at least looked like a part of a living, breathing armored fighting team.

Chandler rode atop his own monster and looked down the road at his battalion as his driver sped to take his place in the middle of the procession. Chandler was suddenly able to appreciate just for an instant some small measure of the consummate horror that would be felt by those who might meet his tanks, most with puny weapons that could never hope to penetrate their flat, honeycombed sheets of Chobham armor layered with steel, aluminum, and ceramics. Chandler committed that feeling to memory for use later on the battlefield: the terror of infantrymen left alone to oppose the enemy's monsters. *I can't let that happen to my infantry*, Chandler thought, *but I've got to make it happen to theirs*. For tanks – Chandler's forty-four M-1s and the Russians' T-72s and T-80s – were indeed monsters. They were also the keys to the kingdom that lay ahead.

PHILADELPHIA, PENNSYLVANIA
July 7, 1500 GMT (1000 Local)

The delegation from the Federal Reserve Board of Governors sat waiting on the President in the ornate paneled conference room. Lambert followed the President in, uncertain as to why his presence at such a meeting had at the last second been requested. The Governors rose and shook the President's hand, and then shook hands with or nodded at the Secretaries of Commerce and Labor, the director of the Office of Management and Budget, the chairman of the President's Council of Economic Advisers, and Lambert. All of the President's men looked somber, and the representative from the Congressional Budget Office who stood and introduced himself from where he sat at the end of the table as an observer could barely manage to look anyone in the eye. Something was up, and Lambert wasn't in on it yet.

As soon as everyone took his seat, the President said, 'Okay, gentlemen. You've got my attention. What is this about an economic catastrophe?'

The chairman of the Federal Reserve's board said, 'I appreciate your attention to this matter, Mr President, and I understand you have a busy schedule these days so I'll be brief. As you know, we haven't had any reliable broad indicators on the economy since the nuclear exchange, and we won't have any for several more weeks. In order to guide us in formulating our monetary policy, therefore, we have had to conduct a poll of our regional Federal Reserve Banks. We asked them to compile estimates for their districts of measures such as Gross Domestic Product and wholesale and retail prices, and then we generated a very rough Index of Leading Economic Indicators. What we learned, sir' – the elder man, a noted economist and academic, sat upright in his chair as he drew a deep breath – 'is that we are heading for an economic depression of unprecedented magnitude.'

'What are you talking about?' the President said slowly in a tone both confused and challenging. He looked at his people and said, 'What is he talking about?' Nobody ventured a comment, and they looked as if they might as well have been seated on hot griddles as they tried not to fidget with their pads and papers or books filled with the latest printouts.

'Mr President,' the chairman of the independent 'Fed' said, 'our estimates are rough – plus or minus five or even ten percent – but we're looking at, this month, a drop in Gross Domestic Product of between twenty-five and thirty-five percent on an annualized basis. Now we haven't dealt as a country with anything like this since the Great Depression, and this one could very well be worse. Our estimates put the Index of Leading Economic Indicators somewhere in the twenties. Anything under fifty is a recession, and the twenties is uncharted territory.'

The President looked as if he suddenly saw a speeding bus bearing down on him, and he began to shake his head. 'No, no.' He looked again at his own economic advisers whose jobs hung now by a thread. 'You people told me that the war damage from the nuclear strikes and contamination might – *might* – give us a slight negative growth, like one or two percent, but this is totally unexpected. Totally *unbelievable!*'

'The problem with the numbers we've been using,' the Fed chairman said, 'that you, we, everybody has been using, is that they look only at the physical damage to the country's plant and equipment and the human losses. That ignores the psychological damage. Sir' – he leaned forward and rested his elbows on the table as he stared down at his clasped hands, – 'nobody is working. Oh, we've got reasonably good production coming out of the critical armaments industries, but it's the butter side of the "guns and butter" equation that is the problem. The emergency census figures had a huge blind spot. They only looked at the disaster sites, and meanwhile the populations of our major cities just up and fled, abandoning their homes, their jobs, everything. They're living in the country with relatives, or in inns and motels off of their savings.' He shook his head. 'It's as if the population of our country has just made one mass suicidal economic decision. You see, sir, consumption has remained more or less steady, but incomes are plummeting. The shortfall is made up by disinvestment, by people spending their savings. We need those savings, sir, to invest in the reconstruction of our damaged areas.'

'But I don't understand. Why? Why is this happening?'

'Fear, sir. Fear of an all-out nuclear war, or, what do you call it, "general" war. Fear of the Bastion.'

The President buried his head in his hands and grabbed his scalp as if stricken by a sudden migraine. 'What's the bottom line?' he asked dejectedly, ignoring now his ashen advisers.

'The bottom line, sir, is that if we don't get people back to work soon – September, October at the latest – the situation is going to be irreversible. Businesses already laboring under the new taxes will fail, increasing unemployment and decreasing tax revenue. The budget deficit will mushroom, shooting interest rates up as Treasury's borrowings chase money at ever higher rates of interest. That will push even greater numbers of businesses and individuals into bankruptcy. Banks will fail, and up the deficit will go again as depositors are bailed out.'

The President raised his head and sighed. 'What can we do? What can *I* do?'

'Talk the people into going back to work. Use the "Bully Pulpit" and get them back to their jobs.'

'If they're scared shitless of another round of nuclear exchanges, what do I tell them? That it's impossible? Go on home, and if I'm wrong they won't be around to vote against me next election anyway?'

'You could alter your war aims,' the Fed chairman said. He shrugged and raised his hands. 'It's not my place, obviously, but tensions seem to me to be growing, not easing. Chemical weapons, radioactive fallout – anything seems possible now, the whole Pandora's box. If you were to back off the demands that the Russians have found most objectionable, then maybe people would trickle back in before it's too late.'

The President's eyes drifted, and slowly his head began to shake. 'I'm between a rock and a hard place, but I can't back off on the war just to see if people go back to work.' He was gazing off into space, his voice barely penetrating from the depths.

'Why don't we just win it quickly?' Lambert asked, and everyone turned to him. 'If it's a timing thing, if we've got a couple of months, let's just pour it on and get it over with.'

There was silence for the next few moments.

'Could we actually do it in that time frame?' the Fed chairman asked.

'How quickly could we go if we pulled out all the stops?' the President asked. 'If we cut some corners and took some risks, could we finish it up by the end of September?'

'Well, we've discussed the "quick-win" strategy at the staff level, sir,' Lambert said. The 'Karelian Variant,' Lambert remembered the planners had called it. 'It would entail substantial risk, and the Joint Chiefs unanimously rejected even recommending it to you, but if it worked we could win by the end of August even, if we get a couple of breaks,' he said, going out on a limb.

The President looked over at the chairman of the Federal Reserve and cocked his head. The chairman shrugged. 'Well,' the President said, placing his hands palm down on the table, 'I'll take to the "Bully Pulpit" and do what I can. I'll try to calm everybody down and get them back into the cities. I'll set up a team of people to study and work on the problem – it'll get my highest priority. And Greg,' he said, turning to look at Lambert, 'I want a full NSC meeting in four hours and a complete briefing on this "quick-win" strategy.'

As they filed out of the room, all Lambert could think was how angry General Thomas was going to be when Lambert informed him he had told the President about their high-risk contingency plan, the Karelian Variant.

OUTSIDE ROVNO, UKRAINE
July 10, 1400 GMT (1600 Local)

'Who's next?' Chandler asked as he and the other two officers, the captain who commanded Alpha Company and his lieutenant who commanded 2nd Platoon, walked toward the next of the widely spaced M-1A1 main battle tanks.

'Two-three,' the lieutenant said. 'That's Adams in command, Martinez is loader, Hartley's the gunner, and Ross drives.'

As they strode purposefully toward the tank, the captain and the junior officer to Chandler's left both matching Chandler's pace and in step, Chandler's eyes strayed over the irregularly patched camo netting of the massive vehicle. The dark green matched the green of the trees that filled the woods across the rolling hills in the distance. If it wasn't for the thick barrel of the main gun, whose muzzle extended from the net and pointed toward the treeline, together with the open hatches and two machine guns left free to fire on top, it would be difficult to tell that it was anything more than a natural protuberance, even at close range. It would, however, still be warmer than the soil; it would glow on the sunny summer day in the perpetual darkness of enemy gunners' thermal sights.

'How's it going, trooper?' Chandler asked the thick-necked, muscular sergeant who protruded from the top of the vehicle he commanded, shirtless but wearing his tanker's helmet with the three chevrons mounted on front.

'Afternoon, M-m-m-major,' the man said, stiffening as the three officers stepped up to the treads. He looked ill at ease.

'I cain't git the thing unstuck,' a skinny soldier said, poking his head and sweat-soaked T-shirt out of the loader's hatch and dropping the heavy wrench he carried onto the flat deck of the turret with a clank as he saluted awkwardly with greasy hands.

Chandler returned his salute, and the sergeant looked down from his commander's hatch and kicked with his foot. 'Hey, get on up here. We g-g-got comp'ny.'

'Say c'mon, ma-a-n. I ain't finished my dessert yet,' Chandler heard from the tank.

'It's the M-m-major,' the sergeant whispered, staring down and kicking again.

'Yeah, right. And is General Thomas hisself out there too?'

'Git on up here, Martinez!' the second man yelled.

'You t-too Ross,' the vehicle commander bent over and shouted down into the tank.

Finally, the other two crewmen popped up, each saluting in surprise as they saw the entourage. One carefully put his plastic cup and spoon on the turret and pulled his Walkman headphones from his ears, the strident tones of loud music the only sound audible in the silence.

'You men getting all you need?' Chandler asked.

'Yes, sir' came from all of them at once, and Chandler smiled. This was his first 'walk-around' through Alpha Company. These men had been on perimeter his first full tour around the battalion while on the road and, during his second, off on a 'parade,' a drive through the center of one of the smaller villages the allies were not permanently occupying in order to put the fear of God in the natives.

'Any w-w-word on when we might get some f-f-fuel, sir?' Adams asked. 'We barely got enough t-to keep the batteries charged.'

'Supposed to get some tomorrow, as a matter of fact. Then we'll be off on down the road.'

'You'd th-think we could take some from that pipeline down there,' Adams said, and everyone turned to watch as the American civilian workers laid a pipe roughly parallel to the line along which they had advanced. The pipe, everyone knew, was one of several massive projects to run fuel from refineries in Romania and Italy directly to the front. Even with the effort, however, the gas-guzzling mechanized armies of the West were barely averting disaster, so great was their need for POL – petroleum, oil, and lubricants. Chandler, like the other field commanders, had taken to issuing chits of paper to free-lance

Eastern European drivers who filled their decrepit tanker trucks full
of low-octane fuel in the West and somehow negotiated the war-torn
roads of Ukraine to sell their loads at outrageous profits. He had no
idea whether the army would honor the chits, but he didn't feel too
bad about the horse-trading given the problems the fuel's impurities
regularly caused in his tanks' high-tech turbines.

'How long till we see some action, Major?' the skinny kid from the
loader's hatch asked. 'I thought we were supposed to be halfway to
Kiev by now.'

'Don't know. According to the last map I saw at brigade,' Chandler
said, pointing off to the southeast, 'the Russians are about forty miles
that way' – he turned to the northwest – 'and about thirty miles that way.
But we're still headed that way,' he said, pointing to the northeast, 'and
we got a way to go before we can expect any contact.'

'That's the way to M-m-moscow, i'n't it, sir?'

'It's up that way somewhere,' Chandler nodded, slapping his hand
on the fender. 'Okay, you men carry on. If you need anything, just let
me know.'

They all grinned from ear to ear for some reason at his comment, but
they saluted respectfully and Chandler and the others turned to head
off to the next tank. After walking a short distance, the lieutenant
whispered, 'Adams has a little stuttering problem, but it's not usually
that bad. He was just a little nervous, I guess. He's really fine on
the radio.'

'Hey, Major, sir!' they heard shouted from the tank. 'How 'bout
some beer?' The crew broke out laughing.

'When we get to Moscow!' Chandler shouted, turning around.

Off to the right in the distance behind the tank, a small black disk
rose up above the treeline, the treetops behind it smudged in the heat
of its exhaust before it fell gently back to the nape of the earth. Behind
it, barely visible almost a mile away, hovered a helicopter, peeking out
around the side of a hill.

'Holy . . .!' the company commander said just as a hollow, thudding
boom crashed into the opposite side of the tank, forcing Adams and
Hartley to grab hold of the hatches.

Blue fire shot thirty feet straight out of the hatches on the turret and
the driver's hatch in front as the crashing wall of noise and lick of heat
broke fiercely across Chandler. Hartley was shot clear out of the tank
and did a somersault in the air to land limply head-first on the ground
in front, tangled in the shredded netting. The driver lay draped over
the glacis half out of his hatch as the fire from inside began to consume
him. The third man had just disappeared somewhere under the netting.
It was Adams who commanded the attention of the stunned officers.

He was screaming in a pitch so high that his voice sounded like the cry
of an animal as he crawled out of his hatch, each lung full of air and shriek

ending with a shuddering quiver like a child's sob. The man looked insane with pain as he slid off the turret, his body, the very skin of his naked torso, ablaze in a white fire tinged with yellow – a human torch.

The lieutenant screamed, 'Adams!' and bolted for the burning tank from which a popping, crackling noise began to sound ominously. The captain leapt out to tackle the young man from behind. '*No!*' the senior officer shouted as he rode the kicking platoon leader to the ground. Several jets of white smoke began to shoot from seams in the rear deck of the tank as Adams flopped to the ground but then rose quickly to stumble away, slapping at his chest and head as if being attacked by a swarm of bees.

The rear deck of the tank blew sky high in a fountain of pure flame. Chandler's head wobbled as he tried to regain his balance and realized then that he was lying on his back propped up on his elbows. The heat burned at his exposed skin and the violence of the roar scraped painfully at his eardrums as his eyes were forced closed by the heat of the fire from the tank's ammunition, which cooked off through the rear deck's blow-out panels a hundred feet into the air.

In a few seconds the fire had consumed all of the highly flammable propellant and explosives, and the rattle of heavy machine guns fired from nearby tanks filled the relative silence left by the slowly burning remnants of tank number twenty-three.

'*O-o-o-h, God!*' Chandler heard, and he sat up to look at the smoldering, unmoving body of Adams. '*Oh my God! Oh my Go-o-od!*' It was the lieutenant, and the company commander was no longer holding him down. He sat up next to him, wrapping his arm around the young officer whose face was buried in his hands. The heavy drumbeat of .50-caliber fire from the other tanks died down, and Chandler quickly scanned the treeline. A small column of smoke rose from the woods about half the distance from where the helicopter had hovered, the helicopter crew guiding a second missile's flight obviously having been driven off by the machine guns.

Chandler rose to sit on the heels of his boots, his legs underneath him and his hands grasping his thighs. *All dead*, he thought looking at the three men visible on or around the tank. *All four of those men, dead*. He knew it from the furor of the blast he had felt at almost sixty yards but in which they had been standing. It didn't seem real. They were just there, alive. At that distance it was as if all he had to do was yell, 'Everybody up!' like in their recently completed live-fire exercises and they would all rise up, brushing the dust from their clothes.

Adams's body still smoked, and none of the tank's crew showed any signs that they would ever move again. As other men began to run up from the widely spaced vehicles, Chandler rose to his feet and walked toward the tank. It got hotter the closer he got. It grew more real as the mortal wounds suffered by the men became increasingly visible.

*   *   *

Chandler watched as his first tank crossed the bridge. It was the bridge spanning the Goryn River, a huge hole opened in one lane from a bomb, but the other lane passable even by the wide tanks. Chandler realized that his boots were unlaced, and as he knelt to tie them he saw in confusion that they were not boots at all but were the black wingtips that he wore to work.

He looked up to see the entire bridge bumper to bumper with traffic, with every tank and armored fighting vehicle and truck in his battalion jammed onto the bridge from one end to the other.

'One at a time!' Chandler shouted, repeating the words of the MP on the opposite side.

As if on cue, Chandler's fears materialized before his eyes as a flight of Russian jets roared over and geysers of black water shot up from the base of the bridge. In agonizingly slow motion, the span collapsed and the entire battalion sank toward the water. 'No!' Chandler shouted, as one of the men whose voice he did not recognize said, 'Major Chandler,' not comprehending his coming fate as he fell through the air.

'No!' Chandler yelled.

'Wake up, sir!' Barnes said, and the late evening sky that appeared as he opened his eyes immediately gave Chandler his bearings. 'Bad dream, sir?'

Chandler puffed out his cheeks and let out a sigh. The cold sweat under his several-day-old uniform made him uncomfortable, and he wiped his brow and neck with his sleeve.

Barnes looked off over the clumps of camouflage netting under which Chandler's vehicles were parked and said, 'You'll do okay, sir. Everybody's tight, but it'll pass once we get a scrape under our belt.'

Chandler stared down the hill toward the treeline. The smell of the charred tank was still with him. It was on his clothes, in his hair, up his nostrils. And there it was, a blackened monument to the senselessness of it all, a huge recovery vehicle hoisting one end up as a trailer slipped under it, winching it slowly up onto its carrier.

'It's amazing,' Barnes said, watching also. 'They'll pro'bly have that thing back to us in a coupla days.' He shook his head. 'Here's those files you asked for, sir.'

Chandler sat up and took the folders and Barnes left him alone.

He opened the first folder. It was Adams's personnel file. Flipping pages, he skimmed the man's last few performance evaluations and recommendations for promotion to sergeant and before that corporal and private first class. He was above average. Everybody liked him.

Next was his application for financial aid for college. It was stamped 'Approved.' 'July 1st,' written in Adams's own hand on the form, caught his eye. He was due to get out of the army ten days ago and go to college in the fall. Chandler heaved a deep sigh, laying his head back against the hard metal of one of his tank's road wheels and closing his eyes. After a few moments, he forced his eyes open, pulled out his clipboard, and lay it on his lap as a writing surface.

'Dear Mr and Mrs Adams: It is with deepest regrets and sympathy that I write this letter to inform you of the death of your son' – he looked down at the file – 'William. Although I did not have much of a chance to get to know him, I met with William just moments before his' – he looked up at the darkening sky and thought about what to write: *being burned alive, screaming, gruesome agony* – 'passing,' he wrote. 'His tank was hit by a missile as we were stopped for routine maintenance' – *because there's not enough fuel to keep us going* – 'and he and his three buddies' – he went through the other folders, writing down the full names of each of the other men – 'were killed.' He toyed with writing the word 'instantly,' but it was not true for poor Adams, so he saved the word for the other three letters that he would have to write next.

'I cannot tell you that I know the depth of your pain on hearing this news, which probably will have come already by wire or visit. I can, however, tell you that . . .' *Tell them what?* he thought. He had written the words, but he looked down at the paper and then at the files and could find nothing that would fill the blank space awaiting his pen. He looked around as the dusk settled in on the quiet countryside of Ukraine, a country about which he had known nothing before and knew little more now.

Why am I here? Chandler suddenly thought. *My wife and the child whom I have never seen are at home in a war-ravaged country, and I am here.* It didn't make sense anymore, not any of it.

The words on the page beckoned. 'I can, however, tell you that' – his pen hovered over the white paper before continuing – 'there are good men and women here, decent people like your son. They each have a life, an identity, an existence stretching back over all those years during which their parents raised them. For some it ends, in the most profound of tragedies, in the care of someone whom you do not know and have never met. Although I feel in my heart that there was truly nothing that could have been done to save your boy, I will bear for the rest of my life the burden of having lost what was for you, I know, the most precious thing in the world. But please know one thing. You did your job. I am certain it was not your design to raise a young boy to be sacrificed in service to his country but you nevertheless raised a fine son who became an able soldier. He should have been with us on this earth for longer, but you may thank God or fate that he visited at all.'

He looked down at the charred, inert tank being carted away slowly on the low-slung trailer. It would be repaired and returned to service good as new. But it would not be the same tank, because the crew would be different. It was the crew inside that brought the tank to life.

'With my deepest sympathies' – he paused, the next line written with a solemnity he was certain he would not have appreciated just a few days before – 'David W. Chandler, Major, 2/415 Armor, Commanding.'

THE KREMLIN, MOSCOW
July 11, 1900 GMT (2100 Local)

'A third crossing of the Dnepr has been reported,' Filipov said. 'Two kilometers to the north of the last. They're armored cavalry units, but heavy armor formations are staging on the west bank to follow. They have at least six pontoon-bridges operational, with three more bridging operations under way, one opposed.'

Razov just nodded.

'Sir,' Filipov said, continuing plaintively as if Razov had missed the significance of his report, 'we've already confirmed the crossing of one entire armored cavalry regiment to the south. Crossing the *Dnepr*!' Filipov said, as if Razov was unaware that the river was the last major water obstacle before Moscow. 'The appearance of a second at a different location would tend to corroborate intelligence assessments that—'

'That they've succeeded in moving their V Corps up to join their III Corps,' Razov completed his sentence. 'Thomas is a classicist. He's "reinforcing success" by merging the two prongs of his advance into the one northern, more successful one.'

'But they have two cavalry regiments and a couple of armored brigades across,' Filipov said shaking his head. 'How can they move their logistical train so quickly?'

'These aren't the Chinese!' Razov snapped. 'I want at least two of their heavy divisions across plus whatever separate elements they have attached to them. We've got to catch as much of their combat strength as possible in the Dnepr-Sozh Triangle or we won't hit *their* flanks, *they'll* hit ours.'

As Filipov went to work at his desk, Razov looked at the map. It was a delicate game. Letting an enemy take ground cheaply in order to put them in the position that you wanted was one thing. Letting them cross a major natural barrier, the last before your capital city, was a true gambit. *But it's a barrier in both directions*, Razov thought. *Once over, we'll sever their crossings, launch tactical counterattacks to pocket them on the defensive, and then . . . the 'right hook.'* He drew the phrase not from his favored game of chess but instead from the less subtle sport of boxing.

The broad, dashed arrows on the map showed Razov's forces sweeping boldly to the north past the American spearhead. The Americans' advance was a narrow one, along just one highway. Initially intended, it appeared, to be a broader but slower two-pronged and mutually supporting advance, Thomas and his field commanders had abandoned the safer approach in favor of a dagger straight at the heart of Russia. The rate of advance had been phenomenal, far outpacing Razov's ability to react, especially given loss of control of the air over the front.

But there were risks. The American advance was all neck and no shoulders. And Razov had marshaled the remaining bulk of his mobile forces undetected to the north of the American line of advance. Once the tip of the American spear crossed the Dnepr, General Mishin's strike aircraft would cut them off, and a holding force would delay them in between the Dnepr and Sozh rivers. At the same time, Razov's forces would themselves cross the Dnepr to the north in the opposite direction and mount their own narrow advance alongside the American penetration. Wheeling into the Americans' northern flank, they would slice cleanly through the thin 'neck' defended by Polish troops and pocket the bulk of the American and British heavy combat forces just short of the Russian border. By cutting off the steady stream of supplies on which the Americans and British depended, they would halve their combat strength. In the stalemate that would follow, peace talks could ensue.

The risk? The risk was the same as that of the Americans. Razov was putting his own 'neck' on the line. Like the Americans, his line of advance would of necessity be narrow. Like the Americans, it too could be severed. It was a ballet of delicate moves and finesse, at this level at least. Razov knew that at the lowest level it was nothing like ballet, or chess, or anything that most humans had ever seen before.

There was a meek knock at his door. It was a woman, the first he had seen in several days. She was a private, her presence a recent concession to the war. She wanted to enter his office but hesitated uncertainly at the door.

'Come in,' Razov said, half stuck between sitting and rising on her entering. He restrained himself, awkwardly sitting with his back away from the hard wood of the chair. Instead of approaching his working area she went to the map and began to wipe away old markings with her rag and draw on the map with a blue grease pencil.

Razov looked back at the papers; their last satellite had been reduced to a pile of junk by another American intercept. He felt completely blind now. The woman turned to leave, glancing timidly over at Razov before she walked toward the door. Razov looked up and saw the map. 'Just a minute,' he said, getting up and walking over to the map. 'What's this?' he asked, looking at the American unit symbols she had drawn, all east of the Dnepr, and the new frontier of the enemy advance that they represented.

She looked down at the sheet of paper from which she had copied the data onto the map, stricken with fear. 'New position reports – from . . . from Operational Intelligence – Fifth Directorate of the GRU,' she said. 'I . . . I copied it exactly from the big map in the Operations Room.'

'When did this come in?' Razov asked.

'Uhm . . . just a few minutes ago, I think, sir,' she answered in a quivering voice.

Razov felt suddenly energized. A broad smile broke over his face. He looked down at the young woman – pretty but a little too soft.

She smiled back but then looked away.

'Wonderful!' Razov said. 'Excellent!' His mind spun with plans and timetables. 'Pavel, come look. The American 4th Mechanized Infantry Division is crossing here, and the two brigades we saw earlier were from the 1st Armored Cavalry. It's time. Send the order.'

Filipov ran to the door as Razov was pressing the ruler onto the map, estimating distances and writing on the map the times of day by which each objective so measured – towns, road junctions, rivers – should be taken. Razov had one hand gingerly holding the ruler on the map and the other making tick marks and writing deadlines along the projected line of advance.

'Get me a one-to-ten-thousand scale map of the Dnepr-Sozh region,' he said without looking up as the woman turned to leave. 'Fill it in with latest unit locations and TOEs. We don't have much experience with the 4th Infantry,' he muttered to no one in particular, although the woman stayed and listened, 'and I don't want to take the threat they pose to our flanks lightly. And I want all position updates up here *immediately* – no delays! And have General Mishin report to me as soon as the first strikes hit the Dnepr bridgeheads. I'll even take pilot reports. I don't want to wait on poststrike recon.'

'Sir?' the private said in a high-pitched voice.

'Oh,' Razov said, looking up and shaking his head. 'Never mind that last part. Just get me the map and make sure, make absolutely certain, that this map on this table is updated without fail and as quickly as the new position data comes in, is that understood?'

'Yes, sir,' the woman said, and Razov worried for a moment from the look on her face before she left that he had been too harsh with her, but then he returned to his map.

He was in his element. No more paperwork. No more internal security matters. No nuclear or chemical warfare concerns. Just armies, tanks and infantry and artillery, clashing in a titanic battle in the field. *And we're stepping off undetected*, Razov marveled. *With all the Americans' satellite and aerial and electronic intelligence assets, a few weeks of lying low under several thousand camouflage nets and 'Hel-l-lo.'* 'Andrusha, my friend,' he said aloud and in English, 'I've caught you with your pants down.'

'*Murphy's Law*,' he thought again, smiling.

DNEPR-SOZH TRIANGLE, 365 MILES SW OF MOSCOW
July 12, 0500 GMT (0700 Local)

The railroad bed was elevated a good four feet the entire length of the line to their left, Chandler saw with satisfaction. High enough to cover up the top of the armored skirts of the M-1s, fully half the height of the low-slung tanks.

The rumble of explosions was clearly audible over the idling engine and the drone of the precombat checklist read out over the intercom by his gunner. Bailey's M-3s were climbing the ramps that the engineers had scraped up to the railbed, returning from a scout mission on the opposite ridge to add their firepower to Chandler's infantry company. Both the battalion and brigade nets had fallen silent after Bailey's report of a regimental-size Russian tank force pursuing a company-size American armored cavalry unit.

Everything seemed set, but Chandler fidgeted. From the tone of Colonel Harkness's voice on the brigade net and the black smoke belching high into the sky at their backs from around where the bridging equipment they had just crossed was, something bad was happening. Chandler twisted to look to his rear. Their assigned support elements – medical, maintenance, and supply units – were digging in behind the low hills about three quarters of a mile away. They would be bracing for the coming clash just as frantically as his men up at the railbed were. If the Russians broke through Chandler's task force, the support elements would become the new front line, however briefly. There would be dozens of women, prohibited from serving in 'ground combat units,' in those support elements, Chandler knew, who lay now in foxholes with M-16s pressed to their shoulders.

Chandler's plans were simple. The railroad track would not be the logical place from which to mount a defense. The treeline behind them, or the stream that ran through the woods behind it, or up ahead at the ridge across the open farmland in front, but not the train tracks. Their maps wouldn't show the critical advantage it offered: the four-foot elevation of packed earth. That meant the Russian artillery plots would 'prepare' one of those other terrain features that the instructors and manuals advised him to avoid, or so Chandler hoped. In the end, he would not let his patchwork unit get fixed in their first engagement, so all three maneuvers he had worked out were 'retrograde operations' – retreats.

A double boom followed by a jetlike howl of main gun rounds cooking off from inside a destroyed tank redirected his attention to the front. The geyser of flame was barely visible over the ridge, yellow and white sparks shooting high into the air. Chandler looked up and down the rail embankment as he felt jittery all of the sudden. The tanks were spaced very close for combat: every 150 meters or so along the line instead of up to 400 meters apart in wide open terrain. Chandler had concentrated here for two reasons: first, hoping to guess right and give the Russians a strong blow before withdrawing, second, wanting to keep things tight to prevent the unit from unraveling in the shock of action. They had arrived with just enough time to dismount and pull their camouflage netting out of the bustle racks, staking them out with support poles and spreaders to make the tanks appear from a distance to be a shapeless bulge.

The inaction gnawed at him. He looked down the barrel of his massive machine gun, loaded and in the FIRE position. Beneath it, the thick barrel of his tank's M-256 German Rheinmetall 120-mm gun pointed toward the onrushing Russians.

'Let's load the big bullets up,' Chandler said to Jefferson in the hatch next to him, swallowing the foul taste of acid that had boiled up from his now nauseous stomach. Jefferson dropped into the crew cabin. 'Gunner, stand by to engage,' Chandler said over the intercom. 'Loader,' he continued, 'load sabot.'

Looking down through his tank commander's hatch, Chandler saw the gunner's back as he sat at his sights. To the gunner's left, Jefferson hit the large button at the rear wall of the cabin with his knee. The door to the ammo locker slid open immediately with a bang.

The gunner turned the switch on his gun panel to SABOT and then pressed his face to the padded blinders of his gunsight to ensure that it indicated the same on the imaging screen. Accidentally inputing the wrong type of round would cause the light, high-velocity tungsten dart of the sabot round to sail several meters over or plow into the ground short of the target, the gun's computer having loaded the wrong ballistics into its aiming computation.

Slapping the steel-plated base of the sabot round with the flat of his hand to make it pop out slightly, Jefferson grabbed the lip of the baseplate and pulled the heavy round out into his free hand. The strange-looking burnished metal penetrator dart made of dense depleted uranium protruded from the front of the shell, and Jefferson slid it into the breech. He then slapped the padded breech handle closed and backhanded the large button to close the armored door to the ammo locker in a long-drilled routine. The main gun's 'big bullet' was loaded.

'Up!' Jefferson said over the intercom.

'Gunner, stand by,' Chandler said. He looked down through the hatch to see that the man's eyes were on his sight. The gunner's hand rested on the 'pistol grip' joystick that turned the turret and elevated or depressed the main gun and its co-axial machine gun.

A growl from behind Chandler caused him to flinch. Half a dozen American helicopters flashed by low overhead in two lines toward the melee ahead – four AH-64 Apaches in front and two OH-58 Kiowa Scouts behind. The helicopters settled even lower as they passed the railbed and rushed across the flat ground in front, the wheels of the Apaches only three or four feet off the ground despite their high speed. The Kiowa Scouts, scanning for the enemy ahead with optics and thermal imagers contained in large orbs mounted on masts atop their rotors, flew along behind at an altitude of about twenty feet.

As the Apaches approached the ridge, the Kiowas dropped their tails in unison, their main rotors throwing up billowing clouds of dust in front. The scout helicopters shot skyward as their forward progress halted. The Apache gunships nosed up and began to slow as they tracked the rise of the ridge ahead, one so low, Chandler saw from a puff of dust, that it bounced its rear wheel off the ground. By the time they were at the crest, they were at a low hover with only their rotors and cockpits peeking over the top.

With the Kiowas now high in the sky above and bobbing and weaving through the air – nervously moving about to make themselves more difficult targets while exposed at altitude – the Apaches suddenly popped up about ten feet over the crest of the ridge, and jets of smoke began erupting from their wing pylons. *Hellfire missiles*, Chandler thought as the *who-o-oshing* sounds reached his ears. Each helicopter was armed with sixteen of the tank-killing missiles, and they unloaded them as rapidly as they could. A chill swept over Chandler as he realized how many targets they had found.

Suddenly, the Kiowa Scouts hovering high over the valley in front fired first one and then two missiles each. Chandler watched as the large missiles quickly accelerated and sped off beyond the ridge. The Kiowas, as best Chandler remembered, were armed only with Sidewinder air-to-air missiles, so . . . The Apaches at the ridge ahead scattered, and Russian Mi-28 Havoc gunships, seven of them, Chandler counted, stormed over the ridge with their chin guns blazing. Shells exploded on the flat floor of the valley in long rips as the Havocs' guns missed the agile Apaches.

The Kiowas high above began spitting brilliant white flares from their bellies and spun and dived to race back toward Chandler's line. Two missiles rose up from beyond the ridge, their wiggling white trails of smoke seeking out the scouts. Chandler twisted in his hatch to the left to see one missile dive at a falling flare and explode harmlessly behind the helicopter high above the railbed, a rain of shrapnel pelting the soil beneath it. A sharp BOOM, however, from behind caused Chandler to turn in time to see the wreckage of the second Kiowa falling from the sky. The slowly spiraling Plexiglas-enclosed cockpit was sickeningly intact. It enclosed, Chandler knew, two men for their long and helpless ride to earth. Chandler closed his eyes just before it smashed into the ground with a great rending and crunching sound not two hundred meters away. A moment later, he opened his eyes and watched as the helicopter burst into flame with a whump.

The Apaches and Mi-28s were now wheeling in a dogfight, climbing ever higher into the air as their engines and the chop of their rotors produced a cacophony of sound. The Apaches' 30-mm chin-mounted guns pivoted wildly and spit flame in short bursts as their targets flashed briefly within the wide angle of their fire. After several seconds of battle, Chandler saw the tail boom of one Russian Havoc kick violently to the side. The Apache behind it pulled up and streaked by the helicopter, which went into a full spin and edged over onto its side. It finally turned completely upside down and plunged into the ground with a thunderous explosion.

The Apaches began disengaging and whirling free of the 'fur ball' to speed back toward friendly lines. The slower Russian helicopters turned to give chase in disorganized fashion – a course that drew them toward Chandler's men sitting immobile under their netting. *Blobs of green at regular intervals along a straight line*, Chandler thought in horror as he imagined for the first time how they might look not from the ground, but from the air.

'Juliet Lima One, this is November Mike Two,' a voice came over the brigade net, the sound of the helicopter's engine over the radio almost completely drowning out the pilot's words, 'do you read, over?'

'November Mike Two,' Chandler replied woodenly, 'affirmative, over.'

'You got at least a tank regiment headed your way,' the pilot said. 'We've done everything we can. They're all yours. Watch out for the friendlies in front. Good luck, out.'

Chandler watched as the American helicopters sped over their heads, the Russians still hot on their heels. Closer and closer the Russians came. *Surely they can see the tanks by now*, Chandler thought in a daze. He stared at them frozen as they approached. Suddenly, the slower Russian helicopters broke off their futile chase and began to turn, not to attack Chandler's men but to return toward the battle raging now beyond the ridge.

Chandler sensed movement and glanced over to the right. Off in the distance, one of the Stinger crewmen protruded from a hatch in his Bradley, the missile's sight to his eye.

'*No!*' Chandler yelled, but the missile shot out of its tube and its motor ignited. Chandler toggled his radio back to the battalion net but froze as another missile popped out of its launcher and sped toward the Russian helicopters.

'*Shit!*' Chandler shouted. His mind reeled with the enormity of the disaster that awaited them now that their positions were revealed. '*Goddamn!*' he shouted again as he slammed his hand down onto the turret. Chandler noticed the upturned faces of the gunner and loader staring at him through his hatch. He grabbed the handles to his M-2 heavy machine gun, his tank's only means of air defense. *Ninety-five percent invulnerable*, Chandler thought as he watched the two Stingers home in on two unsuspecting Havocs. *They're completely invulnerable to 7.62-mm rounds, and ninety-five percent invulnerable to 12.7-mm rounds.* Chandler's M-2 was .50 caliber – 12.7-mm on the metric scale. *And the Havocs have – what? – a 30-mm cannon, forty unguided rockets, and sixteen AT-6 Spiral antitank missiles on their wing pylons.* The Russian helicopters were now banking radically.

First one and then a second helicopter burst into flames and plummeted to the ground. Chandler watched as the other helicopters turned suddenly . . . and raced away. After a moment's elation, however, Chandler realized that the damage was done. The element of surprise was lost, and he began to consider withdrawal.

Almost unheard over the din of battle and low whine of his M-1's engine, Chandler's mind registered a faint whistling sound overhead. His heart skipped a beat as he dropped into the turret, scraping his back painfully along the hatch. Thunderous explosions erupted outside the tank, and Chandler looked up through the open hatch at the sounds. In the pause after the first volley, he climbed back up and peered cautiously over the top of the hatch. The hatches of his tanks and Bradleys were dropping shut as his crews buttoned up. Another crashing wave of explosions caused him to duck back down, but when no shrapnel struck the tank he rose up to look toward the sounds of the explosions. He had guessed right. The Russian artillery was now pummeling the empty woods behind them. That, however, would change when the helicopters reported in.

Chandler slipped down into the turret again and told Jefferson to close his loader's hatch as Chandler dogged his own shut. He called brigade and gave them the SHELLREP, reporting the artillery attack so that the ground radar team could find the shells with their radar in midflight and plot the locations of the guns that had fired them by reversing the trajectory. Once pinpointed, the battery of sixteen M-109 155-mm self-propelled howitzers assigned to them – one section of eight always on standby and the other moving or setting up in a new position but available – would rip the Russian guns to shreds with counterbattery fire.

Should we displace? Chandler wondered, knowing that the fire would shortly adjust onto their positions. As he pondered the question, Chandler saw through the battlesight extension vehicles, friendly vehicles, appearing at various places along the ridge and streaming in Chandler's direction. U.S. M-1s and M-3 scouts. Armored cavalry. Chandler's heart pounded so hard that his breathing grew labored.

'All units,' Chandler said over the battalion net, almost surprised that he had keyed the radio to speak, 'this is Juliet Lima One, those are friendly, I say again, friendly units.' He swallowed to wet his throat before continuing. 'Be prepared to fire at follow-on vehicles, but hold fire until my command. Out.'

The remnants of the covering force from III Corps' 2nd Armored Cavalry Regiment trailed clouds of dust and billowed smoke from diesel shot onto hot exhausts by their smoke generators as they roared back across the farmland toward them, all of their gun barrels pointing to their rear except one, its gun at an odd angle to the side. *It's been hit*, Chandler guessed, *and the turret motor's out*. Chandler radioed brigade that they were 'passing the line.' *Not much of a line*, he thought.

The artillery still shredded the empty forest to their rear. *Surely the Havocs have reported in*, Chandler thought. *Or could it be . . .?* he wondered. The notoriously cumbersome Russian command and control system, which right now would be under a barrage of U.S. attacks both electronic and high explosive, might be so disrupted that the helicopters could not talk to the artillery, one of the 'force multipliers' that U.S. Army doctrine sought to obtain.

When the friendly tanks were about halfway to their line, the first Russian tanks crested the ridge. Chandler was stunned at the sight even though he knew they were coming. They were T-72s, one generation older than the Russians' best tanks, the T-80s, but still formidable in the hands of good crews. *They'd be fighting at under a thousand meters!* Chandler realized as he calculated the distance between the American and Russian units. *Hand-to-hand for tanks!*

The armored cav tanks opened fire immediately, and their Bradleys spewed out TOWs toward the seemingly countless Russian combat vehicles pouring over the crest of the ridge. The slope was coated dark green with the moving Russian hulks, some suddenly erupting into flames, and Chandler began to fear that his unit would be overwhelmed before he could disengage.

When the first of the Russian tanks fired from the bottom of the ridge, Chandler watched as great sparks flew off the side of an M-1's turret and then saw a tree fall out of the corner of his eye from behind his own line, its trunk sheered in two. The American tank continued its high-speed retreat, and Chandler decided he could not hold his fire any longer for fear of the losses that the cavalry would take.

'What the hell's goin' on, man?' the driver asked, his field of vision ending at the embankment about ten feet in front of the tank. Chandler fingered the PUSH-TO-TALK button of the radio as the gunner, whose eyes were glued to the main gun's sight, described the sight to the driver and Jefferson.

Now we'll see, Chandler thought almost sick with worry, and he keyed the radio. 'All units, all units, this is Juliet Lima One. Commence firing, I say again, commence firing.' Chandler then quickly told Loomis, his executive officer, to report the contact to brigade, watching as Russian tanks began to explode in flame.

As the first of the fleeing M-1s reached the railbed, a huge display of sparks engulfed it. The tank's treads quickly rolled to a stop as flame shot skyward a hundred feet into the air. Amazingly, the commander's hatch on the turret flew open. A man tried to get out but was forced back inside by the tremendous violence pouring through the blow-out panels on the back deck of his tank.

Chandler flicked on the intercom and locked down the PUSH-TO-TALK button. 'Gunner, three tanks descending ridge – one o'clock.' The tank that he was looking at, along with several others, exploded before the gunner had acquired it. 'Gunner, two tanks and BDRM – bottom of ridge – one thirty!' Chandler said. 'Right tank!'

'Identified!' The gunner, who had chosen to slide the thermal sight shutter into place because of the growing smoke on the battlefield, had a target in his sight. Chandler glanced down at him. His face was buried in the padded walls of his sight, staring at the small optical/thermal imaging screen with its ghostly green images of the battlefield. Chandler looked down into his own gunsight extension and saw the familiar green world of heat and cold, a duplicate of the gunner's. The gunner was fine-tuning the turret's rotation and the gun's elevation.

'Fire!' Chandler yelled.

'On the way!' the gunner replied, and the cannon erupted – *WH-A-A-A-NG*! – jarring the sixty-ton tank violently and instantly unsettling Chandler.

'Hit!' the gunner shouted almost instantly. 'She blew – turret's in the air!'

Chandler saw it himself through his own sight. Sure enough, the turret of the rightmost tank was falling lazily to the ground off to the side. The tank itself spewed a ferocious yellow fire skyward as the ammo locker burned off. Unlike the M-1 he had seen earlier, from which now scrambled two men, one assisting the other, the Russian tanks did not have Halon fire-suppression systems or armored bulkheads separating the crew compartment from the ammo locker and fuel cells.

'Gunner,' Chandler shouted, 'next tank – bottom of ridge—!'

The gunner interrupted, 'Identified!' and Chandler saw the cross hairs settle onto the correct target.

'Load sabot!' Chandler yelled. He looked down to see the baseplate of the large 120-mm round ejected, as usual, not into its special bin but onto the floor of the cabin. Chandler watched as Jefferson, his hand covered in a thick mitten, picked up the metal baseplate, smudged black and smoking, and dropped it in a bin. The baseplate was the only part of the long propellant cartridge not fully combustible, and you had to make sure to account for each one. At several hundred degrees, they would ignite the propellant casing of an unexpended round if they came in contact with each other.

'Up!' Jefferson shouted.

'*Fi-i-re*!' Chandler ordered.

'On the way!' The main gun blasted another round out, shaking Chandler's internal organs. His ears began to ring.

'Yeah, baby! We bad, we *so-o-o* bad!' the gunner yelled as Chandler saw the target roll to a stop, black smoke erupting out of the point of impact on its turret. Chandler called for more sabot as he watched the tank, suspicious that it might not be dead. All of the sudden, a hatch blew off and flames as bright as sparks spewed out in growing intensity.

'Yeah, baby!' the gunner said again as Chandler directed him to fire at will. Chandler watched as the last of the fleeing armored cav tanks smashed up and over the railroad embankment and the few remaining Bradleys found the ramps hurriedly built by the engineers. Chandler could see that the Russian force was being reduced to a burning junkyard, at least twenty or thirty vehicles killed already. He contemplated withdrawal to their second line at the stream but hesitated, agonizing.

The gun roared again and the tank bucked. 'Reach out and *touch* somebody, baby!' the gunner shouted, and Jefferson replied, 'Treat 'em rough!' as he slammed the gun's breech closed. *WHA-A-ANG*! Chandler was getting used to the rhythm – he no longer jumped at each round fired – but the smell of cordite from the spent shell casings burned his nostrils and he coughed. The number of live targets dwindled.

Just as Chandler prepared to report to brigade that the attack was faltering, a second echelon of Russians rolled over the ridge. As their numbers grew and grew, he saw that it was even larger than the first, and it roared forward firing. Chandler turned to see huge chunks of the railbed blown skyward, the twisted rail bent up into the air at an angle.

Chandler's own tank blazed away. The gunner no longer cheered each kill, the sight of the new wave having noticeably chilled his enthusiasm to a quiet resolve. Each time the guns of the approaching Russian tanks shot fire and smoke seemingly straight at Chandler's tank, his nerves braced for the crash of the kinetic energy penetrator even though he knew that their muzzle velocity was so great he'd never see it coming.

Forcing himself to pay attention to his job, Chandler nervously eyed the Alpha Company tanks. None of them seemed out of action, but one in the near distance had an ugly black streak down the side of its turret and its netting hung from it in tattered panels. When its gun blazed, dust shaking off the hull and from the ground around it, Chandler saw that it was still operational.

Still watching Alpha Company to his left, Chandler saw first the barrels and then the hulls of numerous M-1s edging up to the railbed from the treeline. Their guns fired quickly, some even while on the move forward. *The armored cav*! Chandler realized. *The bastards came back*! Chandler counted over twenty M-1s as they pulled into the spaces between Alpha Company's tanks, their fire more than doubling that of Alpha's fourteen tanks. *Is that enough*? Chandler wondered as he looked back at the smoking field ahead.

His own tank's gun continued its steady beat, the gunner firing rounds as fast as Jefferson could hump them into the breech. The heavily sweating Jefferson asked, 'How we doin' out there, man?' but the gunner, his eyes pressed to the sight, didn't answer. They were firing at their maximum rate of fire, about eight aimed rounds per minute. *Jesus*, Chandler worried. *What's our ammunition gonna be like*? – doing the math in his head as the fighting raged.

He looked back to the front. Pyres burned from every spot. As the second echelon weaved its way among the previously destroyed vehicles on the valley floor, some using the burning wreckage as cover, a third echelon crested the ridge and Chandler's heart fell. He knew now that he would have to order disengagement and withdrawal, and he pivoted to measure again the distance to the cover of the light woods. Tree trunks, each threatening to cause a track to be thrown, littered the floor of the woods where the artillery had fallen.

The armored cav! he thought suddenly. *I don't even have their frequency*! He couldn't just leave them. He'd have to call brigade, who would then either try to raise their regimental command post directly or maybe have to go up through division or even corps and then back down. *How long would that take*? he wondered, panicking. *Would it even work*? *What if some link in the communications chain was gone, destroyed in the fighting they'd just been through*? He measured the distance to the first tank. He could dismount and run for it, or better yet drive over and just hop down.

Artillery burst just behind one of Alpha Company's tanks as he watched, shredding its camo netting to tatters. 'Shit!' Chandler said as he looked back around at the front. The artillery was light, but up ahead the killing continued apace. How many more waves would there be? Chandler nervously called up his other three companies to the right and was told that all was quiet. Chandler considered pulling Bravo Company off the line and moving it over to the left to lend its firepower, but . . .

CH-A-A-A-N-N-G-G! Chandler felt the pain in his knees first. After a second or two, his head cleared and he looked over at the gunner and Jefferson. They both looked around confused, and Chandler realized that he had fallen onto his knees on the floor of the crew compartment. It had been a near miss, and it hadn't penetrated.

'Everybody okay?' he shouted. They all reported in, sounding shaken. 'Systems check,' Chandler said, climbing back up to his post and doing the radio check on the brigade and battalion nets himself. The radios worked, but Chandler had to refuse Harkness's request for a report when checking in with brigade because of his need both to fight his own tank and to make his decisions as battalion commander.

'Computer's rebooting,' the gunner said. 'Manual fire only till . . . wait, it's back up!'

'Resume firing,' Chandler said.

'Gun's hot,' the gunner said, but kept firing. Chandler knew the heat was warping the barrel, but the reference mirror mounted on its muzzle would precisely measure the warp to allow the tank's computer to make minute compensations for the shells' trajectories.

'We're runnin' through ammo at a good clip, sir,' Jefferson said. He looked at Chandler as the gun exploded with the firing of another round. After slamming another sabot round into the breech and yelling, 'Up!' Chandler felt Jefferson's eyes on him again. 'How . . . how're we doin' out there?'

Chandler looked back out at the battlefield, feeling sick with the thought of wasting time in confusion over what to do. *My God!* he thought in amazement. *They're . . . we stopped 'em!* Chandler could see only one vehicle, a Russian BTR filled, presumably, with infantrymen, as it scurried from behind one burning hulk to another. Gunning its engine and then stopping behind cover, chased by several shots each time but protected by what had to be over a hundred wrecked vehicles, all belching smoke.

A crashing noise and a spattering of pings from outside reminded Chandler that the artillery still fell. He turned to see the artillery bursts erupting from all around the railbed. Chandler looked again back at the ridge and saw two new vehicles, one BTR and one T-72 with its turret blackened and gun at a steep elevation, dashing back up the slope. The BTR that had played hide-and-seek when last he looked lay on its side burning. No new vehicles appeared at the ridge, and as he scanned the battlefield for signs of life the retreating tank and BTR exploded almost simultaneously.

'Gunner, cease fire!' Chandler yelled. 'Stand by.'

The artillery raining down around Chandler began to diminish. At any moment, however, a lucky direct hit could kill one of his tanks, or a near miss could riddle a Bradley and the infantry inside. At a minimum, the shrapnel might scrape off an aerial or smash a sight.

Chandler's throat was dry. The main guns of his and the armored cav tanks had fallen silent, replaced by the smoke and heat from the muzzles of their machine guns and the spillage of the spent cartridges from the sides of the guns' chambers as they peppered the few pitiful human figures scrambling desperately about the battlefield.

Is that it? Chandler thought. *No more?* The situation, the doctrine, screamed at him from the books and lectures. The seconds ticked off, and he sat there uncertainly. There would never be a situation more clear cut, but still he struggled with the decision. It was so clear! *If only I had an out*, he thought. He remembered the plaque outside the Command and General Staff College at Fort Leavenworth. *'Audace, audace, toujours audace'* – 'Audacity, audacity, always audacity.'

Chandler switched to the battalion net. 'Victor Whiskey, this is Juliet Lima One, do you read, over?'

'Juliet Lima One, this is Victor Whiskey. Affirmative, over,' the Fire Support Officer commanding Chandler's FIST, his Fire Support Team, said.

'Smoke – Objective Mercedes – fire, out,' Chandler ordered.

'Smoke – Objective Mercedes – wilco, out,' the young officer responded, plotting the fire from inside his modified M-113 armored personnel carrier and directing the mortar platoon to target the ridge across the battlefield.

In just seconds, the first mortars exploded on the crest of the ridge ahead.

'Splash – over,' the FSO said to report first impact.

The smoke quickly obscured the hill from Chandler's view. The Russian artillery had died off completely, smashed to pieces, undoubtedly, by counterbattery fire or air attack. Chandler considered changing his plan, calling it off, but the adrenaline of the fight had pumped him up so much that his grip on the handholds was painfully tight.

'All units,' Chandler said, keying the radio and swallowing to wet his dry throat, 'this is Juliet Lima One. Advance to contact, I say again, advance to contact. Out.'

Chapter Fifteen

THE KREMLIN, MOSCOW
July 12, 1500 GMT (1700 Local)

'What should I do with the colors?' the commander of the 104th Guards Airborne Division asked, barely audible on the shortwave radio over the swirling electronic howl of the distance between Iceland and Moscow. 'Should I present them to the Americans, or burn them?'

Razov looked down the table at the other STAVKA officers and held out his hand in question. Most averted their eyes, and the few who returned his look glared at him without answers.

'Burn them,' Razov said, and before the general could answer there was the sound of an explosion and a series of popping sounds over the radio. 'General Trifonov?' Razov said in a raised voice. 'General Trifonov?'

'Yes, yes!' he replied angrily as the popping noise continued in great ripping bursts. 'It's just their damned gunships, those transport aircraft – AC-130s – that they've converted into weapons platforms.' There was another loud boom. 'Ever since we ran out of antiaircraft missiles they've just been circling up there and firing directly down on us. They apparently located our signals unit about five hundred meters away and are tearing it to pieces.'

'You have my permission to surrender at any time, General Trifonov,' Razov said. 'You've done your job. Your part in this is over. Make contact and call a cease-fire.'

There was a long pause before the acknowledgment came. With it came something else. 'Before I sign off, there's one more thing that I have to get off my chest.' Razov looked up at Admiral Verkhovensky, who raised his eyebrows at the tone of voice used by the field general. 'When you sent us to this godforsaken island, did you intend to leave us here with no support or supplies, or was it just a miscalculation?'

Admiral Verkhovensky flared and raised his hand to punch the speaker button and disconnect the impudent officer. Razov grabbed his wrist, and Verkhovensky stared at him angrily before Razov said, 'He deserves an answer,' in a low voice. Verkhovensky drew his hand back, and Razov turned to the speaker and said, 'We sent you there knowing that we would not be able to supply you for long. By forcing the Americans to fight there, you have tied up some of their best infantry units – their 82nd Airborne and Rangers, plus a light infantry division and a Canadian brigade group. We thought they might also introduce their marine forces in the Atlantic to Iceland, but that was not to be. You have fought well and hard, and the people of Russia will long remember your sacrifices.'

Again there was a pause, but then the general commanding Russian forces in Iceland said, 'Well, we tied them up for almost three weeks, but they're all yours now. Watch out, because they're good, especially their Rangers and paratroopers. They never backed off an engagement. They're fine light infantry. It would have been a good fight, if only we had the ammunition to give it a go.'

As soon as the line was disconnected, Air Force General Mishin shouted, 'We never should have pulled our support of those troops!'

'And what would you have us do?' Admiral Verkhovensky snapped back. 'If I operated my forces much longer in the Norwegian Sea with the American carrier battle group sitting astride my fleet's lines of supply in the Barents, I would have lost them also. Besides,' Verkhovensky said, his eyes narrowing as he stared at his accuser, 'we committed five of your air wings to Iceland, and how long did it take the Americans to brush them aside? Four days! Four days of air cover, and then complete air supremacy for the Americans after that!'

'And how long do you expect your precious ships in the Barents Sea to last,' Mishin said, 'with an American carrier battle group bearing down on them at last report?'

'Iceland is a sideshow,' General Karyakin, commander of the rebuilding Strategic Rocket Forces, said calmly, and both the admiral and the air force general appeared satisfied with letting the argument drop. 'We have more pressing concerns.' Karyakin looked over now at Razov. 'Like how to recover from that stupid attack at the Dnepr.'

'It was a calculated risk,' Razov said.

'It was a *foolish* risk!' Verkhovensky said, rising to the opportunity to vent his frustration on somebody else.

'In the Far East,' Razov responded calmly, 'their marines and their army's I Corps are pushing up the Sikhote-Alin mountains cutting off the bulk of our combat power to the south. It's all we can do to hold the Chinese off our remaining supply bases inside Occupied Territory and mount a few tactical counterattacks. To the south of Moscow, their armored cavalry spearhead should be at Bryansk in a couple of weeks, with an entire corps of their Army Reserve and National Guardsmen moving forward, barely three hundred and fifty kilometers from Moscow. Unless we can get fuel to the 19th Tank Army in Ryazan, we will have no mobile forces with which to counterattack. And they now have mobile forces freed of their commitments in Iceland. We have no satellites to tell us what they are doing because they have all been destroyed, as have our launch facilities.'

'We have raised Provisional Troops from every town and city on the road to Moscow,' General Abramov, commander of the Provisionals, said. 'They're mainly building defensive works now, but as the Americans approach we'll arm them. The Americans will pay in blood for every one of those towns. Plus, there is the "Moscow Line." We'll have two hundred thousand men at work there shortly, with a hundred thousand of them under arms.'

Razov just looked at him, forcing himself to mute his sarcasm, and then continued. 'The Americans have air superiority at all points north, south, and west of Moscow, and south and east of Khabarovsk in Siberia. Outside of coastal waters,' Razov said, 'the navy has no, *no* surface units responding except for the battle group in the Barents Sea and just five attack submarines. The American carrier strikes from the Black Sea at our oil transport facilities in the Caucasus and the cessation of oil deliveries from secessionist Siberian republics has seriously reduced our fuel supplies. On all other materials, we are operating on stocks only; military production is almost at a standstill. Desertion rates are rising and morale is plummeting. We are losing entire combat formations on first contact with the American armored units.'

Razov looked around the table at the officers, but they averted their eyes. 'And have any of you left the Kremlin recently?' When no one responded, Razov said, 'I thought not. Colonel Filipov' – Razov turned to see Filipov rise from his seat behind him – 'would you please give us a report on the civil situation?'

Filipov stepped up to the table. 'There is no food. The people are starving,' Filipov said in a grim tone. 'Estimates are that by the end of August, Moscow will be losing between five and ten thousand dead per day from starvation or diseases related to malnutrition, primarily among the very old and the very young. The apartments and public buildings are jammed with refugees. The power is on for six hours per day on a rotating basis around the city, but it is uncertain how long we will be able to sustain even that level of power generation. If the Americans ever come back at us with something more than the occasional cruise missile they now use for harassment of operations, or if they break their self-imposed moratorium on attacks of our nuclear reactors after the contamination incident at Lyubertsy No. 2, there will be only emergency power. The anarchists are operating completely openly, organizing block committees and holding public demonstrations, especially in the smaller cities to the east and around Moscow University here in the capital. Their membership is swelling dramatically.'

'Where the hell is the Minister of Security?' Verkhovensky asked, looking around the table for the usually silent 'civilian' minister whose forces were in charge of maintaining domestic political order.

'He is on an inspection tour of their units in Nizhni Novgorod,' Razov replied.

The old commander of Construction Troops loosed a raspy laugh that metamorphosed into a hacking cough. 'The little KGB weasel is inspecting his vital facilities to the east, eh?' and several other men laughed, the pattern from the last world war repeating itself. The old man ended by pulling his handkerchief out and coughing until he was red-faced.

Razov felt the tension break in the room. After a moment's hesitation he said quietly, 'I propose a cease-fire.'

There was silence in the room. Finally Verkhovensky asked, 'On what terms?'

Razov stared back at him without answering.

'Impossible!' Mishin shouted. 'We still have two army groups in the Urals and one in the Baltic countries that have yet to fire a shot! Plus the 19th Tank Army at Ryazan, and the St Petersburg garrison that we can pull back to join up with the Provisionals around Moscow! We can regroup, fight all the way back to the Urals if we have to.'

'And if they attack on a third front?' Razov asked. 'We have forces deployed around St Petersburg and in the Baltic States, yes, but after they have run through their stocks – or the ten percent of the stocks that are left after the American air and Special Forces attacks – with what will we supply them? And how do we plan on moving, engaging, fighting these army groups without fuel? Do we bury them up to their turrets like Saddam Hussein and hope the Americans waltz by within range of their *guns*?' Razov was shouting, exasperated and frustrated at his rapidly diminishing ability to control events.

'We've got huge caches of supplies,' Mishin insisted.

'But we can't move them!' Razov shouted. 'We can't move them, not by rail, or by truck, or certainly by air, General, not unless you have some secret weapon to wipe the Americans from the skies.'

'We couldn't even move them if we had air superiority,' the commander of Transportation grumbled, 'not without reprioritization of fuel deliveries so that I can get fuel to *my* people.'

'Reprioritization from what?' the commander of the Western Front asked. 'From tanks? BTRs? BMPs?'

'Moscow will fall,' Razov said quietly.

Nobody said anything. Finally, after the silence had turned oppressive, Verkhovensky said, almost in a whisper, 'Yuri, we can't give up Moscow without a fight.'

'An open city!' Filipov blurted from behind Razov. 'We can just declare Moscow an open city, like the French did with Paris in World War Two. Pull back everything we can salvage to the Urals and keep fighting like in 1812!'

Even though Razov knew his young aide was only getting started,

Filipov fell quiet. There followed an awkward silence, and in that silence Razov knew that the worst would come true. To give up Moscow would be defeatist, and one of two things would happen: either the army would unravel, or some young Turk from lower levels of command would blow STAVKA to kingdom come and assume national command. Everyone's memory was mired in the Great Patriotic War. Hitler had been stopped by stiffened resistance and resolute leadership. None of the others here would dare give up Moscow without a fight. Neither would he.

'But we have fallen into a trap,' General Karyakin said, and Razov was instantly on guard. 'We are thinking *defensively*.' He turned to stare at Razov. 'What we need to do is start thinking offensively, strategically.'

'Like your plan to use chemical and biological weapons?'

'The disease from the biological weapons has yet to manifest itself fully in the Chinese troops,' Karyakin said in a nonchalant tone. 'Once it does, the effects will be debilitating and it will be quite a while before they pose a threat. *Strategic* thinking, don't you see?'

'And your nerve gas attacks against the Americans and British have produced, what?' Razov asked. 'Two, three hundred dead, most of those by accident in that one mobile field hospital?'

'I wasn't talking about chemical or biological weapons for the Americans.'

'What would you have us do, General?' Razov said coolly. 'Fire the Bastion's missiles? Bring them down to defeat with us?'

'"Minimize the maximum gain of our opponent"?' Karyakin said, smiling. 'It sounds a bit like those newspaper accounts of Livingston's decision to retaliate. The "Prisoner's Dilemma," I believe they called it.' He smiled again and shook his head. 'No. There is more that those missiles can do than simply destroy and kill, you know. You're simply not approaching the problem creatively.'

'What are you talking about?' old Admiral Verkhovensky demanded.

'The Americans are not without their own problems. Judging from their news reports and from our human intelligence, there are large numbers – tens of millions – of people who are refugees from their cities. Just listen to the public exhortations of the President in his television and radio addresses and of his traveling minstrel show of Cabinet officers sent out to calm the natives. The Americans have an Achilles' heel.'

'And what might that be?' Air Force General Mishin asked, shocking Razov by showing interest. Suddenly he feared that out of desperation Karyakin might be reeling in the principal members of STAVKA.

'Colonel Filipov,' Karyakin said, turning to Pavel. 'You are our expert on the United States. What do you think underlies the President's exhortations to return home to the cities?'

'They're concerned about falling rates of production.'

Razov began to sense the broad outlines of the plan that Karyakin now leaned forward to explain, and he realized that getting Filipov, Razov's most trusted aide, to supply the plan's factual underpinnings was an artful ploy.

'The very thing that makes them so powerful,' Karyakin said, 'their productive capacity, is also their Achilles' heel. Our boys – these Provisionals, for example,' he said, pandering to General Abramov, who nodded in gratitude for even some recognition, 'can fight if you throw them a few sacks of potatoes and a stackful of old Kalashnikovs. But the Americans,' he said, leaning forward conspiratorially over the table with a glint in his eye, 'their vaunted "systems" – these complicated mechanisms that require every third soldier to be a computer programmer whose job it is to get every last nut and bolt into bins at the front for ready access – they rely on an extraordinarily complex chain from factory to field. If any one of those little nuts or bolts – or more likely computer chips, or exotic hydraulic fluids, or little plastic sheaths on their bombs' laser designator kits, or whatever – if any one of those supplies falls to the critical stage, we start peeling back their "force multipliers." Stripped of all those systems, it becomes tank vs. tank, soldier vs. soldier. The game is leveled, and we are, shall we say, on our home field.'

'Look, Karyakin,' Mishin said angrily, shaking a finger in the air at his face to the relief of Razov, 'we've done absolutely everything we can to interdict and reduce their logistical effort. My boys have been flying off to their death by the thousands attacking their rear areas in a conscious, and might I add somewhat short-sighted, attempt to shut down the flow of supplies to the front. If I had been allowed to contest control of the air by attacking their airfields like I wanted, we might still have—'

'I'm not talking about interdiction of their supplies on the way to the front,' Karyakin said, interrupting. 'I'm talking *strategic* thinking! Shutting down their production at the source. *Fear*, gentlemen. I'm talking about instilling *fear* in the American populace, the working population of ordinary citizens. If we can force them from their cities, we can force them from their jobs! If there are no workers, there are no factories! How long,' Karyakin shouted, 'how long can they maintain their current level of combat effectiveness if their production comes to a standstill? Two months? One month? One week, even? *Fear* – instilling a crippling fear in your enemies – that's the key to winning *battles*, and that's the key to winning wars.'

WEST OF UNECA, 290 MILES SW OF MOSCOW
July 12, 2300 GMT (0100 Local)

'Breakout!' Captain Loomis said as he jerked Chandler's hand left and right and then pulled him into a hug. Chandler warmed immediately and broke into a broad grin as the male celebration continued with the arrival of each new officer. The COs of the three armored companies, Chandler and Loomis, the battalion Executive Officer, punched each other's arms and laughed, as much an emotional release as a gaudy display of their incredible victory.

'Like shootin' turds in a toilet,' the commander of Alpha Company said to the laughter of all. At twenty-nine tanks, forty-four other armored vehicles, nineteen unarmored vehicles, and countless infantrymen, Alpha Company led the task force in kills.

'And how many did we lose?' Bravo Company commander asked for the benefit of Loomis, who had just arrived.

'*Ze-e-r-o-o!*' the three men shouted in unison, laughing.

'Oh, oh,' Charlie Company commander said, almost choking on the big swig of water that he had taken from his canteen as if it were champagne. 'I had one of my loaders hurt his wrist when they hit a bump,' he said with a grin on his face. 'Sprain, they think.'

They laughed, and Alpha Company commander asked, 'Did you Medevac him out?' and they all laughed again, the Charlie Company CO trying to pour water on the head of his questioner but missing as he dodged and shoved him back.

'Oh, uh, Major Chandler,' Charlie Company commander said, 'my tank's barrel count is one seventy-one. We may need a replacement before we get to Moscow.'

'Hey,' the Bravo CO said, pushing him with his open hand, 'I got one guy who's cracked three hundred shots.'

'Well, we aren't getting any new barrels,' Chandler said. 'Just aim higher.'

They laughed again and the banter continued, Chandler reveling in it. Hesitant to acknowledge just how spectacular their action had been, he'd listened in succession to the captains below and the colonel above. Harkness had practically raved, telling him the whole division was now doing some 'broken field running' through 'Chandler's Hole,' as some staff pukes called it at division.

It was Chandler's massacre of three regiments, weakened by the armored cav whose guns also contributed mightily to Chandler's own firepower, that had poked open the hole through which he had put his entire task force. For three hours they had run amok among lightly armed command, supply, and support troops. Finally, in a dash for the Iput River, Chandler had gotten there late, but had rolled right up on a Russian crossing operation. Every shot was a kill as the exposed vehicles swam at four miles per hour or crawled over the narrow floating bridges.

Two of the bridges had been seized intact, and after one of HQ Company's recovery vehicles had managed to drag the flaming hulk of a T-80 off one bridge, Harkness had ordered Chandler across. *That one was simple*, Chandler thought, recalling the ease with which he gave such a risky order. Only Loomis knew that it was brigade's order, however; the rest of the armored company commanders' confidence in Chandler-the-warrior-king reigned supreme. Chandler had issued the order to cross without a second thought, but he never would have crossed if left to make his own decision.

His entire task force and the support elements rolled or swam the Iput, and the turkey shoot began again over the next ridge. Despite having taken time to restock ammunition and refuel, Chandler's tanks had switched to machine guns for most of the killing. No need to waste main gun ammo on trucks and dismounted troops. Chandler had even learned to remain calm as the light and totally ineffective missiles streaked his way. Just keep your eyes open for the brilliant flare of the missiles' motor, train the .50 caliber on the source, and squeeze the trigger. Bullets fly faster than antitank missiles, and the missiles almost immediately went wildly out of control, the hand of its operator jerked off the joystick by fear or by the spasms of death.

Finally, when Chandler made another call for fuel and ammo, division passed a new brigade to continue the advance. Now they stood at the center of the battalion's Maintenance Collection Point, basking in self-congratulatory adulation at the fenders of their four tanks.

Troops hustled all around, their spirits high as their accomplishments were clear to all, to set up a massive camouflage net over the group of Headquarters Company vehicles that ringed Chandler's Tactical Operations Center. The net was necessary even at night because of the vision devices of modern warfare. In the distance, barbed wire ringed the area and two sentries stood, M-16s at the ready, at the one break in the strand.

Chandler glanced over at the wall-mounted map in the battalion's Command M-577, a converted M-113 armored personnel carrier, which was clearly visible through the vehicle's open door under a canvas tent extension. The spike of his battalion's penetration had turned into a bulge as the trailing units had pushed out the flanks, the blue area marked with greasepaint on the map's plastic overlay expanding at an impressive rate. The company commanders would soon be copying the lines and symbols from his map onto theirs and returning to celebrate with their tired platoon leaders, who would take the good news down to the sergeants, and so forth.

Their 'hasty defense' had quickly become a 'supporting attack' to the advance that corps had planned. When it became even more successful, it was upgraded to the 'main attack,' and Chandler and his Fire Support Officer had suddenly received incredible volumes of artillery and air support, surprising even for the main attack given the depth they had penetrated into enemy territory and the logistical difficulties that constantly made their every move uncertain. They had used the firepower wantonly, blasting the earth ahead of them with rolling torrents of fire. A suspicious copse of trees here, a slight rise over which lay the unknown, a small group of farmhouses in which infantrymen could be hiding – Chandler and his FSO blasted them all to smithereens.

They had seized objective after objective ahead of schedule, each of which Chandler had been told was defended but none of which amounted to a fair fight. Chandler's record of successes grew with each slaughter. But he knew the successes were less than what they appeared to be back up the chain of command. He knew it from the dazed Russian infantry that stumbled from their holes, their weapons not even fired against the armored onslaught. But when the commendations had poured in over the radio, Chandler had remained quiet. *'If it's a fair fight,'* Chandler recalled from his training days way back in Officers Candidate School, *'you haven't done your job.'*

Truck after truck rumbled by in the darkness outside their pool of light. The supply train of the main attack was well stocked with materials. Logistics was a martial art at which Americans excelled.

'Did you guys realize we're in Russia?' Loomis asked.

'You're kidding!' the Bravo CO said.

'Nope,' Loomis said. 'Morrison told Dave that we were the first unit into Russia, right before we crossed the river.'

'Well,' Chandler said, 'those jarheads over in Vladivostok might disagree.'

After a momentary pause, the company commanders exploded in laughter and began heaving shit onto Loomis, and Loomis tried unsuccessfully to defend himself. 'He meant . . . he meant . . . he meant in Europe!'

Just then there appeared in the glow from outside their circle a new face. They all turned to admit Captain Wade, the commander of Delta Company that had been borrowed from Colonel Honig's neighboring infantry battalion.

Everyone fell quiet. 'Jerry,' Chandler said in an even voice, holding his hand out to shake. Wade ignored it, and looking into his grimy face and bitter eyes Chandler didn't ask why.

'They told me to join back up with you,' he said with almost a sneer on his face, 'so I'm here.'

Delta Company had reported contact in the woods right after the initial fighting at the railroad tracks, and Chandler had detached them to clear the woods. Chandler was told to expect them to reattach at the Iput, but they were nowhere to be found when his task force effected its crossing and resumed its killing.

'You have anybody combat ineffective?' Chandler asked.

'*Dead*, Major?' Wade snapped. '*Dead and wounded*?'

Chandler had only meant to use the broader term for both, but he realized how inappropriate the euphemism was. 'How many?' he asked.

'Thirty-nine dead, twenty-six wounded,' Wade replied. 'Five of my thirteen Bradleys destroyed, two damaged and recovered. I can field one platoon and my headquarters section.' He looked around at the other officers, and Chandler was glad for the reprieve from his gaze.

'What the hell happened?' the Bravo Company commander asked in a soft voice, the other officers all looking down or away.

'We-e-ell,' Wade said with a deep resentment evident, 'while you boys were out winning the war by gunning down cooks and supply clerks, we dismounted 'cause the woods were too thick for the Bradleys and ran smack into a battalion of infantry. Had to call Lieutenant Colonel Honig to come over an' pull our chestnuts outa the fire.'

'But why didn't you call me for help?' Chandler protested.

'I told you we were in contact!' Wade snapped.

'*Everybody* was in contact!' Chandler snapped back, angry at the implication that . . . that those deaths were . . .

'By the time they threw the second company at us,' Wade said quietly, 'and we realized what we were up against, you people were miles away.' Wade went on, describing his later 'mop-up' actions against units that Chandler had bypassed, each of which bled casualties from his company. The Russians' light antitank missiles, it appeared, worked perfectly well against the infantry's Bradleys.

Chandler ached to explain himself to Wade, to describe the huge victory that had ensued, to suggest that there was nothing more that he could have done without dismounting his tankers and marching them into the woods on foot. But in the end, he just asked, 'Where are your casualties?'

Chandler's Humvee skidded to a stop in the loose dirt. When he opened the door, the four aerials of the battalion commander's vehicle were still swatting at the air from the driver's abrupt use of the brakes.

Oh, my God, he thought as the muffled sounds of agony easily penetrated the inflated polyurethane walls of the field hospital. Wade waited for him; Chandler hadn't realized that he had stopped walking. He looked at Wade, but Wade's face showed no sympathy. Chandler resumed his walk toward the sounds. Every step brought him closer, and with every step he heard a howl or a cry.

Over the next two hours, Wade introduced him to each and every man, wounded or dead. Wade knew his men well, and he told Chandler their dreams, most of which ended that night on a cold, stainless steel table.

FIVE MILES EAST OF LAKE KHANKA, RUSSIA
July 13, 2100 GMT (0700 Local)

Monk fell to the ground as the tearing sound of incoming shells cut through the air overhead. With his hands he kept clawing at the soil for depth right up until the shell burst in the treetops to his left. The force of the blast left him momentarily dazed.

Still, no death found him, and he rose quickly to his knees to pick at the soil with his entrenching tool. Looking over toward where the dark smoke from the shell still hung in the high branches, he saw that a tree lay shattered under the thinning cloud. Monk at first thought that it had miraculously missed the line of marines of which he was a part.

Digging as fast as he could into the slight rise that formed the only usable elevation in the thick woods, Monk looked back up to see one of the new guys pulling up a branch from the fallen tree. The kid sprang straight up and then recoiled backward several steps, tripping onto his butt. Rising to his knees and staring into the tree, he grabbed his stomach and vomited what had to be the entire lunch they had just completed two hours earlier, their first hot meal in a week.

Wood splinters, Monk thought and he shouted, 'Who was it?'

'Tolleson!' one of the other cherries yelled back. *Tolleson*, Monk thought, trying to remember which one of the new guys Tolleson had been.

Another tearing sound approached from above, and they all dropped flat. This time the round fell short, but Monk heard the rustle of brush just to his left as a fragment came close.

Climbing back to his knees he saw the new guys standing around the area where Tolleson lay. 'Dig, you stupid motherfuckers!' Monk screamed at them, incredulous that their work had come to a halt because of a casualty, with a Russian motorized rifle division not a quarter of a mile away and bearing down.

He looked down the line to the right to see the new lieutenant fresh out of platoon leader's class on the radio, the receiver pressed to his ear under his helmet. The woods in front of their positions erupted in fountains of searing hot flame and explosions, and the earth and air all around them rumbled. From flat on his stomach Monk heard over the explosions the roar of jet engines burst to full scream and then rapidly recede into the distance. The bombing run was so close he couldn't decide whether the jets were American or Russian, and he lifted his head to see clouds of black smoke and flame rising into the air in the distance, only the very tops of the clouds visible through the thin upper branches of the trees. Wave after wave of attack aircraft came in, repeating the violence and erecting a wall of fire some five hundred meters to their front. *A-6s*, Monk thought, listening and digging. *Nothin' else carries so much*.

Monk looked over at Mouth, who grinned and nodded, obviously pleased to have someone else doing the job for them.

When the screeching whine of the last pair of aircraft had gone, the only sound from the woods in front was the loud crackle of fires. A heavy curtain of black smoke boiled high into the air all across the broad front. From his left, cheers and whistles sounded from the cherries, and Monk looked over, aghast, to see that they were kneeling and standing, holding their weapons over their heads and pumping their arms into the air all around the fallen tree.

'Get the fuck *down*!' Monk yelled. 'Stay low and dig!' *What could they be thinking*? Monk wondered in anger at their stupidity, watching as they began to scrape at the ground from a prone position, glancing up at him as if he was about to shout at them that they were doing even that wrong.

The first of their Claymore mines tripped. Falling flat and wiping his hands on his trousers, Monk knew now the Russians were only two hundred meters away. He heard the screams of agony from the wounded, their bodies torn by the hundreds of steel pellets unleashed by the Claymores that stood on tiny stands an inch above the ground and sprayed an arc to their front, THIS SIDE TO ENEMY written on them clearly in block letters. They'd only had time to lay trip wires for warning, not a good thick belt for area defense.

Monk brought his weapon up to the ready, his field of vision reduced as he sighted, one eye closed, down the length of the black barrel. Slowly he traversed the weapon left and right, searching. Like other times before, Monk knew that the first man he saw was dead. He'd train his weapon on him until the platoon opened fire, and the first squeeze of the trigger would end the man's life. For some reason, the thought troubled him more than ever this time.

There! Monk thought, seeing a stooped figure moving forward cautiously to his right. He brought the SAW around and put the man's chest right atop the iron front sight. The sight, which wobbled all over the place at great range or from a standing position, was dead on and steady at sixty meters from the prone position. The man would die a few seconds from now. A great wave of depression swallowed Monk with the realization.

There were more figures moving forward up and down the line, but Monk stared at his man, so close that Monk could see his face clearly. It was black with grease or ash, but his eyes were wide and white. Monk closed his left eye again and aimed the heavy automatic weapon. He was so close that suddenly the man – the kid – became real. Nobody had told the boy that his life would end in these woods in Siberia. Nobody knew it, nobody but Monk.

Was he ready? Monk wondered looking at the Russian with both eyes open, torturing himself with the thought. *Has he said his good-byes? Did he know how important, how vitally important, these next few seconds were to him? They were all he had left, and he shouldn't waste 'em. Did he see the trees, the blue sky, how green the summer forest was?*

Monk could clearly see the Russian boy's eyes. He was scared. He closed one eye and aimed down the fixed iron sights.

Monk jumped at the sound of an M-16 firing a three-round burst to his right. Still looking down the sight, the entire line opened up. He half expected to see his guy disappear from his sights in a dive to the ground. But he stood there frozen while all around him men bucked and jerked before they fell or spun to the ground in the hail of thunderous gunfire.

Monk added a tiny amount of pressure to the trigger, so slight that he was surprised when the gun roared and bucked against his shoulder. When the shimmer of heat cleared from the gun's muzzle, the boy was gone.

Monk sprayed bullets from left to right now at the anonymous targets that jumped up and ran or crawled through shaking brush. He felt amazingly calm; it was a repeat of numerous previous firefights. All were bloody and violent, but all were the same. His mind was a blank.

On and on they came, and smoking hand grenades soon sailed through the air or bounced along the ground toward their line, exploding relatively harmlessly in the gaps in the line or thrown short or long.

'*Pull back!*' Monk heard screamed from his right. '*Everybody back!*' the new lieutenant yelled, and Monk looked up to see him standing on the reverse slope of the small hump waving his arm frantically to retreat.

No! No! Monk thought. *That's wrong! Not now, no!* But all up and down the line the firing died down and men began to pull up and head for the rear. To Monk's right, Bone let go a long burst from his M-60, the remainder of a 100-round belt flopping wildly through the new loader's hands as it fed the chamber with bullets until the end of the belt whipped up like a tail and the smoking gun fell silent.

Bone looked over at Monk as he rose, shaking his head and yelling, 'Shit!'

Monk looked back to his left. The new guys blazed away from their positions around the fallen tree. They hadn't heard.

'*Hey!*' Monk yelled, but not one looked over at him. To his right, the line was emptying; the marines retreated from the approaching Russians across the open forest floor at a dead run. Mouth yelled, 'Come on, T Man!' from behind the line and resumed his run.

Monk looked back over at the cherries, who fired with singleminded ferocity from their positions. 'Shit!' Monk said as he pulled back off the crest of the long, low hill and ran toward his three men on the left. A grenade came bounding over the hill in front and he dropped. The grenade went off and a jarring thwack sounded off his helmet as the helmet's brim hit his jaw like a boxer's jab and his neck was jammed and instantly sore. He rose again to rush forward with the newly acquired agony of a headache, and by the time he got to the cluster of cherries, their heads were up and looking all around.

'*Where the hell is everybody?*' one of them yelled back at Monk as he slid into the dirt behind them.

'We're pullin' back!' Monk shouted as the men ahead fired and a grenade went off over the hill in front of them. 'Come on!'

'They're too close!' one yelled as he fired burst after burst from his M-16. Monk crawled up to the hill and peered over. There were Russians everywhere, almost to the line on both the left and the right.

'Ho-o-o-ly *shit*!' Monk said, and two of the cherries looked over at him in horror. Monk heard the scraping of dirt behind him and spun around to see Mouth.

'What the fuck's goin' on?' Mouth shouted.

'We're in the shit, man!' Monk shouted as he ejected the nearly empty magazine and loaded a full 200-round box. 'Keep firing, Goddammit!' he said as he slid down the hill to where Mouth was. The tree that had fallen from the barrage earlier now lay across the middle of the position held by the five of them.

Monk yelled to Mouth. 'You take left, I'll take right!' They waded out into the thick, leafy branches at the bottom of the hill and sank down, back-to-back and separated by the trunk. 'What are you doin' here?' Monk asked.

'Fuck, I don't know, man. I was just followin' *you*!'

'Shit, Sarge!' one of the men screeched as his shaking hands tried to seat a new magazine into his rifle. 'They're comin' over on the right!' Dirt kicked up all around his position as the *zi-i-i-ng* of bullets flew over Monk's head. *This is it*, he thought in frozen terror. *End of the line*. He brought his weapon up and waited. It's a simple thing to die.

'They're comin' up on the left too!' another yelled. 'Oh, Jesus. Oh, Mother-of-God-Je-e-e-esus!' *What's it gonna feel like?* Monk wondered. He cut the first men over the hump to pieces as he heard the thump of Mouth's grenade launcher and then the boom of its grenade almost simultaneously on his left.

The cherry about ten meters away on the left pulled out of his fighting hole and scrambled back over the trunk of the tree into the middle of the small group. *It hurt like shit when my ribs got busted*, Monk thought, but he remembered the agony of the wounded and knew it would be worse. His panic vibrated through him, his body shaking uncontrollably. He tried to swallow, but there was no moisture to be found in his parched mouth.

'They're all over the place!' somebody else yelled from in front as Monk fired down the slope and saw two men tumble.

'Sarge! What the hell's gonna . . .? Oh, man, *S-a-a-r-ge!*'

'Shit!' Mouth screamed over the din from behind Monk. 'We done bought it now, T Man! We in this shit too *deep*, man!'

Two grenades exploded almost at once from just in front of the hill, and Monk heard the screaming of one of his men. *'Red's hit!'* somebody yelled. Russians poured over the rise to Monk's right, and he sprayed the air with bullets from a weapon now shaking noticeably in his quaking hands. *Our Father, who art in Heaven* . . . Monk loosed a long burst as one of the men in front kept up a running commentary on 'Red.'

'Oh, shit, Sarge, he's hit bad! He needs help, man!' . . . *hallowed be Thy name*. Wood splinters sprayed Monk's back and cut into his neck. Mouth's gun fell silent. *Thy kingdom come, Thy will be done* . . . Monk spun the SAW over the trunk. Mouth lay in the branches pawing wordlessly at his flak jacket, jagged holes ripped up the front. Monk blasted the Russians who rose to creep closer. He glanced back down at Mouth, who seemed unable to seize the grip to unzip his jacket, clawing at the zipper instead and staring up at Monk with glassy eyes . . . *on earth as it is in heaven*.

Russians poured over the hill right in front, and Monk raised his SAW and let go a long burst, emptying his magazine. He fell to the ground to reload. Whole sections of wood along the trunk shattered with loud claps, and bullets buzzed by Monk's ears like angry bees.

'Oh, God,' Monk said as his hands fumbled with the heavy magazine and he began to cry. 'Please help me! Please, God! Plee-ease!' The magazine wouldn't seat in the SAW, and his eyes were too blurred by the tears to guide it home. A fierce storm of bullets filled the air all around and tore through the branches of the trees as finally he felt the magazine connect with the weapon. Someone grabbed his legs. He looked up to see one of the cherries, the one who had left his hole, crying in agony.

'Oh, God, o-o-o-h Go-o-od it hu-u-u-rts!' His face was contorted by sobs, and his legs and pelvis were splotched and sopping wet with angry red smears.

Monk loosed a panting, tearful shout and raised his weapon just as the back of the cherry's head was cleaved off right in front of his eyes, splattering Monk in gore. A split second later, a sledgehammer blow shook his right thigh. Monk's SAW fell to the ground as he seized the burning hot fire that shot through his leg and let loose a scream of pain.

The world spun and blackened, and he coughed – warm liquid surged through his sinuses and out his nose. Holding his leg tightly, the agony ripped at his senses. He hurled vomit that rose to burn its way up from his stomach to clear his air passages with a long grunt.

He battered the back of his head against the ground as the pain shot through his nervous system like electric fire, crowding out all of his senses. First searing hot, then burning cold, Monk struggling to get breath into his heaving chest and with each draw panted a short scream, pausing only to heave as his stomach emptied and then just cramped violently. He felt a thousand pinpricks spreading across his skin as he broke into a sweat. The cold slick fabric of his trousers and the warm spurt of blood through his fingers as his heart pumped connected despite the pain. *I'm gonna die*.

He reached up to rip the first aid pouch off its familiar place on his belt. Without being able to see through the narrowing tunnel of his vision, he grabbed the thick packet inside. His hands slipped several times before he was able to tear open the slick cover.

His head wobbled and he dropped it back to the ground. With hands shaking wildly, he pressed the bandage to the spurting blood and began to wrap the gauze around and around his thigh, careful to cover both the entry and the exit wound, which he found with his fingers through the rips in his pants leg. His hands shook so badly that he almost couldn't pull open the adhesive end.

When he'd done all he could, he collapsed back, his skin clammy from head to toe. His shoulders began to quake, the first of the shakes that quickly seized his entire body with a cold so complete that he thought he would freeze to death. He couldn't remember what had happened. Pain, he remembered pain, but he couldn't feel it as he drifted in and out of consciousness.

He shook hard from side to side. A large figure blotted out the sky above Monk. Monk flinched as he felt drops of liquid fall to his face. Focusing as best he could, Monk saw Bone shouting, one hand pressed to his neck, which dripped blood through his fingers, the other grabbing Monk's flak jacket and shaking as he hovered over Monk's face.

'*Corpsma-a-n*!' Bone yelled as he stared down at Monk. 'You're gonna be okay, man,' Bone said, followed by something else. Monk shook again and he opened his eyes. 'Stay with me, buddy! You gotta stay awake! *Co-o-o-rpsman*!'

At the top of the hill behind Bone, Smalls shouted, 'First Squad! Advance by Fire Teams! Alpha, let's go!' and then he waved his arm forward and disappeared.

Bone kept up a constant chatter. '. . . go home now,' Bone said, followed by '*Corpsman*! Where the fuck are you, God-*dammi-i-i-it*!' The ground gave way beneath Monk's back and he spiraled through, only to be caught by Bone and shaken awake again, and again, and again.

I'm so tired, Monk tried to say. *Lemme go, man. Lemme go*. Monk never felt the moisture from Bone's tears that fell onto his face or heard the wail of the big man's anguished cry.

PHILADELPHIA, PENNSYLVANIA
July 13, 2300 GMT (1800 Local)

General Thomas took to the podium in front of the large crowd of officials, and Lambert listened as the dozens of conversations in the room died down. It was only the second major briefing of the war, and everyone was tense.

'Good evening, ladies and gentlemen,' General Thomas said. 'I would like to welcome all of our foreign guests from the coalition countries to these new and somewhat more plush accommodations.' There was a buzz of nervous laughter, and Lambert looked around at the hardwood floors, chandeliers, and ornate crown molding, which truly stood out in stark contrast to the spartan underground bunker from which they had emerged ten days earlier.

'When Operation Avenging Sword began seventeen days ago, the plan for our principal attack in Europe was to advance along two parallel and supporting drives into Ukraine. As you all know, the Southern Prong's attack was spoiled by a cross-border incursion of Russian motorized infantry troops, the last pockets of which inside Slovakia surrendered three days ago. What that spoiling attack has done, however,' Thomas said as he looked up, 'together with the remarkable success of III Corps and I British Corps in the north is to force us to rethink our early campaign strategy.' There was a slight stir in the crowd.

Thomas walked to the map and pulled his laser pointer from his jacket pocket. Thomas's aides pulled the curtain back, revealing a huge wall map. There were gasps, and the red dot from Thomas's pointer flashed onto the map of Ukraine, a huge arrow sweeping from the south and meeting the Northern Prong. 'Three days ago, V Corps was passed through III Corps' lines to merge the old Northern and Southern prongs into one main thrust.' Thomas waited a few moments for the commotion to die down. 'The *results* . . . have been spectacularly successful.'

There was an outpouring of noise – some laughter, some applause as confusion reigned. 'From the point at which III Corps – the old Northern Prong – crossed the Polish border into Ukraine, Moscow lies six hundred and thirty-five miles as the crow flies. In road miles along the intended route of advance, Moscow is about seven hundred and forty miles. Assuming a general ten-miles-per-day rate of advance through Ukraine and Byelarus, we had anticipated crossing the Russian

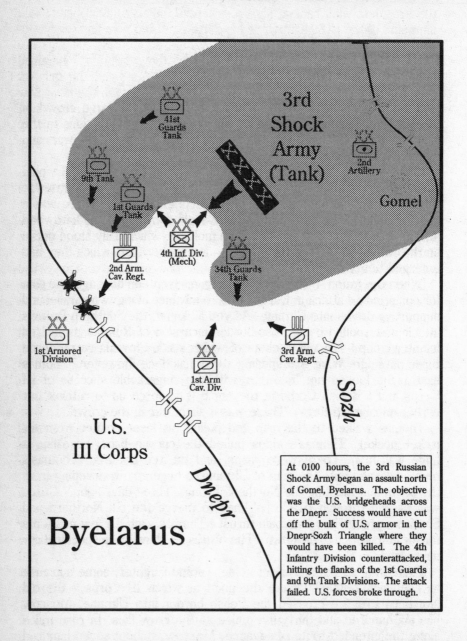

41st Guards Tank

3rd Shock Army (Tank)

2nd Artillery

9th Tank

1st Guards Tank

Gomel

2nd Arm. Cav. Regt.

4th Inf. Div. (Mech)

34th Guards Tank

1st Armored Division

1st Arm Cav. Div.

3rd Arm. Cav. Regt.

U.S. III Corps

Sozh

Dnepr

Byelarus

At 0100 hours, the 3rd Russian Shock Army began an assault north of Gomel, Byelarus. The objective was the U.S. bridgeheads across the Dnepr. Success would have cut off the bulk of U.S. armor in the Dnepr-Sozh Triangle where they would have been killed. The 4th Infantry Division counterattacked, hitting the flanks of the 1st Guards and 9th Tank Divisions. The attack failed. U.S. forces broke through.

border at approximately H plus fifty-two, or on August sixteenth, a little over one month from now.'

Again General Thomas paused for effect, and Lambert turned to see the President wink back at him from across the aisle. 'Last night, lead elements of the U.S. Army's 2nd and 3rd Armored Cavalry Regiments and 4th Mechanized Infantry Division crossed into Russia west of Novozybkov.' Cheers rose from many of the nearly two hundred people present. Some actually stood on their feet, and the military men seated around Lambert and even Lambert sitting in the front row had their backs slapped by the Congressional leadership in the row just behind. Costanzo rose and waved his clasped hands in the air in victory as if the applause was for him, and the crowd settled slowly into a mere buzz of conversations as Thomas held his hand up for quiet.

'Having averaged not ten miles per day but twenty-five, we have achieved rates of advance we had not dreamed possible before the war. With the advantage of superior mobility, we have managed to achieve local superiority on the ground in almost every engagement. In every major engagement, in fact, except in yesterday's Russian counterattack in the Dnepr-Sozh Triangle along the Russian-Byelorussian border.'

There was a stir from the crowd as everyone expected the proverbial 'but' to drop from the story of success to date. Again Lambert looked at Costanzo, who was agitated and searching the front row for one of the cognoscenti with whom to exchange significant looks. Again he winked at Lambert, who smiled back. 'Unbeknownst to us, the Russian High Command had managed to conceal a rather sizable maneuver force, something on the order of five divisions of tanks and mechanized infantry, just north of Dobrush, Byelarus.' The agitation in the crowd was palpable now, and Lambert had to smirk at the way the poker-faced Thomas played the stunning victory they had just achieved for all it was worth. 'The forces had largely remained in place under simple physical concealment – netting and the like – and they achieved a surprise crossing of the Sozh in the early morning hours yesterday. The Russian forces struck a thin screen of V Corps' 2nd Armored Cavalry Regiment, which we were resting after almost a full week of action, and achieved a breakout.'

Thomas did not let the commotion deter him from continuing. 'They were met by fresh units of the just-arrived 4th Mechanized Infantry Division from the old Southern Prong' – the crowd fell quiet again – 'and were routed in a counterattack so successful that it has become our main line of advance. The Russians gambled, and now they are suffering the consequences.'

Only now did Thomas get applause, the crowd's comprehension of what would probably be the greatest victory of the war having been slow to develop. 'Because of those successes,' Thomas said, shifting gears and sifting through the papers atop his podium, 'our planners have rapidly accelerated the objective timetables. The toughest stretch of road still lies ahead. We have met the Russian Army in noncombatant countries, and the results to date are encouraging. But there are many factors working against us as we continue our advance. Our supply lines grow longer and theirs shorter, which will translate into more and longer pauses for resupply. In addition, the Russians will have had the time to prepare their defenses with Provisional Troops, and major river crossings and reductions of city garrisons loom as increasingly daunting tasks.

'As a result of the lengthening of our lines of communication and the expected increase in Russian Army and irregular resistance upon crossing into Russia proper, our estimates are for only a twelve-and-one-half-mile-per-day rate of advance until we reach Tarusa, sixty-five miles south of Moscow. There we will hit the tougher, denser defenses currently being erected, and the rate of advance is then projected to slow to about two and one half miles per day, which, together with a six-day hold at the capital's outskirts, would put us another month away from finally assaulting Moscow. In conclusion, ladies and gentlemen, what we're looking at is about one month to get to Tarusa, and a final month to encircle and attack Moscow proper, which puts us in mid-September.'

'Isn't the one-prong advance risky?' Lambert heard called from the row behind him. There was a stirring in the audience as Lambert turned to see the chairman of the House Armed Services Committee. 'I mean, I thought the whole point behind having two prongs was to keep from being blindsided by a Russian attack. Won't this mean that single prong has to watch out on both flanks, will leave both flanks totally undefended?' Lambert glanced back at the President, who stared at the floor as if not listening. *Public support for the war slips to sixty percent and out come the sharks*, Lambert thought. *The honeymoon with Congress is over.*

'Not undefended,' Thomas replied. 'There are troops – coalition troops, mainly, from Poland, Slovakia, the Czech Republic, and, soon, Italy – all along the flanks of the advance being conducted by forces of the United States and Great Britain. In addition, as the advance gets deeper we will expend some effort to push out the flanks, primarily using the more mobile Italian forces. We also intend to use the National Guard's VII Corps to provide not just a theater reserve but to form the "shoulders" of our deepest penetration. They should be in position to assume that responsibility in a week or so.'

'How long do you expect the fighting to last in Moscow itself?' Lambert turned to see the silver-haired man from the Italian delegation sit after asking his question.

Thomas arched his eyebrows and drew a deep breath. 'Well . . . that's difficult to say. There is really no precedent for any of this, for an urban war with turn-of-the-twenty-first-century arms and tactics. If the Moscow Campaign remains true to our experiences so far, it will be mobile and quick.'

'But as I understand it,' an influential Republican Senator from Texas said – and Lambert turned to look at the woman whose name was being whispered for the next Presidential campaign, 'one of the reasons for the high rate of advance so far has been because you bypassed the Russians' fixed defenses in "end runs." You won't be able to do that when you go into Moscow or any of these other big cities.'

'That's not entirely correct, ma'am,' Thomas said. 'I have given you rates of advance of twenty-five miles per day as an average for an entire army corps. Individual combat units' rates of advance have sometimes been spectacular – fifty, sixty miles per day, rivaling the rates from the 1973 Arab-Israeli or the 1991 Gulf wars, both involving flat-out running along desert terrain. The slower twenty-five-mile average accounts for consolidation of positions, reduction of pocketed Russian troop concentrations, and moderations of advance due to logistical constraints. What I'm trying to say is that once we have everything in place – armor, infantry, artillery, support and supply, everything – around Moscow it could very well go quickly. Under twenty-four hours, possibly.'

'What's the worst-case, General?' the Texas Senator pressed.

'A month.'

The audience immediately broke into a caldron of noise, the general sounds of restlessness and anxiety so obvious that the President rose to his feet and said, 'Let's not get the cart before the horse here. We're talking about something that's at best case well over a month away.'

'Wouldn't the casualties from fighting in a city like Moscow be tremendous?' the Minority Leader of the Senate stood and asked as the Republicans began to double-team Thomas.

The President looked to Thomas, and Thomas said, 'Do you mean civilian casualties, or ours?'

'Both.'

'The answer to both questions is yes, the casualties would be high.' The buzz from the room was renewed.

'I think everybody here remembers Stalingrad,' the Minority Leader said, turning to work the crowd. 'I don't think anybody wants to—'

'This is not the floor of the Senate!' the President snapped angrily, cutting off the opposition political leader. 'This is a military briefing for members of Congress and our allies.'

'What are our casualties now, General?' another Republican, this one from the House, rose to ask.

'To date,' Thomas said, shuffling his papers, 'in the first sixteen days of fighting we have had 11,316 Killed in Action, 21,476 Wounded, and 516 Missing.'

'So about' – the Congressman paused to do the math – 'over two thousand Americans killed and wounded per day. That means, if this war takes three months, we're talking a quarter million killed and wounded?' From the rise in the tone of his voice on the last words of his sentence he indicated incredulity at the estimate.

'It doesn't work that way,' General Thomas protested over the stirrings of the crowd. 'Casualty rates are nothing like rates of advance. They occur in bunches, around offensives, ours or theirs. Most of the casualties we've had to date are disproportionately among the marines in the Far East, who had an opposed landing north of Vladivostok. They also include several major naval losses, and the toughest part of the air campaign.'

'How many casualties do you expect by the time we take Moscow, on all fronts?' the Minority Leader asked, picking up the baton from his colleagues. 'What is this war going to cost us in lives?'

Thomas stared down at the podium. 'We have or will have something in excess of about three hundred seventy thousand U.S. ground troops – Army and Marine Corps – and about an equal number of personnel in the aggregate from the U.S. Navy and Air Force actively engaged in or around the periphery of the Russian Republic. Our estimates run, on the low side, about twenty-eight thousand dead and fifty-six thousand wounded among the ground troops, and about half as many killed and wounded from the other two services.'

'So about . . . forty-two thousand killed, and eighty-four thousand wounded – total?' the Minority Leader asked.

'That's a rough estimate.'

'That's not just a rough estimate, General. That's on the low side, you said. What's the high side?'

Thomas took a deep sigh. 'Assuming that we remain non-nuclear,' he said, pausing to let the implications of that assumption sink in, 'then the high side would be something on the order of double that, with most of the increase coming in casualties among our ground troops.'

Again the voices, in heated comments, boiled over from the restive audience. This time, however, it was the Minority Leader's voice that quieted them. 'If my math is correct, General, what you are suggesting is that there is a possibility that we could lose upwards of two hundred thousand of our three hundred seventy thousand ground troops in this fight. And that assumes, I might add, that the Russians stop fighting after we take Moscow, which nobody has suggested will be the case.' He was arguing now to the crowd, and he had their complete attention. 'Just what, General Thomas, is the reason for the widely varying estimates of casualties from your low to your high end?'

Thomas stared back at the Senator, and all eyes were on him. 'It depends, sir, on how the fight goes in and around Moscow.'

Again the crowd exploded in raucous conversation. The President finally rose and said, 'We may never get there. They may agree to a cease-fire.' The noise level diminished. 'Or they may declare Moscow an open city.'

'And monkeys may fly outa my butt!' the Minority Leader shouted, and the crowd noise that followed signaled to Lambert a shift in sentiment to that expressed by the Minority Leader. 'How, General Thomas,' the Minority Leader continued, 'do you plan on replacing the losses of over half of your ground combat forces if the worst, or even the *average*, turns out to be the case?'

'Well, sir, the only way casualties could go that high in a non-nuclear scenario would be if the fighting in Moscow dragged on for some time, several weeks to a month. During that time, a lot of the wounded, especially those wounded in the early phases of the operation, would be ready to return to action. Some of the people wounded in the first days, those with broken bones or flesh wounds, should start returning to light duty this week. The majority of the replacement personnel, however, would come from new inductees.'

'You mean from draftees?' the Minority Leader said.

'And the volunteers, of which quite a few who joined in the big influx after the nuclear attack are already in basic training,' Thomas replied in a level voice. 'We've shortened both the basic and advanced training courses by a week by working everybody 'round the clock. That puts total training time for, say, Infantry at ten weeks. And we're thinking about trying to shave off another week or so. Add to them the recall of everyone we've discharged from service in the last twenty-four months, who we don't think need any retraining, and there's a steady stream of personnel coming on line.'

'But we're talking about taking nineteen-, eighteen-, even seventeen-year-old kids, sending them through a couple of months of boot camp, and then putting them into a meat grinder on the city streets of Moscow – isn't that right, General? Isn't that what fighting in an urban environment would be like – a meat grinder?'

'The casualties . . . would be . . .' Thomas, an articulate and educated man, Lambert knew, could not find the words. 'I suppose a meat grinder is an apt analogy, if the worst-case scenario were to be true.'

Lambert saw the President flinch and clench his jaw, looking away angrily.

'What about the Russian civilian casualties in this worst-case scenario?' the leader of the Czech delegation interjected into this otherwise purely American political squabble.

'In a worst-case scenario?' Thomas asked. 'Assuming no formal evacuation of Moscow, and a month or more of conventional warfare through the streets and buildings . . .' Again he hesitated, the words clearly getting stuck in his throat. He resumed on a different tack. 'In a worst-case scenario, naturally, we would be hard pressed not to be less . . . less conscious of the risks of collateral damage. Our unit commanders would have to be freed to target artillery or air strikes at buildings, which are the main "natural" obstacle in a city. If those buildings still housed their prewar tenants—'

'Answer the man's question, General Thomas,' the President said in a quiet tone as he sat slumped in his chair, his chin resting on his hand.

'If we fight our way through Moscow block by bloody block,' Thomas said in a slow, deep voice, 'somewhere between one and two million Russian civilians could die.' There was no outburst now, only silence.

Chapter Sixteen

LOS ANGELES, CALIFORNIA
July 17, 1800 GMT (1000 Local)

'London Bridge is falling down! Falling down! Falling down!' Melissa sang as Matthew screamed at the top of his lungs. 'London Bridge is . . .!' The microwave beeped, and she said, 'It's ready! Here it is, baby!' She rushed over to the chair that sat in its reclined position on the countertop and shoved the nipple into his mouth.

Melissa's eyes fell shut as she tried to calm her jangled nerves. The television that she'd been attempting to monitor during the non-stop network war coverage blasted at a volume that now seemed grossly excessive. 'The addition of the U.S. Army National Guard forces of the III Corps to the main drive toward Moscow represents the last full commitment of U.S. troops immediately available to coalition forces. This has led defense analysts to conclude that President Costanzo has ordered a "blitzkrieg" toward the Russian capital in an attempt to end the war as quickly and decisively as possible. Sources at the Defense Department confirmed that the reservists of the 107th Armored Cavalry Regiment have made contact with Russian Army forces in Byelarus at Petriko approximately four hundred thirty-five miles southwest of Moscow. There is no word yet of any fighting from the III Corps' two main combat divisions, the 38th Infantry headquartered in Indianapolis, or the 49th Armored out of Austin, Texas.'

Chi-r-r-r-p. The phone! Melissa's heart leapt, as always. She spotted the cordless handset on the coffee table, just out of reach, she discovered, from her post where she held the bottle in Matthew's mouth. Debating the next move for an instant, she pulled the bottle from his powerful, sucking lips and he immediately spluttered, turned red during a short buildup, and then began his howl, even more outraged than before.

She picked up the phone in that maelstrom of noise and said, in the shaking, expectant voice with which she always answered the telephone now, 'Hello?'

She jammed the nipple back into Matthew's mouth, and he made a long, loud slurp as he reacquired suction on the rubber.

'. . . of the Army. May I speak to Mrs David Chandler?' a woman's officious voice asked.

In the background, the news footage was of burned tanks along a road in western Russia and of U.S. and British army troops standing atop one with their rifles raised high in a cheer.

'Just a second,' Melissa said as time stood still. She put the telephone down and picked up the remote control, muting the announcer's glowing description of the capture of Lesozavodsk in the Far East.

Moving mechanically, she put the remote down, wiped her free hand on her blue jeans, and reached for the phone. Closing her eyes, she thought, *Oh, God, please, God, please no, God.* 'I'm . . . I'm Melissa Chandler – Mrs David Chandler,' she said, finishing the last just before the tears choked her.

'This is the Department of the Army, Mrs Chandler,' the woman said. 'There's a problem, and we need to let you know about it.'

Suddenly, she was acutely aware of everything around her. The sucking sounds of Matthew. The whine of rushing water as the ice maker filled itself. She was making all new ice despite the denials by city authorities that any radioactivity contaminated L.A.'s water supply.

'There was a foul-up with your husband's pay last month,' the woman said in a tone barely polite. 'We're gonna have to cut a check 'cause when they changed pay grades they put in the wrong account number for the direct deposit and it's too late to fix it.'

Melissa listened in complete confusion. The woman read off her home address and asked if it was correct. 'You mean . . . this is about some stupid check? David's army pay?'

'Yes, ma'am. Is that your correct address?'

'Well . . . yes,' Melissa said. 'Look, where is my husband now?'

'Well, uh, I don' know,' the woman said as if it was the strangest question in the world.

'You are talking about David Chandler, right?' Melissa asked. 'You got his address right, so it's David Winston Chandler?'

'David W. Chandler,' the woman said, obviously reading, 'Two thirty-one West—'

'If they're paying him,' Melissa interrupted, 'then he must be alive – isn't that right?'

'Well, not 'zactly,' the woman said, and Melissa's soaring hopes plummeted to earth. 'They keep payin' the widow for ninety days.' There was silence, and then the woman said, 'But I guess they wouldn't be promotin' him if he was kilt.'

'What do you mean?' Melissa asked. 'What are you talking about. David got a promotion?'

'Yes, ma'am,' the woman said, 'O-4 to O-5. It's on account of the change in pay grade that they screwed up the—'

'What's an O-4?' Melissa asked.

'An officer,' the woman said. 'A major.'

Melissa waited, and then rolled her eyes and asked, 'And an O-5? What's an O-5?'

'Lieutenant colonel,' the woman said. 'Anyways, the check'll be a coupla weeks late. If you haven't received it by—'

'Do you know anything else?' Melissa asked. 'Anything, anything at all? Where he is? What unit he's with? Anything?'

There was a pause. Finally, the woman said, 'Well, I'm not really s'posed to—'

'Please,' Melissa said. 'Oh, please. I don't know anything. I haven't heard from him since the war started, and nobody can tell me where he went, what unit, or anything.'

'Well,' the woman said, and then lowered her voice to a whisper, 'all I know is that the Pay Grade Change Run – the computer printout we get showin' all the changes, you know – well, the one fer yer husband was from Seventh Army.'

'And they're' – Melissa thought back to the hundreds of hours of news coverage that she'd watched and the magazines and newspapers she'd read – 'they're in Europe. Isn't that right?'

'Heh!' The woman laughed. 'They ain't in Europe – they's halfway through Russia 'bout now, God bless 'em.' She laughed again.

Melissa broke into a smile, and she laughed through the tears that resumed flowing. 'Thank you,' Melissa said, 'oh, thank you so very much.'

'It'll be all right, ma'am,' the woman said. 'I got two boys over there my own self. Jus' trust in the Lord Jesus – it's all gonna be okay,' she said, and then she hung up.

Melissa jumped in the air and screamed, 'Yes! Yes! He's alive, Matthew. Daddy's alive!'

Matthew, who had almost finished his bottle, let go of the nipple and broke into what almost looked like a smile. He burped loudly, and Melissa rapidly dialed the number for David's parents.

DEEP-UNDERGROUND COMMAND POST, THE KREMLIN
July 19, 0400 GMT (0600 Local)

Filipov knocked on Razov's door. 'Enter,' he heard, the groggy sound of a man whose sleep was interrupted regularly in the same manner.

Filipov's eyes were not adjusted to the darkened quarters, and he stared generally in the direction of the cot in which he knew Razov must lie. Razov switched the desk lamp on. He sat in his swivel chair in the dark behind his desk.

'What is it, Pavel?' he asked, and Filipov closed his mouth, managing a neutral expression on his face. On the desk next to Razov was his pistol.

'There has been a raid by U.S. forces in the far north – on the Kola Peninsula.'

'Where?'

'Murmashi, the bridges across the Tuloma. And east of Murmashi at the bridges across the Kola.'

'Were the bridges destroyed?'

'No . . . no, sir. Captured. Initial intelligence is that the unit is from the Americans' 82nd Airborne Division.'

Razov was out of his chair immediately and heading toward the map. By the time Filipov joined him, following his finger to the map as it rested on the town fifty kilometers inland directly south of Murmansk, Razov was already cursing under his breath.

'Goddamn them. *Goddamn* them.'

'It was a raid in force. The Murmansk Garrison commander sent out a regimental-strength team to counterattack, and they were ambushed seven kilometers from their objective. Admiral Strelov is probing now for the edges of the Americans' forces.'

'They're coming in,' Razov said, turning away from the map. 'A third front – they're going to open a third front in Karelia.'

Filipov was shocked at the suggestion. He followed Razov back to his desk arguing, 'But what for? They've already destroyed practically all of our facilities at Murmansk. And Polyarnyy was obliterated in the nuclear exchange.' Razov picked up the phone and said, 'Get me Mishin.' 'And they've just begun to work Arkhangelsk over with carrier aircraft attacks,' Filipov continued, hoping to save his boss the embarrassment of a grossly inaccurate assessment. 'There is practically nothing left of strategic value on the Kola Peninsula for them to—'

'General Mishin,' Razov said, 'the Americans are landing on the Kola Peninsula, and I want you to give me all the air assets available to you for one massive strike at their landing ships before they put ashore.'

He listened for a moment and then burst, 'It's not Kola they're after!' He was speaking to Mishin but looking at Filipov. 'It's St Petersburg! They intend to come in behind our defenses!'

But the distances . . ., Filipov thought.

'I know it's a thousand kilometers, but we have all our St Petersburg defenses to the south and southwest of the city. We have practically nothing to the north! I'm going to shift everybody I can, but we have almost no transport available for them.'

He listened again, again growing impatient. 'We're using horses now to transport food and provisions! It will take a month just for the move from the Baltics, and then a couple of weeks to prepare defensive works. Do you know how far the Americans can go riding atop tracked vehicles in six weeks? To tell you the truth, I cannot tell you standing here right now who will get to St Petersburg first – the Americans, who have to fight their way a thousand kilometers, or our own troops, who are practically on foot three hundred kilometers away!'

He slammed the phone down with a crash. In the silence that followed, Filipov contemplated the American move. It still made no sense. They had their main forces out of Poland and Slovakia poised, it seemed, to cut the roads between Moscow and St Petersburg, dividing Russian forces in Europe in half. What now would their heavy armies in the south do?

Filipov looked down at Razov, whose bloodshot eyes rose to meet his. It was not like this before, Filipov thought, in the last Chinese war. They had been down, but always Razov had exhibited confidence. When the Chinese had shattered a front-line division with wave after wave of infantry, opening a major hole in their lines and threatening envelopment of an entire army group, Razov had slapped him on the back and said, 'Opportunities, Pavel! Now it gets interesting!' His exuberance had infected even the cautious General Thomas, who was always there, always getting supplies through from the ports despite the bitter winter weather. It was the same cautious General Thomas who had just invaded Russia from the north, from the Arctic Circle, in what to Filipov seemed a foolhardy gamble. *What are they going to do when winter comes*? The problems posed by winter operations in Karelia, for their own forces as well as the Americans, were too many to consider, and only one answer came. They intend to finish this before winter.

'Uh, one more thing, sir,' Filipov said as Razov's eyes darted across the papers on his desk in seemingly random fashion, his lips and nose hidden behind hands clasped in front of his face. 'The Lvov Garrison in Ukraine.' Razov looked up at him. 'They have informed us that they will surrender today.'

'"*Informed*" *us*?' Razov said, sitting up and dropping his hands to grasp the front edge of his desk, his knuckles immediately growing white from the force of his grip. 'Informed us? Since when do we get informed that army groups are surrendering to the enemy?'

'The commanding general of the garrison reported that . . . that . . .'

'Spit it out, dammit!'

'The commanding general is being held under arrest. It appears that some of the junior officers, divisional commanders and below, were in disagreement with your . . . with STAVKA's orders to continue resistance, and they went to Army Group Headquarters and arrested him. They allowed him to inform STAVKA of their intentions, which are to parlay with the Americans for an immediate surrender.'

Razov's face was white, and Filipov grew suddenly chilled. Razov looked frightened, and it had been mere words, words from Filipov's mouth, that had caused his fright. Razov swallowed and licked his lips, his jaw setting then as he issued orders through teeth almost clenched shut. 'I want the names of those mutineers, I want a court-martial, and I want an order issued for their arrest and execution. I also want an order prepared for STAVKA approval at today's meeting for the summary execution of *any*' – he slammed his hand down on his desk, then regained a greater measure of composure, a cooler tone to his voice – 'any soldier exhibiting insubordination. And I want those executions publicized, beginning today.'

Filipov was jotting down notes, and when he came to "today," he was at a loss. 'What do you mean by "today," sir?' He asked the question in a low voice, afraid of this new Razov. Not afraid for himself, but afraid that his mentor, his idol, would crumble further in front of his very eyes. 'It will take some time for arrests, then summary trials, then—'

'Zorin,' Razov said in a tired voice. 'Execute Zorin and his men, and put the tapes on television.' Razov seemed thoroughly deflated, and Filipov took the orders as his cue to leave. 'And Pavel,' Razov said, 'start making contacts with the American news media. I will speak to them tomorrow.'

Filipov stared slack-jawed at Razov, whose eyes were red and had lost their focus. 'See to it Mishin's Long-Range Aviation is ready to go.' Filipov nodded slowly and turned to leave. As he opened the door, he heard the click of the desk lamp and turned to look once more into the darkness of the underground room, at the sleepless Razov, sitting at his desk in the dark with a pistol lying ready at his side.

LEFORTOVO PRISON, MOSCOW
July 19, 1200 GMT (1400 Local)

Zorin heard the crunching footsteps, his ears attuned to every sound.

'Get that thing off my face!' he heard Captain Melnikov yell.

The footsteps crunched on, receding farther down the line. 'Yes, please,' he heard another of the men on his last security detail say quietly, making the same choice as Zorin.

The footsteps sounded again, this time a long, extended march away from Zorin. The fabric of the cloth hood was sucked into his mouth by his next breath, and he gasped for the air it seemed to deny him. He felt alive, every sound tingling nerve endings all over his body. Somewhere way off he could hear the faint rumble of a train, and when the footsteps came to a crunching stop and turn, he heard the sound of a faint whimper from one of the others in quaking spasms poorly controlled.

'*Tselsya!*' the army officer commanded, and Zorin heard the rattle of rifles in unison.

Suddenly, Zorin heard no sounds but those from the prison courtyard. He took a deep breath, bowed out his chest and raised his chin from within the black sack covering his head. '*Ple-e-e-e!*' was shouted from the distant officer. Terror gripped him for an instant before the sledgehammer blows hammered his chest, abdomen, and cheek. Consciousness drained from him, and he was gone.

PHILADELPHIA, PENNSYLVANIA
July 19, 1300 GMT (0800 Local)

The President's breakfast was laid out before him on his desk with the propriety of a four-star restaurant service. Lambert's mood was upbeat – the first good day since . . . He shut it from his mind.

'Okay,' the President said with his mouth full, wiping his lips with a thick linen napkin, 'shoot. How goes Operation White Knight?'

'Very well, sir,' Lambert said. 'Just after sunset yesterday evening, which occurs at about eleven o'clock at night local time during the summer in the far north, two Ethan Allen-class attack submarines delivered one hundred and twenty men from Naval Special Warfare Unit One onto the Kola Peninsula northwest of Murmansk. Four hours later, the remainder of NSW Unit One together with six battalions of the 7th and 11th U.S. Special Forces Groups – about four thousand men – and Navy SEAL Teams Two and Four seized a beachhead at the landing site just outside Liinahamari. Shortly afterward, the first of sixteen thousand marines and sailors of the 4th Marine Expeditionary Brigade began landing and are right now pushing inland along the Swedish border against light resistance.

'At the same time, sir, Royal Marines began landing on the opposite side of Murmansk also against reported light resistance, and the 82nd Airborne Division's 505th Airborne Battalion dropped behind the city straight out of Pope Air Force Base. We tried to do everything we could from the Continental United States for strategic surprise. The Strategic Projection Force's 57th Air Division of six B-52Hs departed Chicago's O'Hare Airport and is bombing right now between Murmashi and Murmansk to keep the Russian Garrison in Murmansk buttoned up. Another eighteen B-52Hs out of New Orleans International Airport will pick up the harassment/interdiction after the 57th departs the target area.'

'When do the rest of the ground forces go in?'

'The Division Ready Unit of the 101st Airmobile is going in by helicopter from marine landing ships as we speak, and 1st Battalion/75th

Ranger Regiment has taken an old World War Two-era airfield that our Special Forces units visited last week and is apparently still in usable condition because the climate prevents excessive vegetation buildup.'

The army and marine officers exchanged looks and then laughed.

'What's so funny?' the President asked wiht a smile, clearly anxious for amusement and diversion from Lambert's terminally dry briefing.

The army colonel cleared his throat and said, 'Well, sir, it's just that there was some high grass' – he chopped at his legs with the blade of his palm as his face contorted with a laugh barely held in – 'about knee-high.' He burst out laughing now, as did the other officers who were in on the story. 'So we parachuted' – he laughed like a schoolchild trying to tell his first joke – 'I'm sorry, sir.' The President was beaming, waiting. 'So we parachuted the Green Berets back in ahead of the Rangers with these John Deere riding lawn mowers.' He collapsed into laughter, and Lambert and the President both laughed also.

'You mean to tell me that there are Green Berets riding around on John Deere lawn mowers in the dark on a deserted Russian airstrip?' the President asked, and as the apoplectic army officer nodded, the President rolled back in his chair howling with laughter.

'Anyway,' Lambert said, feeling like a spoilsport but racing against the clock before the President's new appointments secretary stuck his head in to rob Lambert of the President with the briefing only half over, 'anyway, sir . . .' The unruly crowd didn't seem to be getting back into the briefing. 'To try to wrap it up, sir,' Lambert said, glancing at his watch, 'by the time the first heavy equipment goes in later today – the 82nd's division armor and the remainder of its three brigades – they should have a major airhead operational to the south of Murmansk.

'Then, in three days, we'll begin airlifting the 7th Light Infantry Division in. Following that, we've got another thirty-two thousand marines and sailors who'll mate up with the First Maritime Prepositioning Squadron out of ports along the Norway coast and the former NATO-designated Marine Amphibious Brigade whose supplies were prepositioned onshore in Norway.' The appointments secretary stuck his head in the door and pointed at his wrist. 'It's the 24th Mechanized Infantry Division, however, that we expect to do the main heavy lifting on the road south all the way to St Petersburg. They'll be followed in about two weeks by the 194th Armored and 197th Mechanized Infantry brigades from their respective training schools at Fort Knox and Fort Benning. We've restaffed the training schools for the incoming recruits with army retirees who've been recalled to duty.

'That'll put the entire XVIII Airborne Corps ashore by early August,' Lambert said as the President rose to walk over to the suit rack where his jacket hung. 'And the allied forces will bulk up our forces significantly.' Lambert looked at his notes and spoke hurriedly. 'One corps of Royal Marines, one armored division from the British, plus

the one regiment of Special Air Service and two parachute battalions that are already engaged. Then, of course, in about ten days the Finns will take the two Russian border garrisons farther south when they "come out of the closet."' The President was brushing his coat with a lint brush. 'Once they commit, the Russians will have to concern themselves with the Finnish border just north of St Petersburg. The Finns don't constitute an offensive threat, fielding the equivalent of about four Eastern European divisions, but when the Polish Amphibious Assault and Airborne divisions get put on the border in southern Finland, the Russians will have to respect that pressure point and divert some of their resources.'

'Good, good, good,' the President said, tugging at the lapels of his coat as he straightened the jacket's lie. 'All sounds according to plan,' and then he was off to a stormy meeting with labor leaders and a delegation from the Federal Labor Relations Authority over the Executive Order canceling all vacations, sick and maternity leaves, and other excused absences from work.

'Mr Lambert?' the President's personal secretary said as he left the office. 'I have a FLASH call to you from the director of the NSA. You can take it on line seven,' she said, pointing to the telephone on the end table of the small waiting area.

'Lambert here,' Greg said on picking up.

'Greg, this is Bill Weinberg. You're not going to believe this one.'

'What?'

'About ten minutes ago we intercepted a call to the NBC News bureau in New York, and then a second and a third a few minutes later to the CBS and ABC bureaus in New York, and we're currently monitoring one to the CNN studios in Atlanta. All the calls appear to be coming directly from the Kremlin, Greg. From your old pal Filipov, as a matter of fact.'

'You're kidding. What do they want?'

'It appears they want to set up a television link through a German telecommunications satellite. At ten o'clock Eastern Time tomorrow, Razov himself intends to address the American people.'

'Jesus Christ,' Lambert said, feeling a chill of excitement and hope. 'Did they say what the subject matter would be?'

'Not a word.'

There was a pause. 'Are you thinking what I'm thinking?' Greg asked, his expectations skyrocketing.

'Let's keep our fingers crossed.' Lambert could sense the smile on Weinberg's face. *We won*, Lambert thought. *It's over.*

LOS ANGELES, CALIFORNIA
July 20, 0300 GMT (1900 Local)

'The excitement is building in anticipation of the address,' the NBC anchor said as the picture cut from him and the two commentators with him to the screen with multicolored bars and lines. Melissa herself was chilled with anxiety as she watched, waiting. 'What you're seeing now is a test screen that is being broadcast live from Moscow Television directly to us via satellite. In a couple of minutes, we expect General Yuri Razov, the commander in chief of the Russian High Command, in what will surely be a historic moment not only for television but for our two nations, no matter what he has to say. Jim,' the anchor said as the screen switched back to the studio, 'you've been noncommittal. What do you think he's going to say? Is this the olive branch that so many of us have been led to expect?'

The silver-haired man couldn't help but smile. 'It would make sense that an offer of peace comes at a time like this. The U.S. Army appears to have broken cleanly through the defenses at the Russian border and is in a headlong rush for Moscow. Although the Russians have sizable forces remaining, most are tied down in the east facing off against U.S. and Chinese armies in Siberia. Their other forces in Europe have yet to really do anything, which has led the military experts with whom I've spoken to conclude they can't get the supplies through to mount any major operations. You add to that the Third Front in Karelia in the far north, the secession of Yuzhno-Sakhalinsk, Tyumen, and Irkutsk – major oil-producing regions in Siberia – from central Moscow control, the surrender of Russian forces in the Kuril Islands to the Japanese Defense Forces, and the Russians surely must know that it's just a matter of time. It may therefore be the point to cut a deal.'

'Oh, ple-e-e-ase,' Melissa said, burying her clasped hands between her knees as she sat arched forward on the edge of her seat. 'Please-please-please-please.'

'But why take the unusual step of this television address?' the anchorman asked.

The analyst shrugged. 'He'd have to think he could cut a better deal by going over President Costanzo's head directly to the American people. If he were, for instance, to propose some sort of timetable for mutual nuclear reduction with a quid pro quo, the President would have a tough time politically if he decided to press the military options and U.S. casualties were to mount significantly. The polls have already shown some flagging support for the almost unconditional surrender demanded by the administration, and some polls for the first time are showing support for the war falling below the fifty percent level.'

'We go now to General Razov,' the anchorman said abruptly, and

Melissa's heart leapt at the sight of the man in full dress uniform, medals across both breasts, in front of the ornate yellow walls of the Kremlin room. The picture was fuzzy – it was old NTSC standard, not high-definition television to which she had grown accustomed.

'Citizens of the United States,' the heavily accented man began slowly in English, and Melissa raised her clasped hands to her face, pressing her thumbs to her lips as she sank back into the sofa to watch, 'my name is General Yuri Razov, commander in chief of the Russian Supreme High Command. I come to you directly tonight for the first, and last, time with a matter of great importance.'

Melissa was already falling from her high perch of expectation. This didn't sound right. His tone, his demeanor, the look of the man himself. He did not look defeated.

'Half a century ago, our country and its people suffered destructions of which you knew little. Entire cities were reduced to rubble. Block after block of buildings that once rose to the sky were left standing no higher than a man's waist. Buried in that rubble were the people of those cities. Millions died.' He paused, and Melissa shook her head weakly in silent plea for him to stop. 'It cannot happen again.'

She took a deep breath and sat up. 'A conventional war, carried into the streets of our great cities, would destroy those cities as certainly and as horribly as would a hydrogen bomb dropped directly into its center by your warplanes. Despite that fact, which is well known to your leaders, it is, it appears, the plan of your government to carry the war onto the streets of our capital, Moscow.' Again he paused, and Melissa's gaze fell to the floor before the next words. 'This we will not allow.

'I have, therefore, just issued the following orders to the commanders of our ballistic missile submarine force.' The Russian general picked up a piece of paper as Melissa watched through the tears that flooded her eyes. 'If American ground forces cross Moscow's Okruzhnoye Koltso, the loop road that rings the city' – Melissa heard through the blurry vision – 'or if any of your country's forces threaten the imminent attack of our submarines in the Kara Sea Bastion,' Razov said as Melissa sniffed and began to bat her eyes to clear them, 'the commanders are to launch their missiles at preprogrammed targets. Those targets,' Razov said as Melissa rose from the sofa, 'are five hundred and thirty-six U.S. military installations around the globe and the following additional "countervalue" targets: New York City, one hundred and three warheads; Los Angeles, ninety-two warheads; Chicago, eighty-one warheads.'

Melissa walked around the sofa to the writing desk in the kitchen. 'San Francisco, seventy-one warheads; Philadelphia, sixty-seven warheads.' Melissa sat at the desk and opened the drawer above her knees. 'Detroit, sixty-three warheads; Boston, sixty-two warheads; Washington, D.C., sixty-one warheads; Dallas, sixty warheads.' Half listening, she began to fill her largest purse. 'Houston, sixty warheads;

Miami, fifty-one warheads.' In her purse she placed the thick envelope of ten- and twenty-dollar bills held closed by a rubber band. 'Atlanta, forty-three warheads; Cleveland, forty-two warheads.' Melissa dropped their passports, birth certificates, social security cards, and computer disks with financial data and tax returns into the open purse, her vision totally obscured now by tears. 'Seattle, forty warheads; Minneapolis – St Paul, thirty-nine warheads.' Melissa sniffed and wiped her face as she pulled out the thick bundle of photographs – from her earliest childhood through college, the honeymoon, Matthew's first days – and dropped them in also. 'St Louis, thirty-seven warheads; Baltimore, thirty-six warheads.' She closed her eyes and reached deep into the back of the drawer. 'Pittsburgh, thirty-five warheads; Phoenix, thirty-five warheads.' The pistol fell from her hands into the purse on top of the photographs, and she pulled the straps to close the heavy bag.

'Tampa – St Petersburg, thirty-one warheads; Denver, thirty warheads,' Razov read as she hoisted the bag onto her shoulder for the walk upstairs to wake and dress the baby. 'Cincinnati, twenty-seven warheads; Milwaukee, twenty-six warheads,' she heard as suddenly the windows rattled. 'Kansas City, twenty-three warheads.' The draperies lit with flashes like lightning in the early evening and the glass shook again. 'Sacramento, twenty-one warheads.'

Melissa ran out onto the back deck of their house and listened to the thunderous booms from over the hills. Bright flashes lit the wispy clouds above as the bombs – she was sure that was what they were – shook the air around her even at great distance. Off to her right, one of her new neighbors stood on his deck with a camcorder hoping, she assumed, to catch a shot of the Russian bombers. His wife came out and shouted, 'What are you doing?' – her hands filled with an ice chest that she hoisted into his grip for hasty delivery around the side of the house, presumably to their car in front. She saw Melissa and waved once before running back inside.

Melissa went back in to get Matthew. 'Orlando, eleven warheads; Salt Lake City, ten warheads.' A high-pitched beeping on the television caught Melissa's attention, and she stopped to look at the screen. 'Rochester, ten warheads; Nashville, ten warheads.'

The text of a message, like a weather advisory when a storm threatened, rolled by on the bottom of the screen. 'Memphis, ten warheads; Oklahoma City, nine warheads.'

Melissa read the text of the message as Razov's deep voice droned on. 'Los Angeles Civil Defense authorities have advised Channel Five that a Russian air raid is currently under way. It is *not* a nuclear attack. To repeat, this is *not* a nuclear attack. Citizens are advised to remain calm and not to venture from their homes or use the telephone lines except in cases of emergency.'

Melissa shook her head in disbelief as she heard the *crump* of bombs and the rattle of the clock on her mantel. 'Greensboro, nine warheads; Birmingham . . .' The TV and all the lights went dead as a boom rolled over the hills. In the darkness, she went upstairs to get her baby.

PHILADELPHIA, PENNYSLVANIA
July 20, 0315 GMT (2215 Local)

'I appeal to all Americans,' President Costanzo said as Lambert watched from behind the television camera, 'to be calm in the face of such evil threats by our enemy. Our nation is at war, and that war requires a maximum effort by all Americans, soldier and civilian alike. It is the belief of many analysts that the threat issued by General Razov is merely a ploy to sap our productivity and weaken both our recovery from their perfidious attack and our support of our fighting forces.

'Already, our Gross Domestic Product has suffered in a manner disproportionate to the losses in the disaster sites as workers have chosen to remain away from their homes, away from their jobs, out of fear of renewed Russian attacks. For those of you who now join the ranks of the fearful, I beg you to consider your country and return to your jobs, and I also want to make this point perfectly clear.'

The director cued the man behind Camera 1, and the President waited for the zoom to complete the close-up shot and the director to cue him to continue. 'The only people in whose hearts fear should rage are those few military dictators who preside from the Kremlin like terrible tsars of the past, for they are tempting the gods when they issue their threats. But if it is threats in which the commerce of our day traffics, let me add to that commerce one that all the world should heed.' Again he paused. 'If Russian missiles should once again be launched at our nation, at any part of our great but bloodied country, let there be no doubt that I will, on warning of such attack alone, order the annihilation not just of Russia's military-industrial complex and its repressive military government but of Russia itself. Its cities, its culture, its economy, and, yes, with heavy heart, its people. Let there be no mistake, General Razov. You will lose Moscow one way or the other. It is up to you whether all of Russia is taken with it.'

'Well, obviously, sir,' General Thomas said, 'I think we ought to reconsider our plans.'

'Solely because of Razov's *threat*?' the President asked as if Thomas too were one more person to be convinced of the threat's hollowness.

'Mr President,' Thomas said staring back at the President, who did not bat an eye, 'if Razov is telling the truth . . . if he orders those subs to fire . . .'

'And what would you have us do, General, at this point? Just stop? Stop, when the Russians have an entire army group being withdrawn from the Far East that is due to arrive in Europe in a few weeks? You said yourself that the introduction of those forces to the defense of the Moscow region could force us to halt our current drive, until our European theater troops are reinforced. Reinforced from where, General? We have only a few National Guard and Reserve units left stateside to commit. Do we form the new draftees into units – just send them over instead of patching them into existing units and throw them against prepared defenses? Or do we wait, wait through the Russian winter, all the while under the threat of nuclear attack from those Russian subs?'

'It's a political question, sir,' Thomas said.

Costanzo nodded. 'We're at that brick wall again, are we?' He looked down the table and began polling the civilians – the Secretary of Defense first. 'What should we do, Arthur? We've known all along that those submarines were down there. Here we are maybe five or six weeks away from taking Moscow, fifty thousand killed and wounded in action to get here. Are we going to stop based on Razov's threat? Do we back down now?'

The Secretary of Defense shook his head. 'It's a damn tough call.' He shook his head again. 'If only we knew whether he was bluffing.'

'Well, we don't know,' the President said, angrily looking to the Secretary of State. 'What do you say we do, Leonard?'

Again there was hesitation, anguish over the question, but the Secretary finally said, 'I don't see how we could stop now.'

The President nodded, polling the director of the CIA, the head of the NSA, the director of White House Communications, others. By the time the President approached Lambert, the answers had fallen into a pattern: men and women telling the President what he wanted to hear. 'They're bluffing,' the Vice President said just to Lambert's right. 'They wouldn't dare fire those missiles. They know what we'd do to them.'

Lambert thought the President wasn't going to ask him as he looked at the Secretary of Defense, waiting for the man to jump onto the bandwagon. When the Secretary said nothing, the President said, 'Greg,' without looking his way. 'What do you think?'

'I think we should halt our advance and sue for peace.' A grin, more of a frown, broke out on the President's face as he stared at the table. Lambert prepared his arguments. It's too great a risk. Razov might just have no choice if the consensus on STAVKA developed to use nuclear weapons. But the President never looked his way.

'I've made my decision.' He looked over at General Thomas. 'We will proceed with our plans to seize Moscow with two modifications. First, before breaching their ring-road defenses, you will complete the city's encirclement, or what was that word you used when we discussed the options last week?'

'Envelopment,' Thomas said.

'Right. You are to envelop Moscow prior to entering the city. How much time does that buy us?'

Thomas said, 'About four or five days after we get to the outskirts of the city a month or so from now.'

'All right. Now I've got a meeting with the people at Labor and Congressional leaders,' the President said to his Chief of Staff as he rose. 'We've got some major damage control to undertake to prevent production from coming to a standstill. That speech I just gave isn't going to do shit.'

'Mr President,' the Secretary of Defense spoke up, 'you said there were two modifications to our plans for attacking Moscow.'

'Oh, yes,' Costanzo said, turning to Admiral Dixon, the Chief of Naval Operations. 'I want it timed so that when the army goes into Moscow, you go into the Bastion.'

LOS ANGELES, CALIFORNIA
July 20, 0320 GMT (1920 Local)

'Los Angeles city authorities are pleading with its citizens to remain calm,' the radio announcer said as Melissa tried unsuccessfully to pull into the tiny space between two cars in the left lane. Interstate 210 heading up into the San Gabriel Mountains was jammed. 'Their pleas don't seem to be working, however. We go now to our KRZY traffic helicopter.' A car horn blared, startling Melissa, who turned to see a family pull up next to her and pause to glare at her before continuing on.

They were gone before she could find her own horn so she gave the car's rear bumper the finger as it disappeared from view behind a large truck just ahead.

'This is Chopper Man aboard the Party Copter hi-i-igh over West L.A., man,' the familiar voice of the rock station's drug-addled traffic reporter came over the sound of his helicopter, almost all of the dopey 'Cheech and Chong' routine gone from his voice. 'It looks like all of the freeways leading out of Los Angeles are parking lots, man: I-10 is backed up all the way from Pomona into town, man, and the same from I-5 all the way out to Irvine.'

'Is there any route that you would say is better than others, Chopper Man?' the DJ asked.

'Well, for those of you who loaded the van up with, like, guns and liquor and soybean seeds, it looks like some of the roads heading north up to the San Gabriels are still clear.'

Melissa moved forward about two feet, barreling down the 'clear' road and still trying to edge out into the left lane. Matthew stirred, and she held the bottle to his lips. He latched onto it without opening his eyes.

'Bats! Bats are attacking L.A., man! They're hu-u-uge! News flash! News flash! Radioactive bats from Riverside attack L.A.!'

Melissa wanted to change the radio station, but with one hand holding the bottle she saw a small opening between the two cars coming down the left lane. She turned the wheel in anticipation, edging the nose of her car to the left.

'All right, Chopper Man,' the DJ said, 'just take a deep breath, man. It'll be over soon.' The bottle slipped from the sleeping Matthew's lips just in time for Melissa to put both hands on the wheel and begin her move into the open space. The car coming down the left lane slammed on the brakes and then edged forward to cut her off – a family station wagon with gear strapped down to their roof and covered with a tarp. They weren't going to let her in, and as Melissa began to cry – the nipple spilling milk as she held onto the steering wheel with the bottle turned on its side. The woman in the passenger seat said something to her husband, and the man waved her over.

'Thank you,' she said, squeezing into the lane. 'Thank you,' she waved, realizing that they had seen the bottle. *The bottle,* she thought, slipping it into the elastic pocket by the door for future use.

'And now, a blast from the past!' the DJ said. 'The year was 1992. The song, "She's Unbelievable." This is KRZY, your station for Golden Oldies!'

Up ahead Melissa saw the mountains as she crept along at five miles per hour. Between her and her refuge there stretched, bumper to bumper on the three outbound lanes for as far as the eye could see, ten thousand cars.

PHILADELPHIA, PENNSYLVANIA
July 22, 0300 GMT (2200 Local)

'I would like to ask everyone other than the principals to clear the room,' the director of the CIA said in a raised voice.

There was a brief commotion as papers were rustled. Because the clearing of all but the principals had never been requested before, the 'Wallflowers' – senior aides and advisers both military and civilian – rose uncertainly, staring at their respective bosses to ensure that this request applied to them, then slowly streaming from the room.

As the door was closed behind the last of the departing aides, Lambert looked around the table at the 'principals': the secretaries of State and

Defense, the directors of the CIA and NSA, the Joint Chiefs of Staff, and the President and Vice President, all of whom sat in silence waiting for the CIA director to explain his request.

'In the early morning hours today, Moscow time,' he began, 'a foreign-national operative whom we maintain in residence in Moscow picked up a package that our Seoul station had been informed would be left at a "dead drop." The package contained a letter, in Russian, giving us the last known location of a stray Russian ballistic missile submarine that we had reported as a probable kill. I forwarded the list to the CNO.'

Admiral Dixon said, 'So that's where you got that data.' He looked at the President. 'A P-7 got a positive MAD, Magnetic Anomaly Detection, just west of Meighen Island in the Arctic Ocean and launched a torpedo attack. The submarine surfaced on fire with a massive reactor leak, broke up, and sank before we could get Search and Rescue to them. All hands died, including the twenty-four who made it to life rafts but were dead of radiation poisoning by the time of our arrival.'

'So we've got an agent on the inside?' the President said.

'We're not so sure,' the director of the CIA said, and the President waited while the director dialed the combination into a lock on a black leather pouch and pulled a thick red folder from it. 'The main thrust of the letter – the whole point of it, in fact – was to tell us that the warning passed to us previously by Filipov about the submarines' fail-deadly orders was for real.'

'What do you mean "for real"?' the President asked.

'Let me read for you the English translation of one excerpt.' The director found the passage for which he was looking and grasped the edge of the page by it with his thumb. '"The ultimatum that was broadcast to your country from STAVKA stated that the order to fire missiles from the Kara Sea Bastion *would be* given."' The director looked up and said, 'The ending putting the Russian verb into the future tense was underlined by the writer.' He resumed reading. '"The orders have, in fact, already been given. Our ballistic missile submarines in the Kara Sea received nuclear control orders that your nuclear strategicians call "fail-deadly." Unless recalled, those submarines will fire their missiles under either of two conditions. They will fire if so ordered, or they will fire if attacked."'

The director looked up. 'He goes on to say that the target package given in Razov's address is accurate, and that more information will follow.'

'Who is this source?' the Secretary of Defense asked.

'His code name is Damocles.'

'You mean like the Sword of Damocles?' Lambert asked, and the director nodded. 'I guess that's appropriate,' Lambert said. 'The Sword of Damocles: "an impending danger that causes anxiety."'

'The source chose the code name himself,' the director said. 'I guess he's got a flare for the dramatic.'

'But who the hell is he?' the President asked.

'We don't know. We suspect, however, that Damocles is nothing more than a STAVKA disinformation program. It's clear that STAVKA wants us to believe that the submarines have a fail-deadly policy. We discussed that at length after Colonel Filipov's meeting with Mr Lambert just after the war began.'

'But if we keep getting intelligence that there is a fail-deadly policy in effect,' the Vice President asked, 'shouldn't you reevaluate your assessment that it's improbable? Maybe they really *do* have orders to fire if attacked.'

'But we have only one source,' the director said. 'Filipov, Damocles – we believe they're both mouthpieces for STAVKA. They aren't separate, mutually confirmatory reports. The Russians' GRU boys are playing to a very simple psychological phenomenon that if you hear something enough times you begin to believe it, even though, if we're right, it's just the same thing being repeated over and over by the same source.'

'And that's *if* this Damocles is who you think he is,' the President said, 'and not some modern-day Oleg Penkovsky.'

'Our profiles people did a run on who he might be,' the CIA director said. 'Assuming Damocles is for real, then profile's composite says he is more likely than not to possess most of the following attributes.' The director turned to another page in the folder. 'Young, meaning under fifty. Western-oriented, meaning he's not one of the "Red-Brown" coalition of anti-Western xenophobes. Speaks English, which is based upon the use of one American idiom set out in quotation marks in the text – "that's the ball game" – which he used when he said that no matter how well our conventional forces perform, if the Bastion fires, "that's the ball game."'

A charge of electricity shot through Lambert, and he sat up. General Thomas looked over at him as the director continued. 'Finally, a recent or impending professional setback or adversity along a career path within the military or security establishment, meaning the guy is disgruntled. In addition, he is almost certain to have or be the following. Access, obviously, to classified information at the highest levels. Damocles would be Russian, of course, and not an ethnic minority. And he would be male; there is no reported instance among Western security agencies of Russian females having any inclination to embark upon a program such as this.'

'Does anybody fit that profile?' the President asked.

'We're waiting on a block of computer time later tonight to run—' the director began, but Lambert interrupted.

'Pavel Filipov,' Lambert said, and all eyes turned to him.

The director shook his head. 'We discussed Filipov, naturally.' He shook his head again. 'He's a good soldier. He does what he's ordered to do. The fact that he may satisfy some or most of the profile does not make him Damocles, and the fact that he came to us a while back under purportedly clandestine circumstances does not make him a spy.'

'He said STAVKA didn't know about his visit,' Lambert said. 'He said he came on orders of Razov alone.'

'Has anyone here seen any evidence that there is a difference between Razov and STAVKA?' the director asked. 'Razov *is* STAVKA.'

'He lost his wife,' Lambert said, and the room fell silent. 'He lost his wife to an accidental nuclear war. His motivation is simple. He wants to avoid a recurrence, perhaps a devastatingly tragic recurrence.'

The director's voice was low, calm, persuasive. 'He was sitting right here, in the United States, in our safe house speaking directly to you. His delivery was canned. He refused to answer additional questions.'

'Look at the tape!' Lambert said. 'He used the expression, the idiom, that was used in the message Damocles delivered. He used the expression "that's the ball game"! Can't you see? He's telling us who he is, but in a way the Russians could never figure out if they intercepted the communication.'

'But if you peel back the onion, Mr Lambert,' the director said, 'who's to say this isn't part of the same disinformation scheme? We're not dealing with rookies here. The Russian GRU is as good as it gets. They don't miss a trick. Add to that, Mr President,' he said, taking his case to him directly, 'that in our entire history we have had exactly one – *one* – agent placed this highly in the Russian, at that time Soviet, defense establishment, and that was Penkovsky. We have had, however, during the Cold War *and* since literally *hundreds* of purported sources that turned out to be managed disinformation. Against that backdrop we – and I think I can speak for the NSA as well,' the CIA director said, nodding at his counterpart from the National Security Agency, 'are *not* inclined to believe *any* source, much less one that merely reiterates what we have previously assessed to be the STAVKA party line.'

'NSA would have to concur with that assessment,' the NSA director said, 'on first blush, sir.'

The President nodded. 'Okay, so this Damocles is really STAVKA. That means that STAVKA wants us to believe that the submarines have a fail-deadly policy. But we don't think that they really do, because our wargames tell us that it would be a stupid mistake to program in a fail-deadly policy.'

'Do we have a fail-deadly policy in our nuclear control system?' the Vice President asked the director of the CIA.

Admiral Dixon answered. 'In peacetime,' he cleared his throat, 'no, sir.' He looked over at the CIA director. 'But after the nuclear attack, when our principal nuclear opponent became established with such clarity, we began injecting from tapes a fail-deadly control option into the computers of Ohio-class boomers that established data links for routine computer maintenance. The update injections should be one hundred percent complete in about three weeks. The National Command Authority would have to issue an Emergency Action Message, however, to activate the control orders, but once issued the verification committee on the subs would have authority to fire at their preplanned targets in Russia under certain conditions such as nonresponsive command channels, heightened levels of radioactivity in air samples, cessation of normal civilian and military electromagnetic emissions such as radio, TV, microwave, et cetera.'

· 'But would you *use* it?' the CIA director asked. 'That's where the wargaming scenarios answered no. It's too brittle. The chance of inadvertent firing in any given month is x percent, and over y months – one minus x raised to the y power – the chances of inadvertent firing become unacceptable. Isn't that correct, Admiral?'

'I would never counsel activating the option, sir,' the Chief of Naval Operations said. 'We just put it in because we had it, and wanted to give you the widest variety of potentially relevant options. The only time it would make sense would be if we were in the late stages of a nuclear conflict and it was unclear whether or not *any* viable command structure would survive the next incoming attack. In that case, if decapitation were to be successful, then you might want the system to fail deadly. You might want the submarines to fire if over the weeks and months that followed they surfaced to find nothing left.'

'But the Russians are control freaks, sir,' the CIA director said. 'They have – they have always had, back into the old Soviet days – the most rigidly centralized command and control system in the world, *especially* when it came to nuclear weapons. Hell, that's why Zorin was able to fire in the first place. They removed all the human links in the chain down the line from their nuclear communicators. They're paranoid. They don't trust anyone. Why the hell would they program in and then actually *use* an option that delegated the authority to destroy us and invite retaliatory destruction of their own country to a bunch of completely autonomous submarine officers, for God's sake?'

The President stared down at the table trying to digest it all. 'So you think Damocles is a STAVKA disinformation campaign,' he said looking at the CIA director, 'and you agree,' he said to the head of the NSA. 'And you,' he said to the CNO, 'say we have a fail-deadly policy, but it isn't ordinarily programmed into our computers. Plus you wouldn't advise using it under all but the most extreme of circumstances.' Admiral Dixon nodded. 'And you don't think the Russians would even have a fail-deadly option,' he said to the nodding confirmation of the CIA director.

'Anybody else?' The President turned to Lambert. 'Are you persuaded, Greg?'

Lambert shook his head. 'I think Razov went behind STAVKA's back to warn us off the Bastion.' He leaned forward to put his elbows on the conference table. 'I think Filipov is Damocles, doing his damnedest at extreme peril to avoid destroying the world in an all-out nuclear war. And I think Zorin, who we've gotta remember is the nut who pushed the button on their end to begin with, screwed up not once but twice: first in firing their ICBMs at us, and then in issuing fail-deadly orders to the subs in the Bastion.'

'If he's such a nut, why didn't he just fire the missiles in the Bastion in the first place?' the CNO asked.

'Plus, Greg,' the CIA director said, 'if Razov is so damn concerned about the risk of a hair trigger on those missiles in the Bastion, why doesn't he just issue a recall?' He looked around the table. '*Any* sensible system would have a recall option built into it.'

There was silence. Finally, the President said, 'I'm sorry, Greg, but the weight of the reasoning appears to me to be on the side of discrediting the intelligence as a Russian bluff designed to scare us into backing off going for an X in the win column. You know me,' he said, turning now to look up and down the table. 'I will not be bluffed into backing off. The American people want this win, and I aim to get it. Now' – he leaned back and took a deep breath – 'let's bring all the others back in here and get down to business.'

Lambert shut his eyes. '*Please, God, let me be wrong,*' he prayed as General Starnes opened the door to readmit the Wallflowers.

Chapter Seventeen

PHILADELPHIA, PENNSYLVANIA
July 28, 0315 GMT (2215 Local)

'So this is it?' President Costanzo asked. 'A Defense Mobilization Order?' he read from the cover of the thick sheaf of paper. The Secretary of Labor nodded. 'And with this order I will be drafting all workers, nationwide, and ordering them to report to duty at their places of employment?'

'There's no other way to keep production going,' the Secretary said.

'Jesus.' The President shook his head. 'You know what this looks like, don't you? It looks just like what's going on in Russia.'

'There's no other way. Look at those industrial production numbers the Bureau of Labor Statistics just came out with. They're as bad as we feared. Down twenty percent! Only five percent of that is due to war damage; the rest is from absenteeism. And it would be worse, sir, if the workers who have stayed on the job weren't working nearly double their normal shifts, which is unsustainable over the long haul. Look at the population figures from the top ten Metropolitan Statistical Areas. More than half of the population of the ten largest metropolitan areas is living outside the cities where they're not only *not* adding to our production but are a drain on our resources.'

'But how the hell are we going to implement something like this?' the President asked.

'Temporary national ID cards for everyone over age eighteen. They'll identify the citizen as either a worker – and give their place and hours of employment – or unemployed. If employed, they are subject to arrest if authorities determine them to be absentees.'

'How will you know who is employed, and who isn't?' Lambert asked.

'We'll have citizens boards conduct interviews, with interviewees under penalties of perjury. We'll also computer match using Social Security numbers against W-2s, and we'll have employers submit lists of absentees under criminal penalties. Most people, however, are honest and will comply with the order.'

'Let me get this straight,' the President's Chief of Staff, Sol Rosen, said. 'You want the President to draft every working American, people who have fled their homes with their families in fear of nuclear war, and force them back to their jobs? And if they don't comply it will be desertion during time of war under the Code of Uniform Military Justice?'

'Well,' the Secretary said, squirming in his chair 'most of those people are still working on their jobs, and it won't have any effect whatsoever on them. And if they have a good excuse – illness, death in the family, that sort of thing – then they're okay. All we're talking about really even if they're picked up is that they'll be returned to work. The way you put it, it sounds like we'd be shooting them on sight or something.'

'I'm just putting it the way the press is going to put it,' Rosen said.

'I've got to tell you, Mr President,' the Labor Secretary said, 'if something isn't done, and soon, the pipe is going to run dry, and those stocks that our people count on are going to start dropping. Do you realize that from the time a 120-mm tank shell rolls off the factory line in the U.S. to the time it's ready to fire in a tank gun is four days! Four days! We fly the damn things over every night. Now, that's a credit to our phenomenal supply systems, but what I'm saying is: we may have the best transportation network in military history, but if the private sector can't provide the products, we might as well just paint BANG on a flag to pop out of the gun barrel.'

'The press is going to tee off on this one, Paul,' Rosen warned.

'They've done it before, and they'll do it again,' Costanzo replied.

'Yeah, but this time you're talking about something that really affects people. National ID cards? Jesus Christ, what's next – national police?'

'Is this even constitutional?' Lambert asked.

'My legal staff tells me no,' the Secretary of Labor said. 'But they also tell me that the Supreme Court knows the score. They'll slow-play this one all the way up from the district court. We won't get a ruling until after the war.'

'All right,' the President said. 'I've made my mind up.' He pulled out his pen. 'Where do I sign?'

DISPLACED PERSONS CAMP, GORMAN, CALIFORNIA
August 4, 2300 GMT (1500 Local)

'Thank you for meeting with us this morning, Mrs . . .' the old lady looked down through her reading glasses at her paper, '. . . Chandler.'

'They told me that I needed an ID card to get food,' Melissa said, fuming over being rejected at the mess hall for lunch and then forced to wait, unfed, for three hours in line for the interview. Matthew squirmed and cried out, and Melissa shifted him from one sore shoulder to the other, glaring at the five-person citizens board in front of her.

'You do realize why you're here, don't you?' the old man to the old woman's left asked.

'To get an ID card so that I can eat,' Melissa replied, wondering incredulously at why none of the five 'citizens' seemed to be under eighty years old.

'It's so that we can determine whether you're an "absentee,"' a third octogenarian said.

'Now we're going to ask you some questions,' the first old lady said, 'and you do understand, of course, that you are under oath.'

Melissa just stared at the woman, who waited unsuccessfully for a reply. She cleared her throat and asked to see a driver's license and credit card. Melissa handed them over, and a clerk began to type.

'Now, Mrs Chandler, are you currently employed.'

'Yes.'

The old lady looked at the man in the middle. 'You are telling us that you do have a job?' he asked.

'Yes. What part of my answer lost you?'

The man nodded. 'What kind of work do you do?'

'I'm a lawyer.'

'A lawyer,' he repeated.

Melissa stared back at him. She was about ready to explode, but felt she was doing a fairly good job of controlling herself.

'What kind of law do you practice, dear?' the old lady asked, unperturbed. 'Wills, divorces, things like that?'

'Mergers and acquisitions.'

'O-o-oh!' she said, smiling at her colleagues.

'Would you give me my fucking card?' Melissa snapped. 'I'm starving!'

'Now we'll have none of your profanity, young lady,' a previously silent man chastised.

'Give me my card,' Melissa said, enunciating each word.

'You, missy, are an "absentee,"' the man in the very center said, filling out a form that sat in front of him.

'I, Grampsy, am on maternity leave.'

He chuckled, staring back at her over the page that he held up in the air in front of him. 'All leaves are canceled, Mrs Chandler. All vacations, all sabbaticals, all leaves of absence of any kind whatsoever other than acute illness.'

She stared back at him, incredulous. 'So you're drafting me?' she shouted.

'We're not drafting you,' the man said, 'the President is.'

'And you think I'm going to trundle on back to L.A. with my newborn son and wait around to be blown to smithereens?'

'In some families only the workers have been going back into the city, and they're joining their families for the weekend,' the first old lady supplied helpfully, obviously a policy she felt more comfortable suggesting. 'Is there a Mr Chandler, dear?'

'He's in Europe, fighting the war.'

'O-o-oh,' she said.

'Being that as it may,' the old man in the center said, 'you've got a job, and so we've got to report you as "employed."'

'I quit.'

'What?'

'I don't have a job, because I quit. Right now. I'll sign whatever papers you want. There! Are you happy now? I'm unemployed, now where's my unemployment check?'

'It doesn't work that way,' the man said. 'There's no quitting after June eleventh. If you were employed on June eleventh, you're employed today. Now I remind you, you're under oath. Were you employed on June eleventh?'

'Look, you might as well throw me in the draft-dodging jail or line me up in a ditch and machine-gun me or whatever it is you do with people who are incorrigibly addicted to life, because I am not going back into that city – no way, no how.'

'It's not up to us, Mrs Chandler,' the man said. 'It's a matter for the police.'

'Come on! Look, do you think my job is vital to national security? How many mergers and acquisitions do you think are going on right now in L.A.? And I have a six-week-old baby to take care of.'

'We could give her a dispensation,' the old lady said, almost whispering the last word.

'Gloria!' the man next to her snapped.

'What's a dispensation?' Melissa asked. 'I want it. Give me a dispensation.'

The man was trapped between the stares from Melissa and Gloria, and he looked from one to the other and then at the rest of the board, finding no easy out. 'Oh, all right!' he growled. 'But you have to keep this under your hat, you understand me, missy? We're gonna give you a dispensation for hardship on account of your baby, but don't you go blabbin' this all around 'cause we can jerk it just as quick as we can grant it, you understand?'

'Yes, sir'

The typewriter clattered for a few seconds, and then they presented her with her ID. 'Okay, young lady, you're officially in the U.S. Army on special *unpaid* leave with the rank of private. Now go get yourself some chow.'

PHILADELPHIA, PENNSYLVANIA
August 8, 1100 GMT (0600 Local)

Lambert swung the door, but just before it closed, it banged into his secretary. 'Why don't you just kick me in the teeth next time?'

'What now?' Lambert said, waving his hand across the papers spread all over the office, covering every square inch of his desk, chairs, and sofa in neat little piles. Yellow tabs were stuck onto each pile with one- and two-word descriptions of what lay underneath. 'I've got about two weeks' worth of reading to do today.'

'You've got a visitor,' she said, her voice rising on the last word as if he would be cheered by the interruption.

'I intentionally cleared my calendar to catch up on these reports. Now, I don't care who's out there, just blow him off.' She stared back at him unmoving. 'Well, what would you have me *not* read?' He picked up the pile of papers nearest him on the rumpled blanket under which he had slept every night since they had gone aboveground. 'Maybe this: "Russian Anti-Satellite Threat to Manned Shuttle Flight"? Or this,' he said, bouncing the thick report off the sofa to point at the one next to it, '"Risk of Radioactive Contamination of Ogalala Aquifer from Disaster Area Run-Off"?'

'You know, you really need to work on your people skills if you want to grow up to be President.' She held the door and lightly swung it against her nose, her face only half visible behind it.

'Who is it?' Lambert asked, frustrated.

'Nancy Livingston.'

'President Livingston's daughter?'

'The one and only,' the secretary said before disappearing, not bothering to wait for him to respond.

When the young woman came in, Lambert almost didn't recognize her. Her hair, normally shorn short on one side, was growing out and she wore jeans and a T-shirt instead of the floor-length skirt and black leather jacket.

'Miss Livingston,' Lambert said, shaking her hand and making room for her to sit in a chair. He walked around behind his desk and sat. 'What can I do for you?'

Looking at her as she sat slumped in the chair, he felt like her grandfather.

'I wanted to ask you for a favor,' she said, with no hint of either animosity or friendship in her voice. 'You know, I've read about you in the magazines and newspapers and all, and you seem like you're an okay guy. And I'm sorry about your wife and all.'

Lambert nodded at her. She sat up, her shoulders still hunched over and her hands squeezed between her knees. 'It's just Mom and Dad.'

She looked up. 'They went home to New York, you know, to their apartment.' Lambert nodded but realized, feeling guilty for it, that he had not known what had happened to President Livingston and the First Lady. Nancy looked down again. 'Well, it's just, well, they, like, dismissed the Secret Service people after the Russians threatened to nuke us again, and decided that they'd just stay in Manhattan, you know.'

Lambert nodded.

'And I was just wondering' – she was on thinner ice now, and uncomfortable – 'well, Dad is always saying how much . . . well, I mean, he thinks you're a good guy. A good, you know, whatever it is you do. He thinks you're good at it, and, well, he likes you. They both do.'

'You want me to call your dad and see if I can talk him into leaving the City?'

She shrugged, looking at the ceiling and opening her mouth to speak but just dropping into a huff, her shoulders caving in about her again. 'I don't think they'd leave with just a phone call,' she mumbled.

'You want me to go up to New York?'

She looked up, hopeful.

'You know, of course, that we're trying to keep people from leaving their homes,' Lambert said, thinking of the spin the press would put on it if they caught wind of the story. '*National Security Adviser Quietly Advises Former President to Evacuate*,' he imagined the headline to read.

'Nobody's paying any attention to that. I mean, get real. Everybody's seen those pictures from the war sites.' She smirked. She was in her early twenties, but she looked younger just then. 'You're from New York, aren't you?' she asked, and Lambert nodded. 'The article said your dad is, like, some big stockbroker or something?'

'Investment banker.'

'Are your parents still in Manhattan?'

Lambert shook his head. They had talked to him about the situation after Razov's ultimatum, and they had left for Maine where Lambert's brother and sister and their families had joined them. All of them worked in the financial industry; his brother an analyst, his sister's husband a merchant banker. They just hooked up their computer modems to the phone and avoided absentee status as they watched the market plummet.

'All right, look,' Lambert said, leaning forward in his chair to rest his elbows on his desk. 'I've got a trip to the U.N. next week for the debate on their relocation to Ottawa. I'll give your parents a call – I've been meaning to anyway – and try to stop by and see them.'

She smiled, sort of – baring none of her teeth – and stood to leave. It was just then that Lambert realized why he felt so drawn to the girl, so interested in what she was wearing, the way she looked. For weeks, now, his only contact had been with military and civilian workers, none of whom was from the real world, from the world as it now was outside their cloistered existence. He rose and walked around the desk.

'Excuse me, Miss Livingston?'

'Nancy,' she said, holding her hand out and giving him one vigorous handshake before dropping her eyes.

'If you don't mind me asking, what's it like out there? I mean, what are people saying? What are they doing? What's life like?'

She shrugged. 'Well, I dunno. When they finally let me get off that ship after the nuclear attack, I hitched a ride across the country.'

'You hitchhiked across the country after the nuclear war?' Lambert asked, astonished.

She looked up for a second to show him the face she made before looking back down at her shuffling feet. 'Not really hitchhiked. I rented a car in Palo Alto.'

'And drove across country to New York?' She nodded.

Lambert shook his head, but she didn't see it. He felt like reaching out and pulling her chin up, but instead just repeated his question. 'What do the people think? I want to know. I need to know.'

She looked up at him when he said that, intelligent blue eyes flitting across his for a second before they skirted off to stare to the side, her head still raised. 'They're scared, mostly. They're pissed off and all, at . . . at the Russians' – *and your father*, Lambert thought – 'and they want to win the war, but they're scared that . . .'

'Scared of what?'

'You know,' she said, her head dropping again.

'What?'

'Armageddon,' she said in a voice barely audible.

90TH STRATEGIC MISSILE WING, WARREN AFB, WYOMING
August 12, 2100 GMT (1400 Local)

Stuart could hear his breath hissing through the gas mask as he climbed. His flashlight swung across the metal wall of the cylindrical access shaft. NO LONE ZONE was stenciled on the wall marking the point of the Launch Control Center below which no personnel had ever been allowed to be present alone.

Stuart could see the shaking flashlight on the wall below, the light produced by their last batteries dim, as Langford followed him up. Rung after metal rung they climbed.

Finally Stuart reached the large metal hatch on the side wall. He put his flashlight under his armpit and raised the Geiger counter. It immediately began to click. The light rain of particles picked up noticeably when he waved the receptacle past the hatch, but the ferocity of the radiation detected had died down noticeably in the two months since the attack.

Stuart looked down at Langford.

'Let's do it!' Langford said, his voice muffled through the gas mask.

Stuart hooked the handle of the device onto a higher rung of the ladder and reached out to grab the large wheel on the door with both hands. The wheel moved with surprising ease due to its diameter, but with each turn it emitted a whining metallic squeal. After a quarter turn, the hatch popped open slightly with a deep metal clack, and a handful of sand trickled down the wall of the shaft. Stuart pulled the hatch open all the way, and even more sand fell.

He reached into the side tunnel and began to scrape the sand out by hand. It fell down onto Langford, who ducked his head against the downpour. The soil was soft, and with every plunge of his gloved hand another ledge collapsed in an avalanche. Stuart dug until he had uncovered the pole that had been buried in the escape tunnel.

He pulled the pole back, and another wall of sand broke and slid to the tunnel floor. Working the pole back and forth he loosened huge volumes of sand and scraped it out of the tunnel into the shaft. From behind, Stuart heard the clicking of the Geiger counter and turned to look at Langford. Langford swung the wand toward the tunnel and the clicking turned into a steady buzz.

Fuck it, Stuart thought, and he turned and jabbed vigorously at the sand. A ray of light suddenly blazed into the tunnel and caught him by surprise.

Stuart stared at the bright light. It had been so long that he had forgotten just how different natural light was from artificial illumination. They clawed at the last of the sand without speaking. Finally Stuart crawled out the end of the steel tube and stood up on the earth's surface.

There was nothing. Anywhere. Langford stood up beside him. He turned on the Geiger counter, and its buzz was so steady that it sounded like a hum.

'Let's get outa here,' Langford said, and they began to jog to the southwest, as agreed – the shortest distance to the edge of the base and opposite the direction of the wind on the day of the war, according to the meteorological printout on their teletype.

The grass crunched under their feet as they ran. It was not just dry: it was ash frozen in place. Each step sent a puff of dust flying out from under the soles of their overshoes. They passed the foundation of the Alert Maintenance Facility. There were some fixtures and wiring protruding from the cement pad, and the stubs of walls clearly demarked the various rooms, but there was nothing else. Rubble was strewn all around but it was unrecognizable.

They ran in silence for what had to be almost a mile. Stuart and Langford now both labored for breath in the hot suits. Although he had been fit before the war, Stuart now felt lightheaded and faintly nauseous from the exertion.

After ascending a gentle hill, one of the few elevations within the huge base, they stopped to rest. Two round, black overlapping disks – craters – lay just ahead. 'Number Four,' Langford said, but the Number Four Silo was not anywhere visible, sealed somewhere under the thin layer of black glass into which the silicates in the top-soil had melted.

Stuart looked back around from where they had come and slapped Langford with the back of his hand. A charred crater dug into the earth several hundred meters to the north of their launch center. Similar craters dotted the landscape all around for as far as the eye could see across the scoured and scorched terrain. At Stuart's feet, however, he noticed a green shoot of grass, the first sprout emerging from the post-nuclear plains of Wyoming. *There's still life*, he thought staring at the slender blade.

'Come on,' Langford said, and they resumed their jog down the hill, skirting the crater directly in their path. Sweat poured from Stuart, and his boots made a squishing sound in their overshoes. He licked his lips under the mask, but the salty sweat did nothing to quench his thirst.

Mile after mile they jogged, slowing finally until they were running at a pace no faster than a brisk walk. Back down on the flat Wyoming plain, they saw the twisted remains of the base's fence ahead at quite a distance. As Stuart lowered his head, his mind began to wander. *How much radiation are we absorbing*? He didn't worry about it; he just wondered. He mentally calculated their time exposed and decided that it shouldn't be too bad yet. Maybe higher cancer risk years down the road, but nothing to worry about now.

What's out there? Did they hit the cities? Has the government survived? Has America survived? How many people? He thought about all his relatives and friends and where they lived. Close friends, old college girlfriends, whoever came to mind – he arranged all by city and probability of survival.

The fourteen-foot-high cyclone fence was seared black and bent and twisted at tortured angles. Stuart and Langford simply walked over it gingerly, and resumed their run away from the radiation.

They saw their first car half an hour later. It was off in the distance, but it turned off the two-lane highway toward which they headed and sped down a dirt road, kicking up huge quantities of dust behind it. Stuart and Langford both had the same idea, and Langford pulled the Geiger counter from his belt. Langford hit the power switch just as the car disappeared behind a low hill ahead. The device was nearly silent except when waved over the two men's dusty protective gear.

They removed their suits, which were coated in radioactive ash. A second car headed down the narrow road and squeezed by a canvas-covered army truck that it met coming in the opposite direction. Stuart hiked the pistol belt and holster higher up onto his thinning waistline and they both began to run again, this time much more briskly. The cool air against Stuart's sweat-soaked uniform and filling his lungs felt incredibly refreshing. They headed straight for the hill beyond which ran the road that carried so much traffic for such a remote area.

As they climbed the hill, Stuart's spirits were rising. They had watched as more trucks, cars, even buses came and went down the highway in the distance. There were lots of people, and they would soon be among them. Stuart dug his toes into the dirt of the uphill slope despite the cramping of his calves.

They topped the hill and stopped in their tracks as they looked down on the scene below. Row after row after row of bodies lay in the dirt. Lone men and women and small groups of people walked among them, paper surgical masks on their faces. They were viewing the bodies, many of the distorted shapes clearly not more than just pieces of bodies, it appeared from that distance, and here and there among the thousands of corpses was a collapsed woman with friends comforting her or a single man kneeling in front of a corpse. But mainly it was just a parade of people slowly walking by the dead, looking but not finding, searching but not wanting to find.

Langford headed down. Stuart started to call after him but knew he wouldn't hear. Langford had a family in town.

NEW YORK, NEW YORK
August 15, 1800 GMT (1300 Local)

'Can I make you a drink, Greg?' Walter Livingston asked in a jovial voice.

'Oh, uh, no, thank you.' He walked into the large apartment, his Secret Service detail remaining in the marble foyer, looking at the lavishly decorated sunken living room with corner views out over the park. 'This is a really beautiful place.'

'Oh, well, thank you,' the First Lady said, beaming as she fluffed up a pillow that lay against the armrest. She placed it back on the sofa in its correct place against the corner of the seat back. *No maids*, Lambert realized. *Everybody is gone from the City.*

'I don't suppose you had any trouble with midday traffic?' the

President asked smiling, shaking a mixer containing martinis for himself and his wife.

Lambert laughed. 'No, sir,' he said, shaking his head and taking the seat to which the First Lady directed him.

'Bet we could get a court no problem,' Lambert heard coming from the hallway as the President and First Lady took up places around him.

'I just ran. It's too hot.'

'C'mon, Nance!' Nancy Livingston appeared in the room toweling her hair, stringy from the shower, with her brother Jack nipping at her heels. 'We can just go right across to the city courts and play one set.'

They saw Lambert, and Nancy turned and said, 'It's too *hot*,' in a low voice.

Jack Livingston, the President's son, glared at Lambert, slipping the earphones of his CD player on his head and heading back toward what must be the bedrooms. Nancy walked past the living room and into the kitchen. Lambert saw the First Lady sitting on the edge of her seat, turning first to see that her son had disappeared and then to look at the kitchen door, where her daughter was rattling around. The First Lady smiled at Lambert, obviously calculating how best to manage the problem social situations regularly caused by her children.

'So, Greg,' the President said, licking the spilled martini from his fingers as he settled in. 'How goes it? Tell me everything.' He sat with his back away from the cushions, leaning forward and ready to talk. Lambert grew anxious, knowing he had only a few minutes and that the President was ravenous for news.

Nancy plopped onto the sofa next to her father, a bowl of grapes in her lap and a towel draped modestly around her neck to cover the front of her thin T-shirt. 'Mr Lambert, you have met our daughter Nancy, of course,' the First Lady said as Nancy crossed her barefoot legs underneath herself, placing the bowl in her lap and feigning a quick smile at him, not baring her teeth. Out of the corner of his eye he could see the First Lady, wearing a dress and pearls, looking at the girl who wore baggy khaki shorts and on whose faded shirt was a picture of a plateful of food held in two bony hands and the caption 'Visualize World Peas.'

'Good afternoon, Miss Livingston,' Lambert said as she brushed a wet strand of hair back from her face and dropped the first grape into her mouth.

'Well,' the President said, 'are we going for Moscow?'

Lambert considered the classified nature of the information he possessed and the propriety of a social chat on the subject of war plans, but he knew that the answer was obvious and that the President was just breaking the ice, and so he said, 'Looks like it. We took Kaluga yesterday, and we're knocking on the door at Tula.'

'Any sign those tanks in Ryazan are going to make a move?'

'It's beginning to look like they're out of gas,' Lambert said. 'They've been positioned to the southwest of the city in what looks like an "armored pillbox" defense.'

'God bless those carrier boys in the Black Sea, hey? They really cut those oil shipments from the Caucasus.'

'They did at that, sir.'

'What about the other fronts? What about Siberia?'

'We're just south of the Khor River about fifty miles south of Khabarovsk, which is of course their Far East Army Command headquarters. We're also sprinting up the coast from Vladivostok virtually unopposed and are crossing the Samarga River today.'

'What about Sakhalin Island? Did the local Russian commanders just roll over and play dead?'

'Well, there have been some scrapes along the way, but most had more to do with the Russian Army commanders calling themselves the new Sakhalin Defense Force and demanding to retain their arms, or outright demands for money for the weapons, than anything like loyalty to Moscow. As we go into all those little towns on Sakhalin, our people are reporting that even the Russian soldiers and airmen are hungry. When the people with the guns can't keep themselves fed, you know the unarmed civilian populace is in bad shape. It's that way all across Siberia. Russian government has just broken down, and the loyalties to Moscow among the rank and file draftees of the army on Sakhalin, a lot of whom were recently rotated from the Chinese front and are pretty war weary to begin with, is at a fairly low level. They were ready for somebody who could give them three hot meals a day.'

'What about in the north – Karelia?'

'They're going at it tooth and nail in Petrozavodsk today. That's the largest city left before St Petersburg itself.'

'Are you going to try to hook up the Karelian Front with the troops in the south?'

'They're still a long way away. If this thing drags on, then we probably will try to open the road through Novgorod, but right now it's a tough row to hoe just to get down to St Petersburg.'

'What about the Polish and Finnish troops? Any chance they'll come down from southern Finland?'

'Not right now. The two Polish divisions are very light infantry – an amphibious assault and an airborne division. And the Finns can only field about the equivalent of four infantry divisions. They're doing their job – tying down about an equal number of Russian motorized infantry divisions – but it's pretty much a push. The armored and mechanized infantry divisions the Poles sent into the semiautonomous Kaliningrad Oblast did a really fine job, though, and they're tying down four Russian divisions in Lithuania, two of them armored.'

'I don't guess that British air power had anything to do with it?'

Lambert laughed. Livingston really had been following things closely, he realized. He noticed the comfortable-looking but out-of-place leather armchair off to the side of the room, a muted television set playing on in front of it and newspapers spread all around. It was a far cry from the Oval Office briefings.

'What about "The Ultimatum"?' the President asked with a voice suddenly gone lifeless. Lambert frowned. 'Let me guess. CIA and NSA think he's bluffing.'

Lambert looked up and gave Livingston the most subtle of nods.

'And if they're wrong? Does Costanzo have any tricks up his sleeve for that contingency?'

Lambert shrugged.

'So they're just going to go charging into Moscow – and into the Bastion too, I suspect – and call his bluff? My God, that's just a massive game of chicken: just see who swerves first!'

Lambert needed to look at his watch, but he resisted the temptation. 'Sir,' Lambert said, looking up, 'don't you think it would be . . . prudent to consider relocating? Maybe heading up to your place in New Hampshire?'

'So that's it?' Livingston snapped, his old fire burning through his hospitality. 'Just clear out in case Razov's serious. That's the plan? Have you talked about a formal evacuation?'

'Yes, sir, it's been discussed. Over sixty percent of the big-city population is already in the countryside anyway.'

'And you know who's left, and who would always be left despite how much effort you put into any evacuation. The underclass. The tenements full of people who've never been more than ten city blocks from their homes in their lives. And the National Guardsmen, police, firemen, city workers, and all the others who are needed just to keep the cities standing in case the Russians don't blow them to pieces. And what about the workers that Costanzo is drafting?'

'All the workers in noncritical jobs would be relocated.'

'So how many are we talking about remaining behind if there's a formal evacuation?'

'A report by FEMA and the Census Bureau estimated five, maybe eight percent,' Lambert replied. 'A few million, maybe ten million people.'

'And then there's radiation.'

'The relocation camps are mostly placed upwind of the likely targets,' Lambert said. 'Assuming the prevailing winds, of course.'

Lambert felt Nancy staring at him. He looked over at her. She tilted her head and shook her hair away from her face, meeting his gaze with a stare.

'Sir,' Lambert said, 'it just makes sense to play it safe. If you don't have to be in a major city when the time comes, *if* the time comes, why put yourself there? And there is your family, sir.'

'Oh, I'm sending them to their uncle's ranch in Montana.'

'Sending?' Nancy said, and then she laughed, popping a grape in her mouth. 'You're "sending" me somewhere?' she said, smiling and arching her eyebrows. 'To Uncle Bill's ranch, no less?' She laughed again.

'You have to go, because Jack won't go otherwise,' the First Lady said. 'We've told him he needs to take care of you, to talk you into going.'

Nancy stared at her parents, and they stared back.

'Sir, wouldn't it make more sense if you and Mrs Livingston went to Montana with—'

'Give it a rest, Mr Lambert,' Nancy said, still staring at her parents. 'They're as pigheaded as they've ever been, both of them. Nobody can tell them anything they don't already know.' She looked over at Lambert. 'All that crap about the underclass not being evacuated from the city. They were saying that a week ago. You wanta know what else they were saying? Why it is they won't leave New York?' She turned back to look at her father. 'Tell him. Tell him your great reason to stay here and get fried to a crisp. Tell him.'

Livingston looked at Lambert with a humorless expression. 'Because it's that underclass, those poor people, who voted for me all along from the Congress right up to the Presidency. It was those poor people who have never been more than ten blocks from home, according to all the polls before the impeachment, who stood by me to the end. They were the six percent who still had a 'favorable' impression of me.'

Lambert hung his head, then looked up and said, 'You know that everyone will do everything they possibly can to keep it from happening.'

'Everything except one thing, Greg. Everything except the one thing that will work. Everything but swallowing their pride and backing down before it's too late.'

TWELVE MILES SOUTH OF CHEKHOV, RUSSIA
August 21, 1400 GMT (1600 Local)

Almost every bump slammed Chandler into something hard or sharp. Sweltering inside his chemical protective gear on MOPP Level IV, he scanned the radioactive landscape through the cupola's vision blocks. Although the gas turbine engine could produce its rated 1500 horsepower burning diesel or gasoline, it was currently effortlessly turning at 22,500 RPM on aviation fuel from their last fill-up and pushing them along at forty miles per hour over the rough terrain. He was constantly shaken, and the lenses of his gas mask were fogging from his sweat and from the general dampness of the water-soaked suit following decontamination at the last Maintenance Collection Point.

Need to get the mask filters changed again, he reminded himself. *They should have collected a fair amount of fallout by now.*

He felt miserable and confined, made dirty by the repeated radioactive contaminations despite the prompt washes. It made sense they would pick lines of advance that were awash in fallout. The Russians could not defend them with trenches of Provisionals, at least not for long. But he felt unclean and wanted to pop the hatch and stick his head up, to get fresh air and to get a feel for his surroundings. Chandler had been in armored combat in the M-1A1 now long enough to know that the old adage was true: 'If you can see it, you can kill it.' But outside, the terrain was black and packed hard by the near-ground-level burst, and despite the passage of time since the nuclear phase, the NBC-1 report that Bailey's Scout Platoon had worked up indicated fifty RADs per hour. If they stayed buttoned up, with the separate air system just for the crew compartment filtering the radioactive fallout from the air and the thick armor shielding direct radiation, they'd be fine. No heads stuck out on this ride, at least for the next ten miles.

Chandler struggled to maintain his vigilance to his front and flanks. Although he felt fairly safe sprinting across ground zero, they were exposed to fire not only from the front but at the weaker armor protection of their sides as well. Brigade had laid two lines of M-718 antitank mines, fired ahead of their tanks by artillery, to form a corridor through which they advanced. Those mines and a couple of helicopter gunships were the sole protection on their flanks. They had to hurry not just because of the radiation but also because the mines were set to self-destruct shortly after they had passed to prevent risk to follow-on troops. Chandler would've felt better if he and Jefferson were in their hatches as usual with binoculars to their eyes looking for threats.

Buttoned up inside, Chandler was able to see only the occasional scorched stump of a tree or foundation of a farmhouse rush by. *No infantry here. This was high speed country – no stopping, no dismounting.* He glanced down at the torn and crinkled map he had folded and refolded numerous times as they advanced progressively to the northeast. He was thrown again into the wall of the turret, unable to brace himself for the undulating terrain ahead when looking down at the map.

Looking back up, Chandler saw out of the corner of his eye a break in the landscape, an irregular line. He traversed the turret to look directly at it through the gunsights just as the M-1 smashed into the slight rise of a dirt road at a steep angle and caught air. Chandler's helmet slammed into the hatch above his head with a loud thwack and then he floated in air, his knees rising off the seat on which he had knelt. The sixty-three-ton tank fell back to earth with a crash.

The sophisticated hydromechanical suspension system of fourteen road wheels under the tank's armored skirt, together with the steel torsion bars and sixty-three square feet of track area, absorbed most of the blow, but Chandler came down hard on his knees and slipped down to the deck of the crew compartment, pain shooting through the small of his back. Sweat, shaken loose from his brow by the fall, now stung his eyes and blurred his vision, but there was no way to get through the mask's lenses to his eyes to rub them clear so he batted his eyelids repeatedly. His headache from lack of sleep was joined by the new ache in his back. With the gunner's help, Chandler climbed back up to his perch to resume his watch.

Looking out to the right, Chandler saw a jinking missile rapidly approaching, barely three hundred meters away.

'*Driver ri-i-ight!*' Chandler screamed into the open intercom and then felt himself thrown to the side, his helmet smashing on the left wall of the cupola, spraining his neck. '*Missile – missile . . .!*'

A deep *THO-O-O-NK* from just outside the tank and a vibration that Chandler felt clearly through the armor left him holding his breath, waiting.

'*Je-e-ezus!*' the driver said. 'Man! That was fuckin'—'

'Gunner!' Chandler shouted, staring down the length of thin wire that had controlled the missile, which glinted in the sun all the way back to the BTR. 'Battlesight – twelve o'clock! BTR! Loader, load HEAT!' Chandler yelled, ordering the High Explosive Anti-Tank round to be readied for firing.

'Cannot identify!' the gunner yelled.

'From my position!' Chandler replied, seizing the pistol grip, the Tank Commander's Override, and quickly spinning the turret around to center the cross hairs on the object he'd seen earlier: a low, bulky armored fighting vehicle covered by a camo net.

'Up!' Jefferson yelled, and the gunner added, 'HEAT!' to tell Chandler that he had reset the gun's computer to the new round's ballistic profile. A small puff of smoke from the target shot out and from it emerged a small missile jinking up and down before settling in a path straight at Chandler's tank.

The gun and its sight were absolutely still despite the continuing bounds of the tank. Chandler laid the cross hairs right onto the middle of the BTR's metal side and locked it on as the missile closed the distance.

The battalion net was filled with reports of contact with BTRs and BMPs, but no tanks. As the antitank missile passed the halfway point, Chandler lazed the target with the neodymium YAG laser range-finder. Mounted high on a column at the rear of the turret, weather sensors fed wind, temperature, and humidity to the tank's computer. The digital solid-state computer, armed with those data and the tank's speed, now constantly fine-tuned the aim of the gun.

'On the way!' Chandler yelled and squeezed the trigger. The main gun let loose its HEAT round with a *WHA-A-A-NG!*

The target exploded almost instantly despite its range of fourteen hundred meters, and the second missile spun crazily into the dirt hundreds of meters short of Chandler's tank. A new, much larger secondary explosion from inside the BTR tossed the camo netting high into the air and knocked the BTR onto its side, its body a roman candle of pyrotechnics shooting horizontally across the earth.

'*Got it!*' the gunner yelled, having watched through his own sight.

'Cease fire,' Chandler said, exhausted and jittery from the tension.

Seeing one of Delta Company's Bradleys streak through his field of vision, Chandler said, 'Get back up there with Alpha Company,' and the driver turned left to continue their high-speed run at Moscow.

Chandler pulled back the tank tarp, uncovering the dead men. There were six of them – all tankers. All of them were burned horribly, some of them dismembered – their body parts placed roughly in their correct positions relative to the torso. Chandler let the tarp drop. He was exhausted. It was difficult to feel for the men who lay dead under the plastic shroud at his feet. More dead men. He was just going through the motions of visiting all the dead and wounded that he could during lulls in the fighting. Off in the Tactical Operations Center, Loomis, the battalion Executive Officer, was completing the details of the mission plan that Chandler had discussed in broad details with the company commanders and their XOs. Next, he knew, would come the S-1 with personnel matters, the S-2 with the intelligence briefing, the S-3 with the operations plan, and the S-3 Air with the air support plan. Finally, the S-4 would brief everyone on the most important topic of all, resupply, which was mainly where to link up for refueling.

He walked away, passing a small green device about the size of a bread box. The Chemical Alarm, sniffing, constantly sniffing. Sniffing for death in the air. There had been no chemical attacks since the first, but who knew what was coming. Things were bad – the ugliness of it predominated all his recollections of the fighting – but it could get worse. A shout from a single canvas-covered truck that was being unloaded at the bottom of the hill drew Chandler's attention.

'Mail's here,' Barnes said at his side. Chandler looked up to see Barnes staring intently back at him. 'Division Postal Detachment.' Barnes eyed him up and down. 'We got some new two-strand – WD-1 – and some D-cell batteries. Should we string the 312s?'

Chandler shook his head. They had been using the old TA-1 sound-powered telephones instead of radios when not on the move to reduce electromagnetic emissions that might pinpoint their position.

They were out of batteries for the newer model field telephones, the TA-312, and they had also gotten the last of the double-strand wire required by the 312 chewed up by treads. But the battalion was moving out shortly, Chandler decided, and stringing the wire was not worth the time or effort.

'When we move out, should we back off MOPP Three?' Barnes asked.

Chandler tried to make his mind work. MOPP IV was all gear on. If the bread box's shrill buzz, which was audible for half a mile, went off, they'd go to MOPP IV or die trying. MOPP III, which they had been on for hours – suit, gloves, and boots on but mask carried – was hot and draining. He thought about ordering MOPP I and having everybody take everything off, if only to allow the men to scratch the million nagging itches under the thick suits and damp, dirty clothing.

'Take us down to MOPP II,' Chandler said – suit on, boots, gloves, and masks carried. It would take twenty seconds for a tanker to get to MOPP IV from MOPP I inside the confines of a tank – *too long, too many dead*, he decided.

Chandler looked down at the two M-1s that lay in the flat pasture below Hill 422. One tank was charred black in several spots, the blowout panels missing on the back deck, the hatches blackened, and one ugly hole on the side of the turret. The other tank, however, appeared unscathed, still neat and green. The only thing unusual was that its hatches were all thrown open.

'How're the two men from that one?' Chandler asked, pointing to the heavily damaged tank with the missing blowout panels – the only one from which survivors had emerged.

'One's pretty bad,' Barnes said. 'Pro'bly lost a leg, if he makes it. The other one – I don't know. Didn't have a scratch on him, but he could hardly breathe. He was coughin' and red faced and . . .' Barnes just shook his head.

Metal fume fever, Chandler thought, nodding. At the enormous temperatures of penetration, the exotic metals that armored the vehicle burn and are highly toxic if inhaled. And then there was blast lung from the pressure of the hit. That got some. And spalling – molten metal knocked loose by the kinetic energy of the impact, becoming shrapnel in the enclosed space. The guys from that tank in Bravo Company bought it that way. And . . .

'You should get some sleep, sir,' Barnes said looking at him. 'We got an hour or so till stand to.'

How long had it been? Chandler wondered. *He had been in combat for five and a half weeks. He hadn't slept more than a couple of hours at a stretch the entire time.* 'Okay,' he said, and he walked down the slope to his tank, weaving his way between the Russian hulks littering the ground where they had been caught, just short of Hill 422. Chandler's task force had rained death down upon them from the hill – the M-1's superior vehicle speed allowing it to attain the high ground first. Each of the kills was now chalk-marked with a big X on the hulks indicating that the vehicle had been checked and was 'secure,' occupants still lying inside, no longer their enemy.

Almost every M-1 he passed was still also, its crew asleep. Each platoon had designated one man from each four-man tank crew to clean the main guns, and here and there men were manhandling the twenty-foot-long rammer in and out the length of a depressed gun barrel.

'*The horse, the saddle and the man*,' Chandler remembered the old cavalry principle. His vehicles had all been refueled, reloaded, and cleaned before the infantry and tankers had lain down on the ground around them. They were just sleeping, but an odd chill came over him as he saw them lying completely still, some twisted at uncomfortable-looking angles.

He paused and looked carefully at one of the men whose chest rose and fell slowly in deep sleep, then walked on toward his tank. When he got there, Jefferson and the driver were lying by the treads sound asleep.

Chandler went around to the front of the tank. A long black streak to the right of the driver's hatch marked the point of impact of the antitank missile that had been their only near miss. It had hit the thickest armor of the tank, the glacis, along the extreme angle of the glacis's slope and had discharged its warhead harmlessly.

He brushed the black streak with his fingertips and rubbed the soot between his fingers. Snapping out of the fog, he lay down on the dry grass next to the tank and closed his eyes. His head hurt as if ice picks were jammed into it, and he felt a scratchiness in his throat warning of a coming illness. He began to drift off, but a shot of adrenaline woke him when he began to worry whether Loomis was still on the net. *And I didn't look at the companies' positions*, he remembered. *Surely they put out OP/LPs.*

He opened his eyes with effort and raised his head to look around. The infantrymen on the slope of the hill lay asleep on the ground. *Nobody's dug in.* His head fell again of its own weight, and his eyes sank closed. *I need sleep*, he thought. *I can't even see straight anymore.*

But rest would not come. With a frustrated sigh, Chandler willed himself to his feet and headed off to find the companies' Observation Posts, staggering as he drifted in and out of sleep.

SPECIAL FACILITY, MOUNT WEATHER, VIRGINIA
August 24, 1300 GMT (0800 Local)

'Podolsk has fallen, Mr President,' General Thomas said. 'That puts the lead elements of V Corps' 3rd Armored Cavalry Regiment about eighteen miles south of the Moscow suburbs, which they will reach, in all probability, sometime in the night, Moscow time.'

'The army's orders then, sir,' Lambert jumped in, 'are to begin the envelopment of Moscow, all the while skirting the main defensive belts surrounding the city. We will leave the Noginsk road open for evacuation of Moscow as you directed.'

'*And* for resupply,' Marine General Fuller groused. 'Hell, sir. If we're gonna go in there and get blood on our hands, we oughta do it right. We oughta go on and close the noose.'

'I don't want Razov feeling like a trapped animal,' the President said. 'I don't want to back him in there and leave him no avenue for escape.' The President looked at each of the National Security Council members present, clearly intending to reinforce the point. 'Now, what about St Petersburg?'

'Same general plan, sir,' General Thomas said. 'Skirt the defenses and envelop. Our people have taken Tosno and cut the main rail line between Moscow and St Petersburg. They'll cut the last road link to Moscow on the twenty-sixth. Our timetables put the lead elements at the Baltic Sea by the thirtieth.'

'Are there any signs of movement from any of the independent Russian forces in the field?' the President asked. 'From the army groups in the Baltic countries, or from the south or east of Moscow?'

'None, sir,' Lambert answered. 'We feel fairly confident that we can hold off any moves from the south of Moscow with the National Guard's VII Corps. The Moscow operation, Operation Crown Prince, is therefore secure. And neither DIA nor CIA think the independent army group in the Baltics has the POL or spare parts to make a major mechanized move.'

'And everything is quieting down in the Far East?'

'Ever since Khabarovsk fell, the Russian resistance has practically collapsed. We're done on Sakhalin Island, as you know, and we're pushing west along the Trans-Siberian Railroad north of the Chinese border. Along the coast, the marines are moving north and report little more than a rear-guard action by the Russians.'

'I think it's time to consider calling a halt in the Far East, sir,' the director of the CIA said. 'Have you seen our proposal for Operation Bent Sword?'

'You mean rearming the Russians to hold off the Chinese?'

'Yes, sir. We're going to find ourselves in a pretty pickle if the PLA decides it's time to resume the offensive. Are we going to defend Russian territory against the Chinese?'

'We can't afford, politically,' the Secretary of State said, 'to use nuclear weapons in Asia again, Mr President. Everything we do there now is going to be under a microscope. We have to watch our p's and q's if we hope to fashion any kind of security arrangement after the war to prevent the collapse of Russian rule in Siberia.'

'That's a problem for another day,' said the President. 'Right now, I want to know if we have any indications that the two army groups at the Urals are moving?'

Thomas opened his mouth to speak, but he looked at the director of the CIA instead and remained silent. The President followed his eyes. 'You want to talk about it now?' the President asked.

'I think now is the appropriate time.'

'All right,' the President said, sitting upright in his chair at the head of the table. 'I'd like to ask,' he said, raising his voice and looking at the Wallflowers in the second row of chairs away from the conference table, 'if everyone other than the principals could please leave the room. Thank you.'

There was a brief commotion as papers were rustled. The clearing of all but the principals was now becoming common, and the colonels and senior advisers rose quickly to file from the room.

'Okay,' the President said as the door to the nearly empty conference room was closed behind Colonel Rutherford, the last of the departing aides. 'Someone want to tell me about this Operation Samson and why I shouldn't be scared shitless by it? Jesus Christ, if it's for real . . . A Russian plan to fight an all-out, city-busting nuclear war with us? Evacuation of their cities. Dispersion of their troops and productive plants. Temporary earthen fallout shelters for seventy percent of their population!'

'Sir,' Lambert said quietly as much to try to calm the President as answer his question. 'The CIA doesn't buy Operation Samson. They're convinced that Damocles is a plant, a composite fictional agent representing STAVKA, and that Operation Samson is a plan leaked to us to lend credibility to the Russians' threats.'

'But if the Russians really were willing . . .' The President's voice trailed off. 'Is this thing, this Operation Samson, a realistic, workable plan?'

The director of the CIA shrugged.

'I can say that as far as the Joint Chiefs are concerned, Mr President,' General Thomas said, 'Operation Samson is consistent with the Russian Army's tactical doctrines for field deployment in a nuclear environment. The orders for dispersion of the two army groups at Nizhni Novgorod – the dispersion of the units over wide areas – would be appropriate to minimize their vulnerability to nuclear weapons, and it would be exactly the opposite of what you would do if you intended to move those units into contact with an enemy's ground force. To put it another way, sir, if those units begin to disperse, that intelligence will tell us two things: one, they do not plan on moving to engage us, and two, they anticipate the onset of nuclear war.'

The President's eyes sank to the table in worry before looking back up at Thomas. 'I want you to watch those units like a hawk. If they actually do start to move, to disperse, then I suppose we can assume that the Russians have put Operation Samson into effect.' He scanned the table for disagreement and then went on. 'What about the rest of the plan? Burying critical dies and molds from their factories, selective evacuations of scientists and engineers beginning already, all that? Does it sound real?'

'That's all old hat, sir,' the director of the CIA said. 'That's the point about this whole thing. There's nothing new in any of it. Dispersing units in the field; every army since 1945 has known to do that. Burying aircraft molds – big deal. Hell, we ordered Boeing up in Seattle and McDonnell-Douglas in Fort Worth to do the same after the first exchange.'

The President sat forward to the table, shaking his head before lowering his face into his hands and rubbing his tired eyes. 'I don't get it. I never have been able to get it. This is your guy, this . . . this . . .'

'Damocles,' the CIA director supplied.

'This Damocles is your source – either a CIA spy or a double agent, we don't know which. Ever since he came to you, what, a month ago, you've come in here every so often with some intelligence from this . . . this person that you tout as the God's truth. And then you come in here with *other* reports from the same source – vitally, vitally important intelligence like the fail-deadly firing policy for their nuclear submarines and now this Operation Samson – and you tell us that you discredit *that* intelligence completely.'

The CIA director leaned forward. 'You see, sir, Damocles has given us a steady stream of intelligence about the Russian nuclear capabilities and planning. Some of it's little stuff, like the locations of reloaded ICBM silos, the tanker and strategic bomber reconstitution bases, which we knew about from satellite recon anyway, and the last known locations of the three stray boomers in the Western Pacific. All the little things Damocles has given us were verifiable. But neither of the two really big things Damocles has given us – the fail-deadly nuclear control policy of the Bastion's submarines or this new piece, Operation Samson – is verifiable at all. That's the *essence* of a properly run disinformation campaign. Dribble out little stuff that the target can verify to establish credibility of the source, and then lay the completely unverifiable whopper on him.'

'But,' the President said in growing frustration, holding his hands out and shaking his head, 'how do you know which is the credibility-bolstering tidbit and which is the disinformation?'

'That's where the art of it comes in, sir,' the director said. 'Separating the corn from the chaff.'

'"SWAG,"' Marine General Fuller growled in a low voice.

'What?' President Costanzo asked.

'Bob,' General Thomas said in a cautioning tone, but the commandant of the Marine Corps sat forward and said, 'We who are on the sharp end of the stick have a term we use whenever we get "soft" intelligence and assessments like this from back in the rear areas. We call it SWAG.'

'And what is SWAG, might I ask?' the President said.

'Simple Wild-Assed Guessing, sir.'

'Is that what this is?' the President asked, turning to the CIA director. 'I've authorized an attack on Moscow *and* the Bastion that, if your "assessments" about the submarines' fail-deadly policy or Operation Samson are wrong, will result in the thermonuclear annihilation of our nation's cities. Are you just making a wild guess?'

'We've assumed, sir, that our opponent is rational. Once you make that assumption, you can play the "Game" – run it through our wargaming programs. The computers don't give a damn, sir. They'll blow everything and everybody to little bitty bits if it'll win the Game. They indicate a fairly low order of probability that the Russians either employ a fail-deadly policy or would plan anything like Operation Samson.'

'How low of a probability?'

'Well, there's some disagreement about that,' the CIA director said, looking across the table at the head of the NSA. 'We believe it's somewhere on the order of a one to five percent chance that the attacks will trigger a launch.'

'And you?' the President asked the director of the NSA.

'Fifty-fifty.'

The President slammed his hands on the table. '*Je*-sus Christ!' He stared back at the man. 'Fifty-*fifty*?'

'They're assuming, sir,' the CIA director said lurching forward to the table, 'that you believe CIA's source, the very source that we say is a plant. If you back out the weighting that they put on Damocles's credibility, then their numbers are roughly consistent with ours: two to seven percent.'

'Is that true?' the President asked the NSA director.

The man shrugged and nodded, not willing to openly challenge his colleague as Lambert had heard he had done privately, heatedly.

'So it all comes down to this Damocles?' the President concluded. 'If he's lying, if he's trying to scare us into believing a Razov bluff, then we go in there and end this thing before the collapse of our economy.

And if he's telling the truth, we get blown back into the *Stone Ages*?' The President laughed at the last words. It was not humor, Lambert knew, but nerves.

'Sir,' the Chief of Naval Operations interrupted, and all eyes turned to him. 'There's another possibility here. We've got three carrier battle groups plus three submarine, two antisubmarine, patrol and reconnaissance, and two surface combatant task forces up there in the Barents and Kara seas ready to go. That's three carriers, eight cruisers, nine destroyers, twelve frigates, and *thirty-seven* attack submarines. We're operating eighteen of our new P-7 antisubmarine and patrol planes right out of their naval airfield in Arkhangelsk.'

'What are you telling me, Admiral? That you can sink those submarines in the Bastion before they fire?'

'We can sink a whole bunch of 'em,' Admiral Dixon said, 'and every sub we sink before they fire takes about one hundred and seventy warheads with it. That's why they targeted so many warheads at our cities, Mr President. One hundred and three warheads at New York! They don't plan on actually getting those kinds of results.'

'How many submarines do you think you can sink, Admiral? How many of those twenty-two can you put on the bottom before they fire their missiles?'

The CNO sat hunched under his broad, thick shoulders, his gold epaulets bunching up against his neck as he leaned heavily on the table. 'Well, on a clear day, and if we make the first moves and have our land, carrier, and ship-based ASW planes and helicopters on station over the Bastion – and if we get submarines on the five boomers our experimental blue-green lasers have pinpointed from space – we might be able to get fifteen, maybe seventeen, clean with no missiles fired. They gotta come to a hover, which is a tricky maneuver, at firing depth just under the surface. And they've been under a long time so they'll probably stick their periscope mast up for a final bearing check before the first missile breaks the surface. That'll be visible on radar, and they're sitting ducks during that maneuver.'

'Won't you tip your hand when you go in with the aircraft and submarines?' the Secretary of State asked. 'I mean, we may have run their air force off, but the Russian Navy is still parked out there right on top of the Bastion.'

'Well, sir, we can slip the subs in if you give us a few days. I'm willing to stand by my estimates of fifteen to seventeen sunk without a missile fired. The Russian ships won't pose too much of a threat during the fifteen or twenty miserable minutes of their remaining time afloat.'

'So that leaves five to seven submarines firing,' the President said. 'How many warheads?'

'Now, we'll get some of those before they expend their full complement of missiles. Our guess – our SWAG, as General Fuller would say

– is about half of those remaining missiles would be expended. And of those, there'd be duds and flat-out misses. The Russians' submarine-launched missiles aren't as good as their land-based ICBMs.'

'But a city is not a hardened silo,' the President said. 'If one of those things misses Times Square and lands in Central Park, it'll still blow the crap out of Manhattan. What's the bottom line, Admiral? How many warheads, and how much yield, would strike our cities?'

'Assume, say,' the Admiral sighed, 'six Typhoons firing ten of their twenty missiles on average before we sink them. That's sixty missiles, about four hundred and fifty warheads – two hundred and seventy megatons. About forty percent of the megatonnage expended in the first strike.'

'And they would hit the vast majority of our three hundred largest cities,' the President said in a far-off voice.

'More or less,' the CNO said. 'We could get luckier than that.'

'What? Four hundred warheads lucky? Three hundred and fifty? Just how much good luck can I count on?'

'You can count on none of that happening at all,' the director of the CIA said.

'That's not good enough,' the President replied. 'Is there anything we can do between now and a week from today? Anybody, anything?' He scanned the bowed heads of the principals of the National Security Council, getting no response. 'So it's this or back down?' Nobody said a word. It was a political decision. It was the President's call. He rocked back in his chair and closed his eyes. *Was he thinking*, Lambert wondered, *or praying*? The silence dragged on, but nobody seemed impatient. Nobody exchanged looks. This was it. *'This is the ball game,'* Filipov's words, Damocles's words, whispered from the deepest recesses of Lambert's mind.

The leather seat of the President's chair squeaked as he rocked forward, opening his eyes. 'Okay,' he huffed. 'We go. Admiral, start sneaking your subs in when you're ready. I want you to *try* for perfection; don't hold anything back.'

'Including tactical nuclear weapons, sir?' Admiral Dixon asked.

'Yes, if you have to.' The President scanned the room one more time. 'Anything else before we bring the others back in?'

'What about crisis relocation, sir?' Lambert asked, and everyone looked at him. 'I think the time has come to evacuate the cities.'

'Greg,' the President said, 'if we announce an evacuation, the people are going to go ape shit with panic.'

He stared at Lambert, and Lambert said, 'It may just frighten the Russians enough to bring them to the table.'

'And if the only people it frightens are our own citizens?'

'Then they're frightened,' Lambert said, 'frightened and maybe, just maybe, alive if the worst comes true.' Lambert looked around. All eyes were downcast. It was as if even discussing the possibility, the possibility of death on a massive scale and the wholesale destruction of what generations of Americans had worked their lives to build, somehow tainted them all. It was like a coating of dirt, and Lambert felt it too. 'Sir, maybe the Russians don't plan on implementing this Operation Samson. Maybe it is a plant. But our troops are swinging for a knockout blow. They're headed for Moscow. This is World War Two all over again, but with one huge difference. The genie is out of the bottle. Hitler didn't have ballistic missiles tipped with nuclear warheads. Now we all know Razov isn't Hitler, but none of us knows what's going on inside the closed loop of STAVKA politics. We don't know that it will be Razov down there in that bunker in Moscow when the lights start to flicker and the sound of explosions rumble in.'

Lambert looked around the table again. He had hit a chord. They had talked about it only rarely, every time rationalizing why it wouldn't happen, and then blithely carried on as if the clock had turned back to 1945. But it had not. Even though the vast majority of the two countries' arsenals remaining after the downsizing of the nineties had been expended or destroyed in the nuclear exchange, the two countries were still locked in a death grip. 'If the missiles in the Bastion had fired at our cities in a bolt-out-of-the-blue attack one sunny day last year, FEMA says we would have lost somewhere between forty-five and sixty million dead, most from radiation deaths out to five years. Right now, with the largest cities already largely depleted of their populations and the displaced persons camps generally upwind of probable target sites, the losses would be somewhere around twenty to thirty-five million. We could halve that again by evacuating.'

The President's head began to shake from side to side. 'I can't believe we're doing this. I just can't believe it's come down to this.' He looked pale, his eyes, their pupils wide, giving him a hunted look. He took a deep breath, which he exhaled raggedly. It did nothing to steady the quiver in his voice. 'Okay, I guess the time has come, Greg. You get together with FEMA. Start the evacuation tomorrow.'

ABOARD NIGHTWATCH, OVER WESTERN KENTUCKY
August 30, 1300 GMT (0700 Local)

'Come in, Greg,' the President said. He sat at the small writing desk of his bedroom on the Airborne Command Post to which they had returned for the final stage of the war, for the attack on Moscow and the Bastion, just over twenty-four hours away. Lambert closed the door and walked up to the small group – the secretaries of Defense and State, the director of the CIA, and General Thomas.

'You called for me, sir?' Lambert asked.

'Have a seat.' Lambert pulled up a chair and sat pressed into the tight space between Thomas and the director. The President took a deep breath, and let it out as a sigh as he clasped his hands on his head. There were rings on his shirt under his armpits from several successive sweats, with a new dark spot forming in the center. He ran his hands down to his face, messing up his hair and dragging open the eyelids of his tired eyes.

Lambert quickly surveyed the faces of the other men present. They all were drawn and introspective.

The President picked up the papers before him, and the Secretary of Defense tossed a copy onto the desk in front of Lambert.

'What you've got, Greg,' the President said, 'are the terms of a peace proposal approved on an "Eyes Only" basis by the heads of government of each of our alliance partners. I apologize for not bringing you in on this earlier, but you now make' – he looked around – 'the seventh person to know about it in this country, after the people seated here, and my wife, of course.' They all laughed.

'Greg,' the President said holding the paper, 'I'm just not satisfied in going forward with our attacks on Moscow and the Bastion based on probabilities and opinions and assessments; I never have been. We've been working on this since I approved the plans last week.' The President appeared apologetic and defensive. *Eyeball-to-eyeball*, Lambert thought, *and he blinked. Thank God*.

'What are the terms?' Lambert said, looking at the multipage memo.

'We are proposing,' the President said, sitting back again and clasping his hands over his head, the dark ring at his armpits now wider than before despite the chilly air of the aircraft, 'to completely denuclearize Russia. In return, we would extend a nuclear "umbrella" – a firm pledge to retaliate with American nuclear weapons against any country attacking Russia with nukes – for a period of five years. Thereafter, we would either extend the umbrella for subsequent five-year periods or lift the cease-fire restrictions on Russian development of nuclear weapons, depending on what state Russian affairs are in at the time.'

The mind trained in law school immediately saw the flaws from the Russians' perspective. 'What about conventional attacks? The Chinese?'

'We would guarantee reconstitution of Russia's prewar borders,' the Secretary of Defense said, 'and would grant them a five-year pledge to defend Russia from Chinese aggression. That should give them time to get back on their feet.'

Lambert remained unconvinced that the Russians would go for it.

'We'll also agree to withdrawal schedules for our troops in Europe' the President said, 'but you can read those later.' They all looked at Lambert as he considered the proposal. 'Do you think the Russians will go for it?'

'How good is this nuclear pledge of ours, this umbrella? First of all, we're the ones holding the nuclear stick over their heads. We won't nuke ourselves for our own strikes against Russia. But over and above that, would we really launch nuclear strikes against another country for firing at Russia? Would the Russians believe that we would strike, say, France or Germany or Japan, if they went nuclear? What if the Russians were the aggressors? Why would they believe us when we make that pledge?'

'They don't have much of a choice,' the President said, 'do they? They'll just have to trust us. That's where you come in.'

Lambert resisted shouting '*Me?*' and instead looked around the desk at the inquiring eyes. He felt his face turn red, blushing without knowing why.

'Somebody has to take this to them,' Thomas continued. 'Somebody, preferably, who has an entrée to STAVKA. I know Razov, but I have been ruled out because the President thinks this should come from the civilian side. We could just send a grunt, a courier. Hell, we could just fax it to them, or get them on the phone.' Lambert was already shaking his head: it was far too important for that. 'But we all feel that this may come down to a sales job, and the main thing that's going to entail is cultivation of a sufficient level of trust among the Russians to cease fire around Moscow *and* to recall their submarine force.'

'You speak Russian,' the director of the CIA said. 'Our linguists say your accent sounds like a Russian comedian imitating an American tourist, but your grammar and vocabulary are adequate to go without an interpreter.'

'And more importantly,' the President said, 'we want you to make your case directly to STAVKA. You're also a lawyer, and although you have no courtroom experience, most of us here have seen you hunker down like a badger on one point or another.' They all laughed.

'But to complete my earlier comment, Greg,' Thomas said, 'we need somebody to go who has some stature, who can speak with some authority and make promises, if necessary, on smaller points that may be what it takes to push them over the top. We need someone with all the attributes that we have described, and that someone is clearly you. But there is a downside. There is a very big downside.'

'If things go sour,' the CIA director said, 'if they turn on you, out of desperation or even as a result of simple, cold decisions made according to the exigencies of their deteriorating situation, we understand that we are delivering into their hands a supercomputer,' he said pointing with his index finger at Lambert's head, 'a supercomputer filled with facts and charts and tables and plans that would be absolutely invaluable to our enemy in time of war.'

'We would temporarily suspend your clearance to any classified information,' the President said, 'to let what it is that you do know grow as stale as possible over the day or so it would take to insert you into Moscow.'

'But even so,' Thomas picked it up, shaking his head, 'even so, Greg—'

'You want me to pull the plug on the "supercomputer" if they threaten torture,' Lambert interrupted to conclude for him. There was silence. Greg thought about it for a moment. His parents, of course, would be devastated. Who else? When no one else came to mind, Greg nodded.

'We'd implant a tiny crown on your molar,' the CIA director said. 'If you exerted maximum force combined with a grinding action of your teeth, the cap would crush between your upper and lower jaws. The concoction, which is a strychnine derivative, is tasteless, but our people put a bitter-tasting additive in for confirmation purposes, and you would also feel a pretty instant numbing of your jaw, I'm told. Death would be by respiratory failure within seconds.'

Greg listened distractedly, his mind stuck on his last thought. *Absolutely no one.* He had absolutely no one waiting for him, even if he did come back. And they knew that.

'It's as much,' Thomas said, his head hanging, 'it's as much for your own protection, Greg, as anything.'

'They would come at you quickly,' the CIA director said. 'You'd have very little time before they got the chloroform on your face and you lost consciousness. While you were out cold, they'd find the crown and remove it. You'd be . . . helpless, then. They'd come at you from behind, but what you need to watch out for is—'

'Two or more men coming at me from the front,' Lambert interrupted, 'looking at a newspaper together and talking, or carrying something heavy between them, or doing anything that explained why they were so close together. One man would grab my upper body from behind and then apply the chloroform to my face, the two men approaching from the front would secure my arms, and people would speed up in a car or come out of hiding and grab my legs from the sides to carry me to a car or van.' Lambert looked at the silent group who stared at him. 'When I went to the Defense Intelligence Agency just out of school they let the analysts know when there were vacancies in CIA classes. I was in my twenties, and it seemed like a neat thing to do, so I took Evasive Driving, courses like that, at "The Farm" in West Virginia. One of the courses was Bag "n" Tag, the course on kidnapping.'

'I know, Greg,' the director said, and there was an awkward silence for a few moments. *That's another reason I was chosen*, Lambert thought. *My résumé fits the job description*:

'So I go to Moscow,' Greg said. 'I can set that up with Filipov. He's still Razov's aide-de-camp.'

'And Greg,' the President said, 'this is very, very important. If you don't contact us within two hours after you pass over to their lines, we're going to have to assume the worst and begin our assaults on the Bastion and on Moscow ahead of schedule, before you might reveal anything of value to them. Is that understood?'

'Yes, sir.'

'Just tell them you've got to call us as soon as you cross over,' the director of the CIA said. 'Two hours, Greg. That way they won't be able to act on intelligence they might have extracted from you before we step off. And when you do call in, if there is any foul play, anything untoward occurring of which you need to alert us, just say, "Would you please repeat that? I didn't catch what you said." If we have any doubts as to duress on this end, someone will ask during the communication, "Can you supply more details?" in as appropriate a place as possible. If you respond in any manner other than "I am not under any duress," then we will assume that you are and will disregard all statements made by you or by the Russians.'

'Just one more thing, Greg,' the President said, 'and this is very important too. You need to tell the Russians what we will do if they fire at us from the Bastion.' The small group fell silent, and in the stillness Lambert's skin crawled. 'If – *if* they fire at us from the Bastion, we intend to evacuate the populations of every Russian city we have captured, including Moscow and St Petersburg. We will then mine the cities with nuclear demolition munitions and destroy them. All of Russia's principal cities that we have not captured would simply be destroyed by submarine-launched missiles or bomber attack, population and all. Every last one of them. If it at all seems an issue, if STAVKA appears in any way to be considering this Operation Samson or anything of the sort, you should make those intentions perfectly clear. It's "the stick," Greg, in our "carrot-and-stick" proposal.'

Greg nodded.

'And Greg,' the President said, staring intently at him now. '*This* – what I'm telling you now – is not a bluff. I will do it, as God is my witness, I swear to you, I'll do it.' A chill washed over Lambert completely now as he stared back at the President. This was it – this was 'the ball game.'

PART FIVE

Creation sleeps! 'Tis as the general pulse
Of life stood still, and Nature made a pause
An awful pause! prophetic of her end.

—EDWARD YOUNG
Night Thoughts
Night I, line 23

Chapter Eighteen

OKRUZHNOYE KOLTSO, MOSCOW, RUSSIA
August 31, 1400 GMT (1600 Local)

'Looks like a company, maybe more,' the reconnaissance platoon leader said to Lambert and Lambert's escort as his heavy binoculars rested on the sandbags piled in front of the observation post. The fluttering of the large white flag held with some difficulty in the stiffening breeze by the soldier standing next to Lambert was the only other sound along the quiet front line. On the way up to the FEBA, the Forward Edge of the Battle Area, Lambert had passed hundreds of huge M-1 tanks and Bradley armored fighting and scout vehicles placed all along the sides of the road into the city. All sat poised under heavy camouflage netting and were surrounded by crews busily making last-minute repairs or handing main gun shells up to the turret in a human chain. He looked up at the gray sky to see the huge ledge of dark clouds coming in from the north. There was a storm gathering.

'I got movement,' the platoon leader said, and the major who had escorted Lambert up to the last observation post before the Russian lines said, 'Any vehicles?'

'BTR-80s – about a dozen of 'em – back by the road.'

Lambert looked over at the major standing beside him, whose chafed and wind-dried face wrinkled around his eyes as he squinted, looking off in the distance. 'Paratroopers' was all he said to Lambert, not taking his eyes off the Russians.

There were guns, Lambert realized, pointed at them that very second from across the few hundred meters of charred and pitted earth. *'No-man's-land.'* As the lieutenant reported the details of the disembarking Russian airborne company, as much for the crews of his platoon's heavy weapons as for Lambert and his escort, Lambert felt again the sense of missed timing, of choices made and options passed, that had led him to this place. They had been through war. He had not.

He looked down at the men in the Observation Post, which had been dug into the dark soil at the edge of the treeline and obviously improved over the few days of the 'envelopment' of Moscow to the east and west. They lay behind their weapons – one man with an M-16 atop which was mounted a massive night sight, another two behind an automatic 40-mm grenade launcher, and two men with Squad Automatic Weapons. All were filthy, covered in artificial foliage with weapons to their shoulders, their fingers on the triggers and their minds on killing.

Lambert wore a dark gray business suit. His tongue was sore from running it nervously along the new addition to his molar. The taste from his visit to the CIA dentist lingered.

All my life I've studied war, Lambert realized suddenly, *from the time I was a child. I even made it my chosen career*. But when it came time to decide whether to go into the military, he had gone to graduate school instead. He had feared most wasting his time training and preparing to fight a war – the 'big one' against the Soviet Union – that seemed virtually certain would never happen. *Who the hell would have guessed?* he thought, tracing the origins of this war, each step of which seemed so logical, almost preordained, when viewed retrospectively, but so improbable when viewed prospectively.

He looked over again at the major standing by his side. His face was dirty or tanned and leathery, he couldn't tell which. Two months of war – of World War III. *I could have done what you've done. I could have risked what you've risked. I could have seen what you've seen.*

The major looked back at Lambert. His eyes were bloodshot and glassy, his gaze focusing on Lambert for only a moment before dissolving into that look, that 'thousand-yard stare,' that Lambert had seen in the faces of hundreds of men and women on his way up to the front. They were exhausted, emotionally as well as physically. It had to end here, at Moscow. They could not go on.

I would have joined, Lambert thought as he looked back across no-man's-land toward the Russians, *if only I had known it would happen*.

'There they are,' the major said.

'Got 'em,' the lieutenant replied.

Lambert saw the white flag unfurl in the distance across the open field.

'Let's go, sir,' his escort said, and the three of them – Lambert, the flag bearer, and the major – began the slow walk from the tree-line out into the open.

They had to walk slowly because of the effort it took the soldier carrying the large flag into the stiff wind, which cut into and through Lambert's light summer suit and left him with a distinct chill. Up ahead, the Russian flag bearer was having the opposite problem, digging his heels in as he stumbled in front of the tide of cool air.

'Careful,' the major said, his hand slapping back against Lambert's chest to stop him. 'Unexploded submunitions,' he said, nodding at the small silver disk that lay half buried in the dirt. They skirted the disk and kept going, the only sound the vigorous snap and rustle of their flag's fabric. Lambert searched the charred and cratered ground ahead as did his escorts, looking for anything unusual.

As they neared the group of three Russians, Lambert glanced up to see that the man in the center was Filipov. He was wearing full combat gear.

They stopped about ten yards apart. 'Greg,' Filipov said in a raised voice.

'Hello, Pavel.'

Lambert could feel the eyes of both the major and the flag bearer glance over at him, barely turning their heads for the look. 'Come with us,' Filipov said, and Lambert walked across the open space dividing the two armies – alone.

As they walked back to the Russian lines, Filipov said in English, 'How are you doing?'

'Fine,' Lambert said. 'Busy.'

'I can imagine.'

'How are you?'

'Fine.'

Lambert tried to think of something more to say, but they walked on slowly and in awkward silence. Lambert thought the silence would hold all the way to the opposite treeline, which they approached slowly walking into the wind, but he was wrong.

'Greg, why is your country doing this?' Filipov stopped and faced Lambert.

'Doing what, Pavel? You mean the war?'

'I mean invading my country, destroying our towns and villages, killing our people?'

It was a simple question, and Lambert was the national security adviser to the President, but he could not seem to formulate an answer that was appropriate for Filipov, his enemy and his best friend. From Filipov's expectant look, Lambert realized his answer was somehow critical.

They stood in the field on the outskirts of Moscow, the capital of Filipov's country. He had come all the way across Filipov's homeland but had not asked the Russians' permission for the visit. He hadn't any need to, for the land was, however temporarily, U.S. territory now. Taken, not given, but paid for in the blood of tens of thousands and the shattered lives of hundreds of thousands more.

'If you mean the moral justification for it, I would point to the eight million Americans who have died or are dying from the grossly negligent safeguards you maintained over weapons aimed at my country,' Lambert said, sounding more bitter than he felt at first, the bitterness rising, however, with every word spoken. 'If you want the statement of a policy goal, I will say to disarm you of the nuclear arsenal of which you have proven untrustworthy custodians. But if you want a geopolitical analysis, Pavel,' Lambert said, turning to face Filipov full on, 'if you want an answer that the historians many years from now will write, it is because our two countries were bound to each other with a strange attraction, fascination mixed with mistrust. We were bound so closely for so long, war was never far away, and when it happened, we were strong, and you were weak. We win, you lose – that's the way of it.'

THE KREMLIN, MOSCOW
August 31, 1415 GMT (1615 Local)

There was a soft knock on the door of Razov's office. 'Enter!' he said, not lifting his head from the report on the U.S. naval buildup in the Barents Sea until he realized that someone was waiting on him. He looked up to see a female soldier, the same woman who had come several times before to update his map, standing at the door. 'Come in.'

She walked over to his map table. 'New data?' Razov asked, looking back down at the report.

'Yes, sir, General Razov,' the soft-spoken woman said. 'It's from Nizhni Novgorod – straight off the imager, just like you ordered.'

He glanced up at her, she was smiling at him. Razov flashed a smile back, having trouble concealing his rising fear that despite all his efforts the Americans were deploying for an assault on the Bastion.

'They said I needn't bother, but I officially went off duty a few minutes ago,' she chattered on, 'and I told myself, "Lyudmila," I said, "you'd better get these up to General Razov right away before he evacuates with the rest of them."'

'Possible sonar contacts from Sensors CX-51 and CX-27,' Razov read, flipping pages to find the sea-floor sensors on the map. He looked up at the woman, who was carefully drawing on the plastic map overlay. 'What did you say?'

She looked up petrified.

'Who told you not to update my map? And what is this about an evacuation?'

She was speechless, her eyebrows knitted over worried eyes.

Razov rose and went over to face her. 'Answer my questions.'

'I . . . it was . . . it was the duty officer. He . . . I said maybe I should come up here and update your maps, and he said no, but I was going off duty, and so I came up anyway.'

Razov looked down at the map on which she had been writing. 'What evacuation are you talking about?'

'They're packing everything up downstairs. We all just assumed . . .'

The division markers of the army groups around Nizhni Novgorod were being replaced by brigade and, in some cases, battalion markers as the unit symbols spread out over the landscape beneath the plastic. The divisions were splitting up, dispersing, and Razov had given no orders for the move. 'What the hell is this?'

The private's mouth hung open, and she closed it to swallow, but no words came out of the stricken face.

'Do you know,' Razov said in as soothing a tone as he could muster, 'why it is these units are being redeployed? Why they are dispersing?' *To be of no further use as a threat to the Americans*! he wanted to rage.

She shook her head.

Razov knew. *Operation Samson*! Someone had ordered the troops in the field to thin out. It was a major deployment. It was consistent with the details of Operation Samson, the supposed 'deception' plan STAVKA's staff had developed. He imagined how this would look on the American satellite photos. *What would their intelligence analysts conclude about Russian intentions?* he thought. The answer was so clear it sent ice water through his veins. *They'll see us preparing. Nuclear war*! 'Do you know anything?' he snapped at the woman. 'When did the evacuation begin?'

Her eyes lit up. 'The duty officer was talking last night with a general.'

'Which general?'

'I don't know.'

'What service? What uniform?'

Her eyes lit up again. 'Strategic Rocket Forces.'

'General Karyakin?'

'Yes – *yes*! They said "Operation Samson" over and over. I was working at the map while they talked, and . . .'

Razov strode toward the door, leaving her alone at the map.

Walking through the underground offices Razov saw that they were indeed being packed. He felt the eyes of startled aides standing at printers as he walked down the long corridor for the closed double doors of the conference room at the end. He burst through them with a loud noise from the latches, and General Mishin fell silent midsentence. Karyakin sat at the head of the table, in Razov's seat.

'General Raz-*ov*,' Karyakin said in an upbeat voice.

'What's the meaning of this?' he asked, although he already knew the answer.

'I'm sorry, Yuri,' Mishin said. 'We took a vote. We've decided to go in a different direction.'

'And what direction is that?' Razov sensed more than heard the approach of the two men who appeared at his elbows. He turned to look at the soldiers at either side of him. They would not look him in the eye.

'Please leave us, General Razov,' Karyakin said. 'We have work to do.'

Abramov and several of the others loyal to him were missing.

Razov scanned the table. No one returned his look except Mishin. Even old Admiral Verkhovensky couldn't bring himself to look up at him.

VARSHAVKSKOYE SHOSSE, MOSCOW, RUSSIA
August 31, 1420 GMT (1620 Local)

Lambert passed the Russian firing positions, so like their American counterparts. The Russian soldiers stared at him with white eyes gouged out of dirty faces. Small clumps of previously unseen, brush-covered soldiers rose on a sharp 'Let's go!' yelled in Russian and rushed into the open hatches of the dozen armored vehicles just behind the lines. The vehicles were lying low on either side of the blackened and artillery-pitted road and started their engines as Lambert's small entourage climbed into the open rear door of their own BTR-80.

As the ramp clanged shut and Lambert took a seat on a bench, the engine turned over and the lights came up. 'Granite Forty-two, this is Canyon Seventeen,' Filipov said in Russian and Lambert translated silently, listening. The vehicle lurched to a start as the wavering signal of a man speaking Russian answered.

'This is Granite Forty-six, go ahead, Canyon.' Lambert could barely hear over the loud whine, a storm of constant American jamming.

'Inform Granite Forty-two that our guest has arrived,' Filipov said into the microphone. There was silence. 'Granite Forty-six, can you hear me. Respond.'

'Canyon Seventeen, there has been a change. They have taken Granite Forty-two.'

The look on Filipov's face confirmed Lambert's translation. '*Vzyali*,' the word had been – the Russian conjugation of the verb 'to take' meaning 'they have taken,' only without a pronoun or noun to identify who 'they' are. '*Vzyali*,' Lambert remembered, a word at once as familiar to Russians as it was terrifying. Never '*arrestovani*,' 'arrested.' Only '*vzyali*,' 'taken.'

'Who?' Filipov asked.

'STAVKA' the response came. 'Karyakin.'

'Where to?'

'Lefortovo by motorcade. They have him downstairs right now making a videotape for broadcast on television about the change in command, and then they will take him to Lefortovo.'

Filipov signed off and looked over at Lambert. 'STAVKA has . . . has arrested General Razov.' His face was ashen.

'Do we go to the Kremlin?' Lambert asked. 'Should I try to talk to the others on STAVKA?' Filipov looked lost. 'Karyakin – he's the commander of the Strategic Rocket Forces, right? Can I talk peace to him? Is it worth a try?'

Filipov shook his head slowly, clearly in shock at the news.

Lambert grabbed Filipov by the shoulders, and his friend looked back at him. Lambert spoke slowly, enunciating each word carefully in Russian. 'Then let's go get Razov.' The vehicle's commander and gunner standing in front and a lieutenant and a half dozen men who had piled in after Lambert all stared at Filipov, who hesitated. Filipov's eyes, however, slowly focused and he closed his mouth. He turned and began barking orders to the driver.

SIX MILES SOUTH OF OKRUZHNOYE KOLTSO, MOSCOW
August 31, 1530 GMT (1730 Local)

Chandler and his men were exhausted. Twice his driver had strayed off the road onto the shoulder of the highway. Both times they had been lucky: no mines. The MPs had said that there was a belt every few hundred meters and that they had cleared only the road itself, not the shoulders or fields around it.

His battalion had been pulled off the line and sent one hundred miles over dirt roads, highways, and the streets of towns small and large down the main route of the American advance, never knowing from turn to turn whether the next copse of trees or building might hide Russian Spetsnaz waiting in ambush. The MPs never knew anything more than what the next turn was or which road to take the next few miles. When they ran through the northern edge of their last map and pulled out the new one, it became apparent where they were headed. Centered on the next map, covering the middle third in gray rather than the green and brown of rural terrain, lay Moscow.

M-113 ambulances and M-88 recovery vehicles were parked in the open along the sides of the road as Chandler's tank rolled by. The wreckage of war grew more stark and fresh the farther they drove, and when night fell the images along the side of the road became shadows to the naked eye or glowed bright green, otherworldly, in the thermal gunsights. By morning, two-and-one-half-ton trucks with canvas ripped and burned bumped along toward the rear on rims in plowed dirt tracks

parallel to the main highway. Carcasses of Russian MTU bridge tanks
and ZSU 23–4 antiaircraft gun carriers lined the shoulders, the sickly
sweet smell of decaying corpses fouling the crisp, cool air. It was the
Russian BMPs and BTRs, however, that spooked Chandler most – the
personnel carriers presumably filled with their dead cargoes.

There were few live Russians to be seen. Several times they passed
columns of prisoners, but there were no civilians. Every village was
dark, most windows smashed or boarded shut.

As the day wore on, sounds of fighting had become audible in the
distance, like thunder but not random. Soldiers gathered during a
maintenance stop to comment on the rumbles and to speculate what
they portended, while company first sergeants streamed to the rear
in search of hot food for the troops. Crews refueled their vehicles,
replacing finicky parts. And, of all things, they turned in their laundry and
got clean uniforms. Chandler delivered a SITREP, or Situation Report, to
the Brigade S-3; a LOGREP, or Logistics Report, to the S-1 and the S-4;
and then met with Colonel Harkness for a briefing. They were going
into Moscow, the colonel said simply. The objectives now were not
hills and streams and villages and road junctions, but streets and blocks
and city parks.

Chandler twisted back around on his seat, his butt itching and 'saddle
sore' from the ride. He was roughly in the middle of his task force's
road formation – Bailey half a mile in front, the trailing tank of Charlie
Company a half mile behind. The haze on the horizon was becoming
visible as individual columns of black smoke clustered around the sites
of separate battlefields. That was where they were headed. They were
headed into hell.

Chandler called the subordinates on his battalion net and ordered
them to halve their formation spread from twenty meters per vehicle
to ten. They were too dispersed for ground combat, and they would
have to risk getting caught bunched up from the air.

The breeze streamed by at twenty-five miles per hour. They had
been lucky mechanically: only two minor breakdowns. They were at
about three-quarters fuel, and had full ammunition loads. They needed
rest and a hot meal, but Chandler didn't count on getting either.

He twisted around to ensure that the formation was tightening its
spacing. When he looked back toward the front, he could clearly see
boiling orange flame from the source of one billowing black cloud of
smoke, and the first faint and familiar crack of tank cannon echoed
across the landscape. He remembered, suddenly, the day that he
first rode atop that old M-60 to the tank firing range at Fort Knox
so many years before, the sound of tank guns audible in the distance
on a hot Kentucky afternoon. The wind chilled Chandler suddenly, and
he considered breaking out his field jacket. He had never imagined in
his wildest dreams that it would come to this.

Rolling over a small hill and through another desolate village, their highway ahead crossed open brown fields of some sort of farm. The tilled soil had been churned up by the treads of the massive self-propelled artillery pieces that lay in lines on either side of the highway inside of the tennis-ball-yellow streamers fluttering from iron rods demarking the area swept of land mines. *Heavy guns*, Chandler noted, looking at the huge, thick guns pointing toward the gray sky ahead. *Corps-level battery*.

As they passed, Chandler looked at the twelve eight-inch howitzers. Mounted on the M-110A2 treads, the guns had been modified since he'd last seen them at Armor School over a decade earlier by the addition of a Kevlar and aluminum Crew Ballistic Shelter covering the previously exposed breech of the gun and its gun crew. Backed up to the rear of each of the guns was a tracked M-548 cargo carrier. A conveyor belt ran out of the cargo carrier and into the Crew Ballistic Shelter.

Chandler watched as they passed gun after gun before he caught sight of the first crewman. When he did, his heart skipped a beat. A soldier was hoisting a vented cloth bag of propellant, with small disklike bags inside that could be removed to fine-tune the charge, across the open space between the M-548 and the howitzer. The man wore heavy protective clothing, a hood, and a gas mask.

ABOARD NIGHTWATCH, OVER SOUTHERN OHIO
August 31, 1615 GMT (1115 Local)

Thomas's eyes roamed from screen to screen in the recently updated E-4B's main conference room. The planes had been long overdue for a technology upgrade, in a day and age in which many home entertainment systems' capabilities were superior, and Congress had, since the nuclear attack, appropriated the necessary funds. Real-time pictures of the Moscow skyline were projected onto one flat, wall-mounted LCD screen, the camera low to the ground across a brown field strewn with antitank obstacles, girders welded together to look like giant jacks from the old child's game. Another shot of the city, a picture from an aerial reconnaissance aircraft under a low gray sky, contrasted starkly with the crystal blue sky and water on the screen next to it, the picture on the latter being of the flight deck of the aircraft carrier *United States* in the north Kara Sea. Small streams of steam from the catapult streaked from its groove down the flight deck toward the stern. The ship had turned into the wind. All was ready.

The door to the conference room opened, and the muted conversations ceased. Even the Vice President on his own aircraft and the RAF general serving as liaison from his Fylingdales bunker in England, whose pictures appeared on a split screen beside each other, looked up at the entering air force officer.

'We've checked all channels, sir,' the officer said to General Starnes. 'We have received no communications from Moscow.'

'Damn!' the President muttered, and Thomas watched as the director of the CIA angrily tossed his control book to be used for Lambert's mission in the growing pile of outdated papers that littered the aircraft's deck behind the chairs of the busy men.

'Bastards,' Fuller said. 'He went in under a fuckin' white flag.'

'What are your orders, sir?' General Thomas asked, in the back of his mind hoping for an extension. *We could use the time for preparations*, he reasoned, even though he knew the real reason for his secret urging: his fear of the unknown, of the Bastion.

'Well,' the President said, looking wistfully off into space. 'We did everything we could in sending Greg.' He winced, his eyes shutting as his thoughts took him someplace he cared not to be. He shook his head and said, 'It's been well over two hours. You've got your orders, gentlemen. Let's get this thing over with.'

The sound of half a dozen telephones being lifted from their cradles signaled the beginning of the end.

LEFORTOVSKAYA NABEREZHNAYA, MOSCOW
August 31, 1615 GMT (1815 Local)

'Son of a bitch!' Lambert shouted as he slammed the pay telephone back down onto its cradle, growing desperate.

'Doesn't work?' the paratroop lieutenant asked in Russian.

'*Nyet!*' Lambert shouted, casting his eyes about the streets of the suburbs for another. 'Na remont,' he thought. *Everything in Russia is* 'na remont' – *out of order*.

Just then they heard the eruption of automatic weapons fire from the direction of the Yauza River, where they had left the main force one block away.

'Let's go!' the lieutenant shouted, and Lambert and the small group ran toward the sound, the paratroopers with weapons raised into the air and skirting the walls of the buildings, Lambert feeling naked and out of place in his suit as he followed at a trot. By the time they worked themselves down the side street to the smoky intersection ahead, the gunfire had ended and Filipov's men rounded up the last of the Russian soldiers from the three-vehicle convoy, two of which were army trucks that had crashed into a kiosk and the wall above the riverbank, and one of which was a limousine whose engine smoldered from under its pockmarked hood in the center of the road. At the next intersection ahead, Lambert saw the reason for the convoy's sudden stop: two BTR-80 armored fighting vehicles with cannon pointed in his direction, pulled out from a side street and blocking their route.

The movement of curtains from several windows on the mid-rise building across the street from the river caught Lambert's eye. Tenants of what must be an apartment building furtively looked down at the scene of combat on the streets below their homes. There were people in most of the windows, Lambert realized; the building must be packed. *What will it be like for them if the attack begins?* the thought occurred to him, and he immediately bolted out into the street to find Filipov from among the busy and agitated paratroopers, his 'escorts' – the squad of six soldiers and the lieutenant – hurrying after him.

On the other side of the truck that had slammed into the kiosk, Lambert saw Filipov, still in full combat gear, standing next to a man in dress uniform having blood dabbed from his forehead and cheek by a medic. To the side, the prisoners from the ambushed convoy stood with hands on their heads – their rifles, packs, and helmets being stacked on the pavement next to Filipov. Lambert ran up to the group.

'Pavel, the phone didn't work,' he shouted in English. 'I've *got* to make contact!'

'General Razov,' Filipov said in Russian, 'I have the pleasure to introduce to you Mr Gregory Lambert. Mr Lambert, General Yuri Razov.'

Greg looked at the familiar face of the man, in his late forties but tanned and hard like an athlete, and shook his hand. 'It is a pleasure,' Razov said in English with an accent much heavier than Filipov's.

'My pleasure,' Lambert replied in proper Russian. 'General Razov, I am here on a mission of vital importance. May we speak?'

'Proceed,' Razov said as the medic sewed stitches into a cut just above his right eyebrow, the pain causing a flutter of Razov's eyelid but no sign of a wince in his eyes or mouth.

'I am here to offer terms of peace. My country does not wish this war to continue, and this private offer is contingent on a prompt and immediate reply.'

'What are these terms?'

Lambert told him as the medic finished his job, finally taping across the stitches.

'These terms,' Razov said, 'are acceptable.' *That's it?* Lambert thought, but then Razov said, 'To *me*,' completing his sentence. 'Unfortunately, as you have seen, I am no longer in a position of authority with our government.'

Lambert's heart raced as he looked at his watch. Two hours and ten minutes had elapsed since he crossed the Russian lines. 'There is one more thing. I must get to a radio, or a satellite phone, or something – immediately! Please, you've got to help me.'

Razov and Filipov both stared at Lambert now. 'What is it that you are not telling us, Mr Lambert?' Razov asked.

The words hovered at the edge of Lambert's breath. They were secrets, the most vital military secrets of the war, and he was agitated and could not force himself to decide whether to tell them, whether to trust them.

'Please, you've got to trust me,' Lambert pleaded. Razov hesitated, and then nodded at Filipov, who motioned the unit's radioman over. The paratrooper turned to face away, and Filipov fiddled with the controls on the radio backpack. The squeal and howl of an electronic maelstrom blanketed the dial. Burping bursts of static through which barely distinguishable sounds of shouted Russian could be heard but not understood. 'Jamming,' Filipov said softly as he concentrated.

'Arc Light, Arc Light,' they all heard clearly, in English. Razov and Filipov both shot looks at Lambert.

All at once, a rumble so deep and resonant that it sounded elemental in its source erupted in the far distance – individual, distant thuds forming the ragged conclusion to the unearthly growl. It was a sound that Lambert had never dreamed could be made by any force even in his darkest nightmares.

'Get down!' Filipov shouted as he, Razov, and the hundred-odd paratroopers and prisoners all scattered at once to the shelter of walls and sides of armored vehicles. Lambert was grabbed by his escort, the lieutenant, who hauled him bodily to the side of a stoop of an apartment building. He collapsed into a heap of soldiers who threw themselves for the same cover a split second ahead.

All was quiet save the ragged popping sounds randomly, briskly piercing the calm now from their great distance. All about the street the last movements of the paratroopers ceased as arms folded over their heads and the last legs were drawn into fetal position.

Oh, my God, Lambert thought. *What in God's name is . . .?*

The world erupted in stunning, hot concussions, tidal waves of air and fire that burst over Lambert and tore at him from the very concrete on which he lay. *It's the end*, Lambert thought as from a thousand windows down the street fell shattered glass, and in one great rain it inundated him. He could feel on his head, neck, and hands the slicing cuts of the tiny shards as the breath seemed kicked from his lungs like a jarring blow on the sports field.

He struggled for breath as he raised his head, seeing instantly from across the river trees falling and half a dozen red fireballs rising quickly into the air from a park, the boiling red flame quickly turning into black smoke, whose rise continued hundreds of feet into the air. Another series of stunning blasts literally shook the sparkling glass as it lay on the street and cracked huge trees in the park in half before Lambert's eyes, the shock waves like a thin cloud of vapor pushing outward from the newly rising balls of fire and disappearing in an instant as dust choked Lambert's lungs and he coughed.

'Mount up!' he heard shouted in Russian, and soldiers began to rise amid the storm of high explosives and brush the glass from their uniforms. Lambert felt his arm being tugged to pull him to his feet. Shattering explosions and smoke rose from all corners of the city around him. A screaming roar burst overhead and soldiers ducked reflexively, standing suspended in a stoop until the wall of noise had passed. Lambert never saw the jets that had passed low overhead, and the soldiers began to run toward their vehicles.

Another grip on his biceps jerked him roughly around. It was Razov, with Filipov at his side.

'Are they attacking the city?' Filipov shouted, the shock evident in his voice. 'You are assaulting the city on the *ground*, aren't you?' Again an accusation, the anger palpable.

Another stunning burst shook the park across the river, and Lambert saw the first of the Russian self-propelled guns displacing from their firing positions where they had been unseen to Lambert but not, obviously, to U.S. reconnaissance.

Slightly light-headed from the shock waves battering his body and his ears as another shell threw water from the river up onto the street in the distance, Lambert still managed to shout, 'Yes!'

'What are the other plans?' Razov shouted, his eyes boring holes in Lambert's. He waited only a second before grabbing the taller Lambert by both arms and shouting, 'Tell me what your plans are!' as he shook Lambert out of his daze.

Lambert's tongue found the slight rise on the molar of his lower jaw and probed the small crown. He knew he shouldn't talk, that he should go to his death without revealing vital secrets, but the realization of the enormity of the mistake came rushing in to him at once.

Razov's eyes widened and his jaw dropped. 'The Bastion,' Razov murmured, his eyes opening in shock. His grip grew soft as he looked straight through Lambert into the distance.

'*Goddammit*!' Filipov yelled as another shell ripped into the park across the river and a roaring series of secondary explosions rattled Lambert's chest with puffs of hot air. Lambert ducked involuntarily but could not take his eyes off Razov's pale face as the general stood there, unmoving. 'We *told* you not to attack those submarines, damn you!' Filipov shouted. 'Have you gone *mad*? What could you *possibly* have been . . .?'

Behind the two officers, the column of armored vehicles was forming, turrets unlimbering and riflemen at their firing ports ready for action, ready to fight the invading Americans to the death in a meaningless gesture during the last hour of the two countries' greatness. Standing close beside Lambert with his assault rifle unslung and pointed loosely in his direction was Lambert's escort.

As the rain of artillery continued to fall around the city, a pair of jets whined by at slightly higher altitude – British or Italian Tornados–drawing Lambert's attention as they flashed across the river in a steep bank dropping brilliant white flares. Razov picked up an assault rifle, an AK-74, from the pile of prisoners' equipment and turned to face Lambert from a distance of about ten feet.

Lambert's escort edged away as Filipov turned to watch the scene from off to the side. Lambert stood there all alone as the armed Razov faced him, Lambert's jaw firmly clenched, prepared to grind. Razov raised the rifle, fingered and then looked at the selector switch just above the trigger housing, and looked back at Lambert.

Lambert took a deep breath and lowered his head as he saw Razov raise the rifle out of the edge of his field of vision. He looked up just in time to reach out with both hands to shield himself from the flying weapon, which banged against his chest and neck with a painful blow.

'To the Kremlin!' Razov shouted to an officer jutting from the lead BMP's hatch. Lambert looked at the Russian Army helmet that Filipov was holding out to him and at the heavy black assault rifle still clutched awkwardly to his body, and then mounted the armored fighting vehicle for the drive to the Kremlin.

OKRUZHNOYE KOLTSO, MOSCOW
August 31, 1700 GMT (1900 Local)

'Up!' Jefferson yelled over the open intercom, the wind rushing by Chandler as he stood high in the commander's hatch but not penetrating the folds and mask of his chemical protective suit, providing no relief from the sweltering heat.

'Fire!' Chandler yelled.

'On the way!' the gunner shouted, and the main gun punched out another round, the roar tickling Chandler's abused eardrums.

'*Hit*!' the gunner said over the intercom.

Chandler loosed a burst of .50-caliber rounds at a canvas-covered truck that came into view from behind a small building as the tanks of Chandler's battalion rushed headlong toward the imposing earthen defenses, toward the Moscow Line. The truck's engine began to smoke as three men jumped from the back. 'BMP!' Chandler yelled as he caught sight of movement from a construction site. 'Ten o'clock! Load HEAT!'

'We're low on HEAT, sir,' Jefferson said. 'Down to four rounds.'

'Squash Head, then – *load it*!' Chandler shouted as the gunner called out, 'Identified!'

'Up!' Jefferson said.

'Fire!' Chandler ordered, and the gunner replied, 'On the way!'

The tank shook as the two-ton main gun recoiled against the gush of flame that erupted from the muzzle. Chandler pulled his binoculars up to his eyes to pay special attention to this shot. The HESH round, High Explosive Squash Head, was not highly favored because it did not usually give as dramatic a read on its results as a HEAT round or sabot. The opposite of a penetrator, which focuses its energy on as narrow a point as possible, a Squash Head has a soft casing that is designed to spread out on impact. A fuse then detonates the charge, and the dull but powerful force of the blast fragments the interior lining of the vehicle's walls and knocks loose scabs of metal at high speed. That 'spalling' kills or maims a crew as the hot, jagged metal ricochets inside a vehicle, but only rarely detonates ammo or fuel to give a nice, loud secondary explosion to confirm the kill.

The Squash Head had clearly struck the vehicle's side, and the BMP stood still, its nine occupants presumably dead or dying from the shrapnel of their own armor.

'You want another shot, Colonel?' the gunner asked.

Chandler looked over at the burning column of trucks on the road to the left. Some trucks were pulling off the road to get around, trying to escape the noose they were speeding to close around the slower Russian retreat before they made it back to the main belt of defenses. 'No,' he said, again traversing his gun to the road. 'Just keep your eyes peeled.'

He rattled out another burst, this time getting a thunderous explosion from the back of a truck and seeing it flatten to the ground, its axles, wheels, and suspension giving way under the downward force of the detonating ordnance carried under its canvas.

'You want me on the sixty, sir?' Jefferson asked as they approached the line of trenches ahead, the Provisionals' Moscow Line. 'No!' Chandler shouted just as he saw one of the M-3 scouts ahead burst into flame right at the trenches and roll in agonizing slow motion onto its side. 'Stay ready down there!' Lining up a new target, this one a small truck much like a Humvee, Chandler squeezed off another burst and saw flames begin to lick the ground from the holes punched straight through the metal vehicle. Chandler swiveled the heavy machine gun now to the earthen bunkers of the trench ahead whose black slits they were now rapidly nearing. He squeezed the trigger again, hurling the heavy bullets through the thick earth and log supports of the bunker's walls as dust rose from all around the fist-size holes punched into the soil.

He stole a glance back to his right where his team still engaged the remaining armor emerging from their fighting holes with tell-tales puffs of exhaust from their aging engines. The streaking missile was almost on them, fired from the BMP that they had shot with the Squash Head round.

'*A-A-A-H-H*!' Chandler yelled over the open intercom, involuntarily pulling his legs up into the hatch as the missile hit the lighter armor on the side of the M-1. Burning pain shot up from his legs as a flash of heat radiated out of the tank's crew compartment. The jarring explosion shook his grip loose, and he fell into the inferno below.

Within 250 milliseconds, the M-1's fire suppression system flooded the crew cabin with Halon gas. By the time Chandler's helmet smashed against the deck, the fire was out. Chandler tumbled forward along the cabin floor as the treads of the now stalled M-1 ground to a halt, and he lay there dazed, coughing from the Halon that had temporarily evacuated the oxygen atmosphere from the cabin. The effort of coughing sent pain shooting from a hundred places. 'Je-e-ze,' he heard someone hiss through clenched teeth from behind his gas mask, and Chandler managed to struggle up onto his elbows.

'O-o-o-o-h,' Chandler heard from his left, from deep in the throat and inhuman sounding. Jefferson lay on his back staring blankly up through the lenses of his mask at the white ceiling of the interior. It was dark and still.

Chandler's mind cleared and he lurched for the smoke dischargers, squeezed first one and then both triggers, blowing the two six-barreled M-250 smoke dischargers on either side of the turret front. Chandler waited as the gunner crawled over to Jefferson and the driver asked, 'Everybody . . . everybody okay?' as he tried unsuccessfully to restart the engine.

Jefferson continued to moan as the smoke grenades popped all around the tank's front and sides, enshrouding them, Chandler knew, in the only protection they had left. He kept his eyes peeled at the sky above through his open hatch, holding his breath behind the gas mask without realizing it. *Motionless on a battlefield – sitting ducks*, he thought. *We have to get outa here.*

'Oh, man,' the gunner said as his voice was forced through the mask. He sat over Jefferson, the loader. 'Colonel Chandler.'

Chandler was focused on the hissing of the smoke grenades and the random sounds of fighting coming through the open commander's and loader's hatches. He looked over his left shoulder. Sunlight poured through a perfectly round hole, one inch in diameter, in the turret.

'Colonel!' the gunner cried, and Chandler crawled over to Jefferson. He thought he heard something outside, but when he heard it again he realized that it came from Jefferson's chest. A sucking sound.

'Oh, God,' Chandler said. 'Get something – a poncho! Something airtight!' Chandler stripped Jefferson's torso. His chest was shiny with frothy orange blood straight from his lungs. Every couple of seconds a horrible sucking sound emanated from the wound as he slowly suffocated.

'Here!' the gunner said, handing Chandler the muzzle cover. Chandler pressed the vinyl fabric tightly down onto the open wound.

Under Chandler's hands Jefferson began to buck, to convulse.

A sudden whoosh from outside ended in a rocking thud and thunderous explosion felt both in Chandler's knees and in his lungs. For a moment afterward, as he gasped for breaths of the oxygen that flooded back into the cabin, it seemed to be all over but for a crackling sound like dry wood in a fire. He jumped at the first explosion, which set off a string of ferocious bursts like enormous firecrackers as the main gun rounds began to cook off in the rear of the tank, each one sounding like the end of the world. The explosions grew in violence and intensity to a continuous roar.

Vibrations rattled the men's insides, the driver's screams as he lay strapped into his seat sounding as if someone was thumping his chest. Through the open hatches, Chandler looked up to see a brilliant white fire of pure burn as the propellant vented through the blowout panels, a fire that he had seen before from a distance. The noise and heat suddenly doubled as the fuel burst into flame from the rear of the tank, and Chandler tucked his chin down, his face frozen in a grimace and his eyes watering and squinting closed against the heat. It took all the effort he could muster to keep his hands pressed down on Jefferson's chest and not to clamp them over his ears as the gunner and driver did.

He glanced up, not at the fire jetting a hundred feet into the sky above them but at the armored bulkhead that separated them from the furnace on the other side. As the noise and heat and vibration plateaued, he had only one focus: that bulkhead. The white paint began to turn brown right in front of his eyes, and smoke rose from it. Chandler gave up his battle to force his eyes open and let them close, the moisture that had welled up in them trickling down his cheeks as tears. In that darkness, the sounds clawing at his eardrums became a series of painful tones, and the radiant heat from the ammo locker grew on his chemical gear, which seemed to scorch his skin even through the fabric of his uniform underneath.

With surprising quickness, the vibrations through Chandler's knees faded to a stop. He opened his eyes. The ammo door was now black other than in several places in which it glowed a grayish white. He looked up through his hatch to see a pall of black smoke blotting out the sun. Chandler jumped when he felt hands on his arm. It was the gunner, and he repeated something obviously in a loud voice.

'*What?*' Chandler yelled, but he could barely hear himself over the ringing in his ears. He felt dizzy and nauseous, and a sudden flash of cold sweat made him just want to find a place to lie down, to ride out the feeling.

'It's no good!' Chandler heard through stabs of pain in his ears. 'He's gone!'

Chandler looked down, and then eased his pressure on Jefferson's chest, his arms and shoulders and neck aching from the frozen strain of his effort.

As the sound of the fires from the back of the tank died down completely, Chandler listened for the rattle of Bradleys' automatic cannon that should have been bunker-busting at the trenches ahead by now. There was fighting, but even with the deadened acuity of his tortured ears he could tell it was receding into the distance.

'What's it like out there?' he shouted at the driver, who was twisted around in his seat looking back at the dead Jefferson. He looked around to his front through vision blocks and then turned to say, 'The trench is about sixty meters ahead!' Looking back he said, 'There's a Bradley up there that's been hit!'

Chandler thought for a second, then said, 'Okay,' reaching for his gear and rifle. The driver popped his own hatch, and as Chandler climbed up to his position the gunner rose up from the dead tank to Jefferson's. The rear of the tank was blackened and smoking from the open and burned out ammo and fuel compartments.

'You get on the fifty!' Chandler ordered as he slid down to the ground, mindful not to tear or pull out of place any of his chemical protective gear. They had sent the orders down from brigade. MOPP IV – full chemical protective gear – for the assault into the city. It was the first such order from on high of the war.

The gunner reappeared from the tank at Chandler's hatch and swung the .50-caliber machine gun toward the trenches. He quickly released the handles and then gingerly grasped them again – they were obviously hot to the touch.

The last few tanks from his battalion were disappearing up the highway and through the thinly wooded hills just behind the bare dirt cut in their path ahead: the trenches of the Moscow Line. The overturned Bradley lay just short of the line. Looking back around, the crackle of small-arms fire and *pum-pum-pum* of Bradleys' 25-mm cannon could be heard over the low hill behind them as the second echelon of infantry engaged targets bypassed by Chandler's speeding tanks. The battlefield was still very dangerous. He flicked the M-16's selector switch to 'Burst' and raised the assault rifle to his armpit, walking slowly down his tank's treads toward the M-3 and the men inside. His men.

The driver was lying flat on the ground with his M-16 pointed at the bunker and ready. Chandler eyed the burned patch of ground ahead where the engineer's 'snake,' a long hose filled with explosives and shot forward to detonate the land mines ahead, scorched a path twenty meters wide for them to follow.

'Come on!' Chandler yelled to the driver, and they spread out for their walk up toward the trenches. Chandler placed each step carefully even though the snake had burned a path. Twice he saw unexploded land mines partially unearthed by the engineers' blast. With each step, he tensed in anticipation. The sounds of tank cannon were now nearly a mile ahead as they sprinted through breeches in the Russian lines. The gray sky above was crisscrossed with helicopters. The occasional fighter-bomber dived down through the ceiling of gathering dark clouds to release the black cargoes under their wings and then pull back up into the protective overcast sky. First one and then two smoke trails from antiaircraft missiles shot up into the sky and clouds ahead. A strobe lit one patch of clouds from inside for an instant.

He returned his attention to the trench and blackened bunker. The huge holes punched into the wall of the bunker by his M-2 machine gun attested to the damage it would have done to the bunker's occupants, none of whom were visible. Chandler and the driver neared the Bradley at a crouch now, their rifles raised to firing positions on their shoulders and Chandler's finger pulling firmly against the trigger.

Two bodies in chemical protective gear lay sprawled in front of their hatches, and smoke poured through a grapefruit-size hole in the vehicle's side armor. As Chandler's driver crawled halfway into the hatch to peer inside, Chandler inspected the two men on the ground.

The first was legless and dead. Chandler lifted his hood up. He was a soldier Chandler recognized from the Scout Platoon. He retrieved one of the man's dog tags and inserted the other into the dead man's mouth. He moved on to the other man. His legs were also mangled. Both men's lower bodies had been in the inferno inside the vehicle while their torsos stuck out of the hatch; he had seen the same before. *The gunner and the vehicle commander*. Fire had raged however briefly to leave the suit of the dead man below Chandler still smoldering.

'Oh, man,' the driver said, backing out of the overturned Bradley, his flashlight shaking as he plopped to the ground on his rear. He said nothing, sitting there motionless as his chest rose and fell in panted breaths. He had found the rest of the cavalrymen still inside the Bradley.

Chandler pulled back the protective suit. The man inside was burned badly. He reached inside his tattered blouse with gloved hands but could not find the dog tags. He glanced nervously back up at the trench and saw no one. He would confirm this man's identity and move on; the others inside the vehicle would have to wait.

A piece of paper, scorched along its edges, protruded from a ragged tear seared through his breast pocket. Chandler pulled the paper through the tear. It was folded neatly into a square, but its surface was crinkled with a hundred creases. He looked down at the hooded face of the dead soldier before slowly unfolding the paper. He already knew what he would find.

Woven into the swirl of vines and red roses atop the pink stationery was the name and address of Jennifer from Dallas.

Chandler refolded the sheet and replaced it in Lieutenant Bailey's pocket. He rose. Before him lay the trench. The battlefield was not safe if there were still Russians there. He motioned for the driver to get to his feet and looked back to ensure that the gunner still covered them from the .50 caliber. Chandler and the driver raised their rifles to their shoulders and approached the dark brown cut in the soil, advancing in a crouch.

As they neared the trench, they dropped to the ground to crawl up the slight slope to its lip. Slowly, tentatively, Chandler raised his head and rifle up over the slightly elevated wall. Bodies lined the trench floor where they had poured out of the bunker, the bunker's opening waist high with corpses. None showed the slightest sign of life.

Chandler and the driver both slowly rose, first to their knees, then to their feet. Spread out up and down the trench in ones and twos and at various other places on the dirt road behind were dead Russian Provisionals. They were contorted, twisted in odd positions. Their hands ripped at the neck of their shirts or grabbed their throats as if they had choked themselves to death. None showed any signs of wounds, the only characteristic common to all being their eyes. They bulged as if straining at the sockets, wide open in the peculiar agony of death by gas. There were hundreds, thousands of them in a thick line of death stretching over the hills and out of sight to both sides.

The driver sank to the ground again, dropping his rifle and burying his masked face in the dirt in front before rolling onto his side and hugging his knees to his chest. He rocked slowly from side to side. He had seen enough for one war.

Chandler stood there, safe and secure on this still lethal patch of earth inside his thin charcoal suit, memorizing without realizing it sights that would remain with him for all his days. They were sights that would forever frustrate the efforts of his son Matthew when he asked the inevitable questions a young boy asks of a father who had been to war.

Chapter Nineteen

THE KREMLIN, MOSCOW
August 31, 1715 GMT (1915 Local)

In the confusion of helicopter gunship and fighter-bomber attacks all across the center of Moscow, the column of BTR-80s drove straight through the gates of the Kremlin. The vehicle commander and a soldier with an SA-7 antiaircraft missile on his shoulder dropped down into the armored vehicle in front of Razov and Lambert and pulled the armored hatch closed on top of them, dampening the rattle of the guns and the whoosh and quick boom of helicopters' aerial rockets that had knocked out one of their convoy's armored vehicles already.

The lieutenant on the bench just ahead of Lambert shouted something that Lambert did not understand, but all of the soldiers in the vehicle suddenly began to load their assault rifles. Razov did likewise, and Lambert fumbled with a pouch mounted on the webbing he wore to extract a magazine heavy with thirty rounds of 5.56mm ammunition, the new Russian standard.

As Lambert rammed the magazine home in the rocking vehicle, he felt Razov's hands loosening his chin strap, which cut tightly into his chin to hold it on. 'It is better this way,' he said. 'In case it is hit, it . . .' He made a sweeping gesture with his hand to indicate the helmet flying off his head and then reached for Lambert's rifle to ensure the safety was on.

By the time the engine noise from their BTR died down, the rapid-fire cracks of small arms fire could already be heard up ahead.

'You stay back with me,' Razov said as the side hatches opened and the BTR's occupants poured out onto the smooth, rounded cobblestones of the ancient Kremlin street. Lambert lay flat on the ground, watching as paratroopers rushed a nondescript structure ahead that sat amid all the ornate, brightly colored Kremlin buildings. They entered the smoky doorway, their rifles blazing.

'Let's go!' Razov said, rising to run toward the doorway along the column of vehicles now staggered on either side of the street. The whine of a jet engine caused everyone to dive to the pavement, and

Lambert scraped his knees and elbows in the dive, ripping his suit as he felt a stabbing pain from his hipbone against the stone. He rolled onto his side to see a U.S. Tomahawk cruise missile banking lazily to the left, the tracers of Russian antiaircraft guns streaking up into the sky all around the stubby-winged pilotless jet. When it reappeared in the distance from behind the gold 'onion dome' cupolas of an old monastery on the Kremlin grounds it was nearly completing its turn. Lambert imagined the radar and television images being processed for matches in the sophisticated computer brain of the missile's TERCOM, its Terrain Contour Matching guidance system. All watched in silent fascination as the missile's jet engine powered it slowly in, the engine's sound falling to an idle whine. All of the sudden it waggled its wings and the engine roared to life. Its cruising descent signaled that a match had been found. It was coming in. Lower and lower the accelerating missile came, and the thought suddenly occurred to Lambert: *Nuclear or conventional?*

It sped past him not sixty yards away at treetop level, much larger than he had imagined it to be. The missile angled down sharply just after passing the last building and headed straight through the double doors of the Congress of People's Deputies across the large open square.

It crashed through the doors, and at first Lambert thought it was a dud, but suddenly three floors of windows lit up with a flash and the facade of the beautiful old building shattered onto the few cars parked in front. The explosion echoed from the buildings enclosing the large central square of the Kremlin grounds. As the smoke quickly dissipated, a four-story hole split the building open – rooms of each floor cleaved open and strangely dissected for the naked eye to see.

Razov, the lieutenant, and their men rose quickly and sprinted toward the open door to the building which their comrades had just assaulted. Lambert followed. All along the skyline to the south and west rose a black curtain of fires, and the sky was alive with darting, weaving specks of distant aircraft. When the men reached the door, the strange, hollow sounds of gunfire from somewhere deep in the building could be heard. Paratroopers dug holes in the manicured lawn just outside the building's door. Lambert followed Razov and the others in. The soldiers ahead rushed past a receptionist's desk and through a set of double doors. Lambert and Razov were right behind, and they stepped out onto a darkened metal stairwell. The sound of fighting rose up the shaft from deep in the earth below.

Down the metal stairs ran Razov, Lambert, and his escort. Smoke and the metallic smell of spent gunpowder wafted up as they passed bodies ripped open and bloody on the stairs, some being tended by medics, others lying alone, dead. A bullet clattered up the shaft, sending sparks off the concrete walls and clanging into the metal staircase above. It had passed too quickly, too unexpectedly for Lambert to react. The staircase seemed to go on forever, and the deeper they went the

louder the booming rips of gunfire and occasional deafening explosion
of a hand grenade sounded. Lambert's ears popped and he grew short
of breath as he, Razov, and the half dozen soldiers in their party rapidly
descended the stairs.

Sparks flew again as clanging bullets ripped through the metal steps
and a soldier in front of Lambert howled and fell, tumbling to the next
landing as Lambert was pulled down painfully onto his back from behind
by the lieutenant. Soldiers appeared on either side of Lambert with
rifles pointed straight down through the gaps around the stairs' railings,
but they held their fire. The medic brushed past Razov on the steps
below Lambert to tend to the fallen soldier ahead as still more bullets
ricocheted up the concrete-encased stairwell, fragments of the wall
exploding in puffs of dust at the randomly sprayed automatic fire.

Lambert felt his entire body exposed, suspended there on the thin
perforated metal of the staircase as the narrow channel conducted
strings of bullets straight up the concrete shaft. Soft flesh and brittle
bone would do nothing to stop the high-powered rounds that shattered
concrete and clanged unhindered through steel. Another burst tore
across the risers just below his feet, holes blown into the metal right
before his eyes. One of the paratroopers dropped his rifle and sat down
on Lambert's legs, hugging his forearm to his chest as he gathered for
a scream.

'Let's go!' Razov said as he pulled Lambert to his feet. They were
headed down toward the muzzles of the guns below.

'*A-a-a-ah!*' the soldier cradling his shattered arm shouted as Lambert
edged past, his eyes squinted shut in the agony of pain, of realization
at what had happened to the limb that he held limply in his good hand.
More bullets flew by with clangs and the still more ominous *z-z-z-i-p*
that puffed lightly against Lambert's cheek, the kiss of the bullet's wake
deceptively gentle as it tickled the soft hairs of his face above the line
of his razor.

Down they went into the hellish depths. Lambert nearly turned an
ankle on the puckered hole from a bullet on the metal step as a
brilliant flash lit the semidarkness of the shaft. The blast from the
concussion grenade pounded Lambert's eardrums, and he instantly
grew woozy. They used concussion grenades, he realized despite
the light-headedness, instead of fragmentation grenades. *You don't
use frags in a stairwell.* Down they ran into the choking smoke from
the grenade's blast, the sounds of fighting now hammering constantly
into Lambert's aching ears and head.

By the time they made it to a large landing at the bottom along which
lay piles of bodies, the fighting had died down. They rushed past the
wounded, leaving them unattended as they sped to catch up with Filipov
and came upon soldiers crouching and lying on the floor to fire around
corners. The handful of soldiers remaining in Lambert's little group

raised their weapons and took up standing positions along the walls by the intersection of passageways. They were the front line now.

On shouted command by the lieutenant, Lambert watched in horrified amazement as four paratroopers leapt into the corridor to be met with a storm of bullets, firing their rifles on full automatic from their hips. Two of the men fell dead or grievously wounded almost instantly, the other two disappeared in a rush into the smoke through which they fired, emptying their magazines as they ran.

Lambert saw now Filipov and another man across the corridor. Filipov shouted 'Up!' and the few remaining men rose, two moving slowly and leaving large wet patches of blood where they had lain. They followed the lead men down the hall toward the sounds of their guns, leaving only Razov, Lambert, and the lieutenant. Razov nodded at the corner, and the three of them rushed into the smoke toward the flashes of the guns ahead.

They passed doorway after doorway, most filled with soldiers who stared anxiously back at them, crouching or lying behind map desks, tables, and radios in rooms filled with files or computers, taking no part, no side, in the intramural fighting. The large double doors ahead were kicked open, and light flooded the semidarkness of the hallway. Suddenly seeing the smoke that billowed along the low ceiling, Lambert coughed reflexively.

With the opening of the double doors, the fighting ended, and all fell quiet save the ringing in Lambert's ears.

As Lambert, Razov, and the lieutenant passed the bodies of the last two soldiers from Lambert's little detail and walked briskly up to join Filipov, who stood with rifle leveled in the open double doors ahead, Lambert realized just how close it had been. He stole a glance over his shoulder. They had started down with one hundred men, less the few who were killed up top and the few others left to block the stairwell entrance. They – Filipov, Razov, Lambert, the lieutenant, and three wounded soldiers – had made it with almost no one to spare.

Razov stepped into the brightly lit room past Filipov and one of the wounded soldiers propped against the doorframe. Lambert looked over the shorter Filipov's shoulder at the long conference table and at the men – generals, admirals, older men – who stood to the sides of the room away from the doors that were riddled with stray bullets.

All eyes were on Razov, but Razov's were on the two devices at the end of the table, like bulky portable computers, at which sat two younger army officers.

'Out!' Razov shouted with one pass of his assault rifle past the group of senior officers. STAVKA, Lambert realized as Filipov and his few soldiers herded the men out. They filed past studying Lambert and were led into a room next door to the main conference room as a few additional survivors from the fight filtered down the long corridor. Filipov began his walk down the hallway past the faces of the staff crowding the open doorways shouting in Russian, 'General Razov is now in command! Return to your duties at once! General Razov is now in command! Return to your duties at once!' As he met the incoming paratroopers, he issued orders and pointed, sending the men running off.

'Mr Lambert!' Lambert heard in English from behind and he turned to see Razov opening a thick notebook on the table next to the seated officers. Without looking up he said, 'Get your President on the line now!' and jabbed a finger at a row of telephones on a credenza at the side of the room. 'Dial nine for an ordinary line.'

Lambert lifted the telephone and dialed 9. Pulling his wallet from his pocket he heard the click and then dial tone. He dialed the telephone number dedicated by AT&T International solely for this one call. After a rapid series of clicks he heard the distant sound of an operator. 'Nightwatch.' It was amazingly simple.

'This is Greg Lambert. Let me speak to the President.' It was then that Lambert realized the two devices on the table were the nuclear communicators and that the book through which Razov looked, his pointed index finger running down each page in a search, was a binder torn from the side of the communicators.

'This is Costanzo. Greg, where the hell have you been?'

Lambert quickly told him, keeping his eyes on Razov the entire time.

'What is he doing now?' the President asked.

'He's . . . I don't know,' Lambert replied as Razov frantically searched page after page in the codebook. Lambert lowered the phone and said, 'General Razov, I have the President.'

Razov was muttering to himself as his finger traced the page, his eyes and his attention completely focused on the book.

'What the hell is he doing?' Lambert heard the tinny voice come from the phone's earpiece.

'General Razov?' Lambert asked. 'What are you *doing*?'

Razov did not respond, and Lambert raised the phone. 'He's standing behind the . . . the nuclear communicators and looking through a book. General Razov!' Lambert shouted, the officers seated at the devices staring back and forth between the two with wide eyes. Lambert raised the phone to his ear. 'Just a second, sir.' He placed the handset down and walked over to Razov.

'I've got the President on the line. What the hell is going on?'

Razov kept repeating under his breath the Russian letters for MSGRMG. Lambert looked down at the book, Razov's finger running down the columns of seemingly random letters and numbers. *Codes*, Lambert realized.

'Answer me, Goddammit! What the *hell* are you doing?' Lambert demanded.

Razov took time off from his mumbling to say, '*Doverayte mnye* – trust me, Mr Lambert.' His finger then resumed its tracing of codes down the page. He quickly flipped to the next page in the thick book, the columns of twelve-character codes flying by under his finger.

Lambert went back to the phone. 'He says trust him. He's searching through what appears to be a codebook.'

'Open the code cases,' Razov said, and Lambert watched stunned as the two officers opened up the covers.

'He's ordered the nuclear communicators activated,' Lambert said into the phone.

'Jesus Christ,' he heard in the background of what presumably was the Nightwatch conference room, the voice sounding like that of the Secretary of Defense. Razov turned the page and his finger ran down the column.

Razov's finger stopped in its track. His lips moved, mouthing the code that his finger now traced horizontally. He read it one more time. 'That's it! Enter the following code.'

'He's entering a code, sir. He's entering a code.'

'The letter *M*,' Razov said to the two officers. They each pressed a button.

'He's entering a code, sir!'

'Lambert,' the President said, his voice urgent, 'stop him. Stop him, Greg!'

'*S*,' Razov read from just above his fingertip, and the officers entered the code.

Lambert set the phone down and raised his rifle, clicking the selector switch on full auto.

The two officers looked up at him in shock.

'*G*,' Razov said, not looking up. '*G*!' he snapped when the men did not respond. Tentatively they each punched another key.

'General Razov,' Lambert said, 'step away from the table.' The rifle was leveled at him.

'Faster, faster!' Razov said, intentionally not looking at Lambert. 'Zero!'

'Razov!' Lambert shouted, shouldering the rifle and aiming at his head.

'Goddammit, Greg, don't let him enter that code!' he heard faintly from the telephone.

The officers punched another key. *How many digits was that?* Lambert tried to remember as Razov said, 'Six!' – still hunched over the book.

Lambert pulled the trigger, the rifle exploding with hammering blows into his shoulder as the plaster walls above the three men's heads showered dust and debris down onto them.

The two seated men ducked, their faces frozen in terror as they stared at Lambert. Razov's finger remained planted firmly on the page but he looked up at Lambert. 'Zero.' When the seated men hesitated, still staring at the rifle in Lambert's hands, Razov said, 'Faster! Zero!'

'Don't move, Greg,' Lambert heard as the officers punched the keys on their devices. Out of the corner of his eye he saw Filipov, his own rifle raised to his shoulder and pointed straight at Lambert's head.

'Greg! What's going on? Are you there?' the President shouted.

'The letter *R*!' Razov said, and the two men punched the letter *R* in, the seventh character of the twelve-character code. '*M*!' Lambert watched through the fixed iron sight of the rifle as the eighth digit was entered.

'Put down the rifle, Greg,' Filipov said. 'Put it down right now.'

'*G*!' The ninth digit went into the two communicators as Greg heard the President shouting, 'Is that a launch code? Is he entering a launch code? Greg, are you still there?'

'Zero!' The tenth.

'Greg, for the love of God, if you're there stop that bastard!'

Razov said, 'Five,' and then looked up. 'I'm trying to save the world. Do you trust me, Mr Lambert?' Lambert looked over at Filipov, who shouted, 'Greg! I'm warning you, put down that rifle! Now!'

Lambert looked back at Razov. 'It is your choice, Mr Lambert. Your choice.' He looked back down at his fingertip. One of the officers seated below him closed his eyes. 'Six,' Razov said calmly.

The officers raised their fingers to press the keys and Lambert's finger tightened on the trigger. The twelfth character was punched into the devices. '*Kommanda podana*,' the two officers both said in unison. 'Code accepted.'

Lambert lowered his rifle, and Filipov skirted the credenza to jerk it from his hands, holding his own rifle one-handed and pointed at Lambert's chest the entire time. Greg's jaw hurt from its grinding clench, and his heart skipped a beat as his tongue probed his lower rear molar for any taste of bitterness or numbness. The crown seemed intact.

'Let me speak to the President,' Razov said walking over to the telephone.

ABOARD NIGHTWATCH, OVER CENTRAL OHIO
August 31, 1735 GMT (1235 Local)

'I have just entered a code, Mr President,' Razov's voice came over the speaker, 'that was first input into the code banks on orders of Soviet President Gorbachev after the abortive coup against him in August of 1991. During the coup, his nuclear code case and that of Defense Minister Yazov both came under the plotters' control. In the final stages of the coup's collapse, Yazov threatened use of nuclear weapons against the Soviet air base from which General Shapashnikov organized the military resistance to the plotters.'

Thomas saw the President's eyes shoot over to the director of the CIA, who shrugged and shook his head, rising to his feet to walk over to the President's side.

'The code was maintained as a secret from the military and passed from Gorbachev to Yeltsin upon collapse of the Soviet Union. Upon the arrest of President Poltavsky in the military coup earlier this year – which I personally undertook, as you know – Poltavsky asked for a moment in private with me. He disclosed to me the code, which is perpetually on a long list of "reserved" codes that are set aside for use by our system and are ordinarily for various command, communications, and training purposes. "Reserved" codes are excluded from the set of codes available to be randomly generated every day to serve as the active launch codes.'

The director of the CIA reached over the President's shoulder and hit the MUTE button. 'We have no idea if what he's saying holds water, sir.'

'The code bore the initials and ages of Gorbachev and his wife Raisa.'

The President brushed the director's finger off the mute button. 'What does the code do?'

'It is intended to prevent the possibility of unauthorized use of nuclear weapons, Mr President. Specifically, of use in a Russian civil war – to prevent a nuclear civil war.'

'Does it work?' the President asked.

After a long pause, Razov said, 'I don't know.' There was another silence during which the President stared back at the faces of the men down the conference table, all of which were turned his way.

'You must,' Razov said, 'you absolutely *must* call off your attack on the Bastion. The fail-deadly policy, sir – it was not a ruse. It was not disinformation. It *is*, it truly *is* the nuclear control policy that became effective for those submarines upon Zorin's choice of launch control orders.'

'I'd like to speak to Mr Lambert,' the President said.

During the momentary pause, Thomas looked at his watch and then over at the Chief of Naval Operations, who was doing the same. The Kara Sea naval and air forces were over their targets or very near them.

'Yes, Mr President?' Lambert said.

The director of the CIA held up his hand to silence Costanzo. 'Lambert,' he said, 'did you hear Razov's story?'

'Yes, I did.'

The President started to speak, but the director held up his hand again. 'Were you with Razov the whole time he went through the launch authorization procedure?'

'Yes.'

'Can you supply more details?'

Thomas stared at the speaker during the pause. 'No, Goddammit,' Lambert replied, slow to remember the coded phrase. 'I'm not under any duress!'

The director nodded at the President. 'Greg,' the President said, leaning forward closer to the speaker, 'you were there. You watched him. What do you think?'

There was no pause this time. 'I believe General Razov, sir. I believe he is telling the truth.'

Thomas watched as the President puffed his cheeks out and blew into his hands as if they had grown cold. Holding them clenched, he looked up at the CNO and said, 'Admiral, call off the attack on the Bastion.'

As the CNO repeated the reports fed to him over the two telephones planted to his ears and the Secretary of Defense kept track on a yellow legal pad, Thomas's eyes were glued to the one screen showing the flight deck of the *U.S.S. United States*, the newest of the Nimitz-class of nuclear supercarriers, as she plied the Kara Sea.

'Destroyers *Laboon* and *John Rogers* acknowledge abort,' Admiral Dixon said, and the Secretary of Defense wrote their names under the 'Destroyer' heading. The aircraft carrier was growing busy again, having spent over half an hour launching eighty-odd aircraft at breakneck pace from the four catapults down each of its two angled flight decks as the attack began. Now Thomas watched as an F-14, its wing and fuselage pylons still heavily laden with unexpended air-to-air missiles, came roaring in, its tail hook snagging just past the center arresting cable in the controlled crash that was a perfect landing.

'Attack submarines *Salt Lake City* and *Indianapolis* and frigates *Robert G. Bradley* and *Stephen W. Groves* acknowledge abort,' Dixon said, and the Secretary wrote.

'General Razov,' the President asked in a raised voice, 'are you still there?'

'Yes, Mr President,' Razov said over the speakerphone.

'*Chancellorsville* and *Leyte Gulf* – cruisers – acknowledge,' the CNO said in a lowered voice.

'What about the remainder of the terms?' the President asked.

'They are acceptable, Mr President.'

'And you represent to us that you can speak for the entire Russian military establishment?'

'Yes, sir. I am confident my orders will be obeyed.'

The door opened and an air force sergeant walked around the table with a message for the director of the NSA. The President muted the telephone and turned to Thomas. 'Should we call off the ground attack on Moscow too?'

Before Thomas could answer, the NSA director said, 'Just a second, sir.'

'Cruisers *Philippine Sea* and *Vincennes*, destroyers *John Paul Jones* and *Deyo*, frigates *Ford* and *Klakring*, and attack submarines *Albany*, *Jacksonville*, *Tucson* and *Newport News* report acknowledged,' Admiral Dixon said as the NSA director walked around the table to stand beside the CIA director behind the President.

'We just got satellite imagery in from a pass over Nizhni Novgorod,' he said as Thomas listened, his eyes fixed on the carrier's flight deck for the landing of the ungainly E-2C, its props on full power in case of an abort and its huge radar dome like an umbrella over its thick fuselage. 'The Russian Army groups in the east are dispersing. Units have left their staging areas and displaced into the countryside. Initial analysis is consistent with action orders called for under the Russians' Operation Samson.'

The President's finger remained firmly fixed on the mute button. Thomas's previously dark feeling about aborting the attack grew black. 'What's the status of the recalls, sir?' Thomas asked the Secretary of Defense.

He counted down the list. 'All the attack subs report aborts,' he said, his pencil tapping down the vessel names. 'All the frigates are okay.'

'The carriers, of course, reported back immediately,' the CNO supplied.

'We have the *Comte de Grasse* still out,' the Secretary said.

'They're not in any shape for offensive operations,' Admiral Dixon said but pulled the mouthpiece of one of the telephones to his lips and said, 'Frank, get me an acknowledgment from the *Comte de Grasse*.' He listened for a second before saying, 'She turned turtle four minutes ago. Search and Rescue is on the scene.'

'That means all the destroyers have reported or are nonoperational, Mr President,' the Secretary of Defense reported, 'but we still have one cruiser – an Aegis class, the *Anzio* – from which we've heard nothing.'

'Frank?' the CNO said. 'What's the deal with the *Anzio*?'

'One of her LAMPS helicopters reported a few minutes ago that she was engaged in an attack run,' the Secretary of Defense said. 'Her communications were knocked out in a missile attack from a Russian cruiser, which she in turn sank with Harpoons.'

'We've got to stop her,' the President said.

'The *John S. McCain*,' Admiral Dixon said, the hands holding the two phones sagging to the table, 'one of the reporting destroyers, is signaling the *Anzio* with lights and has fired a warning shot across her bow.'

'What's her range from target?' Thomas asked.

'She's getting close.'

'Sink her,' the President said. Thomas and the CNO looked at him, and he said, 'Order the *McCain* to sink the *Anzio*.'

Admiral Dixon froze, staring back at the President. 'Do it!' Thomas ordered.

'Frank,' the CNO said, 'do you have the *McCain* on— ?'

The CNO fell silent mid-sentence. From the look on his face as he listened, his eyes falling closed, Thomas knew it was too late. He looked back at the screen with its scene of the busy carrier deck. In the background, the deep blue sea met the light, crisp blue of the sky. It was almost as if it were a dream, a nightmare. One second, the smooth blue sea was cut only by the white spray from the bow of a distant frigate. In the next, there erupted the first white streak from the horizon, a fiery arrow riding its blazing tail into space as the first of the Russian submarines fired.

'The *McCain* reports eight ASROCs fired by the *Anzio*,' Admiral Dixon said.

'Mr President,' Thomas said wearily, 'I recommend that we resume the attack with all possible speed and you immediately authorize the use of tactical nuclear weapons.' He nodded at the screen on which had appeared half a dozen streaks from various points along the horizon.

'Oh, my God.'

THE KREMLIN, MOSCOW
August 31, 1750 GMT (1950 Local)

'Mr President,' Razov said calmly.

The President's shouts poured from the telephone as Lambert stood to the side of the credenza, still staring down the rifle muzzle pointed loosely at him by Filipov, who leaned against the conference table.

'You must not fire your missiles at my country,' Razov said in a raised voice. 'Mr President! Mr President, if I could—' Razov grimaced. 'I am aware that the submarines' missiles are headed toward the United States, sir, but if we are to discuss an allocation of responsibility for this crisis – moral, political, and otherwise – do I need remind you that you were warned of the fail-deadly firing orders under which the Bastion's submarines operated?'

Lambert could hear the President's shouting die down as Razov listened. 'I understand completely that your attacks into the Bastion will continue, Mr President, and under the circumstances it is with the heaviest of hearts that I must hope for your success against the submarines that still have unexpended missiles.' Again the President's shouts interrupted Razov, and again Razov listened patiently. 'No, sir, I do not call dozens of warheads falling onto your military installations and cities to be "success" in any absolute sense of the word, and I must tell you that in all probability that number will grow into the hundreds, if not thousands, before your submarines and antisubmarine aircraft can again maneuver into firing positions.' He listened again. 'I understand, but even if you use tactical nuclear weapons the submarines will still launch more missiles.'

This time, the President's shouted interruption drew a clench from Razov's jaw. 'My communications with you earlier were *not* a trick to convince you to call off your attack on the Bastion so that I could order the submarines to fire!' The squeaky sound of shouting could be heard through the tiny speaker of the earpiece. 'Mr President, those submarines fired because they were attacked, *not* as a result of the codes I input into the communicators!'

Ice water shot through Lambert's veins at the possibility that such a thing might be true. That Lambert had stood by, rifle in hand, while Razov ordered the launch of the submarines' missiles at hundreds of U.S. cities. His mouth went dry. He looked at Filipov, and Filipov stared back at him past the black, open hole of his rifle's muzzle.

Razov held the telephone out to Lambert with a sigh, cupping the mouthpiece as the President's voice could be heard shouting, '. . . want me to do then? Another *mistake*? My country is destroyed, a few million more of its population killed, and I'm supposed to chalk it up to another Russian *mistake* and hold my *fire*! Goddamn you, Razov, why didn't you recall those submarines if you were so stupid as to give them fail-deadly firing orders? What am I supposed to think? How am I supposed to believe that you didn't sucker us into this murderous endgame because you had just lost the war, huh?'

'Your President is about to order the launch of your country's remaining nuclear arsenal for the purpose of destroying the population of my country,' Razov said, holding his hand over the phone. 'If he does this, I will fire the two hundred ICBMs that have been reloaded by our Strategic Rocket Forces, which have a separate code set from the old control system and are quite unaffected by the command to the submarines' missiles I entered earlier. I want you, Gregory Lambert, to convince him to hold his fire.'

'Well, it's not going to work, you son of a bitch!' Costanzo's shouts came over the phone. 'I am not going to go down in history as the biggest dupe to have ever lived! Even Livingston had the guts to launch on warning and not wait for those *first* thousand or so warheads that your people "accidentally" fired to impact.'

Lambert took the phone. 'Mr President?' Lambert said.

'Tell him that the first strikes were counterforce,' Razov whispered.

'What?' the President snapped.

'Tell him that he has nothing to lose by waiting this time,' Razov coached, 'that these warheads aren't armed at your weapons and he can always counterattack if those warheads do in fact detonate.'

'Razov says you have nothing to lose by waiting,' Lambert said, unconvinced.

'Nothing to *lose*!' the President screamed. 'Nothing to lose? How about three quarters of our productive *base* and sixty or seventy million *people* if the winds are all wrong?'

'Tell him that the missiles will not detonate,' Razov said, 'that their fusing circuits have been safed – locked by the codes I put in – so that they cannot detonate their warheads.'

Lambert cupped his hand over the telephone as he heard the President, in the background, shout, 'Open that thing up!'

'What if that inhibit code you entered,' Lambert said – thinking, *If that was what you did* – 'didn't get through in time? Or what if it just doesn't work?'

'Mr Lambert,' Razov said, 'what difference does it make? In twenty minutes, your country will either be destroyed or it will not be destroyed. In either case, your nuclear arsenal, the several thousand nuclear devices that sit atop missiles in your submarines, or in bomb bays in your airborne bombers, or in cruise missiles aboard practically every combat ship in your navy, will remain intact and ready for immediate use. And, Greg, your troops will still be fighting their way block by block through the capital city of my country.'

Over the phone, which was pressed to his ear, he could hear Admiral Dixon reading out the target list. 'Saratov, thirty-seven warheads. Omsk, thirty-one warheads. Yaroslavl, thirty warheads. Kaluga, withhold. We'll use ADMs, Atomic Demolition Munitions, on Kaluga after we withdraw our troops and evacuate it.'

'Mr President,' Lambert said. He heard the CNO saying, 'Vladimir, twenty-eight warheads.' 'Mr President!' Lambert shouted.

'What?' Costanzo replied angrily.

'Sir, there is only one hope. There is only one chance that this is not the awful end we all feared. And that is if General Razov is telling the truth, and that the one final safeguard of all the checks and measures that have previously failed works this time and saves us from the ultimate tragedy. If you launch now, that one chance will be given up forever because General Razov will fire his reloaded missiles before our missiles strike their silos. And if Razov *is* telling the truth, and the system does work, then whom, Mr President, whom will history view as the villain in all of this? If those Russian submarines' warheads do not detonate over our cities, sir, but our weapons incinerate tens of millions of Russians and their ICBMs' warheads hit our cities and do explode, what will the final mistake be, and who will have committed it?'

'Greg, *Goddammit*,' Costanzo shouted, 'I don't know if they've got a gun to your head, or if you're just more inclined to trust these bastards

than you have any reason to be, but if what you're asking me to do is
trust Razov, that argument doesn't fly anymore.'

'Sir, you have no choice.'

'That's where you're wrong, Greg. That's where you're wrong. I've
got a whole book full of choices right here! A whole book of choices!'

'Mr President!' Lambert yelled, but the line went dead.

Lambert looked at Razov, still holding the phone to his ear. As the
seconds elapsed and Razov realized that the line had been cut, his face
grew more and more set in a bitter mask. The weather lines around
his eyes deepened, and his clenched teeth grew visible through slightly
parted lips. 'Where are the codes for the reloaded missile silos?' he
snapped in Russian at the two officers manning the still open nuclear
communicators.

'General Razov!' Lambert shouted. 'He hasn't made a decision!' Razov
walked over to the two devices and looked down at the small notebook
pulled from the side pouch of one of the communicators. 'You know
General Thomas! He can talk the President out of launching! The same
arguments that you used on the President apply to *you*!'

'That he should trust us?' Razov asked with a sneer as he looked up
from the book. 'And you ask now that I trust a man who out of nothing
more than a fit of anger is willing to kill tens of millions of people, of
my people. Or do they not count, Mr Lambert, because they are only
Russians?'

Lambert looked at his friend Filipov, Razov's trusted aide and
Lambert's last hope. Filipov's rifle was on his shoulder, its aim straight
at Lambert's face.

'General Razov,' Lambert pleaded, trying desperately to organize the
jumble of thoughts against a rising tide of panic. 'We do not know that
the President will order a launch.'

'And without the satellites that you destroyed we won't know that
he did until our remaining missiles are destroyed in their silos, will we?'
Razov spit out commands to the two officers in front of him, his voice
filled with hatred.

Lambert's heart thumped in his chest, and his throat felt constricted.
'No. No, sir, we won't.'

Razov slowly looked up at him.

'And if the President does fire, you will have disabled your submarine
missiles' warheads and lost your last remaining land-based missiles if
you hold your fire.' Lambert licked his lips and swallowed.

Razov clenched his jaw and looked down at the two officers. 'Initiate
the sequence!'

'General!' Lambert said as he took a step toward him. He heard the
metallic click of the safety from Filipov's rifle, but he remained focused
on Razov. 'What will you lose? What possible advantage will be lost?
Your country will be in ruins. Would you have my country destroyed

also? For what purpose? The only nation with the means of providing for your recovery would be in flames, the hearts of its population seared closed in bitter enmity toward your people for a *hundred* years!'

The orders hung on Razov's lips.

'He might not have fired!' Lambert shouted in Russian.

First one, then the other officer at the table, their fingers on the TRANSMIT keys of their code cases, looked up at Razov. Razov's gray eyes burned into Lambert's. Time stood still.

ABOARD NIGHTWATCH, OVER CENTRAL OHIO
August 31, 1800 GMT (1300 Local)

'Enter the code!' President Costanzo ordered.

'Are you absolutely sure, Mr President?' Thomas asked, standing in front of his chair.

'Look, we were told by this Damocles, whoever he is, about their fail-deadly firing policy. You people were convinced it was a hoax, that the subs wouldn't fire without new orders from Moscow. But they damn sure fired, didn't they? Didn't they?' the President shouted, rising to his feet to pace while lost deep in thought, his hair increasingly unkempt as he ran his hands through it over and over again. 'Either Razov fired those missiles at us when he input that code, or this Damocles was telling the truth all along about the fail-deadly policy. And if Damocles *was* telling the truth, he must have been telling the truth about Operation Samson too. They've been *preparing* for this! They've buried their industrial equipment, dispersed their army, done all the things Operation Samson called for! Razov fired at our cities *knowing* we'll fire back at his! He's playing out some un-*fucking*-believable endgame from which he somehow expects to gain an advantage!'

He grabbed the back of his chair as if to steady himself. Thomas looked into the man's haunted eyes. In the theater of Costanzo's mind he could imagine what was playing: the end of the world.

The President's gaze rose to the room's display, which had switched from the Moscow assault to a map of the earth looking down from the North Pole. NORAD's computers plotted the second-by-second passage of the twelve hundred warheads that had escaped the caldron of thermonuclear detonations atop the Kara Sea and were confirmed inbound across the ice cap. Narrowing circles on the map of the United States were their probable points of impact. From the general outline of the U.S. borders and the location of the hundreds and hundreds of circles all across it, one thing was eminently clear: the warheads were heading for the cities.

'Enter the Goddamn code,' Costanzo ordered, and Admiral Dixon picked up his telephone. In a few seconds, it was done.

U.S.S. NEVADA, BEAUFORT SEA NORTH OF INUVIK, CANADA
August 31, 1805 GMT (0805 Local)

On hearing the muted throb of a siren, Captain Bill McKenzie's pulse quickened. He opened his eyes and immediately swung his feet to the floor. The red light over the hatch to his compartment was flashing – *EAM* written diagonally across its face.

His mind began reviewing the procedures to come as he quickly slipped into his shoes, brushed his hair, and straightened the uniform in which he had slept. Had he awakened to a normal routine, he would have dropped the uniform into his laundry bag before showering, but this was not normal. This was why he slept in his uniform.

Before he opened the hatch, he cleared his throat and pulled the muscles of his back erect. Turning into the corridor, he strode quickly to his post.

'Captain's on the conn,' he said loudly as he reached the crowded bridge, lowering his voice to achieve the resonant quality to which his crew was accustomed. 'Officer o' the Deck, report.' The words were long rehearsed, rapidly spoken.

'Comm's receiving FLASH traffic, Captain,' the OD said, his eyes glancing up to catch McKenzie's and then back down. No one else saw the look.

McKenzie felt all his senses grow keenly alert, catching the subtle differences in the man's behavior. He jerked the microphone off its cradle and said, 'Comm, this is the captain.'

'Uh, Captain, this is Comm,' the tinny voice came back over the small speaker above the cradle. 'Emergency Action Message is: NCA Control Order. Recommend Alert One.'

McKenzie could feel the eyes of his men turn toward him. With a conscious effort to avoid any visible reaction, he pulled the mike back up to his lips and said, 'Convene the EAM Team.' Reaching up to turn the ship-wide intercom on, he said, 'All hands, all hands, now hear this,' his words sounding in the background. 'Alert One, Alert One.'

Replacing the mike in its cradle, McKenzie avoided the openly staring faces of the men on the conn and said, 'Officer of the Deck, proceed to launch depth and prepare to hover.'

'Aye, sir. Dive,' the OD said, turning to the control room at the side of the conn, 'proceed to launch depth and prepare to hover.'

McKenzie headed to the Communications Room without acknowledging the men's stares.

'Cap'n's off the conn,' a sailor called from behind him.

McKenzie walked down the long corridor, oblivious to the sailors as they now poured from their compartments, their artificial eighteen-hour day interrupted in the middle of the 'night,' and braced with heels against the bulkhead just long enough for McKenzie to pass before hurrying on to their stations. He was lost in his own world, doing his job in his head over and over. By the time he got to the Communications Room, he had all the reassurance he needed. He would be cool, professional. He would excel where he had always excelled. He would measure up in the eyes of his crew by the one criterion by which he measured them: he would do his job.

When he opened the hatch to the Communications Room, the three officers all flinched at the sudden noise and then stiffened to attention. Commander Pearcy, his second in command, said by way of greeting, 'Ready for format verification, sir.'

McKenzie got a rush of satisfaction, a feeling of comfort that everything to come would be familiar and expected. Ordered. This was his crew. They were molded in his image. McKenzie turned to the two lieutenants standing on either side of a small table. 'Mr Williams, Mr Barnett, verify the format.'

As the two lieutenants ripped open the sealed authentication packages, McKenzie looked at the copy of the EAM that Pearcy handed to him. The code of numbers and letters appeared normal in all respects. It was a control order – the hundredth, the thousandth time he had seen one in drills. This was the first time he had seen it, however, without clear, safe THIS IS A DRILL qualifiers printed in boldface across both the top and bottom. He checked the printout carefully and found both the beginning and end of transmission indicators. There was no qualifier on this EAM.

McKenzie pulled a mike from the bulkhead and said, 'Control, this is the captain. This message requires Battle Stations – Missile. Man Battle Stations – Missile.' He flicked the intercom to monitor, and against the normal background noise heard the Officer of the Deck say, 'Chief of the Watch, sound the general alarm.'

Almost immediately a low horn began repeating its digitally produced sound from all corners of the boat.

Pearcy stood up from the table with his copy of the EAM in hand and said, 'Captain, the EAM Team has a properly formated message. Request permission to authenticate.'

'Mr Williams, do you concur?' McKenzie asked the lieutenant on his left.

'Yes, Captain, I concur.'

'Mr Barnett, do you concur?'

'I concur, Captain.'

It was quick, and it was efficient – good.

'You have permission to authenticate,' McKenzie said to Pearcy.

'Authenticate – aye aye, sir,' he responded as he again hunched over the table. McKenzie breathed slowly – in through his nose, out through his mouth. Filling his lungs, he smoothed out the ragged edges of his nerves.

'Captain, the message authenticates,' Pearcy said.

'I agree, Captain, the message authenticates,' Williams said.

'Captain, I concur,' Barnett said in rapid succession.

'I concur,' McKenzie said formally. 'It is an authentic message. Executive Officer, break out the CIPT.'

'Break out the CIPT, aye aye, sir,' Pearcy said as McKenzie opened the hatch and returned to the conn.

When he arrived, he said in a loud voice that drowned out all the others, 'Attention on deck, this is the captain! I have the deck and the conn.' He stole a glance at the depth and speed indicators. All was ready. 'Engines, all stop.'

'Engines, all stop' was repeated from the control room.

'Diving Officer,' McKenzie continued in his deep command voice, 'prepare to hover.'

'Back one-third,' the Diving Officer said as he stared over the shoulders of the two drivers seated at wheels like the pilot's yoke of a large airplane. After a moment, the Diving Officer straightened and looked at McKenzie. 'Diving Officer prepared to hover, sir.'

'Diving Officer, commence hovering.'

'Commence hovering,' the Diving Officer replied, 'aye aye, sir,' and the massive steel vessel began what for it was the most difficult maneuver of all, remaining motionless just beneath the rolling surface of the ocean.

McKenzie grabbed the mike from the console next to him and said over the boat's intercom, 'Set Condition 1-SQ. This is not a drill, this is not a drill. Set Condition 1-SQ.' He didn't identify himself. The crew knew his voice.

'Set Condition 1-SQ,' McKenzie heard in reply over the speaker from the Missile Room. They were now on the highest state of alert possible. The hammer was cocked on the 560-foot long, 18,000-ton submarine.

Lieutenant Commander Pearcy and the third-highest-ranking officer on board arrived, and McKenzie removed the keys hanging from the lanyard around his neck and reached over to open his safe. The other two officers immediately went to open their own safes at different places around the conn.

Unlike the firing procedures of the air force, whose nuclear-capable units were in constant contact with the National Command Authority, the procedures on a boomer were elaborate. Cut off from contact while on firing stations by the few feet of water through which high-frequency radio waves would not penetrate, and under standard orders not to risk raising an aerial during time of war, the subs were given broader discretion to fire than any other unit. The only messages they got were a slow series of extremely low frequency radio waves passed through the earth itself, which were picked up by an antenna trailed miles behind the submarine but now reeled in for the hover. The rate of transmission was so slow that all they had gotten was a short code, an Emergency Action Message, which interrupted the normal, continuous transmission of weather reports, enemy position data, and personal messages from family that were constantly emitted in order not to alert the enemy of a sudden burst of activity.

The number of officers required to concur in a launch decision was five: the two junior officers of the EAM Team and the three most senior officers who stood at the launch console. Any one of them, if they did not concur that authorization was valid, had one other order unique to submariners. They were ordered to resist a launch by all possible means, including deadly force, and they had access to personal sidearms at all times for that reason.

The two other senior officers converged on McKenzie with the firing keys they had removed from their safes, which the three men then exchanged with one another. Each then unlocked one of the three separate weapons locks.

'Cap'n,' the Officer of the Deck, who had been watching their progress, said, 'pursuant to Battle Stations – Missile, Dive is in Condition 1-SQ.'

'Very well,' McKenzie replied. 'Weapons Conn,' he said to the sailor standing next to him, 'the printouts have been validated.'

'Weapons Conn,' the sailor said into the mike that was strapped around his neck and hung under his chin, 'the printouts have been validated.'

'Mr Pearcy,' the captain said, 'what are the instructions in the CIPT?'

'The instructions are to launch on detection of electromagnetic pulse consistent with detonation of a nuclear device over North America,' Pearcy said.

Pearcy handed McKenzie the new fail-deadly orders printed from the laser printer after the last computer maintenance link with fleet headquarters, not one of the more rehearsed control orders. After hesitating a second, McKenzie raised the mike to his lips.

'Missile Room, standby Fire Order.'

'Standby Fire Order,' the Missile Room repeated over the speaker. The safety was off.

'The Fire Order will be: "One through Twenty-four,"' McKenzie read from the CIPT.

'The Fire Order will be,' the Missile Officer repeated over the speaker, 'One through Twenty-four.' McKenzie could picture the Missile Officer quickly tapping the vertical row of twenty-four buttons, each in turn changing from a dim orange HOLD to a bright green READY. Each button opened the firing circuit to a single D-5, a Trident II submarine-launched intercontinental ballistic missile. Atop every one of the twenty-four three-staged, solid-fueled missiles were eight W88/Mk5 reentry vehicles, each with a 475-kiloton thermonuclear warhead. Six thousand miles away sat 192 targets. The warheads would land within 400 feet of their targets.

'Fire Order verified, sir,' the Missile Room acknowledged.

McKenzie stared at the weapons console. The READY lights on the missiles all shone green. 'Weapons Conn,' he said, 'prepare to initiate fire.'

There was silence, and it was electric. It seemed like an eternity before the tinny voice came over the speaker on the weapons console, the tone low and mechanical, the speaker sounding as if he were miles and miles away. 'Prepared to initiate fire.' Silence, stillness, and then the voice over the speaker: 'Prepared One through Twenty-four.'

'Officer o' the Deck,' McKenzie said without turning, 'raise the mast and monitor for electromagnetic pulse.'

'Up periscope,' the Officer of the Deck said as McKenzie and the four other officers of the firing committee who would vote on a launch waited on one stray pulse of electromagnetic radiation from a nuclear detonation to tickle the antenna on the submarine's mast and trigger launch of the boat's 192 warheads.

DISPLACED PERSONS CAMP, GORMAN, CALIFORNIA
August 31, 1815 GMT (1015 Local)

The scene reminded Melissa of a Fourth of July picnic as she searched for a seat on the crowded hillside. If it hadn't been for the whimpered tears into tissues and the radios blaring the horrible hum of the Emergency Broadcast System, everyone might have been awaiting a fireworks display, their heads tilted back and their hands shielding the afternoon sun from their eyes. She found an exposed rock and sat down not far from an old couple who held each other in their arms. The woman smiled sadly at Melissa, looking up at her from a quickly stolen glance at little Matthew.

Melissa scanned the hazy sky in the general direction of L.A. She pulled an increasingly restless Matthew up onto her shoulder and said, 'It won't be long now, sweetie,' as the first tears rolled down her cheeks.

It was surreal. She felt like screaming – she thought she might at any second just stand up and scream at the top of her lungs like a madwoman – as she looked out at the sea of heads raised to the sky, searching for the first sign. *Why is this happening?* she raged. *What has gone wrong with the world?* The radio in her tent had that morning reported the war almost at an end, St Petersburg and Moscow surrounded, and then the special bulletin.

'Turn that thing off!' someone shouted, and the loud hum from the radio fell silent.

It was peaceful, now – hundreds of people all huddled together, black, white, hispanic, Asian, all sitting calmly on a hill in the country on a Sunday afternoon.

'There!' a man seated down the hill shouted, his arm upstretched and pointing into the haze.

'There they are!' a woman cried, and there began a general buzz from the crowd, the most dominant comments heard being the sobbing cries of, 'No, oh, no.'

Melissa looked up. The white vapor trails of the warheads broke into irregular dashed streaks as they passed through the wispy upper atmosphere – some patches dry, others wet. The farther the dozens and dozens of warheads fell, however, the thicker the water vapor and the more solid the contrail. With the exception of two or three outliers, most of the fifty or more warheads streaked down in a dense pack toward a single patch of earth in the far distance. Los Angeles.

The crowd all watched the climax of what, Melissa realized, had been building now for months, maybe for all the decades since nuclear weapons were invented. She looked at the couple next to her, locked in their embrace, and wondered whether she would ever see David again. *Just once*, she pleaded. *I want to see him again just one more time.*

As the first of the distant warheads sped down behind the tree-line on the hill opposite their ridge, she thought, *Why, God? Why did you run out of miracles for us?*

Behind it followed the dozens of others. When nothing was left in the sky but the contrails that dissipated slowly in the winds, it was over. The couple in front of her rose from their place on the hill and brushed the dirt from their seats. The man looked at Melissa and her baby and said, 'Not with a bang but a whimper,' about the anticlimactic conclusion to the show.

Everyone began to rise from their places, the 'fireworks' over. She and the elderly couple hugging to Melissa's right stayed put: no place to go, nobody to see, nothing to do. The hillside cleared of people rather rapidly, some still with ears pressed to transistor radios, ever deluding themselves despite what their own eyes had told them.

Melissa kissed Matthew's head, which had been warmed by the sun. 'It wasn't like this before,' she whispered, her lips pressed to his smooth skin and fine hair. He had that baby smell, his skin fragrant. 'There were crowds of people who would go to concerts and baseball games and . . . and the circus.' Her tears left wet trails down her face. 'And we had a house with a spe-e-cial room for you called the nursery.' Her lips quivered and she faltered. 'And . . . and there were balloons on your wall, and clowns and sailboats!' She lay Matthew on her thighs, and he stared up contentedly at her face. 'There was music, and laughter.' She forced herself to smile. She wanted him to see smiles.

The elderly couple next to her rose and gathered their heavy bag, still clasped in each other's arms as they walked off not up the hill toward camp but down the hill toward the mountain stream below.

'You forgot your purse!' Melissa called to the woman as she looked over at their place on the rock.

'You can have it, dear,' she said with a smile. It was a strange smile – peaceful, contented, fulfilled. Melissa watched them as they headed off, right and not left at the steep path to the water, and disappeared behind the outcropping of rock that jutted from the grassy patch of hill on which everyone had sat. Melissa looked over at the woman's purse. The man had even left his eyeglasses sitting on the rock, something that might prove difficult to replace in the changed world of the new millennium. She picked them up and started down the hill after them.

A gunshot rang out and echoed around the valley below. Melissa stopped in her tracks, holding the eyeglasses gingerly in her hands. A second and final shot rang out, and Melissa dropped the glasses and turned to stare off at the streaks in the sky.

NEW YORK, NEW YORK
August 31, 1815 GMT (1315 Local)

Walter Livingston leaned out over the balcony to look down at the National Guardsmen on the street below. The shots had brought the former President and his wife out onto their balcony just before the first special bulletin on CNN's Headline News. They had watched from their perch high above the abandoned city as two dramas played out. One below: the men in combat gear rushing from doorway to doorway as they chased a looter. The other above: the end of the world.

Twice they had seen the Guardsmen's prey, a young man with a bag filled with possessions he would never live to enjoy, as he peered out from around doorways and dumpsters. The Guardsmen even passed by him once, and he almost slipped away before they doubled back.

All of that had come to an end with the first eerie wail of the air raid siren. One by one the troops gathered on the street below, removing their helmets and dropping their packs and rifles as the persistent and unmistakable sound droned on.

All of this the Livingstons had watched, the only interruption being Walter's one departure to make martinis.

'Did I miss anything?' he asked as he handed Margaret her cool glass.

'They said that it looked like every major city was going to be hit,' she said, turning to nod at the television.

'No, I mean down there?'

'Oh!' She smiled, and they both leaned out over the flower pots lining the railing. 'He's down there, just behind the park wall beside the kiosk. Do you see?' She took a sip.

'Oh, yes! I see his back.'

'Walter, I think this is the very best martini you have ever made.' She smiled again, leaning into him on that flimsy pretense for a kiss. Her lips were cool from the drink, her soft mouth so familiar.

'And now,' the Livingstons turned to look at the anguished anchor-woman on television, 'we here at CNN Studio in Atlanta leave you and sign off to these scenes of America from before the war and to the music of Beethoven's Ninth Symphony. Good bye, and good luck.' The stirring music began, and Walter Livingston turned away from the first picture, a smiling young girl eating cotton candy on a sunny day at a country fair.

'Look!' they heard shouted from below, and they leaned over the rail to look down. The boy was running at top speed across the green, now overgrown grass of the park, but the soldiers paid him no attention. One man's arm was raised, pointing into the sky overhead.

Walter and Margaret Livingston looked up in unison. He felt her hand clutch his and a coat of rime cover his chest, sending a shiver across his shoulder blades. Dozens and dozens of wispy white tails trailed the plummeting warheads toward the island.

'Oh . . . my . . .' Margaret's voice sounded distant and frail.

He turned her and hugged her tightly. Some would detonate midair, he realized. They didn't have much time. As she buried her head to his chest, he caught a brief glimpse of the smile that had been a constant with her throughout let go into a ragged quiver of her jaw and twisting of her lips. In the background, Beethoven's Ninth played on.

On the street below, a hollow thonk drew his attention, and he leaned over the railing. One soldier's helmet lay spinning on the pavement. The bareheaded man standing over it twisted free of his rucksack and let it drop straight to the ground. Throwing his rifle down with the sound of a clatter delayed by the distance, he wound up and kicked his helmet down the sidewalk into the empty street.

Margaret squeezed her husband tight. He looked up into the sky one last time. *The end of the world*, he thought staring at the white vapor boiling fiercely off streaking warheads. *So this is what it looks like*. He buried his head in her white hair, which smelled of some fragrance, as it had for all the time he could remember.

He thought he had time to ask her what the scent was when a stunning BOOM echoed through the canyons of the still city. Margaret jerked, and he felt her sag in his arms. 'I love you,' he said in a voice loud enough to carry over blast after blast after blast that shook the air with great shock waves. He held her against him to keep her from falling, as glass shattered up and down the street and picture frames fell from their mantel. A large vase atop a pedestal in their foyer shattered against the marble floor as the explosions across the city outside sounded as if an enormous drum were being beaten all about them.

The last of the echoes died down, and all was quiet. Margaret twisted slightly in his arms and he realized that he was hurting her. He loosened his grip. 'There he is!' someone yelled below, and the two of them looked down at the soldiers resuming their chase through the park, one Guardsman first running the other way to retrieve his helmet before racing to catch his buddies. From around the city rose dozens of columns of black smoke. The first sound of a siren – a new siren, this one from a fire engine – rose up to their balcony as the air raid siren slowly wound down and fell silent.

Margaret looked up at him. Her face was paper-white, but her eyes filled with tears and her lips quivered in the first of what were both sobs and giggling. Walter smiled and felt tears flood his own eyes. She laughed, and he let loose a long, side-splitting cackle. 'They . . . they didn't work!' she exclaimed, the look on her face part incredulity, part joy at the miracle that had saved them. They laughed and laughed, the tears still flowing.

'We'd better go inside,' he said finally as he eyed the black smoke, which would contain radioactivity, he realized, even though the warheads had failed to explode. When he looked down, he saw Margaret, the smile again on her face, as her lips moved in prayer. He bowed his head and said his own thanks as the reporter on television exclaimed, 'This just in to CNN Headquarters in Atlanta . . .!'

THE KREMLIN, MOSCOW
August 31, 2200 GMT (0000 Local)

Lambert, Filipov, and Razov stood on the Kremlin wall staring out at the thousand fires that lit a line across Moscow, roughly marking the forward edge of the coalition advance. While arranging for transport to friendly lines, Lambert had asked the commander of the 1st Cavalry Division to allow Russian firefighters access to the blazing buildings, but either the fires or the sporadic fighting that still flared around the city were dangers deemed too great by the city's workers, and the fires raged undiminished. The wind licked also at the smaller flames around Red Square below, which was pock-marked with shell holes and dotted with blazing vehicles. The ferocious popping sound of a firefight erupted here and there as the two sides still rubbed against each other. Men on each side were still dying, Lambert knew, despite the cease-fire.

Lambert shivered as the cool wind cut right through the filthy, tattered summer suit he wore, and he looked over at the two Russians, comfortably warm in the wool overcoats they had donned.

Filipov returned Lambert's gaze. Lambert searched for words that might bridge the gap that had formed between them. Suddenly he had an idea. 'I guess "that's the ball game"?' he said, watching Filipov for any sign of reaction to the query.

'"Ball game"?' Filipov snapped as he straightened to face Lambert square on. 'You call that a game?' His arm swept out over the fires, sneering as he shook his head.

'It was just an expression, Pavel.' Lambert was confused. He had been convinced that Filipov was the source, Damocles. 'Look, if you want,' Lambert said as he faced Filipov, 'we can talk about this and see if there is anything left of our friendship, or we can just go our two ways. It's your call.'

Filipov stared at Lambert with hatred in his eyes. 'It's this way with Americans every time, isn't it?' he asked, his eyes dropping to look Lambert up and down as his lips curled in animosity. 'You come rolling in killing and destroying and then say, "Now it's time to be friends."' He shook his head again, barely containing his anger. 'You used nerve gas on the Moscow Line,' he said nodding toward the southwest. '*Nerve gas* – on undefended Provisional Troops whose sole crime was defending their homes!'

'You used it first,' Lambert replied, growing angry at the insinuation that there was something criminal in the act.

'On troops who at least had a *chance*,' Filipov shouted, 'who had the equipment to defend themselves! Troops who were *invading* our country! We were acting out of desperation, but still we held back, didn't we? *Didn't we?* We disarmed our missiles before they were fired!'

'Do I have to remind you, Pavel, how this whole thing got . . .?' Lambert began, but Filipov was shaking his head and turning angrily away, not interested in listening.

In Red Square below, the lights of a convoy – Russian Army BTRs leading and trailing three American M-1 tanks – rolled up the hill and into view.

'There's your ride,' Filipov said, his jaw clenched. 'I'll go make arrangements for your departure.' Filipov turned to face Lambert. '*Proshchai*, Greg.'

Lambert stared back at him. No hand raised for a shake, no hint of any friendship remaining. 'Proshchai,' Lambert thought, *not* 'do svidaniya.' *He had used the word for 'farewell' instead of the more common 'until we meet again.'*

'*Proshchai*, Pavel.' Filipov strode off, revealing Razov who leaned in a relaxed manner over the wall and stared at the American tanks below. Lambert felt another chill as the wind whipped up, and he saw the wry smile on Razov's face.

Together they surveyed the amazing scene beneath the Kremlin walls.

'Once again Moscow burns,' Razov finally said. It wasn't a bitter charge. It was simply a tired statement of fact, a historical reference.

'The last time was 1812?' Lambert asked, realizing the moment the words left his mouth that the subject was probably too sensitive, and his handling of it too cavalier.

'Napoleon,' Razov said, apparently taking no offense. 'Yes, 1812.' He looked at Lambert. For an instant, Lambert thought he was going to continue the history lesson, make another historical analogy. After his victory, Napoleon had retreated from Moscow during winter and, in the bitter cold and under constant harassment from Russian troops, had lost his Grande Armée in the thick snows of Western Russia. 'What a terrible century this has been,' Razov said instead.

Three world wars, Lambert thought, *at the beginning, middle, and end of the century*. He nodded. 'I'll be glad when it's over,' Lambert said. 'A fresh start in a new century, without all the blood that stains this one.'

'A new millennium. A thousand years. How many armies have risen, how many soldiers have fallen, over the last thousand years?'

'Too many.'

Razov heaved a sigh, or possibly just breathed deeply the chilly air, Lambert could not tell which. 'Unfortunately,' he said looking down at the American tanks whose commanders waited warily in their hatches, 'this millennium is not quite over yet.' He looked back at Lambert, and again Lambert waited for what he thought might be something significant, some point that Razov seemed on the verge of making. 'What did you want to be, Greg, when you grew up?'

'Pardon me?'

'When you were a boy, what did you want to be? Let me guess. President of the United States?'

Lambert eyd him before shaking his head. 'Most Valuable Player in the NBA.' Razov squinted and cocked his head, not understanding. 'The National Basketball Association,' Lambert translated, and Razov looked up at Lambert's head, judging his height, and nodded, looking out again into the wind.

'I,' Razov said, looking down now at his gloved hands, 'I wanted to be a soldier. A general.' Lambert waited again, but that was all he said, his eyes roaming now across the brightly burning skyline. Lambert's eyes dropped down to the tanks, whose commanders were speaking to a delegation of Russians headed by Filipov.

'Do you know the legend of Damocles?' Razov asked suddenly, and Lambert turned to stare at him for a moment in growing surprise. Razov returned his stare just long enough to confirm that his question was no coincidence, and then continued. 'Damocles was a Greek nobleman who frequently expressed his awe and envy at the power and apparent happiness of the king.' A wistful smile washed over his face. 'One day, the king grew tired of his flattery and held a banquet. At the banquet, the king seated Damocles under a sword that was suspended from the ceiling by a single hair.' His eyes squinted as the wind blew cold rain into his and Lambert's faces. 'The king wanted to demonstrate, you see, that the crown brought with it fears and worries as well as pleasures.'

Razov looked back down into the square, and Lambert followed his eyes. Streaking through the flickering light of flames from a Russian armored vehicle, Lambert could see the air thick with the precipitation that stung his face. He shivered and wrapped his arms tightly about himself. When he looked back at Razov, he saw that his face was turned up into the sky and that he inhaled the cold air and moisture deeply. Not returning Lambert's gaze, Razov said, 'America lies at a southern latitude,' as if he were instructing a pupil in the fundamentals of geography. 'The latitude of New York is about the same as that of Rome, if I am not mistaken. You know of our winters here, of course,' he said, turning to look at Lambert briefly before his eyes were drawn down to the crackling flame below.

'Ah!' Razov said, holding out his gloved hand. Lambert looked down at the flame and saw in the air the downward drift of what could only be snow. On the outstretched palm of Razov's gloved hand there gathered large, wet flakes.

'The first snow of September.' Lambert felt Razov's eyes. 'The snows have come early this year,' he said slowly in his mellifluous voice as a gust of wind blew the snow from his hand and sent a new shiver down Lambert's spine.

> Nothing except a battle lost can be half so melancholy as a battle won.
>
> —ARTHUR WELLESLEY,
> DUKE OF WELLINGTON
> *Dispatch from the field*
> *of Waterloo (June 1815)*

Epilogue

LOS ANGELES, CALIFORNIA
December 2, 2000 GMT (1200 Local)

David squeezed Melissa tightly to his chest as he smelled Matthew's head, inhaling the soft, fragrant baby hair with every breath. 'I love you so much,' Melissa kept repeating as her arms encircled him and her face was buried against his camouflage blouse.

Standing just inside the front door, David marveled at how everything seemed the same. The nuclear war. The fight all the way to Moscow. The steady decline of the Russian civil situation and rise of the anarchists as the violence rose with every new snowfall. Six months. All of that in six months. Here, at home, everything seemed the way it was before for most. But it was not the same for some. Everything had changed for those who had lost someone in the war, and for those who feared for loved ones in the now burgeoning armed forces.

Melissa looked up, tears streaming down her face. Matthew cooed, and both looked at him and then back at each other in pride over what only parents could perceive as an accomplishment. David kissed his son's cheek.

There was a brief tap of a car horn from the driveway, and David kissed Matthew again and handed him to Melissa.

Melissa looked stricken. David hoisted the arctic white bag filled with heavy cold weather gear onto his shoulder and opened the door. The cabdriver got out to open the trunk.

'Can you call when you get there?' she asked, her voice shaking.

He started to tell her about the difficulties still involved in getting an international line from Moscow but said instead, 'Sure. I'll call.'

'And you wrote down everything I need to know to get in touch with you?' she asked. 'I can just write "Army Post Office – Russia?"' David nodded as he turned to hug her, but she lowered her eyes and kept talking. 'And . . . and it's only for a few more months,' she said, intentionally avoiding his gaze. David looked back at the cabdriver, who had obviously seen his uniform and bag with its helmet covered in snow-colored white cloth and was leaning against the hood patiently.

'They still say we'll withdraw completely from Western Russia,' she said as her eyes flitted across David's in question, but as he opened his mouth to speak she rushed on. 'They won't transfer you to the occupation forces in Siberia,' she asked, and her voice broke in open fear, 'or . . . or to the Chinese DMZ?'

'No, no,' David said, shaking his head. 'We tore up the Trans-Siberian Railroad so bad it's easier to ship troops from here than to cross Russia from Europe.'

'And once the anarchist thing is under control in the cities . . .?' she asked for the hundredth time.

'Then we'll withdraw in the west. A few more months,' David repeated the official policy with much greater certainty than he felt. 'Honey, I've gotta go. My flight leaves in an hour.' He shifted the heavy bag to relieve the cramping in his arm and she looked distractedly at it. She had seen him pack. White Gore-Tex snowsuits, white boots, white body armor, everything white and heavily insulated. Even the new rifle stocks were white plastic. Everything was white, including the five chemical warfare suits in the bag that would deteriorate within hours in the subfreezing temperatures of the Eurasian plain. Melissa's eyes stared at the bag. She had seen him pack.

David again wrapped his arms around his wife and son, holding them close. 'Two weeks, David,' she said, shaking her head. 'Only two weeks at home. It's not fair.'

'Honey . . . oh, honey.' He started to tell her how many favors he had called in to get the leave and how Harkness, his brigade commander, had approved the request in stony silence. David decided to let it drop, however, as his mind drifted back to his battalion, to his men who had not had the luxury of a two-week leave at home. David had called Moscow once while on leave, and Barnes had told him of the attempted looting of the battalion food stores. Two of their sentries had been wounded. They had been lucky, but the Russians had not. Fourteen civilians dead, another thirty wounded. All of them hungry. Most of them college students from Moscow University nearby their encampment above the Russians' former strategic command bunker in the Ramenki District.

There would be mass rioting that winter. Food riots. It had probably already started. And it was David with his M-1 tanks and other soldiers like them in the American Sector of Moscow who would have to stop the rabble. Russia was awash in the light weapons that remained around after the war and Russia's arming of the Provisionals, but they were no match for ceramic armor, 120-mm cannon, and heavy machine guns. David worried about sniping, but his greatest concern was not for his men but for the angry crowds of the starving who out of desperation might rush his soldiers. They had no rubber bullets, and their tear gas worked poorly in the cold. It was an old problem for armies charged with maintaining civil order. You either did nothing or you slaughtered the defenseless in numbers that within seconds of an order to fire could mount into the hundreds, even thousands.

David kissed Matthew one last time. The baby squirmed impatiently, oblivious to his father's presence. He leaned over and kissed Melissa, whose face immediately contorted to suppress her tears. She bit her lower lip and looked up, and then stood on her tiptoes to kiss his mouth and face over and over, leaving his cheeks smeared with her tears.

'I love you with all my heart,' he said, and then he left.

Walking to the cab, he began the transformation in his mind. Civilian to soldier. Soldier to civilian. Now, civilian to soldier again. *It wasn't supposed to be this way*, he thought. His mind roamed back to his life just before the war. Everything had seemed so normal. It was as if history's steady and stable progression had turned on a dime and swept him down a course that he would never have imagined possible. Was history's course so volatile, or was it just unpredictable?

By the time the cab's door closed, however, all such thoughts were gone. He looked out the window as the taxi backed onto the street and saw his wife and child as if through a lens, waving at them mechanically as he busily walled up those parts of him that were vulnerable to the crippling emotional pain. The pain was unavoidable, like bullet wounds or burst eardrums, but it could be managed. It could be managed.

'Where to, Colonel?' the driver asked.

The question hung there, unanswered, and after a moment the cabbie looked back over his shoulder. David completed the strenuous task of his transformation and issued his first order.

Acknowledgments

For their willingness to take a chance on a first novelist, my heartfelt gratitude goes to my agents, Jay Garon and Nancy Coffey of Jay Garon-Brooke Associates, Inc. For the patient editorial care of Michael Korda at Simon & Schuster, who turned my manuscript into a book and me into a writer, I am forever indebted. And for my earliest readers Boyd Carano, Vladimir Matlin, Larry Campagna, and Charles Frost (Lt. Col., USAR), and the men and women of the Army Reserve's 417th IMA Detachment, who wargamed the book and provided insightful commentary and advice, I offer my thanks for all your help and encouragement.